SIMONE'
TUSCANY THE SAGA BEGINS

BOOK ONE : SECOND EDITION

CARLOTTA MARIA SHINN-RUSSELL

TABLE *of* CONTENTS

CARLOTTA MARIA SHINN-RUSSELL

SIMONE'

TUSCANY THE SAGA BEGINS

BOOK ONE: SECOND EDITION

Printed in the United States of America.

PROLEGOMENON

Romance is wanted, needed, and desired by all. Time is a preserver of romance. With time, understanding of romance becomes crystal clear. Romance is a juxtaposing of the heart. It is a side-by-side intrigue of two hearts and minds or the one heart and mind. It brings within its proximity fascination, intrigue, a liaison of passion and desire.

Romance is an affair of the heart, an idyll melodrama within the mind, a story, a tale long told by many in different ways, but with, if you will, the same aim or plot. It satisfies our hearts and minds and gives us a safe-place we can go to create and live without interruption the ideals which beset our hearts and minds we crave to become reality

Romance is a romantic sentimental, idealistic, picturesque, and quixotic notion of a poetic visionary adventure of the mind and heart borne between two people in a relationship with time as the keeper and preserver. There are no bounds for romance, the two people or the one set their bounds or live and love in a boundless way with the risk and mystery they choose to venture therein.

Romance is a tender Shangri-La of our needs, desires; a driving passion that wishes to be free and not caged within us; still, it is a separate being that wants to live and be free to express itself and to be understood by the recipient. As time and maturity come, so does the true meaning of romance and being romantic. Like a child, romance starts as a small seed and grows to full maturity into a beautiful blossoming Rose. The husband and wife can cherish and admire their Shangri-La for the extravagance and elegance it brings into their life as it did to Simone' and Roberto' in this novel. It, like Simone's legacy passed on from generation to generation, became a recognizable trait in the Bandaci, Giovanni, Moretti, Meriwether, and Madison families, especially in the 1900's at the turn of the century and events which followed their lives over the years.

Romance is a bathetic experience that permeates the minds and hearts of the male and female. It is an immersing flood of endless needs and desires. Some allow it to live free without bounds; some cage it and set bounds. Roberto' allowed his romantic desires of self to live free and boundless; contra wise, Simone' under duress, caged her romantic desires because of fear. At the end, though belatedly, she removed the bars of the cage and set it free to live and blossom. Her seeds of romantic desires, like a bird in a cage, when the bars of fear were gone, took flight and blossom in the end into a beautiful Rose of many colors. Like a waterfall that refreshes, her love and romantic warmth and intrigue refreshed the heart of her husband and gave their lives a new beginning of true passion linking them completely for the first time. Roberto' and Simone' walked side-by-side demonstrating and living the romantic ideals of their marriage for the remainder of their lives.

Time is a true preserver of romance. Neither years nor age can kill our need for romance in our life. It, like the soul that lives within us, is an eternal, youthful and thriving being.... waiting to live, why not let it?

In life, there are times, situations, actions taken, when decisions made has an impact on our future at a higher degree than can be imagined especially decisions made by inexperienced innocent young adults, who only see the "now" in front of them. Simone' Noelle Angelu'cia Giovanni fits this description as a fourteen years old girl living in a small close-knit farming community surrounded by Wine Kings in the Tuscan Valley in Italy early 1900's. The dilemma she faced mostly was innocence and inexperience.

The Vegetable Farmers and Wine Kings were the most prominent families in the Tuscan Valley in the early 1900's.

Simone' Angelu'cia Giovanni was 14 years old when she met Vincenzo' Alessandro Moretti 17 years old. They became friends. In the process of time, they became more than friends, lovers.

As Simone' approached her maturing years her Father Franco, chose Roberto' Man 'son Bandaci, son of a vegetable farmer, as a husband for her. Franco Giovanni, and Roberto Bandaci Sr., agreed that Roberto', Jr would be a good match as a husband for Simone' and Simone' would make a good wife for Roberto'. This became a binding agreement between the Bandaci and Giovanni families that would stand if both parents were alive at the time Roberto' and

Simone' came of age. The agreement would be void, if either of the two men were not alive when they became of age. Neither Roberto' nor Simone' knew of the agreement, it was not the proper time to discuss marriage they were both too young, especially Simone'. The Giovanni and Bandaci families were two of the wealthiest vegetable farmers in the valley.

Tragedy struck the year Roberto' turned 19 years of age. Roberto's Father died from Pneumonia because of exposure after getting wet during a heavy rain at the age of 69. Francesca', Roberto's Mother heartbroken, died six months later, at the age of 64.

Therefore, the agreement with Roberto's parents could not stand, but Franco was determined that Simone' would marry Roberto' as it had been planned. The choice of a husband according to the Italian custom was not one that Simone' could make, even though at that time she wanted Vincenzo'.

Roberto' soon to be 21 years old, on market day, July 1905 met and fell in love at the first sight of Simone' Angelu'cia Giovanni. That moment in time began a journey that lasted through three generations of Bandaci women. She was pretty, small, with long black hair that fell in curly locks down her back, and she looked fragile as china. Her long legs and hauntingly mysteriously, sexy watery eyes, gave Simone' an exquisite, otherworldly look to Roberto'. He had to make her his. Her love to Roberto' would be like the spring of the year, when Mother Nature comes alive and everything is new; it would be a new beginning to Roberto'. Simone' became an obsession with Roberto'. They were, in Roberto's mind, simpatico.

Roberto', having a romantic nature made him a formidable suitor. He courted her in the way that a Tuscan Gentleman does his future bride. The evening walks to their favorite hill overlooking the valley after Roberto's long days on his farm, the fresh flower bouquets he bought from the market, and quiet dinners at the local restaurant, were romantic to Simone'. Roberto's sweet disposition gave him a charm that Simone' could not resist; she was overwhelmed by his mannerism, she respected him, and cared for Roberto' it was hard not to care for him. He was so kind and loving to Simone'.

On the contrary, even with all the care and respect she had for Roberto', Simone' loved Vincenzo'. The farmers in the community, as phrased by the wine kings of the little valley were "not in their class." The Moretti family's winery produced the finest wines in the Tuscan Valley. Though the Giovanni's did well financially, they and the Moretti's were not in the same social class. To the Moretti family the farmers were beneath their class; therefore, no marriage would take place with someone from the farming community. To the wine kings of the Tuscan Valley only the farmer's vegetables were good enough for them. A farmer's daughter married to a wine king was out of the question! With this custom looming in front of them, Simone' and Vincenzo' kept their friendship a secret from both their families. Roberto' determined to make Simone' his, asked her Father for Simone's hand, in marriage. Franco told Roberto' that he and his Father made a marriage arrangement when they were younger. Roberto' saw this as an act of fate. With this revelation, Roberto' knew that he had Simone's parents on his side. He expressed his love for Simone' and the desire to have her as his wife. Franco knew that fate was with him and God had answered his prayers. Franco gave Roberto' his permission to marry his daughter.

A date was set for the wedding, October 13, 1905.

However, Simone', even with the marriage date approaching continued to see Vincenzo'; they rendezvoused once a week, until the time Simone' was married. They had been passionate lovers only three times during those years of friendship. Neither Vincenzo' nor Simone' could get those nights of passion out of their minds, especially Vincenzo'. Simone' was a fever to Vincenzo', one he did not want to cure.

Simone', met Vincenzo', for one last time October 10, 1905, before she married Roberto' three days later October 13, 1905. So much life had happened to Simone' to be so young and inexperienced, but yet, she was experienced in matters of the heart, she thought!

The bond that Simone' and Vincenzo' formed in the three years they were together could not be easily broken. Later in life, both would regret their earlier actions that caused more hurt and pain to their families that became hard to endure.

The journey of life started at 14 years of age, would take Simone' and her family into a maze of pain, heartache, and separation because of choices in love and decisions made while she was young and inexperienced even to the decisions made after her marriage to protect her family. She found herself in an endless vortex, a downward spiral laced with fear because of the fervent love she had for her family; she felt trapped like a bird in a cage. These decisions were almost detrimental to her daughter and her husband whom she loved with all her soul. Instead of protecting those she loved, her decisions had painful consequences rather than healing remedies.

The influencing actions and devastating circumstances all surrounded and involved one woman, who wore a veil of mystery, even to her Father.

As Simone' looked back over her life and the mistakes she made in love, especially, in her choices, in relations to the heart, and becoming a Mother before she was 20 years of age, never dreamed it would have such a profound outcome on her family.

Even with her running away to America, her past mistakes and Vincenzo' both followed her. Her life would become a nightmare of secrets, deceit, half-truths, and blackmail from someone she thought she once loved. Her Legacy to her daughter Carmeli'ta' and great grandchildren, especially her great granddaughter greatly influenced the decisions years later about life and love.

In her Diary Simone' wrote of her journey through infatuation, the love affair with Vincenzo', heartache, marriage, unbridled passion, desire, and finally true love. Her Diary would bring her family full circle and especially affect her great-granddaughter who would inherit her name. The Legacy of the way she lived her life and, the way she loved, the raging passions that burned within her, and especially the decisions she made causing huge amounts of pain was unintentionally passed on to her daughter and great granddaughter; would be the legacy they inherited from her.

Decisions we make in life in an effort to protect those we love will adversely cause more pain and heartache than protecting those we love especially, if secrets and fear are in the mix overshadowing the ability for truth to be the healing factor. In the decisions, Simone' made to protect the ones she loved, created a false sense of security for her and her family. Keeping secrets are usually detrimental to those we love and those who touch our lives and those who our lives touch.

Simone's decisions caused pain and heartache for her husband, daughter, parents, and friends; and at the end of the day, her. The mental pain and guilt she bore since her marriage to Roberto' took its toll.

Simone' never imagined that her decisions would take her on a journey of secrets, pain, and heartache. The legacy of a 17 years old naïve girl begins in the Farming Community in Tuscany! There were many colures to Simone's personality resembling a rainbow. Like the Rainbow, the world around her was painted with both beauty and mystery. Comparable to the Rainbow, the beginning, and end of which she is depth was unsearchable as it was deep.

Finally, Vincenzo' declaration of love for Simone' had become a Yesterday's Timepiece. As she matured into adulthood, realized she had passions, desires, and values that far descend a 14 years old girl's understanding of love. With Roberto', she had true unconditional love. Her desires and passions were true, strong, and focused. She had the feelings of a mature woman desperately in love with her husband. She lived each day, first, for her God and Savior and then, for her husband and daughter. They were her life. Vincenzo' was like a misplaced page in a book; she had replaced his page in her life with a page with smooth edges and that fit opposed to the one she tore from her life with clichéd edges. He was a misfit, a man out of time and space there was no room for his page in her life anymore, but like a bad penny, he kept turning up.

Her decision to run away from Vincenzo' to America did not take her far enough from her dilemma neither did her decision to run away from Roberto' back to Tuscany where it all begin twenty-four years earlier when she met Vincenzo' Alessandro' Moretti. Can Simone' began again!

Loved by two men, Simone' was torn by her love for one and to her fear of underserved retribution by the other...her love for one became the dictum for her actions and decisions made in life after marriage and then motherhood. Though her avowal, of faithfulness to herself first, her husband and child stood strong, that avowal suffered blows along the way. Life gets complex when trying to protect your loved ones from hurt and pain, as it did for Simone'. Vincenzo' added one last step to her ladder of life she did not seem to be able to climb above, the last step, near tragedy caused the ladder to finally break, falling to pieces as her life seemed to before her eyes. The journey begins...

CHAPTER

ONE

Roberto' Man 'son and Simone' Angelu'cia Giovanni Bandaci emigrated from Italy to the United States the year 1911 when great influxes of immigrants were coming to America settled in South Carolina for Roberto' to continue in the trade he loved, farming.

At the turn of the century, South Carolina was a rich, fertile area in the Southeastern United States in the early 1900's.

Roberto's cousin Amelio' Bandaci, had come to America a few years before, on the RMS Lusitania in 1906, soon after Carmeli'ta' was born. He wrote Roberto' that, South Carolina was a good place to farm any types of vegetables and encouraged him for five years to come to America, then bursting with prosperity with the Industrial Age appearing with the growth of a new country.

Roberto' and Amelio' were two brothers' sons. They only had one son each and no other children. Roberto' and Amelio' were close; their relationship was more that of brothers than cousins. They loved each other dearly and were best friends that spanned a lifetime.

Before immigrating to America, in the little valley, Roberto' and Simone' made their living by raising vegetables and selling them to the local markets in the beautiful city of Tuscany and other surrounding cities. The luscious hills and valleys of Tuscany's Farming Community sat against the eastern sky resembling a picture painted hanging in a beautiful frame. The greenery that surrounded the city, like the beauty of the sea, leant its splendor each day to the farming community. The hidden Tuscan Valley, with its grandeur, made its home at the foot of the Apennine Mountains. The mountains were a rock of dependence and hope like a Mother, poured riches into the soil yielding the farmers bountiful produce each year. The richness of the little valley was not its grapes or its vegetables, which of course gave them bountiful booty but the noticeable riches were the closeness, devotion, love, respect, support, and care the people of this farming community had for each other.

The Tuscany Wine Country surrounded the farming community. The beauty of the vines loaded with grapes supported by stands gave a three-dimensional look to the valley and wine country like stairs were being climbed all set against the mountains; a look that no artist could capture on canvas. The beauty of Tuscany's cultivated hills and animated elegance with blue mist rising over the mountains captured the heart and drew you close like a lover. A smoky haze hung over the farming community and Wine Country, giving the farms the appearance of being suspended in the clouds. The wine country was not mingled with the farms; like the people, the vineyards stood above the farmers; they were in two different social classes.

Roberto' and Simone' often took walks while courting to the hillside to enjoy the beauty and magnificence that graced their eyes.

The cottages that sit above and below the fields lined the skyline. The white embellished cottages like diamonds in the rough with flowers planted in window boxes stood against the skyline as if to guard the peaceful little valley.

Roberto' fields, each year, produced Petroselinum (Curly-leaved Parsley), Fluted Costoluto Genovese Tomatoes, Locanda Delia Valle Nuova (found in most foods in Italy), Tropeana Lunga Onion, Listada de Gandia, Purple Top Milan-Heirloom Turnips, Chioggia Beets, and Firoi di Zucca. Roberto' and Simone' Bandaci did well financially in their hometown of Tuscany during the first five years of their marriage.

Roberto was born in in Tuscany December 24, 1885, to Roberto' Man'son Bandaci, Sr. and Francesca Elena Bandaci, an only child. Roberto', Jr. was born when Francesca was 45 years old and Roberto' Sr. was 49. Roberto' and Francesca tried for years to have children; unfortunately, Francesca miscarried three times before she was able to carry her only child to full term. Francesca called Roberto Jr. her little miracle because he was born on Christmas Eve.

As Roberto' grew, Francesca noticed he was a sweet, considerate, loving, humble, loyal, devoted, hardworking, grounded, respectful, and a kind child. He was strong, muscular built like his Father Roberto', Sr. They both loved their son and gave him the best they could in life. Roberto', Jr. worked hard on his family's farm and learned from his Father the art of farming and raising vegetables. He was astute in his studies in school as well. His parents added to his educational background the English language.

His cousin Amelio' Bandaci was born October 26, 1881, to his father's brother and sister-in-law Ernesto Franz Bandaci and Aryanna Contessa Bandaci. His parents noticed he was quiet, but deliberate in everything he did even as a small child. He was aware of his surroundings at all times. His father watched Amelio' become mature in mind and actions before he became a teenager. As a child he was strong, handsome, and had a pleasant smile on his face endearing him to everyone he met. He and his cousin Roberto' as they grew become closer than brothers rather than cousins they were best friends. Theirs became a lifetime relationship and bond that was never broken. Amelio', a few years ahead of Roberto' in age, parents added the English Language to his educational background also. Amelio' quick and astute in his studies, graduated from high school when he was 16 years of age.

Simone' Angelu'cia Giovanni was born in Tuscany March 6, 1888, to Franco Luigi Giovanni and Catarina Elena Giovanni. Simone' was an only child. Her parents were farmers as most families were in Tuscany.

When Simone' was three months old, her Father Franco noticed that she had mysteriously watery beautiful eyes that were framed by her long eyelashes. She had an ethereal look about her. The long keen nose that refined her face as if it has been sculptured, her black almond-shaped eyes so deep in her head, with a perfect heart-shaped mouth gave her an otherworldly look. She was a quiet child growing up she always had a look of being in deep thought.

Lots of mystery surrounded her, which worried her Father and Mother. Franco knew that his beautiful daughter had a dark side to her. To Franco, Simone' was elusive and quizzical, with enchantingly mystery-filled eyes. He noticed that she displayed a deep-seated passion for any task that he gave her, part of the mystery to her personality, which frightened Franco for his daughter.

He knew her thoughts ran much deeper than an ordinary child's thoughts.

Simone' was sensitive and attached to her parents; she loved being home on her Father's farm where she felt safe and loved. Franco would soon realize his daughter, as she grew, had deep personal strength and resilience, a capable person. With the stamina and persistence, she portrayed as a child, he knew that she would be even more of a mystery as an adult. Franco and Catarina kept these things in their heart as they watched their daughter become a young woman. At the age of 14, she became more enigmatic and indefinable.

Simone' Mother raised her to observe decorum and respectability a young woman should have in dress, mannerisms, and speech. They taught her Italian, as well as the English language. She had all the necessary qualities of a Lady. Simone' learned well; her bent of mind, far-reaching, absorbed her training like a sponge, but there were still those mysteriously watery beautiful eyes she had her Father could not understand.

As they pondered the idea of moving to America, Roberto' naturally, was a little unsure about the move to a strange country. At that point, Roberto' and Simone' thought only of the opportunity their daughter would have in America rather than being a farmers' wife, which is how most families made their living. Roberto' and Simone's reasons and concerns for and about their daughter's future were at different ends of the spectrum of life. With fears of the unknown nagging at them, Roberto' and his wife of 6 years and their 5 years old daughter, Carmeli'ta', packed their belongings after getting approval from the American and Italian Embassies, came to America and settled in Charleston, South Carolina near his cousin Amelio'.

Roberto' and Simone' were young and had time to start over. Roberto' six years later is 26 years of age and Simone' is 22 years of age. Roberto's parents left him the farm when they were both gone to Heaven. Roberto' sold the farm and all his possessions when he decided to live in America.

Roberto' decision to leave his home and farm in the little Tuscan Valley and move to South Carolina was based on Amelio's promise that he would help him get his farm going and get on his feet financially. Even though Roberto' was not a poor man; he had done well in Tuscany, but would need Amelio's assistance in raising vegetables in a new country and getting use to the culture there, especially in South Carolina a posh southern society with people entrenched in culture passed down hundreds of years.

Roberto's sale of his farm increased his wealth. Therefore, money was not a real issue, only starting over. Amelio' built his farm and business into a successful enterprise. He supplied all the people and restaurants in suburban Charleston and in other surrounding cities. The large-scale vegetable business had become more than his ability to supply from his farm. He thought of his cousin Roberto', knowing that between the two farms they could supply the needs of the citizens especially citizens that lived in the city of Charleston and those who did not have gardens.

Amelio' purchased two hundred acres of land and a house for Roberto' three months before he arrived. He cultivated the land and prepared it for planting. This effort would put Roberto' ahead and lay the foundation for a successful start. After Roberto' and his family's arrived in America, Roberto' and Amelio' worked to get Roberto's fields planted with vegetables. While Roberto' waited for his first year's crop, he helped Amelio' on his farm.

Leading up to the time that the vegetables would be ready for harvest, Roberto' called on the citizens of Charleston, restaurants, and grocery stores and secured their business. As Roberto' secured contracts from the citizen of the city of Charleston; of the families on his list of clients he would deliver fresh produce too, were, the Madison's and Meriwether's. They were the two most prominent families in Charleston employing the greatest number of people in the Madison Iron and Steel Mill, and Meriwether Textile Plants.

Simone' worked equally as hard to make their little nine-room house into a comfortable home and get Carmeli'ta' prepared for entering school the next year. The first year they moved to America, Carmeli'ta' was too young to attend school, Roberto' and Simone' continued their daughter studies at home writing, reading, spelling, arithmetic, and the English language. Simone' added to her training etiquette, which was always an important part of a young lady's training, which Catarina, her Mother, expressed over the years to Simone' as she grew.

In September 1912, when she was 6 years old, Carmeli'ta' entered Charleston Elementary School setting her feet on a path and journey that would enrich her life, as well as cause her an enormous amount of pain and heartache. Like the heat from a low burning coals over the years, the heartaches and pain grew unnoticed until it burst into a large flame that burned out of control.

Therefore, the mystery and heartaches begins ...

CHAPTER

Two

Roberto' just turning 20 years old when his father died, June 1904 within six months of his father's death, January 1905, his mother died also. Roberto' mother told him before she died he needed a wife and should consider one of the local girls in the Tuscany farm community since she nor his father would be there to guide his choice of a wife.

Roberto' six months later, at 20 old, met Simone' on Market Day, a warm Thursday morning in July 1905. When he saw her, he fell in love with Simone' Angelu'cia Giovanni, 17 years of age. Simone' 5'7" tall with long legs, long black curly hair, beautiful almond shaped eyes, small, contoured body, and a peaches and cream look to her skin was captivating with a look of intrigue about her that Roberto' could not resist. She was the most beautiful young woman he had seen in their community. He could not take his eyes off her. Roberto' inquired of his neighbors about her family and found that she was the only child of Franco and Catarina Giovanni. At that time, he did not know she was chosen, years before, by his Father, Roberto' Bandaci, Sr. to be his bride and he had been chosen by her Father to be her husband.

Roberto' soon found, after his talk with Franco, Simone's Father, chose her years before to be his bride.

Simone's parents, farmers as well, this fact, Roberto' thought, "It will give Simone' and me a common bond for our marriage and one which we can build a life on together."

Roberto' and Simone' had a short courtship before they were married. (Simone' did not have a choice of who she married, her Father chose Roberto' for her because he was successful and his daughter would have a home and security after he and her Mother were gone.) Simone' did not love Roberto', but was in love with a local executive, who ran his family's business in Tuscany; they met secretly and neither of their parents knew.

Years prior, summer of 1902, Simone' met Vincenzo' Alessandro Moretti when she was 14 and he was 17. He was a twin who missed his sister. When they met he told Simone' he had a twin sister he lost years before. They met and spent time together every day they could find time away from their families. After three years, Vincenzo' became an executive of his family's wine business. Vincenzo' loved and wanted Simone'. However, he would never get his parent's approval to marry Simone'. Simone' was as not in their social class. His parents had chosen another young woman to be his wife.

Vincenzo' Alessandro Moretti and Valantina Teresa Moretti, identical twins, were born May 26, 1885, to Francisco Paolo Moretti and Concetta Lu'cia Moretti. Valantina and Vincenzo' were close as they grew; but Valantina was not as strong as a growing child should be. Vincenzo' was protective of his sister and loved her with all his heart. As he grew, he was a handsome child with black curly hair. Valantina had beautiful long black hair with locks that fell around her face and shoulders, she was proud to have Vincenzo' as a brother. They went everywhere together. However, tragedy struck early in Vincenzo's young life when he was 10 years old. It seemed as if he tried to replace Valantina with Simone'.

Choosing in life is hard. Simone' was loved by Vincenzo' and Roberto' but only one could have her for his wife. She would marry Roberto'.

Roberto' loved Simone' from first sight of her in July 1905; four months later in October 1905, Simone' 17 and Roberto' 21, were married in the Church of the Saints, a community church, located near his vegetable farm. Roberto's thoughts of Simone' as they courted for the few short months were, not only did he want a wife, but he also wanted Simone' for her mind, intelligence, beauty, body, and long legs that never seemed to quit and her mysteriously fluid eyes beneath those long eye lashes.

Her smile moved something in Roberto' that he could not explain. Simone' had that woman scent, captivating, inviting, and alluring. Roberto' unable to fight his feelings could not resist falling in love with her. Being in love with a beautiful woman was a renewal to him of spirit and heart; giving him a new outlook on life; he would not be alone any longer; she became his world, and his passion. To see a life with Simone' as his wife was all that he could ever want. Simone' was everything he hoped for in a woman and a wife and she was even much more than even he could explain to himself.

Roberto' driven by the passion to live and be successful so he could provide for his beautiful wife was the only thing on his mind. This yearning to provide the best for Simone' became a driving force behind his very being and every decision he made. The only thing that confused and baffled Roberto' was her mysteriously haunting eyes that lived behind long, beautiful lashes which held her eyes like a picture in a frame. All of his hopes lay in those beautiful eyes and captivating smile he thought she had only for him.

After being told by her Father of the marriage arrangement to Roberto', Simone' struggled with telling Vincenzo' her Father had chosen a husband for her to marry, a local farmer. Vincenzo' angry and heart-broken she was marrying, knew that he would not have the chance now to convince his parents to agree to a marriage between him and Simone' now she was being married to another.

The bond that Simone' and Vincenzo' formed in the three years they were together could not be easily broken. Simone' and Vincenzo' later in life would regret their earlier actions that caused more hurt and pain to their families than either could bear. Simone' continued to see Vincenzo' until she married Roberto'. They met once a week. Over the years of friendship, they had only been passionate lovers three times. Neither Vincenzo' nor Simone' could get those nights out of their minds. Simone', met Vincenzo', for one last time October 10, 1905, before she married Roberto' three days later October 13, 1905. The last meeting that Vincenzo' and Simone' had was more than emotional.

The loss of each other was a regret that weighed heavily on both as they clung to each other and kissed in front of the little cabin by the lake one last time before Simone' become a wife and she would then be out of Vincenzo's reach. She would no longer be his, not freely. As they kissed, the passions and love they felt for each other, like amnesia, took away their reasoning. They forgot themselves for a few hours failing this one time to take the usual precautions.

Simone's love for Vincenzo' over-shadowed the fact that she had been promised to another man she did not love, not in the way she loved Vincenzo'. The night and the atmosphere that surrounded their last intimate meeting were more than either could resist. The moon shine, the smell of lavender radiating from Simone's beautiful hair, cool breeze blowing softly off the lake, the taste of her kiss on his lips like fine wine warmed over a flame before it is drank, was irresistible. Her kisses were an aphrodisiac to Vincenzo'.

Vincenzo' held on to Simone' as they stood looking at the reflection of the moon dancing on the water. The kisses tore at their hearts. Vincenzo' pulled Simone' down next to him on the cool soft blanket of grass that lay on the floor of the valley; they made love as they had never before. Simone' loved Vincenzo' with a passion that flowed like a stream from a mountain, this stream of passion swept Vincenzo' away. He could not get enough of Simone'. He felt they could not be separated, their bodies had become one; even with the closeness that was there between them, he wanted more of her; he could not get close enough to her and could not hold her tight enough. He felt as if she was melting away and each time he held her closer.

The passion Vincenzo' felt for Simone' took him to a place within himself that he never knew existed. He knew at that moment in time Simone' was his life, his heartbeat, his being; she had become part of his soul. They loved each other, in the little hideaway by the lake, until their juices of passion drained them emotionally and physically.

Later that evening Simone' walked away from heartbroken Vincenzo' not looking back as he made a desperate plea for her not to marry another. Simone' heard the terrible wounds of pain in his voice as he called her name. She had to prepare for her wedding taking place in three days.

There was, as is the custom in Tuscany, a swirl of activities preparing for the wedding. As the preparations were made, Simone' knew she did not love Roberto' she was fond of him. He was kind, caring, strong, tall, handsome with an unruly curly lock of hair black as a raven tickling his forehead at all times and expressive brownish black captivating eyes.

Simone' respected Roberto' as everyone did in Tuscany. He was intelligent, quiet, and astute in business and above all, a Gentleman. He reminded Simone' of her Father, who was a Gentleman; this quality she loved in him.

At last, the wedding day arrived. Simone's bedroom felt like a gust of wind blew at full force for two hours non-stop as her Mother, and other women of the Farming Community fussed over the beautiful bride. The women slowly dressed Simone' to become Roberto's bride. While they dressed her, she looked out the window into the Moretti Vineyard and with pains of regret looming as large as the vineyard.

The traditional colors in dress for weddings in the community for the Bride and Groom were white and black giving the bride and groom a clean simple, but elegant look.

Simone' finally dressed, Catarina dabbed on 1905 Detaille Cologne.

Catarina left for the church, with other women, of the community. She needed to arrive ahead of Simone' and her Father to check with Richelieu about the music for the ceremony. Richelieu, a violinist, a member of the Tuscany farm community, was the leader of a violinist group. Richelieu & Company provided music for all community events and functions. Richelieu was an expert violinist coaxing heavenly sounding music from his Violin and any other musical instrument.

Simone' and her Father, waited at home for the Bridal Carriage that transports all brides to the Church. While they waited, Franco Giovanni thought of his conversation with Roberto' regarding his daughter's future.

Franco talked with Roberto' the night before the wedding day, as the Fathers of the brides did with the grooms. Roberto' assured Franco he would take care of Simone'. He expressed to him his care and desire for his daughter. His love had grown during their four months of courtship. Franco Giovanni knew he was honest in his sayings. He had known Roberto' from birth and watched him as a child grow into a responsible young man. He knew his parents his father Roberto', Sr., and his brother Ernesto, his cousin Amelio's father, two of his best friends. They provided a good home and raised Roberto' in a loving environment Franco knew he had not, in all of the twenty-one years of knowing Roberto' ever seen or was told of him straying from his parent's teachings. These facts alone ensured him of a successful future for his daughter with a husband who already loved and cherished her.

The bridal carriage finally arrived. Aldo Lombardi and his two beautiful white horses with long tails with hair that had a full fan look and well-groomed neck manes flowing to their left side pulled the White Wedding Carriage decorated with Red Roses looked charming as it pulled up in front of the Giovanni's home.

At last, thought, Franco "The carriage has arrived." Knocking at her bedroom door he said, "Simone', my beautiful daughter, the Bridal Carriage is here, are you ready?"

"Yes Father I am ready." Franco opened the door stood for a moment looking at his beautiful Simone' for the last time as a child in his home stood for a moment and looked at the lovely bride he saw before him, she looked like a beautiful doll. He remembered the day she was born he thought she looked like a baby doll, so fragile and pretty.

Simone' had waited in her bedroom, as instructed by her Mother, until the carriage arrived, so her dress would be in perfect condition when she arrived at the church.

Franco held the tail of the gown and the train as he escorted his daughter to the carriage. Aldo helped Simone' into the carriage and seated her. Franco carefully laid the tail of the gown and train on the floor of the carriage, and entered the carriage on the opposite side.

As the carriage moved slowly towards the little Community Church fifteen minutes away, the prancing of the horse's hooves made a comfortable musical sound. Simone' and her Father had their last Father Daughter talk before she became a bride.

Franco spoke his heart to his lovely daughter, "Simone' my adorable daughter, there is not a better, and more honorable and moral man in Tuscany's farming community than Roberto 'Man' son Bandaci, Jr. He will never hurt you or break your heart. He will always care for you. His Mother and Father, bless them, raised him to be the man he is today. They would be proud of their son, the man he has become, and the husband he will become to you today and always. I am glad that he loves you Simone'. I know I can trust him with your heart my lovely daughter. I also want you to remember your Mother and I love you; you can always come home to us. I want happiness for you. It is hard for me, but I know that I have to let you go. You are a young woman now. It is time you find a future apart from your mother and me. We have held you close these years. You were mysteriously quiet as you grew that about you worried me you my daughter. Remember that I love you always, unconditionally."

"Yes, my Father, I know you love me and want the best for me. I love you and Mother with all my heart. I know that you chose Roberto' Bandaci for me because he is humble, kind, and will be a good husband. I care about Roberto' and I am fond of him. I do not love him, not yet my Father."

"Simone', love is love. Passion is not always there in the beginning; it was not for me when I married your Mother; not the true passion that I feel now. Love, like a quiet breeze blows gently across your life alike the breeze it is cooling, satisfying, and enduring. When you have feelings of unrestrained passion with your spouse consider yourself among the blessed. You are still young my daughter and can easily mistake passion for love, when it is not. Unless there is more between two people than just physical intimacy, you know then it is not love. Passion has its season in a relationship; but like a season; it passes. True passion grows out of love, afterwards settles down into a mature true relationship that is a satisfying, joyful and becomes more the desire to be with that person, to be near them, see them, and talks to them. It grows my daughter into pure ecstasy. I have this with your Mother, my Catarina. I consider myself blessed my daughter, to have known passion, desire and pure joy being married to the most wonderful woman in the world. It is something that stays fresh in your mind always daughter. I want that for you Simone' and you will have it with Roberto' but it takes time and true love from the heart and care. Give yourself time my daughter. Roberto' is a good man and has this kind of true love and passion for you, he told me."

He continued, "Sometimes in life we start without love, but if there is a deep abiding care and respect for a person, eventually love will grow out of the relationship as time passes as the man and woman work to make a life and future together. You will have that with Roberto' my darling. He is the type of man that is easy to love."

"I know my Father. He is kind and gentle with me, always thoughtful and considerate. I will be a good wife to my new husband."

"Your willingness is all anyone can ask my obedient daughter, time will take care of the rest", added Franco.

Franco knew that his good-natured, polite, and gregarious daughter would be a humble wife and good companion to Roberto'. Franco hurt inside because his Simone', in that moment of time between his home and her marriage vows at the Alter, was a child for the last time.

Last times are hard in life and full of regret. Our lives are full of bags of last times. Simone's wedding day was one of those last times. Simone's

Father dreaded this day as he held his sweet daughter. The carriage moved slowly toward the church, for one last time, before she became a married woman. It was breaking his heart to give away his only child, his precious baby girl who he loved with all his being, wanting the best for her in life, knew he had to let her go and give her to another who loved her as well.

Franco thanked God for Roberto' and then praying he could quiet whatever raged in his Simone'; he was not sure what it was at that time, but her Mother Catarina quiets the rages that lives in him.

CHAPTER

THREE

Roberto' and Amelio' arrived at the Community Church at 10:00 a.m.

It was a cool crisp morning his wedding day, October 13, 1905. The wedding was at 12:00 Noon. The day to Roberto' seemed brighter than usual. He felt a happiness that he had lost after his parents died the year before; now he had a new outlook on life with Simone' as his bride-to-be.

Roberto' and Amelio' dressed in the room prepared for the Groom and his Best Man. Roberto' looked handsome in his suit, a black fashionable suit with the long coat, matching vest, and suit pants. His shirt, a white tuxedo style front, with a high collar; a black bow tie looked neat on his collar matched the color of his suit. He wore black and Mother of pearl colored cuff links giving a rich look to his appearance, his Black High Top Italian shoes were made of the finest Tuscan leather. Makalu', the shoe carpenter, shined Roberto's shoes until he could see his reflection in them.

Amelio's suit was like Roberto's; they looked refined. Finally ready. At the cue of the Violin, Roberto' and Amelio' walked out the door and up to the Alter and stood to the left of the Minister.

While Roberto' waited for his bride to appear his thoughts went to his Father and Mother, "I wish you were here to see my lovely bride Father and Mother. She is everything in a woman and wife I have always wanted. You would be proud of your and my choice of a wife for me. You raised me well and I know that you both are here in spirit with me today. I love you and miss you. After today, I will not be alone anymore Father; that was a concern of yours before you died. Amelio' has always helped me since you have gone to be with God. He is the faithful cousin as he has always been. He is my Best Man today, Father; he is standing in for you. I know that he misses his Father and Mother, as I do you".

The horse drawn Bridal Carriage arrived with Simone' in front of the little Community Church, as it did with every beautiful bride in the Tuscany Farm Community.

As Simone' appeared in the foyer of the Church, Richelieu and his group of Violinist played Here Comes the Bride. The guest rose in honor of their picturesque bride.

Simone' looked stunning as she walked up to the door that led into the sanctuary in the Church, on her Father's arm. She wore an extravagant white, long-sleeved gown with lace covering the sleeves and bodice; the matching white lace bridal veil extended down her back to the waist of her gown. The gown generously adorned with lovely, scalloped lace embellished with heart shaped circles on the gown and on the train, gave Simone', as she walked, the appearance of a floating white sea. The lace fell evenly on both sides of her gown allowing her adorable white satin shoes to play peek-a-boo at the tip of the front of her gown. Her black hair sparkled like a diamond-garnished ornament, through the lace eyelets in her veil. Her gloves were made of the heart shaped eyelet lace matching her gown. She held a bouquet of White Camellias dressed in black leaves enhanced with black and white ribbon. Chantilly' the local Flower shop made the bouquet especially for her wedding.

Simone' looked at Roberto' standing, waiting, saw him in a different way today for the first time as she walked on her Father's arm down the aisle toward her future husband.

Simone' knew that Roberto' was handsome. She thought, "He is 6'5" tall, slim, masculine, with a wide chest, and a neat waistline. His skin has a honey color tan to it, a little deeper than my color, but he works in the sun. His black curly hair is always neat and well groomed, even when I see him right after work or on Market days. The unruly lock of hair that falls on his forehead adds precision to his well-shaped masculine face. He is any girl's dream in a husband. He is witty, fun, humble, successful, and respected. He is sensible in business, has a liveliness of mind, and highly esteemed in the Tuscan Farming

Community. I could not ask for more, in a husband. I like the way he holds me. He is so sweet to me. He always has a smile on his face whenever he sees me."

Simone' was very fond of Roberto', she respected him, they had fun together, enjoyed the same things in life, but she did not fall in love with him, not then, not that day, their wedding day.

Simone' was the most exquisite bride that Tuscany Farm Community had seen in twenty-years.

At the Alter, Roberto' stood with his cousin and best man Amelio' watched as Simone' walked slowly down the aisle towards him; his entire being was overcome with emotions. His love for her grew even stronger at that moment. He was still in a daze at being married to one of the most striking young women in Tuscany. He felt that he had found a treasure, a gem of great value. She was as the Ruby Ring to him his Father gave his mother years before, precious. Roberto's mother had given him her treasurable gem. He kept the Ruby Ring, with the intentions of giving it to his wife.

Roberto' thought, "I could not have chosen a more suitable woman for a bride, than Simone'. She is loved by all, beautiful, kind, caring, outgoing, intelligent, hard-working, and innocent."

Simone' reached the alter Roberto' took her right hand extended to him by her Father their custom. Roberto' continued to hold her hand; they knelt before the Minister of the little Church of the Saints and after they took their marriage vows, they exchanged the simple gold wedding bands chosen by Franco and Roberto' purchased at the local jeweler. Roberto' removed the white laced glove from Simone's left hand and place the gold band on her third finger of her left hand; Simone' placed Roberto's wedding band on his third finger on his left finger. The Minister pronounced them man and wife. Roberto smiling, helped Simone' stand lifted her veil kissed her sweetly and softly on the lips whispered, "Simone', my Simone'." The guest applauded and cheered as the Minister introduced Mr. and Mrs. Roberto' Man 'son Bandaci, Jr.

After the ceremony, as is the custom in Tuscany Farm Community, there was dancing, food, and music in celebration of a charming ceremony and fine start to a long fruitful marriage. The entire farming village celebrated two of Tuscany's favorite young adults, Roberto' and Simone'; the esprit de corps shown by them for the community as they grew into young adulthood was spoken of often among the citizens.

The honeymoon cottage preparation for the bride and groom was an event in the community.

Roberto' borrowed his cousin Amelio's country cottage for thehoneymoon night. Their farms were next to each other.

Amelio' lived in a cottage on the other side of his farm two miles from Roberto's home. It was a beautiful white six-room cottage nestled in a wooded area a quarter of a mile away on a little hill overlooking his vegetable fields. The wooded area hugged and snuggled the cottage as a mother does her children. Amelio' and Roberto' exchanged homes for three days and nights. Amelio' would look after both farms while Roberto' was on his honeymoon.

Simone's Mother and the women of the village prepared the cottage for the wedding night as they do for all brides in the community. Roberto' felt fortunate to have Amelio', three years older than he willing to allow him to use his home, a quiet hideaway to take his beautiful new bride to consummate their marriage and love.

Roberto' and Simone' arrived at the cottage in their beautiful horse drawn carriage, just as the sun was saying goodbye for another day; the night softly and sweetly like the drop of a feather, welcomed the bride and groom into its hidden place where secrets are made by lovers. The farming community following behind cheered as they got out of the carriage to begin their life together as man and wife.

Richelieu and his String Quartet played and sang 'Ave Maria,' a beautiful song a favorite loved and chosen by Simone' and Roberto' for the end of the wedding day. As the song ended, the crowd cheered again. At the last cheer, Simone' threw her bridal bouquet.

Franco and Catarina kissed their daughter and her new husband bye; Amelio' hugged and kissed them both; the three of them stepped into the bridal carriage, as parents of the bride and groom to take the traditional ride home. Roberto' and Simone' stood on the porch, of the little cottage, waving goodbye until the bridal carriage and the wedding party was out of sight. It was getting late in the evening, the sun was just peeking above the dark cloud that hovered, in front, of it.

Roberto' and Simone' watched as the red in the sky turned a dark greyish color then black. The scenes in the sky were the ones watched by them many evenings during walks all through their courtship the few short months before their wedding.

Holding his beautiful wife's hand as the evening breeze began to have a nippy feel in it, moved closer and put his arms around her shoulders to keep away the chill. Roberto' ready to carry his bride into their honeymoon suite, pulled her close kissed her before they went inside, said, "Simone' you are the most striking bride I have ever seen!"

"Thank you Roberto' you are kind."

Roberto' holding Simone' close, tenderly picked her up and carried her across the threshold into their three days and three nights love nest.

He noticed as he picked her up, that she was quiet. She smiled up at him with her beautiful and hauntingly mysteriously watery eyes put her arms around his neck, snuggled her head under his chin as he stepped over the threshold. Her beauty had captured his heart and mind; he could not see anything else about her except her loveliness, sweetness, delicacy, and look of innocence.

Flowers delightfully decorated the Master Bedroom. White eyelet lace bejeweled the bed and chairs. The heat from the fireplace yielded a warm, toasty, comfortable, inviting feel to the room for the lovers on that cool October evening in 1905. The bed was prepared for the young lover's first night. The comforter turned down, they could see garnishing the yellow sheets, and pillows, on the bed, and on the floor, Red Rose Petals of all sizes and shapes. The flickering flames from the lamp light and the flames from the Fireplace intertwining like lovers danced like ballerinas. The room's colorful energy cast shadows of mystery in their surroundings adding life and romance to the atmosphere already laced with the captivating smell of fresh Roses.

Roberto' put Simone' gently down on the bed, sitting down at her side, laid her back put his right arm around her waist, his left hand under her head kissed her gently whispered in her ear, "Simone' you are beautiful. I thank God you are mine. I need you to make my life complete, to make me complete. I want your love. I need your love."

Simone' kissed Roberto', the taste of Strawberry on her lips was sweet and invitingly satisfying. Roberto' eyes searched her face; he could not take his eyes off his lovely bride. She was all his now and no one else's.

Simone' closed her eyes as Roberto' kissed her more and more. His kisses were more passionate each time. He slowly unbuttoned the back of her wedding gown one button at a time and slipped it off her. Slipping her garters off, removed her stocking one leg at a time and finally her corset lying on her waist like skin. He loosens the hooks on her bra and let it drop to the floor and then her lace panty. The scent of her 1905 Detaille Cologne, as he removed her lingerie drifted slowly into his nostrils. Roberto' searching eyes, for the first time, saw the beauty of Simone's small shapely gorgeous mocha colored body.

Eyes continuing to search, saw her long legs, her beautiful breast, like identical twins, sit firmly on her chest; her perfect small hands with long fingers; her small feet; her long neck like an ivory tower and above it her two small ears. Appearance of mystery danced in her almond shaped eyes as she looked up at Roberto' he saw her kissable lovely heart shaped mouth and long keen nose giving her face a look of perfection. The beauty of her entire being was breathtaking. He knew she would be beautiful, but she was far beyond what he imagined. She was sexy, erotic, sensual, dazzling, with the woman scent he could not resist and she was all his!

Simone' ravished Roberto's heart with her beauty, sexiness, and sensuality like a tasty morsel of food, was spellbinding. Looking up at Roberto' smiled slowly returning his passionate kisses. She could taste the passion and desire on his lips. The taste of mint on his tongue was irresistible and sweet.

Roberto' felt the passion in her kisses as his right hand began to explore every inch of her body; slowly he explored, touched, caressed, and discovered his beautiful wife, while holding her until his desire reached fever pitch. Holding her tenderly, he caressed her body and kissed her with long demanding passionate kisses. His kisses said to her what words could not express, of his love, need, and desire for her.

Her body relaxing finally gave in to the passion she felt at the touch of Roberto's hand; the feel of his hand awaken the secret raging passion she holds so closely inside of her. The sweet taste of his lips, the scent of mint on his warm breath as he kissed her forehead, eyes, face, cheeks, and neck, she wanted him to love her. His face close to her, Simone' softly, sweetly kissed her husband; her body responded to his touch and the intense demands of his body as it entered hers; she made love to Roberto'.

Roberto' was not experienced in this area of his life but he knew how he felt; and the way that Simone' felt as a woman, the softness of her skin, the smooth cool feeling her body made him forget that he had no experience in making love to a woman. His body responded to her sweet innocence as they made love. Roberto' closed his eye letting the cravings Simone' made him feel engulf and consume his entire being.

Each time Roberto's body entered hers; the way that his body felt to Simone' awaken the rage even more that lived inside of her. She wanted more of him. Her body kept reaching up to Roberto's for more, until the level of passion he bought her too frightened her. She wanted to love Roberto' with unrestrained hunger, but could not because of the fear that she felt that rippled through her heart and mind like fire.

The level of intimacy that passed between them their wedding night Roberto' could not find words for it could only be felt and not described.

After a while of quiet, Roberto' looked into Simone's eyes, saw an expression of fright, and saw silent tears running down each side of her face. He thought he had hurt her, held her so gently said, "Simone' I never want to hurt you in any way, especially intimately. I love you so. I want you. I have never felt pleasure like I felt being with you tonight. You make me feel a hunger I never knew lived in me. My heart is full of love for you my beautiful wife. I will love you and care for you forever. All I want to do is make you happy as you have made me tonight. I love you Simone' pass my heart and mind; you are part of me. My love and need for you is similar to a string attached from my heart to yours, if cut, I feel I will not survive. Do you understand what I mean?"

"Yes Roberto' my new husband, I understand." As Simone' said this she snuggled closer to Roberto' as a frightened child would their Mother for protection. Simone' lips on Roberto's neck, whispered, "Hold me tight; please hold me tight!"

Roberto' pulled her close to him put his strong muscular arms around her. He held her close to his chest where his heartbeat was slow and strong with the love he had for his wife. Both fell into a peaceful sleep as the fragrance and a mixture of Simone's cologne, the woman scent, with the aroma of their passion floating up from her small body into Roberto's nostrils.

After a while Roberto' awaken franticly calling her name, dreamed Simone' had left him she was never his. His movement and the sound of his voice he cried out, "Simone' please don't leave me. I love you", awaken her. Simone' held him' close said, "I am here Roberto'! It was only a dream. I am here! I will not leave you!" Roberto' held on to his Simone' pulling her closer to him.

A few minutes later, Simone' turned from Roberto's arms lay on her stomach, looking into her husband's eyes pushed back the unruly black curly lock of hair that even lying down, always danced on his forehead. She ran her hand through his hair, her hand moving slowly, carefully, downward tracing his cheeks, nose, and mouth with her fore fingers. Gently she explored Roberto's body, her hand feeling the hair on his broad strong chest, the tightness of his arm muscles, his neat stomach and waistline, his tight thighs, and buttocks until Roberto' felt as if he were afloat and would explode with the desire she made him feel as she touched every inch of his body.

Her touch raised him to higher and higher levels of passion. The warmth of her touch was magic to his skin; his body trembled and ached from the way it made him feel. Nibbling on his neck, cheek and nose, her mouth found his, kissed him intensely until she was unable to control the rage within her, wanted him to touch her, and make love to her repeatedly.

Her body cried out for his touch, until Roberto' was unable to control his desire, at the same time not wanting to control his desire, he made love to Simone' with fury and depth until they were both exhausted and out-of-breath.

Simone' still had not given him all of her, yet.

Roberto' with passion and emotion in his voice said, "Simone', my beautiful Simone', what I feel when we make love is beyond words my darling. I want you more and more. I want to feel the touch of your hands, your sweet lips kissing me, and your warm sexy body next to mine. I could not bear for you not to make love to me. I need you!" Kissing Roberto' softly on his chest, "I will always be there for you when you need me. I will never refuse you my body or my love. You make me feel so deeply. It is a wonderful feeling."

Roberto', overcome with emotion at Simone's words, knowing that he could please his wife, pulled Simone' closer to him until there was no air between them, held her tight, and kissed her until night turned into day again. The night had passed unnoticed while they made love and discovered each other's bodies, needs, wants, passions, and desires.

Roberto' whispered, "There is a something enchanting about our love; it is hard to explain. I feel like I am in a trance needing you to love me more. I cannot get enough of your body, my darling, your entire being."

He knew that his beautiful wife had deeper passion than he reached on their wedding night thought, "In time, I will know that unreached passion that lies within her. I want to know. I need to know. I need to feel everything about her. I want to know the whole of her; all the intensities of her passion."

Simone' did not comment only held on to Roberto' pulled him even closer once again aroused his passion for her, as he made love to her in the early dawn of the morning, his body, with precision invaded hers over and over again; it gave him a renewed appetite. It was something about the way she felt that he could not describe to himself; he just knew he wanted to be near her for the rest of his life.

Finally, in the grey dawn of morning, the lovers fell into a deep satisfying sleep. They slept until noon after a passionate wedding night. For three days and night, they loved and discovered each other. They laughed, walked, swam in the pond near Amelio's cottage, prepared meals together, ate, and snuggled in blankets by the fireplace on chilly evenings and nights.

The wedding night was a budding of two hearts and bodies that would bond the lovers together in a love that would last for a lifetime through all the struggles and heartaches that came with it.

The last night approached of the honeymoon for Tuscany's Farming Community two favorite young people, Roberto' still afloat with the joy and ecstasy he felt having Simone', his dreams had come true; she was his wife.

Sitting quietly, with closed eyes, echoes of her words resounded in his mind of the past three days as romantic scenes danced before him warming his heart thought, "The warmth and tenderness of her heart is home to me. No one can leave their home; it is a safe haven, a place to go where there is love, care, and acceptance. The warmth of her heart would be the foundation we will build our home, life, and love upon."

Roberto' held Simone' naked body close to his, sitting beneath a blanket in front of the Fireplace watching the last embers sputter, twinkle, and shimmer, let the blanket fall from their shoulders turned and hugged Simone'.

She said, "You are quiet tonight. Is there something wrong? You can tell me."

Roberto' had been in deep thought as he sat with his lovely bride looked at her smiling reached for her right hand kissed it slipping his mother's Ruby Ring on her finger. Simone' speechless, because of the emotions flooding her as the twinkling light from the Fireplace captured the sparkling beauty of the ring said, "Roberto' this is beautiful, where did you get it?" He replied, "It is my mother's Ruby Ring. My Father gave it to her many years ago. I want you to have it Simone' as a further symbol of my love for you. It means so much to me because it is all that I have left of my mother. I loved her with all my heart."

He continuing, "So no, my lovely wife there is nothing wrong. You make me happy Simone' you are adorable in every way. I wanted this ring to say how much I love you. You are to me O' Sole Mio."

"I am happy to know that I am your Sunshine. You are so sweet and kind to me. I will treasure this ring and wear it always."

Looking at her for a long-time eyes searching her face after a while said, "I have made this covenant with my heart my beautiful wife, I am glad that you are so young. That will give us many years to love and time to enjoy each other. I want to live and love you forever. What you make me feel is beyond my ability to express with words. You are young and beautiful my darling. Your love to me is like breathing fresh air. I do not ever want to know what it feels like to be without you, the breath of fresh air in my life. Your love is what keeps me knowing you are mine and you love me only. I know that you do not love me as I do you now, but I know you will, in time, love me, as I love you. I chose you Simone' even before I knew our parents arranged our marriage years ago. After my parents died, which made the arrangement void, I still wanted you. The first time I saw you in the Market, I fell in love with you even before your Father told me that you were the wife my Father had chosen for me."

"What are you trying to tell me, Roberto?" He responded, "I did not marry you because of an arrangement. I married you because I fell in love with you. You are the joy and sunshine in my life Simone', not just your enchanting body, which is ahead of and beyond joy, my beauty, but you the person makes me complete as a man."

Roberto' paused then continued, "I want to know that you are there for me at end of each workday. I want to know you are there when I go the sleep at night; there when I wake in the morning; there when I want to talk about my hard days; there for me when things on the farm will not go right; then again, my darling knowing you are there; just simply there."

"You make me so happy with your words. I will be all those things for you. I do want to make you happy."

"You married me Simone' that made me happy. I want to walk with you, hold you, talk with you, and feel your presence in the room, even, when I am not near you. I told you our wedding night your love to me is a string tied from my heart to yours if cut, I do not think I would survive. What I told you tonight of how I feel is what I meant. I want you to know your love is as precious as the Ruby Ring on your finger. My mother told me all my growing years according to the Bible: *He that findeth a wife findeth a good thing, and receiveth favor from the Lord, Proverbs 18:22*. I know that I have found a good wife Simone'. I love you for this simple fact among the many fine characteristics that makes you who you are."

Roberto' thought deeply how to tell his wife how he felt and how he saw her as his wife. He knew the scripture well, loved the Song of Songs Chapter 7:1-9. He said, "This is how I feel Simone' my beautiful wife". As they sat, he looked into her eyes and quoted these verses to her:

How beautiful your sandaled feet,
O prince's daughter!
Your graceful legs are like jewels,
the work of an artisan's hand.
Your navel is a rounded goblet that never lacks blended wine.
Your waist is a mound of wheat encircled by lilies.
Your breasts are like two fawns, twins of a gazelle.
Your neck is like an ivory tower.
Your eyes are the pools of Hebron by the gate of Bath Rabbim
Your nose is like the tower of Lebanon looking toward Damascus.
Your head crowns you like Mount Carmel
Your hair is like royal tapestry, the king is held captive by its tresses.
How beautiful you are how pleasing.

O love, with your delights!
Your statue is like that of the palm, and your breasts like cluster of fruit.
I said, "I will climb the palm tree;
I will take hold of its fruit"
May your breasts be like the clusters of the vine,
the fragrance of your breath like apples,
and your mouth like the best wine.

Simone' quietly listening intently to her husband as he quoted the verse of the beautiful Song of Solomon to her, did not say anything just smiled snuggling closer to him. His strong naked body as it touched hers felt captivating. His hands, strong, firm, demanding, held her, as if he would never let her go.

With the deeply felt love that Roberto' had for his beautiful wife, he wanted to spend the last night in their quiet hide-a-way making love, enjoying the beauty of her body, glad for the bond formed between them as husband and wife.

Roberto' took Simone' in his arms held her close once again, said, "Love me my darling, love me. I want to feel everything about you. I will always need you, make love to me. You are like a dayspring to my heart my darling, so refreshing and sweet. Love me Simone'. I need your love so much."

She heard the passion and plea for love in his voice, which touched her heart to her very soul. Smiling at Roberto' as the last flame of fire died in the fireplace her kissing and nibbling on his bottom lip ignited the flame of passion. To Roberto' the look in Simone's eyes was more mysterious and enchanting than ever and had an otherworldly appearance to them. Her warm moist lips were exciting, tantalizingly, and enticing as she kissed his eyes, checks, neck, and chest lit burning flames of desire in him. Roberto felt intense delight as he lay back on the floor pulling Simone' gently down on him felt the silkiness of her body caressed her triggering his longing until his entire body was on fire. Roberto' made love to Simone' repeatedly; the pleasure he felt at the response of her body to his need, put him in a daze.

In the quiet still of the night he whispered, "I love you. I never dreamed that love and intimacy would be so wonderful with you. I find so much pleasure being with you in every way."

He heard the soft faintly whispered, "Thank you my sweet husband; I find pleasure in your love, you make me feel wonderful."

Love and romance floated in the air leaving a taste of pleasure an aroma that would linger unendingly; these moments of impact begin the bonds in their hearts and minds; a bond that would be lasting, with a hold as strong as death. A love Roberto knew he would never be able to let go. She possessed his heart. Oneness of a woman and man is not easy to understand. He knew someday she would love him as he does her.

Experiencing first times and moments, those indelibly etched in your memory, as a brand burned into flesh, it remains for a lifetime. The first time with Simone' was one of those times. The vows they took were serious to Roberto', giving his heart away, he gave his life away. To him there was no distinguishing between the two.

As the last spark in the fireplace finally died, Roberto' rose, helped Simone' to her feet, lifted her and carried her to their bed, gently lay her down, and lay beside her, pulling her to him their bodies became interwoven. Wrapped in each other's arms in a world of passion and desire lit a flame that would burn hotter and brighter as the years passed before them. At that moment in time, they created a world with their love only the first-time intimate yearnings of a man and his wife could welcome and understand.

Roberto' and Simone' awaken early the morning of October 17, 1905, packed, and prepared to leave their private hideaway. They felt as if they were in a fantasy world with the intimacy that had passed between them with secrets levels of love and passion that exists only between a husband and wife. Simone's father arrived at 1:00 p.m. as planned and took them to Roberto's home two miles away.

Roberto' and Simone' honeymoon was a beautiful time in their life they would never forget; they would talk of their honeymoon and courtship many times over the years of their marriage and it would ultimately remind Roberto' of the love that he had for Simone' and would start the healing of his heart in the later years of their marriage.

CHAPTER

Four

Two months after Simone' married Roberto' she noticed that she was gaining weight around her waist thought it was because she was happy and eating well each day with her new husband. While preparing breakfast the morning of December 20, 1905, she felt a dizzy sickness. Simone' did not tell Roberto', before he left for work she felt sick. Young and frightened after breakfast, went to her parent's home told her Mother her feelings and commented, "Mother I am gaining weight especially around my waist and I felt dizzy and sick this morning what do you think it is?"

Her Mother, smiling told her. "Simone' my lovely young daughter you are going to have a little one."

"A little one mama, what does that mean?"

"A baby Simone', we have talked before about women having children."

"I just got married Mother; it is too soon. I know nothing about having a baby or being a Mother."

"When a man and woman are intimate in their marriage my daughter having a child from that love is a natural thing. You will learn being a Mother comes naturally to as you carry your child even more so, after the baby is born."

"This is wonderful news for your Father and me our only child having a child."

"What will I tell Roberto'. He will be angry with me Mother; It is so soon?"

"Of course, he won't be my sweet precious daughter, angry about what? Tell him he is going to be a Father. I will tell Franco when he comes home tonight he will be pleased."

Simone' left her Mother returned home and nervously waited for Roberto' to come. She just knew he would be angry her having a baby so soon after they were married. She prepared a nice dinner for Roberto' his favorite, Veal cutlets with Au jus, sliced tomatoes, green beans with red peppers, Olive Oil sautéed potatoes with Parsley, and fresh baked bread. Simone' was a wonderful cook; Mothers in the farm community taught their daughter the art of cooking at an early age.

Roberto' arrived home at 5:00 p.m. He looked forward to seeing his

beautiful wife each day. Simone' always bathed and dressed for dinner to greet Roberto'. He loved the smell of her 1905 Detaille Cologne and the fresh look she had when he arrived home.

The kitchen door opened and Roberto 'walked in, smiled at Simone' and said, "Hello my beautiful bride. How was your day?"

She walked to Roberto' reached up and put her arms around his neck

pushed back the unruly lock of hair said, "I had a good day. I visited my Mother today for a while, did some of the farm errands, and returned home to prepare dinner. I made your favorite dinner tonight."

"My favorite dinner my beauty, you are very kind and thoughtful of what I want."

"I want to please you and make you happy Roberto'."

Roberto' kissed Simone hugged her tight said, "You make me happy my beauty, more each day that you are mine."

He walked over to the kitchen sink, washed his hands, and returned to the table and sit at the well-decorated table each evening for dinner, said, "I am ready for my favorite dinner. I am hungry and it smells delicious."

Simone' smiled and served Roberto' his dinner. As they ate, they chatted about his day. After dinner, she cleared the table standing near the kitchen sink turned and said, "Roberto' I have some news to tell you."

Looking at Simone' smiled, "News? Yes, I am listening tell me the news my lovely wife."

Hesitating, Simone' quietly said, "I have noticed that I have gotten a little larger since we have been married my husband."

Roberto' smiled and said, "My beauty is gaining weight is that what you are worried about? You are beautiful and I have not noticed. You look lovelier than ever in the last few weeks my beauty. Your hair glows and so does your already beautiful skin. I would love you even if you were not petite any more my beauty so don't worry about a few pounds we will walk more if that will ease your mind."

Simone' looking worried said, "I am getting larger my husband. I am going to have a baby. I was sick this morning before and after you left. I visited my mother and told her about how I felt. She said I was going to have a little one."

Roberto' leaped up crossed the room gently hugged his lovely Simone' held her tight kissed her passionately; this was good news to Roberto' in his mind a baby further consummated their love; he loved Simone' even more. Simone' held on to Roberto' because she was frightened at the idea of first being pregnant, then second becoming a Mother, and lastly them becoming parents, which neither of these things, she nor Roberto' knew nothing about.

"I am frightened Roberto', I don't know anything about babies"

"Simone' my precious wife, I will take care of you and your Mother is near us. You will be fine; I will see to your comfort. You will not come to the farm to help me any longer I want you to rest and take care of yourself."

Simone' went to their farm on Monday, Tuesday, and Wednesdays and helped their workers prepare vegetables for the Thursday, December 22, 1905, Market day. On Friday's she did errands for the farm.

"I feel fine Roberto'. I can still come to help you or be there with you. I am strong" She insisted.

"No, my lovely wife, I will take care of the farm and I get someone to cook and do the housework for you my darling Simone'. I will ask Amelio' if he knows of a good housekeeper to clean and cook for us. I love you my beauty, I cannot bear for anything to happen to you." "Yes Roberto' I will do as you say. Thank you. You are good to me." "I would do anything for you Simone'.

I would give my life for you. Your news today has made me an even happier man. I am going to be a Father. I look forward to watching you each month as our baby grows my beautiful wife, fat no, beautiful, yes."

"Thank you for being happy about the baby and for saying that you love me even if I get fat because I am carrying a baby."

"I love you my darling wife don't worry you will always be beautiful to me."

Simone' smiled at her husband. Even though she respected and cared

about Roberto' never said to him "I love you!"

On Thursday, December 22, 1905, Market Day, Simone' met Vincenzo' at in their special place. Simone' told Vincenzo' she was going to have a baby. Vincenzo' picked up Simone' whirling her around. He thought the baby was his. They had been together the month Simone' and Robert' were married. Simone' told him, "No Vincenzo', the baby is Roberto's."

Vincenzo' was not convinced; he would not believe the baby she was carrying was not his. A baby would be proof of the love and passion he and Simone' felt for each other. Vincenzo' was single-minded when it came to Simone'. She walked away from Vincenzo' with doubt as to who the Father was after his statement to her that, he could be the Father as well; immediately, the wall of fear begin to build within her. The possibility of Vincenzo' being the father had not entered into her mind but...?

Simone' went through a metamorphosis in the three months after

marriage. She was no more the girl not understanding her drives, desires and feeling but had become a woman with a different level of passion bought to the surface by Roberto' her husband. She began to understand herself more with each month that the child she carried grew in her womb...not knowing this birth would bring into her and Roberto's life joy and pain all living within the same emotional universe.

Simone' was even more beautiful to Roberto' as she carried his child. She had a glow to her that Roberto' loved. Her pregnancy gave her beautiful black hair a look of blue luster. Roberto' and Simone' decided on a name for their baby; if a girl her name would be Carmeli'ta' Noelle Angelu'cia Bandaci; if a male his name would be Michelangelo De Pasquale Bandaci.

Carmeli'ta' Noelle Angelu'cia Bandaci was born a week early, August 5, 1906, one of the happiest days in Roberto' and Simone's life.

Carmeli'ta' was a beautiful baby. She was 21 inches long, weighted 5lbs, an olive brown color to her skin, and a head full of curly black hair. She looked like a baby doll lying in her crib in the nursery, Roberto' could barely contain his excitement. She was so small and precious to Roberto' and Simone'.

Roberto' thought he loved Simone' as much as possible until he saw the beautiful daughter Simone' have given him; he loved her ever more than he could possibly explain.

Roberto' was overcome with such pride and joy tears flowed as he held Simone' close to him and said tearfully, "I love you my darling Simone', I adore you, you have given me the greatest gift of love that a woman can give her husband besides herself, a beautiful child that was born from our love. She is so like you my beautiful wife. I think she will be tall like you and very tiny."

This statement made Simone' cry, tears rolled down her beautiful face. She held tight to Roberto' said, "Thank you my kind husband you are sweet to me thank you."

Franco and Catarina, when visiting them at Tuscany Valley Memorial Hospital Simone' was holding Carmeli'ta' when they arrive, when seeing their granddaughter for the first time exclaimed, "Simone' she looks exactly like you did when you were born our daughter. There is no difference in the way she looks and the way you looked, she is the same length and weight you were this is so amazing."

Roberto' smiled and said, "Thank you Franco and Catarina she is beautiful like her mother. I could not be prouder of my daughter and I love my sweet wife even more for the beautiful gift she has given me. I feel very blessed."

Tears flowed from Simone's eyes in gratitude for having a loving husband and supportive parents that both loved her.

As Carmeli'ta' grew and the years passed and Roberto' and Simone' with Amelio', coaxing, decided to move to American sold their farm, March 1, 1911. During these five years before they moved to America, Vincenzo' would see Carmeli'ta' whenever he could. He and Simone' argued each time about

Carmeli'ta' and who was her Father. Vincenzo' loved Carmeli'ta' when he saw her, she was his little angel. Vincenzo' loved Simone' even more because she gave him a beautiful daughter, which came from their love, he thought.

Simone' told Vincenzo', she would be moving to America with her husband and daughter. Vincenzo' became angry with Simone' because he wanted to be close to his daughter and not have her come to America most certainly not have another man claim her and raise her as his daughter.

Vincenzo' said, "Simone', I lost my Valentina; I cannot bear another loss of someone I love so much. You and Carmeli'ta' are being snatched away from me how am I to bear this pain and loss?"

Simone' begged, "Vincenzo', please we have discussed this over and over, Carmeli'ta' is not your daughter, and she is Roberto's daughter. Please let it go for both our sakes."

Though uncertain about who the father was of her beautiful daughter she stood on her conviction to Vincenzo' that Carmeli'ta' was Roberto's daughter and not his.

Vincenzo' insisted, "No, Simone', I will not let it go, this is not the end. I will follow you and my daughter to the ends of the world. Tell me you know for sure that Carmeli'ta' is not my daughter."

Her heart beating out of control, "I will not discuss that with you Vincenzo' it is useless."

"You are not sure Simone', if you were you would say it with more conviction. I know you Simone' the look that you have on your face tells me you are not sure who is the Father, your husband Roberto' or me."

"Goodbye Vincenzo'."

Simone' walked away from Vincenzo' and did not look back. She could not bear to look back, her heart, like Vincenzo's, was breaking because they had to part forever. She would have to see him once more before they left; she now loved him as a friend and did not want to lose his friendship. Simone' knew that it would be hard for her to shift gears in a sense, because she was leaving all the life that she knows and a man who loved her would be staying behind. She would be leaving with the man she married and cared for and the husband who loved her.

Simone' became a "mixed" bag of feelings as she walked away from Vincenzo'. She was happy in one sense that they were moving to America; but, then again, it made her sad as well. Doubt hung in the atmosphere as thick as the early morning fog that hung over their little valley; blurred her vision in reference to the possibility that her husband was not the Father of their daughter.

Their leaving Tuscany would be somewhat of a relief because she would not have to see Vincenzo'. Little did Simone' know that Vincenzo' would not let her leaving Tuscany stop him; distance in love is but a short walk across the street when you truly love someone, as he loved her.

Simone' was heartbroken when Roberto' told her his decision after they discussed moving to another country. However, she could not give him a sound reason for them not to leave Tuscany so their daughter would have a better chance at a life she chose rather than have it chosen for her.

CHAPTER

FIVE

The Mauretania scheduled to sail for America, June 11, 1911, Roberto' purchased the tickets and gave Simone' the date they would sail in two months.

Simone' knew she needed to get the opportunity to see Vincenzo' before she left and tell him she was leaving for America in eight weeks. Simone' and Vincenzo' met for the last time on Thursday, April 19, 1911, market day for the village to tell him they would sail on June 11. All the husbands went to market day to sell their produce; the wives who had children stayed home. Simone' left Carmeli'ta' with her housekeeper and cook, Rosetta. Thursday was the day Simone' took care of some of the errands for their home. Roberto' would be gone until 10:00 p.m. that night when the market closed.

Simone' and Vincenzo' argued their last meeting before she boarded ship. Simone' said once again "Vincenzo', for the last time, Carmeli'ta' is Roberto' and my daughter."

Vincenzo' insisted, "No Simone' you know she is my daughter, your silence affirms my suspicions that you are not sure. How can you take her and break my heart? I am losing you and her both at the same time, this is unbearable to me."

"Vincenzo' we have enough pain to live with why make it more difficult? You and I would have never been married your parents made that clear enough. I am not good enough for your family remember," said Simone'.

"You are good enough for me. I am the one that loves you Simone' have you forgotten the passion we felt the first time we made love in the cabin by the little Lake in my Father's vineyard?" he asked.

"Vincenzo' I have to leave. There is much preparation for me to attend to for the trip to America; I cannot see you again", replied Simone'.

Vincenzo' called after Simone' as she walked away, "Simone', please don't leave me. I love you. I need you. I want you in my life."

Simone' with tears in her eyes and overcome with regret ran to get away from him and the pain she was feeling not seeing him again was causing and his insisting that Carmeli'ta' was his and not Roberto's.

Vincenzo' had seen Carmeli'ta' when she was born in the hospital. He had fallen in love with who he thought was his beautiful baby girl. Simone' had begged him not to come to hospital again her husband; Father or Mother might see him.

Vincenzo' said, "Your husband, Father and Mother have never met me; they would not know who I am."

"But they know who you are Vincenzo', everyone in Tuscany knows the Moretti family", she said.

"I will not come here again, if you promise to allow me to see my Carmeli'ta'."

Two weeks before sailing, at the last meeting, May 25, 1911, Simone' and Vincenzo' had said a reluctant goodbye Vincenzo' clung to Simone' with passion and regret.

Vincenzo' begged Simone', "Please let me love you before you go."

"No, Vincenzo' the price would be too high to pay. Vincenzo', please, let me quietly leave don't make this harder for us than it already is, and I am married now, you know that." Vincenzo' with tears in his eyes still clinging to Simone' said, "I will not say goodbye I will see you again."

"We cannot Vincenzo' and I will not", said Simone'. "It would be too dangerous and we promised each other never to make love again before I was married and now that I am married, it is not possible"

"You insisted on me making that promise Simone', I did not. You do not love him. You made me promise, I did not want to promise; because the promise did not come from my heart; I only promised we would not make love again to please you."

"I do care about Roberto' Vincenzo'." "We have a daughter; I cannot hurt my child." Vincenzo' retorted, "this is not the end of it for me Simone'. Kiss me once more!"

"No Vincenzo' It only makes it harder, I have to leave we are sailing in two weeks. I will not get a chance to see you again after today. I have to make final preparations for leaving."

Simone' heard a dangerous sound in Vincenzo's voice and noticed a different mannerism she had not known in him. She felt the chill of his words as a threat like sharp arrows pierced her mind and heart. She knew somehow that Vincenzo' could make her life difficult. She was glad to be leaving knowing that she still cared for him, she thought, yet the sound of his voice instilled fear in her.

Simone' and Vincenzo' parted with their futures unsettled in reference to their relationship. Two weeks later, Simone', Roberto' and Carmeli'ta' boarded the Mauretania, June 11, 1911, and sailed for America arriving two weeks later after leaving Tuscany. Roberto' made sure that his wife and child was comfortable. They had a nice comfortable cabin onboard ship. Roberto' had noticed for months now that Simone' did not seemed happy, her eyes seemed to Roberto' as if she were hiding something. It worried Roberto' but he kept silent; he loved her so desperately.

They arrived in New York, Friday June 24, 1911, and traveled on to Charleston by bus, arriving there June 26, 1911. After arriving to Charleston, and getting settled in, the first year Roberto' did well with Amelio' advising him on what vegetables to raise and which ones would sell in the markets in Charleston. Roberto' raised Turnips, Beets, Parsley, Tomatoes, Sweet Potatoes, and Italian Green Beans, not much different from the vegetables he raised on his farm in Tuscany.

In the process of time, other families from Italy moved to South Carolina the Italian community grew. Carmeli'ta', a beautiful little girl with long ponytails on each side and a smile that melted her father and mother's hearts was a happy child with a delightful personality. She grew up on their farm and played with the other children in the community especially two close friend Alberto' Gambani and April Chambers. Alberto' family's 150-acre livestock farm was next to the Bandaci's; they raised basically cows, chickens, and horses on one side of the farm and watermelons on the other half.

April's parents owned the local grocery store. Carmeli'ta', April and Alberto' were together a lot during their growing years as well as through high school. Carmeli'ta' was a happy lovely child in every way. However, abroad tension in relationships heated up with Germany, hints of war was dancing on the horizon. In spite of the War tension taking place abroad, the Bandaci's did well during these turbulent years with raising and supplying food to local and neighboring communities.

In 1914, as the war progressed and the years grew longer, food was in short supply, with the bulk of it shipped overseas to feed the American troops and other neighboring allies, this fact increased the demand for food from the Bandaci's farms, thereby increasing the wealth of both Roberto' and Amelio' and other families.

Roberto' wanted more of an education opportunity for their daughter, more than they had, so she would not have to work the land as they did. Simone' wanted choices for her daughter in matters of the heart. Both parents got what they wanted for their daughter; success came at a higher price neither imagined they would have to pay. As the war raged in Europe, there was a war raging below the surface in the unseen shadows in the Bandaci family.

Carmeli'ta', April and Alberto' graduated when they were 16 years old from Charleston High School in June 1921. Carmeli'ta' attended Charleston Business School for a certificate in Office Management and Secretarial Science. Alberto' attended four years at North Carolina College, in Raleigh. He majored in Business so he could eventually run his family's farm; he worked in the summer months on his Father's farm. April chose to leave home and attended Anderson College in the next city. April was gone for four years and was only at home for the summers. April, Carmeli'ta' and Alberto stayed close friends through the years. But as they matured, Alberto' loved Carmeli'ta' as a friend, but he always felt a tingling in his stomach when she was near. Conversely, his feelings for April was only friendship, though he lover her dearly.

Alberto during the summer spent time with Carmelita and slowly he stopped seeing her as his best friend, which she still was but also as a woman; a beautiful woman and he slowly fell in love with Carmeli'ta'. Nevertheless, he knew that their families would not approve of his marrying her before he finished college, so he kept his love hid from everyone, including, Carmeli'ta'.

Carmeli'ta' spent eighteen months working hard and studying Office Management and Secretarial Science. She graduated with honors when she was eighteen years old in October 1922.

CHAPTER
SIX

Carmeli'ta' Noelle Angelu'cia Bandaci applied for a job at Madison Steel and Iron Works, one of the oldest and largest businesses in Charleston. Her success in getting a position so quickly surprised her. Hired from a pool of twenty applicants; she would be Jason Madison, Jr. Assistant; CEO and owner of Madison Steel and Iron Works Manufacturing. Carmeli'ta's boss, impressed with her hired her for both her ability and amazing beauty. Carmeli'ta' like her Mother, was beautiful with long black hair, amazingly sexy and mysterious eyes. Long legs seem to run in her family; her Mother had long legs, like eternity, they never quit.

Carmeli'ta' was accustomed to hearing her Father tell her Mother he

married her for long beautiful legs and long luscious black hair. However, Carmeli'ta' always noticed that her Mother said very little when he complimented her, she only slightly smiled, but always a frown came across her forehead and her eyes had the look of pain in them. Carmeli'ta' was not sure what her look meant.

Jason Madison, Sr. came from old Charleston money. His family gained their wealth by starting the only steel manufacturing company in the Charleston area. The Madison family was from South Carolina. They formally owned Madison Lumber and Supply Company before the O'Malley's arrived in America. The O'Malley's shortly after arriving in South Carolina, invested in the Madison Lumber Company, and become equal partners. In the process of time, as the demand for lumber lessen and the demand for steel went up the Madison's, and O'Malley's invested in the growing steel industry, thereby increasing their wealth. Her father solidified the contract by choosing Jason Sr. as a husband. Jason Madison, Sr. married Juanita O'Malley Madison, June 10, 1898.

She was an only child, inherited her family's interest in the business. Jason, Jr. was born March 4, 1902, in Charleston, South Carolina to Jason Madison, Sr. and Juanita O'Malley Madison. The Madison and O'Malley families owned Madison Steel and Iron Works. Moreover, Madison Steel and Iron was borne out of the turn of the century need for iron and steel. The Madison and O'Malley families were "Salt of the Earth" citizens in Charleston.

The Meriwether family owned the Textile Mills in Charleston.

Both Meriwether and Madison families' wealth started in early 1830's. Charles Bienville Meriwether's Father was born May 8, 1855, in Ireland his family migrated to America in 1856, with the remainder of his families' wealth. The Meriwether's, Madison's, and O'Malley lived in the same neighborhood in Charleston and their children all grew up together. Charles Bienville Meriwether, Jr. was born May 10, 1872; Jason Madison Sr. was born January 15, 1871, and Juanita O'Malley was born March 15, 1874.

Charles Bienville Meriwether, Jr. and Juanita O'Malley had grown up together, though he was two years older, thought even as a child, 'she looked like a beautiful picture in a frame.

The Madison, O'Malley, and Meriwether families were not slave owners. They disdained the act of slavery of another human being, hired labor for their companies, thereby adding to the economic wealth of Charleston and surrounding towns and neighborhoods.

Both Madison and O'Malley families had suffered a few loses during and after The War between the States, but had rebounded during reconstruction by being part of the reconstruction era supplying lumber to mills and all construction industries during this period. However, the Meriwether family business, because of the nature of it did not suffer many loses, textiles were a needed commodities.

America was bursting with prosperity in the roaring twenties. The war had ended a few years earlier and America was coming into its own and growing almost overnight. Carmeli'ta' did well; she worked for a CEO of Madison Steel and Iron Works in Charleston.

Jason was pleased to have Carmeli'ta' as his assistant. After a few months of working with Carmeli'ta', Jason realized the abilities

Carmeli'ta' possessed would be an asset to him and his family's business, promoted her to Office Manager. He was her direct supervisor.

Jason's first task for Carmeli'ta' was to hire him a new assistant since he promoted her to Office Manager, one of the many duties she performed, interviewing, and hiring new employees. After the application process, Carmeli'ta' selected ten applicants from a pool of fifty; of the ten, three applicants made the final cut. Carmeli'ta' interviewed all three and chose Daisy Horne.

Daisy Horne graduated from the Charleston School of Business with honors. Ms. Horne was forty-five years old and a widow with one grown son. During a 1916 bombing raid of Germany, flying shrapnel mortally wounded her husband. Carmeli'ta' knew that Ms. Horne would be an excellent assistant for Mr. Madison. She graduated from the same business school that she had few months earlier. Ms. Horne was a polished, efficient, and professional with a pleasant personality. Carmeli'ta' knew she would be a good "fit."

Mrs. Horne's first day was March 15, 1923. After a month working with Mrs. Horne, Jason was pleased with her performance knew that Carmeli'ta' had made a sound decision in hiring her, especially since she seem to have the astute ability through observation in choosing employees that would be an asset to Madison Iron. Carmeli'ta' in this respect was like her mother she could read people.

Jason moved Carmeli'ta' into the office he used the years he served as Vice President while learning the business under his father's guidance. He moved into the President's Suite down the hall from her. Her office spoke to her status in the company and her position of authority. Carmeli'ta' was overwhelmed with the new office and increase in salary she received, but as always remained humble money and position did not change her sweet personality and regard for authority.

Jason, the day he moved her into the Vice President's Suite, said, "Carmeli'ta', I am pleased with your choice of an assistant to fill the position you held in my office. Your decision to hire Mrs. Horne was an excellent choice, you read people well, thank you."

"Thank you Mr. Madison. I like Mrs. Horne; she is efficient", she said. Carmeli'ta' knew she was efficient she was Ms. Horne's supervisor.

Jason over the months, continued to observe Carmeli'ta's people skills. He noticed that the clients his company dealt with preferred Carmeli'ta' assist them with their steel and iron needs. Jason thought, "Carmeli'ta' would be excellent as social Hostess for Madison Iron; yet, I do not know how it will go over with Mother, she is so particular about status."

Juanita Madison is a 120 pounds, 5'6" tall, beautiful woman with tan skin and expressive blue eyes shoulder length Auburn colored hair, with a heartwarming smile, and melodious voice. Her look was one an artist would sculpture. She wore Florida Water for years until Chanel 5 became popular in 1921, which was a more enthralling scent. Jason, Sr. loved this scent on her and so did her son Jason, Jr. He thought his Mother was the most beautiful woman in the world until he met Carmeli'ta'.

On the other hand, Jason thought, "Father is a different story, he would probably embrace the idea of her being Hostess; at least he will be willing to give it a run. I will see." Jason put the idea on the back burner until he found a convenient and opportune time to speak to his parents. When Jason Sr. met Carmeli'ta' for the first time, after watching her was impressed by her beauty, and the business savvy she had and her ability to work with people.

Jason grew fonder of Carmeli'ta' each passing day. After six months, Jason admitted to himself that he was falling in love with Carmeli'ta'. Nonetheless, he played it cool and did not let his feelings be known; but was motivated by his love for her and became more protective of her in the business arena. It was not an immediate feeling, but a slow process as he was around her. Her southern lady-like manners, and the professional way she conducted herself added to the already strong feeling he felt for her.

Jason observed that Carmeli'ta' had a soft kind way about her. All the workers in the plant loved Carmeli'ta'. Any employee issues that surfaced she was the person contacted soon became well respected and loved throughout the plant, even the men on the line in the plant looked forward to her visits twice a week to check with the Quality Control plant supervisor.

CHAPTER
SEVEN

The Madison's, because of their prominence, in Charleston were members of the Charleston Country Club hosted social functions for their business as well as for their personal social life.

Juanita Madison said to Jason, "Son, you need a Hostess for your social functions for the business. I can no longer manage both; handling both has become a burden for me."

Jason thought, "This is the opportunity I needed to get their opinion on asking Carmeli'ta' Noelle Angelu'cia Bandaci to serve as my Hostess."

When Jason considered asking his parents their opinion of Carmeli'ta' as Hostess, did not know how to approach the subject, especially his Mother Juanita, he knew her views on family status in the community.

Jason said to himself, "My Mother is kind and loving, but sometimes she is as hard a nut to crack as Charles Bienville Meriwether." Jason faced the fire bravely.

Sunday, October 20, 1923, Jason asked his parents their opinion of his idea of asking Carmeli'ta' to be Social Hostess for Madison Steel and Iron. After a heated discussion especially on his Mother's part, which he expected, defended his reasons for choosing Carmeli'ta' as Hostess. Jason unwilling to budge on his decision to appoint Carmeli'ta' as Hostess, said, "Carmeli'ta' has a broad business perceptive, she is well-informed and knowledgeable of the day-to-day operations of the business, she as senior management, is liked and respected by the other management staff and employees."

After hours of discussion, Jason won the argument, backed by his Father, who loved Carmeli'ta' and thought she was a gem. Once he had their approval, his Mother suggested he buy her a wardrobe befitting the Madison family's social status showing it as a business expense.

Jason had one difficult client that he was trying to win over to allow him to supply steel for his Textile Mills in Charleston. Charles Bienville Meriwether was the richest man in Charleston. His Father and Mother had come from Ireland during the late 1850's and obtained their wealth in the textile industry. Though he was not an old man, in his late 40's, was a hard nut to crack. Jason's Father had tried for years to get Meriwether to let Madison Steel and Iron be his principle supplier; would only buy shipments from Madison Steel and Iron Works on an as needed basis.

Charles Bienville Meriwether said to Jason Sr. and Jason Jr. when asked about contracts between their companies said, "Madison, I would rather spread the wealth around and not give it all to one company."

Jason Jr. decided to put together a proposal with all the specifications that proved to Mr. Meriwether that buying local would benefit not only both their companies, but the local economy of Charleston. After meeting with Jason, Jr. and hearing the proposal, Meriwether was still not completely convinced.

Later that afternoon, October 22, 1923, arriving home, Jason, Jr. felt as if he had been beaten-up by the meeting with Charles Bienville Meriwether. He came in the door as if he could hardly put one foot ahead of the other.

Jason, Sr. sitting in the den observed Jason, Jr. as he seated himself on the coach and took the iced tea served to him by their cook, Ms. Overton, who had been with them all Jason's life. She was from Clayton, Tennessee. Her parents had moved to Charleston when she was a small girl in the early 1865. She was like a member of their family. She had raised and cared for Jason, especially when he was younger, while his Father and Mother worked to get Madison Steel and Iron Works operating at a profit.

She observed Jason, Jr. and retorted, "Jason, sit up; don't slump. Here, drink your tea; it will help you feel refreshed."

"Yes, Mrs. Overton, thank you", said Jason, Jr.

"How did the meeting with Meriwether go son?" Jason Sr. asked.

"Not well Father, we are still at point zero with Charles Bienville Meriwether!"

His father advised him saying "Son allow Carmeli'ta', Hostess for Madison Steel now, to talk with Meriwether about the proposal."

Jason knowing how he felt about Carmeli'ta' did not want to use that avenue annoyingly, said, "Father, Carmeli'ta' is not a good business match for Mr. Meriwether; she does not have the experience."

Jason Sr. rose, came from behind his desk, and stood face-to-face with Jason. Jason's Father weighed 170 pounds, stood 6'4' tall, slim, with silver, and black peppered hair was a handsome figure of a man. Jason, Jr. was the young image of his Father in every way.

Jason Sr. said in a most adamant tone, "Son, I am not suggesting that you allow Carmeli'ta' to be alone with Charles Bienville Meriwether. What I am suggesting is that you allow her to talk with him as the company's Representative and Hostess about the proposal at the next business or social function you have with your clients, it cannot do any harm. Then again, her talking with him might put the ball in our court."

Jason Jr. frowned looking annoyingly at him said, "Father, I am just not sure, about this."

Jason Sr. looked at his son and asked, "Jason why does my proposal for getting the textile business from Meriwether bother you so? Is there something you would like to share with me?"

"No Father, I just want to protect Carmeli'ta'. However, I will try your suggestion!"

He replied, "I see." He did see. He knew Jason was falling in love with Carmeli'ta', but he did not press the issue any further.

The next morning, Wednesday, October 23, 1923, Jason asked Mrs.

Horne to buzz Carmeli'ta' and check to see if he could come to her office. Mrs. Horne informed Jason she said she was free at that time. Jason walked down the hall to her office and knocked lightly on the door.

Carmeli'ta' opened the door and said, "Good morning Mr. Madison come in, please have a seat."

Jason sit in front of her desk and asked if she would call and invite Mr. Meriwether to their company's annual Thanksgiving banquet and ball, November 7; a few weeks away. While sitting and waiting he observed her professional manner and soft skills when she called Mr. Meriwether's office.

She spoke with his assistant; she put it on his calendar as she did every year. No one in Charleston refused invitations to a Madison's social function.

Jason sat and discussed with Carmeli'ta' his proposal of Madison Steel's official Social Hostess.

He told her, "My parents approved the proposal of my hiring a Hostess for the company's business and social functions. Also, included in this proposal, is a wardrobe at the company's expense." He continued, Carmeli'ta' would you consider serving in this position? Naturally, your salary would increase."

Her breath was taken away by his invitation surprised answered, "I will graciously accept the job assignment as Hostess. Thank you for the honor, Mr. Madison", said Carmeli'ta'. She added, "However, Mr. Madison it is not necessary to buy me a wardrobe I can purchase my own."

Jason objected, "Absolutely not, I will not hear of it; this is a company's expense; I do not want you to spend your money. The company has an account at Toni's at One Gaslight Alley on Riviere' Du' Chein Plaza and

Galleria. Are you familiar with Toni's?"

"Yes, I am familiar with Toni's, Mr. Madison. My Mother has an account there. She buys her and my clothes from Toni's."

"That is good Carmeli'ta'. I have noticed that about your outfits", said Jason. "It is good to know you are familiar with Toni's and thank you for your willingness to be Hostess."

"You are welcome, Mr. Madison."

Toni's was the most popular Woman's boutique in the 1920's for the Charleston Country Club Society.

"I will have Ms. Horne call and make an appointment for you to be fitted for your wardrobe," commented Jason. "In addition, Toni will be given the budgeted amount and will outfit you with all your clothing and accessory needs. Furthermore, Carmeli'ta', take the time you need to choose your outfits for your social responsibilities here at Madison Steel. I will instruct Toni to have the wardrobe delivered to your Townhouse and hung properly. Toni's assistant will take care of hanging your outfits and gowns for you. I will have Ms. Horne and others pinch-hit for you until you are ready. Can you be ready in 5-7 days Carmeli'ta' from the date you get your outfits?"

"Thank you, Mr. Madison; I am humbled by your kindness. Yes, I will be ready; 5-7 days gives me ample time."

"No, Carmeli'ta', it is I who need to thank you. You have taken a huge obligation off of my Mother's hands."

When Carmeli'ta arrived home, she informed her parents of her increase in salary and her additional duties as Hostess. Simone' was happy that her daughter career was progressing. Roberto' worried she may have taken on too many responsibilities, but did not voice his thoughts instead he congratulated his daughter and commented her progress was impressive with one so young and said how proud Simone' and he was of her.

At Jason's instructions, Ms. Horne called Toni's and made the appointment for Carmeli'ta' wardrobe fitting on Thursday, November 1, 1923, at 10:00 a.m. Jason asked Toni privately to allow Carmeli'ta' to choose any clothing items she desired without a limit on price and charge it to his personal account.

Toni' came from Paris, France in the early 1900's and opened up a ladies' boutique in Charleston, which carried the latest fashions from Worth's in London, fashions from Rome and New York. Toni' a petite 5'0' tall, friendly woman in her early 50's, with a pleasant tone to her voice, was a Fashionista. Toni's boutique was Tre' Chic and the atmosphere said "Upscale".

Carmeli'ta' arrived at Toni's Boutique for her fitting and selection of garments for her Hostess position at 10:00 a.m., November 1. Carmeli'ta' had exquisite taste she had been taught about fashion by her Mother, Simone'. She chose with Toni's assistant, ten long Worth's gowns (Black, Dusty Blue, Brushed Pink, Yellow, Beige, Pale Green, Orange, Spanish Grey, Red, and Hunter Green).

She chose five semi-formal Worth's gowns (Red, Royal Blue, Burgundy, White and Beige). All the gowns, smartly embellished with an array of sequins, were appropriate for any occasion and were in keeping with the standards that Juanita Madison had set for her company in reference to fashion and taste. The gowns, where they were fashionable and attractive, did not show a lot of skin. Showing too much skin was not proper, for a woman, of class and position. The necklines were classy and just low enough to "whet" any male's appetite. Carmeli'ta' selected evening shoes and bags to complement each gown. The jewelry selected were pearl earrings and necklace (black, white, and beige), which would match any of the gowns, formal or semiformal. She also chose a selection of suits for business functions for day and night with the blouses and accessories and array of multi-colored brooches and sling backs heels. She would use the pearls for accessories as well. Lastly, she chose a Chocolate colored Mink Stole and a Grey and Black Full Length Mink Coat with Black Leather Gloves with Grey and Black Mink around the cuff.

After her advanced in position, Simone' leased a Townhouse at Albemarle Point on Château Le Arman Avenue. Carmeli'ta' lived one mile from Madison Steel and Iron Works. The Townhouse complex was five minutes from the Madison's Mansion on Madison Drive. Simone', had chosen this area in town for her daughter to be safe and close to her work. In addition, that area of town in Charleston spoke volumes of her position and to her status. Her parents furnished her Townhouse and paid her rent for the first year giving her an opportunity to build her finances. Simone' worked hard to get the Townhouse ready for Carmeli'ta' to move in. She had moved from her parent's home, October 30, 1923, one week before she became Hostess for Madison Steel and Iron. Carmeli'ta' kept in touch with her parents daily, especially her Mother, who advised her in adulthood as she did when she was a growing child.

Toni's assistant, Gabriella Paquette, arrived at 4:00 p.m. the evening of November 1, 1923, with the wardrobe chosen by Carmeli'ta'. Driver and delivery supervisor for Toni's, Manuel Thibodeaux, transported the gowns and Minks up to her townhouse wrapped in garment wrap. Gabriella unwrapped and hung the gowns one at a time; then hung her short Mink Stole and full-length Mink Coat. She positioned the shoe rack over the door unboxed and placed the shoes in the slots. The pearls and brooches were in a jewelry case with five drawers and French doors on front, she placed on the dresser. Carmeli'ta' was ready for her Hostess duties. It was almost 7:00 p.m. before Gabriella completed hanging and assembling her wardrobe. Gabriella also, rehung and coordinated Carmeli'ta' suits, blouses, jackets, dresses, dressing gowns, and her lingerie' to flow in harmony with her new wardrobe.

Carmeli'ta' did well as Hostess for Madison Steel and Iron Works Manufacturing social functions. She became the company's "darling". However, never letting all of her accomplishments and accolades received for her business shrewdness go to her head stayed humble and continued to work hard, this factor impressed Jason; it was evident to him she would be able to handle money and success.

As the time approached, Jason informed Carmeli'ta', "We have a business client whose business we are trying to acquire; yet, it has been difficult to obtain his business. He is the President and CEO of Meriwether Textiles, Charles Bienville Meriwether. My Father suggested that I asked you to speak with Mr. Meriwether on November 7 during the annual Thanksgiving Dinner and Ball; however, if you are not comfortable with talking with him at the Thanksgiving Company dinner, we will try another strategy to get his business."

"Mr. Madison, I will be glad to speak with Mr. Meriwether and it does not make me uncomfortable."

"Thank you Carmeli'ta' I am grateful to you for being willing to take on this task without question, it is a lot to ask. Also, I have another favor to ask of you", added Jason. "Yes, Mr. Madison", she said. "Would you please call me Jason and not Mr. Madison; we are not far apart in age are we?"

"No, I don't believe there are but a few years difference in our ages. Thank you, Jason. I will call you by your first name only when we are not in the presence of other employees or at social functions."

For a moment Jason looked intently at Carmeli'ta' 'thought, "She is consistent in being a professional and a Lady. I like that!"

"That will be fine, thank you."

Jason wanted to put Carmeli'ta' at ease to ask her for a dinner date, but not if she continued to call him Mr. Madison, he would feel uncomfortable asking her.

Carmeli'ta' became Jason's right hand growing in favor with everyone, even Jason's family, especially his Father, Jason, Sr. His Mother, Juanita, when she first began to be host for their company's functions, did not warm-up to Carmeli'ta', but over time Juanita grew to respect Carmeli'ta' because of her ability to help move their steel business to the next level. The respect Juanita Madison had for her abilities won her over at Madison Steel and Iron Works, but her abilities only. With her opinions and thoughts of family status, like the Wine Kings in Tuscany, would not entertain the idea of Jason Jr. having any other relationships but business with Carmeli'ta'.

The whole of Charleston Society, as well as all employees' and their guests received invitations to the annual Madison Steel Thanksgiving Ball and Banquet; the dress was formal. As the Madison Steel and Iron Works Thanksgiving Holiday party approached, the excitement at the plant grew among employees. This was one of the two times a year that the employees had the chance to dress "swanky" for an evening.

The evening for the ball finally arrived.

Carmeli'ta' chose the full length Soft Yellow Evening Gown with silver accessories to wear. It was fitting for the fall of the year and complimented the Thanksgiving Holiday season. The ornate centerpieces for each table were the Horn of Plenty, embellished to give each table a sparkle; enhancing the already glazy smoky look to the room the candlelight provided the room.

Simone' came to help her dress for the first formal occasion at Madison Steel. After dressing and her hair and jewelry in place asked her, "How do I look Mother? Is my choice of dress and accessories appropriate for the season?"

"Yes my sweet daughter your loveliness is sparkling tonight and beautifies your outfit."

"Thank you Mother, I am thankful that I have you to help guide me until I am comfortable in my position as hostess. I do not want to disappoint Jason."

Simone' smiled noticing that she called her supervisor by his first name she did want to assign any meaning to it. Carmeli'ta' was nervous enough without more pressure on her; therefore, she decided to wait to allow her daughter to tell her about being on first name basis with her supervisor replied, "You look "smart" my lovely daughter. Jason Madison and all at the function tonight will be more than impressed. You will be one of the highlights of the evening."

Decorum has always been a priority with Charles Bienville Meriwether. Being appropriate in all occasions was "a must" in his company part of what made him so mythical and elusive. He seldom met anyone who he thought was completely appropriate, until he met Carmeli'ta'. Charles Meriwether could only think of one other woman, in Charleston who met his requirements of Decorum, Juanita Madison, who he wanted to be his wife. Instead, Jason Sr. captured her heart after their marriage arranged by her father. This fact kept him over the years from conducting business with Madison Steel.

Nonetheless, now time and logic dictated that he change his prospective and put aside pride. To continue on his quest of never doing business with Madison Steel would prove costly.

Strategy is a necessary component!

CHAPTER
EIGHT

Carmeli'ta' said, "Mr. Meriwether you are seated at my table. May I escort you there?" "Thank you", he said. Carmeli'ta' placed her left hand on the back of his right arm and guided him to the round table, which seated eight.

As they did each year, the employees and the supervisors in the plant were seated strategically around the room, so that there was a supervisor or manager at each table to give the employees an all-inclusive and comfortable feeling. Jason, Jr. stressed this fact to his management staff, "Showing appreciation to all employees no matter their job duties, is vital to the success of any business, but particularly my company and its business success."

When they reached the table Carmeli'ta' introduced him to everyone seated there and the ones at the table directly behind, across, and in front of them.

"Pleased be seated Mr. Meriwether", said Carmeli'ta'.

With a slight bow, smiled and said, "Thank you, Madam Hostess."

Carmeli'ta' did not want to lose the momentum of the moment, smiling replied, "Mr. Meriwether, as a way of giving back to the community, Madison Steel and Iron has a proposal for a Job Creation Project Initiative for citizens to help build the community. We are encouraging the businesses here to join in partnership with us to supply the needs of the industries unless there is not a company that sell that particular product in the local area. Likewise, this fact will encourage our citizens to buy and sell locally. I would like to discuss this point with you further if you don't mind discussing it before dinner is served."

The Country Club orchestra played softly, couples danced, as the evening started and the social hour began before dinner.

Beguiled by her charm and beauty he replied, "I would not mind listening to your Job Creation Project Proposal Initiative for the community. Increasing my profits and building Charleston both are important to me. May I have this dance before we discuss, Madam Hostess?" She said, "Yes, it will be my pleasure."

Rising, he held out his hand, Carmeli'ta' placed hear left hand on his right hand and walked with him to the dance floor. The orchestra played, "Liebestraume", by Liszt.

Jason, Jr. watched Carmeli'ta' as she danced with Charles Meriwether. The music played and Meriwether danced with Carmeli'ta' smiling and talking, Jason, Jr. felt a knot form in his throat and his green-eyed monster rose. He wanted the Meriwether account, but not at the costly price of losing Carmeli'ta' before he told her he loved her.

As they danced, he thought, "I like Carmeli'ta'; she has so much business savvy in one so young and lovely. I am twice her age, but she is such a gem."

Charles Meriwether toyed with the idea that Carmeli'ta' would say yes to his asking her for a dinner date. However, he would wait to see how the meeting went.

Now, Meriwether did not know that Jason, Jr. loved Carmeli'ta' at that point and later Jason would find that it did not matter to Charles Meriwether that he loved Carmeli'ta'. He would try to compete with him for her heart.

While they danced, Carmeli'ta' smiled and made light conversation with him. She felt the ice break and the walls come down that he had built around himself as a successful businessperson. The danced ended, he bowed and said, "Thank you Carmeli'ta', I enjoyed dancing with you, maybe another before the night is over?"

"Yes, I would love to dance with you again, thank you" she replied.

The proposal presented to Charles Meriwether, would go far better than either Jason or Carmeli'ta hoped.

After returning to the table, Carmeli'ta' discussed the proposal for the initiative with Meriwether. She knew it back and forth all the statistics, specifications, and details. He listened closely impressed with the knowledge of this beautiful young woman with competent skills and abilities anyone with a discerning eye could see.

Charles Meriwether, after an hour's discussion before dinner was served said, "Carmeli'ta', I would like to get your people and my people together after this holiday function and let's see what we can do to make this thing happen. I am hard, people say, when it comes to business, but I am no fool. I know a good business deal when I hear one. I had not heard the proposal in details like you explained it. Madison did not give me the insight that you did or it could have been I was not listening to him closely." With that statement, he smiled and said, "There again, maybe, they sent the wrong person!"

Smiling again, Carmeli'ta' responded, "Thank you Mr. Meriwether. I will call your assistant personally Monday, November 18 and set up the appointment time and place." He nodded and replied, "I will be waiting for your call Carmeli'ta'. Now, let us eat. I saved my appetite for this dinner tonight. Andrea's did cater dinner did they not?"

She confirmed, "Yes, Andrea's did cater the event for tonight, Mr. Meriwether; everyone at Madison Steel and Iron loves Andrea's Thanksgiving and Christmas dinners."

Carmeli'ta' motioned to the waiter and his staff to begin serving the food.

Glancing across the room at Jason, Jr., smiled, lightly nodded a half-moon, yes. Jason knew by the smile and nod that they were on their way to a business contract with Meriwether Textiles. Jason thought, "She did it! She did it! Wow, Carmeli'ta' is a winner."

Andrea's was the most famous restaurant in Charleston. The population of Charleston loved the soul food served at Andrea'.

Andrea', came from Tennessee in search of his dream of having a restaurant.

Andrea' was Ms. Overton's, the Madison's cook and housekeeper's, cousin (the Madison asked Andrea each year to cater their Thanksgiving and Christmas dinners for both home and Madison Steel Annual Ball). The Thanksgiving dinner went well. Turkey and Dressing, Green Beans with Pimentos, Garlic Mashed Potatoes with Sour Cream and Bacon bits, Giblet Gravy, Honey, and Butter Yeast Rolls, and for dessert Sweet Potato Pie a la Andrea's. Pitchers of Iced Tea were on each table. It was a mystery to Andrea's customers one they could not figure out why a traditional dinner tasted like a dream. Everyone eating at Andrea' wanted his recipes, which he never shared. The taste of the food came from a combination of spices used by Andrea's; the taste was his creation.

While wait staff served the food, Carmeli'ta' walked to the podium to welcome everyone.

"Good evening, everyone, it is good to see each of you tonight. Thank you for coming. The social hour has been lively and enjoyable so far. The music is beautiful tonight. Please give the Charleston Country Club Orchestra a hand. On behalf of Madison Steel and Iron Administration, thank you Ladies and Gentleman for helping make this a memorable evening. It is also my hope that you will enjoy the meal. Andrea' would you please join me at the podium, please give he and his staff a hand for the wonderful meal and excellent service. Thank you Andrea".

Carmeli'ta' ended her welcome, "Everyone please help me welcome Jason Madison, Jr. the President of Madison Steel and Iron Works."

Loud applause rang out in the large ballroom in the Excelsior Hotel at the Charleston Country Club. "Mr. Madison, would you please join me at the podium and give the invocation and a few comments?"

Jason, Jr. made his way to the podium smiled and kissed Carmeli'ta's hand, as any Southern Gentleman would do.

"Thank you Ms. Bandaci. Bow with me please for a prayer of thanksgiving and blessing for the food. 'We thank you Heavenly Father for each blessing, for our jobs, food, health, and strength. Bless each family here tonight.' As we depart later, please keep us safe. Amen."

Further, "I would like to welcome everyone to the Madison Steel and Iron Work's Annual Thanksgiving Dinner and Ball for employees and guests. Credit and recognition, for the hard work went into arranging this social event goes to Carmeli'ta' Bandaci and Daisy Horne, they are an unstoppable pair. Thank you, Ladies! It is my pleasure to give this function each year, so without further delay, I know you are hungry, I am, the food is served, enjoy your meal. Please enjoy your evening, the orchestra is playing. Feel free to dance throughout the evening. Thank you."

Jason did not ask Carmeli'ta' to waltz during this function. He knew his feeling for her would be apparent to everyone, especially tonight, the way he felt and the way Carmeli'ta' looked would give his feeling for her away too soon. He did not want that for Carmeli'ta' or him before he knew how she felt and they were ready to reveal their relationship if she cared for him as he did her.

Charles Bienville Meriwether took the opportunity to dance the entire evening with Carmeli'ta'. As they danced, his mind went back to Juanita Madison and the beauty that he loved in her, secretly all the years that he known her. He thought, "Carmeli'ta' is a beautiful young woman though, I am old enough to be her Father, I would love for her to be mine; it would complete my life. I have always loved Juanita Madison. Carmeli'ta' is the only other woman I know that could fulfill my desires and complete me as a man. I know that I would not have a chance. But, then again she is not romantically involved with anyone as far as I can determine."

Charles Bienville Meriwether had quietly asked his closet contact in the city of her family and her relationship status. He toyed with the idea of asking her to dinner and dancing. He loved to dance and she was a good partner. "But dare I?" he said to himself. As they waltz, he smiled at Carmeli'ta' and she smiled back. He thought to himself, "She is so lovely, exotic, and sensual. If intimacy with her at other levels is like they are in conversation with her, she would be irresistible."

He pictured scenes in his mind of intimacy with Carmeli'ta; saw himself holding her, kissing her perfect mouth, looking into her beautiful enchanting, enthralling, and captivating eyes, thought, "She is intriguing; she wears intrigue as if it were a garment. The smooth silky feeling of her soft skin just being near her, scenes of her tears at me; no other woman has since Juanita Madison. She could provide me with a renewed youth, she is at least 20 years old hopefully older and a beautiful young woman; she could revive and keep me alive sexually. If only I could make her mine?"

Carmeli'ta' noticed the strange look on his face as they danced, she asked, "Mr. Meriwether, are you okay?" Carmeli'ta' calling his name, bought him back to that moment in time and away from the fantasy, he lived in the few brief flashes as he held her and danced.

"Yes, of course Carmeli'ta' why do you ask?"

She said, "You have a worried look on your face, Mr. Meriwether."

He replied, "I am well Carmeli'ta' thank you for asking. It is just a business thought that is running through my mind." Knowing that this was not true, he made light conversation with Carmeli'ta' as he whirled her on the floor.

Carmeli'ta' had not noticed the look on his face as anything except business, but Jason, Jr. sitting across the room noticed he had a look that a man has when he is interested in a beautiful woman. This was a moment of panic for Jason knowing his reputation of charm in the community among the females in the Charleston society. His Father told him he was in love with his Mother Juanita as they grew up, but did not win her heart.

Jason realized Carmeli'ta' was beautiful enough to attract any man could not protect her though he had tried, it would be impossible, because she was not his. He needed to try to change this by letting Carmeli'ta' know his feeling of love for her, how she has improved his life and added so much richness to it that filled his days and nights with joy. He decided not to wait any longer; he would ask Carmeli'ta' to go to dinner with him. He prayed and hoped against hope that she felt the same way about him. He had to find out!

Jason became determined after the Thanksgiving Ball and Dinner to ask Carmeli'ta' to have dinner with him next Tuesday, November 12. Rochelle's was open even though it is the Thanksgiving Holiday season with all the social activity in Charleston this time of year. The restaurant crowd being light because of the holiday season would be a plus. He wanted to be as quiet about his love for Carmeli'ta' as possible until he knew she loved him; and it would risk her position in the company and threaten his authority, so as his father reminded him often the quote by William Shakespeare, *"Discretion is the better part of valor."*

Jason after the dinner guest departed, pulled Carmeli'ta' aside, took her hands in his, and said, "Carmeli'ta' thank you for the giant steps you made tonight. I do not know how to thank you. Tonight, I saw walls fall Charles Bienville Meriwether built around his self-years ago. This in-and-of-itself is an accomplishment on your part; but to get him to agree to put our people together and come up with a lucrative and fluid contract deal is more that I could have hoped. You are a winner Carmeli'ta', thank you." Jason thought, "This is a perfect time to ask her to dinner."

While Jason held her hand, his touch sent a sharp bolt of lightning through her body. She was unable to move for a short period-of-time he said, "Carmeli'ta' are you free to have dinner with me next Tuesday night, November 12? Rochelle's is one of my favorites. May I call for you at your Townhouse at 8:00 p.m.?" Jason knew exactly where she lived, not too far from him, which, of course, made him happy.

Carmeli'ta' surprised by the invitation said, "I am free next Tuesday night, Jason. Yes, I will have dinner with you. I like Rochelle's."

"You have eaten at Rochelle's before?"

"Yes, my Father, Mother, and my two close friends April, Alberto' and I eat there once a week."

"I am glad to know that you like Rochelle's. The environment in Rochelle's does make the subject I want to discuss with you next Tuesday easier."

Carmeli'ta' heart racing as she thought, "What can he want to tell me, is it too much to hope that he cares for me as I do him?"

"It is set then, next Tuesday at 8:00 p.m." Jason confirmed verbally and mentally for his peace of mind. Carmeli'ta' had cared for Jason for months, but work ethic, which was paramount to Carmeli'ta', was the roadblock, she faced.

Jason's feelings growing for Carmeli'ta', wanted her to know how he felt even though he was her employer. She was to him more than a manager, but a vital part of his everyday business dealing. However, above all that, he was falling in love with her.

CHAPTER

NINE

Jason was approaching 27 years of age and wanted a wife to complete him. He was good at business and societal necessities, but he was a passionate man and needed what every man and woman at a mature age needs, that special someone to love. Equally he knew only someone he truly loved could satisfy his desires, passions in life, or sexual needs; he learned this from his Father. Definitely, he could not put himself out there with any woman just for the physical gratification, though it was tempting. His parents, raised him in a Christian home, instilled in him intimacy in love, no matter the level, sexual love should be shared with someone you truly love. In reality, Jason knew if Carmeli'ta' agreed for them to date would depend on whether she cared for him. Then again, they would need to be discreet because of the employee/employer relationship. Jason wanted to protect her reputation, position of respect, and authority in his company.

Until Jason met Carmeli'ta', no woman kept his interest. Carmeli'ta' moved something in him in a way that he could not explain. After Church, on Sunday November 10, Jason shared with his Father his feelings.

"Father, may I speak with you in private man to man?"

"Yes son, of course, let's go into my office." Jason's Father had moved his office to their home, so he could assist Jason only when he needed it. He wanted to spend more time at home with his Juanita.

His mother, Juanita, standing next to his father had been silent inquired, "Jason, darling can I do something to help?"

"No Mother, thank you for asking, but I need to talk with Father."

Jason and his Father had a close open relationship; he could talk about any subject with his Father, even sex. Jason, Sr. said, "Juanita my lovely, I will not be long we will spend our Sunday afternoon together as we always do."

Jason, as he grew watched his Mother and Father and the way they loved and cared for each other over the years, even though his Mother seemed hard sometimes, but only in business. At home, she was a completely different person with his Father, who seemed to worship her almost. He saw her touch and caress his Father; kiss him softly, her tone of voice would turn his Father's frustration into cheerfulness. His Father came home many times from a hard day at Madison Steel in a bad mood when Jason was in school at Charleston High. His Mother would touch him, hold him, speak softly in his ear, and in no time, he was a different person. Jason saw how tightly his Father held on to his Mother when she was near him as if he could not get enough of her closeness.

Jason asked his Father when he was eighteen years old what made the difference in his mood after he arrived home from a hard day, "Your Mother son, she is a good woman. All men need the type of woman your Mother is for a wife. What you see in business about your Mother is not the real woman to whom I am married. You will understand better as you grow and learn about women and life. We will discuss this again if you want sometimes. Nevertheless, it will be more meaningful to you if you discover this fact on your own."

Jason, Sr. closed the door quietly behind his son turned to talk with him. Jason stood looking out the French doors leading to the beautiful garden and patio his Mother loved so much.

"Jason, what is troubling you son? I have noticed for a few months now that you have something that is bothering you. Are you ill?" "No, Father, I am not ill, not physically or mentally anyway." "Is it the textile business we are trying to get from Meriwether? How did the meeting with Meriwether go Thursday evening? We have not discussed that yet. Did Madison Steel and Iron Hostess have an opportunity to talk with him?"

"Yes she did Father. The meeting went well. Carmeli'ta' got Mr. Meriwether to agree to get our people and his people together. Carmeli'ta' is arranging the meeting on Monday, November 18. Mr. Meriwether liked her approach and explanation of the Job Creation Initiative Proposal and what we are trying to do to increase "loyalty" from all Charleston's major business owners to build our city's economy and provide jobs for its citizens."

"I am glad to hear that son. I knew Carmeli'ta' would be successful in getting us to first base. Now it is up to us to get the home run. In this light, it will have to involve everyone working as a team, including and especially Carmeli'ta'. She seems to be the key."

"Thank you Father, Carmeli'ta' is a winner for Madison Steel."

Jason, Jr. quiet again still with a faraway look in his eyes with a frown dancing across his forehead, paced back and forth in front of the patio doors.

"Son what is the matter with you? This is beginning to worry me a little. I know the company is solid financially, you are a good manager and CEO."

Jason stopped pacing and looked at his Father commenting, "Thank you Father. It is not Madison Steel I am worried about or thinking about, not at the moment anyway."

Jason, Sr. understanding asked, "Is this a problem of the heart son?"

"Yes, Father. It has been for months." Continuing, Jason, Jr. said, "When I am around this woman she moves something in me that I cannot explain. I have never felt like this before, it is an overwhelming feeling of passion, almost lustful, Father. I know that we are Christians, and what you taught me about relationships, but these feeling are uncontrollable when I am around her or even just think about her. I need her Father. I have fallen in love with her. I know that our love could be problematic. Nevertheless, what can I do? I cannot tell my heart what to feel, I have tried, it does not listen."

Jason, Sr. listening until his son finished said, "Jason, son, this feeling that you are having for this woman is natural. It is these feelings that a man should have, for a woman he loves. The woman should have the same feelings for the man she loves. Unless a woman can move you in the way she has, is the only way that you will be with someone and be completely happy and satisfied. I told you when you were eighteen years old it would be more meaningful to you if you discovered this feeling on your own. This is what I meant!"

"Father, can I ask you a personal question?"

"Yes, son we are both grown men."

"Father it is about you and Mother."

Jason, Jr. paused and looked out the doors into the garden and thought, "Are you crazy Jason? You cannot ask your Father about your Mother and his sex life!" He said finally, "Father, I am sorry I cannot ask you, please forgive me. I will…well I don't know how to say it!"

His Father knowing what he wanted to ask allowed him to put it in his own words, "Yes son ask the question."

Jason Jr stumbling over his words said, "Father, you, and Mother, ah, ah!"

Jason could not get the question to come from his lips, he felt embarrassed asking about his Father about his Mother and his sex life.

Jason, Sr. turned away smiling gained his composure turned again to Jason remaining straight faced, "Yes, Jason, your Mother moves me in the way that this woman moves you. She still does and we have been married for almost thirty years. She is not just your Mother, Jason, a good one she is to you. She is my wife, my partner, my friend, my soul mate, and my lover. I do not know if I can make you understand how she makes me feel; her love lifts me the heavens. I cannot explain it any better than that. As far as it being wrong to feel and need with all the passion and desires of a man; son, God made male and female for this type of love, it is good and pure."

"Father, I did not want to pry into your and Mother's private business, I am sorry, but I had to know, please forgive me."

"I am glad to talk with you about any subject son. I have never hid the fact that I love your Mother passionately from you. We have tried to demonstrate our love and care for each other around you at all times. To let you know that money and position is not everything. At the end of the day, love is all we have because it is timeless and renewable. Love between a husband and wife is sanctioned by God remember the scripture as it says in [Hebrews 13:2], *'Marriage is honorable among all and the bed undefiled'*, you are familiar with that scripture?"

"Yes, I am familiar with that scripture. Thank you Father, I love you and respect you. I appreciate your talking to me man to man. I feel that I am of men most fortunate to have a loving and kind Father like you. I want what Mother and you have with my wife when I get married."

"Thank you son, it pleases me that you are aware of the example we set for you. If you marry the right woman, you will have this type of relationship. Do you want to tell me who she is or do I tell you?"

Jason, Jr., looked shocked as his Father spoke and said, "No one knows Father, who she is."

"Jason, son, I have known since we talked about Carmeli'ta' being hostess you were falling in love with her. I understand why also, she is a gem. I would be proud to have her as a daughter-in-law. However, your Mother is a different story. We will wait to see, if things pan out for you two before we mention it to my Juanita."

"Our first date is Tuesday, November 12 at Rochelle's"

"Jason son, Rochelle's is a good choice; make it a romantic evening, she is worth every dime you spend and more."

Jason, Jr., almost tearful at this point said, "Thank you Father for your support."

"You are welcome. Now my wife is waiting!" Jason. Sr. opened his office door and called to his wife, "Juanita, my lovely, we are done."

Juanita came sweeping through the open door in a soft flowing green and pink dressing gown went and stood near her husband, holding him around the waist asked, "Is Jason okay? Is there something I need to know?"

Jason noticed that his Mother always looked like a beautiful picture in a frame as long back as he could remember.

His father smiling "No my lovely wife, let us concentrate on each other." He led his wife over to the loveseat and sit beside her. He passionately kissed her and held her close to him, and whispered, "Juanita you make me feel twenty feet tall when I am in your arms."

"Jason my love, your love makes me feel feminine, sexy, and I need you more each day, your love is like the sun it warms my very being. I love you passionately."

Jason walked passed his Mother and Father seated on the loveseat near the French doors heard his Father and Mother's statement to each other and smiled. Jason, Sr. seeing the look on his son's face smiled and winked at him and held his wife even tighter.

Jason imagined what the 'Date Night 'for him and Carmeli'ta' would be like. He wondered what she would say, and how she would respond to his love overtures to her.

The time for their first date was fast approaching.

Monday passed quickly. As "Date Night" approached, Simone' advised Carmeli'ta' on what to wear. She decided to wear a simple black dress with pearls. She, up to now, had always worn an evening dress or other outfits appropriate for the company's social functions. However, tonight, she planned to allow Jason to see her in a simpler more elegant, distinguished light. Her outfit was one of her private selections and not part of her work wardrobe. Simone' taught her daughter, for special occasion, a black dress and pearls were smart. Carmeli'ta' remembered her Mother's words, "smart" was what she said the word used in Italy, when a woman dressed for a special occasion. She dressed for the atmosphere of a special evening in mind. She hoped that Jason's invitation to dinner meant more than a company's social necessity.

Carmeli'ta' thought, "Jason did not say it was not company business when he invited me."

Carmeli'ta' revealed to her mother the same evening "Mother I am falling in love with Jason."

Simone' remembering her own dilemma, warned, "Carmeli'ta' that could be dangerous for you in reference to your job and your heart." She continued, "Carmeli'ta' guard your heart, remember Jason is, first, your employer; and secondly, he might not feel the same way about you; and thirdly, he is wealthy. Where your Father is well off financially, he is nowhere in the wealth ballpark of the Madison's. They are one of the wealthiest families in Charleston."

"I know Mother, that all that you say is true. Jason has asked me for dinner and I will go to see what he has to say. I will not give away my feeling until I know for sure he cares for me as I do him." Carmelita reasoning about the evening asked, "Mother how can two people work as close as Jason and I have for the last year and a half and not feel something? He is handsome Mother, 6'4" tall, educated, intelligent, strong, and sensible in business; and he heads his family's Steel Empire."

"Carmeli'ta' my lovely daughter, he is surely to have a lady friend."

Carmeli'ta' feeling a little annoyed with this statement said, "No matter whether he does or not at the present time; his Mother, Juanita, in a discussion with me said he was single and unattached. She is concerned all he does is work and come home. He is still at home with his parents at their estate, though he has a separate living area in one of the wings of their mansion."

"Even in the face of all of this, my daughter, don't get your hopes up to high." Simone', knew what she suffered in love years ago before coming to America, did not want her daughter to end up feeling what she felt then even though her feeling are completely different now, still carried the burden of a secret relationship and the doubts created from that relationship. She realized a short time after she was married it was not true love, but infatuation and immaturity of a fourteen-year-old girl who did not understand herself and what she was feeling growing into womanhood.

"I will remember Mother and I will not expect too much beyond dinner at Rochelle's."

On the other hand, Jason was a traditional Southern Gentleman raised by his Father and Mother in all the fine southern traditions and etiquettes of Charleston. Jason saw the same qualities in Carmeli'ta' from the beginning. Her mother and Father were well versed in etiquette. They came from Italy, a country where etiquette is a must and part of the culture.

Jason knew that only a woman with fine qualities, with his family's social status in Charleston, South Carolina, would be acceptable, as his wife. His wife would play a huge role in his life, business, and success, not to mention in their finding common ground in marriage. After more than a year, Jason watching and observing Carmeli'ta' under every circumstance, knew she was the one for him, he had fallen in love with her. Tuesday night's dinner, he hoped, would be the start of a life-long journey of passion, love, and marriage.

Carmeli'ta', while dressing, thought about the conversation with her Mother earlier in the evening, wondered if this is the night for six months, she hoped and prayed would happen. Carmeli'ta' dressed meticulously as always, but, tonight, she would put an extra touch on her preparations. Carmeli'ta' basked in her bathtub of warm water with Lavender bubbles dancing and pampering her for an hour not long enough to get her skin swiveled, but to soak and let the bath oil and bubbles penetrate her skin, bring out its softness, and luster. Carmeli'ta' snuggled herself dry in her soft, white fluffy terry bathrobe.

She turbaned her hair so it would stay dry and not get any of the steam from her bath. She left work at 2:00 p.m. on Monday with Jason's approval for a beauty salon appointment since her date was on Tuesday. Her light brown peach colored skin she pampered with Nivea Lotion her Mother had used on her skins all of her life since its introduction in 1911. She thought about the color of Jason's skin, naturally he was a soft pinkish color, much like his Caucasian race.

Carmeli'ta' chose her lingerie' carefully matching her lacy black bra and panties with the heart shape that framed her navel. Carmeli'ta' felt very sexy as any twenty-three years old young woman should feel, is what her Mother taught her.

Her Mother and Father always seemed never to get enough of each other. However, Carmeli'ta' did not know at this point, this has always been true, but there is a secret she did not know. Now she knows why they could not get enough of each other! Her Mother knew the secret to passion and making her husband feel as if he was the whole world and could accomplish any feat.

In the 1920's Carmeli'ta' embraced her mother's teaching the importance of being a Lady. In this light, she kept her thoughts close to her heart and presenting herself as a professional, intelligent, and dignified southern woman. Being a southern bell (not in a helpless sense, but ultra-feminine) is the idea she operated upon and from her upbringing and what she was a part of the southern culture.

Carmeli'ta's mind traveled a thousand miles while she prepared carefully for her date. Since Thursday after the Madison Ball her head was swirling in disbelief, she had a date with Jason that did not involve business; at least, she told herself so; then again, "He did not make that clear." She hoped against hope that he cared for her as she did him. Oh, she knew he cared for her in a business sense, but had never shown the slightest interest in her any other way except professionally. However, she noticed that he always kept here close to him at all times during working hours at or away from the office.

Carmeli'ta' opened her closet and looked closely at the simple elegant black dress she had chosen to wear tonight. The black dress had long-sleeved with a round collar that came right below her collarbone to show her long neck. The sleeves in the dress had French cuffs with lace down the outside of the sleeves showing her arms and ten buttons down the back garnished with cut glass in-sets in each button.

Walking to the dresser in her dressing room in her master bath dabbed Chanel 5, behind her ears, near her armpits, on her wrist, the inside and outside of each thigh, and on her lace panties. On her right hand, she wore a Beige Pearl Ring, and Pearl bracelet, to match her Pearl Earrings; the left hand was free of Jewelry, except for the diamond bracelet her parents gave her for her 21st birthday.

Next, she wiggled into her black lace garter belt slipped her flesh tone stocking on and pinned them to the garter. Finally, to the last three things to compliment her evening, she slipped into her black dress buttoned up except the last two buttons at the top she left unbuttoned so she could easily step into it. The last two button done, opened her jewelry box pulled out a single strand of beige colored pearls matching her earrings, ring and bracelet put them around her neck. The pearls fell above her collarbones on the black backdrop the dress provided, giving her neck a sexy neat look of a standing ivory tower.

She pulled her hair back from her face pinned it in a curly mass on top of her head with strands of hair hanging down in the back and strands highlighting her small ears, slipped her feet into a pair of black sling-back shoes that had become fashionable in the roaring '20's. One last step, she picked up here black evening bag with the beige pearl clutch opened it took out her tube of pink lipstick carefully lined her lips. She looked in her bathroom mirror to see her lipstick was on without a smug.

She did not wear powder; her skins was flawless; she only needed lipstick. "Being endowed with natural beauty is a gift from God. Praise him my daughter for his grace, and mercy toward you," Simone' told her. *"All good and perfect gifts come from heaven from the Father of Lights whom there is neither variableness nor shadow of turning, James 1:17.*

After dressing her mind wandered and drifted from one thought to another, the Bandaci family attended the Charleston St. Church of Christ while she was growing up. Jason, she learned, also grew up attending the Lafayette St. Church of Christ that was near her Father and Mother's home across town. Though Carmeli'ta' and Jason had not discussed their religious beliefs, somehow she knew he was a Christian because of the way he carried himself and the kindness he showed everyone. His workers loved and respected him. He spoke always in a pleasant tone never raising his voice and always with a smile. His very presence in the room commanded respect from anyone he met.

Carmeli'ta' and Jason hoped their first date was sweet; both were nervous and unsure of each other's reaction. Around Jason and social functions of Madison Steel she felt comfortable, however tonight she felt naked and exposed. When it came to her Hostess duties she was a pro but as a female on a first date with, her boss and secondly, a wealthy man who traveled in very different social circles than she and her family, gave her the feeling of being in uncharted territory.

In his wing of the Madison Manson, feeling anxious and unsure of himself wondered what her response to his love overtures would be. He too dressed carefully ensuring everything was in place. Jason dressed flamboyantly, chose his best blue pinstriped suit, a crisp white shirt complimented by a yellow paisley bow tie with his diamond-studded cuff links and watch and chain to match.

As he dressed, his mind drifting, thought about their date, hoped Carmeli'ta' at least would think about a relationship with him and eventually marriage. They were definitely alike in many ways sharing common bonds. She was educated, intelligent, and from a wealthy family as well. Her knowing to the painstaking details the inner workings of the steel business would be even more of an asset to him if they were man and wife.

He thought, "Carmeli'ta' can complete me. She is everything I have hoped for in a woman. I love her! Jason whispering a prayer: "Father in Heaven, you know all things, bless this date tonight allow the outcome to be according to your will. You know my heart. I truly love Carmeli'ta', Amen."

While waiting for Jason to arrive, Carmeli'ta' concluded mentally with a convincing thought, "This date is not in reference to business."

Carmeli'ta', was not being paid for this function it was personal matter, she hoped. Her heart raced as she waited for Jason to arrive. She wondered what he would say or why he wanted her to dress for a special evening and not for a company's social function. Questions whirled around in her head and anxiety slowly crept in. Carmeli'ta' paced back and forth near her living areas' Bay Window looking for Jason's car. She did not know which car he would drive, for this date. He had three different cars according to the employees. He drove the small Ford Fair lane he owned more than any of the other cars. Carmeli'ta' knelt on her Bay Window seat and peered down from two floors up said, "I will call Mother."

Hurrying across the room picked up the phone and dialed her parent's home. The phone ringing two, three, four times finally, after the fourth ring her Mother's melodious voice answered, "Hello."

"Mother it is me. Why do you not answer the phone right away? It rang forever!" Simone' listening and smiling at her daughter's nervous voice said calmly, "Carmeli'ta', my darling daughter; are you okay?"

"Yes, no Mother, I am not. I don't know if I can go on a date with Jason."

Simone' with surprise and question in her voice said, "Carmeli'ta', what are you talking about? You have wanted this for a while now have you not why the sudden cold feet?"

"I did or thought I did Mother. I am so nervous and feel sick to my stomach!"

"Carmeli'ta', sip a few swallows of cool water---you will not function well at your dinner, if you let your emotions get the best of you. What are you afraid of, not Jason?"

With an annoyed tone, "No, Mother, I am not afraid of Jason, but I am afraid of me and what I feel." Carmeli'ta' with a tearful tone continued, "I am afraid he may not care for me beyond business. If he does not, how could I go back to work for him? I would be too embarrassed. He could guess my feelings!"

"Carmeli'ta', your imagination is running away with you. There is no choice for you except to wait and see how the evening flows. If Jason does not care for you, he will still make it possible for you to do your job." Simone' needing to calm her daughter's fears knew it would be hard for her to work for Jason if he did not feel the same way about her she felt about him said, "Carmeli'ta', you will not enjoy your date if you are upset!" During the conversation Jason had arrived unnoticed by Carmeli'ta'. Two short knocks at the door and she realized Jason had arrived.

"Mother, I have to go, Jason is knocking at the door. Thank you for listening Mother" she said, as her voice softened. I love Father and you. Oh Mother, please do not tell Father let me do that. I will call you later, okay? Bye."

"Yes, Carmeli'ta', please call me. Good night, my daughter, have a good time."

Arriving home from work, Roberto' was not met at the door as usual by his wife, walked the hallway between their office and the kitchen heard Simone's voice coming from their suite, walked up the stairs and into the room unnoticed by Simone', overheard the conversation, came stood near his wife asked, "Is daughter okay Mother?"

"Yes, Roberto', she is nervous about her date with Jason tonight."

Roberto' flabbergasted and upset said, "Date, with Jason Madison her boss! Simone', why is this, my first hearing of this date?" No one could say Simone' like Roberto'.

"Roberto', this is our daughter's business, she is grown. She expressly asked me not to tell you because she knew what your reaction would be. She wanted to have the chance to tell you herself, but I could not be dishonest with you when you ask me a question about our daughter."

"I would like to know before rather than after the fact of anything that deals with our daughter and the possibly of her being hurt in anyway." Roberto' heart in pain feeling he was not loved by Simone' in the way that he loved her, did not want his daughter to suffer this in anyway. Roberto' had noticed when he made love to Simone' over the years, she always closed her eyes and never looked at him; her response was not that of a woman passionately in love with her husband. She always held back as if she was frightened just as she did on their wedding night. This pain was eating away at him. He still desperately loved Simone' and could not help his feelings even though he was hurting all those years could not resist making love to his wife and having her near him.

Simone' surprised at her husband's response said, "Roberto', hurt? This is a date my husband! She is not getting married."

"I want her to wait to marry Simone' until she knows that her husband and she both feels the same way about each other and not rush into marriage."

In the intervening time, Carmeli'ta' opened her townhouse door where Jason stood and knocked. Jason looked at Carmeli'ta' and thought how beautiful she was standing there. He had never seen her look as lovely as she did tonight. Her beauty astounded Jason. All he could think of was how she would feel in his arms, to kiss her lips, to hold her near him, to touch her beautiful skin, to smell the soft sexy cologne she wore as he held her close to him. He saw them making passionate love together for the first time, he saw her walking down the aisle, and taking his hand in marriage; her beauty captured Jason.

"Good evening Jason. How are you?"

"I am well Carmeli'ta', thank you for asking. I have never seen you look so beautiful, as you do tonight."

"Thank you, Jason you look very handsome in your pinstriped suit." Jason could not stop starring at Carmeli'ta'. He was frozen, he could not move the first few minutes after she opened the door. Jason finally said, "Carmeli'ta' I have a very special evening planned for us tonight at Rochelle's. I know that you like Rochelle's you have been there many times?"

"Yes Jason, I do like Rochelle's the atmosphere is very relaxing."

"Are you taking a wrap Carmeli'ta'? Rochelle's tends to be a little cool at night and it is approaching middle of the month towards Thanksgiving. The winds of winter are warning us of its arrival as they do each year this time." "Yes, I will get my Mink Stoll." She walked to her coat closet in the foyer, reached among her coats and took the Brown Mink Stoll off the hanger walked back to her sitting room and handed it to Jason. He held it as she slipped her arms through the slits on each side of the Stoll. "This is excellent. The Stoll should be enough."

Carmeli'ta' picked up her black evening bag embellished with black sequins with the pearl claps. When Carmeli'ta' passed the hall mirror in her foyer, she noticed she looked what her Mother called "very smart".

Holding her left arm, he closed the door to the entranceway into the Townhouse. Jason continued holding on to Carmeli'ta' as they walked down the stairs. She thought as they walked, "He is a Southern Gentleman, both at the office and in a personal setting."

They approached his car, she was surprised; he usually drove his Blue Fair lane or Black Roadster AKA as Hot Rod, both smaller cars but not tonight, she stood for a second in awe of what she saw. Jason was driving a Beige and Black Ford Bentley tonight, one that she had not seen before. He had driven the best he had; this said a lot to Carmeli'ta'. She knew he had three cars because of the talk among employees in the office, but she did not know he had a Bentley. Jason opened the passenger door for Carmeli'ta' and held her right hand as she sat in the seat she swung her legs around in the car. Jason closed the door very carefully. He moved swiftly to the driver's side got in and started the motor.

"Carmeli'ta' you are warm and comfortable?" He asked.

"Yes, thank you Jason, it is very comfortable my Stoll is keeping me warm. I am fine thank you."

Carmeli'ta' and Jason on their way to start their evening a low burning flame of trouble brewed between her parents at their home, the moment Roberto' said to Simone', he wanted Carmeli'ta' to marry someone she was sure loved her. His words went throughout her body as an icy December wind does on a cold winter's day in Charleston.

"What do you mean? I do not understand why you are reacting this way.

This is sudden isn't it?"

He stared at her without blinking, angrily replied, "sudden, no, it is not a sudden reaction Simone'. I do not want to discuss it right now. Please let me know when daughter calls and she is safe at home again.

I will go and talk with her tomorrow."

"No, Roberto' please let her make her own choice. Please, I beg you do not take away her ability to make a choice in love." Unmoved by his wife's plea said, "No, Simone'! The matter is closed; end of discussion tonight. Marianna is waiting dinner."

Roberto' was not completely quiet during dinner, but reserved in what he said. He did not smile as much as he normally did during dinner. Finishing their dinner, they said goodnight to Marianna and went upstairs to their sitting room. He prepared for bed as usual then prepared Simone's bath. He returned to the sitting room and saw Simone' standing near the fireplace. Roberto' sits on the loveseat leaning forward looking down at the floor. Simone' concerned about his statement to her and his quietness said, "Why are you so disturbed tonight my husband?" He did not respond, but continued in deep thought for a few minutes.

Across town, after starting the car, Jason sat for a moment before speaking finally said, "I asked you to dinner tonight to discuss a matter with you away from the office. I want to have an evening with you alone in a different atmosphere. I appreciate your accepting my invitation to dinner tonight. I had Rochelle's to prepare a private candlelight dinner in the Blue Room for us tonight. I want to talk with you about something that has been on my mind for a few months now."

"Thank you, Jason the plans sounds lovely that you have made for tonight I enjoy candlelight dinners. My Father takes my mother on a date night there once a week. I have heard him make reservations for the Blue Room before when he takes my Mother to dinner."

Jason said, "How romantic your Father is Carmeli'ta'; a date night is a wonderful idea."

He continued, "I wanted this to be a special evening we spend together."

Her heart racing, thought, "Can this be what I think it is what my hopes and prayers have been the past few months, could it be possible that he loves me as I do him?"

Jason feeling a pressure in his chest he did not understand, put the car in gear and was quiet as he drove after their initial conversation, watching the road, thought, "She is so lovely, and looks so fragile tonight. I pray that she loves me as I love her. I want her to be mine so much it has become painful." Jason whispered a mental prayer to God to have the nerve to tell Carmeli'ta' that he loved her and wanted her to be his future wife.

Carmeli'ta' turned and looked at Jason thought, "He is handsome and intelligent. He could have his pick of any woman in Charleston to take to dinner, but he chose me." Carmeli'ta' whispered a prayer that Jason loved her as she had fallen in love with him.

Rochelle's was near the Charleston Country Club; a 15-minutes' drive from Carmeli'ta's Townhouse. They arrived at Rochelle's. Jason parked the car come around and opened the door for Carmeli'ta'. He reached for her right hand to assist her in getting out of the car. Carmeli'ta' took Jason's hand as she swung her long legs around to get out of the seat. Jason noticed the long, beautiful legs through her flesh-toned stocking. He observed how beautiful she was in the soft light glowing from Rochelle's that fell across his car. He could not control the passion he felt for her. He felt lust, need, and want a man has for a woman he loves, all at the same time. He wanted to take her in his arms kiss her passionately and hold her close to him. But no, he had to resist the temptation to touch her in a personal way until he knew she loved him as he did her or at least she would consider them entering in a relationship.

"Thank you Jason you are kind," she said, as she took his hand to help her stand.

"You are welcome Carmeli'ta'. Are you warm enough? The air has a bitter chill to it."

"I am fine Jason, my Stoll is sufficient to keep me warm, thank you for asking?"

He held her hand while closing the passenger door of the car then offered her his arm as they walked slowly to the front door. Chester, the Doorman, greeted them and opened the door and Jason escorted Carmeli'ta' inside. Rochelle, expecting them, when she saw them approached them said, "Good evening Mr. Madison and Ms. Bandaci; it is good to see you both. I have the Blue Room ready for you. Please follow me and I will get you seated. Carlos will be waiter for you tonight as requested Mr. Madison; he is waiting for you." Carlos, Rochelle's headwaiter was everyone's favorite especially for intimate dinners and business functions.

Carmeli'ta' noticed that Rochelle's was not busy that night. A few couples were scattered around the room, maybe thirty people total.

Carmeli'ta' and Jason walked behind Rochelle to the Blue Room, entering, she noticed the flame from the candle, danced, and flickered giving the room a mysteriously beautiful ambiance. The flame from the candlelight captivated the environment; romance like a ballerina danced everywhere. Carmeli'ta' fascinated by the mood of the room, felt a warm feeling envelope her body standing near Jason while he held her arm so gently. The table was set for two, decorated with beautiful red, yellow, and pink roses adding a festive look to the room. Covering the table was a Royal Blue Velvet Tablecloth shimmering in the candlelight, giving it the appearance that the deep blue lake at the Charleston Country Club has in the moonlight on a bright starry summer night and Blue Velvet chairs continued the flow of blue water matching the tablecloth.

Carlos pulled out the chair and seating Carmeli'ta' took the white napkin with yellow lace trimmed and placed it lightly in her lap. Jason walked around behind Carmeli'ta' and pulled his chair out next to hers, not across the table from her. He wanted to be near her tonight close enough to touch her and look into her eyes.

Carlos served Iced Tea in light blue glasses, garnished with orange slices. Jason sitting quietly, felt butterflies in his stomach while his heart yearned to tell Carmeli'ta' of his love for her; however, not yet it was too soon in the evening.

Carmeli'ta' in wonder and amazement, of the atmosphere surrounding her had not felt this way before when she and Jason were at other company related social events. Her stomach began to tie in knots from the mystery and anticipation the evening held and what Jason wanted to tell her. She wondered if he wanted to tell her he loved her or was this just a romantic evening and intimate dinner for two or an appreciation dinner. She could hardly stand the suspense.

Realizing she had not taken her off her Stoll unbuttoned it slipped her right arm out, Jason immediately rose took her Mink Stoll hung it on the back of the chair she was sitting in and returned to his seat.

"Thank you Jason", she said.

"My pleasure Carmeli'ta', replied Jason.

Rochelle stood and waiting for them to settle down, asked, "Mr. Madison is there anything else I can get you at this minute? Carlos will serve dinner at the 9:00 p.m. hour, as you requested. Please let him know when you are ready or if you need anything further. I will check on you later in the evening. If there is something that you desire before then let Carlos know he will get me for you."

"Thank you Rochelle everything looks fine. I will let Carlos know when we are ready", replied Jason.

Rochelle left the room closing the door quietly behind her. Carlos went to his waiter station across the room out of earshot to wait until they desired his assistance.

"Carmeli'ta' you are comfortable, not chilly I hope?" said Jason.

"Thank you I am fine. I am comfortable. Jason the room is really lovely. I love the tone the atmosphere has this evening. I have eaten here before with my parents and friends, but the atmosphere was not as it is tonight." Jason sit quiet, admiring Carmeli'ta' beauty.

Across town, preparing for retiring after dinner as usual, Roberto' stood and walked to the bedroom door and replied, "It is bedtime, your bath is ready are you coming?"

Simone', with fear gripping her thoughts, "what could Roberto' mean by saying this is not all of a sudden?" She said, "Yes, I am coming, my husband."

Roberto' worked harder over the years than he had to on their farm to allow himself not to feel the hurt and pain of needing Simone' to give herself to him completely in a passionate way; she always held back. This hurt that he felt over the years had begun to make him angry and pain, like a knife cut a wound in his heart.

Simone' was a good Mother to Carmeli'ta', a good business partner to Roberto', a wonderful homemaker (she was good to their employees at their farm, and their Maid and Cook, Marianna Chavez, who worked and lived in their home); she was patient, and always smiled. Then again, Roberto' saw the same look over the years in Simone's eyes that mystery he saw on the ship coming to America and the day before they left Tuscany for America; he could not get these images out of his head.

Simone' still bewildered by her husband's statement, nervous and afraid went into their bedroom suite and prepared for bed. Simone' turbaned her hair took off her dressing gown and slipped into the tub of warm bath water that Roberto' had prepared for her, as he did every night.

Roberto' softly washed her back. His touch was kind and loving on her skin. She thought, 'Roberto' treats me as if I am a piece of precious china.'

She felt her emotions rise at the thought of her past mistakes; she knew they would tear at their family if he knew. She finished her bath and lotion her body slipping into her a beautiful soft pink sheer nightgown with the robe to match and dabbed on her Chanel 5. Simone' did not wear anything under her gowns at bedtime.

Roberto' sitting on the foot of their bed watched her every move as he did each night while waiting for his wife to finish preparing for bed saw her beautiful long tan legs, shapely body, and long curly thick black hair as she brushed it; the locks fell loosely down her back.

Watching her every move thought, "She is so like a chameleon, always ever-changing, heartbreakingly mysterious, and elusive; she is like the morning mist that hang over our beautiful valley in Tuscany before the warm morning sun chases it away."

Powerless to catch and hold the elusiveness of his wife, her nature appeared to be adaptive to everything around her, but she never seemed to adapt to Roberto' and his love and passion for her, this mystified him. He wanted her to return his love and passion. The thought of his need for his wife's complete love, deep passions and desires hurt Roberto' deep within his soul.

Roberto' thought, "The pain, I have felt in our relationship over the years, because, of the place in my being that only she can fulfill and love me as I love her; she is, even after twenty-four years of marriage is still, the most beautiful woman, in the world to me. She moves something indescribable in me. She is sensual, erotic, and captivating all in one sweep of her small, beautiful body."

Noticing the look of pain in her husband's eyes said, "Roberto', please talk to me, why are you so silent tonight? Are you so angry with me about not telling you beforehand of our daughter's date tonight, that it will prevent us from talking to each other as we always do?"

With a demanding and agonizing tone to his voice laced with pain, said, "Simone', you say that you do not keep anything from me concerning daughter, this may be true, but, what about things that concerns you, are you honest with me?"

"Roberto' what do you mean? I do not keep anything from you."

"Simone', can you honestly say that you have you always been truthful with me?"

"I try to be Roberto'. I do not understand the question."

"Yes, Simone' you understand! I am no fool. I know that you..." Roberto' not wanting to finish the statement said, "It is time for sleep. I do not want to discuss it tonight. Please come to bed Simone'."

"I want to discuss it, if something is upsetting you." Simone's fears of past years and terrible dread gripped her entire being. Fear and dread of this moment of her sins in the past was catching up with her and that past was not that long ago.

"No Simone' no not tonight!" He took off his robe, lay down, and turned off the lamp on his bedside table. Simone' with fear and dread still gripping her being, slipped off her robe, turned out her lamp, and got into bed beside her husband. She slide over next to Roberto' as she did every night.

Roberto' felt the warmth of his wife's body as she lay behind him and slipped her arm across him. He yearned to take her in his arms as he did each night. Tonight, he wanted her to make love to him, but it was painful to think of her not loving him in the way he needed her too. Simone's touch tonight bought pain to Roberto' rather than pleasure as it always did. Roberto' felt the pain, like a knife, in his heart plunge even deeper, until his eyes filled with tears prayed to God for relief and peace.

Not knowing what to say or if she should say anything said, "Good night Roberto'." Overcome with pain and emotion, Roberto' did not respond, but took her small fragile hand in his and kissed her it lightly on the inside.

The opening of a Pandora's Box.

CHAPTER

Ten

Finally, at Rochelle's, Jason felt nervous, butterflies fluttered in his stomach, "Carmeli'ta' I wanted this night to be exceptional; the atmosphere to be special. I have something I wanted to talk with you about or tell you tonight without interruptions." Jason felt his hands shake and become sweaty heard his voice slightly tremble as he spoke.

"The room is very nice Jason. I appreciate the compliment it shows great preparation, thank you."

"Carmeli'ta', I did not want this night to be a regular company business night because it is not. I wanted it to be a different night."

"It is a very romantic atmosphere Jason." She did not get a response from Jason when she commented about the romantic atmosphere of the room!

"I know what I want to say to you Carmeli'ta', however, I seem to be tongue tied and all thumbs tonight stumbling over my words." He continued, "When you came to Madison Steel as an employee, it was a blessing for me; you have done so much for the company, employees, and clients. I do not know what I would do without you there. You are one of the best hiring decisions I have made in reference to the company and success of business. Certainly, you can be credited with the Meriwether Textile business alliance and so much more that it would take all night to talk about it."

Carmeli'ta', looking at Jason intently did not comment smiled at his compliments of her skills and abilities thought, "This is a business night, he just wanted to say thank you for my hard work." Carmeli'ta' spirits began to fall, because she realized that Jason did not love her as she did him. She would not be able to work for him any longer, as she and her Mother had discussed before the evening started, because of the love she had for him that had grown and had fully blossomed in the last eight months of them working so close.

When viewed as one-sided that kind of Love is harsh.

The evening was not progressing as planned, Jason thought, "This is not going as I intended it to; I did not ask Carmeli'ta' on this date to talk about business. Jason, stop being a coward tell with her about your feeling." Jason was afraid that she did not feel the same way about him, "If she did no love me and I tell her my feeling, the expression of horror on her face would crush me breaking my heart. It is a chance I will have to take. How can I hold the strong intense love I feel for her inside any longer?" he asked himself.

"Jason, thank you. I enjoy each day that I come to Madison Steel and the work that I do. I appreciate the opportunities that you have given me to advance myself. I will never forget what you have done for me over the past year and a half. I have learned a lot from you about business."

Jason frowning, "Carmeli'ta', that sounded like a resignation. You are not leaving me are you? Have Meriwether offered you a job or more money? I know that he would like for you to be part of his organization."

"No, Jason, I have not been offered a job by Meriwether Textiles or Charles Bienville Meriwether."

"You did not answer my question about you resigning, Carmeli'ta'!" Overcome with emotions tears swelling in her eyes she answered, "I had thought about it Jason, and would return the wardrobe that you have let me use while being Hostess for you."

"Why, Carmeli'ta' what happened or what have I done that you want to resign? I thought you were happy with my company!" She said, "I thought my hostess duties were not needed any further since you got Mr. Meriwether to agree to talk about a contract. "She continued, "I am happy Jason you are a wonderful employer."

"What are these tears for that I see in your eyes tonight?"

"They are tears of appreciation Jason for all the compliments that you have given me, the opportunities that I had to advance myself and sharpen my skills with you. You are a wonderful boss and supervisor. I appreciate everything you have taught me."

"That is good Carmeli'ta'. You frightened me for a second. I could not bear to have you leave me. I would not accept the wardrobe back from you Carmeli'ta'. It is yours to keep. I purchased it especially for you from my discretionary fund with no expense to the company. I wanted the wardrobe to be from me personally."

Carmeli'ta' shocked for a moment said, "Thank you Jason; I had no idea it was a personal gift. Toni did not tell me. I feel humbled by your kindness."

He replied, "I did not want you to know then, it would have changed the outfits you selected. I wanted you to have the best and not chose based on a lesser price." Feeling overwhelmed by the revelation said again, "Thank you Jason for your kindness to me."

The emotions Jason saw in Carmeli'ta' took away his fear of revealing his love for her. With thoughts of losing her to another employer, Jason pictured himself without Carmeli'ta' for the rest of his life was more than he could stand had to tell her now, no more waiting. Jason took a White Italian Linen Handkerchief from the kerchief pocket inside his suit, lovingly dabbed each of her eyes, and afterwards placed the handkerchief in her hands.

Accepting the handkerchief graciously, she noticed his initials J.M. jr. monogrammed in one corner of the handkerchief with beautiful burgundy thread.

"Thank you is not necessary for the wardrobe. It was my pleasure. I meant for it to be a gift from me. I did not ask you to dinner tonight to talk about business. I wanted to tell you how much I care for you and I hope that you care for me as well. Carmeli'ta' that is not my true feeling for you, I love you Carmeli'ta'. I have loved you for more than six months now. I realized it long before you became Hostess for me I was falling in love with you. I hope that tonight will be special. You might consider our dating to give a relationship a chance to develop. I know that you may not love me now, but I think that you care for me. I hope it will become love on your part; I already love you."

Carmeli'ta' with tears swelling in her eyes could not speak for what seemed to Jason an eternity finally said, "Jason, I do care for you. I more than care for you, I love you. I have loved you for so long now, but thought you would never fall in love with me. When you were telling me earlier how much you appreciate my being part of Madison Steel, I thought this was an appreciation dinner. I could not have continued to work for you; because of the love I feel for you, it would have been much too hard."

"Carmeli'ta', my beautiful Carmeli'ta', I love you so. I think about you constantly. Your face is with me in the morning when I wake at night before I go to sleep. I dream of you being with me every day and every night. Carmeli'ta' my darling, I need you. I want you in my life for an eternity. It broke my heart many times within each moment that you spoke when I thought you were leaving me. I could not bear life without you. I want you so much my darling, to kiss, hug, to be near you. I thought, at times, I could not breathe if you were not near me each day. You have become my focus my heart yearns for you. I want to hold you near me for the rest of my life."

"Jason, I feel the same way. I see your face in the mornings. You are my first thought in the morning my last thought at night. I cannot imagine not seeing you each day. You are my heart; it beats for you. I do not want to go through the remainder of my life without you."

"Carmeli'ta', I want you to become my wife and be the Mother of my children. I want to date you; romance you fall in love with you all over again. Each time I see you I want to remember this night. I realized when I thought that you were resigning my life would be nothing without you in it at Madison Steel or being mine, all mine my darling; my heart is yours Carmeli'ta' for now through eternity. When I am near you the passion I feel is irrepressible. It is strong and overpowering. You make me happy my lovely Carmeli'ta'. The joy I feel gives me a new energy inside. I want to tell the world that I love you."

"Jason, the happiness that I feel from your loving me is overwhelming to me tonight. I had hoped and prayed this was not a dinner to discuss business. I wanted to tell you for so long how I felt. It was hard to keep my feeling hid from you sometimes. When you came near me in the office, or stand close to me my feelings were more than I could capture mentally. Being near you seeing you each day, my feeling at time, were so strong and potent they bought tears to my eyes. The love I feel for you is so deeply intense, it is painful to deal with."

This would only be the tip of the iceberg, for Jason and Carmeli'ta'. Their love would not come easily. The relationship would suffer many blows and battles before they would be together finally.

The evening was progressing well for the two new lovers; across town tension was building. It was 8:30 p.m., Roberto' neither Simone' could sleep for a while that night.

Roberto' lay quietly thinking as he felt Simone' soft breath on his back thought, "She was so young when we married, it could be that she was not ready for marriage. She did not have the experience to know how to love passionately. I rushed her into marriage that may have been a mistake. She seemed so inexperienced on our wedding night, almost as if she were afraid for me to touch her; so distant as if she were somewhere else. I wanted her so desperately, I was afraid, if I did not marry her then, I would lose her (Roberto' knew that he had been obsessive when it came to Simone'). She was so beautiful and sweet I could not resist falling in love with her, now I suffer for it. I should have given both of us more time."

The thoughts swirling around his head tortured him as he lay next to his wife, "but then again, it has been years since our marriage. I have tried to teach her my passionate needs in the way that I make love to her."

Roberto' saw his love for Simone' through eyes of rose-colored glasses. He still saw her as a 17-year-old inexperienced girl. He did not want to face the mystery in her eyes. He told himself over the years, "If I love her enough it would change, but the pain has kept that knife plunging deeper into my heart."

Roberto' suffered because of the love he had for his beautiful Simone'. He had given her everything and did everything he could to change that look of mystery in her eyes. However, never was there an indication in the smallest way she cared enough to share with him the mystery enshrouding her very being. Lying quietly, he decided, "I cannot fool myself any longer. I love her so desperately it is destroying me not knowing the mystery that surrounds my wife."

Roberto' knew only the truth could alleviate the pain within him decided, "Even if it causes me more pain, at least, I will know the truth. There has to be a truth to the mystery surrounding my wife and only she knows what it is." Simone', unable to sleep, lay still praying to God for peace and mercy knew this dreaded moment would come in her life and she would have to tell Roberto' what has kept her from making passionate love to him at the level he needed and wanted all the years of their marriage.

But then again, she thought, "He does not realize that I do love him and want to give him the passion he makes me feel. The fear of what I did, before I met Roberto' the days before I was married, what I did after we arrived here, for years, are the burdens I carry. I am afraid that somehow, he will find out about me and this will destroy Carmeli'ta' and him both and the love they have for me. I could not tell him all the years before, now I may not have a choice."

Simone' pondered what to do, where to go, who could help her, thought, "Tomorrow while Roberto' is away attending to farm duties I will visit our Minister." Simone' had shared with Steven Meriwether, the Minister of the Charleston Street Church of Christ where she and Roberto' obeyed the Gospel a few years after they were settled in America, all the events that took place before and after her marriage.

She heard the voice of their Minister, Brother Meriwether and the last conversation and his advice, "Simone' tell your husband about you and Vincenzo' Alessandro Moretti, and what has transpired between you since you have been here in America. Simone' if he never finds out, it will always be a there between you and ultimately will cause your marriage to fail. You and Roberto' will be married and living in the same house, but that is all that you will have. Roberto' and my knowing his passion for you Simone', will not be able to live with this the rest of his life. Not the way that he loves and cares for you, it is destroying him slowly, tell him Simone'! You and he can work this out if you truly want to, but living a lie each day, as you have done for years now, will destroy you as well; it is eating at you already, unless we would not be having this conversation today."

As Simone' rose from the chair in his office at his home, he said, "Tell Roberto' Simone' don't keep waiting it will only get worse. I will pray for you and Roberto' and our sweet Carmeli'ta' it will destroy her as well.' Simone', one last point I want to share with you, "Roberto' has been coming here for some time now, and has shared with me the pain and suffering he has kept within himself, because he loves you so. You cannot continue this way Simone', not anymore. You are torturing your husband, he is heartbroken because he thinks that you do not love, want, or need him!"

"But that is not true. I love my husband with all my heart and soul."

"He does not think that Simone' and have no way of knowing it. He is going by your actions he can only know what you let him know." "I can't tell him not now it has to be another way to solve this issue."

He added, "Truth is always the only way to solve any issue Simone'.

Being untruthful only brings more need to be untruthful."

"I know Brother Meriwether I will think about all that you said to me over the time I have been confiding in you. Thank you for caring."

Steven Meriwether did not responds to Simone's last statement only shook his head in an okay I understand manner then said, "I will see you on Sunday for Lord's Day Service my dear sister."

Simone' left and drove home contemplating all he said and what steps she could take.

She went back in time and continued to play the past events in her mind, as she lay next to her husband unable to sleep. In June 1913, two years after Simone' and her family moved to America Vincenzo' came to see Carmeli'ta and her. Carmeli'ta was 7 years old when he saw her again. He contacted Simone' when he arrived and asked her to meet him. He was staying with an old friend, Charles Bienville Meriwether. Simone' was not known in the next town, Sedalia, a suburb of Charleston, as she was in Charleston, so she met Vincenzo' at a little restaurant there. They talked for hours. Vincenzo' wanted to see Carmeli'ta'. He insisted, "I did not come to America to be denied my child." Simone' agreed to take Carmeli'ta' to the park near their home and Vincenzo' met them there under the pretense he was taking a walk in the park. He sat and talked with Simone' as he watched his daughter play happily, near where they sat. As the time approached for Roberto' to come home, Simone' took Carmeli'ta' and left. After a few days visiting with Charles Meriwether, Vincenzo' returned to Tuscany.

More years went by with Simone' keeping in touch with Vincenzo'. He came to America to see them every year even during the war 1914 through 1917 and other times when he could. However, he never let Carmeli'ta' know who he was or that he even saw her. He would observe her from a distance, at school, with her friends, or shopping with her Mother. Events and company business finally prevented Vincenzo' from coming to visit one year in 1915, Simone' felt relief for that year. She had gone along with this farce out of fear and at a loss of what to do because it had gone on so long.

Carmelita was 15 years old when he saw her last before she graduated high school. Carmeli'ta' was 16 when Vincenzo' came to her graduation from Charleston High, June 10, 1921. He bought her two beautiful dresses from Italy. He met Simone' at the park in Charleston and gave them to her before Carmeli'ta' graduation day. Graduation day, he watched Carmeli'ta' march down the aisle; it was a proud "Father moment" for Vincenzo'. Roberto' and Simone' were seated together in the parents' reserved section across the room from Vincenzo', Simone' saw him watching her across the room as the graduation ceremony took place. Roberto' did not see him nor the looks that passed between them; he was looking at Carmeli'ta' thinking how proud he was of his beautiful daughter.

Simone' was still lovely as ever to Vincenzo'. All he could see were they being together. Her face, her body, her beautiful hair, and the scent of lavender, the smell of her skin, and the sweet honey taste of her lips; it was hard for him to control his feeling of wanting to go to her.

Simone' gave Carmeli'ta' the dresses Vincenzo' bought her. Carmeli'ta' assumed her Mother bought them from Toni's as did Roberto'. Simone' let them both believe the lie about the dresses. Three day after graduation, Tuesday, June 13, Simone' agreed to meet Vincenzo' at a little café in the Sedalia suburb city called Justin's. Justin's was a nice quiet cafe', a favorite to the town's people. Justin Tanner was a delightful host and wonderful cook. He had learned from his Mother Marcia Tanner, who was Marianna Chavez's, Simone' and Roberto's cook and housekeeper's cousin, about food as he grew and knew he wanted to own a cafe'. The food was distinctly southern. The taste delightfully tickled the taste buds as it went down as smooth as vanilla pudding. His customer's favorite dishes were his Mother's Chicken and Dumplings, Cornbread Muffins, Four Cheeses Macaroni,

Sweet Potatoes a la Marcia; Fried Pork Salad with eggs and hot homemade Apple Pie, The Apple Pie was Justin's own combination of spices he would not share with anyone, not even with his Mother Marcia.

Simone' was seated in at a small table near a window when Vincenzo' came in. He walked over to her and said, "Hello my beautiful Simone', you are lovelier now than you were at 17 years old."

"Vincenzo' please, let us not go through this each time we meet. This is my last meeting with you; please do not ask to see me again." She continued, "Vincenzo' I fell in love with Roberto', a few months after we were married. I have told you this many times over the years, why can't you believe me?" I will not, for the last time, see you ever again!"

"Simone' what about my daughter Carmeli'ta'?" asked Vincenzo'. "And how can you be so capricious?"

Vincenzo' she insisted, "Roberto' is the only Father she has, when will you admit this to yourself? Secondly, I am not fickle. We were so young then and had no concept of real love."

Vincenzo' feeling a hint of anger, "I know Carmeli'ta' is my daughter, so do you Simone'. I will not give her up, no matter what I have to do. I lost Valentina, I will not lose Carmeli'ta'." This statement frightened Simone'.

"Vincenzo', Carmeli'ta' is not Valentina, you cannot replace your twin sister with Roberto' and my daughter. Please, I will never see you again. You are married Vincenzo' and so am I. I cannot go on playing the hypocrite in my marriage any longer. Please stay away!"

"My wife has not given me children in the twelve years we have been married. It is getting far too late in life for us, she is 35 years old now Simone', we may never have a child. How can I give up Carmeli'ta'?"

Anger, fear, and dread all came out in Vincenzo's voice as he made a plea for being in Carmeli'ta's life. Simone' saw in Vincenzo's face the pain of the prospect of the loss of Carmeli'ta' in his life. She knew within herself that desperate people take desperate measures. Love compels us to do things that we would not do under ordinary circumstances. She did not know what Vincenzo' would do, this added more fear and pressure to an already defeating situation, which she had let run for years, like a train, out of control.

To Simone', Vincenzo's personality had become malignant. His portrait had a different look; it was grossly skewed; disappointments and unhappiness in his life rendered him harshly sardonic, because he could not possess Simone' as he planned and wanted. His spring seemed to have left him and turned to a cold and calculating winter. To Simone', Vincenzo' was the elephant in the room; bringing with his malevolent personality a grey area of ambiguity laced with fear.

Simone' had not seen her Minister, Mr. Meriwether, sitting in the café having lunch. He had come to visit a church member who was sick in a nursing home, with only a few short weeks to live. Simone' looking up saw him looking at her as she argued with Vincenzo'. She was shocked to see her Minister there; not thinking she would see anyone she knew from Charleston, not in this café' it was not on a main street and a good ways from the city of Charleston. Her Minister saw the expression of shock on Simone's face as she glanced up then looked his way once more with a frown forming her forehead. He finished his lunch and walked past the table where she was seated talking to Vincenzo'.

"Good morning Simone' how are you? I am delighted to see you as always."

"Good Morning Brother Meriwether, I am fine today, thank you. It is good to see you too. How are you?"

"Thank you for asking, I am fine Simone'." He looked at Vincenzo' and said, "I am Steven Meriwether."

He replied, "I am Vincenzo' Alessandro Moretti."

"I have not seen you at church. Are you from the community in Charleston?"

"No, I am from Tuscany." Brother Meriwether looked at Simone' with a question in his eyes as a small frown darted across his forehead.

Simone' not letting Vincenzo' know that Steven Meriwether knew who he was and about the past relationship she had with him said, "He is a friend of mine Brother Meriwether from Roberto' and my hometown."

"I see. It was nice meeting you Mr. Moretti. Are you staying long in America?"

"No, I am leaving tomorrow."

"Goodbye, it was nice meeting you Mr. Moretti. Simone', I will see you on Sunday. Tell Roberto' I said hello."

"Goodbye Brother Meriwether. I will tell my husband you said hello, I will see you on Sunday."

Vincenzo' only nodded bye to Steven Meriwether with an intense look on his face.

Simone' could not look at her Minister; felt embarrassed because she thought he could see her thoughts. However, it was only her imagination and guilt working overtime.

Simone', laying silent and still, all the past meetings and conversations

swirled through her head, still pondered Roberto's statement of "honesty" to her…wondered if he had found her Diary. Simone' had kept a Diary since she was a girl of 13 years old. She wanted her daughter to know and understand her so she shared her heart through her Diary. Simone's Mother had kept a Diary and gave it to Simone' to read once she became a married woman. Her Diary contained the secrets of a successful marriage and the heart of the woman that wrote it, her Mother. She added her life and wrote her heart in her own Diary since she was 13 years old. The details were intimate and personal. Simone' thought, "if he has found my Diary and read it, I could not bear the pain that I know it will cause him and Carmeli'ta'. I know that I keep it well hidden in a place that no one knows exist and would think to look."

CHAPTER

ELEVEN

At Rochelle's the evening smoothed out, Jason beckoned Carlos to bring them a bottle of Champagne to celebrate their "Love Confessions" to each other. The character of the room was so lavishly rich with the feelings of love and romance. Jason and Carmeli'ta' sat gazing into each other's eyes for long periods-of-time before they spoke; he held Carmeli'ta' hand while looking at her sweet face; her smile melted Jason's heart.

The romantic mood swirled around them as if they were in a wind tunnel; the dominant atmosphere of romance in the room sent Jason and Carmeli'ta' into a quixotic whirl.

Carlos arrived with the wine, Château Margaux, (archaically La Mothe de Margaux, is a wine estate of Bordeaux wine, and was one of four wines to achieve Premier cru status in the Bordeaux Classification of 1855.) Château Margaux is the most expensive Wine served at Rochelle'. Jason ordered it especially for this occasion. Carmeli'ta' sipped the wine slowly, it was mild and sweetly pleasing to the taste, creating a waterfall of taste in her mouth, giving her a warm sensation of snuggling into a warm bath as she did earlier in the evening. The wine was so satisfying because she could tell the world Jason was hers and she was his. Love was in the air. Jason was in a rare form, Carmeli'ta' had never seen before. He was particularly gentle, kind, attentive, and non-business-like this special night.

"Carmeli'ta', my lovely, I do not want to carry this relationship too fast so that we will both have a chance to get use to the idea of being in love and sharing our love with each other."

"I agree Jason. It is essential we observe protocol with the company as well as our families. We will be careful with the relationship until both our families get use to the idea."

"I agree Carmeli'ta'. I will have to approach my Mother carefully with the idea of getting married or presently having a Lady I am interested in with who I want a future. I do want this relationship to be the beginning of our engagement to be married. First, before all the rest, I want to romance you, date you, know how it feels to pick you up for a date, to see the excitement in your eyes when I bring you flowers. I want the whole of a courtship Carmeli'ta'."

"Jason it is every girls dream to be courted, romanced, and be given flowers. To feel you are that special someone in another's life is very important. A woman needs the feeling she gets knowing she is the love of someone life."

"You are the love of my life Carmeli'ta'. I never thought I would find someone to love me, to understand me, to care about what I care about, to be the joy in my days and nights my darling. I have loved you for so long. I was afraid to tell you. I spoke with my Father about my feeling for you after we came from Church on Sunday. He was delighted I had fallen in love with you. He said that 'I will be proud to have Carmeli'ta' as a daughter-in-law. However, my Mother, Juanita, is a different story. As I told you before, she is a hard nut to crack, tough as Charles Bienville Meriwether."

"And your Mother, Carmeli'ta', what will she say?" asked Jason. "My Mother wants me to have a choice in who I give my heart to in love not have the marriage arranged by my parents. She said, "We are not in the old country anymore." However, "My Father thinks differently. I hope that you understand."

"I do understand Carmeli'ta' my Mother has similar views to your father's; she is from Ireland. In that light, it is good we each have one parent on our side when we are ready to announce our engagement and marriage plans."

"Jason, we will need to talk and make plans so that our relationship will not affect our work or our families before we have the opportunity to tell everyone. Will this mean that I will not be able to work as close with you on a daily basis?"

"No, my lovely, I could not bear that. If the chain of command changes in the office, there will be too many questions; therefore, we will keep our same daily schedules. We can make this work Carmeli'ta'.

I will do everything I can to make sure no one suspects anything. I would not want to compromise your authority or mine. I want to protect you more than I do me. I could not do less; I do love you so."

Carmeli'ta' wanting Jason to understand about her Father, "It will be difficult to tell my Father, Jason. He has the bent of mind that the culture in Tuscany dictates; Fathers are to choose for their daughters and sons their future husbands/wives. My Mother understands and is more open minded. She thinks women should have a choice in the matters of the heart. She has said this to me since I was a small girl."

"You were a younger girl Carmeli'ta' my sweet, you are still very small. I thought I should tell you that I love your size you are so small and petite.

Your size make me want to protect you and cuddle you all the more."

"Thank you Jason your words feel beautiful tonight; I will remember this evening forever; the night you told me you loved me. I have fallen in love with you all over again tonight."

Soft music by Ludwig Van Beethoven played softly in the background throughout the evening starting with Jason's favorite song, "Fur Elise". Jason saw the sparkle in Carmeli'ta's eyes as she talked, and the beauty of her lovely white teeth framed by a heart-shaped mouth.

"Carmeli'ta', please dance with me", reaching for her hand he kissed it.

"Thank you, Jason; I would love to dance with you."

He rose, pulled Carmeli'ta' chair back, and took her left hand; she stood and they walked slowly to the dance floor pulled her to him and held her close. He stood head and shoulders taller than Carmeli'ta' looking down at her beautiful face, he said, "Carmeli'ta', my beautiful Carmeli'ta'."

She snuggled closer to Jason; he held her not wanting to let her go as they moved around the dance floor. The fragrance of her cologne was like inhaling the clean cool breeze after a cleansing rain on a moonlight night. The scent in her hair was like a bouquet of flowers laced with Strawberry. While they danced, the reflection from the candlelight gave her black hair a soft silky glow. Jason felt as if he was of men the most fortunate to have the love a beautiful woman like Carmeli'ta'. He treasured her even more because she loved him. He wanted this night to last forever.

Carmeli'ta' quietly allowed her mind to relax and drift into field of flowers, walking talking, playing, running, and enjoying life with Jason. She had longed for this evening and time with Jason that did not involve business. Tonight was her dream come true. She could feel how strong he was as he held her so close she could hear his heartbeat, slow, sturdy, and strong.

Looking up at Jason after a long while, the scent of his Borneo 1834 Serge Lutens Cologne and Aftershave was so inviting; wanted to get ever closer to Jason; she held him tighter.

Jason feeling the tightness of Carmeli'ta' arms around him looked down at her, stopped moving, slowly lifted Carmeli'ta' off the floor, held her close to his chest, kissed her tenderly and passionately on her mouth. Carmeli'ta', never having been kissed, felt dazed for a short time. Her Father and Mother had kissed her. Jason was her first romantic kiss; it was so pleasant her heart raced out of control. She drew closer to Jason slowly looked at him smiled and kissed him back, so softly almost like an innocent child.

Jason feeling overcome with love and desire to kiss and hold Carmelita, let her tenderly down to the floor, drew her close to him, kissed her longer deeper more passionately until he thought he would not be able to breathe. Carmeli'ta' kisses to Jason was captivating, he could not kiss her enough.

She could feel as she stroked the back of his head, the softy silky smoothness of his hair held her after the long kiss, neither of them said anything.

Jason finally whispered so softly in her ear, "Carmeli'ta', I love you, I love you. I do not want to live without you not a minute. Just knowing that you are mine makes my world blissful."

"I love you Jason, my sweetheart. I always dreamed of my first kiss being special; my first kiss was beyond special, your kiss astounded me. My heart is yours, all yours."

As the evening progressed, and the hour grew late, 9:30 p.m. dinner not requested yet; Rochelle appeared at the door walked over to where Jason and Carmeli'ta' were standing asked, "Mr. Madison and Mrs. Bandaci, dinner is waiting; are you ready?"

Carlos had quietly excused himself from the room when he saw the intimate moments with Jason and Carmeli'ta'. Rochelle noticed Carlos standing outside of the closed door to the Blue Room wanted to see if there was a problem or something Jason and Carmeli'ta' needed other than what they requested.

"We are fine Rochelle, just got involved in conversation and the evening passed quickly. I am hungry Carmeli'ta' what about you?"

"I am hungry as well Jason, it is getting late for dinner. I think that we are ready now Rochelle, thank you." "I will send Carlos in immediately."

"Thank you Rochelle" said Jason as he nodded. Carlos appeared, "Mr. Madison, may I serve you and Ms. Bandaci now?" Jason smiling, "Yes, Carlos, we are famished!"

Carlos walked out of the room, Jason escorted Carmeli'ta' to their table gently seated her while they waited for their food kissed her right hand and smiled. Carmeli'ta' smiled and said, "Jason you are very romantic; this has been a most pleasant evening. I cannot think of one in my life I have enjoyed more; it is wonderful. Thank you for making it special for me; I love your romantic nature."

Jason encouraged by her words said, "You make me feel all these things my love. I want to romance you for the rest of our lives, as we grow older; I know that my feelings will grow stronger as we mature. The need I have for you in my life is already so intense. I look forward to growing old with you my Carmeli'ta'. I cannot think of anything I would rather do than live the rest of my life with you. God has blessed me well in my life; I want to share with you all that I have and everything that I am."

"I feel the same way Jason. God has blessed me in my life. I want to share my blessing of love, care, understanding, and everything I have and I am in life with you my darling the whole of my being. I love you Jason. I never thought I would get a chance to tell you. I had hoped against hope you loved me."

Jason did not say anything just took both of her hands in his, leaned forward, kissed her gently on her lips, and smiled.

Carlos opened the door wheeled in the heated food cart with their dinner. The aroma from their dinner as he approached the table was mouth-watering to Jason and Carmeli'ta'. Neither of them realized, with all the love-energy spent, for the last one-hour and a half, they were extremely hungry. Carlos asked, "May I serve you Sir and Miss?" Jason nodding, "Yes please, Carlos. The food smells delicious." Rochelle prepared the dinner especially ordered by Jason for Carmeli'ta'. The menu included, Tossed Salad with Oil and Vinegar Dressing, Duck A' L'Orange bathed in Sweet and Sour Citrus Sauce, New Red Potatoes, Asparagus, with Hollandaise Sauce, Dinner Rolls, and Iced Tea. The appetizer was Carrots and sliced cucumber with Salt, Pepper, and Red Wine Vinegar. The desserts were Chef Antoine's creation an array of specialty chocolates dainty cookies, cupcakes, and Pinafores with white chocolate swirls with a unique tasting Chocolate and Vanilla Mousse' that Carmeli'ta' absolutely loved.

Jason asked Rochelle the week before what Ms. Bandaci's favorite dishes were when she dined with her family and friends. Rochelle's prepared the favorite of all Carmeli'ta's food including the desserts. The food was perfect, not only was the food delicious, the fact they were in love enhanced every bite for Carmeli'ta'.

Love can enhance or destroy the taste of food. Tonight, it enhanced the taste giving Carmeli'ta' an appetite she never had before. It was as if she tasted the food for the first time, as a baby does, when he listens to discover if it is delicious, I want more, so the baby screams for more. Carmeli'ta' ate savoring every bite. Jason was delighted to see Carmeli'ta' enjoy the dinner he planned so carefully for her in every minute detail.

After dinner, Carlos served Chef Antoine's specialty desserts with Coffee.

"Jason how did you know that these were my favorite foods?" asked Carmeli'ta'.

"I called Rochelle's when you told me that you like Rochelle's and she gave me your favorite foods and desserts."

"Jason my darling this makes dinner even more special just the fact you took time to know what my favorite foods are and have them prepared makes it more than special. Duck A' L'Orange bathed in Citrus Sauce is a long process. Marianna fusses over it the entire day when she prepares it for dinner. Thank you for this exceptional dinner you had prepared just for me; it makes the evening even more beguiling."

"Carmeli'ta' to me you are worth all the special dinners in the world; there is nothing I would not do to make you happy. I want you to know that." The special attention to the evening touched her heart and bought her a joy inside she had not known before. He saw a warm and loving smile on her face. Her eyes danced when she smiled, sparkling likes diamonds.

"Tell me my sweet, who is Marianna?" asked Jason.

"Forgive me Jason, Marianna is my Mothers and Fathers housekeeper and cook. She has lived with us for eighteen years. She helped raise me when Mother and Father worked hard to get the vegetable farm going. I love Marianna; she is so sweet and spoiled me a lot when Mother and Father were not around."

"I will always spoil you my love, you deserve it; you are sweet and humble my darling two of the many things I love about you."

"Thank you, Jason."

Jason and Carmeli'ta' had not noticed after dessert dishes were taken away that it was past 11:00 p.m. Rochelle closes at 11:00 p.m. each night. Carlos came in and asked, "Is there anything else I can get you Mr. Madison before I leave for the evening?"

"No, you have done an excellent job tonight Carlos." Jason handed him an envelope with a $15.00 tip in it. This overjoyed Carlos. This amount in a tip could carry him through an entire week in food, rent and utilities; he would still have money left.

Rochelle appeared at the door and said, "Mr. Madison, please feel free to stay as long as you need to tonight. I will be in my office with my manager taking care of the end of the week accounts. I will put tonight on your account if that is okay with you."

"Thank you, Rochelle that will be fine; I will have Ms. Horne to take care of the account on Monday as usual", he said.

"I will check back with you in a while or if you are ready to leave before then, please let Chester know he will be on duty until you leave tonight. He is also our security for our clients here. Good night Mr. Madison, Ms. Bandaci and it was my pleasure to serve you tonight. I will look forward to seeing both of you again soon."

Jason and Carmeli'ta'bid goodbye to Rochelle. Jason knew that Rochelle would be discreet and not say anything about what she saw tonight. They continued dancing as the music played softly in the background kissing and holding onto each other as if this would be the last time.

New love is so beautiful between two people that feel the way that Jason and Carmelita do about each other. The music put them on a floating cloud, kept them elevated above all the world while they danced and danced for more than an hour.

Jason pulled his pocket watch out to see the time said, "Carmeli'ta' my darling, it is midnight. I will regrettably have to take you home. I want to stay with you here and dance the night away; unfortunately, I cannot keep you out all night."

Escorting Carmeli'ta'back to the table took her Mink Stoll off the back of the chair and put it lightly around her shoulders. She picked up her evening bag they walked out the Blue Room to the front door where Chester was waiting to escort them to their car. Jason held her close to him as they walked to the car, his mind and heart on a merry-go-round, of joy and happiness, swirled in unison because of the love he felt.

Carmeli'ta' noticed Jason's Bentley was the only car left in the parking besides Rochelle's and her staff. He unlocked and opened the car door and waited for her to be comfortably seated, locked her door, walked swiftly around the front of the car, got in started the engine and drove toward her Townhouse. A brief moment of silence invaded the atmosphere as they drove. The silence broken by his concern for the lateness of the hours said, "Carmeli'ta' my darling, it is so late tonight. I have kept you long you will be tired tomorrow at work. I want you to come to the office later after lunch. I will have Mrs. Horne cover for you until you get there."

"Jason that is not necessary. I can come in at my regular 9:00 a.m. time tomorrow. I am not the least bit tired my love; in fact, I am just the opposite. I feel so excited. If I tried, I do not think I could be tired.

If it is okay with you, I will come in at my regular time, I could not bear not seeing you at 9:00 a.m. It feels like I am in a dream; I do not want to wake up to find it is not true. I want to see your face first thing in the morning."

Jason, smiling, "Yes my darling that is fine with me if you can make it that early, but if not, feel free to come in when you are rested or if you feel tired at any point tomorrow I will understand if you excuse yourself and go home for a rest. We do have a date later tonight. It is 12:10 a.m. already my darling. We can change the date if you like to Thursday, November 14."

"No, Jason my darling, I want to go on our date tonight. I will be fine. How are you Jason, you are so concerned about me. Will you be tired tomorrow?"

"No, Carmeli'ta' I am use to this type of schedule. I will rest over Saturday when the plant is closed. Don't worry about me my darling."

"Jason do you think the employees will notice the change in our mannerisms toward each other?" Carmeli'ta' asked.

"Not at all, we will do as we said and not allow our feelings to show, it is important for morale and the chain of command and authority in the company. We can do this. I will make sure there is no change. I have always treated you special in front of the employees it will be no different."

"Thank you, Jason."

Jason's muse for a few minutes was his first date with Carmeli'ta'. He glanced at Carmeli'ta'; she was looking out of the window at the lights as they passed the Charleston Country Club thought, "I want to know the place, and be the only one in that place in her heart no one knows exist except us; Heavenly Father, I love and need her so desperately. Please help us as only you can."

Carmeli'ta' turned, looked at him and commented, "Jason, I have always thought this was a beautiful scene; the lights on the pathway leading to the Country Club. The lights among the palm trees lining the street look as if they are soldiers on duty."

"It is a beautiful scene Carmeli'ta' I have loved this view for years as I pass to go home at night. Carmeli'ta', I will tell you every day for the rest of my life, I love you darling. I told you yesterday; this is another day; it is Wednesday morning, Carmeli'ta' I love you."

"I love you Jason I will tell you every day of my life. I have enjoyed this special evening you planned so carefully for me. I will never forget it as long as I live."

The night grew longer and longer for Simone' and Roberto'. Simone' wrestled with doubt to fear and Roberto' wrestled with doubt of his wife loving and needing him. Sleep eluded them as the moon does a night because of the cloud covering, neither of them could see for the pain they each felt.

CHAPTER
TWELVE

Unable to sleep, her past still wrestling her to the ground, all of the years of marriage flooded Simone's mind while she lay sleepless fearing what the future would hold. Her thoughts fell on her Diary, though well hidden, was the keeper of her most secret possessions: her thoughts, fears, needs, wants, desires, passions, and love for her husband and daughter. Her dairy she kept in the secret compartment of her Negligee' Armoire' she discovered when she inspected the Armoire' before she purchased it. The Lingerie' Vanity was an antique make in England in the early 1500's for Ladies of the Queen's Court.

Simone' found the Armoire' in a quaint little shop in Charleston, Etsy Candelabra's Antiques, named after the owner, Candelabra Antoinette da Molyneux, near their home on Rue de Mellencamp. The Armoire' was a yellowish white stood 5' tall with five drawers and a compartment with French doors. Candelabra informed her, the Armoire' was designed in the time when dashing young English men were great lovers and courted the Duchesses of the English Court; who would hide the love letters there in the secret compartment so their husbands would not find them.

She purchased the Armoire' for its beauty, historical aspect, quaint style, and because she adored antiques, especially from England and France.

She thought about the hiding place for her Diary before she purchased the Armoire'. She kept it in one of her hatboxes in the closet, she knew Roberto' would not find it there. He never plundered through her hats and other personal items.

She determined that the secret compartment would be a good place to put my Diary, just peradventure Roberto' did have an occasion to look in her hatboxes; however, he always helped her get dressed for Church on Sunday. He loved the accessories she wore. Therefore, she decided to change the place and keep her Diary in the Armoire'.

"He could not have found my Diary", she said to herself. "I will check to see if the hidden draw below my gowns has been disturbed." She would wait until Roberto' went to the farm.

Simone' wrote her most intimate thoughts and secrets that only she knew about herself the real Simone' who lived behind those mysterious elusive fluid eyes that were framed so beautifully by her long luscious and sexy lashes.

Simone' wrote in her Diary of the passions and deep-seated needs and desires that she had. It feels like a violent storm raging inside at times. Simone' remembered one excerpt that she wrote ten years earlier, "I feel, at times, and that it will tear me apart. My passion reaches the deepest level of my soul. The love that I had for Vincenzo' was just the tip of the iceberg." (He had only unleashed and ripened her passion and desire).

Her mind raced ahead of her, "However, only one man can satisfy my needs, desires and passion, Roberto'. On the other hand, Vincenzo's love for me, when I was so young and inexperienced was sweet and I desired being with him and wanted him to satisfy that passions that raged within me. I knew the passion and feelings that I had that tore me apart inside, the fires once released only my true love could quench them (one of the lines she wrote in her Diary, I just did not know it at that time). The feelings that I have are so intense that they are painful; to be loved the way that I need and my desires satisfied makes my entire body ache and burn uncontrollably at times. Vincenzo' could never quench the fires that burned so strong within me."

Simone' had written many times in her Diary, but she did not want Roberto' to see what she wrote in its entirety. It would tell him everything about Vincenzo' and her. She felt as if she wrote that she had betrayed her husband and her daughter, truth and honesty was very important to Roberto'.

"I have told my Diary all the things of my heart; things that I could not share with my Father, Mother, Roberto' or Vincenzo'. I pray that he never finds and reads it. If it ever come to the point that I have no choice except to let him read it; I want to tell him about it first, I want him to understand the why, of what I wrote, why I have been so secretive about it."

Their farm was twenty miles from their home; Simone' would check the hiding place when he left. She could barely wait until morning.

Roberto' would be gone to their farm most of the day supervising and working with their Caretaker and Foreman, Peter Meriwether, and his family, who lived in the house that is there. Simone' and Roberto' had lived there for the first five years after them arriving in America while they got their farm on a solid footing. Simone' helped Roberto' with the lighter work on the farm, in early mornings only. She supervised the workers crating the vegetable for daily deliveries.

Not wanting her to work hard anymore only light work decided she had done enough to help him with the necessary work to get the farm on solid financial basis.

After the farm was prosperous and financially sound, he purchased a beautiful house at 15 Rue du Mellencamp, nearer the city with modern conveniences further increasing her comfort. Carmeli'ta' was 10 years old when they moved closer to the city. After they moved to the city, Roberto asked Simone' to be the accounts manager for the Bandaci's Farms, which she did from the office in their home.

Hours later, at 11:00 p.m., which seemed like an eternity Roberto' felt Simone's warm firm body softly relax against his body. He knew she had drifted off to sleep, for this he was thankful. He looked at the clock again later on his bedside table it was 1:00 am; he still had not slept neither did he move it would disturb Simone' and he did not want that. He could not face another conversation tonight, so he lay quietly still and sleepless. At 3:00 a.m. Roberto' finally drifted off to sleep after lying awake for hours thinking about his life with his wife, how their marriage began, the passion and intensity he felt for her, and the need he had for her to love him with the same passion and intensity.

Roberto' knew that Simone' loved him but she did not give herself to him completely. Why when they made love, she did not respond with the passion of a woman in love? He had to know the answer to the secret that Simone' carried behind her intriguingly beautiful and mysteriously watery eyes all the years of their marriage and why she held back loving him was getting more painful as the years passed for him. The pain he felt was a heavy burden;

he could not carry it any longer. There was no panacea that Roberto' could find or think of that would cure the hurt that he felt because he wanted his beautiful Simone' to love him with all her being. The only cure for him would be the truth of what kept his wife from giving herself to him completely.

Across town, Jason approaching Carmeli'ta's Townhouse Community at 12:30 a.m., knew their first date was coming to an end, pulled in front of her building opened his door came around the front of the car waited while she unlocked her door, opened it, took her right hand, and helped her stand.

Pulling her close to him, held her near him for a minute, and whispered in her ear, "You have made me the happiest man in the world tonight; you told me you love me. I prayed to God for your love and I thank Him for your love. I need you Carmeli'ta'; I need you in every way. The intensity of the passion and desire within me burns only for you, my darling." He tenderly kissed her on the mouth and held her tight once more before he took her upstairs. While walking he noticed the moonlight dancing on her silky black hair and the soft feel of her skin felt like a dream. He did not want to awaken from this beautiful dream.

At her Townhouse door, she handed Jason the key, he opened the door escorted her inside closed the door behind them laid the keys on the foyer table next to the lamp, took her Stoll from her shoulder lay in on her lounger, and placed her evening bag on the lounger beside the Stoll. Taking her in his arms, kissed her long and passionately. She returned his kiss just as passionate. Kissing put them in a daze. It was hard to part.

Leading her over to the couch in front of her fireplace the embers still glowed as small flames danced and flickered behind the glass screen, sat down pulled her down beside him, put his arms around her, held her close, and cuddled her next to him. Carmeli'ta' placed her head on his chest and relaxed while Jason leaned his head back on the couch, she felt the strength in his left hand as he held her and said he never would let her go.

His heart beat steady and strong beneath her cheek as it did when they danced. Holding her, Jason became emotional, tears swelling closed his eyes and thanked God for the love Carmeli'ta' and he had for each other; he never wanted to be apart from her.

Feeling Carmeli'ta' move; pulled her closer and said, "Please, Carmeli'ta', I am not ready to let you go, not yet tonight, do you mind if I hold you a little longer? My entire being has starved to be near you for so long; I cannot get enough of your closeness. I know I have to leave, but just a few minutes longer, my darling. I have only one wish not fulfilled tonight."

"What wish is that my darling?"

"I wish we could rewind this night and start all over again."

Carmeli'ta' did not respond immediately to Jason's question or comment. At that moment, moving closer, put her arms around his neck held him and kissed him on his eyes, his cheeks, his nose, his forehead, and her mouth found its way to his mouth and she kissed him so tenderly, and with intense passion in her voice whispered finally, "Jason, I love you and need you so much. I am glad that you stayed with me for a while before you go. I too wish we could live this night all over again. We, my darling, will have many nights like this one. My love for you is so strong."

Jason felt a rush of desire at the sound of the intensity in her voice when Carmeli'ta' whispered so softly and passionately in his ear, drew her closer returning her kiss tenderly with care and understanding. Jason felt himself getting to the point leaving would be almost impossible and that would hurt their relationship.

He could not risk hurting their relationship. He loved and desired her so, at that moment, struggled with the desire not to make love to her. His desire and common sense in a battle, knew he needed to go, sit up looked at his pocket watch, stood pulled Carmeli'ta' up in front of him hugging her tightly said, "It is time for me to leave Carmeli'ta'; it is almost 1:00 a.m."

Jason lived on the next corner near the end of Madison Drive, five minutes from Carmeli'ta's Townhouse, in the left wing of the Madison's Mansion with his parents.

"I know Jason it is getting late."

They walked to the door hand in hand Jason opened the door turned and kissed Carmeli'ta' on the forehead and said, "Good night my precious Carmeli'ta', you have made me a happy man tonight. My days will pass quickly now because I will be anticipating our date later tonight. I probably will not sleep, but will think about you and dream about us being together as man and wife." He added, "Carmeli'ta', I will wait until I hear the lock on the door before I leave, I want you safe."

She responded, "Good night my darling, thank you for caring, and I will lock the door when you leave." Jason closed the door behind him and waited; he heard the latch drop into place knocked softly and said, "Thank you my darling, good night."

He walked to his car, got in, sat for a second to gather his thoughts, and get control of the desire and passions Carmeli'ta' aroused in him before he arrived home. His Mother, Juanita would be waiting for him no matter how late he got home. He did not want to reveal his love for Carmeli'ta' yet. It would mean trouble before the relationship got started good.

Jason finally drove away, Carmeli'ta' stood at the window and watched the taillights until she saw his Bentley turn right at the corner when he arrived at his driveway that led up to the front of the left wing of the Madison Mansion.

Jason pulled his car under the carport near his wing of the Madison Mansion, knew his Mother, Juanita, would be waiting up for him even at 1:30 a.m. in the morning readied himself for her questions. Jason unlocked the door that led to his private suites, just as he closed the door his Mother awakened from the lounger in his living area.

"Jason my darling son, you are so late getting home tonight this is unusual for you. Were you working late?"

"No, Mother, I had a date tonight. I took my date to dinner and dancing afterwards."

"Jason, how lovely for you my son, I am overjoyed that you are finally dating. Is the young lady someone that I know?"

"Mother, it is late and I am tired. I will retire now if you do not mind and talk with you tomorrow after work."

Juanita with insistence in her voice, "Jason, you are avoiding my question?"

Jason said again, most adamantly, "I have to work tomorrow, Good night Mother!"

Juanita Madison, left his living area, returned to her bedroom, and said to her husband, who had awaken because his beautiful Juanita was not beside him, "Jason is just getting in my love. He took his date to dinner and dancing. He was very vague about the date. He would not tell me who she is. Do you know who she might be darling?"

"Juanita, my sweet, come back to bed and let our son make the decision who he wants to date. He is 27 years old; it is time that he found a woman to complete his life as you do mine. When Jason is ready, my lovely, he will share with us the name of the person he is interested in."

Unable to go further with the conversation, Juanita slipped between the sheets next to her husband he held her tight, they drifted into a peaceful sleep.

Jason could not get Carmeli'ta' out of his mind, while undressing relived the entire evening. The Strawberry Scent of her hair lingered in his nose; he noticed the scent of her cologne was on his jacket when he hung it in the closet; both played with the taste buds of his mind.

He could taste the honey sweetness of her kisses and the silky feel of her skin while holding her. Jason was overcome with emotions knowing that Carmeli'ta' loved him something he hoped for so long, could not stop thinking about her.

Anxious for morning and his workday to start so he could see and be near Carmeli'ta'. Jason thought, as he changed into his royal blue silk pajamas, the evening seemed like a dream, brushed his teeth, and got into bed. Carmeli'ta's face was the last thing he saw before he drifted into a peaceful sleep feeling pleasantly tired.

Carmeli'ta', in the meantime, walked into her bedroom and turned down the comforter and sheets on her bed, loosed the buttons on her dress, stepped out of it, and hung it in the closet. She took off her jewelry placed it in the jewelry box on her dresser, removed her shoes and stocking changed into a pink negligée', went in the bathroom and brushed her teeth. She swirled around and around as she came back to the bedroom, finally getting in bed pulled the covers up snuggling beneath them; it was cool in her Townhouse, did not stay awake long she was tired from the long evening and all the Château Margaux Champagne she drank in their love celebration she had earlier last evening. Her sleep was serene. Jason's face danced in her memory as she floated through the open door of love into another dream world.

The alarm clock rang at 7:45 a.m. for another workday. She leaped out the bed and looked out of her bedroom window; the sun was shining so beautifully. She washed her face, brushed her teeth, and went quickly in the kitchen to make coffee and put a bagel in the oven to warm. There was beauty everywhere the day sparked to Carmeli'ta'. She felt light on her feet wanting to soar like a bird in flight. In fact, she did fly around the room as she hurried to dress and have breakfast. She wanted to call her parents to let them know that she was safe and got home okay from her date before she left at 8:45 a.m. for work.

The need or not to know...

CHAPTER
THIRTEEN

Roberto' awaken early that morning at 6:30 a.m. by the sun beaming in on their bed, turned and looked at his beautiful Simone' still sleeping thought, "Do I want to know?" Fear of what he may find out made him want to try to forget, but no, he could not, not at this point, he had to know. His daughter's future was at stake, he could not allow her to marry too quickly and not have the love of her husband she needed and deserved.

Roberto', over the years, had watched Alberto', Carmeli'ta's childhood friend, chose him as a husband for his daughter as all Fathers guided their daughter's future so it would be secure. Franco Giovanni chose the path for his daughter's future by deciding she would marry him.

Mr. Giovanni had chosen Roberto' for her as he chose Alberto' Gambani' to be Carmeli'ta' husband. He was educated, strong, levelheaded, his family was financially secure, they like Roberto' and Simone', had done well after coming to America. Both the Bandaci's (Robert' and Amelio') vegetable farms and the Gambani' livestock and watermelon farms were successful. Roberto' was pragmatic when it came to his daughter.

"Simone's body when we made love", thought Roberto', "says there is something between us but what? Simone' has never refused me when I wanted to make love to her."

Roberto', pushed back the sheet, sat on the side of the bed, pulled the

sheet across his legs. Roberto's slept in the raw every night for the twenty-four years of his marriage to Simone'. He did not want even a garment between them in the privacy of their bedroom. She, on the other hand, slept in a negligee' keeping something between them in their bedroom, even if it was just a sheer gown.

Roberto' saw quiet tears on her face many times after they made love. He thought he hurt her in some way, this thought of him causing his precious Simone' pain was unbearable, he was gentler when they make love; she was so delicate and he was big and strong. Roberto' came home unexpectedly more than once, amidst Simone' crying when he asked her why she said, "It was nothing my darling, women cry sometimes."

Looking back over the years, knew his wife was not crying just because she was an emotional woman thought, "Pain and heartache was causing those tears. She never trusted me enough to share it with me. I would forgive her almost anything because I love her so."

His thoughts went back to his beautiful daughter, "It is urgent that I talk with Carmeli'ta' to see what she was thinking, what her feelings are toward Jason Madison, Jr." He knew the Madison's from dealing with their staff in supplying fresh vegetable to them on a daily basis. He delivered them himself to the Madison's home and to make sure they were of the finest quality and flawless upon delivery.

Roberto' mind filled with a hot burning pains thought, as he looked at Simone' still sleeping "What has she tried to hide behind those gowns all these years? Not her body, I can see it through the sheerness of the gown."

But this sent a message to Roberto' he could not understand, but now, he could not nor would not stop until he knew what it is that Simone' keep between them all the years they have been married. Roberto's mind flashed on his Minister, Mr. Meriwether, "I will visit our Minister today after I make my vegetable deliveries, especially to the Madison Mansion, Peter, can make the rest of the deliveries."

Peter Meriwether was the Bandaci's Farm Foreman and brother of their Minister Steven Meriwether and they were both poor relations of Charles Bienville Meriwether according to their mother when she was alive.

Carmeli'ta' on the way to another Wednesday workday after her date the night before stopped for a few moments after she had breakfast and dressed for work dialed her parent's home. The phone rang four times.

Carmeli'ta' was floating on a cloud when she called her parents.

Roberto' in a quiet tone answered and said, "Hello." Carmeli'ta' in an excited tone of voice said, "Good Morning Daddy."

"Good morning Carmeli'ta' my beautiful daughter, how are you today?

"I am just fine daddy. How are you and Mother? Is Mama awake yet?" "We are fine daughter. Your Mother is still sleeping Carmeli'ta'."

The tension escalates.

In the meantime, Simone' was awakens by the ringing of the phone and her husband's voice lay quietly listing to her husband's response to Carmeli'ta'.

"Daddy asked her to call me when she is awake."

"I will tell her Carmeli'ta'. I want to come see you after work today. Do you have plans for tonight?"

"Yes, daddy I have a dinner engagement at 8:00 p.m. tonight." Roberto' careful not to reveal the fact her Mother told him about her date with Jason Madison, Jr, said, "I will come at 5:00 p.m.; you will be home by then I expect?"

"Yes, Father, I will be home by then. Will Mother be with you?" Carmeli'ta' wondering about the tone of her Father's voice; he never spoke to her in that tone; she heard both a question in his tone and in his tone pain and heartache; it puzzled her greatly. "Yes, I will ask your Mother to come with me."

Carmeli'ta' hearing the seriousness in his voice, reverted to calling him Father. She called him daddy when she was growing up when she was at her happiest. Yet, the tone in her Father's voice did not sound as if the conversation would be just a Father, Mother, daughter visit. Her Father's tone made Carmeli'ta' a little uncomfortable. She wondered if her Mother had mentioned her date with Jason to her Father.

After her husband put the receiver on the hook she said, "Good Morning, Roberto'. How are you feeling today?"

"Good morning Simone', I am okay my lovely wife, did the phone awaken you? I am sorry that my conversation disturbed your sleep. I feeling okay; how are you this morning? Did you sleep well?"

Roberto' lay back turned and faced Simone's stroking her right side supported himself with his left elbow leaned forward kissed her forehead took her right hand gently kissed it on the inside thought, "She is as lovely as the morning sun, what can't she tell me?"

Simone' touching her husband's face so softly, smiled and pushed his unruly black curly lock of hair out of his face as she did each day. "Yes, Roberto' I slept okay. It is not necessary for you to apologize. I am anxious to know if she is okay today, I heard your conversation."

"Yes, she is okay. She sounds happy as usual. I told her we would be to see her at 5:00 p.m. today. You will be able to go Simone'?"

"Roberto', please, I beg of you let us wait to see what Carmeli'ta' tell us."

"No, Simone' I will speak with her today whether you go with me or not is up to you. It is breakfast time; I have a long day ahead of me can we get dressed now? Marianna will be waiting breakfast for us."

"Yes Roberto'." Simone' and Roberto' went in together as they did each morning bathed, dressed, and went down to breakfast. Marianna as usual, fussed with the Bandacai's because they were never at the table exactly at 8:00 a.m. She busy putting the food on the table said, "You are late again today; it is 8:10 a.m."

Roberto' smiled at Marianna and said, "Thank you Marianna our morning clock." Marianna smiled as she did each day. This made her day. She loved the Bandaci's. She had help raise Carmeli'ta', who was like her own daughter.

Simone' after breakfast told Roberto' I will run some of my errands today while you are working and some shopping, so I will not have so much to do on Friday. I will be back in time to go with you to see Carmeli'ta'."

Roberto' rising from the breakfast table reached for Simone's hand to help her get up, pulled her close to him held onto her and kissed her. Simone' holding him tight looked up her husband smiled him and kissed him back.

"Will you leave the money you want deposited and the accounts to collect in its usual place? I will take care as much as I can today?"

"I think that is a good idea my beauty. I will leave everything in its usual place. I will see you after work Simone'."

"Have a good day Roberto'."

"Thank you Simone' my beautiful wife, please be careful driving around town today, there are a lot of people out on the streets. The town seems to be growing at a rapid pace."

"I will thank you." Simone's mind was on checking the Armoire' to see if the secret compartment has been opened, but then she knew if he had seen the Dairy his reactions would be on a different and heightened emotional plane.

However, nonetheless, she wanted to check to make sure it was there for Her own satisfaction and comfort level.

Roberto' left for the farm and mid-week vegetable deliveries, Simone' waited until she heard his car leave the office driveway, walked swiftly went back upstairs, retrieved the Diary key from her purse. She kept the Diary locked and the key in a zipped compartment in her purse on a chain, opened her Armoire' moved her gowns aside and checked the little slide that hid the knob to open the secret compartment where she kept her Diary.

Almost afraid to open the secret compartment, her hands began to sweat, she felt flushed, and her heart raced out of control at what she may or may not find. Hands trembling pushed opened the slide grasped the knob and opened the secret compartment. In her excitement, she imagined that the Diary was gone. Reaching to the back of the secret compartment where she kept the Dairy felt the book; it was still in place. Emotions rising Simone' picked up the Diary, not thinking about what she would find unlocked and opened it flipping through the pages. It was as if she had left it. She immediately thanked God for Roberto' not having found the Diary, yet not yet she thought. Simone' returned the Diary to the secret compartment, pulled the knob, closed the secret compartment, pulled the slide in place, which was almost impossible to find unless you knew where to push to open it, and repositioned her gowns in the neat position she kept them. Simone' picked up the phone and dialed Mr. Meriwether, their Minister's home. Mr. Meriwether answered, "Hello."

"Good morning Mr. Meriwether, this is Simone'. How are you today?" "I am well Simone', you?"

"I am fine Mr. Meriwether. May I come to see you today about the matter we have been discussing?"

"Yes, that would be fine Simone'. Is 11:30 a.m. a good time for you? I will be back from my visits by then."

"Yes, I will see you at 11:30 a.m. today." She hung up.

Simone' looked around the room to make sure that it was neat before she left for her errands. She kept their private bedroom in neat order so Marianna would not have much to do when it came to tidiness; just vacuumed and cleaned the bathroom daily.

In the meantime, Roberto' arrived at their farm office spoke with their Foreman, Peter Meriwether about the priority for the days deliveries. "Peter, I will deliver to the Madison's and Meriwether's homes today myself. I would like you to make the remainder of the deliveries. I have an urgent meeting that I need to attend today."

"Is there something I can do to assist you Mr. Bandaci?"

"No Peter it is something I need to take care of myself. You making the deliveries on time will be a great help to me today. Please ask one of your workers to assist you." Moving quickly towards the door Peter said, "I will take care of it Mr. Bandaci." Peter walked out of the office door and called Jamie his top hand to help him. Roberto' checked his pocket watch for the time. It was 9:30 a.m. He knew Mr. Meriwether and his wife would not be sleeping at this hour. He looked out of his office window to assure himself Peter and no one else was in earshot before he made the phone call to Mr. Meriwether, his Minister.

The phone rang at the Meriwether's home. Mrs. Meriwether answered, "Hello."

Roberto' paused then said, "Mrs. Meriwether this is Roberto'."

"Good morning Roberto' it is so good to talk to you this beautiful morning. How are you?"

"I am well, thank you. How are you?"

"I am good Roberto', thank you. How can I help you today?"

"Is the Minister in this morning?"

"Yes, just a moment I will get him for you."

"Thank you Mrs. Meriwether." Roberto' waiting, Mr. Meriwether picked up the phone, "Hello Roberto'. How are you today? It is good to hear from you as always. I hope you and your family are well."

"Yes, we are all well. I would like to talk with you today about the sensitive and personal matter that we have discussed before."

"Of course, I have only two appointments today. I have a sick visit and then a counseling session I should be done with both by 1:15 p.m. is 1:30 p.m. a good time for you to come?"

"Yes, I will see you then. Thank you, bye." Mr. Meriwether hang up knowing that he had to deal with both Simone' who called earlier and Roberto' both today. He shook his head and said, "Help me Heavenly Father your children need you today."

Simone' knew that with the questions and comments that Roberto' made to her last night, it would not be long before she would have no choice, but to answer his questions. With him talking to Carmeli'ta' later that day, it would almost be impossible for her to hide the fact that she loved Jason. This thought frightened Simone'. What could she do to prevent her husband from finding out about the situation that she created, unintentionally, with Vincenzo' by allowing him to see Carmeli'ta', because of the threatening tone she heard in his voice he might tell Carmeli'ta she was his daughter or tell Roberto' about their relationship. She did not know what he would do.

Simone' picked up her purse and walked downstairs to give Marianna directions for dinner said, "Marianna dinner would be later in the evening at 7:00 p.m. rather than 6:00 p.m. We are visiting Carmeli'ta' at 5:00 p.m."

"Yes, Ms. Bandaci. Tell my sweet Carmeli'ta' I said hello and come to see me soon. I miss her."

"I will tell her Marianna. I am on my way to attend to some of the errands today so I will have a lighter day on Friday and I will do some other shopping. I will be back by 3:00 p.m. Please tell Mr. Bandaci if he arrives before I do, I will be here by 3:00 p.m."

"I will tell him Ms. Bandaci."

"Thank you Marianna. I am off. I will see you later." Simone' went to her office and received the money for deposit and the accounts she could collect on Wednesday, drove to town, quickly attended to the farm business, and deposited the money, picked up Roberto' and her clothes from the dry cleaners, and a few personal toilet items from the drug store for herself.

Simone' did not take the time she usually did to visit with the clerks and others she saw each account collection day, but excused herself as having an appointment, drove hastily to her Minister's home to talk with him about the conversation that took place between she and Roberto' last evening.

It was 11:10 a.m.; she needed to hurry to be at Mr. Meriwether's at 11:30 a.m.; it was a twenty-minute drive from downtown Charleston. Simone' nervous arrived at their Minister's home and knocked softly at the door. Mrs. Meriwether answered, "Good morning Simone' my dear; how are you today?"

"I am well Ms. Meriwether, you?"

"I am doing fine, Simone'. You look beautiful as always. Brother Meriwether is in his office. I will let him know that you are here or did you come to see me?"

Thinking quickly Simone' said, "If the Minister is not busy, I would appreciate seeing him."

"Of course, my dear, wait here for a moment." Charlene Meriwether 56 years old, small, and petite with shoulder length brown hair she wore in a bun on top of her head, a handsome woman with a kind voice and sweet personality. The congregation loved their Minister Steven Meriwether 62 years old and his wife. Mrs. Meriwether opened the door to the office and said, "Simone', Steven said please come in. Have a nice visit my dear. I am off to run some errands as we all do. You have done errands today I take it?"

Simone' smiled said, "Yes, I finish mine before I came here."

"You will be at Bible Study tonight Simone'?"

"No, Roberto' and I have an appointment at 5:00 p.m. today and will not finish in time to make it by 6:00 p.m."

"I understand my dear, have a good morning; I will see you on Sunday."

Steven Meriwether walked to the door as Simone' and his wife finished their short conversation, "Good morning Simone'. How are you today?"

"I am well thank you", Simone' said. A small frown crossed her forehead, the same frown that Steven Meriwether saw in the café in Sedalia, South Carolina said, "Simone' the look on your face tells me that things are not well with you and Roberto'."

"Things are well with us. However, he wants to talk with Carmeli'ta' today about her choice of love. Roberto' wants her to marry Alberto' Gambani. I want Carmeli'ta' to have a choice in matters of the heart. I do not want her to marry someone that she does not love before they are married as I did, because my Father chose for me."

Mr. Meriwether surprised replied, "Simone', you love Roberto'." Startled for a moment Simone' exclaimed, "Yes, with all my heart! I did not love him when we got married. I respected him and cared for him. I fell in love with Roberto', a few months after we were married and now I love him with all my heart and soul."

"Simone', have you told Roberto' about this situation with Vincenzo' Moretti, is his name, as I recall?" Simone' said, "Yes, Brother Meriwether, that is his name and no, I have not told Roberto' yet. I do not know how!"

"Simone', Roberto' is coming here in two hours. He called and made an appointment with me earlier this morning, so we will need to conclude our discussion at least by 1:15 p.m.; he will be here by 1:30 p.m. I am not wanting to go on with you and Roberto' and him not knowing that you come to see me and have related to me the full details of your relationship with Vincenzo' Moretti. It is time that you tell him Simone', you are destroying your husband and your marriage. I know that you realize how much this will affect Carmeli'ta' and her future relationships."

"I have thought about that; I just don't know what to do at this point in my life. What I have done plagues me day and night; now, I know not knowing is torture for Roberto'. I have let it go on to long; the pain has festered in Roberto' to the point of his being angry. He never spoke to me the way that he did last night. I felt the anger and hurt for the first-time last night, like a dagger it stabbed at my heart and soul because I know that he is hurting. He thinks that I do not love, need, or trust him. He questioned my honesty with him last night. What am I to do Brother Meriwether?"

"Simone', you know the solution to the situation and the answer to your question to me. It will take honesty with him and Carmeli'ta'. However, first Roberto' need to be told about the maze that has been created around your marriage. I will pray with you Simone'. The answer is not complicated. On the other hand, hiding the truth and giving your husband the impression that you do not love him or want him in the same way that he wants you, and not sharing your past with him is even worse. I have watched a happy man over the years grow very unhappy trying to go forward. It is a painful to love someone and need them as desperately as he needs you. Simone' you need your husband; stop being afraid. It is only getting worse. I will tell Roberto' today that you came here, may I?"

She felt a sudden weakness from the question, "No please, I need to wait until I know what he will say to Carmeli'ta' later today. I will talk with him after we get home tonight. This will be one of the hardest conversations that I have ever had with Roberto'."

"You will not be talking to a stranger but to your husband who loves you with every fiber of his being."

"I know he loves me is why it is hard for me to reveal the truth of the matter to him. It will only deepen the hurt he feels now."

After a one hour and a half discussion, rising from behind his desk pulled out his pocket watch flipped it open to see the time said, "Simone' it is 1:15 p.m. I will wait to hear from you about the meeting with Carmeli'ta'. I do pray fervently for the best for you and your family. This is a difficult situation at best."

Simone' rose and said, "Thank you."

Simone' shook his out-stretched hand. He walked her to the door and opened it, "Good day, my precious Simone'. I know that you were trying to protect your family. I understand your reasons; it is time to let it go. I heard you tell Charlene, Roberto' and you will not be at Bible Study tonight. I will see you both on Sunday."

Simone' walked down the steps, got in her car waving as she drove off knew she had not shared all the truth with her Minister. She just was not sure about anything anymore not after last night and Vincenzo's had continued his verbal battering insisting that she could be his daughter.

She hurried to leave before her husband arrive. One day she knew she would have to face the truth about the matter of a last-minute poor decision on the desire at that time and what she thought was love for Vincenzo' Moretti. She was marrying a man, she did not love, not that day, her wedding day, but now understood her feelings for Vincenzo' was not love at all, but more friendship. She needed someone to understand how she felt with the raged that possessed her within body and soul. She could not figure out how or why.

Waving at Simone' from the horizon was the dilemma: Flight or Fight!

CHAPTER

FOURTEEN

Simone' gone fifteen minutes before Roberto' arrived at the Meriwether's home, took the long way back across town. A route that she knew Roberto' would not be taking because the farm was on the opposite end of the town from the Meriwether's home. Mr. Meriwether was still standing on his front porch, enjoying the beauty of the day and the flowerbeds that gave bright colors of life to their home and yard. The crispness of the air, as November days are in Charleston, the day felt refreshing, watched Roberto' drive around the circular driveway leading to the porch that encircled their home.

Roberto' loved this view each time he visited his Minister. Mrs. Meriwether had a green thumb. The way she planted the flowerbeds gave the yard a look of a being a Cal-de-sac alive with the colors of daisies, pansies, and purple sunflowers, sprinkled with yellow added a zestful look to the entire yard.

Roberto' opened the door of his Ford Roadster waved and said, "Good afternoon Mr. Meriwether. How are you today? It is a beautiful day. The air has a crisp feel to it today; it is promising us winter soon."

"Good afternoon Roberto'. I am well thank you for asking. I hope that you are also. I was just thinking the same thing about the day and admiring God's creation and its beauty as you drove up. Come in please, I was waiting for you to arrive." Roberto' walked up to the porch replied, "Thank you for seeing me today on such short notice. I hope that I have not come at an inconvenient time."

"Your timing is fine. I did not have but one visit to the sick and shut-in today and one counseling session. I have taken care of both already today.

Your lovely Simone' is well?"

"Yes, Simone' is lovely as ever and she is well, thank you for asking."

Mr. Meriwether and Roberto' entered the door that led to his office from the front porch. Mr. Meriwether noticed Roberto' looking around the room nervously towards the open door that led into his private living quarters, knew he was wondering if they were alone. "Roberto', please be seated here in front of my desk. We will not be disturbed. Mrs. Meriwether has left to take care of mid-week errands as usual."

"Thank you, I want this conversation today to be private."

Mr. Meriwether smiled, "I understand Roberto', and as always it will be private. Simone' and your private lives are not discussed by me with any outside persons."

Roberto' looked at Mr. Meriwether and frowned a little, but did not say anything to his last comment.

"How are things between you and Simone' since we last spoke?"

Roberto' quick glance and facial expression answered the question for his Minister before he spoke, responded, "I became angry with Simone' last night because she kept the fact that Carmeli'ta' had a dinner engagement with Jason Madison, Jr. from me. We had a disagreement about her dating him. Simone' said that. "It was a date; she was not getting married." This statement made me angrier; it bought to surface all the anger I have held in for so long. I questioned my wife as to her honesty with me. 'She said she has always been honest with me about our daughter and she felt my anger was all of a sudden. I told her that it was not all of a sudden and asked her if she could truly say she has always been honest with me?' She said she did not know what I meant, yes, she had been honest with me.' I said to her, "about Carmeli'ta' yes, you have been honest with me, but what about you Simone', have you been honest with me about you?"

Mr. Meriwether patiently listened while he continued, "I know that she is hiding something from me Mr. Meriwether, but I do not know what. I can feel it in her when we are intimate. She holds back her feeling of passion for me, it has become so painful for me. I feel like a knife is cutting deep into my heart and soul. It has become unbearable for me. I love her so much it is driving me crazy not knowing if she really loves me and then thinking that she does not love me."

"Roberto', Simone' loves you with all her heart, I know that she does. I have watched you both for many years now. I can tell by the way she acts when she is at Church and when she is around you at other Church functions we had over the years."

"I want to believe that, but she is so mysterious and I just do not understand her at all. I want her to want me the way that I need her and love me with the same passion that I have for her. I cannot bear the thought that she does not feel the same level of passion for me that I feel for her."

"What do you want to do, at this point Roberto? You came to me for some reason today, why?"

"At this point, I am at a loss of what to do. I feel so angry and hurt it is hard to think. I have never spoken to my wife as I did last night in all years we have been married!" he replied angrily.

"Remind me Roberto' of the number of years you have been married to Simone'. I know you told me once, but I do not know if I remember correctly. With a congregation of four hundred members, I have a lot to recall with all the marriages in our congregation."

"We were married 24 years, October 13th."

"That is a blessing Roberto' only last month!"

"I am proud of my lovely wife; but, she has never been all mine notyet"

"I am confused by this statement, not all of your yet, what do you mean by that Roberto'?"

Roberto' hesitating for a long period-of-time put his head in his hands, groaned in agony not wanting to share his most innermost thoughts about Simone's and his intimate relationship in their bedroom. He could not hold his pain in any longer, knowing that he could trust his Minister as he had for almost twenty years whispered, "Simone' has not let me share her deepest desires and passions. She has kept me on the outside looking in and wanting to get in to share her deepest needs. I know that the needs, desires, and passions that she has goes much deeper and are lot stronger than she has allowed me to share. I can tell by the intensities of the response of her body when we make love, but she will only let me get to a certain point and then she cuts me off, but why?" With torture and distress in his voice Roberto' continued, "I just do not know why! She tells me that I satisfy her desires and make her feel as if she is on a cloud, but she still hold back. I know she needs me as I do her. A few times, she has let me get a little closer where her deepest needs are but then she stops the flow of passion that she feels and will not let me reach that part of her. I want so desperately for my wife to share all of her passion with me. I sometimes think now that I do not satisfy her and she only lets me love her because she is my wife. I do not want her that way; I want her to want me as I want her. I know only she knows and only she can tell me. I cannot bear these secrets any longer, I cannot, I will not, it is destroying me and has bought me to the point of feeling anger and hurt."

Mr. Meriwether embarrassed and shocked by the admission stammered, "Ah, ah, Roberto' I know that it must be agony" breathing stammered again, "I know especially for a man to think that he cannot satisfy his wife. It has been hard for you over the years I am sure, but here and now what do you want to do? What actions do you want to take? And when do you plan to tell Simone' your feelings?"

Roberto' feeling the intensity of his pain and anger replied almost angrily, "I have to talk with Carmeli'ta' today about the matter that has come up with her dating Jason Madison. I do not want to say anything to Simone' before we see our daughter in a few hours. I will see how the evening goes with Carmeli'ta' first. After dinner tonight I will talk with Simone' and tell her how I feel."

Searching for a gentle and kind way to reply to Roberto's apparent anger and frustration, Mr. Meriwether said, "Roberto', please be careful how you approach Simone' this is a sensitive matter. She may be fragile emotionally and you not been aware of it."

"What do you mean by fragile emotionally? What are you trying to tell me Mr. Meriwether?" Roberto asked.

"I have encountered situations of like-nature in my years of being a Minister and Counselor of the Lord's Church. It is not an easy avenue in life to travel down. I just want you to be sensitive to her feeling and listen to what she has to say before you make a judgment or let your anger rule your common sense. You have always been levelheaded in the almost twenty years I have been your Minister. You have given me excellent advice on matters of life when I sought it from time-to-time in my perplexity about what to do or say about the circumstances before me."

"You are asking me to do something that has become very difficult for me and that is control my hurt and anger at this situation!"

"This "situation" and your wife are one in the same Roberto' you cannot forget that. You are still madly in love with her or you would not be coming to me for counseling."

"You are right I am in love with my wife, more now than when I first saw her. I thought I could not love anyone as much as I do Simone'. I guess that is why I am having such a hard time with this. I want her to need me as I need her. It destroys something in me each time she denies me all of her."

At this point, Roberto's voice broke. The sound of his words were so painful it bought tears to Mr. Meriwether's eyes. He hurt for both Roberto' and Simone'. She was suffering as well because she knew she was destroying her husband who she loved with all her heart and soul. Mr. Meriwether with tears of compassion in his voice said, "Roberto' in matters of the heart, hurt and pain are hard emotions to get pass. I will pray for you and Simone' as well as our sweet Carmeli'ta'. I do not want to see her become a victim of this situation."

"How can she become a victim of this situation? This is between her mother and me."

"This could hurt Carmeli'ta' in more than one way. If what you think about she and Jason Madison is true you do think she is falling in love with him, am I accurate in this? This could hurt her in reference to relationships as well as Simone' and you being upset. She loves you both so much Roberto' remember that don't make her chose between you."

Roberto' becoming annoyed, "Mr. Meriwether, I cannot promise you anything right now except I intend to speak with Carmeli'ta' and Simone' both before another day arrives. I will let you know as soon as I can; thank you for seeing me. Please continue to pray for me and my family."

"I will wait to hear from you Roberto'. You will be in my prayers."

Roberto' rose from his chair, pulled out his pocket watch and opened the face. It was 3:30 p.m. said, "I will see you soon Mr. Meriwether. I need to get home by 4:00 p.m. to pick up Simone'. I promised Carmeli'ta' that we would be there by 5:00 p.m."

Mr. Meriwether wanting to reassure him said, "Roberto' the Madison family is one of the finest families in Charleston. They attend the Lafayette Street Church of Christ Congregation across town near your farm. Jason Madison is one of the finest young men I know, well brought up, and he is a Gentleman like his Father Jason, Sr."

Roberto' agreed, "I know the Madison's are good people, I just don't want my daughter hurt, and I need to guide the decision of a husband for her so she won't be hurt." At that point Mr. Meriwether observed Roberto' could not be pushed further said, "Try, and stay calm Roberto'.

Have a good rest of the day and evening. I will see you on Sunday." Roberto' nodded, "Thank you. I will see you on Sunday. Bye."

Roberto' walked out of the office door, down the steps, stepped into his Roadster, and drove slowly down the driveway. It would take him twenty-minutes to arrive home. As he drove, his mind kept going back to the conversation that he had with his Minister. The feelings of torture and pain hung in the air around Roberto' as a night fog does that takes away your ability to see. Even with suffering anger and desperation, on his drive home, knew he still felt passion, desire, love, and need for his wife. He wanted to hold her, see her, touch her, have her touch him, could not wait to get home to see Simone'; he loved her he could not seem to stop.

Roberto' grasped the fact he was jealous of something he could not understand or some part of his wife that she had not shared. The tears that he held back while talking with his Minister rolled down his cheek, blinding tears to the point that he could not see the highway. A car appeared suddenly in front of Roberto'. The car horn was blowing, becoming conscious he was on the wrong side of the road, swerved just missed hitting the other car and was on the shoulder of the road before he was able to stop the car, turned off the motor, leaned his head on the steering wheel, thanking God for his life and safety. He cried tears of pain and heartache, sobbing uncontrollably for more than ten minutes. All the hurt and pain he felt over the years came crashing down on him like an avalanche. He had not wanted to admit to himself that Simone' possibly might not love him the way he loved her. He remembered their wedding night and his thoughts of her deeper passion and desire that she would be share with him as time went on. However, up to-this-point, she had not done so; the mysterious side stood like a barrier he could not get passes nor could he find the missing piece of the puzzle. Her promise, to never, refuse him her body and love hung like a pendulum over his head now. He could not bear to think that she was just keeping her promise to him.

Taking his handkerchief from his jacket pocket, dried his eyes started the car and slowly drove toward home.

A love stronger than pain!

CHAPTER

FIFTEEN

With their home twenty minutes from their Minister, Simone' had driven slowly taking the long way home to avoid running into Roberto, and to think of a solution to the problem, she had allowed to run un-checked and now it was out-of-control, because of fear.

Simone's decisions to hide the truth from her husband and daughter, especially her husband propelled her into rough waters, without a bridge to help her push against the coming tides that would clash and beat on her life as a storm does, those moments of impact's long reaching arms had caught up with her. Those arms were threatening to hold and bind her with the cords of mystery she created with her silence. Drove slowly home to be there when Roberto' arrived, asked herself, "What have you done? How will you ever see your way out of the tidal waves that is approaching? I created a vicious circle because of the love that I have for your family, which made me afraid of losing their love. I am in a no-win predicament!"

Simone's thoughts went to her Mother and Father in Tuscany. They were in their late fifties and early sixties now. They had kept in close touch all the years that she had been in America and they had come to visit them twice. She never, however, mentioned to her parents about the situation with Vincenzo'. The decisions she made to protect her family left her facing a dilemma of which she had no answer. Simone' thoughts carried her back to her childhood when her Father and Mother seemed to have all the answers to her questions and perplexities life presents.

She thought, "If only I could talk with my Father and Mother I know that they could help me to know what to do what path to take from here. In the same light though, they are so far away. How I need my Mother right now. She could understand why I made the decisions I made, not that she would necessarily approve, but she could understand the catch-twenty-two I faced over the last twenty-three years or more."

In the meantime, finally, arriving home at 3:15 p.m., entered through the office door so she could put the paid bills and paperwork of her transactions to-be filed in the paid accounts tray. Simone', at home, attention went to preparing for their visit to Carmeli'ta'. She would check with Marianna about dinner and freshen-up for her husband as she did each day.

Simone' walked into the kitchen and said, "Good afternoon Marianna. How was your day?"

"Good afternoon Ms. Bandaci. My day was fine. I began to worry about you Miss. It is 3:15 p.m. I thought something had happened to you. You are never late from your errands. Did you get all your errands done Miss?"

"Yes Marianna all my errands are done. Thank you for caring about me, I am fine. I had some free time today so I took a long drive to enjoy the beauty of the day. How is dinner progressing? Remember we are having dinner an hour later this evening; we are visiting Carmeli'ta' in about two hours."

"Dinner is coming along okay. It will be ready when you and Mr. Bandaci return from seeing Miss Carmeli'ta'. Mr. Bandaci called Miss and asked if you had returned from your errands. I told him you had not, but said to tell you he would try to be here by 3:30 p.m. and wanted to leave by 4:50 p.m. to visit Ms. Carmeli'ta'." He said tell you Miss that, "If he is a little after 3:30 p.m. when he arrived don't worry about him. He had a stop to make before he comes home."

"What time did Mr. Bandaci call Marianna?" asked Simone'. "It was 1:00 p.m. today Miss."

"Thank you Marianna for the message. I will go upstairs and freshen-up before he arrives."

Marianna smiled and said, "Yes Miss."

Simone' slowly climbed the stairs to their bedroom suite, which took up most of the second floor with the sitting room adjourning their master suite, knew that Roberto' had spoken with Mr. Meriwether by this time. Simone' thought about Carmeli'ta' when she was living at home and Marianna.

Before Carmeli'ta' moved she lived downstairs on the opposite side of the house in a separate suite with her own private bathroom, sitting room, and bedroom. Marianna's room was behind the kitchen near the garden with a private bathroom and private entrance. She loved living with the Bandaci's. She toyed with the idea of leaving going to her Mother and Father before she talked with Roberto' about her past. She just wanted to run away now from the prison she made for herself.

Simone' checked the room to see if her Armoire' had been disturbed by Marianna's when she cleaned their suite. She had become especially nervous in the last twenty-four hours because of the impending storm brewing beneath the surface. It had been years with Roberto' being hurt, feeling, she did not return his love and now he had become very angry; it showed in his voice and body language last night when he was talking with her about Carmeli'ta' dating Jason Madison, Jr.

She thought, "Roberto's always holds me each night before we go to sleep, even when we don't make love. He always caresses my body, kisses me, and whispers he loves me. We tell each other the events of our days in the quiet dark of our bedroom. I miss his loving me last night. I wanted and needed Roberto' so desperately. He was so angry and hurt I did not know how to talk with him for fear of revealing my secret. My love for him is so strong it pains me to think of the hurt I am causing my husband."

Simone' went in the bathroom freshened-up, walked to the closet and chose one of her favorite dresses. She unbuttoned it half-way down stepped into it and dabbed Chanel 5 on her skin. Picking up her brush began brushing her hair, her contemplations were on the situation that she had created with Vincenzo' and what she would tell her husband when he asked her again about being truthful with him.

She did not hear Roberto's car drive up as she usually did every evening; she always ran to his arms when she met him at the door.

Roberto' drove in the yard near the office entrance and parked his car next to Simone's car. It was 3:55 p.m. He entered the office door opened the wall safe and laid the money she had collected for the weekly deliveries in the tin money box he kept there for his business; separate from the personal money. He turned the combination lock on the safe and walked into the kitchen where Marianna was making the bread for dinner and said, "Good evening Marianna. How was your day?"

Marianna replied, "My day was good Mr. Bandaci. How was your day? I will have dinner ready for you and Mrs. Bandaci when you return from seeing Miss Carmeli'ta'."

"My day was fine Marianna, thank you. Dinner smells delicious as usual. I took a long drive today and enjoyed its beauty."

Marianna surprised, "Mrs. Bandaci said she took a long drive today. It is a pretty day."

"Where is my wife Marianna?"

"She is upstairs freshening up for your visit to Miss Carmeli'ta's today."

"Thank you Marianna. I will join her."

Roberto' walked up the stairs to their private suite, through the sitting room, and opened the door that led into their bedroom. Simone' had changed her outfit from the official black suite she wore on collection days and to do her errands Roberto' had seen her in when they dressed for the day. She changed into a yellow and brown long sleeve A-line shift dress with buttons down the front, that looked comfortable and appealing on her. Roberto' stood looking at his beautiful wife as she brushed her long black curly locks of hair in front of the mirror. So involved in reflections of the problem she has caused, did not hear Roberto' enter.

Roberto' waited for a few minutes enjoying her loveliness, before speaking to Simone'. Though angry and hurt, he still loved her desperately but could not resist being near her and finally said, "Hello my beautiful wife, it is good to see you as always. Your dress is lovely it looks comfortable."

Simone' a little nervous, turned ran across the room into Roberto's open arms, put her arms around his neck, looked up at him, brushed the unruly lock of hair out of his face, said, "Hello my darling husband. Thank you for the compliment, I feel comfortable. It is good to see you. I am glad you are home."

Roberto' smiled, holding her tight, hugged, and kissed Simone', "Thank you my beauty, I am glad to be home more so than ever today." He did not want to tell Simone' about his near fatal accident, but just silently thanked God again for his safety.

"Why are you happy to be home today so much more than usual today?" asked Simone'.

"I feel the same way each day, I like being home with you, Simone'. I love you my darling more each day that passes."

Simone' held tighter to Roberto' kissed him softly and sweetly said, "I am always glad to see you Roberto'. I look forward to your coming home to me every day."

Roberto' kissed his beautiful Simone' and held her tight. She felt so good in his arms, the fragrance of her cologne soft and inviting, took Roberto' back to their honeymoon night. He let his mind float, for a second, remembering the pleasure he felt being with his wife. Their love had become so much more mature and satisfying; he wanted to know the rest of his wife's deepest passions and desires. As pictures, of her on their honeymoon flashed across his mind, he felt feverish desire and passion drew her even closer. He kissed her repeatedly whispering softly, "Simone', I need you. I want you so much right now. I want to make love to you, please love you, and hold me for a while before we leave to see Carmeli'ta'. I need to feel your body next to me, your touch that gives me the feeling of uncontrollable passion. I thought about you all day today. I could not get you out of my mind or the way you make me feel. I missed you last night, I wanted you so much."

Simone' whispered softly', "Yes, Roberto', I need you. I want to make love to you and want you to make love to me. I missed you last night. That was the first time in twenty-three years that you did not hold me and kiss me."

Roberto' held Simone' tight for a few second and slowly unbuttoned her dress. It fell to the floor. Simone's body was still beautifully irresistible. She gradually unbuttoned her husband's shirt and slipped it off one arm at a time. Simone' looked at her husband gently ran her hand over his muscular arms and chest. He was strong and handsome. His arms to Simone' felt strong like steel as he held her tight yet so tenderly, led her to the bed still holding her tightly laid her down, kissed her with an intensity Simone' had not felt before in him. The taste of mint on his tongue sweeten his kisses. The fresh smell of his skin was sexy and inviting. They caressed each other's bodies as they kissed.

Simone's hands to Roberto' felt satisfying; could not resist the passions she made him feel while she touched, caressed, and kissed him until his passion was covetous. Roberto's eyes searching her face, she saw the passion he felt; he kissed her repeatedly as he made love to his beautiful wife took her breathe away. Simone' returned his passion. Roberto' felt the warm hungry desire flow from Simone's body. The smooth rhythm of her body as she moved was sweet music to Roberto' his body reached deeper into hers; he loved her; his heart ached with the love that he felt for her and for the love he needed her to return to him. She loved him and gave herself to him, but not completely.

Afterwards, laying snuggled together in their bed, Roberto' lovingly pulled her close, held Simone' with tenderness and care closed his eyes and enjoyed the beauty of this time before they would leave.

Carmeli'ta' lived ten minutes from them; he had time to enjoy being with his beautiful Simone'. Roberto' turned looked at the bedside clock as it ticked away the minutes. It was 4:25 p.m. They still had a while before they would leave at 4:50 p.m. to arrive at 5:00 p.m., the time he told Carmeli'ta'. Simone' felt Roberto' move asked, "is it time to get dressed to leave Roberto'?"

Pulling her closer he said, "We still have a little while my lovely wife. I want to enjoy you near me. I need this so much right now; don't ask me to let you go now, not yet."

Simone', hearing the passion, pain, and need in his voice pulled him close caressed his body with her hands moving little by little across his stomach, his thighs, and his buttocks; in his yearning, Roberto' groaned with intense desire, whispered "love me, I need you, please love me", she made love to him again. The firmness of his body felt so good to her; he was everything she wanted in a lover and a husband. Afterwards, Simone' lay still holding onto her husband and listening to his heartbeat with her head resting against his chest.

She wanted so desperately to tell him her deepest desires, feelings, share all her heart with him, and give her body to him completely. She knew he wanted her to let him into her deepest passions and desires, but fear still kept her unable to voice what she felt for him and why she could not give herself to him completely.

Roberto' looked at the clock once again, it was 4:40 p.m. said, "And it is time to get dressed, my lovely wife." They went in the bathroom freshen-up, dressed and left at 4:50 p.m.

On the ride to see Carmeli'ta' Roberto' glanced at Simone' she sat quietly looking out of the window reached over, touched her hand. She looked at him smiled held his hand in both of hers and kissed it. Roberto' thinking about what Mr. Meriwether said in reference to this situation and Simone' being one in the same did not want to hurt his wife in any way. He decided to talk with her and know her opinion in a calm manner rather than be angry, that would frighten her. She was not use to anger from Roberto' in all the years they were married. She knew he had the capability of being angry, she had seen him at his work.

He said "Simone' I can't express in words what I feel when you give yourself to me. I love you with all my heart and soul; and need you in the same way. I want to know, no, I need to know that I can meet your needs satisfy your every desire."

Smiling, Simone' squeezed his hand and said, "Roberto' you do satisfy me and meet my needs. Your body is wonderful and so desirable to me; you are a sexy man. I want you more than you know my darling husband always remember that no matter what happens or where we are."

Roberto' did not think about what Simone' said "no matter what" at that time, but he would later in pain and agony suffer at the loss of his beautiful Simone'.

"Simone', I want what's best for our daughter. I cannot take the chance she could be hurt in life by marrying someone she is not sure she loves or loves her. Jason Madison is a wealthy man; he could hurt our sweet daughter; it frightens me to even consider it."

"Roberto', I just want Carmeli'ta' to have a choice in love and who she gives her heart to. If we chose for her it takes away her ability to make a choice is all that I am telling you."

"Our parents' chose for us Simone'. We did not do so badly my beauty, what is your opinion?"

"Robert, I could not ask for a better more loving husband than you are. Our Fathers made good choices for us, as was our custom in our country; it is still. Carmeli'ta' was raised by us Roberto', if you remember to have choices in her life. We cannot tell her now she cannot choose for her own heart. She will not understand."

"Carmeli'ta' is young and innocent Simone' she does not know about choosing a husband. Sometimes our hearts will fool us lead us wrong, especially if that person is who we want; those wants can put blinders on allowing us to see only with our heart and that is dangerous."

Roberto' knew he had seen Simone' only with his heart not his eyes and it was causing him pain now. Simone' asked him, "what are you telling me, Roberto'?"

"I am trying to make you understand that sometimes we tell ourselves that this is what is best or good for us; it can blind you to the truth."

Carefully Simone' suggested, "Let us wait Roberto' to see what daughter tells us. It might not be what we are thinking at all."

Roberto' agreed, "What you say is true Simone' my beauty. We will wait. We are almost there."

Roberto' and Simone' could see Carmeli'ta's Townhouse right in front of them as they turned in the gate that led to the front of the buildings at 4:56 p.m. Carmeli'ta" arrived home at 4:30 p.m. and prepared tea for her parents. She knew her Father and Mother both like tea with ice. Carmeli'ta' sitting on her window seat, saw her Father's beige and black Roadster turn into her complex.

Simone' wanting to set the stage for the conversation with Carmeli'ta' said, "Roberto', remember what you told me on the last night of our honeymoon?"

Roberto' smiled and replied, "I remember our honeymoon well my beauty how can I ever forget!"

Simone' smiled lifted her husband's hand to her lips kissed it and said, "Thank you Roberto' for the wonderful compliment. You said to me when we were sitting in front of the fireplace that you did not marry me because I was your chosen bride. You married me because you fell in love with me and not because of an arrangement by our parents."

"I remember Simone' it is still true."

Simone' quietly said, "I ask Roberto' that you remember this when we are talking to our daughter, you chose, can't you allow her to choose?"

"I will keep that in mind my darling when we are talking to daughter."

From her window seat Carmeli'ta' saw her Father's Roadster pulled up in front of her Townhouse and stop. She watched her Father as he came around the front of the car to open the door for her Mother. Seeing her parents together was a pleasant experience for Carmeli'ta'. She loved them both and especially adored her Mother. Roberto' offered Simone' his left hand, pulled her up from her seat, held her close hugging her tightly as he pushed the car door close, smiled at her; they turned arm in arm and walked to the steps that led up to Carmeli'ta's Townhouse.

Carmeli'ta' smiled rushed to the refrigerator to get the pitcher of tea and glasses with ice she had chilling, set them on the coffee table. They knocked at the door she exclaimed as she ran to the door, "I am coming, Daddy and mummy."

Opening the door smiling rushed into her Father open arms. Roberto' held his daughter for a moment kissed her on the forehead said, "Hello daughter, how are you today?"

"I am fine daddy how are you?"

"I am fine my beautiful daughter."

Carmeli'ta' turned looked her Mother said, "I am glad to see you mummy; she kissed her mother on her cheek. You are so beautiful mummy. I love you and daddy a lot. I am glad you came to see me today."

"Thank you Carmeli'ta' my sweet daughter, I love you too, and I am happy to see you."

Roberto' took Simone's Grey Fox Mink coat and hung it in the coat closet in the hallway.

They walked arm in arm into Carmeli'ta' living areas, she closed the door softly behind them. Roberto' commented, "It is always good to see you my daughter. We love you with all our hearts and want the best for you in life."

"Thank you daddy, I have the best. I have you as parents."

Simone' added, "Thank you my sweet daughter. You make us proud as parents." Roberto' noticed the refreshment tray sitting on the coffee table with the chilled glasses with ice.

"I made tea for you mummy and daddy."

"Thank you; that was sweet of you my lovely daughter to make our favorite drink", Roberto replied.

Carmeli'ta' felt a little nervous, yet happy to see her parents. She sat in the huge, oversized chair that faced the sofa as her parents sat down.

Simone' poured the tea in the chilled glasses handed Roberto' and Carmeli'ta' their glasses, took her glass sit back on the coach snuggling close to her husband. She sipped her tea waiting for her husband to start the conversation praying he would not get upset or cause Carmeli'ta' to be upset.

Carmeli'ta' sipped her tea and continued to smile at her parents. Roberto' looked at his daughter sitting in a slightly distant manner, was so precious, and looked so innocence. She was small, with long legs just like her Mother, beautiful long black hair that extended down her back, long eyelashes that framed her eyes, such a beautiful and cherished child to Roberto', his only child. "Carmeli'ta' my daughter, your Mother tells me that you went on a date with Jason Madison, Jr. last evening?"

"Yes daddy, I did. I was waiting to tell you about Jason and my date."

Roberto' set his glass on the tray again moved forward on the coach put his hand together in a firm grip looked at his daughter said in a firm tone, "Tell me now Carmeli'ta'. Was this another business function or was it personal?"

Carmeli'ta' swallowing hard answered, "It was a personal date daddy. Jason took me to Rochelle's last night for a lovely dinner and dancing."

"Are you telling me Carmeli'ta', that you have a deeper interest in Jason Madison, Jr. than business? I know that you are his company's Office Manager and Social Hostess."

"I care for Jason very much daddy. He is a wonderful man and he is a Christian. He attends the Lafayette Street Church of Christ near Mother and your farm."

"I know that he and his family are Christians and where they attend worship my daughter. However, you did not answer my question."

Carmeli'ta' nervously replied, "I am the company's Social Hostess and Office Manager; he is a good boss, but it goes deeper than that. I have fallen in love with Jason over the past months."

Roberto' becoming impatient and agitated said, "Carmeli'ta' how do you know you love Jason Madison? You know nothing about love; you are so young yet."

Feeling a little warm under the collar, and then a cold chill in the same instance, Roberto' picked up his tea glass walked over in front of the fireplace. Carmeli'ta' started a fire earlier because of the coolness in the November evening. Roberto' turned looked at her and said, "Carmeli'ta' I cannot approve this relationship with Jason Madison."

Carmeli'ta' expression changed to a look of dread and horror exclaimed "I don't understand Father, I love Jason and he loves me. We are engaged he has asked me to be his wife!"

Roberto' anger growing even more said, "Absolutely not, Carmeli'ta'. No! You do not know what love is you have only known one man and you work for him; your feelings could be confused it may be infatuation, he is older than you and a rich businessman."

"No Father, I am not infatuated. I know my heart and mind. I am an adult. I know what you and Mother taught me about life and love. You always said. "I should choose for myself, have that changed?"

Roberto' replied, "You can choose in some things Carmeli'ta', but not in matters of the heart. I do not want you to be hurt or marry someone that you do not know well. I want you to take your time. I do not know Jason Madison. He might be a good man and wonderful boss, but he is not for you my daughter."

Carmeli'ta' growing more and more upset, "He is for me Father I love Jason!" Carmeli'ta' fighting back said, "You and mother are rich just like Jason's family."

Roberto' not giving in to her emotions said, "We are wealthy, yes, Carmeli'ta'. Our wealth is nowhere near the Madison family. They have an iron and steel empire."

Simone' sitting listening, saw tears swell up in Carmeli'ta's eyes and run down her cheek could not remain silent any longer said, "Roberto', please, you are upsetting daughter." Simone' set her glass on the tray, sit on the arm of the large wing-backed chair besides Carmeli'ta' and held her close to her side.

Roberto' insisted, "No Simone' we will discuss this matter tonight. I cannot approve a marriage or relationship of any kind between Carmeli'ta' and Jason Madison." Roberto' retorted, "Carmeli'ta' it is the custom for the Father to choose a husband for his daughter. I have watched Alberto Gambani as he matured; he is a good man, his future is secure, he cares for you and he is from the farm community. He will care for you and never hurt you."

Carmeli'ta' countered, "I love Alberto' Father, but I am not in love with him. He is my best friend. I do not feel the same way about him as I do Jason. I am in love with Jason. I cannot marry someone I do not love. We are not in the old country any more my Father."

Roberto' insisted, "We are still Tuscans Carmeli'ta'. I still believe that a Father should choose a husband for his daughter to make sure she is safe and has a secure future as your Mother's Father and my Father chose for us."

Carmeli'ta' still insisting, "I do not love Alberto'! I have never been disrespectful to you, my Father. I have always been obedient and did what you told me, but I want to make my own choice in who I give my heart too."

"Alberto Gambani would love you Carmeli'ta' he would make you a good husband as I have for your Mother; love will come in time. You care for him as a friend already; it will be easy to love him."

"No, my Father, I cannot, I love Jason. Mother please, I do not understand why I cannot make my choice in love. You told me that I should make choices when it came to matters of the heart, you still believe that?"

"Yes, my daughter, I still believe that. Your Father is just concerned about you and wants the best for you."

Carmeli'ta' feeling afraid asked, "Do you agree with Father?"

She said, "No my daughter, I want you to choose who you love."

Roberto' angry looked at his wife and said, "Simone', I will not give my approval for Carmeli'ta' to marry Jason Madison, she will get hurt, I cannot allow that to happen."

Simone' insisted, "Roberto' you made the choice when you fell in love with me. Please allow daughter to do the same, please. Do not hurt our daughter in this way and me."

Roberto' snappishly said, "I understand your comment about hurting Carmeli'ta', but you, Simone', you speak to me of hurt and pain?"

Simone' felt the same chill as she did the night before when he asked her if she had been honest with him about her feeling. "Roberto' please we must not let our emotions get out of hand and you have become very angry."

Roberto' position still the same said, "Yes, I am angry with the whole situation that is unfolding before my eyes."

Carmeli'ta' interrupted, "Father, I do not understand why you are so angry with mother and me. What have I done? What has she done? Love is not wrong. You love Mother with all your heart. I have watched you over the years. I have always wanted the type of relationship that you and Mother has. You are so much in love."

Roberto' said, "It is true I love your Mother Carmeli'ta' with all my heart, but I know what pain loving someone can cause you."

Carmeli'ta' shaking her head with a look of disbelief on her face exclaimed, "I do not understand my Father!"

"I do not expect you to at this point Carmeli'ta'."

Simone' wanting to end the conversation, "Roberto' it is getting late and Carmeli'ta' have a date with Jason tonight in just a while. We promised Marianna that we would return for dinner by 7:00 p.m. It is 6:45 p.m. Roberto' should we not be leaving? Daughter has to get dressed."

"We will leave Simone', Roberto' said, "But this is not the end of this. Carmeli'ta' we will discuss this again in a few days."

Carmeli'ta' insisting on an answer, "Father why are you angry with Mother, she only want me to make choices as she has always taught me?" Roberto' did not want to discuss the private matter in front of Carmeli'ta' of Simone's honesty said, "I am angry about the situation period Carmeli'ta', not just with your Mother."

Carmeli'ta' felt hurt, "I do not want to upset you my Father, but I do love Jason, it is not infatuation, I know what I feel. I need him and he needs me."

He responded, "We will let it go at that for tonight Carmeli'ta'. I will come again in a few days."

Decision time! Fear outweighs commitment....

CHAPTER
SIXTEEN

Roberto' picked up his keys from the coffee table went to the closet put on his coat, took his wife's Mink coat from the hanger held it for her; she put it on and buttoned the front to keep away the November chill. Carmeli'ta' walked over to where her parents stood hugged and kissed her Father then her Mother opened the door held her face up for her Father to kiss her as he did at the end of each visit, "Good night Father and Mother, I will call you later when I return from my date with Jason."

"See that you do daughter", Roberto' said, "I will be waiting no matter the lateness of the hour, please call me."

Hugging her tightly Simone' said, "Good night my lovely daughter; enjoy your dinner tonight. Marianna sends her love and she misses you."

"Thank her for me and tell her I said hello and I will come soon to see her."

"I will tell here my lovely little one."

"Thank you Mother, I will come soon, I love you both." Carmeli'ta' closed the door still pondering her Father's statement to her Mother about "hurt and pain" she did not understand what he meant. Her Mother never hurt anyone; she was kind to everyone and anyone.

Roberto' quiet on the drive home, Simone' watching her husband, reached for his hand holding it gently lifted it to her cheek and said, "Talk to me Roberto', you are angry."

"Yes, Simone', I am angry and afraid for my daughter. You agreed with her in her desire to have love with Jason Madison. She is not his equal. He is a rich man; we are farmers. Our world is different from his. How can you allow this to happen?"

"I did not allow this to happen, Roberto' Carmeli'ta' made the choice not me."

"If you had been honest with me Simone' about the matter it would not have gotten this far." She replied calmly, "Our daughter asked me not to say anything."

Roberto' still annoyed asked, "How long have you known Carmeli'ta' has feeling for Jason Madison? How long Simone'?" She replied, "A few months Roberto'."

"That does not tell me anything Simone', how many?"

"Three months Roberto'."

"That is a long time to keep a secret from me Simone'."

Roberto', "I do not understand your anger Carmeli'ta' is grown; she can decide for herself."

"No, you wouldn't Simone'. You are good at keeping secrets and hiding the truth. I have come to realize that about you."

"I do not know what you are talking about Roberto' please; why you are angry, tell me?"

At 6:55 p.m., Roberto' turned into their driveway and parked his car in the usual place commented, "We will continue this discussion after dinner. We are home Marianna is not to know. We will eat and go upstairs and finish the discussion."

Agreeing she said, "Yes you are right Roberto'; it is private."

Roberto' opened the car door for Simone' helped her rise walked ahead of her to the office door and unlocked it waited for her to enter. They walked through the office into the kitchen Simone' felt another chill that had overcome her while at Carmeli'ta's, and the night before. Fear gripped her heart and mind. How could she have done this, let it go so far without being truthful? Her husband was now questioning her honesty and integrity.

Marianna heard the Bandaci's enter through the office, put dinner on the table. Marianna smiled as they walked in said, "You are on time for a change, and dinner is ready to be served."

"We will wash our hand and be right back Marianna, dinner smells delicious" Roberto' said and smiled. He helped Simone' take off her coat and then took his off; laid them on the Winged-backed Victorian Chair in the Parlor near the entrance.

They went to the bathroom in Carmeli'ta's suite, washed their hands and returned to the table for dinner. Marianna made fresh bread with butter, new potatoes, green beans, a chicken and vegetable casserole with grilled mushrooms, and a deep-dish apple pie for dessert. She served a bottle of Chilled White Cabernet Wine with the meal and made coffee to serve with the dessert.

Their unusual silence at dinner was noticeable to Marianna. Normally they chatted and laughed the entire meal a happy lively couple. Marianna asked, "Ms. Bandaci is Miss Carmeli'ta' okay? Did you tell her I miss her and said hello?"

"Yes, Marianna, Carmeli'ta' is fine. We did tell her you said hello. She said tell you hello; she will come to visit soon."

This news made Marianna happy she smiled and served the Bandaci's dinner. Simone' ate her dinner, but not the usual amount; her taste for food was lost in the confusion of the conversation with their daughter and the impending discussion she faced after dinner. Roberto' ate his dinner as usual. He was hungry and needed his strength to operate their farm each day.

Simone' glanced at Roberto' often during dinner but did not say anything. Dinner finally done Roberto' said, "Marianna dinner was Delicious. We appreciate you preparing it later than usual. We will retire now, good night."

"You are welcome. Good night, Sir and Miss sleep well."

"Thank you Marianna you are very much appreciated by our family", commented Simone'. Marianna smiled.

Roberto' and Simone' climbed the stairs to their suite leaving Marianna with a question in the back of her mind. Roberto' opened the door and went in first ahead of Simone'. She entered and stopped in the sitting room, kicked off her shoes, stood in front of the warmth of the simmering flame in the fireplace lit earlier in the evening by Marianna. Feeling not weak but not strong at that moment, sat in the overstuffed winged-back chair, continuing to enjoy the warm toasty feel the fire gave to the room. Roberto' opened the closet door, took off his shoes, undressed, went to the bathroom showered and prepared for bed. He returned twenty minutes later wearing his robe and slippers and joined Simone' in the sitting room in their suite. She loved the fresh smell Roberto' had when he came near her. He stood in front of the fireplace a few minutes later sit looking at his wife. Simone' dreaded this moment and final showdown she knew would come eventually with her husband.

She never thought their daughter's love for Jason Madison Jr. would trigger the conversation about her honesty and integrity with her husband. Roberto' sit on the loveseat opposite Simone' looked at her for a long time finally said, "Now Simone', tell me, you say you have nothing to hide and you have been truthful with me. There has always been something between us even in our bed, you wear a gown every night Simone', and I sleep in the nude, why Simone'? On the ship, you were distant as if you were sad to be leaving Tuscany. The look in your eyes told me of the regret and the pain you felt. That hurt Simone'. I love you and have done everything I can to make you happy! I have given my life and myself to you completely. Can you say the same of you Simone'? You hold back when we make love Simone' why? Yet, you say I satisfy your needs and desires Simone'! You have deeper passion and desires that you have not let yourself show with me Simone', I know you do; I can feel your body retracting at a certain point when we are together; you cut me off why? This crushes me Simone', I don't think you love me as you say you do."

This statement finally got a response from Simone' who, up to this point, sit looking at her husband speaking the pain and hurt in his heart to her he felt over the years. "I do love you Roberto' with all my heart, you are wrong if you think that I do not love you. I want our daughter to have the chance to choose the man she loves not have him chosen for her. Jason Madison is a fine young man; she cares for him and he cares for her Roberto'. Please, give them a chance. You cannot punish him for being born into a rich family. We know people in Tuscany that think this way Roberto'. We are in a different culture and society; we raised our daughter since she was five years old in this culture of men and women making the choice of who they would marry and not their parents make the choice for them. I did not say anything to you about her love for Jason because she told me in confidence and asked, I not tell you before she knew whether Jason Madison cared for her in the same way. I could not break my promise to her Roberto'. I was not trying to deceive you or hide anything from you just keeping my promise is all, after all Carmeli'ta' is an adult."

Simone' continued, "We know now since our visit that she and Jason love each other. She is happy Roberto' as she should be. Young love is so beautiful. Our young love was beautiful. Now, we are matured our love is even more beautiful. I know how Carmeli'ta' feels she is in love and is more mature than I was when we were married. I do love you Roberto', as she loves Jason. I have never done anything to hurt you intentionally. I have devoted my life and everything that I have and am to making you happy because I love you so."

Simone' still avoided answering Roberto's questions about her secrecy all these years; also, why she had not shared here deepest passion and desires with him.

Roberto' listening intently at his wife waited for her to finish said, "Simone' all you say is true about young love and the beauty of it. I felt and feel that way about you. I need you so desperately in every way. I cannot bear the pain of not having the love I need from you, nor the possibility that our daughter may be hurt because she loves Jason and he may not love her the same way. I cannot bear this added pain. I will not! If she marries Alberto Gambani, I know he will care for her and not hurt her like Jason Madison could and might."

"Roberto', Carmeli'ta' does not love Alberto in the way a woman loves a man, he is her best friend it begins and ends there, Friendship! You are asking her to do something that you are disapproving of with Jason. How is this different Roberto', tell me? The love has to be mutual not one-sided."

"I am glad to know that you realize this Simone'; be it our daughter or you. You are not answering my questions about you and your feelings Simone'. Why are you avoiding answering my question about our love life, why?"

"I do not know how to answer or what to say to you Roberto'. I cannot answer your questions, but I do love you and need you beyond my heart and mind. You make me happy. You satisfy my every need Roberto'; I want with all my heart to do the same for you so desperately."

"Why the secret and why keep things between us in our intimate life? Why can't you give yourself to me completely? I have to know!"

Simone' felt pressure as Roberto's questions and demands grew surrounded by her negative fears, held her prisoner. She felt trapped with no way out. She had to be able to get free from the trap she had been in all these years now it is pulling in others she loved Roberto', Carmeli'ta', Marianna, Mr. Meriwether, and it had to end. The only thing Simone' could think to do was to run away from the situation. How could she answer Roberto's questions without him knowing about Vincenzo'? Sometimes, if she admitted it to herself, the pressure for a long time made her doubt herself in reference to Carmeli'ta'. Who is her father, Roberto' or Vincenzo's? It was a possibility that she could be Vincenzo's daughter. She would allow herself to believe only the probability of it not being his daughter, had totally rejected the notion of that possibility even in Tuscany when Vincenzo' said the baby was his when she told him she was pregnant. Still his statement created fears, these mental and emotional moments of impact has plagued, haunted, and terrified her over the years.

The grips of fear and dread was tearing into her, its strong jaws rendering her unsure of anything about life, except the fact that she loved her family and her husband with all her heart. She knew Carmeli'ta' for sure, was her daughter!

She could not tell Roberto' tonight his vision would be blurred because of the anger and hurt he felt. The truth would destroy him. At this time; she felt as if she were walking on eggshells; the only action she could take to delay his finding out would be to run away. She decided that she would leave and go to Tuscany to her Father; he said she could always come home.

Roberto' waiting for answers continued to look at his wife, his sweet exquisitely lovely wife who would not be honest with him, realized was flawed.

"Roberto', it is getting late it is bedtime. You have to work tomorrow and I want to collect the remainder of our account for the week and make the deposits as well if you don't mind, it will be a long and difficult day for both of us."

"You are right Simone', but this is not the end of this conversation. My daughter is not going to be hurt if I can help it. And I don't mind you collecting the remainder of the accounts tomorrow if that is easier for you."

Simone said, "I do not want our daughter to be hurt, unhappy, or married to someone she only loves as a friend."

"I will prepare your bath Simone'."

She asked, "Are you still angry with me Roberto'?"

"No, Simone', I feel better. I am not angry anymore tonight; this is just the beginning and not the end of this matter" he replied and walked out of the sitting room.

"I will be there in a minute Roberto'."

Roberto'in their bathroom prepared the bath for his wife. Simone'picked up her shoes put the glass screen in front of the fireplace and went into the bedroom.

She undressed hung her dress in the closet, put her shoes on the rack, put on her dressing gown, put her hair up, and went into the bathroom where Roberto's was waiting to help her with her bath. He was sitting on the dressing bench when Simone' entered. She took off her dressing gown and lingerie, toweled her hair and stepped into the warm bath sliding down in the bubbly mile-high suds, leaned back looked at Roberto' and smiled, "My bath feels delicious. You are good to me. I love you with all my heart, never doubt my love for you, and never forget that I love you no matter the circumstances. My love for you will never change."

He responded, "I care for you Simone', thank you is not necessary, you are always welcome. What I do for Carmeli'ta' and you is driven by love only."

"I know you love me Roberto', I have no doubt about your feelings for me. I need you Roberto' always. My life has been richly rewarding because you are in it. I could not imagine a life without you. I have tried and I cannot see a future without pain if I lost you for some reason."

"Lose me Simone', why would you lose me? That is a strange thing for you to say to me!"

"I just want you to understand what I feel. I have that same string tied to my heart that you told me about on our last night before we left our honeymoon hide-away."

Roberto' surprised by this revelation responded, "You never shared your feelings about what I said to you on the last night of our honeymoon, Simone'. I never knew you felt this way or if you really understand how I feel."

"I do understand Roberto', I always have; I am not 17 years old anymore. I have a clear understanding of what you felt then and how you feel now. I need you tonight Roberto'. I want you to love me and I want to love you. I need to be near you, have you hold me and love me before we sleep. Please do not deny me your love tonight. I know you were angry with me."

"I would never deny you love Simone'. I am yours at all times under all circumstances even when I get angry with you my love is still strong, it does not stop because we do not agree at that time. My anger does not last forever. We will see what tomorrow brings. Tonight, I am still your husband. I want to please you and satisfy your needs. I would never or could never deny you intimacy. There are places in my heart that no one can touch except you; it is as a fever, a drive that keeps my love for you growing each passing day and it enriches itself as the years past."

Roberto' reached for the sponge, rose from the dressing bench, sit on the side of the tub to wash Simone's neck and back. Gently he washed her back his hands touched her soft velvety honey colored skin, looked at his lovely wife sitting with her eyes closed enjoying the touch of his hand and the warm water while rinsing the soap off her back and neck. Continuing to massage her neck and back, his hands slowly moved to her throat and the small sink there, the *External Notch* he loved to kiss and touch, could see her pulse beating steady and strong; the collarbone across the top of her chest like a strong rod, giving her neck a graceful luxurious look.

Simone' relaxed in the tub, his hand moved down across her breast, stomach, buttocks, and long slim legs sitting up in the bubbles. Roberto' caressed her entire body as he had done many times over the years while she relaxed in the bath of bubbles. His touch sent hot waves of desire that washed his body. His hands were persistent, demanding, and strong caressing her body; journeying to every inch of it. The feel of the warm water and the warmth of Simone's body made her irresistible to Roberto'. The atmosphere felt different tonight with hints of desire drifting around when he touched his wife.

Simone saw the look of desire in Roberto's eyes, could feel the passion he had for here in the way his hands glided over her body; the same desire and passion she saw in his eyes, earlier before they left to see Carmeli'ta', and their wedding night twenty-four years ago.

These moments and times were like frontlets before his eyes. The memory of intimacy with Simone' gave him a warm satisfying rush that went across him like the flow of the river stream in summer they loved to watch from the hill overlooking the farming community in Tuscany. His touched electrified the desire in Simone' awakening the desire she had to make love to her husband and be near him one more time. Simone' relaxed even more. Roberto' touched her, leaned forward, and kissed her on the lips. Touching his cheeks during his tender kiss, she could feel the strong desire and gentleness of her husband's touch and kiss.

She whispered in his ear when he leaned and said, "I need you Roberto' as you needed me earlier today. I want you Roberto'; your hands are so strong, gentle, and kind." Tears formed in Simone's eyes as her voice broke, whispered, "I never wanted to hurt you. My daily thoughts are to please and make you happy. I am sorry if you think I do not love you."

"Let me help you out of the tub my beauty, the water is no longer warm enough to stay in."

She said, "I am ready."

Roberto' stood took Simone's hand, she rose from the water, pulled the drain plug, and stepped into the large Egyptian Cotton Bath Towel he held for her to snuggle dry. Afterwards she lotion her body, face, neck, put on a short black negligée, dabbed on Chanel 5 cologne, brushed her teeth, gargled, turned out the light, went to the dresser, un-toweled her hair and brushed the long curly locks that falls down her back.

Routinely, Roberto' placed his bedroom shoes under the foot of the bed at the edge, and sat on the foot of the bed waiting for his wife to finish preparing for bed. The lamp light from the bedside table casted a beam across the room to where Simone' was standing in the mirror brushing her hair, Roberto' saw the beauty of her body through the black negligée. She was the most desirable woman and the only woman he wanted in the world. Here sensuality, like a magnet, drew him; moving from the bed, walked over to where Simone' stood, put his arms around her, kissed the back of her neck and then her shoulders. She smelled fresh as a spring morning. Leaning back against his chest, she smiled at him in the mirror.

Roberto' snuggling his wife whispered, "Simone' you are my heart and life, I love you."

"I love you Roberto'. You are my strength, hope, and my entire life."

Roberto' turned Simone' around to face him hugging her tighter said, "Please no gown tonight for the first time in twenty-four years, please!"

Simone' closed her eyes. Roberto' lifted the gown over her head carefully placed it on the dressing table saw his wife's face and closed eyes said, "Look at me! Why do you close your eyes? Are you so shy after all these years?"

"No Roberto', it is because of the enjoyment and pleasure the touch of your hands and the intimacy between us gives me at all levels."

Unable to tell him the truth, felt as Roberto' removed her negligée, he could see the truth of the deceit she hid all the years of their marriage. She was incapable of controlling feelings he could see or might know her secrets. Fear's twenty-four-year grip became her slave master, she was intensely more afraid now after their conversation earlier than before, he was so close to discovering her secrets she had guarded so well all these years.

Simone' saw his naked body while he disrobed thought, "His arms are so muscular, thighs tight, and strong; he is such a desirably attractive man."

Holding his body pressed against her, Simone' could feel the full force of his manhood. She held him tight pulling him close to her. He lifted her off the floor holding her tight, she kissed his neck and chest, looked up at her husband pushed back the unruly lock of hair dancing on his forehead; he put her down gently on the floor, she snuggled closer to him. He could see her embrace in the mirror. Powerless at that moment to look away, he saw the beauty of her naked body picked her up, carried her to their bed, sit with her on his lap, and lay back pulling her down to him.

Lying on her husband she said, "Roberto', I want you, please love me."

With the passion and desire growing, Simone' could feel the firmness of his body. Holding her, he rolled over his hand travelled touching her, kissing her lips, her breast, her stomach; his entire being was demanding, pleading for passion, his firm body entered hers. Simone' moaned gently with the pleasure she felt as his body kept searching hers, begging for more passion, to be let into her deepest desires.

Roberto' whispered, "Simone', please love me, love me, let me in, I want to know and feel all of you."

She gave herself to Roberto' more than she had in all their years of marriage, but not completely yet not yet. Feeling a new level of passion flowing warm and strong from her sensual body bought the emotions of tears and pleasure to his mind and pain to his heart of not having even this level of passion over the year; both emotions flooded him in the same moments.

Holding Simone' tighter thrust even stronger; she groaned more and more with each thrust, her body reached up to him for more, whispered, "Roberto', love me, love me, your body feels so good, it gives me pleasure, that I cannot put into words."

"Simone', love me, as I love you."

Her body responded to Roberto' smooth and strong matching his every move, lifting up to meet his, she loved Roberto'. Her body inviting him in; giving him a feeling of being a welcomed guest with the new level of passion she allowed him to feel. Simone' caressed Roberto's body, he moved closer to her deepest level of passions and desires. She moaned softly; his demanding lips kissed her until she could not breathe. Her soft moaning, drifted in his ears, like drops of warm sweet oil, used to soothe an earache, drove Roberto' speechless with desire, he finally said, "I cannot get enough of you tonight. Love me my beauty, I do not want to stop not now; I want more of you. "

Simone' knew that Roberto' was trying to make-up for all the passion he needed over the years that he had not felt from her, "Roberto', I am yours, my body, my heart, and my mind all yours; love me until you are satisfied; I cannot refuse the demands of your body, I need you too."

Roberto' felt his wife's body grip his as he entered hers each time. She felt as if she would explode as she and Roberto' reached a climax that left them breathless. Tears of joy fell on her cheeks from his eyes, he held her murmured, "I cannot describe the pleasure tonight Simone', our honeymoon was just the beginning of what pleasure I can feel with you. I love you so my beautiful wife." Simone' snuggling next to her husband, he pulled up the covers over their naked bodies, she whispered softly, "Thank you Roberto' for not denying me your love tonight. I will never forget this night. Our love is beautiful to me." Simone' kissed her husband passionately again, he said, "I love you. I would never say no to your needs, my lovely wife." Pulling her closer held her tight; felt sleepy drifting on a cloud of love.

This one-night Simone' slept naked with her husband beside her. Before drifting into a peaceful and satisfying sleep, Roberto thought, "With the new level of passion I experienced my winter of starvation is coming to an end and my spring season of passion is evident by my wife's response tonight."

He was closer to her deepest passion than ever before.

He felt her love and desired to know it fully. It was like a waterfall coming out of a mountain flowing strong and beautiful. Yet, he could not reach it because of the valley and dales he had to cross. He could feel it, yet it was always just of reach, so near and at the same time so far. Simone's love powerful and beautiful, like a stream flowing from her mountain of desire kept him struggling to reach her innermost desires and passion. He wanted and needed her love like a waterfall it is warm, then cooling; her love would replenish and refresh his heart and soul.

To Roberto' this level of love was new...the warmth flowing from Simone's he compared as light to a dark lonely day starving for any ray of sunshine. Roberto' thought, "I waited for this time; I am so close to being joined with Simone' completely with nothing between us."

The vibrancy of this time made a new bold statement. The jubilation, mystery, and ecstasy of sexual love were within his reach. He was not ready for this night to be over; he wanted to make love to his wife more that night, hold her, and be near her.

Would they unite in the true passion they both felt for each other?

Or would there be more horizons for Roberto' to cross?

CHAPTER

SEVENTEEN

At her Townhouse, Carmeli'ta' had prepared for her date with Jason even at the objection of her Father.

Carmeli'ta' dressed for her date in the same careful way she did for their first date the evening before. She wore a beautiful red dress with silver accessories and her hair falling loosely down her back. She waited for Jason to pick her up at 7:45 p.m. for their 8:00 p.m. dinner and dancing at La' Ju'nev'via, the Country Club Restaurant and Ballroom.

Carmeli'ta' decided not to call her Mother since it had only been one hour and a half since she spoke with them. She knew her Father did not want her to see Jason; talking to him would only make the situation worse and anger was something she had not seen between her Father and Mother.

When her parents left at 6:45 p.m. for their home and dinner left her puzzled. Puzzling was a minimal description of the evening for Carmeli'ta' after the wonderful day she had at work.

Looking down the lights below her window provided a view at the pleasant scenery of the flower garden below. Her thoughts went back to the day. Arriving at work at 9:00 a.m. after an overwhelming evening of love and romance Carmeli'ta's head still spinning from Jason's and her new love.

Jason was at his desk when Carmeli'ta' arrived at Madison Steel. He had been at work since 7:00 a.m. that morning with instructions to Ms. Horne to ask Ms. Bandaci to come see him when she arrived.

Ms. Horne saw Carmeli'ta' arrive her office down the hall. Ms. Horne walked down the hall knocked on her door and said, "Ms. Bandaci, Mr. Madison asked that you come to his office when you arrive. He wants to check on the details of the project proposal with Mr. Meriwether that is coming next Wednesday."

"Thank you Ms. Horne, tell him I will be there momentarily." Carmeli'ta' knew that the Wednesday meeting with Charles Bienville Meriwether was not why Jason wanted to see her.

A few minutes later Carmeli'ta' in his office, Jason smiled and moved from behind the desk walking toward her, he noticed she was smiling. Jason reached her side of the room closed the door turned to her and said, "Hello my darling, it is good to see you. I was eagerly waiting for you to get here. I missed you after I left you last night."

Jason excused himself, at his desk, buzzed Ms. Horne and said, "Ms. Horne we are not to be disturbed unless it is urgent. Please ring me if there is an emergency. We should not be longer than an hour if that long."

"Yes, Mr. Madison."

He walked back to where Carmeli'ta' was standing reached for her she slide into his open arms looked up at him and said, "I could not wait to see you my love. I still feel as if I am floating on cloud from last night. I love you Jason, more now that I know you love me."

"I do love you Carmeli'ta'. You have filled my mind both day and night for so long now. I am happy to know that you love me my sweet. You can make my life complete. I can't imagine my days without you."

He pulled Carmeli'ta' close to him and hugged her tight. His arms felt good around her. She felt safe and secure for that moment. She did not feel threaten by her Father's decision she should marry Alberto Gambini her best friend, because he was a farmer like her family. Her Father was still holding to the Tuscan culture, especially where his daughter was concerned. Carmeli'ta' understood how he felt and what the culture was like in Tuscany; however, she was raised in America not Tuscany a culture where women and men chooses whom they love not marry because of a 'Cast' based system of ideas.

Jason looked at Carmeli'ta' lifted her face to his and kissed her. She returned his kiss. She was sweet to him, warm and precious. The taste of his love for Carmeli'ta' was like sparkling wine. Her lips were warms and inviting. He thought as he kissed her lips how well they fit to his.

He wanted to hold her forever.

Carmelita stood clinging to Jason thanked God for the love he has bought into her life. She did not care that he was rich, only that he loved and needed her as she loved and needed him.

Finally, Jason said, "Carmeli'ta', my love it is nearing 10:00 a.m., we better end our meeting." Ms. Horne will be reminding me of my 10:00 a.m. meeting in about ten minutes. I do not want this to end, but we must be careful my love."

"Yes, Jason we must be careful for everyone concerned as we discussed last night. I will miss you as the day's work starts my love. Have a good day. I will see you in a few minutes in the meeting."

Jason smiled as Carmeli'ta' opened the office door and said, "Thank you Carmeli'ta'. I will see you in about ten minutes at the Departmental Supervisors meeting." Carmeli'ta' walked pass Ms. Horne's desk and said,

"Thank you Ms. Horne. Is the Boardroom ready and the Agendas in place?"

"You are welcome, Ms. Bandaci. Everything is ready for the meeting."

Carmeli'ta' mind went forward in time trying to think of what or how she would tell Jason about her parent's earlier that evening. Nonetheless, not tonight, this was their second night of new love she would not spoil it with telling him about the conversation.

Jason finally arrived.

Carmeli'ta' saw his Bentley pull up in from of her Townhouse. She rushed to the mirror in the foyer to check her appearance once more. Her red dress shimmered in the soft lighting in the foyer. She was ready.

A familiar light knock on the door, Carmeli'ta' said, "Jason?" He said, "Yes, my love it is me." She opened the door he walked in close the door and reached for Carmeli'ta' pulling her to him said, "Hello my love it is good to see you. Tonight, did not come quickly enough for me. Are you ready my love? You look lovely tonight. My sweetheart, you are sparkling."

Jason calling her my sweetheart reminded her of what her Father calls her Mother, "My beauty." It warmed her heart to hear the sweet words from Jason. She knew what her Mother meant to her Father. "Yes, Jason darling, I am ready. Thank you for the compliments. I feel happy Jason." Jason and Carmeli'ta' left for dinner then an evening of dancing and romance.

Later that evening, Roberto' awakened at 11:30 p.m. still holding Simone' looked at his sleeping wife. She looked so peaceful. Her long, beautiful hair, black as coal, her smooth tan colored skin, long sexy eyelashes, and perfect mouth with the pillow as a background gave her the look of an exquisite work of art. The love of his life, she was everything he ever wanted, had one flaw, she kept secrets.

Roberto' leaning over kissed Simone' on her mouth and cheeks. Simone' made a satisfying sound, a sigh soft as a whisper, moved her naked body toward his. Roberto' spoke gently, "Wake up my beauty."

Simone' opened her eyes looked at Roberto' and finally said, "I am awake Roberto'. What time is it? Is it time to get our day started?"

"No, my lovely wife, it is 11:30 p.m. still night. We still have a few hours before our day starts. I awaken Simone', I always do, and in the wee still hours of the night to watch you while you sleep. I love to see you so peaceful. You sleep so beautifully Simone'."

"Thank you Roberto'. Tonight was so wonderful. You made me feel a deep and satisfying passion Roberto'. The feel of your body is unforgettable. I need you Roberto' and love you with all my heart, never forget."

Roberto's hands begin to explore Simone's body again, pushed back the covers and looked her naked body lying next to him caressed her kissing her eyes, nose, mouth repeatedly. Simone' looked up at her husband and pulled him close to her.

Roberto' desiring to satisfy his wife and feel her warmth his body again entered hers said, "Simone' don't move just let me feel the warmth of your body hold me close my beauty."

Roberto' felt her body react to his; he felt her gently squeeze his; he pushed his body deeper into her and held her tight, her body squeezes his tighter.

The warmth and pleasure that invaded his being held him emotionally. He kissed his wife. She was so sweet and loving he could not get enough of her, "Simone' you have given me pleasure tonight that I have never known since we were married. I felt tonight as I did on our honeymoon, like it was the first time."

He held her tight smiled and nibbled at her nose. Unable to resist moving at the feel of her Roberto' made love to her. Simone' whispered his name softly, "Roberto', Roberto', I love you." The ecstasy and pleasure that invaded his heart and mind holding him captive did not want the warm flow of passion he felt from Simone' to end.

At long last, Roberto' rolled over on his pillow put his hands under his head, "Simone', I have always needed you, your love, but I want all of you; I have not gotten that from you! You keep me shut out of your deepest passions and desires. I know I can feel it when we make love. I want to know why when you say you love me with all your heart and mind but not with all of your body. Why, Simone'? Why?" Tell me. I cannot accept these secrets between us any longer. I know now Simone' that I am jealous of what I have not felt with you intimately, what I do not know yet about my wife. I cannot bear not being completely one with you in body and mind. Why have you denied me that part of you over the years? Why? Tell me."

"I have always loved you Roberto' from the third month we were married. I always cared about you since they day we met. I give myself to you always. I told you on our honeymoon, I would never deny you love or my body."

"This is true Simone' and you have done that; but was it just a promise? You are keeping secrets Simone' about our daughter, you, and your feeling, why tell me?"

"I cannot answer you more than I did earlier tonight Roberto'. I do love you; and no, it was not just a promise, I give myself to you because I love you my darling husband."

Simone' knew with Roberto', at the present time, when his emotions were running high, needed to measure each word she spoke and not throw fuel on the already raging fires inside of her husband.

"Simone' what is it that you can't tell me?"

Simone', with tears in her yes, "I am sorry Roberto'. Please forgive me. I do love you, please forgive me!"

"No, Simone', you are asking me to forgive you. How can you ask me to forgive you for something I know nothing about, how? Tell me what you are hiding!"

"I cannot answer your questions Roberto'. I cannot!"

All the anger felt earlier that evening returned said in a calm low tone, "Simone', I am leaving for the farm. I cannot sleep anyway."

Simone' knew this shade and the tenor of his voice when he was angry with any issue concerning his family replied, "Roberto', please believe me I do love you. I always will." Not commenting, Roberto' walked in the bathroom showered and put on his shorts and tee shirt, went to the closet took pants and a shirt off the rack dressed to leave.

Simone' sitting in the bed studied her husband thought, "What must he think of me? I hate deceiving him or Carmeli'ta'. I will take care of the business, make the deposits, and check the Airport for a flight to London and then on to Italy. I hope I can get a flight today. I will go back to Tuscany to my parent's home. I need to talk with Carmeli'ta' before I go and call Mr. Meriwether, our Minister, especially to thank him for his help and advice."

Thursday, November 14, 1927, it was time for Simone' to turn the next page of her life. She had stayed on the one path and one page for much too long. Sometimes turning the page in life is difficult. That unfamiliar, the new is frightening...like unchartered territory. Truth is hard to face especially truth of self. This truth of self was hard for Simone' to face. Her life had come full circle; her finger on the page ready to turn it; however, in order for her continue, she had to have the nerve to flip the page, which she, at that time, did not have that nerve. Leaving and going back to her home would be a start to hopefully to gain the nerve to move her finger and turn it to see what is written on the next page of her life ...turning that page would mean revealing the truth to Roberto'?

Roberto' ready to leave said, "Simone', I will leave the week's deposits in the usual place. I will not need breakfast. I will get some later. I will talk with you later. Simone' this is not the end of this discussion; I want an answer to my questions to know this mystery when I return today. You must realize by now Simone', there is not anything you cannot share with me. I am completely open with you. I keep no secret from you, past or present."

"I will make the deposits and take care of the account collections. I love you Roberto', have a good day."

"Thank you Simone'. I love you. When I return from work at 5:00 p.m. today, I want the truth of the secrets you are keeping and why you are not truthful with your words or your body. Have a good day. Please be careful remember traffic is heavy on Thursdays as it is on Fridays."

"Yes, I will be careful Roberto'. Thank you for caring."

Roberto'left the bedroom walked downstairs into the office and opened the safe, prepared the weekly deposits for the business and personal accounts and left both in the usual place for Simone'. She waited to hear his car start and pull out of the driveway. She slipped on her dressing gown and went downstairs to the office and flipped through their business address book for the phone number to the Charleston International Airport. She would call the Charleston International Airport first. If she could not get a flight later that day, Friday, she would call the Airport in the nearest town of Holton, South Carolina. Flying, not the safest way to travel in 1924 but she felt, now, there was no a choice.

Phone ringing at the Charleston International Airport, agent answered saying, "Charleston International Airport, Pan American Airline may I help you?"

"Yes, do you have a flight today to Tuscany or London?"

"I will check for you, please hold on." Agent checked the availability of seats; there were two left; the flight was leaving that day. "Hello Miss, there is a flight leaving today bound for London, England at 3:00 p.m. There is a connecting flight to Tuscany, at 7:00 a.m. on Friday morning.

There are two seats left."

"I want to book passage on this flight today please."

"May I have your name please? I will put you on our passenger list and assign your seat."

"My name is Simone' Angelu'cia Bandaci. How much is the ticket please?"

"The ticket is $100.00, Ms. Bandaci." Hello Miss, I believe I know your daughter, is her name Carmeli'ta'?"

"Yes, I have a daughter named Carmeli'ta'. How do you know her?"

"We went to Charleston School of Business together. She was a very good student the head of our class."

"Thank you for the compliments of my daughter. We are proud of her

accomplishments. Your name, I will tell Carmeli'ta' the next time I speak with her."

"I am Charlotte Overby. Ms. Bandaci, I have your reservation for you. Please check at the tick desk when you arrive, everything will be ready for you."

"Thank you Charlotte, you are kind and have been helpful."

Reservation made. One hundred dollars for an airline ticket was expensive but she did not have a choice. She had to get away from the pain and hurt she had caused her family. It was only getting worse. Roberto' was too close to the truth.

Simone' went back upstairs and pulled her luggage out of the closet. She would only take two pieces and her cosmetic bag. She could buy anything else she needed in Tuscany. Simone' suddenly became home sick or far sick to travel away, far away. The situation escalating out of control, promised to have an astounding effect on her family's life and they were not aware of it yet, not fully aware.

Simone' packed both winter and spring clothes. The weather will be cold in Tuscany in a few days, but spring will be arriving in a few months. She packed all of her Lingerie' and Negligees' opened the secret compartment retrieved her Dairy laid it on the bed with her shoes and other accessories she was taking. Focusing on packing and what to take, she did not notice how quickly the time passed; it was getting late in the morning already 9:00 a.m. She still had to collect their weekly accounts and make the deposits.

Simone' had to create a reason for Marianna to leave the house, but what? Pondering where she could send Marianna without creating suspicion, while she completed the packing of her suitcases. Rushing trying to remember everything she needed did not realize the Dairy had fallen on the floor. Her moving around, without notice, kicked it under the edge of the bed next to Roberto's bedroom shoes and it did not get packed! Simone' dressed went downstairs to send Marianna on an errand.

"Good morning Marianna."

"Good morning Miss. Mr. Bandaci and you did not eat breakfast today. He left early Miss?"

"Yes, he left early, will you take him something?"

"Yes, I will. Before I leave, can I get you coffee and breakfast Miss?"

"No, I will have just coffee, and I will get it. Mr. Bandaci had lots to do today and so do I. If you could take Mr. Bandaci some lunch, that would help me a lot. Take a Roast Beef sandwich with mustard, fruit, and tea. He loves all of those. Oh, Marianna, slice the bread thin; cut the sandwich in half, he does not like thick sliced bread or a sandwich that is not cut in half."

"Yes, Miss, I do remember to slice bread thin and cut the sandwich in half. I am happy to help. It will take a while getting to the farm and back. I probably won't be back until almost 2:00 p.m. not in time to clean the house and prepare an early dinner, Miss."

"That is okay Marianna. We will work it out or Mr. Bandaci and I may eat at Rochelle's tonight, just do your daily cleaning, don't worry yourself with dinner today."

"Yes, Miss." Marianna prepared the lunch tray took it and the tea to her car returned to the kitchen said, "I am off Miss. I hope you have a good day running errands." It would take Marianna an hour and a half to get to the Bandaci Farm and an hour and a half to get back. She was a slow and careful driver.

"Thank you Marianna. I do not tell you often enough how much we appreciate you. We consider you a member of this family. I appreciate you taking care of Mr. Bandaci, Carmeli'ta', and me all of these years. Never forget how much I appreciate you."

"Thank you, Miss that means a lot to me. Bye Miss."

"Goodbye Marianna", said Simone'. Marianna looked at Simone' when she said goodbye something she has never said before...it sounded strange but Marianna dismissed it.

Simone' watched until Marianna's car drove away. She ran upstairs retrieved her luggage and cosmetic case put them in her car, went back into the house into their bedroom straighten it up did not notice the Diary at the edge of the bedspread, left everything neat, went to the sitting room to her desk pulled stationery from the draw sit and wrote Roberto' a note. She left a love letter and poem for him; one of her favorites to express what was in her heart.

Simone' knew that it was not so much the fact that Vincenzo' and her were close friends when they were young. Even the last time they were together three days before she and Roberto' were married, which now looking back was bad enough. The egregiousness was the fact that she kept this a secret from Roberto' of Vincenzo' Moretti's and her relationship before they were married. Nor did she tell him that Vincenzo' thought that Carmeli'ta' was his child and came to America for the sole purpose of seeing Carmeli'ta' and her. Now, doubt about her daughter's Father kept creeping into her mind. She hid these actions out of fear of Roberto' finding out in addition to the hurt and pain she knew it would cause as well as the threat of exposure put forth to her by Vincenzo'. She knew her husband's anger level, but she did not know what he would have done to Vincenzo' if he knew. All of these thoughts kept her bound in an imprisonment of fear.

Simone' left the note in a sealed envelope on the desk in sight where Roberto' would see it picked up her purse, keys, and beige and black hat, with a light jacket to match, went downstairs looked in each room of this house she loved because Roberto' purchased it especially for her. With her emotions running high, picked up the moneybag and left to collect the remainder of the week's accounts and make the deposits in the bank from last week's account collections.

Simone' collected all the accounts briefly chatted with their customer, went to First National Bank of Charleston, and made the deposits in both personal and business accounts. By this time, it was 1:00 p.m. She had to return home and leave the banking information and money she collected; it would be 1:30 p.m. or after; her flight was at 3:00 p.m. It would take thirty minutes to get to the Airport across town. Simone' returned to their home put the deposits receipts in the in-tray and the money collected in the special place for Roberto' to put it in the safe.

Tears forming in her eyes left their home for the last time; getting to the car remembered she had not called Carmeli'ta', unlocked the office door, went to the desk, and dialed Carmeli'ta' office. The Phone ringed at Carmeli'ta's desk but no answer. She tried Ms. Horne. The phone rang three times at her desk, "Good afternoon, Madison Steel, President's office."

"Ms. Horne, this is Simone' Bandaci, how are you?"

"I am well Ms. Bandaci thank you. How can I help you today?"

"Is Carmeli'ta' there? I rang her desk she did not answer."

"Yes, she and Mr. Madison are in his office' they are just returning from lunch."

"May I speak with her if she is not busy?"

"I will ring in to see; would you hold?"

"Yes, I will hold." Simone' looking at her watch it was 1:40 p.m. she had to hurry. Ms. Horne rang Jason Madison desk phone, Carmeli'ta' answered, "Yes Ms. Horne."

"Ms. Bandaci your Mother wants to speak with you, shall I put her through?"

"No, Ms. Horne, I will take the call in my office." She and Jason was enjoying a few private moments together. Carmeli'ta' excused herself, left Jason's office, and went swiftly to her desk. Carmeli'ta' buzzed Ms. Horne that she was ready for the call transfer. "Hello Mother, it is good to hear from you. Is everything okay? How is Father?"

"Yes my darling daughter everything is okay. Your Father is fine."

"Is Father still upset Mother?"

"Yes, my daughter he is still upset, but do not worry he will be calm soon."

Carmeli'ta' waiting for her Mother to tell her the reason she called her since she never calls her while she was at work. "Carmeli'ta', I just wanted to check to see how you are after last evening. How is Jason, did you tell him?"

"Jason is wonderful and loving. No Mother, I did not tell him yet, it is

too early in the relationship don't you think?"

"You will need to determine that my daughter. I can say don't keep it from him too long it will not help the situation down the road."

"I will Mother. I will call and talk with you about it soon to get your advice on how to approach the discussion", Carmeli'ta' commented.

"Okay my daughter. I love you, Carmeli'ta'; always remember that, no matter where we are."

"I will Mother, thank you. I love you and Father too. Please tell him."

"I want you to tell him you love him. Good-bye my sweet daughter; take care of yourself. I love you."

Simone' hung up the phone and rushed to the car. It was now 1:45 p.m. she had to hurry, or she would miss her flight and have to face Roberto's questions tonight. She knew she would not be able to hold back the truth any longer with his insistence. On Simone's ride through the streets of Charleston on her way to the Airport, she enjoyed, maybe for the last time, the beauty of this quaint little town she had grown to love so much.

In the meantime, Marianna arrived at the Bandaci's farm with Roberto's lunch. Roberto' saw Marianna pull up ... his heart jumped in his throat. He thought maybe Carmeli'ta' or Simone' was hurt or sick, flung opened his office door said before he saw the food in her hand, "Marianna is Ms. Bandaci okay?"

"Yes sir. Miss asked me to bring you lunch since you did not eat breakfast. She had me make your favorite: a Roast Beef Sandwich with Mustard, a bowl of mixed fruit with Iced Tea to drink."

Roberto' calming down said, "Thank you Marianna that was kind of you to drive this long way to bring me lunch. My wife is sweet to think of me."

"Yes, Mr. Bandaci, Miss is the finest person I know and she loves Ms. Carmeli'ta' and you. She only thinks of pleasing you."

"Thank you for that compliment Marianna, she is a good wife and Mother. Thank you again for lunch. I will see you at dinner."

"I will not prepare dinner today Mr. Bandaci. Miss said you and she would probably go out since it will be late for me to do my daily house cleaning and prepare dinner when I return."

"That is fine Marianna take care of the house, you know how particular Ms. Bandaci is about the house."

"Thank you Mr. Bandaci you are kind. Bye, see you later."

Robert watched as Marianna drove off went in ate his lunch, prepared to meet with Peter his Foreman about the week's business and the next week's priorities.

CHAPTER
EIGHTEEN

Simone' was nearing the Airport it was 2:15 p.m. She had to park her car, pick up her ticket, and checked her luggage, pulled up to the front of the Airport and gave a Porter her luggage, parked the car, locked the door, and laid the keys under the floor mat. Roberto' would pick it up later she was sure.

Simone' walked back to the Airport terminal to the Porter holding her luggage; he followed her to the ticket counter. She took $120.00 from her purse and paid $100.00 for the ticket, checked the luggage, asked the attendant for change for the $20.00 gave the Porter $2.00, took the ticket, her cosmetic case, and walked to the gate to board the plane.

Pan American flight 2370 was boarding when she arrived at the gate. With regret and relief both looming above her head at once, she glanced back at the Airport terminal across from the entry gate, walked down the steps to the plane, boarded and sit near a window. She felt movement, the plane pushed back and taxied to the Tar Mat for takeoff, she knew her life in Charleston was not over, but "flight" would give her momentary relief. Sometimes it is better to run than to stand and fight. This was a good time to take the run option. The plane now airborne she would be in Italy by 3:00 p.m. on Friday with her parents. She would not have a choice except to tell them the truth, as hard as that was to face, it would be better than facing Roberto'. She could not bear the look of devastation that the truth would bring to his face, not now, eventually, just not now.

Settled into her seat, opened her cosmetic case intending to add to her Diary, did not see it there looked frantically for it in her case under her cosmetics, in her purse, in the jacket pockets; it was nowhere! She replayed her packing in her mind. She saw herself taking the Diary from the secret compartment laying it on the bed among the accessories, putting her accessories in her suitcase accessories compartment, but not her Diary. Her cosmetic case was on the bed next to the Diary intending to put it there for easy access. She could not see herself putting the Diary in the case just her cosmetics.

Simone' remembered she felt something hit her foot, or her foot hit something near the edge of the spread on the bed. At that time, she thought it was maybe one of Roberto's bedroom slippers left under the edge of their bed at night while he sit each night waiting for her to finish preparing for bed. She realized what she hit with her foot was not his slipper, but her Diary. It must be under the foot of the bed hidden by the spread. More fear gripped Simone' the plane climbed to the twenty-five thousand feet altitude. The pilot announced that they would arrive in London at 4:00 a.m. Friday morning, November 15, 1927, Simone's connecting flight would leave at 10:00 a.m. Friday the final leg of her journey to Tuscany and home.

They were out over the Atlantic flying near the coastline. There was nothing she could do except pray that Roberto' would not discover her Diary. Even with the Diary locked and key in her handbag found little comfort in this fact; at this point, neither she nor her secret was safe.

However, knowing her husband, he would not break the lock and read her private Diary... she hoped? Simone' found comfort in the fact that her husband's integrity was above approach, regretted her level of integrity did not reach his, or was even in the same paradigm, but in this instance only. Simone' rationalized her situation, it was hours later, and dinner was being served. She could not eat, but a few bites. She had several glasses of wine served with the Roast Beef w/Au jus, Potatoes and Green Beans. The Red Wine was perfect it helped her relax she drifted off to sleep, praying to God for forgiveness hoping that Roberto' would not find her Diary and read it. She knew Marianna would not find her Diary, the fall deep cleaning was finished and the spring-cleaning would not take place until late April.

In the meantime, back in Charleston, Marianna returned home at 2:00 p.m. busied herself with the daily house chores since she was not preparing dinner for the family tonight. Ms. Bandaci had planned for them to eat at Rochelle's tonight. Marianna singing happily, while she dusted the downstairs then went upstairs and started dusting Simone' and Roberto's suite when the clock sitting in the corner of their sitting room chimed 3:00 p.m., thought, "Ms. Bandaci is usually back by 3:00 p.m., but not today she probably would not arrive until 4:30 today since she got a late start." When she got to the desk to dust noticed a sealed envelope with "Roberto" written on it she knew as Ms. Bandaci said earlier was probably asking Mr. Bandaci to meet her at Rochelle's as they did sometimes when their days ran long. Rather her have Mr. Bandaci to drive back across town, she would meet him at Rochelle's their favorite restaurant.

Marianna left the note as it was on the desk, vacuumed the Persian Rug on the wood floor in the middle of the room and the matching throw rugs on each side of the bed in the bedroom then and bathroom and their dressing room, but did not look in the luggage closet there. She walked past the foot of the bed and the Diary. She did notice Mr. Bandaci slippers just under the edge of the foot of the bed as usual. Everything was in order now. Mrs. Bandaci would be pleased. She ran a tight ship when it came to cleanliness, neatness, and her family's food.

Marianna decided since Mr. and Mrs. Bandaci would not be home for dinner she would go visit her cousin Justin, for the evening in Sedalia, the next town. He owned the popular restaurant, Justin's, known for its Southern Cuisine. Thursday nights were not her night off, but since she did not have to prepare dinner she would change days off as she did sometimes. She would work Friday night and then take Saturday to relax. Marianna dressed and left for the evening it was late sometimes even midnight before she returned.

Roberto' left the farm a little later that evening and headed for home. On the drive, he thought about the conversation he had with Simone' and the fact that he left that morning without hugging and kissing his wife as he has every day since their marriage disturbed him. Even with the secrets, he felt she was holding, he loved and needed her desperately. Expectantly tonight would bring a change; the secret wall around his wife would begin to come down. He could not "cha-cha" or cover this battleground each evening with her it was too hard. Roberto' arrived at home at 7:00 p.m. a little later than usual, but not that late.

Pulling into the driveway, noticed that Simone's care was not in its traditional place. That was a little strange to Roberto'. She could have gone to Rochelle's, but they did not agree to meet there tonight as they did sometimes and Marianna did not say she wanted him to meet there. She said Simone' told her they would work dinner out tonight or she may have run a quick errand. Marianna's car was not in front of her private entrance. It was Thursday, she should be there; but she may have run an errand or taken the evening off as she did sometimes on Thursdays.

Roberto' entered the office checked the in tray for the paperwork from the weekly account collections, the deposit slips for the business and personal accounts, both were there; he checked the special place for the money, it was there. Simone' had taken care of the business. He filed the receipts and put the money in the wall safe.

In his mind, Roberto' reasoned she was fine and would be coming home shortly went upstairs took his shower dressed for the evening of dinner and dancing with his wife at Rochelle's. He began to get hungry; it was a long day; the sandwich and fruit had disappeared long hours ago. Roberto', walked into the sitting room in their suite, over to the fireplace, and lite the well-laid wood. The temperature was dropping; the November wind was announcing the arrival of winter, in the way the wind was hugging Charleston. Roberto' stood in front of the warm fire thinking of his wife and his life from 1905 until now, and this year 1927 was nearing an end; the years had passed fast and 1928 was upon them in less than two months. His daughter was twenty-three now and his wife was forty she was still so young. Robert was forty-three.

Roberto' walked over to the desk picked up Simone's photo and looked at it then saw the envelope with his name on it picked it up, opened the sealed flap, and took out the note. He could not believe what his eyes were reading:

My Darling Husband,

"I cannot bear to hurt you any longer. I love you too much for that. I cannot answer your questions; it would hurt you even more. Never forget I love you with my entire being. You are the only man in the world I want. I wanted you to know how you have made me feel over the years Roberto', and the love that I have for you."

Simone' loved the love story in the Bible, had left Roberto' from the Song of Songs Chapter 5:10–16:

> *My lover is radiant and ruddy,*
> *outstanding among ten thousand*
> *His head is purest gold;*
> *his hair is wavy*
> *and black as a raven,*
> *His eyes are like doves*
> *by the water streams,*
> *washed in milk,*
> *mounted like jewels.*
> *His cheeks are like beds of spice*
> *yielding perfume.*
> *His lips are like lilies*
> *dripping with myrrh.*
> *His arms are rods of gold*
> *set with chrysotile.*
> *His body is like polished ivory*
> *decorated with sapphires.*
> *His legs are pillars of marble*
> *set on bases of pure gold*
> *His appearance is like Lebanon,*
> *choice as its cedars.*
> *His mouth is sweetness itself*
> *he is altogether lovely.*
> *This is my lover, this my friend,*
> *O daughters of Jerusalem.*

"Remember my darling I love you always. Please forgive me.
Goodbye Roberto'; my going will be the best for everyone." Simone'

His wife was not away on an errand, she would not be coming tonight at all; she was gone. Panic hit Roberto' like a ton of bricks with this unexpected occurrence. The room swirled around as Roberto' stood in disbelief his wife was gone; he could hardly wrap his brain around this fact! Why? Where did she go? What could be so bad that she would run away from him? Roberto' felt sick, fell to his knees in uncontrollable tears after the reading the beautiful love letter and at the loss of his beautiful Simone'. After a night of passion more than he had known in their marriage, when he was so close to her deepest needs and desires she run away. How could he go on without his wife, even if there was a secret between them, he needed her! Roberto' played the last night over in his mind. Why did he not see this coming?

Roberto' pondered the dilemma facing him, remembered something she said on the way to see Carmeli'ta' last evening (Wednesday), "No matter what happens or where we are remember I will always love you." He knew she was telling him then; she was leaving he did not listen or hear nor did he think about what she was saying. "What great fear would cause her to leave him not just him but also their home? Where did she go? Why was she running away? Not from him, it had to be the secrets she had been holding so close all these years. What could it be?" Robert' tortured himself with questions and he felt over the years his Simone' did not love him. "And with all this she left me such a beautiful description of a woman's love for her husband from the Song of Solomon we both love so well."

At this point, he did not know what was and what was not true. Simone' had been a faithful, helpful, supportive, and loving wife. "She is a good Mother; our daughter adores her and she loves Carmeli'ta' with all her heart. We have a good life here in the United States. The land has been productive and rich. God has blessed us well, why would she leave?"

Roberto' called Marianna then remembered that she apparently was out for the evening. He picked up the phone to call Carmeli'ta', but he did not want to upset her before he knew where Simone' went. The phone in Carmeli'ta's Townhouse rang three times before she picked it up.

"Hello."

"Hello, my precious daughter, how are you?"

"Hello Father, how are you today? I wanted to tell you that I love you. I told Mother to tell you today when she called me, but she thought that you would like to hear it from me. How is Mother tonight Father, it was strange that she called me at work today, is she okay?"

"I love you as well, my daughter. You are precious to your Mother and me. We both love you with all our hearts. Why do you say it was strange your Mother called you today do you not talk with her every day?"

"It was strange that she called me at work. She had never done that before. She said that she called to see how I was and check to see how Jason and I were doing. She said Goodbye Father that was strange. She always say when we talk, I will talk to you soon my lovely daughter."

"I am sure that everything is okay Carmeli'ta'. Are you going out

tonight, with Jason?"

"No Father we are having a quiet evening here at my Townhouse. Tell Mother I will call her later." Quiet on the other end of the phone Carmeli'ta' said, "Father, are you still there? Are you okay?"

"Yes, I am still here and listening to you. I am okay. I will talk with you soon my daughter." Roberto hung up he did not have the energy to deal with Carmeli'ta' about Jason right then he needed to find out where his wife went. Roberto' called Mr. Meriwether their Minister.

The phone rang and the Minister answered.

"Mr. Meriwether, this is Roberto'. I hope I did not disturb you."

"No, we are just finishing dinner and I was about to retire to my office to study for Sunday Morning Bible Class and Sermon. Did you want to see me?"

"Have you heard from Simone' today?"

Mr. Meriwether getting concerned saw this coming, but did not say it to Roberto' when he spoke with him on Wednesday afternoon.

"I have not spoken with Simone' today. Is there a problem? Is she there?"

"No, my wife is gone. She left a note saying that it would be better for everyone concerned if she left. I do not understand what it meant. I did not want to tell Carmeli'ta' yet, so I thought I would call and ask if she had talked you before she left and you may have a clue where she might have gone."

"Roberto' remembers our conversation Wednesday afternoon when you were here; I told you that this could be a very fragile situation, which makes Simone' fragile. I was afraid that this would happen when we spoke yesterday."

"I do not understand why she left, I know that we spoke about her keeping secrets or at least I accused her of keeping secrets last night, we had a disagreement and I left for work early around 1:00 a.m. this morning. She sent me lunch by Marianna which was strange now that I think about it."

"All these were probably signs; she is apparently frightened of something. I am disturbed that she would run away from her home and family. She must have thought it necessary knowing Simone' as I do for almost twenty years."

"Has Simone' talked with you before?"

Mr. Meriwether hesitated there was a silence, for what seemed like,

an eternity to Roberto'.

Roberto' insisting, "Mr. Meriwether, please if you know something please tell me. I love my wife. I did not want her to leave our home. If she told you something that would give you a clue to where she is, I want to know."

"I cannot say where she is Roberto' neither can I tell you anything about

this situation. I can discuss only what you told me."

"Thank you I will call you when I hear something."

Simone' had forgotten to call Mr. Meriwether in her rush to get to the Airport and catch her flight.

Roberto' hung up the phone and sat for a while thinking, where could his wife have gone? "There is no one in the United States that she knew other than my cousin Amelio', and their church family. What actions should I take? Calling her Father would not be wise at this point; it would only upset him."

CHAPTER

NINETEEN

Roberto' knowing his wife and her closeness to her parents knew that she would probably go to back to Tuscany. He would check the Airports in the two closes cites to see if there was any flights out after 1:00 p.m. today; he knew from the deposits slips and other paperwork she was still in Charleston at 1:00 p.m. Therefore, the Airport had to be close to them, which of course was the Charleston International Airport thirty minutes across town. Roberto' had forgotten that he had not eaten dinner. His appetite like his Simone' was gone.

Roberto' called the Charleston International Airport first. The agent answered, "I would like to get some information about a flight today and the time of departure."

"Yes sir, I can help you."

"What time did the afternoon flight leave for London today?"

"The Pan Am Flight 2370 left for London at 3:00 pm."

"I want to check to see if my wife Simone' Angelu'cia Bandaci was on that flight and not missed it."

"I will check sir. Hello sir, we have a Simone' A. Bandaci on that flight; is she the same person?"

"Yes, thank you; what time will it arrive in London?"

"It will arrive in London Friday morning, November 15, at 4:00 a.m."

"Thank you for the information, I appreciate knowing she did not miss the flight and is safe."

"You are welcome…" He hang up and went downstairs to the office.

Roberto' walked in the office opened the desk drawer retrieved the extra set of keys to Simone's car and drove to the Airport. On the drive to the Charleston International Airport, anxiety gripped his mind as he was thinking and praying that his wife would make it to Tuscany safe, flying was dangerous and uncertain out over the Atlantic Ocean, 3,000 miles was a long way then another 350 miles to Tuscany. He would call her Father and Mother, later, to let them know she is on her way home.

On the other hand, what could he tell them? He would decide what to say when the time came. Finally, arriving at the Airport he drove through the parking lot, there in front of him was his Simone's car. He pulled in a few carrels down took the keys and walked to the car unlocked the door. Chanel 5's scent floated out when he opened the door.

Her keys were probably under the mat if she did not take them with her. He lifted the mat there on the floor was her ring of keys for the cars, house, farm, and desk. Keys to everything they owned. Roberto' sit in the driver's seat for the longest time thinking of Simone', Carmeli'ta', her parents, Marianna, his cousin Amelio', what would he say to keep the situation in check? His minister could easily tell the congregation she was visiting her parents, they would have no questions. Roberto' lived moments of eternity repeatedly as he sat in her car engulfed in silence felt it had been too long since she left, time without end.

All the years Roberto' had wrestled with his feeling of need and desire for his wife to share with him; he never mentioned any unhappiness to Amelio'. To him, he, and Simone' were perfectly happy and had worked hard to create a good prosperous life for themselves in the more than eighteen years they had been in America.

Roberto' left the Airport and drove directly to his cousin Amelio's home to talk with him. He would be his dependence for keeping his farm running well while he went after his wife. Arriving at Amelio', Roberto' explained his visit, shock of the entire situation was overwhelming to Amelio' Simone" would leave her family and possibly return to Tuscany so abruptly without explanation. Roberto' did not share any details with Amelio' just that Simone' was gone. It was even more of a shock because Amelio' had seen Simone' earlier that day as she did her Thursday errands. The usual conversational exchange too place between them as the sister and brother they had always been since she married Roberto'. Exasperation loomed in the air, "She never let on to me at any point she was leaving or there was anything wrong" Amelio' commented to Roberto'.

"Is there something you are not telling me why she left cousin?" Amelio' asked.

"I cannot answer that for you right now until I see Simone', my cousin. I want to ask if you will help Peter, my Foreman, run my operation until I return, is why I am here," said Roberto'. You are already set-up at the bank to make my deposits, as I am yours and make transactions in my accounts. Carmeli'ta' can help if you need her too."

"Carmeli'ta' don't know her Mother has left home?" Amelio' asked.

"I haven't quite decided what would be the best way to tell her. She will have to know something. I will think of some way of telling her to avoid upsetting her too much. I have to go after my wife and bring her home. I can say her Mother went to see her parents for a visit and I am following in a few days," said Roberto'.

"That will only suffice for a while, she will not accept that reason very long if I know my sweet sharp little cousin", said Amelio'.

"I know, but by that time, I hope her Mother and I will be on our way home. I can't be away from my business long a maximum of ten days", said Roberto'.

"I understand your point, but take your time. We have been operating each other's farms for years now. I will be okay", said Amelio'.

"You helped me the month I went back home a few years ago. I had not told you Roberto' that, while I was there, I bought back my little cottage and land", Amelio', told Roberto'.

"No, you did not mention it. What are you planning to do with it Amelio'?"

"I have a Caretaker; he is working my farm right now, but does not live in the house. I did repairs and furnished it when I was there. His wife cleans and cares for it for me. You are welcome to use it while you are there if you need to", said Amelio'.

"Thank you, I will love to do that after I see what the situation is with Simone', commented Roberto'.

"You did not say what your plans are for it, Amelio'", said Roberto'.

"I intend to retire in a few years Roberto' and go back home to Tuscany, find me a wife. I am forty-six now and ready to share my life and fortune with someone."

"It will be lonely here without you, Amelio', but I understand. Except for Carmeli'ta' being here, I think of that for Simone' and me sometimes. Life has been good here, but I long for the old ways sometimes", said Roberto'.

Amelio' nodded in an understanding manner.

In the intervening time, out over the Atlantic, Simone' awaken with a start, dreamed Roberto' had read the Diary----she awaken crying. A few minutes later, as she looked around, realized it was a dream. She carefully glanced at the other passengers; they were all sleeping. No one had been disturbed; there was a dead silence in the plane. Simone' anxious and eager to get to her Father, had lost the sleepy feeling afforded her by the four glasses of wine she drank at dinner.

The stewardess passed, Simone' asked, "How much time before we arrive in London?"

"We have five hours to go Ms. Bandaci, are you okay", asked the Stewardess?

"I am fine, just anxious to get home to Tuscany"

"Try to sleep Ms. Bandaci, the time will pass quickly for you", she said.

"Thank you, I will try", commented Simone'.

Simone' closed her eyes but sleep eluded her.

Climbing the hill of youth to adulthood was not a question of age for Simone'. She left childhood at the age of 14 years old when she met Vincenzo' Moretti. It then became a matter of mental, emotional, and physical development. She walked blindly for those three years not knowing that understanding herself, which is an important part of growing into adulthood; not just giving into the physical, which brings with it the baggage of responsibility, trust, integrity, faithfulness, and most important honesty. The "Truth" is better served, warm; it tastes sweeter; and can be digested eaten in small portions at a time. Truth time-tainted served old and cold becomes sour, distasteful, and hard to swallow. In addition, truth served cold becomes hard to swallow even to the person that has held it enshrouded within them for so long. Truth can be an old faithful friend or a cold and calculating enemy. Truth had become an enemy to Simone'. It was a double-edged sword cutting both ways through her family as well as her.

The only recourse, when she reached her "valley of decision" was to prolong the truth's revelation by running from it; never stopping to consider in all this integrity always demands truth and it followed her back to Tuscany. Simone' felt she was hanging on a scalpel suspended in time between life and death.

Simone' left a person of absolute high integrity behind her, Roberto' her husband. However, she had to prepare for the person of integrity she faced in front of her, Franco Giovanni, her Father. Both men she loved so desperately were men of high integrity. They exemplified nothing less in the way they lived their lives. They had no demands of integrity from anyone, but lived in such a way, which said, "Integrity, a positive characteristic, is a must for the people they loved and the people they dealt with, on day-to-day bases, is of the uttermost importance."

Back in Charleston, Roberto' left Amelio's headed for home to prepare to leave no later than Monday, November 18. Pulling into his driveway noticed Marianna's car parked at her private entrance. Roberto' pondered what or how he could tell her without upsetting her, she loved Simone'. Roberto' walked through the office into the kitchen; he saw Marianna preparing the bread dough for the next day's meal.

"Hello, Mr. Bandaci", said Marianna. "Hello Marianna." Where is Miss, did she go upstairs?"

"No Marianna, Ms. Bandaci is not here, she is on her way to Tuscany", said Roberto. Marianna stood in shock and disbelief, said, "Tuscany, sir? I did not know she was going on a trip. Is something wrong, Mr. Bandaci?" "She went to visit her parents, she had thought about it for a while, decided at the last minute", said Roberto'. Continued, "I will be going in a few days Marianna."

More waves of shock and dismay passed over Marianna, she asked, "When will you leave Mr. Bandaci?"

"No later than Monday, Marianna I will be gone about ten days", he said.

"Does Ms. Carmeli'ta' know yet?"

"No Marianna, I will tell her tomorrow."

Roberto' feeling a little shaky and weak remembered he had not eaten said, "Marianna, I have not eaten yet, please fix me some dinner."

"Yes, Mr. Bandaci, I will be glad to." She busied herself preparing food from the dinner they had last evening.

Roberto' called Amelio' and asked him to come and take him to the Airport to pick up Simone's car. Roberto' went back to the table and sat as Marianna put his plate of food in front of him. He ate hurriedly; Amelio' was only ten minutes away. Marianna busied herself in the kitchen she watched Mr. Bandaci's face, saw pain there. She knew Mrs. Bandaci did not leave just to visit; there was something else. She remembered last night when they came from visiting Carmeli'ta' there was tenseness between them.

"Mr. Bandaci, should I pack your suitcases?" asked Marianna.

"No, Marianna, thank you. I will attend to that chore myself."

Amelio' arrived finally. Roberto' waited in his office for the sound of his car went outside got in the car and they left for the Airport. Roberto' returned with Simone's car and parked it in her space right outside the office door. Roberto' entered their home went upstairs to the sitting room in their suite and lit the fireplace. He sat thinking of the conversation Simone' and he had over the last two days. He knew from their last conversation Simone' was telling him she was leaving. He should have not pressured her for answers. Whatever the problem or issues she faced was overwhelming to her and she did not feel she had a choice except to run away. Roberto' sat with his head in his hands feeling he was partly the cause of his wife leaving.

Brother Meriwether had tried to warn him of the delicate situation and how fragile Simone' was inside. Roberto' knew that Brother Meriwether surely knew what the situation is, but he could not or would not share a confidence. It was not his responsibility to tell him anyway. Simone' only had the answers and explanation he needed.

Roberto' showered prepared for bed. Tomorrow will be a hard day. He had to tell Carmeli'ta'. Sunday he had church then packing. He would call the Airport and check the flights for Monday; there was one every day. Roberto' did not sleep in their bed, but on the sofa in front of the fireplace. He could not bring himself to get in the bed without Simone'.

CHAPTER
TWENTY

Simone's plane arrived in London at 4:00 a.m. early Friday morning as expected. Her flight to Tuscany was at 1:00 p.m. later that day. She had an 8-hour layover, took a taxi to the Hotel of London located near the Corydon Airport and checked into a room to rest while she waited for her flight to Tuscany.

While waiting, Simone' rested on the bed wondering what Roberto' would be thinking and doing it was five hours earlier Thursday night 11:00 p.m. in Charleston.

Her mind went back to another time in her life, she knew, as she sealed the envelope with the note to Roberto' folded inside; she was running from her past mistakes and decisions made during an immature period-of-time in her life. At that time did not understand what the ramifications of her actions would result in later in her life and allowed her feelings and innocence in sexual matters to dictate to her heart what she thought was love.

At their home in Charleston, Roberto' lay awake miserable thinking of his Simone' leaving and trying to reason within himself what could be so devastating she would run away from him and their daughter. Roberto' looked at his watch lying on the coffee table; it was 3:00 a.m. He had not slept well. It would be 8:00 a.m. in London now. Simone' would be safe on the ground. He needed to call her parents in a little while to let them know that Simone' was on her way home. It was 8:00 a.m. in Tuscany as well they would be up and had their breakfast by then. Roberto' decided what he would tell them.

The phone rang at the Giovanni's home three times before Franco answered. "Hello, Franco Giovanni here speaking." "Franco this is Roberto'; I hope I did not call to early."

"Not at all Roberto' my son, how are you? How are my lovely daughter and granddaughter?"

"Carmeli'ta' is doing well Franco she is successful at her company and moving up the corporate ladder in authority everyday it seems. She works for a good company. My Simone' is beautiful and sweet as ever. I am fine as well. I called to tell you she is on her way home. She has landed in London and should be there in Tuscany by 3:00 p.m. today."

Surprised by the fact Simone' was coming, "is there a problem Roberto'? Franco asked. Simone' did not call to say that she was coming home!"

"She had planned to come for a while now Franco, she decided at the last-minute last night; I will be following her on Monday" said Roberto'."

Franco was quiet at the other end of the line knowing Roberto' and Simone' both, did not quite believe this was just a holiday said, "It is so strange that she would come and not call Roberto' this is not like my daughter."

Roberto' did not comment but said, "Franco take care of my beauty until I arrive on Tuesday."

"I will Roberto'. I am anxious to see my daughter it has been a few years since I have seen her."

"She is as lovely as ever Franco, even more so, as time goes on. I will see you in a few days. Please let me know when my Simone' arrives safely."

"I will let you know Roberto' thank you for letting me know; you are a good son to me." Roberto' listening finally said, "Thank you Franco, I will talk to you soon."

Franco hung up puzzled and anxious about his daughter and her unexpected visit to Tuscany. She had not been home since she left. They had visited Roberto' and her twice in the last eighteen years. Each time they were there, she seemed perfectly happy and contented. Roberto' had provided an easy and prosperous life for his daughter. She did not want for anything. He would have to wait until she arrived to know what the problem was if any. He went to tell Catarina their daughter would be there in a few hours. She needed to ready her bedroom Suite.

That same evening, Carmeli'ta' and Jason spent a romantic Thursday evening and night at her Townhouse with dinner and soft music. Jason struggled to maintain his composure and poise with Carmeli'ta'. The way she looked, the feel of her soft skin, he held her, the fresh cologne scent of her Chanel 5 was inviting an evening of passion.

"Carmeli'ta', I love you; it is hard to be near you and not want you close to me. I need you Carmeli'ta'. I want to make love to you. The desires that you bring out in me comes over me like waves of fire. I know that our relationship is new my darling, but my love for you is not. How can I go on like this being near you and not wanting you? The desire that I feel for you is like a pressure building. I feel I will explode." Jason pulled Carmeli'ta' to him and kissed her long and passionately.

Carmeli'ta' quietly listened at Jason pouring his heart out to her took him in her arms, "Jason, I love you with all my heart and it is growing stronger each day. The more I am near you the harder it is for me to be near you. I want you my love so much. I want us to make love. Hold me Jason, hold me."

Jason moved closer to Carmeli'ta' as his passion grew to a fever pitch.

Jason kissed her deeper and deeper until his desire was out of control.

Carmeli'ta's tongue was warm and sweet to Jason as his slide over hers. He wanted more of her kisses. The sweet strawberry taste of her kisses lingered on his lips. Jason pulled her closer; he could not bear to let her go. "Carmeli'ta' please let me love you tonight, I need you, love me please." His plea tore at her heart; she wanted to make love to Jason. He held her tight and close to him.

She whispered, "Jason we cannot my darling not yet, it would complicate the relationship even more than it is now. Please my love, we have to be careful that we do not make a mistake. I love you so Jason, it is hard for me not to give my body to you tonight; you have my heart and mind."

Jason aware she was right, agreed, "Yes, my love, you are right. It is painful being near you and needing you." It took Jason a while to get his emotions, desires, and passion under control. He excused himself and went to the bathroom. Feeling all of his strength drained because of the intensity of the passion he felt, leaned on the wall for support, turned to the sink and splashed cold water on his face toweled it dry, returned to Carmeli'ta' pulled her close to him, "I know you are right Carmeli'ta'. I won't apologize for loving and needing you my love it is a natural feeling when you love someone as I do you."

"I love you Jason my darling as you love me. It is not necessary for you to apologize for loving and needing me. My desire is as strong, but we can't, be intimate not yet." Jason held Carmeli'ta' close aching on the inside with love and the need he felt for her.

They knew this was dangerous and their ability to control themselves would not be possible the next time. Jason had awaken a craving in Carmeli'ta' she did not know she had; a yearning only he could satisfy. She felt she would starve in the desert of passion and loneliness needing Jason could not allow their fires of desire to burn out of control.

In the hotel near the London Airport, Simone' awakens at 12:00 noon; it was nearing the time to leave for her two-hour flight to Tuscany. She freshened up, called the desk, and ordered a cab for the five-minute ride to the Airport, picked up her jacket and cosmetic case, went down to the reservation desk, paid for her room, checked out and waited in the lobby for the cab to arrive.

On the ride to the Airport, her thoughts went to Roberto'. She wondered what he must be thinking and feeling. Simone' felt emotional with tears of regret forming in her eyes. She opened the cosmetic case looked in the mirror and checked her eyes. She did not want to appear at her parent's home red-eyed. Simone' needed the time to decide when would be the best to tell her Father why she appeared suddenly without notice or a phone call. Arriving at the Airport, went to the phone desk, the desk monitor, checked her roster for her ticket number and name, handed her the phone and dialed the number to her parent's home. Calls from the Corydon Airport to Tuscany were free to the passengers.

The phone rang three times in the Giovanni's home, Franco answered, "Franco Giovanni here speaking."

"Father, I am here in London, I know that it is a surprise for you. I will arrive in Tuscany at 3:00 p.m. can you pick me up?"

Franco surprised to hear from Simone' even though he knew she was coming, "Simone' my daughter I am happy to hear from you." Excited Franco said, "Yes, I will pick you up. You will tell me why you surprised Mother and me and why you did not let us know you were coming when I see you?"

Simone' silent for a minute said finally, "Yes, Father we will discuss my visit. I will see you soon."

Simone' boarded the plane at 12:30 p.m. The flight 2370 left on time at 1:00 p.m., arriving at 2:50 p.m. a little earlier than she expected. At the Tuscany Airport, Simone' had retrieved her luggage when her Father Franco arrived at 3:15 p.m. The Tuscany Airport was an hour's drive from the Tuscan Valley Farming Community. Franco saw Simone' looking his way, could not wait to hold his beautiful daughter. She had not changed in looks. She was even more beautiful than when he saw her in 1920 the last time they visited them in America.

Simone' saw her Father coming towards her thought, "His looks have not changed with age. He was still 6'4" tall, handsome, slim, and muscular as all farmers were in Tuscany. Only his coal black hair has hints of grey in his side-burns complimenting his olive color skin."

Simone' ran to him with tears of happiness hugged and kissed him and said, "Father I am glad to see you and happy to be back in Tuscany after more than 20 years! How are you, Father? Is Mother okay? Why didn't she come with you?"

Franco smiling at Simone' commented', "Slow down my daughter one question at a time. I am fine, Mother is fine, she stayed home to prepare the meal for you and wait. How are you my daughter? I am surprised to see you!" He did not mentioned that Roberto' had called to alert him that she was coming.

"I wanted to surprise you Father. I decided at the last minute to come. I had thought of it for a while now", she said.

Franco listening thought, at least she and Roberto's stories match, said, "Your visit is a surprise, and I am happy to see you Simone' my lovely daughter. Mother and I have missed you these years."

"Thank you Father, I missed you, Mother, and our little valley."

Franco loaded the luggage in the luggage rack of the car and opened the door for Simone'. They left the Airport for the drive to the valley and home. On the way Franco chatted lightly with Simone' waiting for her to tell him the reason for her visit. She seemed tense and jittery to her father on the ride home. He noticed she was swirling her hair on the left side, something she did when she was a child during serious parent child discussions knew that this was not "just" a visit. Franco felt trouble brewing. His Simone' was as mysterious as always. What was she hiding?

"Father everything has changed so since I left. It is so modern now, even with a small Airport," Simone' commented.

"Yes, there have been many changes since the War here my daughter and more to come", Franco said. Further, "We have plans to extend the Airport and other surrounding areas to bring more business to our little part of the country."

Simone' smiled and asked, "We Father?"

He continued, "Yes daughter we. I am on the Community Improvement Board of Directors to build and modernize Tuscany and surrounding areas. I stay busy with that and supervising the farm. I have a manager for the farm now. It is doing well financially."

Simone' delighted to hear the news said, "That is wonderful Father, I am proud of you."

Franco smiling glanced at Simone' and said, "Thank you daughter."

Franco drove slowly, chatting with his daughter about Carmeli'ta' and her life in America. However, her Father noticed she had not mentioned Roberto' once since they started the trip. Simone' smiled and talked with her Father, but he saw the same mystery and elusiveness behind her long eyelashes. She had not changed in this aspect.

He wandered to himself, "How can someone so small and beautiful be shrouded in so much mystery?" Franco was as mystified now by his daughter as he was when she was a growing child. This worried him even more.

Catarina waited anxiously by the window looking out on the driveway to see their car pull in the drive. Finally, they arrived, Catarina rushed out opened the car door, Simone' jumped out of the car and rushed into her Mother's open arms.

Catarina said, "My baby girl. I could not have asked for a better gift when Father told me that you were in London. It is good to see you my daughter, you look beautiful."

Simone' smiling with happiness to see her Mother said, "Thank you Mother, it is good to see you and be home. I hope that you were not too surprised and it is not a bad time for me to come."

Catarina looked puzzled at this statement exclaimed, "Simone' you are our child, this is your home, you are welcome here anytime, and that is without a phone call." She took her daughter's face in her hands kissed her on both cheeks and hugged her once more. Franco unloaded the luggage they went into the house for lunch, Simone' had gotten a little hungry on the trip to Tuscany.

After eating, Franco excused himself, went to his office, and phoned his son-in-law. Roberto' did not go to the farm that Friday morning but waited in their private suite by the fireplace looking into the flames waiting for Franco to call to let him know Simone' had arrived safe. The fireplace was Simone' and his favorite place in their suite. At 11:00 a.m., the ringing of the phone interrupted his solitude. He rushed to the desk, picked up the phone, anxiously said, "Hello".

Franco voice quiet, "Roberto' my son" this is Franco. Simone' has arrived; she is safe with Mother and me."

Roberto' breathed a sigh of relief and said, "Thank you Franco for calling me. I will speak with Simone' later. I will see you on Tuesday."

Franco said, "You are welcome my son, I look forward to seeing you Tuesday, safe travels. I will pick you up at the Airport."

"No Franco, I will get a car and drive into the valley or hire a taxi. Take care of my wife please is enough" said Roberto'. They hang up Roberto' went back to the comfort of the fireplace and lay on the couch where he had been sleeping sat for a while then went down to lunch before leaving for the farm.

Franco returned to the kitchen to join his wife and daughter did not question her although tempted, decided to allow her to tell him in her own time. "Rest and relaxation is probably what she needs; tomorrow will be time enough" he thought.

Roberto' as he readied himself to turn the next page of his book of life wondered with one question in his mind what would be written. His page was not one surrounded by fear, but wondered what train had wrecked his life?

CHAPTER
TWENTY-ONE

Roberto' resolved to tell Carmeli'ta' on Sunday afternoon, November 17, after church rather than Saturday. She would have two days to question him about her mother and he did not want that. Roberto' tossed about in his mind what he would say as he made his plans for his visit to her to let her know her Mother had gone to Tuscany.

He called the Airport on Friday afternoon from his farm office to check the availability of seats on the flight to London and Tuscany on Monday, November 18. The Pan Am Flight 2370 to London left at 3:00 p.m. Roberto' booked a flight with the last vacant seat on the plane. He would arrive in London at 4:00 a.m. Tuesday morning with a few hours layover. His connecting flight to Tuscany would be earlier that morning at 7:00 a.m. He only had a three-hour or less wait in London, he would arrive in Tuscany at 9:00 a.m. He planned, as mentioned to Franco, to get a car and drive into the valley or take a taxi. Roberto' would be at his in-laws' home by the time Simone' awaken. He could not think of what he would say or what she would say. He just wanted to wait. He had to focus on his conversation with Carmeli'ta' now before he left.

Roberto' got through a miserable and lonely Saturday. Sunday finally arrived at Church. Brother Meriwether avoided speaking to Roberto' about Simone' and the escalating situation. Carmeli'ta' phoned her parent's home as she did each Sunday morning before she met them for service, "Father is Mother awake yet? Is she okay today? I wanted to tell you and her I will be attending Church with Jason today and I hope she and you will not be disappointed."

"Your Mother is okay Carmeli'ta', I will tell her you said hello and you are attending Church at the Lafayette Street Congregation today."

"Thank you, Father", said Carmeli'ta'. "I will call you later after Church."

"Okay my lovely daughter, have a good day. Are you and Jason having lunch afterwards?"

"Yes, Father, we are. I hope you and Mother understand, bye for now."

"We understand, Bye."

Carmeli'ta' hung up the phone and wondered why she had not been able to speak to her mother in the last few days. Her Father answered the phone each time she called. She thought, "Mother must be busy. I will try and reach her later." Her thoughts went back to her and Jason's new love relationship.

Roberto' thankful Carmeli'ta' was occupied at the time with Jason was a blessing. He would go to talk with her later that evening after he could get a logical reason in his mind to tell his daughter why her Mother was not at home.

After Worship Service, Roberto' spoke privately with the Minister. He told Brother Meriwether he would be traveling to Tuscany to see his wife.

He said, "I am glad that you are going after Simone' Roberto' she needs you. Please remember how delicate and fragile of a situation like this can be. Please be gentle with Simone', she loves you."

"Is there something you know about my wife you want to share withme Brother Meriwether?"

"No Roberto', just remember your wife loves you with her entire being."

Roberto' not commenting held out his hand, "Thank you Brother Meriwether. I will see you when I return to America. I will be gone for about ten days."

Brother Meriwether shaking his hand replied, "Thank you for telling me Roberto'. I will let the congregation know Simone' and you are on holiday."

"Thank you for your support Brother Meriwether."

Roberto' left the building and returned home. Marianna, as always, leave before the Bandaci's, arrived home before Roberto' prepared lunch as usual each Sunday as she did for he and Simone'.

Upon arriving home Roberto' had lunch. After lunch called Carmeli'ta'. Her phoned ranged five times before she answered, "Hello".

"Carmeli'ta' it is Father, how are you this time? I hope that I did not get you at a bad time."

Carmeli'ta' smiling at the sound of her Father's voice said, "Not at all

Father, I am just getting in from Worship Service and lunch. How are you? Is everything okay with you and Mother?"

"Everything is okay Carmeli'ta'. I want to come over to see you. Are you planning to be home later this afternoon; if so, what time is good for you my daughter?"

"Three o'clock is a good time for me Father. If you want to come earlier, please do so, I have no plan to go out before evening Worship Service. I will be going to service again tonight with Jason and Father. He thinks it is a good idea for me to attend their service as a guest since I am the host for Madison Steel. Is mother coming with you today?"

He replied calmly, "Not today Carmeli'ta'. I will see you at 3:00 p.m. Bye for now."

"Bye Father, see you soon."

Carmeli'ta' noticed her Father's voice had a worried tone to it not his usual "sure" self. Roberto' went upstairs to pack for the trip. He only took one large suitcase. He pulled ten pairs of slacks from the closet with shirts to match, two pairs of shoes (black and brown) two belts (black and brown), shorts, tee shirts, pajamas, he chose a Black Suite, white shirt and black bow tie for church, his toiletries, and other personal items; his bedroom slippers would be the last thing he pack.

Simone' kept his slacks and shirts matched hanging together. He took his coat and laid it on Simone's dressing bench. It was cold in Italy as it was in South Carolina. Roberto' packed remembered his favorite bedroom shoes under the foot of the bed lifted the bedspread and reached for his slippers to pack them. There on the floor next to his slippers was a medium size book, he thought. After picking it up realized it was a black leather case, and he held what he thought was a book. He noticed the front of the case had a clasp with a lock on it. There on the front was a window in the leather case with "Simone's Diary" on the title line. In almost twenty-four years of marriage, he never knew his wife kept a Diary, another secret! He never saw her in all the years of marriage write in it. Where had she kept it? He knew every crack in his home! He attempted to unbuttoned the case realized after he tried it was locked. Roberto' knew Simone' had left her Diary un-intentionally. It had fallen on the floor and kicked under the bed. He laid the Diary on the bed and sit down by it.

Simone's Diary can tell me what I want to know or at least give me an idea of what she has been so secretive about over the years. He struggled within himself whether to open it. He would have to break the lock. Locks always say "private". What is there? I may not want to know! Nevertheless, if I break the lock at least I will know. After a long while Roberto' put the Diary in his suitcase to take to his wife. He could not violate her privacy. If it were a matter of life or death, he would, but this was not, he did not think; he hoped against hope it was not a life-or-death matter. He rather Simone' tell him and not read it.

Simone' was right about her husband, his integrity was above reproach, though tempted, in the final rinse of a matter his integrity came out unwrinkled; it always shined.

Roberto' looked at his watch it was 2:30 p.m. He prepared to leave to talk with Carmeli'ta' went downstairs to the kitchen, "Marianna, I am on my way to see Carmeli'ta'. I will return in a while."

Marianna responded, "Yes, Mr. Bandaci." She was cautious about what she said to him, he seemed different to Marianna. The tone in his voice was not the joyful one she has known in the eighteen years she had worked for them.

Roberto' drove slowly to his daughter's Townhouse thinking deeply what he would tell her. He decided on the strategy he would use. Carmeli'ta' waited, feeling a nervous anxiety while she waited for his arrival thought, "He did not say Mother would be with him on this visit."

He visited her often without her Mother at the end of his workday on his way home from their farm. Carmeli'ta' knew this would not be just a friendly visit. His voice had that tone in it she heard growing up when trouble was abounding. She paced back and forth in front of her Bay window looking for her Father's car to arrive. She had iced tea with chilled glasses as usual for him.

Carmeli'ta' saw her Father's Roadster approaching at 2:55 p.m. He stopped, parked his car, and climbed the stairs reluctantly, to Carmeli'ta' Townhouse. This would be a difficult conversation with his daughter. He was not accustomed to lying to his family; but he could not tell her all the facts either; presently they were as elusive as his lovely wife's personality.

Roberto' knocked on her door, Carmeli'ta' said, "Father is that you?"

"Yes, my daughter it is me."

Carmeli'ta opened the door and smiled and said, "Hello Father it is good to see you today, how are you?"

"I am fine" he said and kissed his daughter on her forehead.

"I made your favorite tea. Have a seat Father."

Carmeli'ta' poured a chilled glass of tea and handed it to her Father waiting for the lecture about marriage and seeing Jason Madison. Roberto' sipped his tea looking at the blue and red flickering in the fireplace.

"Father why Mother didn't come with you as she usually does? Is she okay?"

Roberto' glanced at Carmeli'ta' and said, "Yes my daughter, she is fine. Actually, Carmeli'ta', your Mother went to visit her parents on Thursday. She has arrived safely in Tuscany."

Carmeli'ta' surprised, "Gone Father? I spoke to Mother Thursday. She called me at work but she did not say anything about going to Tuscany. I don't understand why she would keep it from me my Father?"

"She decided at the last minute, she had thought about visiting them for a while. I will be going tomorrow my daughter to join her for ten days. I asked Cousin Amelio' to manage the farm while I am away and that you could assist him in making deposits and other business accounts if needed", said Roberto'.

"Of course, that will be no problem for me Father. I just don't understand why she did not tell me you and she was thinking of visiting my grandparents!"

"She had not decided when we saw you on Wednesday Carmeli'ta', she decided after we went home Wednesday night. She did not want to tell you over the phone so we decided that I would tell you. She did want to talk with you before she left so she called you at work", explained Roberto'.

Carmeli'ta' felt tenseness in her Father she had not seen before. She somehow knew it was more to her Mother leaving than a visit. Roberto' sat his half empty glass of tea on the tray rose and said, "The tea was delicious as always my daughter; however, I need to finish my preparation for my trip. I will call before I leave. You remember the process for business don't you?"

"Yes, Father. I know the special drawer for the money and I will get the collected accounts from Amelio' if I need to" she said. "I think he will be okay Carmeli'ta', but you are his backup. He has taken care of the business before when Mother and I went on vacation to New Orleans in 1921", Roberto' reminded her.

"Please be careful Father. I love you. Ask Mother to call me please. Please call me also when you arrive safely. It will feel strange with you and Mother out of the country", said Carmeli'ta'.

"Take care my daughter, I will see you in ten days", said Roberto.'

"Mother is not coming back with you Father. You said you will return in ten days". Roberto' reassured her. "Your Mother may want to visit a little longer, if so that will be okay my lovely daughter. It will be her first time going home in many years we will let you know."

Roberto' smiled at Carmeli'ta' hugged her tight and kissed her on the forehead, left for home to finish the last-minute preparation for his trip. Arriving home parked his car entered the kitchen, "I am back Marianna."

"Yes, Mr. Bandaci", she said.

"I will finalize my plans. If you need anything for the house, you can let Amelio' or Carmeli'ta' know. Please feel free to go to the market as usual for any food you need. Take care of yourself and our home while we are away Marianna."

"I will Mr. Bandaci. Tell Miss it will be lonely here without her," she said.

"I will. Thank you for all you do" said Roberto'.

In Simone's office, Roberto' left a list for Amelio' of the business transactions to be taken care of while he was out of the country. He would leave the paperwork in the in-tray of any accounts collected and bank deposits. Carmeli'ta' would meet him and get the money he collected if he did not get a chance to deposit it and put the accounts in the safe.

Upstairs he checked his luggage to make sure he remembered everything saw the Dairy, picked it up, tempted to break the lock and read it, held it for a minute; yet he could not bring himself to violate his wife's privacy no matter the circumstances. It was not a life-or-death situation even though it felt like it. Roberto' put the Diary back in his suitcase closed it. He was ready for his trip.

In the Monday morning, November 18 meeting, he would set the next ten days priorities with Peter, his Foreman. It was necessary that he returned home by 11:00 a.m. for Amelio' to take him to the Airport. Eagerness and anxiety hung over Roberto' like a cloud. He was eager to see Simone' but felt anxiety; he was not sure he wanted to know, but had to know the secrets she held. A rock and a hard place was not a comfortable place to be right now. He felt pulled and pushed at the same time.

Roberto' knew that Franco would not mention to Simone' that he was coming. He did not want her to run-a-way again; he may never find her. Roberto' had not planned to go back to evening Worship Service, it was getting late in the evening, looking at his watch noticed it was 7:00 p.m. knew Marianna had returned from evening worship, and went downstairs for dinner.

Marianna was patiently waiting until he came down for dinner. Roberto'

said as he walked in the kitchen, "I am here Marianna and ready to eat." "Dinner is ready Mr. Bandaci", she said.

After dinner Roberto' called Amelio' and asked if he would take him to the Airport at 1:00 p.m. on Monday. Roberto returned to the kitchen, "Marianna, I am retiring for the night. I will want breakfast at 6:00 a.m. in the morning. I will return by 11:00 tomorrow to leave for my trip to Tuscany", he told her.

"Yes sir, it will be ready for you good night", she said.

Roberto' climbed the stairs to their suite lit the fireplace and prepared for bed.

Earlier that Sunday evening, after dinner, Simone' walked on her Father's farm but not near the city; for fear that, Vincenzo' or someone she knew would see her. Word would get around she was there. News in the valley spread like wildfire in a dry vineyard, quickly. She wanted her presence to be unnoticed. She returned home as the grey sky began to turn black that evening around 9:00 p.m. While she was walking, Franco and Catarina discussed their daughter's visit. Franco said, "There has to be more to Simone' being here than just a visit Mother. She is so mysterious even more so now than she was as a child. I am afraid that trouble is brewing." Franco continued, "When Roberto' called he did not want to speak to her. He said he would speak with her later; he has not called Mother. It worries me."

"Franco, please wait let Simone' tell us. She seems so fragile and unsure of herself. She is not the Simone' that we know. If Roberto' is on his way and she does not know, then it is obvious to me she left without telling him or Carmeli'ta'; so, say nothing unless she does."

"You think she might run away again, if she knows he is coming?"

"I think so Franco, it is Simone' that the issue is with and not Roberto'. I noticed that she has not mentioned him once since she has been here."

Franco looked amazed at the revelation his wife called to his attention, "You are right Mother! I had not thought about that. I do know daughter is troubled. She acts like she did when she was growing up."

"Yes, Roberto', she does", said Catarina.

Franco asked, "Catarina my lovely, do you know something I don't know about daughter?"

"No Franco, just a woman's intuition" she said.

"What does your intuition tell you Mother?"

Catarina answered, "I would rather that I not give you my thoughts, but remember Franco Simone' has the same rages inside that you do. She went off by herself a lot when she was young, that is all I will say on the matter."

Franco felt like a balloon with the air let out. He knew his sexual urges were strong. Catarina looking out of the window saw Simone' coming said, "She is coming up the path Franco we cannot let her know we were discussing her in depth. I will make tea Franco, as always, it is 9:00 p.m. We will have tea and dessert now as I promised her before she left for her walk. Help me Franco. Get the cups for me. Look busy my husband; remember Simone' does not fool easily. I do not want my Simone' to be uncomfortable. I love her no matter what the problem is."

Franco commented, "Of course Mother that goes without saying, we will wait."

Simone' opened the kitchen door, smiled, and said, "I had a wonderful walk Mother and Father. The valley is as beautiful as always. I am glad to be home. I was just thinking of the tea and dessert Mother. Can I help you?"

"No daughter, it is ready. Franco helped me. Seat yourself and relax this is a visit. We do not want you to work." Catarina smiled and put the tea and Strawberry Tarts on the table Simone's favorite dessert.

She looked at her Mother said, "You are beautiful Mother. You never seem to change." Catarina responded, "Thank you daughter, neither do you."

Franco said, "I have the two most beautiful women in the world. How

much richer can one man be?"

Catarina, 5'7" slim petite with olive tone skin at fifty-eight looked twenty years younger than her age. Simone' had inherited her looks, hair, legs, and overall beauty.

They laughed and chatted while they ate their dessert and drank their tea. Simone' talked with her Mother while she washed and rinsed the cups, the dishes, and placed them on the drain board.

Franco went to his office to complete some paperwork.

Simone' said, "Mother I think I will retire for the night. I am a bit tired from the long trip. I will see you in the morning. I will say goodnight to Father on the way to my bedroom. Thank you for preparing my bedroom suite it is just as I left it."

Catarina said, "You are welcome my daughter. Sleep well, good night."

Simone' passing her Father's office stopped at the door said, "Goodnight Father. I am tired; see you in the morning."

"Good night my daughter, sleep well." Simone' continued, "Oh Father, I am glad to be home. I want to thank you for not questioning me about my trip."

Franco did not comment just smiled with a slight wave of his hand thought, "Mother was right, she is as sharp as ever, and seem to have grown sharper with time and maturity. She only looks fragile; she always did, even as a child!"

After preparing for bed Simone' lay sleepless and looked at the clock it near 1:00 a.m. She thought of Roberto' needing him to be near her, hold her, love her, thoughts went to her walk. She needed to decide what she would tell her father why she suddenly appeared in Tuscany.

Life becomes even more mysterious.

CHAPTER
TWENTY-TWO

In Charleston, Roberto' lay on the coach in front of the fireplace thinking of all the events that had taken place in just four days. He felt as if he lived two lifetimes all pressed into a few hours. His life had become an upside-down merry-go-round. He felt a loss of direction, security, and his wife was gone. In addition, he had not been exactly truthful with his daughter and did not know what Tuesday would hold for him when he reached Tuscany.

For Roberto', the earth spun around in intervals more than once while he contemplated the possible loss of his Simone' forever. The love they shared, the bond created through their physical, emotional, and psychological intimacy; all he could think of was drinking of her love. Her touch lit passion in his mind and heart. The look in her eyes, the warm kisses that lingers on his lips was smooth and sweet as wine. The way she moves as she walks across the floor in the privacy of their bedroom in her negligee', like a picture frame, captured the beauty of the cream-colored skin on her body, her hair black as coals flowing down her back and a smile that captures his heart each time in a different way.

The images of Simone' dancing in his memory would not allow him to rest. The passion, love, and desire he felt for her madden him. Pain enveloped his mind as he fell to his knees and prayed for relief and strength to go forward and rid his mind of the terrible pain that held him captive as Simone's love does. He could not get out of his mind no matter how hard he prayed. when they made love she was a different woman, the taste of her kisses and love was like sweet honeycomb on his lips; the feel of her body moving against him smooth as silk; her lips so soft as they kissed his skin; the beauty of her being possessed him as his own soul.

Simone' had left a trail of mystery in their lives. Over the years, the mystery surrounding his wife as time passed grew in complexity. He felt his wife was an unread book with many unanswered questions. No matter how much of her he read, the answers never came.

He said out-loud, "Simone' is my strongest weakness."

His love for Simone' came over and over him like the waves crashing against the rocks from the river that twisted and slumbered its way through their little valley in Tuscany. Roberto's sleep was fleeting and illusive. How could he go on with his Simone'? His love for his wife was like music to him; it bought peace and joy to his mind, though he knew there was a part of his wife he knew nothing about. The Dairy found on floor under the bedspread at the foot of the bed further intensified the mystery of her, locked with no key to open it as his wife deepest passion locked inside of her and he did not have the key to open it.

Earlier in that evening while packing, had struggled with the temptation that invited him to open and read it. He thought, maybe this will tell me the mystery that enshrouds my wife; that part of her I cannot reach. These thoughts gave him the feeling of being behind a closed door. He felt shut out of part of his wife's inner being. He had to know the mystery she hid so well. He picked up the Diary repeatedly before leaving for Tuscany...but honor and integrity kept him from breaking the lock...he still trusted his wife. Opening it would say to him he did not trust her and that would break another trust in his life.

Simone' his one weakness in life; loved her beyond even his comprehension. He loved his daughter Carmeli'ta', but realized they raised her to live in the world. Her life would be separate from his but not Simone'. She was in his heart and mind; a part of him, even with the feeling of that terrible knife cutting deep within his heart, could not remove his need and desire for her. As the farmer grafts the limbs of one fruit tree to another to change the flavor, enhances it, makes it more desirable to the taste, she had become grafted into his heart; the taste of love made life sweeter with Simone' by his side. Together they were complete like the circle of time; apart it felt like part of him was pulling to the point of pain. That string tied from his heart to hers if broken he knew it would destroy a part of him that only she possessed.

The true treasures were hidden inside Simone'. What she allowed him to see and know of her was only a prologue to who the true Simone' is he married. She was to Roberto' like a "Silhouette", he could only see shadows of the true person inhabiting her beautiful body. Who was she?

The last ember flickered the fired died, Roberto' pulled up the covers and drifted into a peaceful sleep. He was one day closer to seeing his Simone'. They had never been apart since they were married almost 24 years ago.

Roberto' awakens at 5:30 a.m. showered, dressed for his trip, and went downstairs for breakfast at 6:00 a.m. Marianna, as usual, had breakfast ready. He left for his farm at 6:45 a.m. Roberto' met with Peter and went over the list of priorities for the ten days he would be out of the country. Roberto' and Peter completed their meeting at 10:00 a.m. He left for the drive home arriving at 10:45 a.m. went upstairs got his luggage and placed it in Simone's office. While waiting for Amelio' to arrive he returned to the kitchen to say bye to Marianna. As he entered, Marianna was drying her eyes.

"Marianna are you okay?" asked Roberto'.

"Yes Sir, I will miss you and Mrs. Bandaci. I hope everything is okay Mr. Bandaci," Marianna said with hope in her voice.

"Yes, everything is okay Marianna. I am leaving now I heard Amelio's car. I will call you when I arrive in Tuscany. Please call Carmeli'ta' or Amelio' if you need something or have questions." He added, "Marianna, Ms. Bandaci, and I feel fortunate that you are part of our family for the last eighteen years. Your loyalty has been and is a blessing to us."

Marianna was surprised and humbled by Roberto's compliment. He had never made this statement to her before, as Ms. Bandaci had many times. She said, "Thank you Mr. Bandaci it pleases me to be here and be considered a member of your family. I love Ms. Bandaci, Ms. Carmeli'ta' and you. Take care of yourself Sir and bring Ms. Bandaci home soon."

He did not comment nodded and smiled with a half wave of his hand, went to the office to the secret draw and retrieved Simone's note and put it in his inner pocket of his jacket. He placed it there so Marianna would not per chance read. He opened the safe took $500.00 from the personal cash box, put it in his billfold, picked up his suitcase, and walked to Amelio's car and placed the suitcase on the back seat.

"Good morning", Roberto' said when he got in the car.

"Hello cousin you got everything set?" asked Amelio'.

"Yes, all set" said Roberto'.

Amelio' noticed the stressful look on Roberto's face out of the corner of his right eye and asked, "Roberto' you want to tell me what all the mystery is about? Maybe I can help you?"

"I can't answer your questions Amelio' I don't have the answer for me yet", commented Roberto.

Amelio' felt the pain in his cousin's voice and knew it was more than a visit to Simone's parents. There was trouble he could feel it. Giving leave way to his cousin said, "I understand Roberto' I will not press you any further."

"Thank you Amelio', I really don't want to talk about it. I appreciate your care and concern for me. You can help me by taking care of my farm and my business", said Roberto.

"Done", commented Amelio'. He continued "Roberto' I called my Caretaker to let him know you might be using the cottage while you are in Tuscany. I instructed his wife to prepare it for you and stock the kitchen with food if you need her to. Here are the Caretaker and his wife's name and his number," he said handing Roberto one of his business cards with the contact information on the back.

Putting the card into his shirt pocket replied, "Thank you, Amelio' I will let him know if I need it. I want to take Simone' there again since it is where we begin out marriage."

Amelio' nodded in his understanding as they reached the Airport. He parked the car, pulled Roberto's suitcase from the back seat; they walked into the Airport. Roberto' paid for his ticket, checked his luggage it was 2:15 p.m. went to the boarding area to wait to board; they had 30 minutes.

Amelio' sat leaning forward with his hands together in a prayerful way. He thought about his cousin, he had not seen this level of perplexity in him since his Father and Mother died twenty-four years ago. Amelio' had taken the place of his parents in his life. He worried about Roberto'. He could feel his pain. He knew how sensitive his cousin was and how desperately he loved his wife. Tears formed in his eyes. He hurt for Roberto'. He wanted to help him and did not know how.

Roberto' sat by his cousin and said, "I have always had your support Amelio' and it has meant the world to me. I hope you know that. Thank you for your care and support all these years."

"I know that Roberto', thank you is not necessary. You and I are all we have left of our immediate family. I will always be here for you as you are for me", said Amelio'. As he finished his statement, the technician calls for the passengers to board. Amelio' and Roberto' stood, he smiled and shook his hand and said, "I will see you in a few weeks cousin take care of yourself. I will call you when I arrive."

"I will wait to hear from you Roberto'. God bless you my cousin", said Amelio'.

Roberto' showed the technician his ticket, walked down the steps to the outside, across the walkway, and up the steps to board the plane turned saw Amelio' standing waiting near the window waved, Amelio' smiled and waved back. The Pan American Flight 2370 left at 3:00 p.m. on time. Roberto' settled in his seat. He was finally on his way to Simone'. It would be a long flight!

Earlier that Monday morning in Tuscany, Simone' had awaken at 9:00

a.m. She slept a long time; she was tired from the long weekend and the last two days without sleep. Emerging after dressing, Simone' walked into the kitchen where her Mother was waiting breakfast. Her Father left early as he always does to check on their farm and the delivers for Monday.

"Good morning Mother."

"Good morning daughter." Catarina walked over to Simone' and hugged her and said, "Are you ready for breakfast?"

"Yes, Mother, but fruit only. My stomach is still a little sensitive and I don't know why maybe from the long flight or the restless weekend. I don't like missing Lord's Day Service but, I feared I would not stay awake. I slept while you and father were at service yesterday."

"I knew you were tired on Saturday and Sunday."

Simone' sat at the table while her Mother filled a bowl with fruit and poured her a cup of coffee. "Thank you Mother, will you join me?"

"I will for coffee Simone'. I ate breakfast with Franco at 7:00 a.m. as usual daughter." Catarina sipped her coffee and watched her daughter as she ate her fruit.

Simone' finished her fruit, picked up her cup sipped her coffee and looked at her Mother, "When will Father return Mother?"

"He will be back at 5:00 p.m. today my daughter as always. He says staying busy and working hard gives him more energy. He does not have to work. We have a Farm Manager. The farm business is doing well. I know that this is not just a friendly visit my daughter. I wanted you to rest over the last three days since you arrived. You want to tell me the real reason you are here?" She asked.

"You are right Mother you could always read me, but never said anything."

"You are right my daughter, I did not, tell me what you are running from."

"My past and myself."

Looking puzzled, Catarina said, "Your past and yourself, Simone' explain!"

"Mother when I was 12 years old, I realized I felt different. At age 13, I knew that I did. I had such rages and feelings that invaded my body and mind that I did not understand. When I was 14 years old, my feelings and desires were almost out of control. I did not know how to tell you then; I was so young. I know what you had taught me about women and growing up, but you never told me I would feel like a storm rages in me. The passion I felt overwhelmed my body. I was trapped Mother! I did not know what to do or how to tell you. I wish now I had. I was embarrassed to tell Father, that was impossible at that time and it still is."

"I wished that you had felt that you could tell me Simone'. I always made sure you knew you could come to me, or thought that I did anyway!" Catarina said in an upset tone.

"Mother you did. I am not saying you did not. I was not mature and did not have the words. Besides all that, there is no way that you could see inside of me or know for sure what I was feeling", Simone' reassured her Mother. Rhetorically Simone asked, "Mother you know the Moretti family?"

Catarina responded surprised by the question, "Yes, Simone' everyone does!"

"Vincenzo' Alessandro Moretti and I met and became friends Mother when I was 14 years of age."

Catarina's heartbeat faster and her head felt hot while Simone' talked revealing her childhood experience of becoming a woman She was right about Simone' going off by herself, "Oh my goodness," she thought and put her hand over her heart. Catarina said, "Continue Simone'."

"Mother, Vincenzo' was always there when I needed someone to go to. He understood the rages in me."

"What are you saying to me Simone?" Catarina asked.

"Vincenzo' and I was lovers' Mother during the three years before I married Roberto'."

Catarina trying to maintain her composure said, "Simone' what were you thinking daughter?"

She said, "I was not thinking Mother, just feeling I did not understand all my feelings. We were only together three times those three years. We talked, took walks, swam in the lake, and enjoyed each other's company."

"What Lake Simone'? Is there a lake on the Moretti property?"

"Yes Mother, it is not visible nor the little cabin sitting there unless one knows exactly where to look. The Vineyard is so massive it is hidden beneath the overhanging vines."

"Go on Simone', it must be more to this, why did you run away from Roberto'? What did he do? Did he ask you to leave? Did you tell him about Vincenzo' Moretti?"

"No Mother, Roberto' is a wonderful man; he treats me with love and care at all times. I told my Diary; it is all there and I left it on the floor under the bed. I realized when I looked for it on the flight over. I know Roberto' has found it by now. It is locked if I know Roberto' he will not read it. His integrity is unquestionable Mother. He is a wonderful husband, good Father, and excellent lover."

Catarina said, "If he is all those things, why is it so hard to tell him? It must have caused problems between you two over the years."

Simone' looked at her Mother feeling the uncomfortable pain she carried with her and said, "Yes, Mother it has. I did not realize it until three days ago. He has been angry because I never let him into my deepest passion and desire."

Catarina dumbfounded at her daughter's frank revelation to her about her intimate life with Roberto', "Simone', this is surprising my daughter in one way and then it is not in another. I suspected and somehow knew there were rages in you like they are in your Father!"

Simone' looked at her Mother, "That is what he always had to be near you Mother! I always loved to see you and daddy together, it reminds me of Roberto' and me. He loves me so Mother, I could not ask for a better husband."

"I know that you not telling Roberto' about you and Vincenzo' Moretti, is not the worst thing, in the world, my question to you Simone' is why Vincenzo'? He was not a farmer and his family would not approve of a relationship with a farmer's daughter!"

As a group, the farmers socially disenfranchised in the Tuscan Valley; the Wine Kings did not want to mix classes.

"They never knew Mother, no one did we made sure of that."

"Simone', my daughter, what must you been thinking, I ask this once again?" stated her Mother.

"I could not understand myself and over the years Vincenzo' and I grew close. I thought at one time I loved him, Mother; it was hard to give him up when Father told me he arranged for me to marry Roberto'. I was not in love with Roberto'. I respected him, I cared for him, we had fun together, he was charming and such a Gentleman. I saw Vincenzo' during the time before I married Roberto' Mother, I did not want to give him up then."

Catarina listened patiently to her daughter. She did not want to show any disapproval lest she become silent or run away again. "Go on Simone', I am listening tell me all of it daughter don't hold this in you any longer."

"Three days before I married Roberto', I saw Vincenzo' Mother and we, Simone' paused, Mother, she finally said, "We made love for the third time in three years."

Catarina closed her eyes for a moment then asked, "And daughter what else?"

"Roberto' thought I was a virgin on our wedding night I did not let him know that I was not a virgin. I felt so shy that night and afraid is why he thought I was innocence. I was really, I did not know that much about intimacy. Vincenzo' was sweet to me and tried to teach me, but he was not that experienced either."

"Simone' what else my daughter? I want you to tell me all before Franco arrives."

"When I knew I was pregnant at the end of November or beginning of December, I saw Vincenzo'. I told him Roberto' and I was having a child. He assumed it was his. I tried telling him it was not, but he never believed me. He came to the hospital to see Carmeli'ta' when she was born. I begged him to stay away. He refused. I was happy and sad when Roberto' said were moving to America. I thought that would end it but distance did not matter."

Catarina feeling afraid to hear more said, "Simone' did Vincenzo' Moretti follow you to America?"

Simone' quietly said, "Yes Mother. He came almost every year to see Carmeli'ta' and me even during the War and then at her graduation. I never told Roberto' Mother. I was trying to protect my family and I have made it worse. Roberto' is so angry because I have not allowed him to feel all of my levels of passion and let him in to my deepest desires. It has gotten to the point he cannot accept the mystery, secrets, and denials anymore. I will not go into details any further Mother; I think you understand."

"I do", said Catarina.

"When I told Vincenzo' the last time he came I would not see him again nor would he see Roberto' and my daughter, he threatened me Mother."

Catarina angry said, "What do you mean threatened you with harm to your person Simone'?"

"No Mother, he said he would see Carmeli'ta' and I would not keep him for his daughter no matter what he had to do. I was frightened Mother that he would tell Roberto' Carmeli'ta' was his. He could have caused a scandal in Charleston; it would have destroyed Roberto's and my business and Carmeli'ta' career. She is so happy now. In addition, I was afraid of losing Roberto' and my family Mother, what can I do? I will have to face Roberto' eventually, I know. I feel like running further away."

Catarina bewildered said, "No Simone' that is not what you need to do, running is never an answer my daughter. It is more than a difficult situation, I know, but staying and facing the problem is the only answer daughter." Overcome with the thought of Vincenzo' and his threatening her daughter, Catarina did not process the fact at that moment that Vincenzo' thinks Carmeli'ta' is his daughter; her concern was his boldness to follow her to America.

Simone' felt sick with the idea of facing her Father and her husband asked. "Mother what was I to do? When you make decisions to try and protect your family it backfires on you."

Her Mother said, "Simone', truth is always the best avenue to take. I understand your reasons for doing what you did."

Breathing a sigh of relief Simone' asked, "Mother you are not angry or disappointed in me?"

"I am concerned about you daughter and wish your decision had been different. I love you daughter, I do understand. I can't say I would not have done any different."

"Mother what will I tell Father or how can I tell him what I just told

you?" Catarina shaking her head, "I don't know Simone'. Franco will be heartbroken my daughter."

Catarina and Simone' had talked all day. The day had passed quickly almost unnoticed. It was nearing 4:00 p.m. Catarina looked at the clock on the wall; it was near dinnertime. She went to the stove checked the Chicken and Vegetable Casserole she made for dinner, placed the bread on the cookie sheet for warming, and finished making the salad.

Catarina turned to Simone' and said, "I will talk with Franco first my daughter. He will be hurt and angry when he knows the truth of your being here. You can talk with him later after dinner. He will have time to digest it by then."

"Thank you Mother, it will be hard to face Father."

"Simone' if you don't ever know anything else about your Father Franco, remember that he loves you unconditionally no matter the circumstances; you are our only child. We will always support you and come to your aid my daughter."

"Yes Mother. I think I will rest before dinner if you do not mind. I suddenly feel very tired."

"Yes, Simone' rest, I will call you at 6:30 p.m. that will give me enough time to speak with Franco about this situation."

Catarina thinking as she said this to her daughter turned to her and said, "Simone', before you go, I want to say, this to you. I have thought about what to tell Franco in the last few minutes. I will tell him that you and Vincenzo' Moretti were friends for three years before you met and married Roberto'. You saw him after you were married, not intimately, but to tell him that you were leaving Tuscany to live in America. He will be angry with Vincenzo' Simone'. He does not care for the cold and calculating personality he has developed in the last eighteen years." She clarified her statement about Vincenzo', "Over the years, Vincenzo' has grown very hard and unfriendly. Now, I understand why his personality has changed so much. He does not have the woman that he wanted in his life nor a child. Vincenzo' is like an animal with a wound that will not heal. He strikes out at the people of the valley as if he is in terrible pain. If I tell your Father all the details you shared with me today, there may be trouble tonight. You are his only child and he will see this as Vincenzo' taking advantage of an inexperienced 14-year-old child that you were at that time. What I tell him before you speak with him will only break the ice for you Simone'." Catarina warned her, "Measure your words with you Father tonight. Tell him only what is necessary."

"Mother, I felt as if I was in a spiral...a spiral of silence. I could not share my feeling with you or daddy. I could share them with Vincenzo'. I was 14 years old Mother and afraid that I was not normal with the rages in me. Vincenzo' seemed to understand. We drew close as I told him about my feelings. I know that he cared for me."

"Apparently, he still do daughter; he more than cares, I know now that he is still in love with you. He is not a happy man even though he is a married. I am at least thankful for one thing; he was there to listen to you then."

"Mother, I could not tell Roberto' when I met him about my feelings or about my relationship with Vincenzo'. As time went on the spiral of silence got worse. I found security within myself by holding my feelings close to me. I wanted to tell Roberto' on many occasions. I was on the verge so many times. It would be on the tip of tongue but I could not get it to come out. I felt if I told him it would compromise our relationship and damage our love."

Simone's confession bought tears to Catarina's eyes. She hugged Simone' tightly and said, "Let it all out my daughter don't keep this terrible pain bottled up in you any longer. I feel that your Father and I are the blame for the pain you have suffered over the years; I wish I could turn back the hands of time, my daughter."

"No Mother, I do not want you to feel that way. I have been grown for more than 23 years but lived in fear. I wanted you to know the absolute truth no matter how it ends for Roberto' and me." Simone' continued, "I knew my judgment day would come for the secrets I held for so long. By running, I thought I could delay the inevitable Mother."

"Daughter running has never been a solution for heartache when you stop the heartache and problem it caused is still there and in your case, you have run back to where it all started."

Simone' agreeing, "You are right Mother. I guess when you run the other way for so long you have to turn and face the sentence that pronounces you guilty."

"Simone' I would not say that your sentence would be one of a guilty. It would be one of not making a wise decision or a wise choice in the matter. We can all make unwise decisions or choices in our lives."

"You are supportive Mother and I love you and appreciate your kindness and the compassion shown me today. I will rest now; it is after 4:30 p.m."

Roberto' after one hour and a half into his flight, settled in his seat and gazed into the mid-afternoon sun as they headed out over the Atlantic, wondered what his wife was doing and what would he say to her once he saw her. All he wanted to do was to hold her and know she was safe in his arms again. He envisioned them back at their honeymoon cottage together making love. He needed her. These last few days without her were worse than physical starvation; it was a starvation of the heart, mind, and soul where he needed her most.

From sheer mental weariness, Roberto' drifted into sleep as he heard the Stewardess serving afternoon snack and drinks. He had no appetite for food just for his wife.

In the interim, in Tuscany, Simone' after tossing and turning for a while finally was able to rest until 6:30 p.m. when her Mother awakens her for dinner.

When her Mother awaken her, she told Simone', "I spoke with Franco daughter about your visit to us. I cannot say he is upset as much as he is confused with the entire matter. I mentioned that you knew Vincenzo' Moretti when you were younger and you were friends before you met Roberto'. I think my daughter, he has put the rest together in his mind about your relationship, not Carmeli'ta' just you and Vincenzo'." Catarina continued, "I also said, "You kept your friendship from everyone including your husband before and after you were married. My advice to you is to let him, my daughter, ask the questions he wants to know. It will be less painful for him."

"Yes Mother, I will do as you say" Simone' said in an obedient tone.

"Come daughter, your Father is hungry it is past dinner time for us."

She freshen-up and prepared to face her Father.

Simone' and her parents chatted and laughed at dinner as always. Franco looked at his lovely mysterious daughter as she chatted and wondered what made her run. He did not want to know all the details; whatsoever the situation he loved her and would support her. In contrast, he could not think well of Vincenzo' Moretti, that fact made him boil on the inside. She was 14 years old and he was 17 years old; he should not have been around his daughter at any point. The Wine Kings in the valley made it clear they would not go out of their class to have any kind of relationship with the farmers other than buying vegetables. And additionally, Simone' had been sheltered and he had not.

Finishing dinner, Franco walked outside into the beautiful patio garden Catarina loved and put much time in tending. "Simone' my daughter come walk with me. The evening is still young."

Simone' pushed her chair back from the table and answered, "Yes Father, I would love to join you."

Simone' looked her Mother as she rose from the table. Catarina nodded smiled and said, "Take heart my daughter remember he loves you."

Simone' replied, "Thank you Mother you are both kind and supportive of me in this dilemma I face." Simone' walked out on the patio and joined her Father.

"Simone' my daughter, tell me of Vincenzo' Moretti; what was the relationship?" Simone' commented, "We were friends, Father. He seemed to understand me and was always kind to me. Over the years, we grew close and then we fell in love, at that time, I thought it was love. He helped me through a difficult time in my final years of puberty, my Father."

ranco commented, "I wish you had come to Mother and me."

"I wanted to Father, but did not have the words. He was near my age and understood, or seemed to anyway."

"I am sorry for that my daughter, but thankful you found an outlet for your feelings, someone to share your thoughts with."

Simone' replied, "Mother said I am like you inside Father." This statement bought tears and emotions to Franco's eyes. He understood fully what she meant. He felt pain for his daughter. He understood how lost he was and the feelings of isolation it bought to him when he was a teen and then a young man. He hugged Simone' tightly she sobbed into her Father's shoulders, he was heads and shoulders taller even at her being 5'7" tall.

Simone' said tearfully, "I have made mistakes and bad choices and wrong decisions surrounding my relationship with Vincenzo' my Father. I wish I could live those times over and change my decision."

Franco said, "You cannot change the past my daughter, so we go forward. The only other question is Simone', why did you run away from Roberto, did he do something that would make you want to run?"

"Roberto' is more than good to me. It is all me, Father. He got to the point to where he could not live with the pain of not having the love he needed from me."

"I am afraid to ask what that statement meant my daughter, but tell me anyway."

"I never allowed him to reach my deepest need and desire because I was afraid of him knowing the truth of my and Vincenzo's relationship."

Franco stopped and became as cold and silent as stone, the color gone from his face and said, Simone' are you telling me Vincenzo' took advantage of you at 14 years of age?"

"No, my Father, he did not we were both to blame for the three times we were intimate" she said.

Franco anger and disbelief growing, "That is not the worst of it, Simone' why did you run? Even though you were not a virgin on your wedding night, why did you run?"

She commented, "Father I don't want to hurt you anymore, I really rather not say." Franco frowned and said, "Why Simone'? It will come out eventually."

Simone' paused for an infinitesimal amount of time what seemed an eternity to her Father finally said, "Vincenzo' thinks Carmeli'ta' is his."

Franco shocked asked, "how can this be possible Simone'?"

She said, "We were together three days before my wedding."

Franco said under his breath, "God in Heaven, how can you and he have done this Simone'? What makes him think she is his?"

She responded, "It was so close to the time that I was married from October to December."

"But Carmeli'ta' can't be his, can she?"

"She could be, but I believe in my heart she is Roberto's daughter Father, then again at this point I am not sure, it is a possibility; I could not convince Vincenzo' of that fact. He would not take no for an answer."

Franco said, "I saw him at the hospital when you were there. I thought he had someone in his family that was ill." He came to see Carmeli'ta' and me. I asked him to stay away but he would not. Even when I went to America he followed us and saw Carmeli'ta'."

Franco exasperated asked, "You agreed to this?"

She said, "I didn't know what else to do. I wanted to protect my family. I love Roberto' so desperately now Father. Three months after we were married, I realized he was the only man for me and what true love really feels like."

Franco asked, "Why did he not stay away?"

Simone' responded, "He said, he would not allow me to deprive him of his daughter. So, to keep him quiet, I allowed him to see Carmeli'ta' and me."

"Oh, my daughter, my daughter" Franco said as he groaned within himself.

"I could not tell Roberto' and as time went on, I became more afraid and it became impossible to tell him. Then, Vincenzo' threatened me in so many words."

Franco growing angry again, "Threatened you Simone'? Vincenzo' Moretti threatened you, my daughter! I will see him on this matter."

Simone' with a worried tone, "No Father, please."

He insisted, "No Simone'. I will speak with him about his actions. What about Roberto'?"

"I could not bear for him to know Father, so I ran away when he got too close to the truth. I didn't know what else to do, so I ran."

"Truth will out itself Simone'. It is better to tell Roberto' than, let him hear a twisted version."

She nodded and replied in agreement, "You are right Father; however, I couldn't bear the pain in his voice and eyes any longer. He is kind, gentle, and caring; I cannot say anything bad about Roberto'. Integrity is so important to him and I have not displayed it with this matter in our marriage."

Franco, fearing that it was a possibility that Carmeli'ta' may be Vincenzo's child and not Roberto's felt panicky because it could be true and that would make the situation even worse. The one that stood to be hurt the worse would be his sweet granddaughter asked finally, "Does Carmeli'ta' know anything?"

"No Father, she adores Roberto' and me, as we do her."

"This is good news daughter. Let us go back to the house. Mother will be waiting tea and dessert for us."

"Father, I have not told Mother that it is a possibility that Carmeli'ta' could be Vincenzo's. It is a possibility, but not a probability my Father, I am just no sure not any more at one time I thought I was, but with the pressure and the confusion over the years, I just don't know anymore, I just don't! Tears forming in her eyes and a desperate plea in her voice, what am I to do?"

"Come my daughter, let us go Mother is waiting, we will see what tomorrow looks like."

Simone' did not know that he meant Roberto' was on his way. He knew she would run again if he told her Roberto' was coming. It was almost 10:00 p.m. and darkness was setting in.

Subsequently, Vincenzo', after marriage, to Antonia Amoretti, and no other children to claim as his own, was still single-minded when it came to Simone' and Carmeli'ta'.

His Father, 65 years old thought it was a good investment to expand their business and holdings to America since the war ended a few years earlier, had bought prosperity to the states; it was abounding in America during the roaring 20's. During the war, Francisco Moretti met Charles Bienville Meriwether, while traveling abroad in reference to his textile business and supplying textiles product to the English government to assist in World War II.

Francisco Moretti and his son Vincenzo' ran the business together for years until Vincenzo' was trained and could handle the company. Francisco advised Vincenzo' to look for other investments to bring in to expand his holding and wealth. Charles Meriwether and Vincenzo' were about the same age and became friends over a 10-year period. Vincenzo' for the times he went to America to see Simone' and Carmeli'ta', told his wife and his parents he was on vacation and visiting Charles Meriwether. Antonia Amoretti, when in the valley, was involved in the Tuscan society activities and never cared to go.

Vincenzo', and Antonia had not done well over the years of their marriage, she like Simone' did not love her husband when she was married, but married Vincenzo', out of family obligation and because her parents insisted she marry Vincenzo', for status. When his Father made the expansion idea, Vincenzo', jumped at the idea to go to America on a fact-finding mission, especially in South Carolina and this would give him the opportunity to see Carmeli'ta' and Simone' without being questioned by his wife and family. Francisco wired Charles Bienville Meriwether and arranged for his son to come to America. He would stay with Charles Bienville Meriwether for 2 weeks while looking into investing in textiles.

Vincenzo', could not think of anything except Simone'. He could not get her out of his heart or mind and she is the Mother of his only child. Vincenzo's wife had not given him any children in the years of marriage.

Vincenzo' did not get married until four years after Simone' went to America in 1911. He married Antonia in 1915 during the war.

The winds of changed blew strong in their lives!

CHAPTER
TWENTY-THREE

Four hours into his flight, Roberto' awakens looked at his pocket watch realized it was almost 7:00 p.m. The Stewardess was serving dinner. In a few hours, they would cross the International Dateline and time would catch up with the time in London. He had eight more hours before he reached London, Tuscany, and his Simone'.

Simone and her Father returned home from their walk, wanted to freshen-up before she ate her dessert, walked towards the door leading into the living area and her bedroom "Please excuse me, "I will be right back."

Franco walked over to his wife Catarina and asked if there were any phone messages. Catarina told him that the phone had not ring during the day. Franco breathed a sigh of relief. Looking at her husband knowing that there was more to his question asked, "Franco is there something that I should know?"

He looked at her for a few moments and whispered, "Roberto' is on his way. He will be here by the time Simone' awakens in the morning."

Catarina surprised asked, "Do you think it is a good idea not to tell daughter Roberto' is on his way, Franco?"

Franco thought for a moment, "I think so my darling, she would leave if she knew. This will be best for her and she needs to stay and face Roberto' not run away again we may never see her again would be my greatest fear." He continued, "Did daughter tell you Mother that there is a possibility that Vincenzo' could be Carmeli'ta' Father."

Catarina feeling sick, commented, "I got that feeling from what she said. She is not sure right now about anything Franco. This is a difficult situation at best; but I will not think that way we have to remain positive so we can help our daughter."

"You are right Mother. I have faith in our daughter. I think that she knows who the Father is. She is just upset and confused right now. But if Roberto' is not we will have to be strong for our daughter and granddaughter. Roberto' would hurt Vincenzo' Mother; it would be too much pain for him to bear after all the pain and heartache he has been through thinking Simone' do not really love him. We need to brace ourselves for the coming turbulence of this situation."

Simone' walked back into the kitchen and looked at her parents with a question on their faces, "Mother and Father is everything okay? You both look so strange. I am sorry that I upset you today."

Franco said, "Please don't apologize. We are fine daughter just concerned about you. You did the right things by coming home and then telling us Simone'. The situation will work itself out, but you will have to make up your mind to face Roberto' eventually; sooner is always better." She did not comment just asked, "Mother, are the tea and scones ready?"

"Yes they are ready."

Simone' parents kept her talking late into the night until 1:30 a.m., to make sure that Simone' would sleep later on Tuesday morning and Roberto' would be there when she awaken.

Simone' droopy eyed, finally said good night to her parents, and retired for the night went to her suite, drew her bath water, and stepped into the warm bubbly suds that danced red, yellow, and blue images of the light from the lavender fragrance candles garnishing her bathtub. She sat in the tub of bubbles and let the warm water kiss and caress her body like a lover. She could feel the soothing caresses of the water as it slowly swished against her body as she moved her legs. The warm caress of the dancing water gave her the feeling of being in front of their fireplace each night in Charleston; the flames slowly warmed and soothed the cool chill of the evenings for Roberto' and her. The bubbles felt like Roberto's arms, enveloped her entire body holding her captive, loving her body as Roberto' does each time he made love to her...taunted herself with questions: "how could I have let this situation with Vincenzo' go so far as to jeopardize my entire life and those that I love so desperately?"

Thoughts invaded her mind, induced by the warmth of a bath in the quiet of her private bathroom. Her early loss of innocence and virginity flashed across her mind. At the time Vincenzo' and she became lovers, did not know the long arms of her actions would reach across time and space as history does. Indeed, she had a history, like a bad penny it kept turning up. She thought of a scripture Brother Meriwether, their Minister quoted to her many time during their tell-all sessions, while he counseled her to be honest with her husband said, "you and he are one", quoted [Ephesians 4:22], *"Therefore, having put away falsehood, let each one of you speak the truth with his neighbor, for we are members one of another."* She knew that this was true and he cautioned her eventually Vincenzo', in time, would act upon the threat he made.

She continued to weigh the ramifications of her poor decision. "The level of intimacy that existed between them, there are no inhibitions on Roberto's part. He never held back his needs, desires, and passion he felt for me nor did he hold inside of him the love he needed from me, but expressed it to me. There was no ego or pride on his part in our intimate life. As a man, he never allowed his ego or pride to cause him to hold his feeling for me inside, but took the chance to put his heart and needs out there, so I would know that terrible love he feels for me that tore at his heart and what it took to soothe the ache he felt. I know now the pain tortured him over the years, how he must have hurt; how I must have hurt him!"

Simone' finished her bath, lotion her body, slipped into a peach color negligee', freshened her mouth, brushed her hair, and slipped between the warm sheets on her bed, seeing images of her husband in her head slipped into a weary, but peaceful sleep. Disclosing the reason to her parents at the sudden arrival at their home has drained every ounce of her energy mentally and emotionally.

Monday morning, November 18, in Charleston, Carmeli'ta' had awakened at her usual time and began preparing for work. While bathing, her thoughts went to the conversation with her Father on Sunday. She was still perplexed about her mother going to Tuscany and not saying anything to her. She and her mother had a close mother/ daughter relationship. She was open with her mother. Moreover, her mother did not keep any secrets from her.

It became apparent to Carmelita that she did not know her mother as well as she thought. She was anxious to hear from her Father, he said he would call when he arrived, she knew he would be traveling for a long time and reminded herself she needed to be patient, Tuesday would come eventually. Marianna came to her mind; she promised herself, "I will call her later in the morning to see if she needs anything."

Carmeli'ta' finished her bath dressed ate breakfast and left for Madison Steel and Iron at 8:45 a.m., as she did each day. On the short drive to work Carmeli'ta' mentally planned what she would say in the phone conversation with Charles Meriwether's office in the effort to get Madison Steel and Meriwether Textiles managers together.

Jason was eagerly waiting for Carmeli'ta' to arrive at work. Arriving at Madison Steel Carmeli'ta' went to her office. As she passed Mrs. Horne's desk she spoke, "Good morning Mrs. Horne how are you?"

Ms. Horne smiling pleasantly said, "I am well Ms. Bandaci. How was your weekend?" She replied, "My weekend was beautiful thank you for asking."

Carmeli'ta' walked down the hall to her office and called Mrs. Horne asked if she would check to see if Mr. Madison was free to see her before she called Charles Meriwether. Mrs. Horne opened Jason's door said, "Excuse Mr. Madison, Ms. Bandaci asked if you and she might speak before she calls Charles Meriwether?"

He replied, "Definitely, Mrs. Horne, please tell Mrs. Bandaci I will be there shortly, give me five minutes."

Mrs. Horne called Carmeli'ta' and informed her that Mr. Madison would be there in five minutes. Jason did not want to appear too eager even though he was desperate to see Carmeli'ta'. Occupied with the day's priorities she replied, "Thank you Mrs. Horne. We will let you know when the meeting is over, please hold all calls, and tell the Quality Control Manager I will come to the plant as soon as I have finished; it should be no more than an hour."

Mrs. Horne replied, "Yes Ms. Bandaci."

Carmeli'ta' called her Father and mother's home the phone rang three short and one long, Marianna answered, "Hello, Bandaci residence."

She said, "Good morning Marianna. How are you today?"

Excited to hear voice, Marianna exclaimed, "Ms. Carmeli'ta' it is good to hear from you. Are you okay?" She said, "Yes Marianna, I am fine. I wanted to see if you needed anything for the house or from the market?"

"No, Ms. Carmeli'ta' I am fine. Everything her is going okay as if Ms. Bandaci was here."

"Thank you Marianna", Carmeli'ta' replied. "Please call me if you need anything and I will take care of it."

Marianna said joyfully, "Thank you Miss Carmeli'ta', Mr. Bandaci said that I could get what I needed from the market as usual. I do not need anything right now. I am glad to hear from you. I miss seeing you. I hope you can come soon to see me."

Carmelita promised, "I will. I have to go now Marianna. See you soon. Bye."

Jason walked slowly down the hall with a tablet and pen in his hand. He approached her office door and knocked. Carmeli'ta' was hanging up the phone as Jason knocked on her office door. She opened the door and smiled. Jason walked in closed the door behind him pulled her close and kissed her and at length said, "Good morning my love. I was eager for you to arrive. I am glad to see you. He stroked her silky hair and whispered in her ear, "I love you Carmeli'ta'. I am happy to have you in my life."

She smiled hugging Jason tightly, "I love you Jason. I feel so happy knowing that you love me and we have each other in our lives."

They stood holding each other for a long while. Carmeli'ta' felt safe in Jason's arms relishing the moment, leaned her head against his chest on his pristine white shirt. He smelled so fresh. After a while Jason said, "Let us make the call to Charles Meriwether it is getting late in the morning we don't want to keep him waiting too long."

Carmeli'ta' walked around her desk picked up the phone and dialed Charles Meriwether's direct line to his office. Ms. Gooding, his assistance answered, "Good morning, Mr. Meriwether's office may I help you?"

"Yes, Ms. Gooding this is Carmeli'ta' Bandaci at Madison Steel and Iron, Mr. Meriwether is expecting my call today."

She answered, "Yes Ms. Bandaci, Mr. Meriwether is expecting your call. Please hold I will get him on the line."

"Thank you, I will hold."

Jason observed the professional manner in which she handled herself in a business setting while Carmeli'ta' stood holding the phone waiting for Charles Meriwether to pick up. She smiled and waved at Jason. He and blew her a kiss, proud of her in both settings, personally and professionally.

A few minutes passed, Charles Meriwether answered, "Good morning Ms. Bandaci I was expecting your call. I trust that you are well today."

"Yes, Mr. Meriwether, I am well and hope the same for you." "I am well, thank you."

Carmeli'ta' wanting to siege the moment came back with, "Mr. Meriwether can we coordinate our calendars for a date for Meriwether Textiles and Madison Steel's people to get together in reference to the discussion we had at the Thanksgiving Ball, Thursday night, November 7 concerning the economic growth of the community and job creations?"

"Yes Ms. Bandaci, I was just looking at some dates before I answered the call. I have two dates on my calendar that we could meet if your calendar will allow."

"Please give me the dates Mr. Meriwether, I have my calendar in front of me", she replied. Looking at his Calendar, Charles Meriwether said, "November 20 and the other is December 5. Which date will be more convenient for you Ms. Bandaci?"

Carmeli'ta' wrote down both dates and turned the tablet where Jason could see and placed a question mark by each. Jason smiled and formed with his lips "Either, the sooner the better". Carmeli'ta' circled November 20 Jason nodded in agreement.

She said, "November 20 is good for us Mr. Meriwether." He answered, "That is good Ms. Bandaci, and November 20 is perfect for me. Now to the time, 10:00 a.m. should give everyone involved time to get to work and set their day's priorities."

Carmeli'ta' agreed 10:00 a.m. is good." She looked at Jason and he nodded yes. "Where do you want to meet Mr. Meriwether?"

"Your plant would be fine if that is okay with Mr. Madison."

"Our Boardroom is available that day." She looked at Jason he smiled and nodded yes again.

"That would be perfect Ms. Bandaci. I have not been to Madison Steel in a few years. If I remember correctly your Boardroom is very elegant and conducive in providing an atmosphere that encourages the success of any meeting, correct?"

"Yes, you are correct. Our Boardroom does provide that atmosphere. I will plan for refreshments. We will see you on Wednesday November 20, Mr. Meriwether. Please call me if you have questions or suggestions for the agenda."

"I will look at the topic areas and let you know Ms. Bandaci. I look forward to working with you."

"Thank you Mr. Meriwether, I am looking forward to working with you. Have a good day. Goodbye."

"Thank you Ms. Bandaci. Have a good day. Bye for now."

Carmeli'ta' had gotten the proposal to Meriwether Textiles so Charles Meriwether and his staff could be up to speed on the intricate details of the proposal and job initiative process Monday November 11.

Charles Meriwether thought after he hung up the phone, "This is my foot in the door and a chance to ask Carmeli'ta' to dinner, at first in a business manner of course. After this meeting, I can, if I plan carefully, not appear ungentlemanly like, invite her to a business dinner, and go from there with a relationship hopefully. She is the epitome of a southern woman, much like Juanita Madison."

Charles Bienville Meriwether was obsessive in his mind in reference to Juanita Madison, he tried to make Carmeli'ta' a replacement for her, or she would become Juanita Madison to him.

Carmeli'ta' hung up the phone. Jason smiling admired the successful way she handled herself in getting the meeting scheduled noticed she did not make any final decisions without his approval. He liked this characteristic in Carmeli'ta'. The fact she is always respectful in reference to his authority impressed him. She did not allow her position in the company to change her mannerisms. She smiled back, walked around her desk, and stood in front of Jason. He said, "Thank you Carmeli'ta' you and your skills are a wonderful asset to this company."

She smiled, "Thank you Jason I enjoy my job."

Jason looked at his watch realized it was almost an hour later, held Carmeli'ta's hand and walked toward the office door. "I have another appointment at 10:30 a.m. Carmeli'ta'; I need to complete my preparations."

"I am on my way to my weekly Quality Control Meeting Jason. I will see you after lunch."

"Thank you again my love. Enjoy the remainder of the day; until later tonight."

"Thank you Sweetheart. I will be ready at 8:00 p.m. Jason smiled and walked down the hall to his office. Carmeli'ta' left for her Quality Control Meeting, after informing Ms. Horne of her schedule for the next two hours.

Tension on both sides of the Atlantic grew.

CHAPTER
TWENTY-FOUR

Roberto' now across the International Dateline would be landing in three hours in London, was awake and ready to get to Tuscany. At 3:00 a.m., the pilot announced their descent into Corydon Airport, London. His connecting flight to Tuscany would be at 7:00 a.m. or earlier as the Stewardess announced. This thought made Roberto' happy; earlier would be better.

Upon landing, Roberto' noticed, everything was different from the last time he saw London eighteen plus years ago before when he moved to America. It was modern and well lite now. He picked up his personal case and walked off the plane into the Airport terminal went to the information desk and asked to reserve a taxi or a car once he arrived in Tuscany. The agent checked the Tuscany Airport and said yes, he could rent a car or hire a taxi. Roberto' decided to hire the taxi. He anxiously waited for the flight to Tuscany to board his thoughts went to Simone' and hoped he arrived before she awaken. The wait in the Croydon Airport in London was not a long one. The technician called for passengers boarding at 6:00 a.m. This was wonderful for Roberto'. It would get him to the Tuscany Airport by 8:00 a.m.

Two hours later his flight arrived on schedule at the Tuscany Airport, Roberto' went to the Imperial Airways desk and asked for the reserved taxi to drive into the valley. In the interim, he picked up his luggage while the agent called for the taxi. The ride into the valley would take forty-five minutes. On the ride into the valley, Roberto' felt anxious but eager to see his wife to be near her again hold her and love her. He took the note Simone' left from his jacket pocket and read it again. At the Giovanni's home Franco had risen for the day, planned to go to his farm later after Roberto' arrived.

He and Catarina had breakfast at 7:00 a.m. as usual.

Franco sat and sipped his coffee with an intense look on his face that worried Catarina, "Franco what is worrying you today? When will he arrive? You think he will be here before daughter is awake! It was late when we retired so she may sleep later today."

"Let us hope my lovely. It will be better if Roberto' is here when she awakens."

"I do hope that we made the right decision in not telling her."

"It is done now Mother. He should be arriving in a short while."

The taxi approached the farming valley, Roberto' saw the haze hanging over the little valley giving it a look of a hanging paradise bought back memories growing up in his beautiful valley. He gave the driver the address to his in-laws home. It was now 7:45 a.m.; the taxi pulled in front of the Giovanni's home, he paid the fare, removed his luggage from the seat beside him, walked up to the front door, and knocked lightly. Franco watching for his arrival rushed to the door and opened it before he knocked again. Simone's room was on the back of the house she would not hear the light knock for anyone coming in the front door, but then again, he did not want take the chance of her being awaken by the knocking.

Franco smiled and said, "Roberto' my son it is good to see you again it has been four years or more since we were there to visit."

"Hello Franco, it is equally good to see you. How is my Simone'? Did you tell her I was coming?"

"No Roberto' we did not think it was for us to tell her. You did not call; we thought it best to wait to see what you wanted to do."

Feeling a sigh of relief Roberto' said, "Thank you Franco, thank you."

Catarina appeared from the kitchen and rushed to Roberto' and hugged him saying, "Hello my son-in-law it is good to see you."

Roberto' smiled and lightly kissed Catarina on the cheek thought how much Simone' looked like her mother, she inherited the same beauty, but his Simone' was prettier said, "Thank you, I feel the same. Is Simone' still resting?"

"Yes, I checked before you arrived she is sleeping peacefully. She was tired from the long trip and the long weekend." She continued, "Please have some breakfast Roberto' or at least coffee it is early for her yet. We all went to bed after 1:30 a.m. I kept her talking intentionally so she would sleep late today. I prayed that you would arrive before she awakened. I don't expect she will be up before 10:00 a.m."

"Thank you I will have breakfast; I could not eat on the plane. Now I know that my wife is safe I will eat." Roberto' had fruit, baked Italian Sausage, bread, and coffee. He chatted with his in-laws for a while and said, "Is Simone' in the same room?"

Franco commented, "Yes my son. Go to her she needs you. Be gentle with her Roberto' she is very fragile."

Roberto' stopped, stood paused for a diminutive moment of time, turned, and looked at Franco and Catarina with understanding for their concern for their daughter, finally said, "I love Simone'. I would never hurt her in any way. I realize that something is bothering her. I want to know what it is; only she can tell me. I will go to her now if you will excuse me. Thank you for what you did to keep my beauty safe for me."

Roberto walked towards Simone's bedroom beyond the Parlor of the Giovanni's home to the end of the hallway where she slept. During her teenage years, she could see from her bedroom window, the Moretti's vineyard, and winery. Roberto' walked quietly to her door and opened it; sit his suitcase on the floor near the lounger. Simone' was sleeping peacefully on her left side dreaming of Roberto' did not hear him enter the room. He removed his sports coat, took a mint from the side pocket, put it in his mouth, laid his coat on the Chaise Lounge, walked over to where she was sleeping, softly sit on the bed besides Simone,' leaning over said, "Wake up my beauty."

Simone' moved and said in a fretful tone, "Roberto' I want you." Simone' still sleep did not realize Roberto' was there thought she dreamed she heard his voice said again, in a tone of desperation, "I love you Roberto'. I want you Roberto', please don't leave me." Simone' dreamed Roberto' left her and she felt as if she were groping in a dark place, reached out find him could not see him nor feel him, called his name aloud in a frightened tone, "Roberto', Roberto'." Awaken by the sound of her tearful pleas; sat up in bed with her eyes still closed both hands reaching out in front of her pleading for her husband not to leave her.

Her plea tore at Roberto's heart; he reached and pulled his wife to him said, "Wake up Simone' I am here my beauty. I will not leave you. I love you. I am here; open your eyes look at me!"

Simone' opened her eyes and could not believe there before her was Roberto'. She made sounds like a frighten child clung to him for dear life. Her mother and Father heard the outcry, rushed to her room, and opened the door, saw Roberto' holding their daughter consoling her and, kissing her face repeatedly saying softly, "It was only a dream my beauty, only a dream. It is I. I am here. I came after you. I cannot live without you Simone'. I need you. Why did you leave me?"

Simone' crying almost uncontrollably held tighter to Roberto'. He pulled Simone' closer to him, lifted her small body onto his lap, held her close, spoke to her in a soft loving tone, "I love you Simone'. I am yours always. Please do not cry my beauty. It is breaking my heart to see you so upset. What have I done to make you want to leave me?"

Simone' after a long while calmed down and said, "I did not know that you were coming Roberto'. I could not hurt you any longer. I could not bear the pain in your eyes and agony in the tone of your voice that told me how much you were suffering almost since we been married. I did not know what to tell you Roberto', how to answer your questions."

Simone' still avoided answering Roberto's questions. Franco and Catarina quietly backed out the room, closed the door, and went to the kitchen to give them the privacy they needed.

Simone' held onto Roberto' for dear life, he caressed her after a long time until she stopped the fretful crying. Moving slowly from his arms as if she regretted leaving even a minuscule amount of time went into the bathroom. She wanted to freshen-up before she kissed him, returning a few minutes later to the bedroom and her bed, Roberto' sitting on the bed watched his wife walk across the room to where he was waiting for her, could still see the same elusive mysterious woman she had been since they married. He went in the bathroom freshened up returned to his wife waiting in bed, sat on the side of the bed near her, took her right hand kissed it softly, "I love you Simone'. I missed you. My days have been miserably long and lonely since you left five days ago. All I could think of was getting to you and knowing you were okay and being near you."

Simone' leaned forward and kissed her husband sweetly. Pulling her to him, kissed her passionately caressing her body. Seeing her beautiful body through the sheerness of the negligée aroused his desire. Roberto' stood, undressed, walked across the room to the bedroom door, and turned the lock so they would not be disturbed, returned, removed her negligée, lay beside Simone,' and pulled her onto him, his hand stroked her shoulders, and then moved down to her buttocks. He felt the passion and physical pressure of his need for her growing she kissed him and whispered, "I need you Roberto'. I have also been miserable without you coming home to me and having you near me at night. I ached for you to love me, to feel your touch, hear your whispers in my ear as we caress each other."

"I want you desperately Simone'. I was eager to see you be near you, please love me. I want to feel the warmth of your body, please love me. I cannot think of anything else right now." He, at that moment, only wanted to drink of her love when their bodies mold together and become one to soothe and please every fiber of his being. These memorable times, through the years, had burned themselves into Roberto's heart and soul.

Simone' looked down at her husband saw the passion in his eyes let her fingers slide lightly over his chest and arms, kissed his eyes, mouth, cheeks, and neck. She saw the craving for her his body showed, caressed his legs, and thighs. Roberto' trembled with passion and desire while she slowly moved her hands across his body, he closed his eyes and gave in to the pleasure she gave him, felt as if he would lose his breath with the level of passion he reached with her touch bringing with it a new pinnacle of desire and pleasure. She whispered, "Roberto' you are so desirable. You are the only man that I want, the only man I need, hold me tight."

He pulled Simone' closer until there was no air between them; their bodies became molded and entwined together. Her hands continued to explore his body. Roberto cupped her small face in his hands looking into her eyes said, "Simone', love me my beauty." He gently lay Simone' down and caressed her body, she felt as if rays of sunshine were streaming inside of her, wanted Roberto' to make love to her. He did not yet. He continued caressing her, kissing her whispering uttering barely heard words of his love and need her ears. He wanted to bring her to a higher level of passion, kissed her until her mind and body burned with desire.

The taste of his kisses were sweet; she did not want him to stop kissing her pulled him closer held him tight and kissing him more. Simone's kisses to Roberto were a drink of water to a thirsty soul on a hot summer day in July in Charleston. He heard soft whimpers of pleasure, felt her body on fire as his body slowly entered hers fulfilling the loneliness that had invaded her very being in the few days she was apart from her husband. She gave herself to her him, Roberto' searched every inch of her as he did the first night of their honeymoon exploring, probing, and reaching in pursuit of its hidden treasure. Roberto' softly called her name, "Simone', Simone'" holding her tighter and yet so tenderly.

The rhythm of her body moved to his, she loved Roberto' still afraid, she could not allow him to reach her deepest passionate needs. Roberto' thrusts were asking for her unleased passion, reached farther and farther wanting to know all of his wife's passions and desires. Each time he entered her body gave new pleasure to Simone' she had not felt before with him.

The passion Roberto' felt for his wife was evident in the way he loved her. To Roberto' this moment in time was like discovering his wife for the first time again.

The joy he felt relieved the pressure from his body, heart, and mind. The painful aches felt while parted from his wife, were all gone. Being with her again in a different environment and the city where it all begin gave him a wonderful comfortable feeling that was delightfully satisfying.

Roberto' and Simone' held on to each other. She felt good in his arms once again. Even with all the joy felt being with Simone' again that knife cutting into his heart and soul was making the wounds deeper because of the mystery enshrouding Simone', his heart still ached with the pain felt because of the unanswered questions and the secrets she held from him. Even now, he could feel her body retracting, as he got closer to her deepest level of passion. Roberto' lifted Simone's face to look at him and asked, "Tell me Simone' what you are keeping from me? Why do you not let me feel all of you? I cannot bear to see you in pain. I never imagined that you were suffering at this intense a level. What is so bad that you cannot share it with me? You don't think that our love is strong enough to get through this problem?"

"I know our love is strong Roberto'. And I believe that it can get us through any problem, but I am afraid of losing you."

Roberto' with a question in his voce said, "Lose me? This is the second time you said that! What are you referring to?"

She responded, "It is best not to talk about it now Roberto'. Please let us join Mother and Father; they are waiting. It has been almost three hours since you arrived."

Even though he wanted to know the problem Roberto' agreed, "Okay for now Simone' later then. Let us dress and join your parents." Even with the pain that he felt, his concern for his wife and her suffering outweighed for that time, his need for answers to his questions and his own pain. He could not bear to see her suffer even in his suffering.

 After bathing and dressing, they walked down the spacious hallway side-by-side, Simone' held Roberto's hand as if to prevent him from leaving her. Roberto' noticed the frighten look on her face and felt the tenseness of her grip as she held his hand, they joined her parents. Franco and Catarina were waiting in the kitchen. Catarina poured coffee for everyone and put a small bowl with two spoons of fruit in front of Simone said, "Eat my daughter it is getting late in the day after 11:00 a.m. we will eat lunch later today maybe 1:30 p.m. you should be hungry by that time."

"Thank you Mother, I will be; I am hungry now, but will wait for lunch with my family."

Franco continued playing the part of the uninformed Father-in-law as if Roberto's coming to Tuscany was a surprise. He did not want Simone' to know that he was aware of his coming. A certain amount of anxiety was in atmosphere in the kitchen though Roberto' was happy to see his wife. While chatting with her parents, Roberto' observed his wife. She did not seem to be there with them in mind, but present somewhere else at that moment. Simone' was thinking of the past few days and wondering if she would see or run into Vincenzo' hoping and she would not while in Italy.

Franco and Catarina looked at each other. Simone' felt the tenseness in the kitchen coming from her husband and parents asked, "Is there something I am missing? What is this quiet and tense feeling I am getting about between you?"

Franco quickly responded, "No daughter, not that we are aware of. Why do you ask?" Looking at them Simone' declared, "Well, you are not talking to each other!"

Roberto' quickly said, "There is nothing my darling wife that I am aware of that is wrong. After you finish your breakfast my lovely, I want to take a walk and see the countryside again, visit our little river we liked so well; also go back to the cottage where we had our honeymoon. Amelio' purchased his farm back and offered it to us if we wanted to go there."

Simone said excitedly, "Yes Roberto', I would love to visit the cottage again. I cannot think of a happier time in my life. Can we stay there for a few days?"

"Yes, my darling wife we can stay as long as you like. I planned to be gone ten days from the farm." This made Simone' happy she smiled and kissed her husband's hand.

Franco and Catarina sat quietly and listened at the conversational exchange between them, looked at each other hoping that they would not say anything to give their daughter's secrets away too soon. Simone' still feeling tension wondered what the issue was, but did not say anything. She remembered the conversation she spurred with Roberto' when she mentioned Carmeli'ta's dinner date with Jason Madison. She was not ready for another conversation of why she kept secrets and did not fully give her husband the passion he needed from her. She wanted to avoid answering his questions as long as possible.

Roberto' looked at the kitchen clock 11:45 a.m. said, "My lovely wife I promised Carmeli'ta', Amelio', and Marianna I would call when I arrived and let them know that we are safe after the long flights. If you will excuse me, I will make those calls now. Franco may I use your phone? I will pay the cost of the overseas calls."

Franco a little annoyed, "Roberto' my son, there will be no charges to members of my family for using the phone in my house. Mother and I can afford the calls to America. Please feel free to talk as long as is necessary. This is your home as well as Simone's. Please, I want you to feel comfortable, Mia casa è tua casa."

"Thank you Franco' I do feel comfortable and appreciate that your home is my home. I hope you have felt that way when you came to visit my beauty and me, Mia casa è tua casa."

"Yes my son, my Catarina, and I have felt more than welcome each time we visited thank you."

"You are more than welcome. Please excuse me, I shall not be long."

Roberto' walked into Franco's office over to the desk picked up the phone and said, "Operator I would like to make three calls to America. Is it possible that I could be connected to each person as needed?"

She answered, "I can try sir, please give me the phone numbers that you want connected. There will be an additional charge for connecting you sir."

"That will be fine. I can pay for the additional service." Roberto' gave the operator the numbers: Amelio' (928-768-8543), Carmelita (928-876-3548), and his home to call Marianna (928-568-9087) his housekeeper.

After a few seconds, the phone rang three long rings and one short at Amelio's, "Hello, Amelio Bandaci speaking."

"Hello Amelio' my cousin, Roberto' here. I am in Tuscany and my Simone' is safe."

Amelio' excited to hear his cousin said, "Hello Roberto', it is good to hear that you are safe. I was getting concerned; it has been a while since you left. I was waiting to hear from you before I leave for the farms."

Roberto' in an assuring tone, "I am fine now that I see and can hold my Simone'."

His cousin grateful for the good news, "I am relieved my cousin everything is fine."

Roberto' changing the subject asked, "Is the farm business going okay Amelio'?"

"Everything is okay Roberto'. There are no problems so far, enjoy yourself. I will take care of everything until you return."

"Thank you my cousin, have you seen Carmeli'ta'?"

"Not in the last few days. I spoke with her; she called to see if I needed help. She is okay working hard as usual - like her Father."

"Thank you for staying in touch with her."

"Thank you is not necessary, we are family."

Roberto' wanting to get to the next call said, "I need to talk with Carmeli'ta' and Marianna, so I will say bye for now."

Amelio' said their native tongue, "arrivederci, per ora prendersi cura (goodbye, for now take care)."

"Grazie Amelio', lo faro, (thank you, Amelio', I will.)"

Roberto' pressed the button on the phone and said, "Operator, I am ready to speak with Carmeli'ta' Bandaci."

She said, "Thank you I will ring her number Mr. Bandaci." Carmeli'ta' just getting up to prepare to go to work, the phone was ringing, picked it up, and said, "Hello."

Roberto' pleased to hear her voice, "Hello Carmeli'ta', my lovely daughter how are you?"

Excited Carmeli'ta' responded, "Father, it is good to hear from you. How are you? How is mother? Is she okay? How are grandfather and grandmother, are you with them?"

"Slow down my beautiful daughter, one question at a time. I am fine. You mother is fine. Your grandparents are fine. We are staying with them; however, your mother and I are going to the cottage where we had our honeymoon; Amelio' owns it again. We will spend a few days there before we return to America, anyway at least before I return to the U.S. As I told you, mother may stay to visit her Father and Mother for a while."

Carmeli'ta' still perplexed, "Yes Father, I still do not understand mother's sudden decision to leave home and visit my grandparents. That is unusual behavior, so unlike mother then you leave also Father."

"Carmeli'ta', my daughter, it is okay, your mother is fine and so am I; please calm yourself. How is your work? How is Jason Madison? Is everything going well with you my daughter?"

Carmeli'ta' re-joined, "Yes Father everything is fine. Jason is fine. I have not heard from Amelio'; he must not need any assistance."

He responded, "Yes Carmeli'ta', I spoke with Amelio', he is fine and handling everything okay."

She insisted, "Father, when will you and mother be back home? I miss you both!" He replied, "I will return in ten days Carmeli'ta'. I will let you know if your mother is coming back with me or staying longer with her parents."

Carmeli'ta' as always, respectfully answered, "Yes, my Father."

Roberto' ended by saying, "I need to be connected to Marianna, my daughter. I will talk with you soon." She responded, "Thank you Father, I love you and mother, please tell mother for me I love her. I am preparing to go to work."

"I will goodbye for now Carmeli'ta'."

"Have a good time Father."

"I will."

Roberto' asked the operator to connect him with Marianna. The phone ringing Marianna in the kitchen preparing her breakfast answered, "Hello,

Bandaci residence."

"Hello Marianna, this is Mr. Bandaci."

Marianna excited and overwhelmed with emotion said, "Mr. Bandaci, it is so good to hear your voice. Are you with Mrs. Bandaci?"

"Yes, I am; she is doing well. How are you Marianna?

"I am fine Mr. Bandaci. Is Ms. Carmeli'ta' okay? I have not heard from

her since yesterday."

"She is good Marianna. Do you need anything for the house?"

"No, I am good. Mr. Amelio' said he will take care of what I need later today, thank you for asking."

"I will check again with you soon. I will be back in ten days; take care of yourself Marianna, goodbye."

She sadly said, "Goodbye sir."

Roberto' hung up the phone and returned to the kitchen to his wife and in-law's. Simone' asked, "Roberto' everything back in America okay? It is still early there."

"Yes it is my lovely wife. I spoke with Amelio', Carmeli'ta' and Marianna, everything is going well."

After lunch, Roberto' needed to be away from the thick atmosphere for a while said, "I want to walk Simone' and see the valley it has been a while, will you join me please?"

"Yes, I will my husband. Turning to her parents Mother and Father please excuse us."

Franco delighted, "Of course my children; please enjoy yourselves." Roberto' and Simone' walked toward Franco's farm beyond Catarina's Rose Garden.

Roberto' held Simone' around her waist and reflected for a few minutes on how small and petite his wife was, noticing his quietness smiled up at her husband. She had gotten good at hiding her fear and today was no different. The dilemma she faced was before her again. She would need to prepare to answer his questions she had run to get away from five-days earlier. Simone' once again felt tense and her guard went up after letting it down to reveal the situation to her father and mother; her mother more than her father.

Roberto' carried a blanket so they could enjoy the view from their favorite hill overlooking the valley and river that flowed so peacefully beyond Franco's farm. Approaching the hill Roberto' took Simone's by the hand, smiled pulling her along; they ran laughing to their favorite spot. He spread the blanket on the ground and pulled Simone' down beside him and commented, "Simone' you are quiet my beauty, please tell me what is taking you away from me."

Looking at him Simone' said, "I am here Roberto' my love, I was just thanking God you are here. I love you so." He replied, "I could not bear for you to be apart from me Simone'. I had to find you." Roberto' still not letting her know he had spoken to her Father, continued, "I hoped, and prayed you would come to your parent's home, so I came here first. My life is empty without you Simone'. Everything we have worked hard for means nothing without you in my life. When I found your note, it broke my heart to know that you wanted to leave me and you could not share your deepest thoughts with me."

Simone' wanted to run again even if it were just a short distance, rose from the blanket beside her husband walked a few feet from him turned and said, "I know Roberto', I could not endure the look of hurt in your eyes and the painful sound or your voice. I thought it best to go before the hurt got any crueler."

Roberto' rose, walked swiftly to where Simone' was standing and took her by the shoulders looked at her with his eyes dancing in annoyance and frustration, "It could not be any worse than you leaving our home Simone', please, tell me why you ran away?" Simone' had seen Roberto' angry with her before, the night he discovered Carmeli'ta' was dating Jason Madison and she had not warned him beforehand. She had also seen this level of anger when things did not go well at the farm.

Simone' silent for a long period-of-time, finally looked at her husband, "Roberto' I cannot answer your questions. I am sorry just know that I love you."

Roberto' did not press her for an answer in the fear she would run again. He turned walked to where they had sit picked up the blanket holding his wife hand leading her to the edge of the hill overlooking the river pulled her close and kissed her. Simone' relaxed at his touch he felt so strong, she leaned into his kiss. He knew she loved him, but why could she not give herself to him totally? These unanswered questions tortured his mind; he still did not have an answer.

The evening sun had begun to fade, by the time they walked back through the vegetable fields and home. It was nearing dinner. Simone' knew her mother would be expecting them. Nearing the house, an inviting aroma of garlic and fresh baked bread floated gently into their senses from the atmosphere in the garden. Roberto' and Simone' realized they were hungry.

Franco had watched for their arrival saw them opened the kitchen door smiling and said, "Mother, our missing children are here. Did you have a good walk?" asked Franco.

When they walked through the open door, the aroma was stronger and more inviting. Catarina was putting the dinner on the table, Roberto' saw ha vista Il Maglio alto Pasta con basilico e salsa di Pomodoro con pollo e insalata con balsamico e vinaigrette (the mile-high pasta with Basil and Tomato sauce with chicken and green salad with Balsamic and Vinaigrette dressing).

Roberto' said, 'Yes we went to our favorite spot on the hill overlooking Val di Greve (Valley of the River Greve in central Tuscany). It is as beautiful as I remembered. I love watching the waves as they are crashing against the rocks."

Simone' quiet, sinking back behind the protective wall where she trained herself to take refuge. Caterina noticed Simone' and the worried look she saw on her face said, "Please chose a wine my husband and son-in-law from the cellular."

Catarina beckoned to Simone' after they went through the door to the wine cellular went ahead of her into the Parlor turned, "Simone' what is wrong? The look on your face is giving away the fact that you are upset. Eventually, Roberto' not to mention your Father, will notice."

Her voice broke revealing the pain she felt, "Mother I cannot tell my husband right now about my past and Vincenzo' Moretti. I thought I could and tried when we were out walking, but could not bring myself to do so. Roberto' became angry with me because I left our home without telling him why. He is so hurt mother, what will I do, if we cannot get past this situation?"

"First, Simone, you will need to change the expression on your face and act happier to see your husband or it will not be a good evening. You do not need to set your Father off about this situation he is so angry with Vincenzo' he would go there tonight and Roberto' would know the truth of the matter before you are ready for him know about your past. It would be mass confusion Simone' and someone would get hurt and it probably would be Vincenzo'. Moreover, yes, I can understand why your husband is angry my darling daughter, you left with no warning. How did you expect he would feel other than anger? I think it is more fear for losing you than anger my daughter, so smile."

"I know Mother, this is true. He has a right to be angry with me. I will smile thank you for helping me keep my thoughts prospective and in the present."

A few minutes later, Roberto' and Franco entered the kitchen from the cellular with a bottle of White Cabernet Wine for dinner. Simone' noticed the size of her husband and Father. They were both 6'4" and 6'5" inches tall, masculine, fit, and slim due to the nature of their work, thought, "Mother is right, Vincenzo' would get hurt and that would be more trouble to contend with and Roberto' would know, then it would be beyond my control." Simone' went over to Roberto' slipped her arms around his waist looked up at him smiled; he leaned forward she kissed him adoringly on the mouth. He picked her up off the floor and held her near his face, hugged her tight, and whispered, "I love you Simone' please don't keep me shut out of the deepest parts of your heart and your needs."

She whispered softly so her parents would not hear, "I love you Roberto', please know this."

He whispered back, "I want to know all of your love. I plan for us to go our honeymoon cottage after dinner would you like that?"

Smiling she whispered, "Yes my husband, I want desperately for us to be alone tonight. I just want to love you and be near you without my parents being in the same house with us."

He replied, "Yes, my lovely I feel the same way." He put her gently down she hugged him, took his hand, and walked to the table where dinner was waiting. Catarina smiled at them asked after they sit, "Everything okay, my children?"

Roberto replied, "Yes," I called Amelio's caretaker earlier when I called back to America and told him that we would be coming to the cottage later after dinner. He had his wife stock the kitchen with the list of foods I gave him and made everything ready for us. We will stay for a few days."

"That is a wonderful idea my son, please take my car and stay as long as you want enjoy yourself my children", said Franco.

"Grazie, Franco" said Roberto'.

Late Tuesday evening, in Tuscany after dinner, Simone' and Roberto' left for the cottage planned to spend six days together before Roberto' returned to America.

As the hour begin to be late, Tuesday night at the cottage Roberto' sit up on the side of the bed, pulling the sheet across his naked body. Pushing back the beautiful black lock of hair that danced on his forehead could not endure the thoughts that vexed his mind and soul, not knowing what his wife was hiding walked toward the window and the suitcases.

Opening the side-pocket of his suitcase pulled out the Diary he found on their bedroom floor. Simone' sitting in their bed where he left her, observed her husband, turned, and walked back toward the bed. As he approached the bed, she recognized her Diary in his hand her pulse begin to race her heart felt as if it would jump out of her chest. There was no mistaking the look of her Diary.

She asked as calm as possible, "What do you have my husband?"

"I found this on the floor at our home while packing, my beauty. I never knew you kept a Diary. You hid this fact from me as you do your deepest desires, why Simone'? Pausing then continuing, "There are just too many questions in the last ten days. I do not seem to be able to get an answer to; you keep telling me you cannot answer my questions. If you can't Simone' then who can? Does this Diary contain the answers I need?"

He gently laid the Diary on the bed waiting for an answer. "It is locked Simone', I chose not to read your private thoughts; I could not or would not violate your privacy by opening your personal Diary; in the same light, I need answers to my questions. What are you hiding Simone', what?"

She picked up the Diary as if to keep it safe from his eyes knowing that if he wanted to he could easily break the lock and read what she had written between these pages since she was 13 years of age, but particularly the last years they were married. There would be no way that she could prevent the ensuing calamity that would follow. Roberto' saw the tears form in her eyes as she gripped the Diary near her chest to protect it from his eyes, sank back in her pillow with a look of fear dancing in her expressions. Voice trembling, she said barely above a whisper, "Please Roberto' I cannot allow you to read what I have written, please my husband don't ask me anymore questions I cannot answer your questions."

Roberto' felt his heart sinking as he did when he found the note from Simone' last Thursday night. He sit on the side of the bed and looked at Simone' with tears streaming down her face, "I would rather you tell me Simone' or at least agree for me to read your private thoughts. I would never force my way into your Diary."

Simone' did not respond just sat with the Diary still pressed against her chest; she sat still as the atmosphere in the eye of a hurricane; it is the outer winds that are mostly destructive in a hurricane as it would be if Simone' allowed him to read her Diary without explaining first.

"Simone' I want answers to my questions before I leave for America. When I commented, I would be leaving in ten days you did not say that you would be returning with me. Are you planning to return to America with me? You don't need to answer my question tonight but I need an answer in a few days."

Roberto' was past being angry: for that time, he felt exasperation, upset, annoyed, and betrayed by his wife. The pain of that dagger that cuts deep into his heart was rawer than ever. He lay down beside his wife and pulled her close his mind racing with questions and doubt danced on a horizon of pain before him. She lay beside him as a frighten child clinging to him with tears dripping from her chin on his chest, after a while they both drifted into a restful sleep.

Challenges awaited the Bandaci's on both sides of the Atlantic.

CHAPTER
TWENTY-FIVE

Early Wednesday morning, November 20, in Tuscany, at Amelio's Cottage, Roberto' awakens as he did each day 6:00 a.m. turned and observed his wife still sleeping, leaned over, kissed her, and whispered, "Good morning my beauty, did you sleep well?"

"Yes my husband, how was your night?'

"It was restful my love."

"It is time for breakfast my lovely, after we have breakfast, coffee, our morning talk, and prayer, I want to enjoy being back on the farm."

"That is a good idea my husband. I will get dressed and get breakfast started."

Roberto' desired to spend some time in solitude thinking, decided to take a walk around the farm to clear his mind. A deluge of feeling flooded his mind thought of the years of secrecy from his wife. He had a desperate need to know all of her emotionally, physically and in total intimacy with no inhibitions loomed large in his mind, had not held any emotions from his wife, but had been totally open and honest about his needs; only God and she knew the Roberto' that lived in his soul. He felt cheated, betrayed giving him a feeling of being behind a locked door leaving him powerless with no key to open it. Locked like the Diary his wife kept hid, like she did her deepest desires; she held the keys and the power to unlock both the Diary and her deepest hidden passions.

An hour later, 9:00 a.m. Roberto' left for his ceremonial walk around the farm and spend time in solitude thinking.

Wednesday morning, November 20, in Charleston, two days after her Father left for Italy, Carmeli'ta' dressed in preparation for the business marriage between Madison Steel and Meriwether Textiles. She chose for upshots to the outcome, a classic black business suite with flesh-tone stocking, black sling back heels, and her beige pearls earrings, pondered her Father and mother's strange behavior, he left Monday had reached Tuscany; however, she was still puzzled by her parent's behavior. On the drive to the plant reminisced about the romantic evening she spent with Jason even though her desire was to be with her parents to know what was behind her mother abruptly leaving Charleston and a few days later her Father followed. When he called her, the vagueness of his explanation left Carmeli'ta' with an eerie feeling causing a nauseous feeling in the pit of her stomach when she thought of it. Her mother and Father, before her eyes, had always been a loving and kind example to her never once any hint of unhappiness. Oh, she heard her parents discuss and disagree on different points of view, but never saw any outright anger between them. Carmeli'ta' looked at her watch it was 2:00 p.m. in Tuscany, wondered what was happening with her father and mother.

Carmeli'ta' pulled into her parking space at 8:30 a.m. a little earlier than her usual 9:00 a.m. workday for the meeting schedule at 10:00 a.m. in the Board Room. She parked next to Jason, who as usual, was already at work. She exited the car and entered through the door for the plant administration and other plant supervisory staff. Smiling when she reached Ms. Horne's desk said, "Good morning Ms. Horne, how are you today? Good weekend I hope."

Yes, Ms. Bandaci, It was a good weekend!"

"How was yours?"

"It was pleasant and relaxing, thank you."

She turned the conversation to the matter at hand, "The Boardroom set

up Ms. Horne for the meeting?"

"Yes, Ms. Bandaci, all is prepared and the agendas are in place for all the attendees as you instructed and the name plates placed as instructed. Mr. Madison is there now helping the plant manager supervisor finalize the details."

"The refreshments and the lunch Ms. Horne are all prepared as instructed?"

"Yes, Ms. Bandaci...the coffee, juice, Danish, and Fruit are there now with water. Andrea will deliver and set up lunch in the break room to be served lunch at 12:10 p.m. as instructed." Carmeli'ta' smiling,

"Thank you Ms. Horne, please make sure the ice-tea is served in chilled glasses."

Ms. Horne nodded and reassuring obviously nervous Carmeli'ta', "Yes, as instructed Ms. Bandaci."

"This meeting is very important to the success of what we are trying to do for this community. We have finally courted Charles Bienville Meriwether into meeting and discussing a partnership and business venture with Madison Steel now we need to get him to the alter."

"I completely understand Ms. Bandaci. I know the Meriwether family. He is very particular about etiquette and decorum."

"Thank you Ms. Horne. Please let Mr. Madison knows I am here and if he needs to meet prior to the meeting, I will be in my office."

"Yes, Ms. Bandaci."

Carmeli'ta' walked swiftly to her office. It was 8:30 a.m., this would not give her hardly any time to do her final mental preparations to meet Charles Bienville Meriwether and the difficult businessman he is with a 'in charge' Boardroom mentality wanted to be at her sharpest today with all of her wits about her. Carmeli'ta' sits at her desk to collect her thoughts. She would need them over the next hour, glanced over the agenda and read her notes she took during the meeting the Madison group had last Friday concerning the path they wanted the meeting to take to get the results desired.

A light tap on the door bought her thoughts back to the present, "Come in." The door opened and Carmeli'ta' knew for sure it was Jason. She waited in excited anticipation. The door opened slowly. Carmeli'ta' hastily glanced at the clock on the wall it was 9:00 a.m. It was early for the meeting Jason and she would have time to chat for a moment after the morning greetings. Carmeli'ta' rose from her chair, the door opened to full view. To her surprise, it was not Jason. A slightly familiar voice said, "Good morning Ms. Bandaci, how are you?" Startled for a moment then hurriedly gathering her composure walked to the center of the office smiled, extending her hand, "Good Morning, this is an unexpected pleasure, I am happy to see you."

"Yes, Ms. Bandaci" said Charles Meriwether, approaching with the swagger he is known for as he entered a room. He took her hand, kissed the back of it as the Gentleman in him does, for select Ladies he met. He asked Ms. Horne not to announce him wanted to announce himself. In his sagaciously shrewd mind, he first, wanted to see Carmeli'ta'in a natural office setting in her position as Madison Steel's Office Manager, instead of Hostess. Secondly, he wanted to observe her reaction to his unannounced visit to her office said, "Ms. Horne offered to escort me to your office and announce my presence, but I don't feel like a visitor, anywhere I go. Please place the blame on me and not your gracious, elegantly polished, and efficient assistant." Continuing "I must say I envy Madison for his office multi-talented hostess and manager in her dual roles that she performs both to the highest level of efficiency; however, Ms. Bandaci, I will speak with you later about my plans for that role." To what he was referring, escaped her completely! It was too sensitive a time to ask. She did not want to provoke any refusal to do business with Madison Steel.

He added, in addition, "I came early ahead of my people selected to meet today Ms. Bandaci to go over the Agenda so I would have it in my head and to bring the details to the proposal items we are to discuss to be placed on the table so we can begin and end in a timely manner. My team should be here by 9:30 a.m. I have given Ms. Horne the proposal details we spoke of in our conversation earlier in the month as an addition to the items already there. She also tells me that as a gracious hostess you have Coffee, juice, Danish, and Fruit in the breakroom, could I interest you in joining me for a cup of coffee?"

He smiled, his eyes dancing, his demeanor bathed in charm. Carmeli'ta' smiled and said, "It will be my pleasure Mr. Meriwether." In a softer tone he said, "Please call me Charles; may I call you Carmeli'ta'?"

Startled again she said, "By all means, please do call me, Carmeli'ta'.

If you will excuse me, I need to instruct Ms. Horne, give me a moment." Graciously with a half-bow, "Of course take your time."

Carmeli'ta' smiled at Charles Meriwether picking up the phone buzzed Ms. Horne, "Yes Ms. Bandaci." She said, Ms. Horne, Mr. Meriwether gave you the proposals addendums for the meeting would you place them please. I am on my way to the breakroom with Mr. Meriwether."

Ms. Horne with concern in her voice said, "Mr. Madison and the Plant Foreman are in the breakroom Ms. Bandaci; should I will tell him so they can leave?"

Carmeli'ta' grateful for Ms. Horne's alertness said in a cool manner, "Please do, thank you Ms. Horne that is a wise idea. Are you ready Charles?" asked Carmeli'ta'.

"Yes, Madam Hostess, please lead on." He turned and opened the office door, Carmeli'ta' walked pass him into the hallway, her Chanel 5 left a romantic aura heightening his fervor and yearning for her in his life; he envisioned a refreshing and renewing of love could be his with her. Carmeli'ta' looked lovely, tempting; the scent she wore called his needs to the surface; he resisted saying anything about her loveliness because of the business venture. He was cunning as ever in mind.

Ms. Horne walked swiftly to the breakroom and said, "Mr. Madison, please excuse the interruption."

"Yes, Ms. Horne, does Ms. Bandaci need to see me?"

"No, Sir. Mr. Meriwether is with Ms. Bandaci and they are on their way here now Sir."

"Thank you Ms. Horne, I will go into my office."

Jason Madison taken aback by his early arrival felt that this was a sneak attack. His Father warned him how devious and cunning he was he asked, "Ms. Horne did Ms. Bandaci know he was coming early?"

"No sir! He asked me not to tell her; he would announce himself. I did not want to argue with him Mr. Madison; I know how hard it has been to bring about this meeting."

Jason smiled, "Very wise move Ms. Horne, thank you. That is just another reason why I am glad that Ms. Bandaci chose you as my Assistant."

Ms. Horne smiled, "Thank you Mr. Madison, I appreciate the compliment." Jason Madison and the Plant Foreman exited through a side door leading into his office.

Carmeli'ta' walked slowly chatting with Charles Meriwether, giving Jason and the Plant Foreman time to exit the room. Ms. Horne cleared the used cups and plates into the return bus for dishes near the sink.

She was coming out of the breakroom when Charles Meriwether and Carmeli'ta' arrived, "I checked the coffee Ms. Bandaci it is hot and I refreshed the Danish tray."

Carmeli'ta' winked at Ms. Horne, smiled in an "I understand" signal, and said, "Thank you Ms. Horne you are always on top of it."

She smiled, passed them said, "Thank you Ms. Bandaci."

Carmeli'ta' walked over to the refreshments table, "May I get you a cup of coffee and a Danish Charles?"

"Yes, please, I am a little famished. I did not have breakfast."

She poured the coffee and said, "Straight, cream, or sugar Charles?"

"Straight please, I like for my coffee to stand up without any help." Carmeli'ta' put an Apple Danish on a crystal dish and handed it to him.

"Thank you Carmeli'ta'. I understand that Andrea' is catering lunch today."

"Yes he is."

"Andrea's is one of your father's customers is he not?"

"Yes, he is Charles."

He smiled, "Excellent and tastefully done Carmeli'ta'. Andrea' is always a favorite of mine his vegetables are the best and always fresh. You have excellent taste in food as well as business. I appreciate the association and alliance forming between the two major players in the Charleston business world."

In the parallel of time in Tuscany, Roberto' returned after many hours of meditation, it was 2:00 p.m. time for afternoon tea and his Simone' was waiting.

Simone' sitting on the bench under the Rose Trellis watching for Roberto' finally saw him coming through the garden toward her. Thoughts still swirling in his mind, he felt torn between knowing and not knowing; it was costly either way. He questioned himself, 'If I know what she is hiding would I be able to get pass the hurt and pain I know within myself is there, otherwise, why hide like she has all these years?' On the other hand, if I do not know, would I be able to live with the thoughts and questions as I have, for so long, even before I admitted it to myself?' He knew within there was a possibility it would destroy his heart and soul eventually.

His love for Simone', he feared would not withstand his not knowing; he would rather know than to continue to swallow a bitter pill of deceit and secrecy every day for the rest of their lives. Roberto's thoughts gave him the feeling of being on a tight rope over the gorge that spans Tuscany's *Val di Greve River* that watered their little valley. Just as a fall from the tight rope into the gorge would be certain destruction, not knowing the secrecy that enshrouds his wife would be also is certain destruction to him. He had to choose before he left for America and back to their life there.

Time at the cottage passed quickly.

Simone' had been silent on the subject when he mentioned their leaving in a few days. They had been at the cottage for six days. He would need to leave for America in two days. It would take two days traveling to arrive in South Carolina within the ten days, as he promised Amelio'. He had spent the last six days with his lovely wife. She was as warm as always, but secretive and a look of fear had become part of her eyes. He had let the questions of the Diary drop while they were at the cottage after their first night there, when he gave it to her. Now it is decision time!

Simone' smiled when he walked to where she was sitting and said, "Did you enjoy your walk?" He nodded, sat next to Simone, and held her close, for a long period-of-time.

"Yes, I did. It was pleasant and the farm is still as beautiful as it was when Amelio' and I were younger."

"I have made tea Roberto'. I awaited your return to have our afternoon tea."

As Simone' rose to get the tea, the light of the evening sun reflected the beauty of her face. Moments later she returned with the tea and sit next to Roberto' poured his tea and then hers. She snuggled close to him; he held her close to keep her warm as they sipped their tea and enjoyed the afternoon with hints of winter promised by the cool November breeze.

Roberto' could feel the warmth of her as she snuggled next to him for protection from the brisk breeze holding them captive. They did not want to go inside and miss the beauty of the quiet evening.

Roberto' felt as if he was living on hourglass time; it had been turned and the sands of time was running out. Her not returning to America with her husband could hurt too many people involved. Returning to America without Simone' would be more than he could bear. As turmoil boiled like a pot of oil in his mind, he questioned himself, "How could I leave my heart in Tuscany? What would I tell Carmeli'ta' why her mother did not return with me?"

Roberto' did not realize the pain he thought may be caused by Simone' not returning with him would be minimal to the pain that waited to he revealed in her Diary; that pain would almost destroy his family and as a result of the secret, bring his daughter Carmeli'ta' near death.

He felt like he was living someone else' life standing on the outside looking in. He could not figure out how his life became upside down almost overnight; the sands of time in his hourglass would run out in two days. Knowing that he would leave in two days hung like the threat of a loaded bow with the arrow pointed at his heart and soul.

He placed his teacup on the table near the teapot, stood and walked a few feet from where he and Simone' were sitting turning, looked at his wife sitting so still watching him. His thoughts still racing, "She has a confusing enigmatic personality, hard to understand, mysterious, yet delicate, a discreet seductress with apparent romantic intensity and full of intrigue. He felt trying to understand his wife was identical to swimming in an ocean with unreachable depths. She is feminine, responsive, but has a painfully secretive evasiveness about her that is mystifying. Simone' is like a beautiful summer storm that rains misty love, warm and pleasing giving me a tranquil calm feeling afterward of being bathed in her tenderness. She is gentle and patient, with a malleable nature. I know within myself she does not have a vicious personality; whatever it is she must be trying to protect Carmeli'ta' and me from hurt and pain."

Rationalizing Roberto' knew he had to think from his wife's prospective. Knowing her as he does, there seems to be one wall he had to get over was the wall of fear. The fear trail led to one place, the secrets in her Diary.

"I love my wife, she is suffering, and the look of fear in her eyes is just as painful to me as not knowing the secret holding our lives hostage. How can one small Diary cause so much mystery, fear, anxiety, and distance? We have never been as distant as we are now. I have always felt I could be completely open with my wife, now I feel I need a vanguard on my words and the way I say them or she will run away forever. There is a silence that is unbearable; the atmosphere between us is a rocky slope, it could fall at any moment crushing everyone at the foot."

Leaning against a beautiful Weeping Willow Tree, he cried for the pain he felt for his wife inside, weeping, like the tree he leaned on, watched Simone' looking his way, prayed to God for an answer. He knew the entire truth would be the only solution to every ones' healing. He asked himself "Can I face that truth? Will Simone' survive emotionally from that apparent harsh revelation of the Diary? Would this truth affect Carmeli'ta' and her mother's relationship? Or Carmeli'ta' emotionally?"

Simone' stood and pulled at the grass that grew on the rose trellis, bathing in regret, musing, weighted her actions and the price that came with them considered, "Skeletons in the closet and actions taken in innocence haunt you like ghosts. The massiveness of the Atlantic Ocean could not ensure that my past mistakes would not appear in my life again. The long arm of my past has reached into the present and the future changing the complete course of my family's life. I feel like a storm has come ashore, is standing over our life, and will not move. Memories of the past are like treasures that you keep close to your heart or they can be like a beast that devours you; the only recourse you can think of is to run to escape the jaws of its revelation. These memories are a beast in my mind; they have been gobbling my life one day at a time for almost twenty-four years. Now, I have come full circle back where it started." Simone', was so engrossed in thought she sit again on the bench beneath the rose trellis continued, "Fear has a taste, a horrible metallic taste. It chokes, giving you the feeling of having your breath cut-off or the wind knocked out of you when you are hit with a strong blow to the chest."

She recognized one's actions in life always have consequences whether they are positive or negative. The consequences to her actions were the taste in her mouth of her past decisions, like metal, was so nauseating. That metallic taste had begun to change the taste of her entire life. Fear's steel related strength, unbendable, unrelenting, unforgiving, destroys as those feeling grows stronger possessing you, eventually conquer and enslaves you, building bars in your mind and heart hard to cut through to free yourself. We cannot bury our past within us; eventually, emotional distress like acid will eat at your conscious, effects your heart, mind, and the very soul of that person.

She continued not seeing Roberto' intensely watching her, "Fear leaves

you naked and open to the elements. I wore my gowns at night as a protection to keep my fears hid; not for the reasons my husband thinks that I do not love or desire him. He is the most desirable man, the only man I want. In retrospect, Vincenzo' was like a waterfall that cools and bath the body on a hot day, but is only temporal, not lasting."

Simone' chiding herself for the poor decisions she made in this one instance only. She contrasted the two in her thoughts, "How can one person be on point in all other areas of their life with all other decisions they make; then on the other hand, and in just one area if their lives so far off point. This one decision have almost destroyed my husband, maybe my daughter, once she finds out, and hurt my parents. Though they did not say it, they were hurt, nonetheless. I know my parents and the pride they have in me their only child."

Simone' thought, "Love is like a river that starts with a head water of a few drops from leaves; the more it drips the larger the pool of water becomes, and continues to flow more until the pool, becomes a large stream, the stream becomes a river. Eventually, the river flooding over its banks cutting a path and becomes part of an ocean massive and strong. My love for Roberto' grew in this manner and has become an ocean dominant and strong. Taking my love, for my husband, from my heart and mind is as impossible as it is to drain an ocean of all the water. My love for him invades me as the headwaters that ultimately flow into an ocean. It started with respect, admiration, care, and concern. These emotions were along the riverbank in my life. They grew each day over the years into a powerful force even though I cannot always navigate. I love to talk with him, walk with him, eat candlelight dinners on our date night, watch the sun rise or set, and walking over our farm looking at the vegetables grow; just simple things in life makes my husband the most exciting man alive to me. Over the years, we sat all night long talking about nothing laughing and enjoying each other's presence."

She continues, "Love, is simple and complicated, at the same moments in time. This complexity and simplicity is what makes it so beautiful and fulfilling. We had our trouble times as any marriage would; but, never to the point where there was a moment we did not love and care for each other. Alternatively, our marriage had growing pains as any marriage would the challenge of raising an only child, a girl, in this day and time, in a bi-cultural way, and living between two worlds, American and Italian. Roberto' is my life, my hope, and my security. These three things we all needs in life and they all spell Love. It is like operating within a small paradigm on a continuum of never-ending need for the same person as humans need food for health, strength, and life. No one can survive for long periods-of-time without food. I would not be alive without my Roberto'; he is like my food for life. Existing is not living; it is a state of being with no substance. This would be the state of my being without him. My mouth and my heart tell my husband of my deep love for him, but my body does not say the same. Fear is dreadful and unforgiving; reigning over lives and it has become my prison. How can I get past this awful state of terror I built for myself for the last twenty-four years?"

Looking at his wife, questions tore at his mind as the sands of his hourglass of time continue to tick away the minutes! The situation was nebulous at best.

Tenderness and intimate actions connects love. Roberto's love for Simone' produced in him the determination to overcome whatever the underlying problems causing the trouble on the surface of their lives. The trouble, like cream, was rising to the top. Roberto's thoughts were paradoxical in nature, but he realized his wife's need for his understanding and help. How could he reconcile this situation with both sides of the truth? It would not be easy. He would need to put his needs and desires aside for a while, and try to attend to the needs of his family even at the delay of him learning the truth. Pain and discouragement would become second to the needs of his family.

He walked back to where Simone' was sitting, seeing tears in her eyes he pulled her to him, cuddling her in his arms lifting her sitting on the bench with her in his lap kissed her tenderly whispering softly in her ear, "I love you Simone'!" She hugged him tight snuggling in the safety of his arms said, "I love and adore you Roberto'; I never want to do anything to hurt you or Carmeli'ta'. You are my safe place to shelter me from any storm."

"Thank you for that my beauty, I have tried to be everything to you and for you as God wants a man to be for his family."

The most confusing in life are those things we cannot see. As prolific as Roberto' was in all of his dealings with his life and business, this one area he could not grasp. The pain and hurt that invaded his being would prevent this solution from being easy to achieve. There was no mathematical formula to arrive at a solution as he does in his business. He knew love is a state of being lived in whisperings and moments in time.

In Charleston, the meeting time drew near.

After chatting for a while, Charles Meriwether looked at his pocket watch and said, "It is 9:40 a.m. Carmeli'ta'. My people are probably here and waiting; If they could have coffee that would be good."

She graciously said, "Of course, please." Opened the door and asked Ms. Horne to show Mr. Meriwether's team to the break room and make them comfortable. Three members of Meriwether Textiles team were attending the meeting, the office manager, plant manager, and his accountant and finance manager, all sharp as a switchblade knife and just as cunning and deadly, in reference to business deals, as their boss Charles Meriwether.

Charles Meriwether said, "I will take a look at the boardroom if you don't mind and get prepared for the meeting. I believe I can find it. I saw the sign as I passed on my way to your office earlier, is that where you are holding the meeting?"

Carmeli'ta' nodded, "Yes it is. I will see you in twenty-minutes Charles."

"Thank you." He bowed graciously and walked past Carmeli'ta' and his staff standing in the breakroom having coffee and Danish.

Carmeli'ta' tapped lightly at the door of Jason's office and went in, greeted them, "Good morning, Mr. Madison and Mr. Brown, how are you both today". He and the plant manager were discussing last-minute details of the meeting. Jason smiled as Carmeli'ta walked toward the center of the room saying,

"Good morning Ms. Bandaci. How are you today?"

"I am well Mr. Madison, thank you." Peter Brown said, "Good morning Ms. Bandaci. It is always a pleasure to see you. I will excuse myself and go to my office to get my notes and let the Finance Director, Mr. Chasings know we are almost ready as he requested. I will see you both in twenty minutes."

Jason replied, "Thank you Peter." Carmeli'ta' smiled with a half nod before he left the office.

Jason walked over to Carmeli'ta smiled hugged and kissed her snuggling her in his chest for a few moments moved behind his desk and said, "Ms. Horne informed me Charles Meriwether arrived early without notice to the plant and came to your office unannounced."

"Yes he did. I was surprised to see him entering my office after the knock on my door. He is astutely devious Jason and bears watching in this meeting. I suspect he wanted to catch me off guard and see what my reactions to an unannounced visit from him would be."

"You are right my lovely that is exactly what it was I am sure of it. Mrs. Horne and you handled the situation in a professional manner. You are both an asset to this company and to me. He was apparently pleased with the overall reaction. My father tells me that he has been known to do exactly what he did this morning arrive unannounced and if the reaction were not in a professional manner, of the intended business partner, he would leave and not enter a contract with that company, devious and astute is a good description of his character when it relates to business."

"He wanted me to be aware he knew Andrea'is one of my father's customers."

"Just another point of reference to his astuteness and awareness which bears watching but then, so is Rochelle's is she not my lovely Carmeli'ta'?

Jason commented.

Carmeli'ta' smiled replying, "Yes she is a good customer of my fathers, my love; awareness is a powerful tool. I get the point that you are making, I think you are right Jason my darling shall we go to the Boardroom it is 9:50 a.m."

"Definitely we should be there my lovely Carmeli'ta', well before the meeting begins."

Carmeli'ta' noticed the Meriwether staff still in the breakroom and he had joined in a huddle with his Plant Manager, Office Manager, and Finance Manager for the last-minute preparations for the meeting. Jason and Carmeli'ta' walked down the hall and entered the Boardroom. Ms. Horne was there placing a tablet and pens on the table in front of the chair assigned by Carmeli'ta'. She sat on one end of the long Boardroom table and Jason sat at the head of the table at the other end, as Chairman and CEO of Madison Steel. Carmeli'ta' smiled at her and commented with a question to her tone, "Everything looks good as usual Ms. Horne. We are ready then?"

"We are ready Ms. Bandaci."

Jason did not say anything this was Carmeli'ta' area and one of her many duties as office manager; in addition, he knew everything would be in place and efficiently done under Carmeli'ta' supervision.

A few seconds later in walked Charles Meriwether and his team and behind them was Peter Brown and Mr. Chasings.

Jason walked over to Charles Meriwether and extended his hand "Mr. Meriwether, I am looking forward to creating an alliance with your company that will benefit the overall community."

"Thank you Madison, it will be, I believe, beneficial for all concerned including our companies. I want to introduce you and Ms. Bandaci to my Office Manager, John Overstreet, Plant Manager, Winston Dante' and Finance Director, Alexis Handover. They have been with my company for 90 years combined." Charles Meriwether wanted to highlight the strength and efficiency of his team; he ignored his comment, did not allow him to shake him, but remained the gracious host and commander in Chief of Madison Steel and Iron.

The introductions done; everyone sit according to the name placements on the table. Charles Meriwether sat to Jason's left and near the middle of the table where he could see everyone comfortably. Jason wondered before the meeting started why Charles Meriwether wanted him to know the combined years of employment of his top managers wondered if he meant it as a threat.

Carmeli'ta' started the meeting according to the items on the agenda. While she was speaking Jason noticed that Charles Meriwether had the same look on his face watching her he had the night of the Madison Thanksgiving Ball, he felt a surge of anger and jealousy.

Carmeli'ta' noticed the look on Jason's face as he watched Meriwether said, "Mr. Madison will explain the overall plan of the job creation in the community", smiling at Jason. He was thankful for her pulling his thoughts back to the meeting and not on watching Meriwether looking at her. As he begins with the job creation explanation, the attendees relaxed and took notes. He explained the extensiveness of the job creation and the role each company would play.

While Carmeli'ta' and the Madison Steel and Meriwether staff we're having lunch, dinnertime approached in Tuscany for the second time honeymooners.

The meeting for the two powers in Charleston continued until 12:00 Noon. Ms. Horne excused herself and checked to see if Andrea' needed assistance. Lunch was set-up and smelled delicious. The aroma drifted into the Boardroom when Ms. Horne opened the door to the hallway. Carmeli'ta' ordered Tossed Salad w/Oil and Vinegar Dressing, Filet Mignon with Au jus, garnished with Asparagus, Roasted Potatoes with Garlic, Fresh Field Peas with Snaps, Parsley Cornbread Muffins, and Iced Tea and for dessert one of Andrea's specialties, Deep Dish Peach, and Apple Pie with coffee.

The aroma whetted the appetites of everyone in the Boardroom. Ms. Horne returned and walked over to Carmeli'ta' "Ms. Bandaci lunch is ready to be served when Mr. Madison is ready." She went to Jason standing talking with Meriwether Office Manager, John Overstreet touched the left sleeve of his suit coat and said, "Excuse me Mr. Madison, lunch is ready."

"Thank you Ms. Bandaci." Jason walked back to the head of the table and said, "May I have everyone's attention please. We have lunch in the breakroom; please bow with me to give thanks for the food." After Jason's prayer they assembled in the breakroom and were seated; Andrea' and his staff served lunch.

Charles Meriwether noticed it was a white glove and jacket luncheon with Crystal plates and silverware; there were two large round tables well-dressed seating five at one table and six at the other. He noticed as the plates were served Andrea' in his usual manner directed the waiters. The food on every plate was a work of art.

Carmeli'ta's choice of lunch and service, further impressed him, he did not expect a white glove affair to kick off their meeting, done with such elegance and style and she had all of the favorite foods he loved served by Andrea' as if was a special occasion. After lunch, the meeting reconvened the five items on the agenda were completed and the process of the contract creation was set.

In Tuscany at the time lunch was over for the Madison Steel and Meriwether Textile it was dinner preparation time for Roberto' and Simone'.

Roberto', after a time, carried her inside standing her up in the middle of the kitchen, smiled and said, "Time to prepare dinner my lovely." They prepared Pasta with Habanero sauce with Grilled Chicken, grilled veggies, and fresh bread from the Boulangerie Veinnoise, with White Cabernet Wine to complement their entrée.

The Alliance, November 20, 1927

At 4:00 p.m., the meeting ended with the beginning of a successful alliance between the two powers in Charleston.

Charles Meriwether said, "Thank you everyone was attending and making this a successful meeting. I believe that we are on our way to a good marriage between our companies and overall community improvement with the job creations that will come from the initiatives with forming the alliance. Ms. Bandaci, Mr. Madison, Ms. Horne, thank you for the wonderful job today in getting the meeting set. The breakfast was wonderful, the lunch was delicious; Andrea's does an excellent job in preparing Filet Mignon."

Charles Meriwether with his finger together bought them to his lips and in a motion as he was throwing a kiss said, "Um magnifique."

Jason said, "Thank you Mr. Meriwether. I too think this a successful marriage alliance between our companies. I am glad that you enjoyed the breakfast and lunch. The credit for the lunch goes to Ms. Bandaci and Ms. Horne. I believe everyone loves Andrea's Filet Mignon." He turned looking at the table where members of both teams were still sitting said, "Thank each of you for your valuable input today."

Though the day ended in success for Carmeli'ta' and Madison Steel, turmoil, like a beast, loomed large in Tuscany.

CHAPTER
TWENTY-SIX

In Tuscany the same day, after dinner, Roberto' took Simone for a long walk holding her hand they quietly walked through the beautiful fields and around the lake. He did not say anything just walked with her. It was late when they returned to the cottage, sit in the garden, and watched the sun gleam its last ray before it disappeared behind the horizon, went in, and prepared for bed. Roberto readied bath water as usual. Simone' bath water was warm stimulating; he sit on the side of the tub washed and massaged her back and neck. He could feel the tightness of the muscles gently caressed her neck and back, she began to relax regaining her composure.

After a while, he stood held her towel, she stepped into it and snuggled herself dry, lotion her body and begin brushing her hair. Robert did not leave the bathroom, but watched Simone while she combed and brushed her hair as she did each night before retiring. He tenderly took the brush from her hand and slowly brushed her hair. The tresses, like a black sea, flowed down her back, the smell of lavender hovered in the atmosphere from her hair with each stroke. She stood deathly still looking at him in the mirror with no comment.

After a few minutes, he laid the brush down not moving and continued to look at his wife. Simone' wondered what he was thinking as he watched her. She did not want to ask for fear of the subject of the Diary surfacing again.

Roberto' saw his wife watching him and smiled moving closer, putting both hands on her shoulders turned her around and hugged her tightly. She snuggled close to him; he smelled so fresh and felt so strong, then moved away from him took off her robe and reached for a short black negligée. Roberto' stopped her saying, "No my lovely wife, no gown, I don't want anything between us tonight while we sleep." Simone feeling nervous, followed his lead to their bed. Removing his robe, got into bed, and held out his hand for Simone' to join him. She took his hand slipping in beside him, moved into his open arms, he held her tight for a long while finally said, "Simone I want to give you intimacy tonight; I want to hold you and comfort you. I want to make love to you, but it is more important that I hold you. I want you to know you are important to me also. I have no expectations of you tonight my darling. I just want to comfort you and be near you. I want more than your body my love, you are important to me in every way."

Simone did not comment, but snuggled in his arms, he could feel her delicate warm breath flowing from her nostrils onto his chest, caressed and held her to him. Though his need for her pressed his body, did not give in to the need to make love to her. "She seems so fragile to me tonight", he thought. "I want her to know she has my heart and all my love."

Simone felt her husband's body respond to their closeness; she kissed him tenderly. He felt lustfully feverish and warm at her touch and closeness said, "No Simone' let me hold you my beauty." They finally drifted into a beautiful and peaceful sleep.

Later that evening, unable to sleep, Roberto' could not fight the yearning for intimacy with his wife, sat up turned, admiring her beauty while she slept. He touched her cheek, felt the velvety smoothness of her body, saw the frame her hair made around her face, her long full black eyelashes curving upward, exquisite keen nose, heart shaped lips that appeared to have lipstick on them at all times, smiled with thoughts of the pleasure of her, kissed her mocha-colored cheeks. Simone' sighed. Roberto' tenderly kissed her lips, her chin, her eyes one at a time, pulled her into his arms and said, "Simone' my beauty."

She opened her eyes, smiled and just above a whisper answered, "Yes, my husband I am awake."

"I want to love you my beauty, I wanted to give you intimacy earlier, I cannot fight my desire for you any longer my beauty, please love me."

"Yes, my husband, I want to love you and let you know how much I love and adore you; I want you to know how much I need you and desire you. Your love gives me everything I need and fulfill my desires, and you are a wonderful lover. I needed you to love me before we slept my husband. I am pleased that you awaken me."

Roberto' longed for this moment while he walked and mused about their lives earlier, through dinner, and then on their walk after dinner, could not resist any longer, pulled her to him, his lips found hers.

Simone' recognized his burning desire and the distress his body felt, moved closer. Her every move said yes to him. He gently, slowly, with precision made love to his beautiful wife, his body made a desperate plea to be closer and completely one with hers. Later, Roberto' held her and said, "Simone', Simone', I love you."

She heard the pain in his voice when it broke while calling her name replied, "I know my husband. I love you, thank you for tonight, I feel like I am floating on a cloud my husband."

He held her tight to his chest, did not comment, and finally slept. The love that his wife shared with him relieved the pressure and distress his body felt earlier.

Wednesday evening, in Charleston, the same day, a long day of meetings ended in success.

The meeting ended when Carmeli'ta' walked Charles Meriwether to the door and said goodbye to he and his staff. He bowed in a Gentlemanly way kissed her hand and left the plant. Carmeli'ta' returned to Jason's office, walked past Ms. Horne's desk said, "You were outstanding today Ms. Horne thank you."

"Thank you Ms. Bandaci, I appreciate your support."

Jason was waiting for Carmeli'ta' in his office, she knocked and walked in and closed the door, he came quickly to her, lifted her off the floor, swirled her around, smiled and let her down slowly, kissed her commenting, "You are a gem my darling. I love you. How did you know those were all Charles Meriwether's favorite dishes?"

"I learned from you Jason. I had Ms. Horne call Andrea' and ask him. He like Rochelle' will not say anything; he values his customers and is a confidant for them and attentive to their needs; he is discreet and helpful. Plus, Jason, I know Andrea'. I rode with my father on his deliveries sometimes. Andrea' was kind me to. He always had a treat for me each time I went with my father."

Jason smiled and kissed Carmeli'ta' again, "I am learning more about you each day my sweetheart; building relationships overtime is very beneficial, the interest gained like money does will pay off in the end. You are perceptive and wise my darling, thank you. You are an asset to me and to this company, as I expressed to you before."

"Thank you Jason. I am ready to go home and relax for a while. I do not need any dinner since we had such a heavy lunch. I think I will have fruit and rest tonight."

"You are right my darling it time for you to leave and relax. I will miss you tonight my darling."

"Thank you Jason, I will miss you too. Bye. Will you ring me before you retire for the night?"

"Yes, I will my darling. He kissed her, opened the office door, and said in Ms. Horne's hearing, good night ladies wonderful job today."

Carmeli'ta' walked back to her office as she passed the Boardroom door noticed it was neat and organized. Ms. Horne had cleared the table and placed all the chairs neatly. She picked up her purse and walked back to Ms. Horne's desk, who was pulling her purse out of the draw ready to go home for the day Carmeli'ta' said, "I will walk out with you Ms. Horne." They left the building and the parking lot. Jason sat for a moment at his desk thinking of the day's activities and success of the contract alliance. His father and mother would be pleased. He left the plant and went home to relax.

In Tuscany, time at the cottage had passed quickly.

Simone' had been silent on the subject when he mentioned their leaving in a few days. They had been at the cottage for six days. He would need to leave for America in two days. It would take two days traveling to arrive in South Carolina within the ten days on December 1, as he promised Amelio'. He had spent the last six days with his lovely wife. She was as warm as always, but secretive and a look of fear had become part of her eyes. He had let the questions of the Diary drop while they were at the cottage after their first night there when he gave it to her.

Now it is decision time.

The following day, Tuesday, November 28, they would return to her parent's home. His time to leave for America was fast approaching. He would leave in one day with or without Simone'? Only tomorrow would answer his question.

Six days later, earlier that same Monday evening back in Charleston, Alberto'home for Thanksgiving break, decided to see Carmeli'ta'. She arrived home after a long day on Monday. Tuesday, November 28 would be another long and difficult one with the continuation of the contract formation process between Madison Steel and Meriwether Textiles. Meetings prevailed the entire day. Carmeli'ta' and Jason exhausted, decided to stay home, and relax.

Carmeli'ta' bathed and put on a dressing gown for the evening before retiring for the night. Charles Meriwether, sponsored lunch again, from Andre's, decided to eat a bowl of seasonal fruit and have a cup of hot tea. As she sipped her tea after finishing her bowl of fruit, the phone rang, "Hello."

"Hello, my sweet little friend" said the familiar voice from the other end of the phone.

"Hello Alberto, how are you?"

"I am fine Carmeli'ta' and you?"

"I am fine Alberto'. Are you home for the Thanksgiving break?"

"Yes, I am. I would like us to visit before I return to school. This is my last year of studies at the University. I graduate next May 1928."

"That is so wonderful Alberto'. I am proud of you. I know your parents are. How are they? I have not spoken with them in ever so long!"

"They are fine. My Father said, he had not seen you, but hears that you are doing well."

"Yes, yes, I am busy Alberto'. Tell them I said hello. I will visit soon."

"I will Carmeli'ta'. They love you; you know that."

"Yes, I love them Alberto'."

"Yes, I will tell them you said hello and send love. Can we have lunch soon?"

"Yes, of course Alberto' let me know. I will check my calendar tomorrow. I will check to see if April can join us. I think she is still out oftown visiting a relative. Bye, until tomorrow Alberto."

"Bye Carmeli'ta'. I will await your call."

Alberto' called to see if he felt the same about Carmeli'ta'. Her voice was as enthralling to him as ever; the same pain was in his stomach. He knew he loved her. He would talk with his Father about his feeling for her. Mr. Gambani would speak to Mr. Bandaci about their courting and then marriage. He knew she loved him as a friend, but could she love him as a wife? "She is so tiny and beautiful' he thought, so sweet and kind. 'When we were growing up she always smiled and spoke softly to both April and me. We were close, the three of us and we still are; but my feeling is far beyond friendship for her, they have been for a long time. In this light, I must do this the proper way or her Father will not approve. He is still entrenched in Tuscan tradition, which is a beautiful thing, and so are my parents. These traditions do not help my heart in any way, but I accept that way of life because of my parents. Carmeli'ta' is any man's dream of a wife and companion...beautiful, accomplished, independent, sweet, kind, loving and a strong Christian, like her parents. I will see what happens."

Jason paced back and forth in his wing of the Madison Mansion, felt lonely without Carmeli'ta' could not bear not speaking to her or seeing her any longer picked up the phone and dialed her Townhouse.

"Hello," she said.

"Carmeli'ta' my love; how are you?"

"I am fine Jason, how are you my darling?"

"I miss you Carmeli'ta'."

"I know. I miss you too my sweetheart."

"Thank you Carmeli'ta' for saying that it means more to me than you will ever know."

"I say what is in my heart Jason."

Silence for a while before Jason spoke, "Carmeli'ta'." "Yes, Jason..."

"Carmeli'ta' when will your parents be back home from abroad?"

"They are supposed to return on Friday Jason, at least my Father will. Mother may stay and visit with my grands for a little longer, it is uncertain right now; but Father will definitely be here Friday, why do you ask my love?"

"Carmeli'ta' I want to come over to see you for just a short visit. I will not stay long. I know you are exhausted from the long days of contract negotiations with Meriwether Textiles."

"Yes, of course Jason. I will await your arrival."

"I will be there in ten minutes. See you soon."

"Yes, see you soon."

Carmeli'ta' quickly scanned the room for neatness, went into her dressing room and bath to freshen up, checked her hair, and returned to her living area to want for his arrival, wondering the reason for his unexpected request to come over. Jason arrived ten minutes later, knocked lightly at the door.

Carmeli'ta' walked to the door and said, "Jason."

"Yes, my love it is me."

Opening the door there stood Jason smiling said, "Hello, my lovely Carmeli'ta'."

"Hello Jason. It is good to see you as always."

Closing the door, he took her hands and led her to the sofa and sit. Carmeli'ta' still waiting for the reason he came over. Jason's expression said it was a serious matter whatever it was. He sat forward on the coach looking at the floor, and then stood paced back and forth in front of her. Carmeli'ta' becoming perplexed asked, "Jason what is wrong and what has this visit to do with my parents? Is it something with the farm deliveries, or the service?"

Jason stopped pacing and looked at her with a small, perplexing frown appearing on his forehead "The deliveries or service? Oh, no my love no, nothing of that nature, my parents are completely satisfied with the service your Father provides. He and his cousin Amelio' provides the best service and has the freshest vegetables in the surrounding areas."

"You know my cousin Amelio'?"

"Of course, my sweet, he is an excellent businessperson and I met him at a family dinner at Church a few years after he came to America. I was just starting high school."

Carmeli'ta' amazed at the attention he paid to small things.

"Carmeli'ta' when your Father returns I want to ask him for your hand in marriage. I know that we said we would wait for a while; but can we not allow our families to get use to the idea while we are engaged?"

"I had not thought about that Jason. I know you want to marry me as I do you; yet I had not thought it would be so soon."

"Is it too soon Carmeli'ta'?"

"No, my love that is not what I meant. I had not thought you wanted to announce our engagement this soon."

"Do you have any objections to me speaking with your Father when he returns?"

"No Jason, I don't, my Father however, holds to the tradition of the old country, Fathers choosing for their daughters."

"I know the tradition Carmeli'ta'. It is a beautiful one, but we are in America. I respect that tradition nonetheless; traditions cannot dictate to the heart."

"You are right my love. I think the same way. I do love you Jason and want to be your wife. This will not be easy for my Father to accept."

"And your mother?"

"My mother thinks the heart should choose whom it loves."

"Your parents?"

"My Father loves you already Carmeli'ta'. My mother believes in marrying within status. So, you see we have parents that think alike on both sides of the coin."

"Yes, my love we do. My Father will be difficult in this matter Jason so, expect it. We may have to fight for our love."

Jason remembering Charles Meriwether and the way he looked at lunch earlier that day and the first day of the meeting two weeks ago. He looked at her and said, "I am willing to fight for you Carmeli'ta'. Your love to me is worth any fight I have to make. Before I called you tonight to ask if I could come over, I imagined what my life would be without you in years to come. I felt lonely without you tonight. I knew if I were this lonely without you and we are not married, how much worse it would be if we were never married. I knew immediately, I had to make you mine as soon as I can."

"Thank you Jason that is the highest compliment any woman can receive; I am humbled by your love for me. I love you Jason and I will fight for our love as well. You are worth all of my love and devotion."

"I am blessed to have you in my life Carmeli'ta'. I am happy to have you in both my business life and personal life."

Jason took her hand and walked slowly towards the door, "Carmeli'ta' I am going so you can rest we have another long contract meeting with Meriwether and his people tomorrow," Jason continued, "He is indeed as wily as a fox; nevertheless, we are nearing an end with all the proposal points agreed upon you spoke to him about at the Ball earlier this month. I think it will be a lucrative venture for both companies."

"Yes, my love I agree", she said.

At the door, he leaned over and kissed her on the forehead, "Good night my lovely."

"Good night Jason, be careful on your ride back home. I will see you at 9:00 a.m. tomorrow or earlier. We need to get up early to stay ahead of Charles Bienville Meriwether. He is clever and careful, plays a shotgun game. You never know what he will hit with his stray bullets."

Jason smiled and nodded. She closed and locked the door while he waited. Tapping light to let her know he heard the lock slip into place. Carmeli'ta' went into her bedroom and slipped under her comforter as Jason arrived home to prepare for another day with thoughts of Carmeli'ta' and prayers of thanksgiving to God for her wanting the same things in life as he did, she was his soulmate.

That evening at his mansion on 16 Chateauguay Le'Armant Avenue two streets over from the Madison's home, Charles Meriwether contemplated his strategy to win Carmeli'ta's heart. She was lovelier to him than Juanita Madison is, if this were possible. He had one driving reason why he could not get Juanita Madison out of his mind, just one; he loved her desperately and with a passion that tore at his heart; he could not get her out of his head though he tried for many years.

Charles Meriwether a would-be major player in Carmeli'ta' life because of Vincenzo' Moretti and Jason Madison Sr., though not her age, his revenge would prove to be bittersweet as was Napoleon's. He would meet his Waterloo at the hands of Jason Madison, Jr, who would prove to be a formidable opponent in love as he is in business, but not without a fight.

In Tuscany Valley, Tuesday morning, November 28, arrived early for the second time honeymooners. Roberto' was still pondering the dilemma he faced with his wife., took one more walk after breakfast early Tuesday morning to clear his mind before they returned to Simone's parent's home, Roberto' thoughts were always of his wife. Simone' did not have a stoic mentality, though it seemed that way to Roberto'; but was emotional and grieved because of the pain, even through the years, she never complained or demanded...she deals in logic only...no emotions...dealing with Vincenzo' reduced part of her mentality to an appearance of being apathetic.

Her indifference personality, mysterious and logic defying kept Roberto's interest always on high alert. He was not able to undercover the mystery of her being ... a proclivity for secrets ... a Pandora's Box atmosphere surrounded her. He kept peeling off layers but did not find the answer nor did he pare off enough layers to reach the bottom of the mystery surrounding his lovely Simone'.

Roberto' thought of her as a dual person, one loving kind, sensual...the other unyielding, secretive, silent as stone on certain matters. This complexity surrounding his wife drew him in, as well as kept him at arms-length. The beauty of her loving soul kept him wanting to know more at all times. He would watch his wife in an attempt to unravel the mystery that surrounded her. She wore mystery as a garment with no buttons or zippers...He did not know how to open the tightly sealed envelope of her being that held this mystery, nor did he have the key to open the Diary she kept. Her Diary was a better friend to her than he was; at least, it seemed that way.

She trusted the Diary and not him. "Why could she not share her inner most emotions, thoughts, hurts, pains, and disappointments with me?" His happiness of having Simone' as his wife and the life they made in America had blinded him in respect to his wife's complex dualistic nature. He desperately needed to understand her and come to grips with the direction he needed to take in order to help his family.

Mental labor is more taxing than physical labor. Recovering is hardest when it deals with the mental and emotional aspects of humans.

The dilemma of resolution was before him; which led to cross purposes in his actions ... he wanted to know the secrets so he might help his wife and protect his family all in the same moments of time. Whatever his first actions were would greatly influence the results.

He thought, "Simone' and I spent our last night at the honeymoon cottage where our lives began." Later that morning they packed and returned to her parent's home.

Franco saw the car pull into the driveway, rushed out to greet his daughter. His concern for her was growing knowing the reason she ran away from home opened the car door, "How are you my daughter?"

"I am fine Father; how are you and mother?"

"We are okay. Good morning Roberto'."

"Hello Franco."

"How was your stay my children?"

Roberto' responded, "Enjoyable and reflective Franco. It was good to be back at the cottage where our life started. I am grateful for that time with my wife."

"Mother prepared lunch, she is waiting in the kitchen, and will you join us?"

"Yes, of course Father. It has been a while since we ate. I know my Roberto' is hungry."

"Yes, I am hungry my beauty" said Roberto' "shall we go in?"

Roberto' and Franco took the luggage from the back seat entered the house and walked down the hall to put the luggage in Simone's bedroom suite near the other suitcases that were there. Simone' joined her mother in the kitchen.

Catarina looked at her daughter with a question in her voice said, "Simone'?"

"No Mother, I did not tell him. I could not. He will be leaving on Thursday to travel back to America. He wants me to return with him."

"Have you decided to go home my daughter?"

"No Mother if I do it will worsen the situation; he is insistent on knowing the truth. I can't tell him, I just can't!"

"You will have to tell him sometimes Simone'."

"I know mother. I want to stay with you and Father for a few days longer if you do not mind."

"What are you saying Simone', this is your home. You know your Father will want you to stay and so do I as long as you want to or you think is necessary to sort this situation out."

"Thank you mother I am grateful for your and Father's kindness. I just hope I do not run into Vincenzo' Moretti."

"I wanted to tell you later my daughter; but right now, is a good a time as any; I see your Father and your husband are walking in the garden. Vincenzo' knows you are here. I was at the market last Friday, he saw me, and asked if it was true, you were here. One of his employees saw you walking the first day you got here and told him."

A feeling of horror and dread drenching her being she asked with a shaky tone to her voice, "What did you tell him?"

"I told him the truth my daughter that you were visiting with your husband for a few days and would be returning to America on Thursday. He asked if he could see you. I told him you were with your husband out of the valley and would be gone until your scheduled flight back to America."
"What was his response?"

"He said he understood and thanked me and said to tell you he said hello. I told him I would give you his message when you returned. He seemed to accept the fact that you were here only for a while, however, you can never know what he will do knowing how he feels about you Simone' that is why I wonder if you should stay here. Going home with Roberto' would be the least risky for you. If you stay and Franco finds out he knows you are here, it will be dangerous to Vincenzo'. Your Father is really angry about this situation."

Luggage in place, on the way back to the kitchen Franco asked Robert to look at a new fruit tree he had grafted and give him his opinion of the possibility of success. They walked briefly in the garden. Roberto' looked at the red delicious apple and a green sour apple graft.

"The graft looks good Franco that gives me an idea. Let me know if it is successful and I will try with some of my fruit trees in my yard. Simone' loves apples."

"Your main concern has always been my daughter; I appreciate your care and concern for my only child my son she is a treasure to me."

"I care about and I treasure my wife Franco. She is my life. I don't want to know what life is like without Simone'. It hurts too much to even think about it." He continued, "Tell me Franco', how was Simone' when she arrived here?"

"What do you mean my son?"

"Was she happy, seemed upset, what?"

"She was okay Roberto', not the usual, but okay. I did not want her to know you had called me so mother and I acted in total surprise. She has been quiet since she arrived she seemed tired so we did not press her."

Franco did not want to reveal to Roberto' that he knew some of the reason Simone ran away. He knew he would go after Vincenzo' right then; the situation would be completely out of hand; he did not want to think of the end results of Roberto' knowing about Vincenzo' right at that moment. Time and distance takes care of some issues or at least make them less pronounced. He wanted to protect his fragile daughter in this situation as well as Roberto'. Franco knew Roberto's temperament. He would wait until he left for America before he spoke to Vincenzo' Moretti about his daughter and the situation he created with his obsession with Simone'.

Over the years, Vincenzo' had made his self very unpopular with the farmers and other wine merchants in the valley. Franco now knew why, but that was no excuse for his rudeness or his taking advantage of his daughter when she was younger and worse than threatening and blackmailing her with fear of exposing her secret over the last twenty-four years. Vincenzo' behavior was cruel and ungentlemanly; anger rose in Franco while he walked with Roberto' through his fruit trees commented, "It is time we go in I see mother and Simone' waiting at the table."

Catarina sitting where she could see the fruit trees said, "they are coming Simone'. I did not tell your Father I saw Vincenzo'. So, you know how important the decision you make to go or stay will be."

"Yes, I know Mother it is difficult at best. I feel as if I am in dark woods and cannot see the path for thorns and briars nipping at my entire being causing pain and leaving scars."

Roberto' and Franco entered the patio door in the kitchen, "We apologize for the delay Mother. I wanted to ask our son his opinion of my grafting of the apple trees together."

"What was his opinion my husband" Catarina asked.

"He said they looked good and the graft has taken well. Therefore, we will wait to see. Let's have lunch."

After lunch Roberto and Simone' walked in the garden, Roberto' turned to her, "Simone' have you decided to return home with me on Thursday, November 30? The flight to London leaves at 3:00 p.m. There is a five-hour layover before the flight leaves for America; it arrives in Charleston at noon on Friday. I want us to talk about the secrets you hold. I want you to tell me before we leave Tuscany what you are hiding and why your body does not say to me of your love for me as does your mouth and other actions."

Simone' quietly said, "Roberto' I don't want to talk about it now. I cannot my husband. Again, you are wrong about me not loving you. I do with my entire being. My actions were to protect you and our daughter not hurt you; that is all I can tell you my husband."

"All you can tell me Simone'? Are you returning home with me on Thursday? I need to make reservations for you and confirm mine."

"Roberto' if you don't mind please, I would rather stay for a few more days and visit my parents; it has been a lot of years since I visited them; they are in their late fifties and early sixties now."

Roberto' feeling disappointment and annoyance walked a few feet from his wife before he spoke, "your decision does not please me Simone'. I want you home so we can face whatever these struggles are together. You are clearly struggling and in fear, what are you afraid of?"

"Please Roberto' not now, I have to think this through before I talk with you. I cannot think it through with you near me. I love you so desperately it is a distraction. When you are near me all I want you to do is hold me and love me. I can't explain it now to the point where you will understand; not now."

Feeling angry and disappointed Roberto' replied, "I will let it go for now. My question to you is what are you planning to do about the situation? A better question, when are you planning to share why you are running away from me? You say it is not me; then, what is it if not me? I will accept for now your visiting with your parents a few more days, but this has to come to an end Simone'. It has become a constant disruption in our lives Carmeli'ta's and mine. We are on the outside looking in. In fact, at this point, she does not know you are running away, but she is suspicious that your sudden and immediate decision to visit your parents is strange especially when you have talked with her all her life. You are so close your actions are baffling to our daughter; she will not accept what we are telling her long Simone'. I want our lives back to some form of normalcy."

"Thank you Roberto'. All that you say is true and I will tell you my husband one day soon. Please forgive me. I love you. You and Carmeli'ta' are my whole life here on earth my husband, I am just afraid of losing you my husband."

"I do not understand how you can lose me. You will have to tell me my beauty. I love you Simone' you are the sweet taste in my mouth."

"I know you are angry with me Roberto"

"I am more hurt and confused than angry Simone' mostly because I do not understand your actions over the years especially in our intimate life that pain for me is the worse. It destroys me Simone'. I think you love me so I am not sure. You allow me to get close to your deepest desire like a water faucet you cut me off. I cannot tell you the agony of those moments; it affects me on all levels. It destroys me when you deny me all of your love and passion. You give me your heart and not all of you Simone'. The intensity and passion that you feel so deeply that part of your heart is not mine. I want all of your body and your heart not just parts of you my beauty. My heart breaks a hundred times when I feel that you don't need me the way I need you."

Roberto' saying Simone' you destroy me each time you cut me off and deny me all of your bought tears to her eyes the pressure of the pain she heard in his voice and saw in his eyes the guilt and pain finally broke her. She cried out-loud; uncontrollable tears flowed; she felt weak and faint as she reached for the back of the garden chair and sit to regain her strength and composure. Her husband's words like a flood drowned her with twenty-four years of guilt and pain.

Regaining her poise, Simone' did not respond just walked over to her husband and snuggled close to him holding onto him as if she would never let him go exclaimed, "I love you Roberto'. I love you, adore you, and respect you. All my actions are to protect you and our daughter."

He replied, "We as a family need to work our troubles out together not you taking on the problem by yourself. We have always shared and worked together; this situation should not be different."

She did not respond just held him tighter and moved in closer to him; he closed his eyes and held her tight. Roberto's love was palatial to Simone'. as luxurious and lavish as the life he had provided for her.

Franco and Catarina watched Simone' and Roberto' in their garden and could tell from their appearance the conversation was intense, in depth and they were struggling.

Franco wanted to go to his daughter to protect her from the pain he knew was tearing her apart said, "I must help them Mother."

"No, Franco you cannot let Roberto' know you are aware of even a hint of what the problem is with Simone'. Roberto' would hurt Vincenzo', please let it alone for now let them handle their personal problems. Simone' is staying with us for a few more days and we can talk to her about the situation after Roberto' leaves tomorrow. They need this time together before he leaves. Remember my Franco, he loves Simone'."

"I know Mother and I am thankful for his care and love for our daughter." Love is stronger than pain but sometimes pain can overshadow love....

CHAPTER

TWENTY-SEVEN

Finally, Simone' replied, "Roberto' you have given me everything any husband could in life and asked for nothing in return. Your giving was unconditional; like a heavy burden you carried the responsibility for our family always giving! You are brave, kind, loving, exciting, and the only man I want or love in this world; you possess my heart and soul. There is nothing I would not do for you, including running away to keep you from pain. I love you to a painful depth I cannot explain, please remember this."

"I know that you mean that Simone', yet there is something that is keeping you from me this secret you hold seems to hold you hostage. You have confused me, kept me needing and wanting you as a thirsty man wants water. You excite me; your love takes my breath away."

"You are to me Roberto, a lover, and friend. When you hold me, I want to melt and become one with you. You are so masculine, strong, tender, and gentle with me. I know you love me with every fiber of your being. I need and want you. I cannot imagine my life without you. I guess that is my greatest fear."

Simone' felt at that moment that Vincenzo' Moretti had stolen her innocence she should have given her husband their wedding night, continued, "I never wanted to disappoint you but want you to be proud of me as your wife."

"I am all those things Simone'. My life is rich because of you not what

we own, but you. I love Carmeli'ta'; however, she will not be always a part of me; she has never been?"

"What do you mean my husband?"

"We raised her to be her own person, Simone'. We raised her to live in this world differently and apart from you and me. But you, Simone' is that string tied to my heart. I cannot severe it without destroying that part of me that makes me whole."

Snuggling close to him Simone' felt warm. He said, "I need to confirm my reservation my beauty."

He took her by the hand and led her through the French door from the garden into Franco's office, picked up the phone and called the Airport. The attendant answered the phone, "Ciao, Campo di Marte."

"Ciao, I am Roberto' Bandaci, I would like to confirm my reservation and my seat for Thursday, November 30. Is my seat confirmed?"

The attendant, after realizing Roberto' spoke both English and Italian, responded in English, and said, "Yes Mr. Bandaci your seat is reserved. Pan American Flight 2472 leaves for London at 3:00 p.m. Please arrive by 2:00 p.m. There is a five-hour layover in London. The flight leaves for America at 10:00 p.m. I can make a hotel reservation for you Mr. Bandaci."

"Please do, thank you."

"When you flight arrives in London, check with the information desk Sir, they will have the hotel and the reservation for you."

"Grazie'! Arrivederci."

"Sei Benevento addio, Mr. Bandaci." He placed the phone on the hook turned and pulled Simone' close to him; it was getting late in the afternoon; time had passed quickly without notice. It was dinner hour, Catarina had prepared Chicken with Paprika, and Roasted Potatoes, Asparagus wrapped in Bacon, Salad with Italian Dressing and Fresh Bread for dinner.

Franco interrupted them with a knock on the open door to his office, "Dinner my children, mother is waiting for us. Are you ready?"

"Yes, we are Franco", said Roberto'.

"Thank you. We will be right there Father." Simone replied.

Robert said, "Simone'." The tone in his voice said everything.

"Yes, my husband, I feel the same. Let us join Mother and Father for dinner. I will help Mother after dinner with the dishes, if she needs me to while you chat with Father. We will pack your luggage and spend the remainder of the evening together."

Walking into the kitchen, Simone stated, "Mother I wanted to help with dinner. I did not pay attention to the time."

"No that is not necessary Simone' I want you to relax while you are here."

During dinner, the conversation was lively and reminiscence. Franco guarded in what he said, did not want to add fire to the conversation kept it light and festive. The atmosphere was less tense than at lunch; he did not want any little statement to spark a fire and destroy the relaxed feeling floating in the atmosphere and pretty smile on his daughter's face.

After dinner, Roberto' chatted with Franco in the garden while Simone' helped her mother with the dishes. As they cleaned the kitchen Catarina observing Simone' asked, "How did Roberto' take the decision of your staying?"

"Not well mother, at first he was not pleased. Even with his disapproval, he is willing for me to visit for a few more days. I told him I wanted to visit and think about how to tell him what I have kept from him over the years. He is insistent on knowing Mother. I do not know how much longer I can avoid telling him. He will only be patient for just so long. I know my husband's temperament."

"Yes, Simone', I am concerned about your Father and his tempers in this matter. Franco is angry, it is hard to keep him from confronting Vincenzo' before Roberto' leaves."

"Mother, Roberto' and I are planning to spend these hours tonight and tomorrow together before he leaves if you and Father will excuse us."

"Of course, Simone', that is the best idea. They will be apart so there is no danger in Franco saying something Roberto will pick-up on."

"Yes, Mother. My husband is sharp. He does not miss a word anyone says is why I need to stay here and decide how to tell him before I allow him to read the Diary I have kept all these years."

Simone' and her mother finished clearing and cleaning the after-dinner dishes. They walked to the garden where their husbands stood talking with each other. Franco saw them coming, "Here are our beauties my son."

Simone' walked to Roberto' and smiled and put her arms around his waist and said, "I am ready my love to get our evening started."

"Franco if you and Catarina will excuse us we want to spend the last hours tonight, and tomorrow together before I return to America on Thursday."

Franco quickly replied, "Yes, yes, my children please do mother and I will take our evening walk as always we will see you for breakfast. If you need anything before then let us know this is your home. We want you to be comfortable here during your visit."

"Thank you Franco, good night to you both" replied Roberto'.

Simone' and Roberto' walked to her bedroom at the end of the hallway beyond the Parlor. Roberto' opened the door and allowed Simone' to enter first walking in behind her he closed and locked the door turning, noticed Franco had lit the fire went and stood in front of the fireplace. It gave the room a warm comfortable feeling in the coolness of the evening finally said, "Come to me my lovely wife." Simone' walked to where he stood and looked up at him smiling. He took her hands in his and pulling her close to him then led her to the lounger and sit with her besides him, they revealed their hearts to each other.

"Simone I saw you everywhere in our home after you left. I saw you in the mirror, in the tub; I could smell the Lavender scent of your hair, your Chanel 5 so soft floating in my nostrils; I saw you in the bathtub with bubbles kissing your long legs. You were everywhere like the air I breathe. Then you were gone. The pain was more than I could bear still standing; your leaving bought me to my knees. You are my sunshine, my song of life. You presence was in the atmosphere. I heard your laughter, I saw you turn and smile, running to me greeting me with love and warmth as you do when I arrive home from work each day. I heard your sweet soft voice whispering in my ear, as you greet me each day, "Hello my love, I missed you. I am glad you are home."

"He continued, "You said that I had given you a wonderful comfortable life, I gave you that life as a way of showing my love for you. I wanted you to have an easy life, a life that spoke of love, desire, and beauty the way that I see you. I have never loved anyone as I have you my love. I cannot explain the intensity of my love for you; it overpowers and strengthens me both. Our love is an unfinished book. I will return to America with a heavy heart because you are not retuning with me, but then with joy in my heart that you are safe and I found you."

"Roberto' your love to me has created a world of beauty and joy. One that I know I would not have if I were not married to you. You are my joy in life. I thank God for you every day and your abiding love. I missed you my love when I arrived in Tuscany. That string tied to my heart; the pull was so painful because you were not with me. I felt lost without you. We have never been apart before my husband it tore at me like a thorn in my flesh. I could not stop the pain. I cried out for you in the fog. I could not see you. I was groping in the dark reaching for you I could not feel you my love. When I awaken and found you here, it was more joy than I can express. I could not control the tears my husband at the relief I felt. I dreamed you stopped loving me, did not want me anymore. I felt like a dry riverbed with no water, no life; I could not go on. I need you Roberto' my life is rich with you psychologically, emotionally, and physically. The way you care for me makes the intimacy with you like the taste of a sweet honeycomb so pleasing and enjoyable. You excite me my husband, when I see you or am near you the passion I feel is a like fire inside, only you can quench. Hold me Roberto', please hold me. I want you to feel wanted by me my husband. You are so wanted. I want to hold you forever."

Roberto' held Simone' tight and kissed her face saying, "I need you to want me my beauty. I need you Simone' show me how much you love me. I need you desperately. It is hard to think of me leaving without you. I need you Simone'."

"I need you my Roberto'."

"These are precious moments to me my darling wife. I feel as if I will lose my heart tonight and tomorrow; leaving you is hard ... the coming days will not be sweet ones but bitter and lonely for me. I need to feel your warmth and nearness. Just being there or anywhere I am is important to me my love.

I will always want you, Simone, and I will always love you. I have come to know over the years there is no worse pain or absolute pleasure than that which love can bring. It tears you into and then it put you together again and then heals. Love is like a glue; a foundation; a strong force; it drives you ever forward intensifying the desire to be with that one person to know and feel all there is about them." Simone' listened to her husband silently she held on to his hands, her eyes dancing as she cried tears of pain and sorrow inside; his words became her judge, jury, and sentence.

"I love you Roberto. You are a good man and wonderful husband. Your heart is so tender my husband; it amazes and mystifies me. Your tenderness has captured my heart and energized my emotions over the years. I am thankful for the precious memories your love has created for me."

The Curriculum Vitae of Roberto' was full of talent and knowledge of his wife but not complete. "My heart is tender because of you Simone'. You bring out the best in me my beauty. Otherwise, I am just not sure that I am that good at heart. Living with you Simone' is like opening a Treasure Chest. Every day the jewels that your treasure chest holds is luxuriously beautiful and each more desirable than the one before. You wear the jewels in loveliness and mystery every day. On the other hand, I feel different in reference to my business or if someone or something threatens my family, especially you or Carmeli'ta', Simone'. I believe, no I know, I would hurt that person. I cannot bear to think of anything that would affect you or put you in danger. I am not sure what I would do; but I know the end results would not be pleasant."

Simone' knew her husband was right. She saw him when he thought Carmeli'ta' might be hurt. His temper raged at her townhouse and again when they arrived home. She knew Vincenzo' would be in danger when Roberto' found out what he had done over the years coming to America to see Carmeli'ta' and her. Roberto' was just as dangerous a man as he was good. Shivers ran through her at the thought. She had to find a solution that would keep her husband safe and not allow what she did to cause him to hurt anyone. She prayed, "God help me. I created this situation and I cannot see a solution. Please help me have the strength to tell my husband."

While he held her Simone thought, "Roberto' has carried the cross of self-denial all these years because he loved me. He lived with the fact that

I had not allowed him to be fully one with me in body. We are one in everything else in our life, but not one in our intimate life, not yet. He carried the cross for years denying his self the full pleasure that he had a right to know. He has given himself to me without holding back; he demanded with his body in the way he loved me; his body begged to be loved by me fully with no secrets between us, but I could not because of the terrible reigning fear that built this mental and emotional wall. I could only allow him to get to a certain point before the pain of fear took over. He carried this for twenty-four years. What great love he has for me; it is inestimable and unconditional. I cannot bear the guilt."

She sweetly kissed his neck before she moved from his arms and said, "Roberto' let us pack your suitcase my love so we can enjoy the remainder of the evening together. Tomorrow will past quickly and Thursday will be here. I will drive you to the Airport my love and see you off. Thank you for agreeing for me to visit for a few more days."

Quiet for a few second he looked at his wife and commented, "It took every ounce of strength in me to agree with that Simone'! Leaving you will be one of the hardest things I have ever done. It took us being apart for me to say exactly what I have felt over the years the intensity that I feel the need and love for you that invades my mind and heart so immeasurably."

Roberto' and Simone' finished packing and preparing for his long journey home. Long because it meant two days to get there and because his wife was not returning with him, Simone' and Roberto' took their baths as usual. He watched his wife prepare for bed. She was his match in emotional quotient, in intimacy and in depth. He felt feverish, hot, jealousy, stressed at the thought of leaving his wife, regretting his not knowing why she ran away, lots of unanswered question. His love and need tore at him; he wavered between going and staying. He did not know what to think or how to feel in this situation. He had to go take care of his business and see their daughter, but wanted to be with his wife. He whispered, "Simone." She turned from the mirror brushing her hair smiling replied, "Yes, my husband."

Sitting on the foot of the bed, held out his hand for her to join him, she placed her brush on the dresser and walked slowly across the room smiling, her body moving with precision and depth said, "yes to her husband." Roberto' saw the love, passion, and desire in his wife's eyes and the way she moved toward him and the bed. Her movements created an environment in the room of love and desire for Roberto'. He never seemed to get enough of her love and warmth. Simone' felt the rages that invaded her body and being since she could remember beginning at 13 years old. She felt passionate, stimulated by the environment. Roberto' was exciting and thrilling in the way he loved her. Roberto' stood when she came close to him, loosen the ties on her dressing gown, pulled her to him, and put his arms around her waist inside the gown.

Simone' welcomed his firm grip, she kissed his neck, ran her hands down his waist to his buttocks making sounds of satisfaction she sighed softly whispering, "Roberto' my darling husband I need you always, you are sexy and desirable to me my husband and you please me so much in every way. Your body is so strong and gives me pleasure beyond my words to tell you."

"Don't tell me Simone' show me, love me my beauty; just love me. I will miss you while we are apart. It will be lonely nights without you beside me in bed. " He leaned over and nibbled at her long nose so straight and petite on her face, she smelled fresh and inviting to Roberto'. He wanted to love her and feel her love flowing warm and satisfying from her beauty body.

"I know I feel the same my husband, you have spoiled with me your love, desire and need for me over the years."

"I love you and have never wanted anyone else since the first day I saw you. I knew that you would be all I want in life no other. My desire and need is only for you my beauty, only you", he said, laying Simone' softly down on the bed in a cushion of comfort to love her and to be loved by her. Her kisses to Roberto' was warm like the summer sun, her cool skin pleasing he could not get enough of her softness and warmth. Roberto' slowly drifted into fields of pleasure with the way Simone' loved him slow with depth and passion got lost in hunger and thirst in the ecstasy he experienced wrapped in the love of his beautiful Simone'.

The next morning, Roberto' awaken Simone' at 4:00 a.m. with soft whispers in her ear, "Wake up my beauty, let me feel your warmth before it is time to prepare for my last day with you." Simone' welcomed her husband's early morning love with tenderness and warmth; he made love to her in early morning. Her love like the morning in their little valley came softly and slowly arriving, as a stream quietly trickling along its bed. They rose at 5:00 a.m. dressed to take one last walk to enjoy the scenery in their beautiful little valley before breakfast. They knew that after breakfast the morning and the remainder of the day would pass more quickly than either of them would desire. They walked through the garden on the way to their little hill overlooking the *Val di Greve River* below. They ran laughing reaching the top of the hill. Roberto' stood behind Simone' she leaned against him and watched the morning breeze awaken the birds stretching the limbs on the trees, tickling the leaves awake gently blowing softly through the grass like a mother calling to awaken her children; it played the sweet song of nature. It was so beautiful and peaceful they stood for a long time without words enjoying the beauty of nature and thanking God for each other and their love.

They returned to the house; Catarina had prepared breakfast as usual at 7:00 a.m.

"Good morning our children did you enjoy your walk" asked Franco.

"Yes, we did Father, it was pleasant, and nature was just waking upwhen we arrived."

Franco said, "I will return from the farm by Noon Roberto'; I want to spend the afternoon with you and I will return on Thursday by noon to see you off my son. It has been a pleasure having you here after many years not seeing you and my beautiful daughter. This visit has meant a lot to Mother and me."

"Thank you Franco, I have enjoyed my stay. I would stay longer but for the farm. Amelio' has a lot to manage with both his and my farm. You will take care of my beauty while she is here I know; she is precious to me."

"We will, you know that my son, Simone' is our only child in this world."

"Thank you Franco, I know you will; I guess I just feel better saying it out loud. I hope you understand."

"Yes, I do understand Roberto' she will be safe with us."

CHAPTER
TWENTY-EIGHT

In Charleston, Tuesday morning November 28, when arriving at the office, as promised, Carmeli'ta' checked her calendar to plan a day to have lunch with her friend Alberto. Carmeli'ta' called April's parents asked if she was back from visiting relatives her mother said, "No my dear, April will not return for another two weeks around the 15th of December. Is there a message I can give her when she calls?"

"No, I wanted her to join Alberto and Me for lunch before he returns to college after the Thanksgiving Holiday for his final exams."

"I will tell her you asked about her Carmeli'ta'. Alberto and you are well, I hope."

"Yes we are thank you. I will visit soon. I love you. Take care, Ms. Chambers."

"Thank you Carmeli'ta', we love you. Goodbye."

Carmeli'ta' pressed the button on the phone to end the call. Dialing Alberto's home, Carmeli'ta' waited for him to answer. After the third ring he answered, "Hello."

"Good morning Alberto."

"Good morning, my lovely friend. How are you today?"

"I am well thank you Alberto. I called to schedule our lunch, when can you go?"

"I can anytime it is convenient for you Carmeli'ta'."

"I am looking at my calendar Alberto; Thursday of next week, December 7 at 11:50 a.m. is open can we meet at Andrea's? I know you like his food."

"Yes, that is fine Carmeli'ta'." He made a definite statement and both a question, he continued, "I don't leave until December 11, so we may get a chance to see each other more than once!"

"I am not sure that is possible my friend, my schedule is tight with the contracts we are working on now. In addition, my parents will return on Friday. I will spend every minute I can with them. I have not seen them in almost 3 weeks, my Mother especially. I need to go Alberto we can chat more at lunch next Thursday."

"Okay. One more question, Carmeli'ta'!"

"Yes, Alberto."

"Will April join us?"

"No, she is till visiting her relatives, returning on the 15th of December."

"I am sorry to hear that Carmeli'ta' she will be missed."

"Yes, she will be. Goodbye Alberto."

Carmeli'ta' heard a tone of non-regret in Alberto's voice when he said, "April would be missed." She wondered what that sound was about as she placed the phone receiver on the hook. However, she soon dismissed the thought and focused on the terms of the contract on her desk. Charles Meriwether was one to watch closely in business. She wondered how he and their Minister; Mr. Meriwether could be first cousins. There was a night and day contrast-of-difference in them; she knew from her brief experience with him of his mysterious and convoluted way of dealing in business. Jason said his Father stated, "He is there then he isn't."

 Illusive was the word she used to describe him.

Alberto hung up the receiver and shout out loud, "Yes, this is perfect for me."

Ms. Gambani asked, "Alberto is there something wrong?"

"No Mother, everything is wonderful. I just had some good news."

"Do you want to share your wonderful news with me?"

"Not today Mother, maybe in the near future." Ms. Gambani just glanced at Alberto and did not comment.

At his office, Charles Meriwether's mind was not on the contract with Madison Steel and Iron, but on Carmeli'ta'. He thought, "How beautiful and sensual she is; like a rose, lovely and perfect whose petals are fresh and desirable. Her beauty is a gift and I want her to be mine." He contemplated his approach to the subject of relationship with her, "I am twice her age and then a few years. I am almost fifty actually I am older than her parents are. She is young enough to be my daughter. I have wanted Juanita Madison all my life, therefore, if I cannot have her, I will have Carmeli'ta'. I know she is important to the Madison family. I will do everything I can to hurt Jason Madison Sr. because he took the love of my life, the most beautiful woman in the world. Jason Jr. would have been my son. I do not have children because of him. Juanita is like a picture frame of lovely desirability even now; she seems to be ageless. She left footprints of desire on the streets of my heart. She is there at all times walking through my passions and desires. Sometimes I wish I could reach in and tear her image from my mind. I love her and cannot help myself. All the ladies that I have known in Charleston over the years, I have not found one that could rival Juanita, until I met Carmeli'ta' Bandaci."

It would become arguably apparent, Vincenzo' Alessandro Moretti and Charles Bienville Meriwether shared more of a common bond than they knew, Vincenzo loved Simone' and she belonged to another, Charles Bienville Meriwether loved Juanita, and she belonged to another. This common bond once realized by both would be the link of revenge that would exist between them. They loved women that were not their wives and they would never have the pleasure of them being in their lives. Both men angry and in pain from their loss triggered the settling of scores.

It was mid-morning on Thursday, November 30, in Tuscany, Simone' and Roberto' prepared for his leaving. Franco arrived right at noon to have lunch and visit with Roberto' before they departed for the Airport for Roberto's journey back to America. Franco, Roberto', Catarina, and Simone' sit quietly eating lunch hardly looking at each other. They all sit with regret in their hearts, Simone' and Roberto' anticipation of being apart Franco and Catarina because their daughter faced a daunting task of telling her husband the secrets she had held all these years. It was approaching 1:00 p.m. time to leave for the Airport. Goodbyes were hard to say. Catarina overcome with emotion could only kiss Roberto' and hug him tight.

Franco felt pain, anger, sorrow, and regret said after a long handshake, "Roberto' I prayed to God for a Son after my Simone' was born but we were not able to have any more children. I am thankful for my sweet daughter. It was 17 years later but God answered my prayer I have a son. I could not be more proud of you nor love you more if you were my son by birth. Thank you for loving my Simone'. Your father, my best friend, said to me that it was beyond explanation of how full of pride your mother and he was of you. You were born to your mother and he late in their life and he felt as if you were a special gift from God. You have proved him right my son; thank you for loving us as your parents."

Roberto' moved by Franco' statement said, "I feel blessed to be a part of your family Franco and thankful that you think of me as you would your own son. I feel like I am your son, which gives me a lot of pride. I love Simone' with everything in me that will never change. Thank you and Catarina for your kindness to me, I love you both. Take care of my beauty."

Simone' stood quietly listening to her father and husband exchange goodbyes. Catarina seeing the look of pain in her face came and put her arms around her daughter's waist, hugged her, and smiled.

Simone' drove Roberto' to the Airport to board his 3:00 pm flight. Arriving at the Airport, Roberto' walked over to the ticket counter and picked up his ticket checking his baggage went to the Information Desk and asked for his hotel reservation information during the lay-over in London. The minutes, so precious, seemed to be ticking away too fast. The sands in his hourglass of time had run out. He looked at his pocket watch it was 2:40 p.m. nearing time to board the flight to London, pulled Simone' aside and held on to her without speaking. She gripped her husband's waist; tears flowed from her eyes into his shirt. Roberto' lifted her face, looked into her tearful eyes, and said, "Please my love, don't cry; I can't bear to see you in pain it is breaking my heart to leave you."

The Counter Technician finally called for the boarding at 2:40 pm. Simone' looked up at her husband and pushed back the curly lock of hair that danced on his forehead. This, for Roberto' had become endearing. It was not a day passed, she at some point did not push back his curly lock of hair.

He hugged and kissed his wife and whispered, "I will call you when I arrive at the hotel in London my beauty. Take care of yourself."

With tears still flowing she barely whispered, "I will Roberto, I will my love. Thank you for caring."

"Simone', I more than care, I love you period."

Last call for boarding, Roberto' was last to board the plane. Simone' stood at the window waving, watched him across the walkway, climbs the steps, turned when he reached the top step before boarding, smiled, and waved. He was leaving his wife and her Diary containing all the answers he felt had become an antagonist in their lives.

Simone' walked back to the car with a heavy heart, drove slowly while contemplating the next steps to take to resolved this situation and go home to her husband; she loved and needed so desperately.

Simone' drove slowly back to her parent's home, musing, trying to put the facts and her thoughts in the same paradigm. She had to tell Roberto' what she has hidden over the years from him that had caused him enormous amounts of pain and heartache? She still questioned herself, how she could have let this situation escalate out of control and cause emotional damage to her husband more than anyone else.

Vincenzo' was not the man she thought he was; he had become completely different. She thought about what her mother said on Tuesday, 'he evidently still loved her, but that was not important to her. He had become cruel, but then, she knew that from his visits to see Carmeli'ta' and her over the years.' Arriving back at her parent's home, she wondered what solution would be best. Having an opportunity to talk with her parents would make the difference; her Father was wise; he would know how to help her with this solution.

Simone' walked in her mother's kitchen at 4:30 pm. She wanted to be sure she was home when Roberto' called as he promised after arriving at the hotel to rest before his flight to South Carolina.

"Hello my daughter. How was your drive back home?"

"It was good mother. Are you okay now Mother you were so upset before Roberto' left?"

"Yes, I am okay it was hard to say goodbye to Roberto' my daughter because he was hurting from this situation it showed in his face."

Simone' wanting to go to a happier subject commented, "Tuscany has changed so much in these years; so much growth."

"Yes, my daughter, your Father and his Economic Development Committee is making progress."

"Tell me Mother are there any of the Moretti family members on that development committee?"

Simone and her mother continued chatting while she finished preparing dinner, Catarina replied, "No my daughter, they are not; the committee is mostly made up of farmers, merchants, doctors, and lawyers. Vincenzo' refused the appointment to the committee by the Mayor ten years ago. He is very unhappy and angry my daughter, he just does not have interest in the community. His wife is seldom in the valley. They are not on the best of terms. He seems angry all the time."

Roberto' arrived at Corydon Airport in London two hours later at 5:00 p.m., November 30, 1927, checked with the customer service desk to get his hotel reservation for the next five hours. The taxi approached the Premier Inn near London Airport, he wondered if Simone' was okay, she was so quiet and seemed so fragile when he left her. He was anxious to get to his room to call to see how she was doing.

Looking at the clock, Simone' thought, 'it is after 5:00 p.m. and Roberto' should be at the hotel by now.' Catarina observing her daughter said, "He will call Simone'."

"I know he will Mother, I just love him so and hated to send him home alone with all of his questions unanswered."

"It was best this way Simone', it will give you an opportunity to sortout the issues in your mind and know what is the best way to tell him."

Roberto' reaching the hotel room called and asked the operator to make a long-distance call to Tuscany and add it to his room charges. The operator dialed the number given her by Roberto' to Franco's home. The phone rang three times in the Giovanni home, Simone' walked swiftly to the office, picked up the phone and said, "Hello."

"Hello, my beauty, I am here at the hotel and safe. How are you? Did you have trouble getting back home with all the changes in the streets?"

"Hello, my love, No, I was fine. I remembered the directions we took to the Airport. I miss you Roberto' already my love. My days and nights will be lonely without you."

"I miss you now Simone'; please make your visit short."

"I promise you my love I will make my visit as short as possible. I just want to think about what I want to tell you and how before you read the Diary Roberto'. It was never my intention for the situation to get this far. It is because I love you so my darling. I would do anything to prevent your hurt and pain. I will come soon my love, very soon."

"I know that you love me Simone' and I love you. What I cannot bear is not knowing what is causing you so much pain and keeping you distant from me. I want to know what is making you so afraid."

"I know my darling thank you for caring. Are you planning to get dinner before your flight tonight at 10:00 p.m. my love?

"Yes, I need to Simone'. I noticed that there is a restaurant here in the Premier Inn. I will get dinner before I rest. It is getting near my dinnertime. The clerk at the information booth in the Airport informed me there would be only snacks, drinks, and coffee served during the late evening flight and breakfast is the next meal around 6:00 a.m. I cannot make it that long without eating, not successfully anyway. We will have passed the International Dateline by that time and be near New York and from there my flight will take me to South Carolina."

"How long is the wait in New York my love?"

"We get to New York at 8:00 a.m. The flight will leave again at 10:00 a.m.; it is fueling stop. We get to South Carolina at 12:00 Noon. Amelio' is meeting me at the Airport. I will talk with him about our farm maybe then later in the day I will visit Carmeli'ta' or I may wait until tomorrow. I want to get settled in first before I see our daughter."

"Take care my love and I hope that you can rest well before the long flight. One day, I am sure they will have flights that can make it in less time than fourteen hours."

"I am sure they will as time go on my love. I will go now, eat, and rest. I will call you when I arrive home on Friday Simone' that is tomorrow my dear, please don't worry about me."

"I will always be concerned about you my darling. Have a good dinner and rest. Talk soon my love."

"Bye my beauty, I will call you very soon. Stay safe and enjoy yourself."

"Thank you my love. Bye for now."

Roberto' put the receiver on the hook, removed his jacket, picked up his room key, and went to the hotel restaurant for dinner. Simone' placed the phone in the receiver and returned to the kitchen where her mother was preparing dinner.

"How is Roberto' my daughter?"

"He is missing me, anxious to get home to see Carmeli'ta' and checkon our farm; other than that, he is fine. Thank you for asking. "She added,

"Mother I am not sure what to say to Father about Vincenzo', it is a difficult

situation at best, especially because he is so angry with Vincenzo'. After I told him more details, I wish at that moment I had not, it would just be more trouble caused by my poor decision making not to tell my husband about Vincenzo'. I do not want Father hurt or Vincenzo' for that matter. I am glad that Roberto' is on his way home, he would have confronted and hurt him, I know he would. He told me last evening that he does not know what he would do to someone that hurt Carmeli'ta' or me but he know it would not be good. I felt a chill of fear sweep across my mind and body at his statement and the look in his eyes."

"It is a difficult situation Carmeli'ta', but as long as life last and the sun rise, there can always be an answer. It may not be the answer we want or desire but there is a solution to this situation as well. We just need to find the best one that will be the least costly my daughter. When you love in life you will get hurt and hurt others though unintentionally, yet pain is pain. Your husband is hurting and so is my husband because of their love for you. I of all three understand what you are going through and how you made the decision; it too was out of love for your husband and child. I would do anything to protect my husband and you Simone' even be secretive that is the quality of a true loving wife and mother."

"Thank you Mother you saying that mean a lot to me. I am thankful for you as my mother even though you are only eighteen years older than I am it seems so strange to me as it does for me to be eighteen years older than Carmeli'ta'." She looked at her mother and smiled.

To Catarina, she was lovely as any angel in Heaven. She is sweet, kind, loving, caring, and the most wonderful compassionate daughter on earth.

As the evening progressed Roberto' rested for a while as his thoughts went to his Simone' and their last evening together examining the feelings that he had for her and the love that possessed his heart and soul. She was a rare jewel, loving, and kind. He thought of how her body felt as they made love that puts him in a trance; a world of confusion and he knew he did not want to find his way out. He wanted to be lost in her love for an eternity. Roberto' so overcome with emotions could no longer rest looking at his pocket watch realized it was 8:30 p.m. time for him to prepare to return to the Airport to board his 10:00 p.m. flight to New York. He took his personal case went to the bathroom brushed his teeth, combed his hair, and freshened his skin with Boellis Panama 1924 Soap and Aftershave, left the room for the hotel lobby and the cab waiting at 9:00 p.m.

He could not shake the regret like darkness covering his heart having left Simone' in Tuscany.

CHAPTER

TWENTY-NINE

At dinner at 7:00 p.m., Simone' and her mother and Father had dinner and chatted lively as they evening progressed and Simone' thought about her husband and his long flight over the Atlantic Ocean back to America. She prayed that he would be safe and the plane would not crash.

Later in the evening, noticing little frowns dancing across her forehead Franco reached for her hand and holding it tight said, "He will be safe Simone'. God is able to keep him and all others on that flight safe."

"I believe that he will be safe my Father, but I still worry until I know that he has made it home. Thank you and mother for caring so much for me and am sorry to be so much trouble to you." As she said this, tears swelled in her eyes.

"You are not trouble to us Simone' my daughter; mother and I am concerned that you are having a difficult time right now. You are too precious to us to be trouble; so please do not think or say that again." Catarina smiled and nodded, in agreement with her husband, while she held Simone's' other hand.

"Thank you both. I could not have better or more loving parents than you. I love you both so. Roberto' should be boarding now; it is 9:30 p.m."

At the airport passenger waiting area, so deep in thought, he did not hear the boarding call. The Technician announced, "Last call for Roberto' M. Bandaci; we are waiting for you sir". The announcement bringing his focus back, retrieving his Attaché' Case from the seat next him, boarded the plane. Settling in his seat, regret filled his mind, he was leaving his heart behind no matter the situation he loved and needed her.

Pan American Flight 2370 moved away from land, Roberto' pulled the farm accounts from his Attaché' Case to go over the Bank Statements he bought with him since Simone' would be away for a few more days. She had looked at them while they were at the cottage, but did not complete the monthly balancing. While she was away he would have Carmeli'ta' to come over and help him with the accounts so they would not get behind it would take Simone' a long time to update them when she returned since she checked them daily against the journal log of accounts receivable and notes payable for their Farm. After he completed the daily audit and bought them current, Roberto' leaned back in his seat, closed his eyes, his memory played mental pictures of Simone' and he together. His heart felt heavy. He missed her being with him by his side. He needed her with him, just her presence.

The hours wiled away; he thought about his life with Simone' over the past twenty-four years. He thought how pleasant they were, yet so mysterious; they kept him wanting to know more of her, but never knowing. After a long seemingly unending night, at 6:00 a.m., the Stewardess served breakfast. He needed the nourishment and strength to make the last leg of the flight. The plane approached the coast of New York; the Stewardess announced their descent into the New York City Airport. He glanced at his pocket watch; it was 8:00 a.m. New York time and 1:00 p.m., in Tuscany five hours ahead knew Franco, Catarina, and his Simone' were finishing lunch.

Roberto' prepared to disembark for a break and stretch his legs. New York was a normal refueling stop before reaching Charleston. He was excited to reach America again and the anticipation of seeing his daughter and cousin made him smile.

In Italy, after lunch, Simone' prepared the vegetables for dinner while her mother made the bread. Catarina watched her daughter and the expressions of worry dancing across her face commented, "He will be fine Simone' God will keep him safe in his travels."

"I know mother, I believe that God will keep him and all others on the plane safe. I was wondering more of what I would tell him and how I can solve this problem I have caused my family over the years, especially my husband; Carmeli'ta' knows nothing of the situation; however, I think she is suspicious now from what Roberto' said when we were at the cottage." "You will have to allow it to play out Simone' there is just no other choice in the matter. Your Father said we will discuss what to do after dinner tonight and then he will talk with Vincenzo' Moretti about his actions over the years."

"Mother I am so afraid that Father will hurt Vincenzo' he seems so angry about the entire situation."

"He is angry about the entire matter Simone'. He feels you were young and defenseless. He thinks Vincenzo' took advantage of you because of your innocence. In the same light, his actions were of a despicable and viler nature, making the matter worse. He continued to come to America to see you and Carmeli'ta' blackmailing you through a threat of exposing your relationship, how ungentlemanly he is my daughter. His actions are offensive and unforgiveable."

"I know mother, I feel the same way. When he kept coming and insisting on see us, I thought I did not have a choice because I did not want my family hurt: you, Father, my sweet Roberto' and my daughter. I hope I have not destroyed our marriage Mother. I don't know if my husband's love will be strong enough to get pass this situation."

"Have faith in your husband Simone'. I know that it is difficult; but, the fact is that he loves you no matter what the situation is."

"Mother, I have not told you before, with Vincenzo' insisting that Carmeli'ta' is his daughter I am just not sure if she is not."

Simone's statement was a second punch, it was more impactful hearing her daughter say it than her husband Franco telling her the possibility, Catarina felt as if she had been hit feeling weak, and dizzy she turned and looked at her daughter. Simone' saw the surprise, pain, hurt, and disbelief in her face.

"Simone' is that possible?"

"At this point Mother I am not sure of anything, possible or probable, yes it could be both. I had to tell you so you would not be surprised when it comes out. I wanted to know your thoughts; Father knows. I told him the day we walked in the garden but I was afraid to tell you that particular 'maybe'; it was hard for me not to share that with you mother, please forgive me. Father said it would be best if I mention it to you and not him tell you." Even with

Franco mentioning it to Catarina and she got the impression when Simone' talked with her the day after she arrived but could not mentally process the possibility before Simone' said it to her.

Regaining her composure, Catarina said, "I understand Simone' why it was hard for you to tell me. In this instance, I am sure it was easier to tell your Father since you are so alike inside my dear daughter. We will need to think logically about this Simone' and not let it get out of hand with your Father. He is angrier, I am sure, about what Vincenzo' is claiming, and I say claiming, because I simply don't believe it my daughter, it is just a gut instinct, and I have no way of justifying it, just a woman's institution."

Friday December 1, Roberto's flight 2370 arrived in Charleston, South Carolina on schedule at 12:00 Noon. The plane taxied to the passenger disembarking area. Roberto' stood and retrieved his case from the luggage rack above the passenger slowly moved toward the open door. Standing at the top of the steps, he could see Amelio' waving and smiling at him from the window. He waved and smiled back just as he reached the bottom step.

When Roberto' entered the Airport Terminal, Amelio' met him at the door and hugged him saying, "It is good to see you my cousin, I have missed you."

"I know my cousin; I missed you as well. How is everything with you, the farms, Carmeli'ta', Church Congregation, and Marianna?"

"Everything is fine Roberto'. The farms are operating at 100% your Foreman is an excellent manager; he made it easy for me to take care of everything for both farms. Carmeli'ta' is doing well and happier I believe than I have ever seen her. Worship Service is good as always, Bro. Meriwether is a good Minister. He wants you to call him when you are settled. I checked every other day, Marianna is taking care of the house; she manages well, everything is in place my cousin. How is Simone' is she well and happy?

"Yes, Simone' is well and staying a few more days with her parents she had not visited them in a while."

"Why did she leave so suddenly Roberto' did she tell you?"

"I know a little more about it than when I left, but I have not gotten to all the facts yet. I will share with you when I know the facts about the entire matter. But know for now my cousin, Simone' and I are fine. I just want her to hurry home because I love and miss her so much".

"Thank you Roberto', I feel better. I will wait patiently for you to tell me about it. I will not question you any further about the matter."

"Thank you, for understanding Amelio', I appreciate your care and support it means a lot to me and I will call our Minister tomorrow after I see Carmeli'ta'. We can finish our chat in the car; I need to pick up my luggage from the baggage area."

Roberto' arrived home about the time that Franco arrived back in Tuscany from his farm. Amelio's car pulled into the yard Marianna rushed out to meet Roberto' with an out-stretched hand and exclaimed in an excited tone of voice, "Hello Sir it is so good to see you. I am glad that you are home. How is Miss, she did not come with you?"

"No Marianna, Ms. Bandaci stayed in Tuscany with her parents for a few more days. She has not seen them in a few years. She will be home soon. How are you? Thank you for caring for our home while we were away."

"You are welcome Sir; I enjoy taking care of your home. It is my home too and I care so much for Miss, for you, and Ms. Carmeli'ta'."

"Thank you Marianna, we love and appreciate you more than you know."

Roberto' and Amelio' carried his bags inside stopping in the office to go over the accounts for the past ten days. After the accounts rectification was done, Amelio' ready to leave for his farms and then home said, "I am will talk with you later my cousin, I need to get back to the farm and then home."

"Thank you for caring for my farm and business Amelio' everything is in perfect order with the accounts and deposits. I will talk with you tomorrow."

"Yes, do call me Roberto' and let me know how you are doing and if you need help. I will always do whatever is necessary."

Roberto' opened the office door for Amelio' and said, "Thank you Amelio' I will definitely let you know. "Marianna prepared lunch for Roberto', "Mr. Bandaci your lunch is ready."

"Thank you Marianna, I will be there in just a few moments."

After lunch Roberto' went upstairs slowly entering the sitting room where he and Simone' spends a lot of time together in front of the fireplace there. He looked around and it seemed so empty without his wife there. The scent of Chanel 5 drifted into his nostrils when he entered their bedroom. Her scent was everywhere. He could not tell whether it was lingering in the air or invading his memory as everything about his wife does; whether it was real or his memory he could not reason with the fact that she was not there with him. His promise to Simone' to call was first on his mind, walking over to the phone on the desk in their sitting room he called the operator, "I would like to place a long-distance call to Tuscany at 0+1-998-765-4375-46 to Franco Giovanni."

Waiting for the Operator to connect the number, he remembered Thursday morning and the warmth that he felt with his wife before he left for the trip to America. She was warm, loving, and sweet and never said no to him. The phone in the Giovanni's home rang four short rings and one long, Franco picked up the receiver saying, "Franco Giovanni here speaking."

"Franco, this is Roberto'. I am at home safe. How is Simone' is she there?"

"Hello Roberto' my son; it is good to hear from you. I am happy that you are home and safe. Simone' is here; she is in the kitchen with my Catarina. How is everything there with your farm and my lovely granddaughter?"

"Everything is fine Franco so far. I have not seen Carmeli'ta' or the farm; Amelio' tells me that all is well with both my farm and my lovely daughter."

"That sounds good. I will call Simone'."

Franco said, "Simone', Roberto' is calling from your home in America."

Simone' excited and pleased pushed her chair back and ran quickly down the short hallway to the study and took the phone from her Father. He smiled and left the room closing the French doors behind him. She said, "Roberto' my darling you are safe. It is so good to hear from you."

"Hello, my beauty, I am safe. How are you? Are you enjoying yourself?"

"Yes, darling, mother, and I were just finishing dinner and we will be eating in another fifteen minutes whenever Father is ready. He is just arriving home and wants to freshen up first. He has a meeting after dinner and wants to be prepared to leave when we finish eating."

"Amelio' picked me up from the Airport and we went over the accounts and deposits. Everything here is fine with the farm so far. Before I forget, I completed the account rectification on the flight back so all is current. I will do the daily balancing while you are away and will get Carmeli'ta' to assist me if necessary. I have not spoken to Carmeli'ta' yet. I will call her when we have finished our conversation. Also, Brother Meriwether wants me to call him as well."

"I am glad that things are well my husband. Tell our lovely daughter, I said hello and I will talk with her in a few days."

"Yes my beauty, I will tell our daughter what you said. Do you have any idea when you might be coming home yet?"

"No, my husband not yet, but it will not be long I promise you. I miss you so much. The bed was lonely last night without you there to cuddle and snuggle me next to you. I love you so my husband."

"Thank you my beauty. I love you too Simone' and I want you home as soon as possible. It is lonely here without you."

"I will be there soon my darling. I miss you terribly."

"I miss you too my beauty. I will let you eat your dinner and not keep your parents waiting. I need to call Carmeli'ta' and Brother Meriwether. I will call you again tomorrow, maybe tonight after I check the farm and get unpacked if it is not too late. Please call me if you need me my love it does not matter the cost of the phone call."

"Thank you my husband. I will call you if anything happens and I will call you because I miss you. I will talk to you very soon my husband. Have a good rest of the day. What time is it there my husband?"

"It is 1:30 p.m. my beauty. Bye for now."

"Bye my darling."

Hanging up Simone' walked back to the kitchen. Roberto' pressed the button on the phone; then dialed Carmeli'ta' office. Ms. Horne answered, "Ms. Bandaci's office, Mrs. Horne, may I help you?"

"Ms. Horne is Carmeli'ta' there? This is her Father, Roberto' Bandaci."

"Yes Mr. Bandaci, she is. She went to Mr. Madison's office for a minute. If you will hold on I will get her."

"Thank you Ms. Horne. I will hold."

Ms. Horne walked down the hall quickly to Mr. Madison's office and knocked lightly at the door she heard Jason's say, "Come in Ms. Horne."

She opened the door and standing in the doorway, saw Carmeli'ta' sitting in front of Jason's desk.

"Yes, Ms. Horne", Jason said.

"There is a telephone call for Ms. Bandaci."

Carmeli'ta' asked, "Who is it Ms. Horne? Can you take a message for me?"

"It is your Father, Ms. Bandaci."

Carmeli'ta' feeling excitingly flushed at the news rose quickly and said, "Thank you Ms. Horne I will take the call. Please excuse me Mr. Madison, I was expecting my Father's call he arrived back in Charleston at Noon today."

"Of course, Ms. Bandaci we can finish our discussion after you talk with your Father. I will be waiting for you."

"Thank you, I will not be long if you both will excuse me."

Walking down the hallway, almost running, she reached her office and picked up the receiver saying, "Hello Father, it is so good to hear from you and know that you are home. I want to see you as soon as I can. Will you come after I get off from work?"

"I am not sure my daughter, but I will certainly see you tomorrow. Are you working on Saturday? I can come after your work. I need to talk to a few more people, eat my dinner, get unpacked, and rest a bit from my flight. It was long and tiring fourteen hours total time getting back."

"Yes, I have to work for a while tomorrow. The plant will not be open; however, Jason and I need to go over some contracts we have with

Meriwether Textiles. I will be there until at least 3:00 p.m. It is a possibility we may complete our assessment earlier. How is mother, Father, did she come back with you?"

"No, my daughter your mother stayed to visit with your grandparent a few more days. I spoke with her before I called you, she will not be gone long my daughter. How is Jason Madison?"

"Thank you Father for telling me, I hope to talk with mother soon. I have so much to tell her."

"And Jason, my daughter?"

"Jason is fine Father working hard as usual and he is really good to me."

Roberto' did not want to discuss the matter of her and Jason said, "Okay my daughter, I will not keep you long. You have your workday to finish. I will talk with you tomorrow before I come to make sure you are home."

"Yes Father. I will look forward to hearing from you. It is good you are home; I missed you and mother while you were away. I am thankful you had a good time. You needed to get away from the farm and rest."

"Thank you Carmeli'ta' I did have a good time and it was good to get away and spend time with your mother back in our country. I will see you tomorrow my daughter. I love you, bye for now."

"Bye Father, I love you."

Carmeli'ta' returned to Jason's office smiling knocked lightly entered, "My father is back my darling. I am happy to have him back home again. Mother stayed in Tuscany for a few more days to visit with my grandparents. I pray that she is okay; it is so strange that she and my father are apart for the first time that I can ever remember."

"I am sure she is fine my lovely Carmeli'ta'. When will you see your father? We have a date later we can always cancel it and go another day so you can visit with your Father."

"My father is planning to see me tomorrow after 3:00 p.m. Jason. I told him that we were working on finalizing contracts tomorrow. He will call me before he comes. I am looking forward to our date later my love." Time passed quickly while they chatted.

"Thank you Carmeli'ta' so am I my lovely. I will call for you at 7:00 p.m. to make it by our 8:00 p.m. dinner reservation."

"Thank you Jason, I will be ready. It is 3:00 p.m. I have a bit more work on my desk I want to complete before I leave at 4:30 p.m. if you will excuse me. I will see you at 7:00 tonight my darling."

Okay, my sweet Carmeli'ta' I will see you as 7:00 tonight. Have a good rest of the afternoon."

"Thanks, you, Bye."

In Tuscany, Simone' had returned to the kitchen where her parents were waiting dinner. Her mother had put dinner on the table and they were sitting waiting patiently for her to return. She smiled and said, "I feel better now that I know that my husband is at home and he is safe.

I can eat now mother, suddenly I am very hungry."

"Yes, my daughter, eat; we will talk after dinner."

"Are we discussing what I will say to Roberto' before he reads my Diary?"

"We need to talk about Vincenzo' Moretti before that my daughter!" replied Franco.

Simone' grew very quiet and sinking back behind the protective wall of thought, she reverts to when fear of being exposed rages in her mind and heart.

The Confrontation....

CHAPTER
THIRTY

Roberto' after talking with Carmeli'ta' called his Minister, Brother Meriwether. The phone rang four times Mr. Meriwether answered saying, "Hello."

"Brother Meriwether this is Roberto' how are you? I am home from Italy."

"Roberto' it is good to hear from you. How are you? I hope that your trip was good and you relaxed while you were away. How is Simone' did she return with you?"

"Thank you for caring. I am fine. My trip was good and I did get to relax with my lovely Simone' while I was there. Simone' is doing fine; she stayed with her parents for a few more days. She will be home soon."

"I am glad to hear that you have all good news Roberto'. Did you and Simone' get to talk about the subject you have shared with me over the past year?"

"We did talk a bit about it Brother Meriwether, but not to resolution yet. She does have something that is frightening her and I don't know what it is yet, but she will tell me when she returns in a few days."

"I am glad to hear that Roberto'. I thank you for letting me know and calling me as I asked. I have been more than worried about you and Simone' and how this will affect Carmeli'ta'. You have spoken to her I am sure!"

"Yes, I called her first. Thank you for caring. I will let you know when I know more about what is frightening my wife. I plan to do all I can to protect my family."

"I know that without you telling me Roberto'. You are a good husband and Christian Man. I am thankful to God every day that I know you and you work in this congregation."

"Thank you. I will see you on Sunday, Brother Meriwether. Bye."

"Thank you Roberto'. Have a good evening."

Roberto' walked downstairs to the kitchen to talk with Marianna about dinner afterwards left for the farm to check in with his manager and let him know that he had returned from Italy. Arriving at his farm office, his supervisor, Peter Meriwether, saw his Roadster pull up to the office, opened the door smiled extended his hand, "Hello Mr. Bandaci, I am glad to see you."

"Thank you Peter, it is good to see you as well. Amelio' tell me that everything ran smoothly in my absence and you were of great assistance to him. I appreciate that Peter. Though he did not need to tell me that, but I appreciate hearing it anyway."

"Thank you Mr. Bandaci, everything went smoothly same as when you are here. I am ready to go over the accounts with you if you have time."

"Yes, I do Peter that is why I came and to see how you were doing." "Thank you. I have the delivery logs ready for you to review."

In the meanwhile, Simone' and her parents ate their dinner with less cheerfulness to their conversation. Franco sit tensed. The muscles in his jaws moved during the entire dinner. His anger level grew to a heated pitch and finally said, "I will go and see Vincenzo' Moretti after we have finished our dinner. Simone' I will speak to him about his behavior in this entire matter over the years, especially coming to America to see you and then using a threatening tone to try and coerce you into continuing to allow him to see Carmeli'ta' and you."

"I can see no benefit in you talking with him Father, he never wanted to listen to me telling him not to come to America to see us anymore or that Carmeli'ta' is not his daughter. He will not listen to you now."

"I will speak to him about his behavior my daughter; his behavior has been less than gentlemanly and he needs to realize that fact. I cannot allow this to pass and not address it with him. I would be less than a caring and protective Father if I do not speak with him; it cannot be put-off any longer past tonight my sweet daughter. I will leave for the Moretti's home in a few minutes and return as soon as I have finished my conversation with Vincenzo' Moretti."

"Please my Father I do not want any trouble for you over this matter. I do not want Vincenzo' or you hurt. I do not intend to hurt him my daughter, though it crossed my mind. I will speak to him and he can set the tone for what happens after that. I will not have him treating my only child in the manner that he has over the years; I will be back soon Mother."

"Please Franco be careful, remember your temper my husband."

Franco did not comment just held his hand up in a half-wave at his wife and daughter.

He drove quickly the five miles to the Moretti Vineyard and Mansion. Pulling into the Moretti driveway, exited the car and knocked at the front door. The white-coat cladded Butler, Fabia', answered the door said, "Good evening sir. Who do you need to see Mr. Giovanni?"

"Good evening Fabia', I am here to see Vincenzo' Moretti."

"Please wait in the Parlor; I will let him know you are here."

Walking back in the dining room where the Moretti family was just finishing their dinner, entered, Francisco Vincenzo's father asked, "who was at the door Fabia'?"

"Mr. Giovanni is waiting in the Parlor to see Mr. Vincenzo' sir; what do you want me to tell him?"

"Francisco Moretti asked, "Vincenzo' are you expecting Franco Giovanni this evening son?"

"No, I am not expecting any callers Father. I cannot imagine what he wants to see me about. He had asked me before to be on the Tuscany Community Development Committee, maybe that is what he wants to see me about."

"What do you want me to tell him Mr. Vincenzo'?" asked Fabia'."

"I will take care of it Fabia'. You may go back to what you were doing." Fabia' bowed his head slightly in respect and returned to the kitchen.

With a puzzled look on his face Vincenzo' rose laying his napkin on the left side of his plate said, "Please excuse me I will see what he needs of me."

Vincenzo's wife sitting on the opposite side of the table, observed him and the worried look he had on his face, smirks, with a sarcastic tone in her voice commented, "Vincenzo' why do you appear nervous to me my husband? Is there something you need to share with me?" She snarled, "Why is one of the farm community leading members here to see you, my dear husband?"

With each other, sarcasm had become second nature to Antonia and Vincenzo'.

Looking intently at her, putting emphasis on his words, replied sharply and sarcastically, "I have nothing, I want to share with you, my lovely Antonia."The sound of his voice when he spoke and the words he used hit his father like points on an arrow when it makes contact with flesh, piercing and hurtful.

One of the reasons Vincenzo' married Antonia Amoretti, she was a picture of loveliness and immense beauty reminded him of Simone', but not as beautiful as Simone'. However, there was only one of Simone' and she was the love of his life. If he could not have Simone' he decided he would get a substitute for her not knowing that grapes do go sour sometimes; he had suffered the twelve years of their marriage making love to a woman he cared for but did not love.

Antonia was angry most of the time with her husband; she knew he did not love her; and it was only an arrangement between the Moretti and Amoretti families. After the first year of marriage, Antonia unexpectedly fell in love with her husband and suffered since that time waiting and wanting him to return her love.

Vincenzo' walked quickly into the Parlor and pulled the French Doors closed behind him observed the size and height of Franco Giovanni. He was 6'4" tall and weighted at least 180 pounds, realized he was short in statue next to Franco. He thought, I am 5"10" and weighs 170 pounds said, "Good evening Mr. Giovanni. I was not expecting you today, is there something I can assist you with?"

"Mr. Moretti, I am here about my daughter Simone'."

"Simone', I don't understand what you mean. Is Simone' well?"

"My daughter's welfare is no concern of yours. I came here to talk with you about your behavior towards my daughter over the years. First, I was not aware that you knew my daughter when she was young until last week. It came as a complete surprise."

"Simone'and I became friends when we were in our early teens Mr. Giovanni."

Vincenzo' realized Franco was angry; his eyes showed his level of anger, at that point, guarded his words and walked toward the Fireplace away from the French doors so his family would not hear their conversation and Franco would not be towering over him in size and height.

Franco continued, "Simone' has related all of the facts about your relationship to her mother and me, including, the fact that you have been coming to America over the last eighteen years to see her and my granddaughter. She has asked you on more than one occasion not come to see her and your persistent actions and attitude resulted in you making blackmail related statements about your intents in reference to my granddaughter to her."

"What do you mean, I never blackmailed Simone' I care too much for her to do that."

"You said that you would do anything necessary to continue to see your daughter is where she got that impression. My granddaughter's Father is, Roberto' Man 'son Bandaci. I intend for you never to see or speak to either my daughter or granddaughter ever again. I came here to warn you and let you know you I feel you took advantage of my innocence daughter at 14 years of age and many years thereafter. Your behavior has been more than improper, dishonorable, and ungentlemanly. I never want to see you again Vincenzo' Moretti neither do I want you to have any contact with my daughter or granddaughter; this is a warning for you."

"I have always loved Simone' and I love Carmeli'ta'. I believe she is my daughter how can you ask me to let her go and not see my only child in the world?"

"She is not your child Vincenzo'. My daughter said she stated this fact to you a thousand times if she said it to you once. What about this fact can you not accept? You have a wife she is young enough to have children."

"We have not had children in the last twelve years that we have been married. I love Carmeli'ta'. I know she is my daughter."

"I am warning you Vincenzo' this is my last words to you, stay away from Carmeli'ta' and Simone'."

"It is apparent to me that Roberto' does not know about Simone's and my relationship Mr. Giovanni."

"If he did Vincenzo', you would not be safe. Roberto' knows that something is wrong with Simone' and she is frightened and he has grown very angry over the years. I hope that you never cross his path. Nor do I want you to cross mine; in both cases, it will be healthier, for you."

Vincenzo' feeling frightened at his words and the thought of being the recipient of anger from Roberto' and Franco, shook a little, regaining his composure asked, "Are you threatening me Mr. Giovanni? I will not be threatened by you in my home."

"I am not threatening you sir, I am warning you; you would be wise to heed the warning. I am patient because I promised my Catarina and Simone' I would hold my temper while I spoke with you about your behavior toward my precious loved ones. Roberto' would not be as patient with you."

"Simone' is still here in Tuscany Mr. Giovanni?"

His anger raging even more, as Franco started to comment on Vincenzo's question about Simone's whereabouts, at that moment, his father, Francisco knocked on the French Doors to the Parlor and opened one slightly and asked, "May I join you gentleman?" He extended his hand and commented, "Hello, Franco, it has been some years since I have seen you face to face. I hope you and your family are well,"

Shaking his hand as a Gentleman would Franco replied, "Thank you my family is well. I will take my leave now my wife is expecting me. Vincenzo', I hope that you will take thought to our conversation. Good evening gentleman."

Franco was the Gentleman he had promised his wife and daughter to be before he left home, but his temper flared and raged within him while he stood and spoke with Vincenzo'. He drove slowly back home to calm his self before he saw his family.

Francisco looked intently at his son and said, "Vincenzo' what was your meeting about? Franco Giovanni was very angry when he left here. His wanting to see you had nothing to do with the Tuscany Community Development Committee did it son?"

"No Father it did not. I would rather not discuss the reason he came to see me."

"I heard voices through the door and mention of his family before I knocked. What have you to do with his family?"

"Father I would rather not discuss it; please could we just let it drop before mother and my wife hear us talking. It will serve no purpose in your knowing the details of our conversation."

"I will let it go for now my son, but we will visit this again, when my Concetta and your Antonia is not in the house. I feel there is trouble between the two of you and you are trying to hide it son. We will speak of this again and soon. I do not need any trouble with the farmers in this community do you understand? Franco Giovanni is a powerful and respected man in this community. He is the President of the Tuscany Valley Farming Association, as well as the President of the Community Development Committee. It would be trouble if the Farmers and the professional community were raised against us."

"I hear you Father."

"Do you understand? Is what I said Vincenzo'."

"Yes, I understand what you said."

"It is good that you do. Up to now, you have been a good son; I am thankful that you grew up healthy my son, since I lost your twin sister, my sweet Valantina when you both had Scarlett Fever at the age of 10 years old. I am thankful for having one child. I think about that with Antonia and her not having children and I do not have any grandchildren yet Vincenzo'. You are still a good son and descent husband, even though you do not love your wife as you should and treat her with the respect that is due a wife, but you are a good manager of the Moretti Wine and Textiles Industries. We don't need any trouble son, none."

Vincenzo' stood looking at the fire dancing blue and red flames. From its mist he saw Simone's face and remembering how preciously soft and warm she is, fretted in his soul for the loss of her in his life. He thought about his need for her in his life and because of the "system of thought" in a community, two classes of people could not mix. How can you tell a heart that loves someone from another class of people there is a difference? He leaned on the mantel with his right hand holding his head with tears streaming down his face. His entire body shook; he cried out his pain in tears feeling the loss of Simone' in his life and the possibility he may never see Carmeli'ta' again.

His Father still observing his behavior knew his son was perplexed and it had nothing to do with the wine business, was clearly in pain asked, "Son what is the problem why are you crying?"

Surprised he was not alone turned and said in a low voice "Father, I

thought you had left the room. Please can I be alone for a while?"

"Yes, I will leave you alone. Join us for coffee when you feel up to it. We will be in the evening sitting room."

"Thank you I will."

Vincenzo' could not reason with his powerful love for Simone' and the young woman he thought was his daughter. The loss of Simone' in his life made him bitter over the years because of jealousy and envy of a life that should have been his with the woman he loved and child he adored.

Franco arrived home, sat for a minute in his car before entering the kitchen where he knew his wife and daughter were waiting to hear the outcome of the conversation. Simone' and her mother had prayed that he would not lose his temper and hurt Vincenzo' or get hurt.

Franco quietly entered the kitchen through the French doors leading to his wife's garden, "I am here my lovelies." He sat hushed at the table and looked at his daughter so lovely and sweet thought, 'She is so much like her mother, even lovelier and so innocent with a deep and profound intensity within, for one with so much beauty and grace, these facts defies logic.'

"Father what happened at the Moretti home? No one was hurt were they?"

"No, my lovely daughter, I held my temper as I promised. I warned Vincenzo' about his trying to see Carmeli'ta' or you again. I told him how improper, dishonorable, and ungentlemanly he has been over the years not to mention threatening you with exposing what he thinks is the truth of the matter. Simone' are you sure Vincenzo' is not the Father of my granddaughter? He is not willing to give up on it. He is adamant about him being the Father."

Her voice shaking and tears forming in her eyes spoke softly, "I am not sure anymore Father, I am just not sure of anything anymore; he could be. I am sorry to be so much trouble to you and mother."

Catarina angrily said, "No Simone' you are not trouble to your Father and me. Vincenzo' Moretti is the cause of all of the trouble. He should have let the situation stay as it was and not continue to see Carmeli'ta' and you and then threaten you. It was clearly a threat my daughter. You are our daughter and Carmeli'ta' is our granddaughter I am sure of that fact. As far as, who Carmeli'ta's Father is, Roberto' is her Father as far as I am concerned, whether it is true or not true Vincenzo' is the Father, at this point, it is not important. I refuse to accept any other truth, especially Vincenzo' Moretti's version. He is an angry man and acts like a wounded bear."

"Mother is right my daughter that is what we need to concentrate on and how to tell Roberto' what Vincenzo' thinks that is the difficult part we have to deal with."

"It is difficult for me Father, I have to go home in a few days and face my husband, and daughter and I don't know how. I love them so; I could not bear to hurt them and I know that the truth coming out will hurt everyone even our business and Carmeli'ta's position at Madison Steel and Iron."

"I hope that this will only be known between our families Simone'. It would be better if it came out here rather than in America it would only damage Vincenzo's family and not my lovely daughter and her family."

"I can't see how that can be Father. I can't destroy my husband and daughter I just can't maybe it would be better if I did not go back to America then they would be safe."

Franco said, "Simone' your husband and daughter would never accept you not coming home and you would not be happy either with a decision not to return home."

Catarina replied, "We have a few more days to think about this, let's have dessert and coffee and try to relax for the evening and be thankful that no trouble was started between your Father and Vincenzo' Moretti."

"You are right my sweet wife. We will have dessert and relax!" replied Franco.

Vincenzo', after fifteen minutes, joined his family in the evening room. His mother observed his flushed look when he walked through the door, but did not comment at that time. Antonia asked, "What did Mr. Giovanni want of you Vincenzo'? You look flushed and disturbed my husband." Before answering Vincenzo' called Fabia' and asked him to pour him a cup of coffee. After Fabia' handed him the coffee he went and sit next to his Mother finally replied, "It was a community matter Antonia, nothing to concern your pretty head about."

Francisco sat looking straight ahead into the fireplace with no reply, knew that it was not a community matter, not yet anyway. Vincenzo' looked at his father and said, "Charles Meriwether called me yesterday, and wanted to discuss the textile and iron business Co-op that he lately entered in a contract with Madison Steel and Iron to create jobs in Charleston and improve the community. He wanted to know if we were interested in joining in to take advantage of the service he would get from Madison Steel and Iron. I think it would be a good venture and to our advantage to ship some of the highest quality iron made in America."

"We can discuss it with him my son. It sounds interesting and lucrative. Most certainly, if Charles Meriwether is interested and considers a Co-op a good business venture it bears looking into. He does not make business decisions unless it is to his advantage, so yes it worth discussing. We can call him tomorrow, yes Saturday is a good time, and it will be good to discuss and think about it over the weekend and make final decisions next week."

"I will call him around 10:00 a.m. his time since we are five hours ahead of America."

"Sounds good son; thank you for letting me know, it is a good idea to venture into the steel and iron business on this side of the ocean."

In Charleston, Roberto' and Peter completed their examination of the farm shipping and delivery logs and the schedules and he returned home at 6:00 p.m. Marianna had dinner ready and begins putting it on the table when she heard Roberto's car pull in the driveway. Roberto' freshen-up the bathroom in Carmeli'ta' old suite before he entered the kitchen to eat dinner. He wanted to call Simone' before it was any later in Italy; it would be 11:00 p.m. there and she would be retiring soon. He could not bear not speaking to her before she went to sleep, though he said he would call her on Saturday.

"Good evening Marianna, smells delicious as usual."

"Thank you Mr. Bandaci. It is good to have you home to serve dinnerto again. I missed Miss and you being here."

"Thank you Marianna we missed you also. I am ready for dinner. I want to call my wife before she retires for the night."

"Yes, tell her I said hello sir."

"I will Marianna."

After dinner Roberto' went to their private suite and called Simone' while waiting for an operator to connect him, he picked up her picture sitting on the desk and looked at the loveliness that the picture showed, her eyes, mouth, hair, and beautiful honey colored skin. He felt feverish and lonely finally the operator said, "The phone is ringing now sir, we have been busy tonight. I apologize for your wait."

"Thank you."

Simone' had waited in her Father's office; she knew that her husband would call her before she went to bed, picked up the phone and said, "Hello."

"Hello, my beauty. How are you? How was your day?"

"I am fine my husband. I waited for your call before I sleep. Is everything okay with the farm and the deliveries? How is Amelio'?"

"Yes, all is okay my beauty with the farm and Amelio' are doing okay. He is more my brother than my cousin. I can depend on him. Everything with the farm is just as it is when I am here. The logs are accurate of the shipping and deliveries of Bandaci Farms. Peter did a good job of keeping the deliveries on schedule."

"How is my sweet Carmeli'ta'? How did she take the news, of my visiting my parents, a little longer and not returning home with you?"

"I can tell you she was not pleased Simone'. I will see her tomorrow. I wanted to spend a good bit of time with our daughter tomorrow; therefore, I took care of all the farm business today and left tomorrow free. Have you decided when you will be coming home my beauty?"

"Not yet my husband I will let you know in a few days."

"Please do Simone' I miss you; I need you; I want you home with me, my life is nothing without you with me."

"I feel the same Roberto', it will not be long my sweet husband."

"I love you Simone' always remember that my lovely wife."

"I love you my husband, please know that no matter what."

"Good night Simone' sleep well my love. Before I forget, Marianna said hello my beauty and she misses you being here."

"Tell Marianna I said, hello and I miss her as well and I thank her for taking good care of our home and your meals while I am away, Good night my Roberto' I hope that you sleep well to. I will miss you tonight being near me."

"Thank you good night."

Hanging up both Roberto' and Simone' felt the same chill of loneliness trickle across their mind and bodies at the thought of retiring alone for the evening. Roberto' warmed his self by the fire that Marianna lit earlier; it had given the room the toasty comfortable feeling that Roberto' enjoyed each evening during the winter season.

Simone' walked down the hallway to her bedroom into the bathroom and drew her bath relaxed in the warm water for a while dressed, slipping between the warm sheets her mother had for her bed. She remembered the same comfortable feeling of warmth and safety in her parent's home when she was a growing child.

A time of planning...

CHAPTER
THIRTY-ONE

Carmeli'ta' and Jason, as planned, spent the evening in the quietness of her Townhouse snuggling in front of her Fireplace talking about their future. They also discussed what Jason would say to her father when he asked his permission to take her hand in marriage.

Jason looked at Carmeli'ta' sitting so quiet and lovely knew that there would be many evening of his kind in their lives. She was peaceful, loving, kind, understanding, caring, warm, and beautiful. He could not think of anyone that he thought more beautiful than his sweet Carmeli'ta'.

Jason seeing the faraway look in Carmeli'ta's eyes pulled her close to him saying, "Tell me my darling what you have on your mind, you look perplexed."

Carmeli'ta' silent for a moment before she answered, "My Mother did not return with my father earlier today; she stayed in Tuscany with my grandparents for a few more days."

"Why is that so strange to you my darling? Has she seen her parents recently?"

"No, it has been four years since my grandparents were here to visit mother, father, and me. This is their first trip back to Tuscany since they came here when I was 5 years old. Mother never mentioned to me that she was thinking about going to Tuscany even when she called me at work. She said she was calling to see if I was okay. She never calls me at work."

"I am not sure where you are going with this my love."

"My father acted strange when he called me to tell me he was going to Tuscany also. He left quickly; his trip was not planned either and that is the issue I have with both of my parents leaving, and this is strange behavior for them. They always tell me when they are going anywhere out of the city, which is not very often because of the farm."

"Now I see where you are going with this. I understand. That would be strange behavior for my parents as well if they left to go back to Ireland suddenly without explanation. Madison Steel has kept my father and mother from traveling extensively also. If they suddenly left without explanation I would have the same concern and questions."

My father acted so strangely when he left; he barely talked to me and that is unusual for him. He always talks with me each day and visits me at home three to four times a week on his way from the farm in the evenings."

"I can see now what you mean my darling. When will your father visit? I thought he would be visiting you tonight my love."

"He wanted to check the farm and delivery logs and talk with Peter his Foreman and Amelio' about the business while he was away. He will come tomorrow after I arrive home from work tomorrow evening around 4:00 p.m."

"We will complete the Contract review as soon as possible my darling and you can come home to relax before talking with your Father. The deliveries and accounts are set up for Meriwether Textiles. The delivery schedules are all arranged, therefore, there is nothing else we need to do at the present time. Charles Meriwether is being cooperative, to my surprise, and that is a plus for us my darling and it worries me as well; he is too willing to cooperate, I wonder my darling about his sudden and obliging cooperation. He is to be watched."

"Yes, that is a plus my love he is cooperating. Then again, I thought the same about his sudden turn-a-round Jason. I agree he is to be watched but could he have an ulterior motive if so what? On to the matter at hand, I will leave as soon as I can tomorrow and relax before father gets here. It has been a long three weeks of meetings, planning strategy and contract negotiations my darling. I, for one, am happy it is over and the contracts are solid between Meriwether Textiles and Madison Steel and Iron; the co-op and job creation initiative makes a good marriage."

"I agree Carmeli'ta'. It is all because of your major role in solidifying the relationship as well as keeping the lines of communication open. My father and mother are pleased with the progress you made my darling future wife."

"Thank you Jason for both compliments."

It was after 11:00 p.m. Jason looked at his watch and rose pulling Carmeli'ta' up, "It is time for me to go my beautiful Carmeli'ta'. I will see you at 9:00 a.m. tomorrow."

"Yes, my darling. I will see you at 9:00 a.m. I love you Jason."

"I love you Carmeli'ta'. I am looking forward to our wedding soon my love."

"So am I Jason." They said goodnight at the door. Jason waited to hear Carmeli'ta' drop the latch in place. When he heard it, he tapped lightly and left for home.

Carmeli'ta' feeling weary, happy she had taken her bath when she arrived home, went to her bedroom took a pink negligée from her lingerie armoire put it on, slipped between the sheet lay for a moment thinking of her father, mother, Jason, and her future marriage drifted into a peaceful sleep.

After preparing for bed and talking with Simone', Roberto' spent the remainder of the evening thinking about what he would tell Carmeli'ta' why her mother left so suddenly and went to Tuscany. He knew she would not accept that she decided to visit her grandparents at the last minute. Simone' and Carmeli'ta' were close and she would have told her under ordinary circumstance she would be going to visit her parents. He knew that Carmeli'ta' was not convinced of the reason he gave her, felt drowsy, after many hours of going over the events, of the past three weeks and how drastically his life changed overnight thought, "Life is so beautiful one minute like a sunshiny day with no clouds in the sky. Then again, in an instant or moments time, your life changes into an unexpected storm with darkness looming over. The floodwaters of issues rise higher and higher until you feel as if you are drowning caught without a life jacket to stay afloat." Sleeping finally, Roberto' awaken at 6:00 a.m. showered, dressed, went to the desk in the sitting room of their suite and called Simone'. Her father answered, "Franco Giovanni here speaking."

"Good morning Franco is Simone' nearby?"

"Good morning my son, she is in the kitchen with her mother preparing lunch. I will get her. How are you my son?"

"I am well thank you rested and ready to get back to work next week."

Franco lay the phone receiver down, walked to his office door, and called, "Simone'."

"Yes, father, I will be right there." She walked down the short hallway to the office doors and smiled, "I am here my father." Franco replied as he picked up the receiver, "Roberto' is calling from America."

Simone' smiling ran across the room to the desk taking the receiver felt excited said sweetly, "Hello my husband. I was waiting for you to call me. How was your night?"

"My night was restful my beauty. I missed you being here. How are you today my lovely wife?"

"I am well my husband. Mother and I was preparing lunch. It is near 1:00 p.m. here now; we are late eating lunch today. Father did not get back from his Committee Meeting until just a few minutes ago. When will you visit Carmeli'ta'?"

"I will visit with her after work today. She and Jason are finalizing contracts I believe is what she told me. I plan to be there at 4:00 p.m. First, this morning, I will go to the farm and check with Peter and return to relax and have lunch before I face our daughter. I am not sure what I will tell her Simone'. When I spoke with her yesterday, she was insistent on knowing "why" you did not return with me yesterday."

"I know, my husband, she is so like you my darling wanting to know all the details."

"Yes, she is like me my darling. I have known that for years and I am thankful to have her as my daughter. I will never be able to thank you for the beautiful daughter you gave me. The day she was born the first time I saw her astounded me. She looked like a doll. I loved you even more the day she was born."

Simone' with silent tears running down her cheeks, barely whispered, "Thank you my husband."

Roberto' hearing the whispering knew she was crying, "Simone' my beauty, why are you crying? I did not want to upset you with what I said."

"I am not upset my husband just thankful that you love me with a passion and depth that I cannot always understand. I am so thankful to God for you my sweet husband. Carmeli'ta' is a blessing in our life. She is a sweet daughter never giving us one minute of trouble as she grew-up. Marianna spoiled her while we worked to get the farm going, but she does not act like a spoiled child. In that respect she is truly like you my husband; you think of others before yourself and so does she."

"Yes, my beauty and she is beautiful like her mother with a sweet personality."

"Thank you my husband. It is nearly time for your breakfast. I don't want Marianna to wait long, even though she loves for us to be late so she can say, 'you are late again'." Both of them laughed because they knew they were late each day so Marianna would not be disappointed. "Yes, my beauty it is my breakfast time, and Franco is waiting for lunch I am sure. Take care of yourself and I will call you and tell you the outcome of the conversation with our daughter."

Thank you my husband for caring. Take care of yourself and do let me know what my sweet daughter said before you sleep tonight. I will wait for you to call before I sleep my husband. Bye for now."

"Bye my beauty; enjoy the rest of your day."

Simone' and Roberto' placed the phone receivers in the hooks. Simone went back to the kitchen where her father and mother were waiting to eat lunch. Roberto' went downstairs entering the kitchen Marianna said, "It is 8:15 a.m. sir, you are late again."

Roberto' smiling said, "Thank you my time-clock. I am ready Marianna."

After breakfast, Roberto' left for the farm. He informed Marianna he planned to return by noon for lunch and to rest before he visited Carmeli'ta'. He wanted to check with Amelio' also to see how he was doing and if he needed his assistance in any way. As he drove to his farm, his thoughts went to Simone' and how much he missed her wanting to know what secret she held so closely; yet, all the while, wanting to have her home so he could be near her. She was like the air he breathed he could not endure her being gone long; it had already been an eternity after two days.

Saturday morning, December 2, Carmeli'ta' arrived at Madison Steel at 8:45 a.m. her usual time entered the plant through the door for the company's top administration. Jason was in his office when she arrived. Knocking lightly at his door before entering she opened the door, Jason came around his desk and met her halfway the office, "Hello my lovely Carmeli'ta'. I was waiting anxiously to see you my darling. How was your night?"

"Hello my darling. I am fine my night was peaceful. How was your night my love?"

"My night was peaceful and restful as always. I missed you after I left you last night. It tears at my heart each time. I hated to leave you my lovely Carmeli'ta'. I want to marry you as soon as I can get your Father's permission to do so. I love you so my sweetheart and I do not want to be apart from you."

"I know Jason, I feel the same way my darling. I hope that you can talk to Father soon my darling. It will be wonderful to be your wife and have you come home to me after your day ends or we go home together after our workday is over."

"I love both ideas my darling. I want you to continue in your position after we are married. I do not want anything to change that you do. The only change I want is us to move into a home of our own."

"Thank you my darling. I am looking forward to being your wife and us working together."

"Yes my lovely. Now let us finalize these contracts and the delivery

schedules and get you home to rest for the visit with your father."

"Yes, I want to leave at 1:00 p.m. Jason so I can rest and prepare my Father's favorite drink."

"I had begun to check the Contract terms and delivery schedules when I arrived earlier. It will not take long to complete the check list."

Jason and Carmeli'ta' worked steadily completing the last on the checklist at 12:55 p.m. Carmeli'ta' rose from her chair walking towards the coat rack in Jason's office where she hang her coat when she arrived. Jason walked quickly there taking the coat from the rack held it for her to put on, opened his office door and escorted her to the car, kissed her, closed the car door, she smiled, and drove away from the parking lot.

Carmeli'ta' arrived home by 1:30 p.m. freshened-up, made Tea, and put the glasses in the refrigerator to cool and rested before her father arrived.

Saturday morning, December 2, Francisco, and Vincenzo' in the office located in their home called Charles Meriwether as discussed the Friday night before to listen to his proposal for taking advantage of the opportunity to import from Madison Steel and Iron. Plans for the steel and iron was for use in their wine industry plant facilities or sell as a supplier to companies in the United Kingdom, some of the best steel and iron made in America in the 1920s.

The operator rang the phone at 16 Chateauguay Le'Armant Avenue. Jeffrey, the Butler, answered the phone, "Meriwether resident."

"I have a call from Tuscany, Italy for Charles Bienville Meriwether, is he there please?" asked the operator.

"Yes, he is in, please hold and I will get him for you."

Charles Meriwether had walked out in the garden from his office enjoying the view and the flowers he loved so much his mother planted years ago before she died, smiled at the beauty of the day and the garden. The Meriwether's gardens, one of the most luscious in Charleston, with every flower imaginable surrounded a fountain with a stunning statue of a woman reminding him of Juanita Madison, became a tourist attraction, and were visible from the street behind the decorative iron fence around his mansion. He heard the phone rang walked back toward his office reaching the door Jeffrey said, "A long distance call for you sir from Tuscany."

"Thank you Jeffrey, I will take it here, please close the door when you leave."

He picked up the phone after Jeffrey closed the door and said, "Charles Meriwether."

The operator said, "Mr. Meriwether, I have a call from Tuscany, Italy from Vincenzo' Moretti, will you take the call?"

"Yes, of course, put him through."

"Vincenzo', I have expected your call. It is good to hear from you. How is your family?"

"All is well on this end and you my friend?"

As always Charles Meriwether is a get to the meat of the matter man said, "I am well thank you. I wanted to offer you and Francisco the opportunity to buy into the lucrative venture of the steel and iron contracts I have entered into with a major steel and iron player her in South Carolina. The iron and steel produced here in Charleston are of the finest quality. My constituents in Europe are using it to upgrade our plant and be a second party supplier on that side of the Atlantic. I think it will be a good investment; we could partner together in this."

"Yes Charles, my father thinks that it is worth looking at what is being proposed. When can we meet and discuss the venture?"

"Very soon Vincenzo, I will check my calendar and let you know. The shipping begins in January 1928."

"Thank you Charles we will look forward to hearing from you. Bye for now. My father sends his regards."

"Thank you Vincenzo' let him know I appreciate him asking about me. I will call you soon."

Charles Meriwether hang up the phone and smiled. His first step was made in the destruction of Jason Madison, Sr. Being nebulous is a tool he uses in his business, another reason he was so elusive and hard to read, using people was also one of his fortes'.

In Tuscany, Saturday, December 2, the same day, Simone' and her parents talked about how to approach Roberto' with the subject of her being secretive, not allowing her husband to be close to her in the way he desired over the years.

"Father have you any suggestions how I can approach the subject with Roberto'? He will call again tonight; tomorrow will the third day since he left. I told him I want to stay three or four days longer."

Catarina replied, "I don't see anyway except start from the beginning when you were a child and tell him that way; he will better understand and get the full picture of what you mean my daughter."

"I agree my Catarina. Simone', moreover, you will have to be truthful with your husband; it has gone too far for you not to be truthful with him, at this point. As to Moretti's claim Carmeli'ta' is his child will be difficult issue to get past my daughter; nonetheless, you will have to tell him his claim and do not hold anything back from him and remember my daughter it is his claim no matter whether this entire issue has made you question yourself, do not say that to him. He is angry enough as it is. Vincenzo' Moretti would be in danger if Roberto' were here and you told him what Vincenzo' is claiming. He still might be even with your husband in America. I know he would make a trip here just to see Vincenzo' and the results would not be good for Vincenzo' we can be certain of that fact."

"I know father, my husband's temper when something happens that might affect his family; can be dangerous for that person. I will not mention my question in my mind about Carmeli'ta'. I just know that it is a possibility within the period before I got married. He told me once, he does not know what he would do if someone hurt Carmeli'ta' or me, but it would not be good. His statement and the look in his eyes made chills go through me."

"I know you told us that yesterday. He can be dangerous, like his father, Roberto', Sr.; he loved his family as passionately as Roberto' loves his. When will you tell him you will come home Simone'?" asked Franco

"Today is Saturday my daughter. What do you think about Tuesday of next week December 5?" said Catarina.

"Yes, Mother, that will be a good time. I will have a few more days to think about this more and plan what I will say first to my sweet husband. I will wait to see how the meeting goes with Carmeli'ta' before telling him when I plan to come home. I will check to see if there are any seats left on the plane on Tuesday. Thank you Mother and Father, I wish I were not in America when I tell my husband and it could be kept quiet and not affect Carmeli'ta' job or our farm."

"You are right my daughter; it would be better if it came out here and not in America, we would wait to see what the next few days bring my lovely daughter" said Franco.

Catarina had starting preparing dinner; it was getting later in the evening.

On his way home that Saturday, Roberto' stopped to see Amelio's at his Farm Office. Amelio' saw Roberto's Roadster pull up to his office opened the door smiled said, "I am glad to see you my cousin. I did not expect to see you today. Please come in."

"Hello Amelio'. I stopped to see you and thank you again for your help with my farm. Also, I wanted to see if there is anything I can do to assist you with your farm business."

"Everything is running smoothly my cousin, as always. I want you to take care of the matters at hand and do what is necessary to help your family. If you need some additional time off, I can manage both the farms, okay? Our Foreman's' are dependable and good managers. I mostly oversee what they are doing now. I do not work a lot my cousin, mostly handling the financial part of my business."

"I agree Amelio', they are good managers; we are blessed to have them. I will let you know if I need your assistance. You will have lunch with me as usual on Sunday after Church. Marianna always expects you."

"Yes, as always my cousins. We have been having lunch together on Sunday's all our lives. I do not want to change that now. I told you I am thinking about returning to Tuscany my cousin. I had thought about another four years here. I will be 51 years old then. I want to marry and retire in our old country in our little valley."

"Your leaving will be a sad day for me my cousin. I will definitely miss you being here. You have been more than a cousin, but a friend, a brother and a father figure all rolled into one. You have always been more mature than your years even when we were growing up. My father told me once that if he were not here for me I could depend on you and he was right. You are a wise, faithful, and loyal cousin."

"Thank you Roberto'. It has always been easy to help you and advise you. You were always willing to listen and heed advice as we grew and even now as a man. It was not hard for me to be a father figure and friend to you. I will be there for you as long as I live without fail my cousin."

"Thank you Amelio'. I am meeting my sweet daughter in a few hours. I want to eat lunch and rest, before I see her to talk with her about Simone' not returning home. She is a bit upset and I want to try to assuage her fears."

"Yes, Carmeli'ta' is sharp. Trying to fool her or put her off when she wants to know the truth of a matter is not easy. She is like you in that respect Roberto'. She has the same insistent personality just by the look she gives or that silent nature she has, so much like you my cousin."

Roberto' smiling at the pleasant thought of Carmeli'ta' being so much like him said, "Thank you Amelio', I am proud of my sweet daughter and she is persistent in a matter until she knows all details. She is that way in business, is one of the reasons why she has been so successful at Madison Steel and Iron. Amelio' you said that you were wanted to get married, do you have someone in mind?"

"Yes, my cousin. You remember Bibi 'Ana Nunnarelli?"

"Yes, Amelio', she was your High School Sweetheart. She went away to school when she was sixteen. Her parents owned the Allevamento di polli (Chicken Farm). What happen to her? You heard from here again?"

"Yes, a few times my cousin. I loved her then and still love her now is why I have never married my cousin. It broke my heart when she left the valley to go to private school."

"I knew that you loved her Amelio' and I wondered if that was the reason for your being single all these years and never married. I noticed the change in you when I was growing up. You were almost 21 years old when she left, you were quiet and reserved after her leaving. I did not want to ask. I knew that you would tell me why eventually."

"Her parents sent her to a private girl's school in Rome in 1904. After she graduated, she lived and worked in Rome for many years, my cousin. Her father chose a husband for her in Rome a wealthy merchant who owned hotels. He died ten years after their marriage and she has been single since that time. She is now around Simone's age forty-one or maybe a few months older. We have kept in touch over the years and now we are planning to be married and live in Tuscany."

"This is good news to me my cousin. When will you get married? I remember Bibi 'Ana was a beautiful girl when we were in school. She is not as tall as my Simone' but very petite with beautiful, black, straight hair."

"Yes, she is still beautiful, even more so now my cousin. She never had children and neither do I and we have so much in common. She is still in love with me my cousin. We are planning the wedding date now. I will let you know when we get it set. She is finalizing all her property sales in Rome now; she has only the house left, which a potential buyer is looking at now."

"You never wanted children Amelio'?"

"I did Roberto' with Bibi 'Ana and that did not happen so I concentrated on building my future for retirement hoping one day we would meet again. It is not too late for children now, but we want to spend the time together. I have always thought of Carmeli'ta' as mine as well my cousin since we are a close family. I love her she is precious to me. She is my heir. She will get all my property and money." "I know you love her Amelio' and she adores you as well. You were so close when she was growing and she was happy to see you each Sunday at church and then for lunch. It is not necessary for you to leave Carmeli'ta' as your heir she will have more than enough from her mother and me."

"I want to leave it to her. I will always think of her as mine too. I love her as I do you; she is part of me; because she is part of you."

"Thank you for saying that about my Carmeli'ta'. I know she would be in good-hands if anything ever happened to me. I am looking forward to hearing the wedding date. Will you get married here, in Tuscany, or in Rome?"

"I would take care of both Simone' and her Roberto' the same as you do. To answer your question, we will get married here and live the last few years before I retire and move back to Tuscany. We will get married at our congregation here in Charleston. I have already spoken to Brother Meriwether about the wedding. She helped me decorate the cottage when I was in Tuscany three years ago. We met and spent that month decorating and spending time together renewing our relationship and love."

"The cottage is as beautiful now as it was when Simone' and I spent our honeymoon there. It was just as I remember when I was growing up when you and your parents lived there."

"I wanted the cottage to feel like home again so I had it decorated as it was when I lived there. Bibi 'Ana loves the quaint and elegant look; actually, without me telling her the furniture and drapes she chose made it look almost exactly like they did when we were growing up. I was amazed." Pausing for a moment Roberto' looked at him and asked, "When you say renewing your love Amelio" does that mean?"

"Yes, it does my cousin. I know that I love her and did not want to spend any more time alone, but wanted and needed the warmth of a woman in my life and she still is and has always been that woman."

"I understand Amelio'."

"I hope that you do Roberto'. I think you understand what I mean and the Church. I hope you can approve of my Bibi 'Ana."

"I want you to be happy Amelio'. I do understand, I will never judge you in that respect. You deserve it and yes, Bibi 'Ana, like Simone' is now, I remember when we were in school together she was sweet, kind, and always smiled. I am just sorry that I did not know my Simone' then."

"Amelio' smiled, I understand. Simone' is a gem my cousin. You could not have chosen a better wife and mother of your child."

"Thank you Amelio'. I am happy for you and Bibi 'Ana. Tell her I said hello."

"I will tell her Roberto'. She asked about you when I spoke to her yesterday. I told her you were fine. She also knew Simone' when they were growing up. She wanted to know if she would be her Matron of Honor she was an only child as we were and her parents are gone now."

"I am sure that my wife will be happy to her Matron of Honor. I will have a sister Amelio' that is wonderful. It is a small world my cousin. I have to go. It is nearing 11:30 a.m. Marianna will be waiting lunch. I will let you know the outcome of the conversation with Carmeli'ta'. One more question Amelio', you said her parents are gone, what happened to their Allevamento di polli?"

'She sold it to the Moretti family. Her parent's land and the Moretti Vineyards are connected; separated only by a fence. They wanted to extend their Vineyard about three years ago; she got a good price for it; the land was what the Moretti's were looking for, flat and fertile."

"I will tell my beauties hello, for you my cousin."

"Yes, do Roberto'. Tell both Carmeli'ta' and Simone'I said hello. Roberto' after lunch tomorrow I have an idea that I want to talk to you about to make sure that our finances are secure for the future."

"I will look forward to hearing your ideas my cousin. Thank you for always thinking of me when you are planning for future security for our finances. I want to make sure Simone' and Carmeli'ta' are secure."

Roberto arrived home at 12:00 Noon, had lunch and rested for a few hours before he left for the meeting with Carmeli'ta' at 4:00 p.m.

In Tuscany, Saturday evening, December 2, Simone' had assisted her mother with preparing dinner as they chatted about the conversation she would have with Roberto' when she returned to Charleston.

"Mother it will be a difficult conversation to talk with Roberto' about. I do not know how to bear the look of pain in his eyes. When we talked while he was here, his eyes only showed me hurt and confusion about the situation."

"I know that you are concerned about his reaction to the explanation Simone'; it has to be said and you are the only one that can make it easier for him to understand. Roberto' is not a weak man and he loves you my sweet daughter. You made what you thought was the best decision at that time. You did not hide the situation out of viciousness or out of deceit but to protect him and Carmeli'ta'. The truth is the only medicine that will lessen the pain for your husband and start the healing of his heart. If he thinks that you don't love him that is more painful than what you have to tell him."

"I know Mother. I just love him so much and don't want to hurt him anymore."

"You are strong Simone' you have always been. You have a quiet strength that is very apparent to anyone around you, even the ones that does not know you. Pull from that strength and your faith in God my daughter."

"I do Mother that is the only way that I have survived over the years with this and talking with my Minister about the situation."

"I am happy that you had someone to talk to about his Simone'. I am sure, that he advised you well."

"He did Mother. He told me to tell my husband because Roberto' had been talking to him over the time about it. But Roberto' does not know that I have been seeing our Minister."

"It is complicated my daughter but not impossible to deal with. The truth is the only way that you will get pass this problem and get your life back on an even keel."

"I know Mother, being here with you and Father have made it seems less stressful and I have gained new strength to go forward and tell my husband why the mystery all these years. Thank you Mother for your support; I have the best parents in the world." She added, "Roberto' will be visiting Carmeli'ta' today to talk with her about my decision to stay in Tuscany."

It was nearing the time for Roberto' to visit his daughter to talk with her about why her Mother did not return home and why she left suddenly without explanation.

Difficult explanation...confusion of a daughter...

C H A P T E R

Thirty-Two

While dressing in preparation to leave, Roberto' thought, "this will be a difficult conversation to have with my Carmeli'ta'. She is not put-off that easily. My explanation will sound suspicious to her. I will pray that she is not insistent on knowing the whole of the matter it would serve no purpose in her knowing and being upset."

Roberto' walked into the kitchen, "Marianna, I am leaving now to see Carmeli'ta'. I should return between 6:00 p.m. and 7:00 p.m."

"Yes, Mr. Bandaci dinner will be ready."

"I know that this is your night off; I will understand if you want to take Sunday off since you have not had a day off this week."

"I am fine Mr. Bandaci. I was off for ten days while you were in Tuscany that was enough. I am happy that you are home and I can prepare dinner for you."

"Thank you Marianna, you are thoughtful. I appreciate your loyalty."

"You are welcome sir. I will see you when you return. Tell Miss Carmeli'ta' I said hello."

"I will tell her."

Roberto' arrived at Carmeli'ta's Townhouse at 3:55 p.m. parked and sat for a few minutes to collect his thoughts before exiting the car. Carmeli'ta' was waiting at her Bay Window, especially when she knew her father was coming to visit her, saw him exit the car, rushed to the refrigerator, took out the tea with the chilled glasses, and placed them on the coffee table near her Fireplace. The Fireplace had a soft glow to it setting a pleasant ambiance in the room. Slowly climbing the steps, Roberto' feeling at a loss for words, knocked lightly and waited for her to open the door.

"Father is that you?"

"Yes my daughter it is your father."

Carmeli'ta' opened the door smiled rushed into her father open arms saying, "Hello daddy I missed you while you were away. I am glad that you are back and safe. It is good to see you daddy." Carmeli'ta' hugged him a long time, Roberto' smiling, turned closed the door, took her hand, walked over to the Fireplace, leaned forward, and kissed her on the forehead said, "It is good to be home my sweet daughter and good to see you and know that you are safe."

"I made you favorite drink daddy would you like some?"

"Yes, my Carmeli'ta' I would. Thank you for being so sweet my lovely daughter." She poured two glasses of tea and handing her father a glass taking her glass and sit in the oversize chair across from the sofa where she knew her father would sit near the fireplace.

"How is everything with your work daughter? Did you and Jason Madison complete the contracts? He is doing well?"

"Everything is going well at work my father. Jason and I did complete the contract work much as we could at this point, the second phase will start soon. Jason is doing well. He is kind and sweet to me as ever."

Roberto' listened to his daughter, looking at her face, he saw the expression on it when she spoke of Jason Madison as he see on Simone's face when she looks at him. This frightened Roberto' he was afraid that his daughter would be hurt.

"Carmeli'ta' I am happy to hear that all is well for you and your job. Your mother decided to stay in Tuscany a few more days to visit with her parents since she has not seen them for four years. She misses them so much being such a long distance from them."

"I know that mother misses my grandparents my father, but my question is why did she leave so suddenly three weeks ago after you and she came to see me on Wednesday and she left on Thursday?"

"She decided at the last minute to visit your grandparents my daughter."

"Did you discuss it father? You were angry with mother and me when you left that night. Did that have something to do with why she left? I just don't understand all of this mother never goes anywhere   w i t h o u t telling me she always has talked with me about all things."

"She just decided to go at the last-minute Simone'. We cannot argue with her decision of visiting her parents my darling daughter."

"I am not arguing that decision my father it is just strange that she decided to go suddenly after the discussion about my date with Jason. You were angry with us both. I have not seen you angry that way with mother in my life my father. I do not understand yet what she did to make you angry. She only said that she thought that I should have a choice in who my heart loves as you and she raised me to believe."

"I was angry that night Carmeli'ta' the thought upset me, I cannot bear to think you might be hurt my daughter by anyone. As well, I do not like to be kept in the dark about what is happening with my family."

"I asked mother not to tell you my father. I wanted to tell you myself. She was only honoring the request I made of her. You should be angry with me and not my mother. She is so good to everyone and she is the best mother in the world to me as you are the best father in the world to me."

"Thank you my sweet daughter. Your mother is precious to me. Yes, she is a good mother, wife, partner, and friend; she is my best friend. I was only angry for a little while that night my daughter not later after we arrived home we were just fine."

"Father did mother tell you that she was going to Tuscany to visit my grandparent?"

"Yes, Carmeli'ta' she did." Roberto' hoped that she would accept that answer and not ask any further questions. Simone' had left him a note, so he did know, but not before she had gone. He tried to avoid being specific. Carmeli'ta' looked at her father sitting looking at her wondered if he really knew but would not voice her suspicions to her father out of respect and honor. She dared not question him that was just not done in her family and to her father. Her mother would definitely disapprove of her questioning her father. Carmeli'ta' did not say any more about whether her father knew or not.

"Father, when will Mother return home? Have you heard from her today? I miss my mother so much."

"Yes, I spoke with her before I had breakfast she was helping your grandmother prepare lunch. Tuscany is five hours ahead of our time. She was fine and said tell you hello and she would speak with you in a few days."

"It is still hard for me to get the concept Father that Tuscany is five hours ahead of us and it is near mother's bedtime there and we have not had dinner."

"Yes, my daughter it is a bit of a difference in the time zone. It makes a difference in the way that you feel as well after you travel on a plane and then go forward five hours once you are at a certain point when crossing the Atlantic."

"I should visit my grandparents one day my Father it would be nice to see where I was born and where you and Mother grew up. I was so young I vaguely remember my home. I do remember the pretty white cottage that lined the hillside each time I was playing in the yard."

"Yes, my daughter maybe one day I can take you there. It is still the most beautiful place in the world to me. Your mother and I went to our favorite place on the hillside overlooking the *Val di Greve River* in Tuscany whose waters gives life to the valley."

"Oh, that would be lovely my Father. I will look forward to it. Maybe Jason can visit with us and see where I was born."

"I am sure that he will enjoy seeing Tuscany Valley; it is a beautiful place. Your grandfather is the Chairman of the Tuscany Farming Committee and President of the Tuscany Community Development Committee. Under his leadership, the community has seen enormous growth and progress for the future. He is a good businessman with a brilliant mind."

Carmeli'ta' smiled and listened to her father talk about Tuscany Valley thinking, "My father is hiding something from me; I don't know what it is. I know that it has something to do with my mother staying in Tuscany and not returning home. She has never been away from my father at any time. They are together all the time. It is strange what he is telling me."

After a few moments of thoughts about what her father was hiding, Carmeli'ta' settled into comfortably chatting and laughing with her father. Roberto' looked at his pocket it was 6:50 p.m. commented, "It is getting near my dinner time. I need to get home at the time I told Marianna I would be there for dinner between 6:00 p.m. and 7:00 p.m. Would you like to have dinner with me Carmeli'ta' or do you have other plans?"

"I have a dinner engagement my father. I will have lunch tomorrow with you and Uncle Amelio' if you don't mind."

"That would be excellent my daughter. I will look forward to it after we leave Church tomorrow. You are attending Lord's Day Service with me aren't you?"

"Yes, I will attend with you tomorrow my father and then have lunch."

"You have not called Amelio' Uncle in a long time Carmeli'ta'. I am sure that he will be pleased to hear you call him uncle. He adores and loves you more than you realize I am sure."

"Yes, I love him to he was so good to me when I was growing up and now that I am an adult, treats me with respect; and is still sweet and kind always. I am sorry that he does not have a wife all these years."

Roberto' smiling knew Amelio' was to be married soon; but, wanted it to be a surprise for Carmeli'ta' and wanted Amelio' to tell her himself.

"Thank you for the tea my daughter. I will tell your mother I talk with you and you are missing her and want to talk with her. Oh, one more thing, Marianna said tell you hello."

"Tell Marianna I said hi and I will see her tomorrow. Tell mother I love her and miss her for me father and please hurry home."

"I will give the message to your mother. I need to call your mother before she goes to bed. It is almost midnight there; she will be waiting up for me. I don't want to keep her up that long." "Yes, father. It is getting late." Roberto' took Carmeli'ta' by the hand, walked to the door, hugged, and kissed her on the forehead, smiled, opened the door, and left for home. Carmeli'ta' closed the door and stood for a moment in the foyer looking in the mirror wondering why her father did not tell her more about her mother leaving and not returning home with him. Walking slowly back to her bedroom she dressed for her evening with Jason. She would ask more questions tomorrow after lunch while she is spending the evening with her father and her cousin Amelio' who she always called her uncle.

Roberto' drove quickly home, pulling into his driveway, entered the office door, and called "Hello Marianna I am here." Marianna had begun to put dinner on the table when she heard his car pull into the driveway. He washed his hands in the bathroom in the suite downstairs went to the kitchen; Marianna smiled and said, "You are almost late sir it is 6:57 p.m. Your dinner is ready."

"Thank you Marianna my timeclock. I am ready for dinner. Carmeli'ta' said hello and she will join us for lunch tomorrow along with Amelio'. I hope that is enough notice of guests coming for you to prepare since Ms. Bandaci takes care of these matters."

"Thank you Mr. Bandaci for your thoughtfulness. I will be fine. Ms. Carmeli'ta' and Mr. Amelio's are not guests. It will be like old times having them here on Sunday."

"Yes, I am looking forward to it." Roberto' hurriedly ate his dinner. He wanted to call his wife it was near 1:00 a.m. or after in Tuscany. "Thank you Marianna the dinner was delicious. I need to call Ms. Bandaci and then retire for the evening. Do you have everything you need for lunch tomorrow before I retire?"

"Yes, I do thank you."

"Goodnight Marianna." Upstairs, Roberto' walked to the sitting room over to the desk picked up the phone and waited for the operator to answer.

The phone rang a voice said, "Operator, how can I help you?"

"I would like to make an international call to Tuscany, Italy." Yes sir. May I get the number and the party's name?"

"Yes, the number is 0+1-998-765-4375-46. I would like to speak with Simone' Bandaci." Simone' was waiting for Roberto's call in her father's office, she sat near the fireplace reading Shakespeare's Sonnet 116:

> Let me not to the marriage of true minds
> Admit impediments. Love is not love
> Which alters when it alteration finds,
> Or bends with the remover to remove:
> O no; it is an ever-fixed mark,
> That looks on tempests, and is never shaken;
> It is the star to every wandering bark,
> Whose worth's unknown, although his height be taken.
> Love's not Time's fool, though rosy lips, and cheeks
> Within his bending sickle's compass come;
> Love alters not with his brief hours and weeks,
> But bears it out even to the edge of doom.
> If this be error and upon me proved,
> I never writ, "Nor" no man ever loved.
> www.Shakespeare.com

She thought as she sat reading how she and Roberto' were trueminded married people.

However, trouble come, the years that would pass, or the changing of season in their lives, our love will not change, but it is true to the end. She loved him with all her heart no matter what took place and would continue to love him until she took the last breath of her life and then went through eternity. If she has not been truly in love then what have they created all the years they have been together? It was not her imagination or some fallacy of mind. The moment she read Sonnet 116, knew she had to tell her husband and let the strength of their love keep the bonds tight between them. Humans do so many things for the sake of love and devotion.

Deep into thought did not realize that the phone was ringing and her father had answered it. He walked into his office and noticed that she was not aware of the ringing of the telephone picked up the receiver and replied, "Franco Giovanni here speaking."

"Franco, how are you? I was expecting my lovely wife to answer the phone."

"I am fine Roberto'. She is here sitting and reading. She did not hear the phone she is so engrossed in what she is reading my son. Let me tell her you are waiting to speak with her."

Franco walked over to where Simone' was sitting and touched her on her shoulder. When she looked up Franco saw a perplexed and far away expression on her face said, "Yes, Father. I am sorry that I did not know you were in the room."

"It is okay my lovely daughter. Your Roberto' is on the phone waiting to talk with you." Surprised, she said, "I did not hear the phone rang my father were you using it when the call came through?"

"No, my daughter I was in the kitchen talking with your mother while she set the bread dough up for tomorrow meals. You were engrossed in your reading. It must have been interesting you did not hear the phone."

"Yes it was father. I was reading Shakespeare's Sonnet 116 one of your favorites and now am a favorite of Roberto' and mine."

"Yes, my daughter it still is and always will be. Your husband is waiting my daughter. We can discuss more about the Sonnet later."

"Yes, my father let's do discuss later."

Simone' walked swiftly to the desk picked up the receiver and said, "Hello my husband, I was waiting for you to call. I am happy to hear from you. How are you? How is everything and everybody at home?"

"Everything is fine and everyone is doing okay my beauty. I begin to worry when you did not answer the phone. I thought I may have waited too late to call and you had gone to bed."

"No, my darling I was reading and thinking about you and so engrossed in thought I did not hear the phone nor realize father was in the room. I would not go to bed without talking with you my sweet husband. I will always wait for you no matter where we are."

"Thank you my beauty. I appreciate knowing that you will always wait for me. I love you more each day and more heightened awareness of it now that we are apart."

"Thank you my darling husband. How is Carmeli'ta'? What was her reaction to your explanation of my not returning yesterday with you?"

"I do not think she was convinced with the reason that I gave her for you not coming home and you not telling her you were visiting your parents. She was, especially focused, on the fact that, I was angry with you and her when we left her Townhouse three weeks ago. She was insistent on knowing the why of my anger since you only agreed that she should have the choice of who she give her heart to. She was not convinced my beauty, but being Carmeli'ta', she did not argue the point with me, for obvious reasons, due to the way she was raised not to disrespect her parents."

"That is not a good sign to me my husband. She will not let it alone until she has the full details."

"I know, she thought it strange that you sent her a message by me and have not called her yourself. I told her you said you would call in a few days. I did not get a buy-in on that my beauty. Our daughter is not easily put off as you know."

"Yes, my husband, I know. She is like you in that respect. What should we do now my husband?"

"I think that we should wait and see how lunch goes after Church tomorrow. She and Amelio' are coming for lunch as usual on Sunday. We will miss you my darling wife."

"I will miss Carmeli'ta', Amelio' and you. I am glad that you are continuing with our Sunday tradition of lunch after Church and also you will have company my love and not be lonely for someone to eat with."

"Thank you my beauty. I miss you most and our life together. It seems so strange without you here."

"I feel the same way Roberto' I miss you and our life together. Marianna is not taking off as she usually does?"

"No, she said to me she had ten days off while I was gone and that was enough for her right now."

"She is a sweet and loyal to our family my husband."

"Yes she is. I have a surprise for you. Amelio' is getting married my beauty after all these years."

Simone' surprised exclaimed, "Roberto' that is wonderful. I am so happy for him. He deserves to be happy. He has helped us and been there for both of us like a father-figure and true friend, never wavering in his loyalty to our family and he especially loves Carmeli'ta' like she is his own."

"Yes, he said as much earlier when I spoke to him."

"Do we know the fortunate lady my husband?"

"Yes, you remember Bibi 'Ana Nunnarelli?"

"I do remember her, my husband. She was sweet and always smiling. She and Amelio' were truly in love even at their young age. He has always been mature my husband and so was she. Her parents owned the Allevamento di polli?"

"Yes, actually it was the only Chicken Farm in the valley. They did well with their business."

"They sent her to Rome to a private school my husband. I remember her telling me that it was breaking her heart to leave the man she loved. I did not know until later it was Amelio' Bandaci; because he was older and had graduated from high school when we came along."

"Yes he graduated when he was seventeen. I was thirteen then he was always like a big brother to me. He never treated me as if he thought I was a baby under him. He has been kind, understanding, and helpful throughout my life."

"I remember Bibi 'Ana told me that about him. I am happy for them. When will they get married my husband?"

"They have not set the date yet. She is finalizing sales of property in Rome. Her husband died ten years after they were married. She has never remarried. Now Amelio'; and she have a chance to be together as he and she has always wanted. She wants you to be her Matron of Honor my beauty."

"I would love to my husband. Bibi 'Ana and I were friends when we were in school. She was a few months almost a year older than me, but not that much. I liked her a lot. She will be a sister to us Roberto'. Tell Amelio' I said congratulations my husband."

"I will my beauty. He said she was a few months older than you were not sure how many. It is getting late for you my lovely wife; you are attending Worship Service tomorrow morning. I will say goodnight and will call again tomorrow after I talk with Carmeli'ta' at lunch and see what her thoughts are. I love you."

"Yes, we are attending Worship Service. I love you my sweet husband. Thank you for calling me before I sleep. Goodnight."

After finishing his conversation, Roberto' sit on the loveseat in front of his fireplace and thought about the conversations he had with Amelio', Carmeli'ta'; and Simone'. He felt drowsy, went in took his shower and returned to the loveseat, and relaxed drifting into a sound sleep.

Simone' joined her mother and father in the kitchen where Catarina had set the dough for making bread and was sitting and chatting with Franco waiting for Simone' to join them. She entered and said, "Everything is fine at home. Carmeli'ta' did not buy-in to the explanation that Roberto' gave her of why I did not return. He is waiting until lunch tomorrow to see what the conversation will be like after they return from Church. I fear that her reaction will not be one of satisfaction. She wanted to know why I sent her a message and have not talked with her since I left."

Franco shook his head and nodded in agreeance with Simone' said, "Knowing our granddaughter the way that we do she will not let it alone until she is satisfied that she knows the truth; furthermore, I am afraid that we have difficult days ahead in this matter so we need to brace ourselves for what is coming."

"Yes, father you are right Carmeli'ta' is like Roberto' in this respect. He taught her all her life to know the fullness of a matter before making any judgments; never assume. He knows that and has the same concerns that we do about her reaction and what she might do."

"It is time to retire my daughter tomorrow is another day. We need to get up early to get to Church on time and we will wait to see what it brings with it there is no other choice in the matter. We will have to wait and see."

Rising from her chair Simone' sighed saying, "You are right. Goodnight mother and father; thank you for supporting me. Father we can discuss Sonnet 116 tomorrow after Church during lunch if you do not mind. I feel exhausted and sleepy will that be okay with you?"

"Yes, yes, of course my daughter, it is late and we all need some sleep or we will embarrass ourselves in Church tomorrow by nodding or sleeping through the sermon goodnight."

Catarina standing near the sink without saying a word, reached for Simone' hugged her tight, kissed her on the forehead, and smiled.

Simone' walked to her bedroom, drew her bath, afterward dressed for bed, and slept after thoughts of Sonnet 116, Roberto', Amelio', Carmeli'ta', and Bibi 'Ana whirled in her head. She remembered Bibi 'Ana saw her with Vincenzo' once while they walked in the Moretti's Vineyard near their chicken farm, a well-hidden area where the cabin was located on the extreme backside of the Moretti Vineyard where they met each week. However, knowing Bibi 'Ana, would never say anything about what she had seen to anyone. She knew the trouble it would cause and the system of thought that existed about mixing classes of people at that time when they were growing up. The next morning breakfast was fruit and coffee. Simone' and her parents rushed through breakfast and left for the 9:00 a.m. service. To their surprise all three were able to stay awake during the sermon without nodding. It was late when they retired for the night after 1:00 a.m.

Later that evening preparing dinner, Simone' looked at the clock on the kitchen wall, 5:00 p.m. I was 12:00 Noon in Charleston, Roberto', Amelio' and Carmeli'ta' would be having lunch. She walked to the door that led into the garden still deep in thought. Carmeli'ta' after lunch, Roberto' would talk with Amelio' about their finances.

In Charleston, Roberto', Carmeli'ta', and Amelio' gathered in the kitchen and enjoyed lunch after Church Service.

CHAPTER
THIRTY-THREE

Sunday in Charleston, after lunch, Roberto' Carmeli'ta' and Amelio' sat chatting. Amelio' looked at Carmeli'ta' reaching for her hand smiled and said, "My sweet beautiful little cousin, I have some news to tell you. I am excited and I told your father and I wanted to tell you myself, I am getting married soon."

Carmeli'ta' grasped in surprise and finally said, "Uncle Amelio' that is wonderful. I am so happy for you. You have been alone and helped raise me and take care of my father and mother. I am so happy for you."

Tears begin to roll down her face, she rose and walked behind Amelio's chair, put her arms around his neck, and kissed him on his cheek as she does each time she see him.

He held both arms and proceeded to say, "I am happy my sweet cousin. I enjoyed looking after Roberto' and helping to raise you. I think of you as I would if you were my own daughter and I think of your father as my younger brother, and your mother, like a sister, she is a gem. I love all of you. You are the only family I have left in the world that is close to me. We have distant cousins in Italy, but do not hear from them."

"Who is she Uncle Amelio'? She attends Church with us or goes to another congregation?"

"She is not here in America Carmeli'ta'. She was my high school sweetheart and the love of my life. She left Tuscany when she was sixteen and went to boarding school in Rome. After that, her father chose a wealthy merchant for her to marry. He died ten years later; she never remarried. She has kept in touch with me over the years and now we are getting married. We will marry here and live for the next four years before I retire and go back to Tuscany."

Carmeli'ta' shocked exclaimed, "You are leaving America Uncle Amelio'; when did you decide this? I will miss you so my Uncle you are one of my favorite people in the world."

"I know Carmeli'ta' I feel betwixt two worlds and the people I love. I will miss Roberto' and Simone' and you; but we decided to live the rest of our lives in our quiet little valley. I bought back my little cottage and my farmland. When I was in Italy a few years ago, I redecorated the cottage; it looks like it did when I live there 30 years ago. Bibi 'Ana helped me with the decorations and we spent time there renewing our love my sweet cousin."

"What a lovely name my Uncle. I will look forward to meeting my new aunt. I do not have an aunt. Father, Mother, and you are an only child, like me. Is she beautiful my Uncle?"

"Yes, she is beautiful. She has long straight black hair and maybe 5'5" tall, very petite with a lovely smile like your mother Simone'. Your father tells me that your mother knows her and your father remembers her from school though he was a few years ahead of her."

"It is so strange to me that father knew your Bibi 'Ana and did not ever see my mother, she went to school the same time."

"Sometimes in life things like that do happen you see some people and remember them and others you never see though they are in the same place. He proceeded; indeed, my cousin life and turn of events are strange sometimes. In spite of this, your grandfather chose a wonderful man for your mother and her father chose a wonderful woman for his wife. Remember this one thing my sweet lovely little Carmeli'ta', God puts those people in our lives in his time and not ours."

"I do believe that my sweet uncle, yes, definitely I believe that. Thank you for pointing that out to me. What a lovely romanticism."

Time passed while they chatted without notice and the hour grew late. It was 2:00 p.m. and Amelio' wanted time to talk with Roberto' about their business accounts. Rising Amelio' said, "Are you ready to have our conversation Roberto'?"

Yes, I am ready. Please excuse us Ladies. Carmeli'ta' I will talk with you before you leave my darling daughter will you wait for me?" "Yes, I will wait my father."

They left Carmeli'ta' and Marianna in the kitchen chatting and laughing, went to Simone's and his office, closing the door Roberto' said, "You wanted to talk to me about the suggestions you had for the future of our finances Amelio'?"

"Yes my cousin, I have checked into the European banking system and believe that it would be to our advantage to move our accounts to Switzerland. I have researched the system and it will be a lucrative and a wise move on our part. The Schweizerischer Bankverein (Swiss Bank), organized in 1874 is now Swiss Bank Corporation. The name changed in 1917. We have done well here with the interest paid which is really at premium now; however, my instincts tell me that this run, of prosperity will not last much longer?"

"Do you have a bad feeling about the solvency of the business and financial world here in America my cousin?"

"Yes, I do. I have contacted the Swiss Bank Corporation and they would

be glad to make the transfer for us. What do you think my cousin?"

"It sounds like a good plan Amelio', though I have not checked into the system of banking in the United Kingdom. I have noticed that the run of prosperity is high in America and this does worry me. Inflation is high and people are doing well, it is a little scary."

"I am planning to make my transfer on Tuesday, December 5. I went ahead and acted on my gut instinct, I have opened an account in each of our names for our business, personal and saving accounts if that is okay with you. I put $20,000 in each account. They are waiting our final decision."

"I will need to talk with Simone' and get her opinion on moving our major accounts there. Otherwise, yes, I always want to do what is most profitable and financially wise for my company and your instincts have never been wrong. I will let you know what she says after I speak with her tonight. I will call you on Monday. I will only keep what we need to operate successfully here in the states for both business and personal accounts."

"That is wise Roberto' and I think that we will make the right move and will not regret it as time goes on. It is getting late my cousin are you returning to service tonight?"

Looking at his pocket watch Roberto' commented, "It is 4:00 p.m. now and I have not had my conversation with Carmeli'ta' yet. We may not be done by 5:30 p.m. to make that half-hour drive. If we do not make it, please let Brother Meriwether know and tell him I will chat with him later."

"Yes, my cousin whatever it is, I hope that the conversation with Carmeli'ta' is successful. I will make the transfer of the accounts just call me when you talk with Simone' so you can concentrate on your family matters. One more thing, Bibi 'Ana has her accounts there as well; she says it is an excellent bank. Her father opened his account there years before he died and her late husband had his accounts there as well."

"Sounds good Amelio', I will ask my beauty and call you tomorrow. How much would you suggest we leave in our business and personal accounts?"

"I would think that $300,000 in the business accounts and $20,000 in personal accounts should be more than enough to operate on successfully. If we need more, we can always deposit less in the Swiss accounts for what we need. What is your opinion?"

"I think that $300,000 for the business is good, but I will keep my personal at $30,000 since I never know what Simone' or Carmeli'ta' may need or want to buy. One more thing, I will transfer $60,000 back to your accounts on Monday if that is okay with you."

"Noted my cousin, I will do as you think is best for you and your family. It is wise to have more for your family; I do not need as much. It is okay if you transfer the money back into my account, if not that is okay as well that amount does not put me in any financial difficulties as you are well aware."

"I know Amelio' I want to it is only right. Thank you for your all you do to watch after our finances."

Roberto' and Amelio' said goodbye and he returned to the kitchen where Carmeli'ta' and Marianna still chatting and laughing when he entered Marianna rose, poured his after-lunch coffee, and set the cup in front of him asked, "Is there anything else you need before I start dinner Mr. Bandaci?" "No, Marianna, Carmeli'ta' and I will go to her mother's and my sitting room upstairs and chat for a while so we will not disturb you. The lunch was good as always."

Carmeli'ta' hugged Marianna and said, "I love seeing you always Marianna. The lunch was delicious. I sometimes forget how much I miss the meals that you fuss over and prepare for our family. I will come to see you before I go."

"Thank you Ms. Carmeli'ta' it is good to see you and talk with you."

Roberto' and Carmeli'ta' climbed the stairs to his and Simone's suite to the cozy sitting room with the enormous fireplace that Carmeli'ta' remembered as she grew in her teen years.

She loved the room because it was beautiful and smelled like her mother's Chanel 5. Roberto' opened the door and went in ahead of his daughter, stood in front of the warm cozy fire said, "Carmeli'ta' I know that you miss your mother and it has been a long three almost four weeks since you have seen or talked with her. She is doing well and just wanted to spend a few days with her parents as I told you on yesterday. She will be coming home soon hopefully next week. I want her to enjoy her parents she does not get to see them as much as she would like to."

Carmeli'ta' sitting quietly without commenting listening intensely to her father and what he said finally commented, "Father, I just do not understand why my mother will not talk to me or have not called me since she has been away. I did not hear from you but once, that was the day you arrived in Tuscany. This is all so strange to me. We, as a family have never not talked to each other. I just do not grasp yours or mother's behavior in all of this. I know that there is more to this than you are telling me, I want to know what it is. I am mature enough to be told the situation and comprehend."

"I know that you do not understand Carmeli'ta'; right now, I want you to trust your mother and me in this and not allow yourself to worry about it. Your mother is well; we are fine and we love you. Your mother asked me to make sure that you understand that she loves you and will be home very soon. Will you do that for us my lovely daughter?"

"I will do as you ask for now my father and try to understand this is something between you and my mother; if she wants to visit her parents I cannot object. I will let it go for now my father and I will talk with you tomorrow. Will you come after work to see me?"

Time passed swiftly, Roberto' looked at his watch it was 4:45 p.m. knew it was getting late in Tuscany nearing 10:00 p.m. He wanted to call Simone' before she retired for the night.

"Yes, my daughter I will stop by after work to see you as I do on Monday's. It is getting late in Tuscany. I promised your mother I would call her before she retired for the night."

Roberto' and Carmeli'ta' went back down to the kitchen where Marianna was preparing dinner. Carmeli'ta' walked over to the sink where Marianna was standing hugged her and said, "Thank you Marianna for the lunch. I am happy to see you. Thank you for taking care of my father while my mother is away. I love you. I will see you Wednesday night at Bible Study."

'Thank you Miss Carmeli'ta' I love seeing you. You are my sweet baby. I will see you on Wednesday at Bible Study. I like taking care of your father and mother."

Roberto' walked Carmeli'ta' to her car opened the door as she got in,

waved, and drove away. Carmeli'ta' decided to attend evening service at Jason's congregation fifteen minutes away; it was closer to her home than where she and her parents attended.

Roberto' rushed to their sitting room again and called the operator. Simone' waited at her father's desk to answer the phone. The phone ringed at the Giovanni's home, "Hello."

"Simone', how are you tonight my beauty? I miss you my charming wife and could not wait to hear your sweet voice. It is like music to my ear my beauty. I hope that I did not keep you up too long, I know it is getting late."

"No, my dear husband you are not keeping me. I will always wait for you no matter how long it takes. I was waiting anxiously for you my darling to hear your voice and tell you I love you so my husband. How are you? How was your day? Did your conversation go well with Carmeli'ta' my husband?"

"I am fine my beauty. My day was good. Amelio', Carmeli'ta', and I had a good lunch as is our custom on Sunday. Marianna prepared fruit and cheese with fresh bread for lunch. I did speak with Carmeli'ta' my beauty she is not accepting what we are telling her. She insists there is more to this than what we are saying. She does not understand why we did not tell her you were going to Tuscany. She wants to know what the problem is and if it had anything to do with my being angry with you when we visited her. She thought I should be angry with her and not you since she asked you not to tell me about her and Jason Madison. She has never seen me angry with you in all her life. She reminded me that her mother was the best person in the world and was good to everyone. I asked her if she would trust us in this and not allow herself to be worried. She said she would until I see her tomorrow after my workday with my usual visits on Monday."

"She will not let it alone my husband. I do not know what to say to her when I call. I have never lied to our daughter, nor have you. This is indeed a difficult situation Roberto' and I caused it all by not telling you what was bothering me all the years we have been married now it is affecting our daughter, my parents, and you and me my darling. I feel so badly that I have caused my family a problem."

"Simone' my beauty we have to work through the situation no matter what it is. Please tell me what it is so I will know how to handle Carmeli'ta'. I feel like I am on the outside looking in that is a great disadvantage to me. When will you come home so we can get whatever it is resolved?"

"I am thinking this week my husband. I will check the flights tomorrow and see when I can get a seat and return home. I do miss you my husband and want to talk with you about what the situation is and has been for the 24 years we have been married. I want to talk with you before I let you read my Diary Roberto' it will tell you everything you want to know."

"I am still at a lost Simone' why you have kept a Diary and I never knew. I never once saw you write in your Diary that is so strange to me that you would keep a secret or secrets from me. I like to know that my wife trust me and know I love her and would do all I can to protect her even with my life if it would save yours Simone'."

"I feel the same way Roberto' I would give my life for you my husband and to keep you from being hurt I would go away forever."

"Is that what you had in mind Simone' when you left me and our home?" Roberto' heard deadly silence on the other end of the phone said, "Simone' did you hear what I asked you?"

"Yes, my husband I heard you. I had thought about it and decided to come to my parents. I know that this is upsetting to you my husband, please know that I will be home sometime this week and I will tell you then. Will you please be patient with me a little longer?"

"Of course, Simone' at this point, I do not have a choice. I will wait to discuss the matter when you arrive. You can tell me what has been taking you away from me for twenty-four years my beauty. I cannot bear to not know all of you any longer."

"I know Roberto', I will tell you my husband. How is Amelio'?" Did you tell him I would be happy to be Bibi 'Ana's Matron of Honor? I know he must be happy! Did he tell Carmeli'ta'?"

"He said that he would tell Bibi 'Ana that you would be honored to be her Matron of Honor. Yes, he is happy and told Carmeli'ta'. She was ecstatic and thought it the best thing in the world for her uncle who she loves so much. She is excited about having an aunt. You should have seen the sparkle in her eyes as Amelio' told her about his plans."

"That is good to know Roberto' that my Carmeli'ta' is happy for her uncle. He loves her so much."

"Yes, he does. She is the heir to all his property and money. I told him it was not necessary that we would leave our daughter well cared for financially."

"Yes, my husband that has been a concern of mine all her life that after we are gone she will be well-taken care of and not have to suffer or want for anything."

"I work hard for Carmeli'ta' and you to be taken care of if something happens to me my beauty."

"I know my husband and I appreciate you and love you so much because you care with all your heart for your family."

"You and Carmeli'ta' are my life Simone'. Amelio' talked to me today after lunch for a few hours about an idea that he has to secure our finances. His instincts tell him that the prosperity wave that this country is in will not last too much longer; inflation is high, everything is going so well. This nation is in a golden age. He has checked out the Swiss Banking System and it is solvent and thinks it would be wise for us to move our accounts there; personal, business, and saving accounts. He has opened accounts in our names and businesses with $20,000 each. I told him I needed to talk with you before we make the final decision. With all the facts he related to me, I agree with him that the prosperity level is high America is riding on a wave and it cannot last. What do you think my beauty about moving our accounts and leaving enough here to live on and operate the business?"

"I know that Amelio's has sound instincts my husband. How much are we thinking about keeping for business and personal?"

"I think that $300,000 is enough for business and $30,000 is sufficient for my family to survive on. It is not necessary to keep the saving account amount very high just enough so that the bank will transfer the money each month into all the Swiss accounts."

"That is wise my husband; it is a sound idea and worth paying attention to your and Amelio's sense in business and the feel for the financial stability of the America in the near future. Inflation is high everywhere my husband and I want to protect our future we never know what tomorrow will bring."

"You are right my beauty. I will let Amelio' know we agree with him in changing to the Swiss Banking System. He will make the transfer on Tuesday, December 5. Thank you my beauty for caring about our future and our business. We have worked hard to get to where we are in life. Moreover, the money from the sale of my parent's farm and home is there. I want that to go for Carmeli'ta'. We have never used it after we replaced what we used to get the farm started."

"You are right my husband. I agree with you completely. How will we know the transfers are successful my husband?"

"The bank will get a wire stating the transfers are in the accounts and the amounts. We will be okay my darling. The Charleston National Bank has been doing these transfers for many years now so it is safe."

"I will be anxious until I know the money is in the accounts and the correct amounts are there; it is a sizeable amount of money my husband."

"Yes, Amelio' and I will stay on top of the transfer my beauty. Please don't worry."

As Simone' and Roberto' spoke of the transfers Franco had walked in and stood listening to their conversation said, "Simone' ask Roberto' to hold on for a moment I want to ask you a question."

"My husband my father wants to say something to me can you hold on for a second?"

"Yes, I will wait."

Franco asked, "Are you and Roberto' planning to transfer your accounts to the Swiss Banking System?"

"Yes, my father does that make you uneasy?"

"Not at all my daughter, your mother, and I transferred our accounts there 5 years ago it is a wise idea and safe. I have been watching the American financial world and it is dangerous to be as prosperous with inflation as high as it is there now. It can only last another 2 years maybe three my daughter before it fails, so do something while you can."

"Thank you father, I will let Roberto' know your opinion." Taking her hand from the receiver Simone' said, "Roberto' my parents have their accounts there and my father says it is a sound banking system and a wise move on our part. He feels as you and Amelio' does this wave the country is riding will not last many more years before it fails."

"Tell Franco thank you and I appreciate his input. One more thing, my beauty before you go Amelio' tells me that Bibi 'Ana has her accounts there as well, and her late husband used the Swiss Banking System as did her parents."

"Let's move our accounts with all speed then my husband and our daughters as well. Will you tell her tomorrow?"

"I will tell her when I visit her tomorrow after my workday is ended. It is late for you after 12:30 a.m. there; we have talked for two-and one-half hours."

"The phone bill will be much my husband."

"It is worth it to talk with you my beauty. We can afford to pay for times as these. It is not something that I would do all the time, but this is necessary as long as you are away from home."

"Thank you Roberto', for saying I am more important to you than money."

"You are the most important person in my life my beauty. I love you. Good night and sweet dreams."

"Good night my love it is 7:30 p.m. and pass your dinner time, Marianna will be waiting. Tell her I appreciate her seeing after your meals while I am away. You have work tomorrow. I love you."

After hanging up Simone turned to see if her father were still in the room; he had gone to the kitchen where her mother was drinking tea and waiting for Simone' to finish her conversation so they could know the state of things in South Carolina. Simone' joined them, sit for a moment before she spoke, "Everyone is okay there. Carmeli'ta' is not accepting the explanation her father and I are giving her that she will not let it go my husband said. He will see her again tomorrow after his workday has ended. I told Roberto' that I would check the flights to America and when there would be a seat available, I told him I am thinking of this week."

Catarina commented, "It is time my daughter you will have to go sometimes. The longer you wait the worse the situation will get."

"I told Roberto' I wanted to talk with him before I let him read my Diary. He is still mystified that I kept a Diary and he never knew. He questioned my trust in his love, he said as much when we spoke. He told me that Amelio' is getting married. I forgot to tell you on Friday when I talked with him. He is marrying Bibi 'Ana his high school sweetheart and love of his life. You remember her mother and father she was my best friend in school and her parents sent her away to private school in Rome when we were 16 years old."

"Yes, we remember her daughter. I saw Amelio' and her when he was here visiting 3 years ago. He bought back his farm and repaired his cottage, redecorated it, and hired a caretaker to look after it. She is still beautiful even more so now that she is a mature woman. I talked with them for a while when he came to the Tuscany Farming Association to purchase the land."

"Father you have never said anything about it to me all the times we spoke on the phone and wrote letters."

"It was not for me to talk about my daughter. I am the President; discretion is important in my position. They spent the month there decorating and spending time together. I knew that they were renewing their love. He was heart-broken when her parents sent her to boarding school. She could not have chosen a better man to marry. If I had to choose for her I would choose Amelio' for her as I did Roberto' for you. The Bandaci families are moral, ethical, intelligent, and successful people. Amelio's father, like Roberto's, two brothers, you could not find more honorable men than they were and now their sons are just like them; you are blessed my daughter to be married to Roberto."

"I am thankful for my husband and feel blessed. You amaze me my father all this time you know about what is happening in people lives here in the valley. I did not know that you knew Amelio's father so well."

"Yes, I knew him well. We were friends as were Roberto's father and I were his younger brother. It broke my heart when my two best friends died; it is not easy to lose close friends they were to me. Simone' saw her father's eyes water up." He concluded, "It is bedtime. I have to check my farm tomorrow. I will leave around 9:00 a.m. and return for lunch at 1:00 p.m. Are you ready my lovely wife?"

She interrupted her father and mother again saying, "Father I told Roberto' that the phone calls will add up much. He said that I am more important to him than money."

"Yes, that does not surprise me Simone'. What is your point about the phone calls?"

"I want to pay you for them when you get your bill. I have money with me and Roberto' will send whatever I need or have it transferred into your account at the bank."

"Simone', your mother, and I will not hear of you and Roberto' paying for anything while you are with us. We can afford to pay for calls for our children. You are the only child that we have and you have never given us one day of trouble in your life. Besides everything that mother and I have will be Carmeli'ta' and yours after we are gone."

"Thank you mother and father how can I ever repay you for all you do for me?"

Franco looked at her without saying anything smiled and said again, "Ready my wife?"

"I am Franco. Goodnight Simone' we will see you when you wake."

"I will sleep late tomorrow if you and father don't mind." "Not at all, my daughter you need your rest."

Simone' sits for a few moments reviewing the day and her conversations with her husband and her father and mother. She turned out the kitchen light, checked the lock on the patio door, walked slowly down the hall to her bedroom suite, drew her bath, bathed, lotion her body, put on her negligée, slipping into bed before drifting off to sleep, she thanked God for all the blessings He allowed her to have in her life.

Knowing he was late for dinner and Marianna was waiting, Roberto' walked swiftly down the stairs and to the dining area of the kitchen, as he entered Marianna smiled and said, "So you finally decided to eat?"

Roberto' smiled and said, "Yes, my time clock I am ready. Ms. Bandaci said tell you hello and she will see you soon."

"It will be good to have Ms. Bandaci home, sir. I miss her being here."

"I know Marianna it will not be much longer."

Roberto' finished his dinner, went to their bedroom suite, and relaxed in front of the fireplace before he retired for the night. He looked at the flames dancing saw his beautiful Simone's face and the way she smiled. Later that evening, while preparing for bed Roberto' thought about how much her smile made his heart dance like the dancing flames in their fireplace, these thoughts lit flames of passion and desire in his mind and warmed his heart.

Sleep floated across him with thoughts of dealing with the questions Carmeli'ta' would have concerning her mother not speaking to her in the past three week, leaving Charleston without telling her why, and why she did not return with him on Friday. He prepared mentally for the brewing storm he felt his daughter would cause with her questions being unanswered. However, she was sweet, humble, obedient, and kind; he knew that she could be insistent and would not stop until she had a resolution to her questions or she was contented with the response, in that way he knew she was just like him.

Monday again!

CHAPTER

THIRTY-FOUR

Monday came too soon for Roberto'. He dressed and prepared for breakfast. After his usual morning conversation with Marianna, went to check with his Foreman, and set the week priorities for local deliveries and the shipping schedules to Bandaci Farm customers. The day progressed fast; lunch passed as business occupied his day 4:00 p.m. arrived without notice. Leaving his farm, he stopped at Amelio's office to give him and Simone's decision to transfer their accounts.

Arriving at Amelio's office at 4:15 p.m. knocked twice and opened the door saw Amelio' sitting at his desk. By the time he reached the center of the room Amelio 'said, "Hello Roberto' I was just calling you to ask your and Simone' decisions about transferring your accounts to the Swiss Banking System."

"That is why I am here Amelio'. We made the unanimous decision to transfer our accounts with all speed. We both feel that this step to secure our finances is a wise one. Franco Giovanni feels the same way that you do about the economy here in America. He has noticed the high level of prosperity and outrageous inflation; he feels the level at which prosperity and inflation are running will have a negative effect on the economy within the next 2-3 years, if not sooner. We agreed on the amounts that you and I discussed on Sunday. Also, I will speak to Carmeli'ta about her accounts when I see her at 5:00 p.m. today."

"I will take care of the transfer on Tuesday, December 5 as we agreed. Please call me and let me know Carmeli'ta' decision. I will open a $10,000 account in her name tomorrow morning when the Swiss Banking System is open if that is agreeable with you."

"It is agreeable with me Amelio'. It is in the best interest of my daughter. I am sure she will not object. Thank you again for opening the accounts and keeping an eye on the financial status of the country. In addition, I called the bank earlier and had the $60,000 transferred back into your account. Also, I will transfer the money back into your account for Carmeli'ta' as well."

"It will be in everyone's best interest to monitor their finances and watch the economy of this country and not get carried away with all the prosperity that is taking place at this time, a rich run like this seldom last. It has been almost seven years since it begin."

"I need to get to Carmeli'ta's, Amelio'. I promised her I would be there around 5:00 p.m. I like to keep my promises and get home for dinner no later than 6:00 p.m. I will call you later tonight after I speak with Carmeli'ta' and let you know her response to moving her account."

Roberto' waved at Amelio' and drove off to see his daughter. Arriving at her Townhouse complex thirty minutes later to the waiting Carmeli'ta' with iced tea and chilled glasses, Roberto' sat for a minute before going upstairs and said a prayer, "Father, God, help me to say the right thing so that it will assuage my daughter's enquiry and trepidation in reference to her mother."

He exited the car walking slowly up the stairs to her Townhouse door knocking lightly. The same sweet voice came in response to the knock that he knew so well, "Is that you my father?"

"Yes it is." As the door opened, he saw the smiling face that was so precious to him, of his only child. He asked himself, "What will I say other than what I've told her?"

"Hello father how are you today. I am happy to see you. Have you talked to Mother today?"

"Hello, my precious one, I talked with your mother after you left last evening. I will call her after I arrive home and have dinner Carmeli'ta'. I have another subject to talk with you about before we talk about your mother."

Pouring tea into a chilled glasses handed it to him, picked up her glass poured her tea replying, "What is it Father?"

"Amelio' and I think it wise to move our accounts to the Swiss Banking System. The prosperity level and inflation here in America are both high, at the present. Uncertainty of prosperity lasting is slim and questionable at best. Moreover, if this is true, we will lose everything or almost everything. I want to transfer your accounts there as well leaving you enough to live on. What is your opinion my daughter?"

He sipped his tea listening to her response to his proposal.

"I cannot object my father as long as you are comfortable with the move and have checked the Swiss Banking System. I know that Madison Steel and Iron has its accounts there. The accounts here in Charleston are only sufficient for payroll and other items that the company needs on a weekly basis. Jason and his father effected their transfers 5 years ago is what he tells me."

"That is wise Carmeli'ta'. It is apparent everyone's level of thinking is the same in reference to the impending disaster of the economy."

"Jason said that it was a wise move because they do an enormous amount of business in the United Kingdom and need money there to be effective in their business deals. In addition, it is not prudent to use one banking system for a large corporation the size of Madison Steel and Iron. He also has his personal accounts there, as do, their entire family."

"I will tell Amelio' to make the transfers my daughter. He will open a $10,000 account in your name tomorrow, Tuesday and make the transfer to your account on Wednesday. I will call him later tonight to let him know that you agree. How much do you want left in your account?"

"I think $5,000 is more than enough my father. I do not need much. The money that you and mother gave me when I moved to my Townhouse is still there. Rent, telephone, lights, gas, and other personal items are all that I have as expenses, you paid for my Roadster cash and get it serviced when it needs it. Jason pays me a good salary for being Office Manager and Hostess, and Mother and you buy my clothes. Every week, I find new outfits from Toni's shoes, lingerie, and other accessories Mother has purchased. I am so thankful for you as my parents my father."

"We love you Carmeli'ta. That is why I came to see you to reassure you that everything is okay and your mother will be home very soon."

"Father this is becoming increasingly more difficult for me to understand, as you try to explain to me why my mother did not come home with you. She has never acted in this manner, never. She has not called me or talked to me since she left. She sounded so strange on the phone that day she left. She has never said goodbye to me as if her leaving was permanent."

Noticing she was getting increasingly more upset, Roberto wanted to calm her only made it worse said, "Calm down Carmeli'ta' your mother will be home soon, you must believe this."

"No father, why must I believe it? You are sounding so strange also even now, what are you hiding from me? Is my mother sick? Is she really in Italy with my grandparents or you just say that so I will not be upset?

"Yes, she is with your grandparents my sweet daughter and no, she is not sick. Please stay calm and it will all be okay you will see."

"I don't see is part of the problem my father, I just don't see that as being okay. You are not telling me everything I know it." She continued, "Father, I would like to rest now before Jason comes over. I know that you need to be home before 6:00 p.m. as you promised Marianna. I need to think about all of this and decide what I want to do."

"What you want to do like what my sweet daughter?"

"I don't know in this moment but I have to do something. She is my mother. I love and miss her."

"Yes, my daughter. I need to go. I will come to see you tomorrow on my way home from work."

Walking toward the door holding her close to him, reaching the door turned and said, "Take care, my sweet little one, enjoy your evening. I will see you tomorrow." He kissed her and held her tight with a reassuring hug of understanding. On the drive home, thoughts and fears swirled in his mind what she might do or what she was thinking of doing. She has never been impulsive, but on the same wise, she never had a challenge put to her of this nature not having the facts necessary to make a sound decision.

Arriving home, Roberto' stopped in his office and called his cousin. Amelio' just finishing dinner and waiting for Roberto' to call him, still sitting at the kitchen table his housekeeper Juanita served him dessert and coffee, when he heard the phone ring two longs and three shorts rings for his home rose, walked to the hallway answering said, "Hello, Amelio' Bandaci."

"Ciao, mio cugino. Spero di che non disturbare la vostra cena (hello my cousin, I hope I am not disturbing your dinner)."

"No, sto avendo il mio dessert e caffè in attesa per la chiamata con la mia's decisione di cugini poco dolce, (No, I am having my dessert and coffee waiting for your call with my sweet little cousin's decision)."

"Lei crede che sia che una buona idea la sicurezza era la sua unica preoccupazione. Lei ha rassicurato che era sicuro (she thinks it is a good idea. Safety was her only concern. I reassured her that it was safe)." Amelio' reverted to speaking English again.

"She is wise to agree Roberto'. I will open her account tomorrow when I make our transfers to the Swiss Banking System and on Wednesday complete her transfer. What balance does she want her account to reflect?"

"She said $5,000 is enough to leave as a balance. I will add what she needs to her account here if it is necessary."

Amelio' detecting a hesitant tone in his voice said, "Is there something else you want to discuss with me before we hang up?"

"She is not accepting my explanation about her mother and why she did not return with me. She said she had to think about the situation and decide what she wanted to do. That is worrying me. I don't know what she had in mind."

"I understand your fears my cousin. When will you see her again?"

"I am seeing her tomorrow after my workday is over as usual."

"The only suggestions I have for you, if you are asking my opinion, is to wait to see what she says and try and relax Roberto'. She will not do anything tonight. We will see what tomorrow brings."

"Buonanotte mia cugino."

"Buonanotte. Grazie." Roberto' went to the kitchen for dinner, Marianna waiting patiently smiling said, "You are late again."

Amused, he did not respond to her comment. At least this area of his life was normal. Never noticed before, were unappreciated bits and pieces of calm in his life. External small things we take for granted in life are most rewarding when internal struggles and conflicts raise their ugly heads.

After dinner Roberto' rushed to the sitting room in his and Simone's suite called the operator and gave her Franco's number. He mulled over his and Carmeli'ta' conversation while he waited for the call to connect.

A sweet voice finally came from the other end of the line, "Hello."

"Hello my beauty. How was your day? I hope that you are well."

"Hello my sweet husband. I am fine. My day was restful and peaceful my darling. How are you? How is Carmeli'ta'? Did you visit her today? What did she say about your explanation?"

Laughing at the sequence of questions Simone' asked without taking a

breath mystified him. Simone' on the other end of the line was puzzled at his laughing said, "Roberto' why are you laughing did I say something funny my husband?"

"No, my love, it is amusing you asked questions and answered my questions and asked four others before you took a breath my beauty." Simone' calming herself said, "You are right my husband now I think about it. They both laughed.

"I am fine Simone' my lovely wife. Carmeli'ta' is fine. I did visit her today. What was said I will sum it up, she is not pleased with the explanation I gave why you did not return home with me last Friday. She is upset as you can well expect. She said that she would think about what she wanted to do. That is frightening me Simone' I do not know what she means or what she plans to do. Simone' felt nervous twitches in her stomach as if little pins were sticking and pricking her did not comment for a few minutes. Finally, replied, "I hope that she will think before she does anything Roberto', and talk with you before she makes any rash decisions."

"What do you mean by rash decisions Simone'?"

"Think about it my husband, she is like you. What did you do when you found no answer in Charleston?"

Thinking for a moment replied, "Oh no, she would not try and come to Tuscany. Traveling such a distance by herself Simone' she knows nothing about traveling. She knows nothing about traveling abroad. She was five when we left Tuscany. She is too inexperienced and innocence to try that trip alone. It was dangerous for you, but at least you are more mature and have experience in traveling. I need to talk with her as soon as I can tomorrow before she makes any rash moves."

"Please do my husband. I do not want Carmeli'ta' to come to Tuscany alone. Please stop her Roberto'. I know our daughter and that is what she has in mind. She could leave without telling you. She is financially independent and can buy her ticket without us knowing it or she could use another name on the plane my husband to keep us from knowing that she has left Charleston. I am really afraid my husband."

"I know Simone'. I will call her as soon as possible tomorrow. Amelio' will be setting up an account in her name at the Swiss Banking System when he makes our transfers. That will give me a good reason to call her without raising suspicion since I never call her at work."

"I am glad to know that she agrees with you that her accounts will be more secure in the Swiss Banking System."

"Yes, she did as long as it is safe and she trust Amelio' and my instincts. I did not get a chance to mention her decision on moving her accounts. She is leaving $5,000 in her personal account and if she needs anything further, we can always deposit money in her account. Amelio' will make her transfers on Wednesday."

Fear and anxiety bewildered her mother and father. Unpredictability in situations of this nature can be perplexing leaving the people involved with questions in their minds.

"I will try and rest now my husband and you should as well. Tomorrow will be a long day for everyone."

"I will Simone' it is past your bedtime my beauty. Have you decided what day this week you will come home?"

"I was thinking maybe Friday my husband."

"I will look forward to that Simone'. We need you here my beauty. I love you. Goodnight."

"I love you Roberto'. Goodnight."

Monday, December 4, Carmeli'ta' dressed for her dinner date with Jason, she thought about the conversation she had with her father earlier that evening. It just did not seem right that her mother was not calling her. Never during her life has she not spoken to her mother on a daily basis sometimes more than one and her father as well. She felt torn and hurt because she did not understand what was going on with her parents. She said out-loud, "I will check my calendar tomorrow and see what I can reassign to Ms. Horne and others. I will go to Italy to see if my mother is with my grandparents. My father has never lied to me as long as I can remember. However, this time I believe he is avoiding telling me the truth! In addition, my mother not calling me the entire time she has been away and leaving without telling me. I wonder if my father really knew she was going to Italy! I will talk with Jason tonight and get his opinion of me taking some time off." Carmeli'ta' immersed in thought did not hear Jason knock at first. Jason, after waiting for a few seconds did not hear movement near the door, knocked harder and called her name. The sound of his voice bought her thoughts back to the moment in time; she rushed to the door and called, "Jason, is that you my darling?"

"Yes, my darling. Are you okay Carmeli'ta'?" She quickly opened the door exclaiming, "Yes, my darling I am fine. I was deep in thought, my love and did not hear you at first. I hope that you have not been waiting long."

"No, not long Carmeli'ta' only a few minutes. I became overly concerned when you did not answer immediately. You are usually waiting for me. Tell me what is taking you so deep in thought Carmeli'ta'. Is there trouble I am not aware of at the plant?"

"No, Jason it does not involve my job in anyway my sweetheart, not this time."

"Then what is it my love? Can you share with me or is it to personal?"

"No Jason, I don't have anything that I cannot share with you. I will talk with you about it after we have dinner and spend our evening together."

Jason concern growing, his imagination took him two or three ways, in thought of what it might be pulled Carmeli'ta' to him and held her tight. She snuggled close to his chest holding on to him in desperation. Jason feeling the desperation in her hug, held onto her and did not speak praying that she was would not tell him that they could not get married. After a long while, they left for their 8:00 p.m. dinner reservation at Rochelle's and later dancing at the Country Club.

At home, Roberto' nervous and worried sat on the loveseat in front of the fireplace and thought about the conversation he had with Simone', Carmeli'ta' is like me! I raised her to be the person that she is now to think and reason for herself and determine the best recourse to take in any situation. I should have known that she would not stop until she had the absolute truth about why her mother did not return home with me last Friday. If I say too much to her, she will definitely know that there is more to her mother not returning than visiting her grandparents. In the same light, if I let it go, she will not stop questioning her mother's absence. I have no choice except to wait, like Amelio' suggested, until tomorrow. She will not do anything tonight. She is out with Jason Madison for the evening. I will check with her before I go to the farm in the morning."

Simone' sat for a long time, thinking about what Carmeli'ta' might do. She knew her sweet little daughter. She was not impulsive, but overly determined. She thought of her coming to Tuscany. The thought frightened her, without realizing it, she was perspiring her hands were wet, cold, and shaking, "I could not bear the thought of Carmeli'ta' coming to Tuscany. If Vincenzo', find out she is here could possibility result in him telling her she was his daughter." Reflecting back to the conversation her father told them he had during his visit with Vincenzo' and his insisting she is his daughter would be a disaster for everyone. She had to prevent this from taking place somehow. But how? "I need to talk with my parents as soon as they are awake. I cannot sleep late as I thought about earlier."

Simone' worn and torn from the possibility of her daughter coming to Tuscany took her bath, finally slept. She awake each hour and looked at the clock on her bedside table to check the time. She wanted to talk to her father before he left for his farm.

Carmeli'ta' and Jason spent the evening after dinner and dancing at the Country Club. She was quiet during the evening more so than Jason had ever know her to be at any point even when working. Jason observing her every move touched her hand finally said, "Carmeli'ta' what is taking you away from me tonight my lovely. You are quiet. Is there something I said or did that I am not aware of?"

Looking at Jason replied, "No my darling you are always sweet and loving to me. I could not ask for a better friend or lover."

"Can you share with me now what is upsetting you. It is clear to me that you are upset about something."

"Jason my father and mother are keeping something from me. I do not know what. He acted so strange since he returned from Tuscany. I begin to wonder if my mother is really with my grandparents as he said or if he even knows where she is. I have to do something to know where my mother is. I want to know your opinion of my taking leave from work and going to Tuscany to see if my mother is with my grandparents. She could be sick or hurt. Why will she not call me? I don't understand any of this." Tears begin to roll down her cheeks. Jason moved closer and held her to him dabbing her eyes with his handkerchief speaking gently to her, "Carmeli'ta' it will be okay. I am sure your mother is fine. Your father would not keep her being ill from you. It has to be something else if it is anything my lovely."

"You don't think she is sick Jason?"

"No, I believe your father would tell you. It is another issue not illness."

"Do you mind if I take time off and go to Italy Jason?"

"No, my darling I don't mind. I would do the same thing if one of my parents were not talking to me or I was not sure of their location. I am concerned with your traveling to Italy by yourself Carmeli'ta'. Flying is uncertain at best across the Atlantic. I know that the trip have been made there are flights daily nothing has happened so far my darling, but then it was not you that was going, the woman that I love. You are so fragile and innocent my love it frightens me to think of you trying to make your way to Italy having never travel before and a long distance from home."

"I know Jason, traveling that distance alone concerns me also, but I have to know about my mother. I will think more about it and see what my father says tomorrow as I mentioned to you. Changing the subject, a little Jason, my father, and uncle has changed their accounts to the Swiss Banking System. They have watched the economy for a while and feels with inflation and prosperity running so high it will not last. They are thinking this country might be in trouble in two years or less."

"That is true my darling. I am happy to hear that your father and uncle are financially astute and well informed; it is father and my feelings as well. Our nemesis, my sources tells me moved his accounts 5 years ago, both personal and business. Charles Meriwether is always on top of business and finances. We are taking every step to secure our future as much as possible. You mentioned their accounts my lovely what about yours?"

"Mine as well Jason. Uncle Amelio' is opening a Swiss account for me tomorrow and finalizing my transfers on Wednesday. He is leaving enough for me to live on for the next few years."

"That is wise Carmeli'ta' but you will not have to worry about your financial future. I have secured our future financially my love. We will be okay."

"Thank you Jason. I love you more each day. With my and your accounts being secure we will do well if we are careful."

Her mind never off her parents she continued, "I will check my calendar tomorrow morning and assign work to my staff Jason; however, before I do anything. I will talk with my father again and see what he says."

"That is a wise idea Carmeli'ta'. It is always better to take calculated steps rather than act without considering all aspects of a situation."

"Thank you for your support Jason. I feel better knowing that I have your support my love. It is important to me."

"Of course, you have my support Carmeli'ta' I love you in good or bad circumstances. Whatever bothers you belongs to me as well my darling. I want to be your strength and strong rock to lean on my darling. You look lovely tonight my darling."

"Thank you Jason for the compliment and care. I need your strength now."

They sat close to each other not commenting further. Jason held hear hand kissing her on her right cheek. As the evening progressed into the lateness of the hour Jason took Carmeli'ta' home and did not stay as he usually does after their evening out. He made sure she was safe inside her Townhouse kissed her, closed the door, and waited to her the latch fall into place he tapped lightly saying, "Good night my lovely Carmeli'ta'."

Carmeli'ta' prepared for bed slipping between the sheets collapsing into a sound sleep from thinking about the conversation with her father, the overall state of affairs with her parents, and waltzing all evening with Jason.

Sleep was like a stranger, eluded Roberto'!

CHAPTER
THIRTY-FIVE

Roberto' paced back and forth in front of the fireplace as the embers died and the hour grew late, though he was dressed for bed as usual, but could not force sleep to come. He felt restless and helpless at the thought of not knowing what his daughter might do. Finally, lying on the sofa wrestling with thoughts of Simone', Carmeli'ta', and what tomorrow will bring swirling in his head at 2:00 a.m. slept for a few hours. He awaken at 6:00 a.m. his usual time, looking at the clock knew that it was 11:00 a.m. in Tuscany. He rushed to dress and get breakfast before calling Carmeli'ta' to ask if she could take time to talk with him before she left for work.

Earlier Tuesday morning, December 5 in Tuscany, "Simone' had set the alarm for 6:00 a.m. She did not dress, but freshen up and wore her dressing gown to breakfast. Her mother and father surprised to see her so early, Franco asked, "Daughter, are you okay?"

"Father and Mother something has developed since I spoke with you last night. Roberto' talked with Carmeli'ta' as he planned. The conversation did not go well, she is not accepting his reason why I did not return home, nor is she pleased with his explanation why I have not called."

"Why is that a great concern to you Simone'? There has to be more to it than her not being pleased at her father's answers to her questions."

"Yes, it is she said that she had to decide what she wanted to do about the situation."

"What do you mean do Simone'?" What can she do or what will she do?"

"Father, think about it. She is like Roberto' she will not stop until she has the answer. He came all the way to Italy to find the answer."

This possibility never crossing her parent's minds. They looked baffled for a moment before Franco' spoke, "Do you actually think she will try to travel alone here Simone'? She knows nothing about traveling and it is dangerous for her alone so young and inexperienced."

"Yes, father that is number two of my concern for her."

"Number two Simone' you are not clear my daughter."

"Father, if she comes here Vincenzo' will know; there is no way that he would not. This valley is too small to hide anything or anyone. He knew I was here because someone saw me and told him. It will be the same if she comes."

"That will be okay if he knows. What can he do?"

Simone' becoming fearful with tears forming in her eyes replied, "He might see her and tell her she is his daughter. That would destroy Carmeli'ta'. How could I bear up under her knowing that another man might be her father? In addition, just the fact she saw Vincenzo' when she was small when he came and met us in the park as she played and he sat with me talking. She came to tell me different things and show me things she found. She never said anything to him but she always looked at him so strange."

"That thought had not crossed my mind Simone' you are right my daughter that would be a disaster. If he told my granddaughter he is her father, I would hurt him or worse. He is getting older and he and his wife has no children. A man will sacrifice anything for his child and I think that he is at that point."

"Father and Mother, I think I will try to get a flight on Thursday, December 7, rather than Friday. Today is Tuesday it is too late to book a flight today maybe tomorrow."

"Simone' flights are not booked on Wednesday's. It is a day of staff training, planning, and meetings. The Tuscany Development Committee meets with the Airport employees and managers for updates and growth planning, I can check to the flight tomorrow and see if it is full for the 3:00 p.m. departure on Thursday."

"Yes, please do father. I am more afraid since speaking with Roberto' last night than ever before. As desperate as you say Vincenzo' seems and his still wanting me it would be dangerous for her to be here. I think he will go through with his threat he made the last time he was in Charleston to do whatever it takes be part of his daughter's life. I am waiting for Roberto' to call after he speaks with Carmeli'ta' before she leaves for her workday."

Catarina stood silently near the stove preparing breakfast for Franco' finally said, "Simone' this could easily get out of hand and become a storm. You have no choice now except telling Roberto' the truth and allowing him to read your Diary my daughter; the choice has been taken away from you; and made for you in the same instant. We cannot allow this to destroy Carmeli'ta'. Her welfare is more important now than Roberto' finding out; he might be able to prevent her being hurt too much by this. He has to know, that is the only choice."

"It will be painful either way mother. I have allowed my family to come to this point because of fear and my daughter may be hurt and never forgive me for my poor decisions as a child and then as an adult to try and protect my family."

"The problem is not you as much as it is Vincenzo' Moretti. If he had not pursued this insane idea of Carmeli'ta' being his daughter, it would never have come to this point. He should have left well enough alone. You left Tuscany and he followed you and kept coming over the years is the egregiousness of this entire matter and would not take no for an answer that is certainly not the actions of a man that loves."

In Charleston, early that Tuesday morning, Roberto' finished his breakfast and went back upstairs to call Carmeli'ta. He dialed her number.

Carmeli'ta' awakens at 7:00 a.m. as usual, torn in what decision to make. As she prepared breakfast and coffee, she contemplated going to Italy. She knew that she could sail there, but it would take almost two weeks. She could fly lot of danger in that choice, she had never been on a long trip abroad, and flying was still dangerous especially over the Atlantic Ocean. The phone rang while she pondered the dilemma, she ran to her living area picking up the receiver said, "Hello."

"Good morning, my sweet daughter. How was your night? I hope that I did not catch you at a bad time."

"Hello Father, how are you today? My night was okay thank you. No time is a bad time for you. I am happy you call me always. I love you. Have you heard from Mother today?"

"I love you my sweet daughter. I have not spoken with your mother today. I will after I talk with you. I want to talk with you before you leave for work today. I want to come over if that is okay and you can go in later..."

"Yes, that will be fine father. I will call my office and let them know I will be in later. I will wait for you. I will have coffee for you."

"Thank you sweetheart I will be there in a few minutes."

Carmeli'ta' hoped that he was coming to tell her about her mother and why she did not return and have not called or talked with her in more than three weeks. She rushed and prepared the coffee, put fresh bread with butter in the oven to warm. While the bread was warming, she called Ms. Horne's desk. She arrived each morning at 8:00 a.m. Ms. Horne picked up the phone after the third ring, "Madison Steel. Administration, may I help you?"

"Mrs. Horne, good morning."

"Good morning Ms. Bandaci. How are you?"

"I am fine thank you. I hope you are well. I am coming in later this morning. I should be there by 10:00 a.m. if not before. Would you let Mr. Madison know? Please take my calls and all messages. Thank you."

"You are welcome. I will let Mr. Madison know. In fact, he is standing here now. See you soon."

Jason listening said, "Mrs. Horne was that Ms. Bandaci?"

"Yes, she is coming in later. She asked me to let you know she should be her by 10:00 a.m."

"Thank you Ms. Horne. I was expecting her call to let me know if she was coming in later."

Carmeli'ta' walked back to the kitchen removed the bread from the oven and finished her breakfast and the dishes before her father arrived so she could talk without eating. She took the opportunity to finish dressing for work and tidying up her Townhouse. Carmeli'ta' sat in her Bay Window watching for her father so she could get his coffee and have it hot for him. Roberto' arrived at 8:15 a.m. Carmeli'ta' poured his coffee and set it on the coffee table where he sit when he came to visit her. Roberto' knocked lightly at the door. "Father is that you?"

"Yes, my daughter it is your father." She opened the door smiling hugged him and said, "Good morning. I have your coffee near your favorite place to sit when you visit."

He held onto her as they walked toward the couch, "I hope that I am not making it difficult for you being late leaving for work."

"No father it is fine. I called my office and let them know. I have time I can take off if I need to. I have many sick days and vacation days since I have never taken either since I went to work for Madison Steel and Iron."

"That is excellent my daughter and wise only use them if you need them. You learned well from your mother and me."

"Yes, mother and you always work never taking off for just any reason. I appreciate that fact along with many others in the way you raised me."

Roberto' smiled. "Carmeli'ta' I wanted to talk with you about your statement last evening you wanted to decide what you wanted to do about your mother not coming back with me and her not calling you. What did you mean by that my daughter?"

"I wanted to think about why my mother is not here and what I should do if anything about it Father. You have been so vague with me about my mother since you came home. She has not called me. Do you know where my mother is? I feel afraid that something has happened to her and you do not want to tell me. Is she ill or hurt? Where is she at my grandparents or do you know?"

Roberto' saw the tears forming in her eyes thought, she is so like her mother with those mysterious eyes framed by long lashes, so sensitive said in a surprised tone, "Carmeli'ta', of course, I know where your mother is and she is not ill my daughter. She just wanted to visit her parents and rest for a while. She will be home soon."

"When Father, what does soon mean?"

"Carmeli'ta' I wish you would trust your mother and me. She will not be gone much longer."

After a long time talking Carmeli'ta' said, "Father I have to go now. I need to get to work by 10:00 a.m. It is 9:45 a.m. now. The drive is ten minutes from here or more since traffic is heavier this time of day."

"Yes my daughter thank you for taking time and for the coffee. I hope that you feel better now. I need to get to the Farm and talk to your mother before I start my day."

Carmeli'ta' walked her father to the door held her face up for his kiss on her forehead, closed the door, standing for a moment; she was not satisfied with his answer. She left for work and arrived at 10:00 a.m. Mrs. Horne handed her messages as she passed her desk, "Good morning Ms. Bandaci."

"Good morning Mrs. Horne. Please let Mr. Madison know I am in my office."

"Yes, I will." Jason Madison working on the contracts with Meriwether Textiles, phone ringing said, "Yes, Mrs. Horne, has Ms. Bandaci arrived?"

"You are amazing sir, yes she has. She is in her office."

"Tell her that I will be there within the next fifteen minutes. I need to finish reviewing the delivery contract."

In the interim, Roberto' arrived home opened the door to the office and called the waiting Simone'. It was 3:00 p.m. at the Giovanni's resident, the phone rang, she ran from the kitchen picked it up, "Hello."

"Hello, my beauty how is your day? I hope you rested last night."

"Hello darling, my day is going fine. I did not sleep too soundly. I wanted to talk with father before he left for the farm. I set the clock and looked at it every hour. How was your night?"

"It was fine my beauty. I did not sleep long. I visited Carmeli'ta and talk to her before she went to work today. She is not buying into what I am saying my beauty. I am visiting her again after work today."

"I am worried about her Roberto'. I am getting a flight hopefully Thursday to come home. There are no flights on Wednesdays' my father tells me it is a day of planning and growth training for employees. I will let you know when I will arrive if there are any seats left."

"That is wise my beauty. Our daughter is suffering because I cannot answer her questions. I need to get to the farm. Peter will be waiting for me."

"Yes, my darling. I will talk to you later after you speak with Carmeli'ta'. Have a good day."

"Thank you my darling bye for now."

Roberto' left for his farm to complete his workday. He planned to call Amelio' later in the day to see if the bank transfers went well and if he was successful in getting Carmeli'ta' accounts set-up.

Tuesday morning, December 5, at 9:00 a.m. Amelio' arrived at the Charleston National Bank to affect the transfers of the money into Roberto's and his farm and personal accounts and set-up Carmeli'ta' personal account. After three hours, the banking was completed. He obtained receipts and the paperwork for bank transfers for the seven accounts where he transferred money.

In the meantime, Mrs. Horne walked to Carmeli'ta' office knocked and entered, "Mr. Madison is finishing his review of the delivery contract. He will be here within fifteen minutes."

"Thank you Ms. Horne. I have a few calls to make before then." She decided to cancel the lunch date with Alberto on Thursday. She called the Gambani home. Ms. Gambani answered, "Hello."

"Ms. Gambani this is Carmeli'ta' how are you today? I hope that I did not call at an inconvenient time. I need to speak with Alberto' is he there?"

"Your timing is fine my dear. It is good to talk with you. I miss seeing you. Yes, Alberto' is here. I will call him. I hope to see you soon."

"Thank you. I will come as soon as I can. I miss you as well." Silence on the other end seemed like an eternity to her actually was only one minute. Alberto said, "Hello Carmeli'ta'. It is strange that you called me. I was just thinking of you. How are you today? It is good to hear your voice. I am looking forward to seeing you Thursday for lunch."

"Thank you for thinking of me Alberto. I am fine. It is good to hear your voice. Lunch is what I am calling about Alberto." As Carmeli'ta' spoke, his spirits began to sink into sadness, she continued, "I am not able to meet you on Thursday, December 7, can we plan lunch for another time, maybe when you return for the summer break. I apologize for having to cancel. It would have been good to see you."

All his hopes dashed in a moment's time summer break was six months away it was just December 1927 anything could happen by that time. He was at a lost for what to do. It was too early to talk with her father he needed to have graduated and working before he asked for her hand in marriage. Love is a miserable state to be in if you loves someone that does not know, you love them or they might not love you the same way.

Jason was walking in the open door just as she was hanging up from

cancelling her lunch with Alberto closed the door and said, "How are you today my beauty? I was anxiously waiting your arrival. I missed your early morning greeting my darling." Carmeli'ta' walked from behind the desk smiled without answering walked to his open arms and kissed him with a long passionate kiss holding onto him tightly. He felt her small body tremble beneath his hands pulled her closer waiting for her to tell him why she was shaking.

"Jason, I met with my father before I came to work and he is still vague and asking that I trust him and my mother. He said she will be home soon. I do not know what "soon" means. I am not sure he knows where she is, he was not convincing when told he did. I think I want to go to Tuscany to find my mother to know if she is okay."

Jason feeling perplexed at the idea of her traveling alone and so far said, "I understand Carmeli'ta'. I am worried with you traveling alone and so far. You have never been far from Charleston alone. It is just not a good idea for one so young and beautiful to try a trip of this magnitude."

"I could sail on the Mauretania or the RMS Olympic they are both in dock in the New York Harbor. I checked the Mauretania sails for London at 5:30 p.m. Thursday, December 7 and the RMS Olympic on Friday, December 8 at the same time. I checked the flights and there is one every day at 3:00 p.m. I could fly. I would rather make the trip by flight; sailing aboard ship takes seven to nine days, which is too long a time for me. The flight only takes fourteen hours and I will be there by Thursday morning and in Tuscany by 11:00 a.m. The layover in London is only one hour. I will be fine at the Airport. When I get to Tuscany I can take a cab to my Grandparents house or call my grandfather."

Jason not wanting to press her too much with his desire for her safety said, "You have been thorough as usual and checked all the traveling possibilities. I will support whatever decision you make to travel to Italy Carmeli'ta'. I only want what is best for you my lovely one."

Jason felt a little sick as he thought of her traveling so far away from him. He could not go at the present-time since she would be away from the plant. He would only call his father to take the helm under extreme circumstances. He would complete the Delivery Contract review and could go without any problem the following week of December 13. His father would take the helm for a while, however, a question in reference to the contracts might arise, and Charles Meriwether would be the contact person. This would be a problem since he does not care for Jason Madison, Sr. so it is best that he stay and complete this phase of the contracts. The next phase would not start until January of 1928.

"I will decide what I want to do after I talk with my father when he visits me after work today, Jason. It is difficult for me to concentrate on anything else now except my mother and whether she is safe and not ill."

"I understand my lovely sweetheart. If you would like to go home that will be fine. I will call you later before I come by. Would you rather cancel our spending the evening together tonight?"

"I don't want to go home; I will be miserable until I talk with my father. I want to spend the evening with you my love. If I decide to go I will miss you terribly." She snuggled close to Jason. He thought how vulnerable she was, so innocent, sweet, loving, kind, understanding, and trusting, is why he worried about her traveling alone. He also realized that at this point he needed to say a less as possible she was not his wife. Jason held her close to him for a long time and finally said, "I will make this week's visit to the Plant Manager's Office, and perform the Quality Control Check for you

Carmeli'ta'. In addition, I will let the Plant Manager know that you may be out of the plant for ten days or more. You have trained Mrs. Horne well; I will ask her to take care of checking the Quality Control Process while you are away if you decide to go."

"Thank you Jason. Mrs. Horne is an excellent employee. She is knowledgeable of the process that I created for the Weekly Quality Control Check. I will let you know what I decide later when we see each other tonight."

"Yes, my love. I will see you later tonight. I need to complete the contract check before my day ends today. Please make your plans now for the delegation of duties to be done if you decide to go through with your travel plans." Jason smiled held her around her waist and walked to the door and left for his office and the pile of work on his desk.

Carmeli'ta' busied herself with the task at hand, delegation of duties in her absence.

In Tuscany, Simone' heart pounded in her ears as she paced anxiously back and forth in the kitchen as her mother prepared dinner; it was 4:00 p.m. nearing the time for her father to come home and it would be many hours before she would hear from Roberto' and his conversation with Carmeli'ta' after his Monday, workday ends. Noticing her nervousness, Catarina' in a concerned tone stated, "Simone' please my daughter, calm yourself there is nothing that you can do until you hear from Roberto'. He will call as he promised. We hope that Carmeli'ta' will not do anything rash; but it concerns me she is not accepting her father's explanation of why you did not return. I do not want her to come here with Vincenzo' being in the valley and thinking the way he does and insisting she is his daughter that would be more trouble than any of us want."

"I know mother, I cannot sit down and I feel extremely afraid now that this situation is about to spill over into trouble for everyone. How could I have allowed this to metastasize? It feels like a bad bruise on my heart and it worsens by the minute."

"It is good to keep your composure my daughter."

"I will try for father and your sake." Catarina did not comment just looked at her and nodded an approval to her statement.

At her desk Carmeli'ta' planning the delegation of duties, her heart became apprehensive and fretful. The whereabouts of her mother was not clear in her mind or the fact of her well-being. She did not want to call her grandparents, if she were not there that would make them worry they were older and she did not want them to worry; therefore, that was not an option. She would just go there and see without alerting them of her coming or asking them if her mother was visiting with them as her father stated the three times they discussed her mother not returning home. The hours passed quickly as she worked diligently assigning duties, she would leave the assignment list with Jason.

Jason working to finalize the check on the Delivery Contract with Meriwether Textiles mind continued to drift wondering what Carmeli'ta' would do. He could feel her pain of not knowing; he could not understand why; it was so strange. He felt a bond with Carmeli'ta' that was so strangely wonderful to him; one he could not explain if he tried to himself or any other. He began to know within himself what his father meant when he said that he would better grasp the power of a loving woman in your life, in time. It was as if someone punched him in the stomach and put butterflies there all at the same moment. How could he bear to be away from her for any length of time? Love drives a heart, stirs it up, and stimulates the mind and soul.

Carmeli'ta' checked the time, it was nearing 4:00 p.m. her father would be leaving his office and on his way to her Townhouse. She needed to get home, make his favorite drink, and prepare her mind for the direction that their conversation might take.

Later that afternoon, Roberto' on his way to Carmeli'ta's, stopped to check with Amelio' about the success in transferring the funds to the Swiss Banking System and the weekly amount he set to transfer each week into their Swiss accounts. Amelio' prepared each account and the balances with the weekly transfer amounts before Roberto' arrived. Arriving at Amelio's office, sat for a moment thinking of the conversation he would have with his daughter in thirty minutes, was doubtful, he could convince her that her mother was okay. Pondering what to do, he leaned on the steering wheel. Amelio' observed him from the window of his office opened the door, walked to the car, and tapped on the window. Roberto' looked up not realizing he was still sitting in the car said, "Hello my Cousin. How are you?"

"I am fine Roberto' it is apparent to me that you are troubled with the situation with Carmeli'ta' and what to tell her about Simone'."

"Yes, I am. I do not know what she will do next. It is difficult to read my sweet little daughter sometimes, in this way, she is so much like her mother with those expressive eyes of hers hides what she is thinking and feeling. I want to check the success of the transfers and then be on my way."

"I have all the paperwork ready for you Roberto' on my desk." They walked back inside, Amelio' handed him his transfer documents and Carmeli'ta's. The amounts were accurate just as they discussed. Amelio' said, "I will complete Carmeli'ta's transactions December 6, (Wednesday). I will be there when the bank opens."

"Thank you Amelio'. I need to be on my way to get to my daughter's by 5:00 p.m. and I promised to call Simone' as well it will be late there, as you well know."

"I understand Roberto' just let me know the result of your conversation with Carmeli'ta'."

Roberto' picked up the legal documents and walked toward the door replied, "Thank you Amelio'. I will call you after I have spoken with Carmeli'ta' and Simone'."

He left Amelio's office and arrived at Carmeli'ta' Townhouse complex at 4:55 p.m. Carmeli'ta' sitting in the Bay Window looking down as usual for her father's Roadster, saw it come through the gates, went to the kitchen retrieved the Tea and chilled glasses from her Refrigerator/Icebox and placed the tray on the coffee table.

It was approaching 10:00 p.m. in Tuscany. Simone' and her parents waited anxiously for Roberto' to call and tell them what Carmeli'ta' said in response during his fourth visit to reason with her concerning her mother not returning. Simone' paced back and forth on her mother's patio. Her parents sat at the kitchen table looking at each other as their daughter wore out her shoes felt for her and the dilemma facing her. She was dealing with the issue of revealing the twenty-four-year secret she held from her husband and additionally trying to protect Carmeli'ta' and hoping she would not find out about Vincenzo' Moretti's claim of being her father.

Roberto' knocked lightly at the door and said, "Carmeli'ta' it father."

She opened the door smiling he held out his arms, she hugged him and replied, "Hello father I am happy to see you. I made your Tea and I have the glasses chilled just as you like them."

"Thank you daughter I appreciate your thoughtfulness making me my favorite drink in the world."

"Father you never told me how to come to love Tea in chilled glasses."

"Your Mother spoiled me with preparing my Tea this way long before you were born when we lived in Tuscany. It has become my favorite because it reminds me of her each time I drink it no matter where I am and what I am doing."

"You love my mother passionately. That is amazing Father how we grow so much like the people we are around; or how much like them we become when we associate with them on other levels of our lives."

"Were you thinking, of Jason Madison, my daughter?"

As she poured the tea she answered, "Yes, and you as well, my Father. Mother tells me that I am just like you in many ways. It is amazing to me how much Jason and I have in common and how much you and I have in common."

"That is true my daughter. People do grow alike over time as they get to know each other and the relationship bond is stronger. Your mother is right, you are like me precious one; you are my child."

There was silence for a moment between them. Roberto' looked at his lovely daughter so innocent and kind said, "Carmeli'ta' I wanted to talk with you again to reassure you that your mother is fine my daughter, she is not ill, and will be home soon hopefully by this week's end."

"Father that does not answer my questions about my mother and I keep seeing the last time we were all together the evening before she left the next day you were angry with her. She had not done anything and only said that I should have a choice in who I love. Why would that make you angry? I just do not understand any of this; it is such a mystery to me. What are you hiding from me? I feel hurt and lost not knowing about my mother and you are trying to reassure me she is okay, why can't I talk with her?"

Roberto' noticed that she was becoming increasingly agitated and distraught replied, "Please daughter calm down and listen to me. She is well, and with her parents in Tuscany."

Becoming angry she responded, "No my Father I will not accept that answer. There is something wrong I know it and I will not stop until I know all the facts." Carmeli'ta' was crying uncontrollable by this time saying, "No Father, I don't accept the answer and explanation you gave me. It is strange she left and then did not come home; no, I don't accept your answer."

Roberto' held her as she cried into his shirt, "Please my precious daughter, I did not intend for you to be upset your mother is fine." He, at this point, was loss for words. His explanation was not convincing his daughter he knew it was useless to continue. He continued to hold her close to him until she was calmer. Carmeli'ta' calmed herself; he poured another glass of tea and handed it to her. She took the tea, sat down in the oversize winged-back chair, sipping it slowly, and did not comment.

Roberto' observed his daughter saw *Anima Mundi* in her, a pure ethereal spirit. She was sweet and innocent he did not know how to help her or answer her questions simply because he did not have all the answers himself only her mother had all the answers. He moved near his daughter and stroked her hair saying, "Carmeli'ta' I would like for you to come home with me tonight. We could spend the evening together and Marianna is always happy to see you."

Quietly and calmly, she replied, "Thank you for the kind invitation father, Jason, and I have plans for the evening. I will come another time if that is okay with you." She smiled as she set her glass on the tray. Roberto' worried what she might do. She has never been impulsive; but always took calculated steps in anything she did. He was pleased to know that she would be spending the evening with Jason was a comforting thought to him, rose saying, "It is getting late my daughter, Marianna will be waiting dinner for me." He did not want to mention Simone' and risk another upsetting scene. Roberto' took her hand and walked to the door, hugged her, looked down at her, and smiled. "Yes, father. I understand. I will see you tomorrow."

"I do not like leaving you upset my daughter. I will come tomorrow definitely. Please call me later to let me know how you are after your evening with Jason is over."

"If it is not too late I will call you father. Thank you for coming by to see me today." She hugged him tight and held onto him for a long time looked up at him and smiled. He smiled back at her and closed the door. She dropped the latch in place and went to prepare for her date with Jason.

Carmeli'ta' rushed to freshen-up, Jason would arrive soon, thought about what she would do. Tomorrow she would decide.

CHAPTER

THIRTY-SIX

Roberto' arrived home placed the Legal Transactions Papers in the Safe. He would give Carmeli'ta' a copy of her documents later. The documents would be secure in his safe. She had the combination she could get them at her discretion. He washed his hand and went to the kitchen where Marianna was waiting dinner for him. Smiling as he entered he said, "Good evening Marianna, how was your day?"

She smiled back replying, "You are late again. I had a good day thank you for asking Sir." Roberto' hurried through his dinner thanked Marianna and went to the sitting room to call Simone. While waiting for the operator to get the call through to Tuscany, he thought of the conversation with Carmeli'ta' still wondering what action she would take or what she would do. He did not want her to be upset about her mother. He thought, 'I will insist that Simone' come home so we can work through the problem for everyone's sake, especially Carmeli'ta'.

Simone' waited by the phone still pacing back and forth. Her father and mother sit across the room in his office near the fireplace still observing their daughter. The phone rang three long and two short.

Simone' picked up the receiver and said, "Hello."

"Hello, my beauty how was your day?"

"My day was fine my husband, how are you? How is Carmeli'ta'? Did you talk with her?"

"I am fine my beauty. My day was fine. I did see and talk with our daughter she is fine. I will tell you about the conversation I had with her earlier this evening. Firstly, I want to tell you the results of the bank transfers."

"Yes, definitely my husband that has been a concern of mine as well. Did Amelio' get everything taken care of for all the accounts?"

"Yes, I have the legal documents showing the transfers for all accounts including Carmeli'ta'. Amelio' opened a $10,000 account for her today. He will complete the transaction early tomorrow morning. I put all the legal documents in the safe. Our finances are secure and we have the necessary funds to operate the business on a weekly basis. In addition, the bank will transfer the stated amount each week to the Swiss Banking System. If you need any cash my beauty, please ask Franco to give it to you and I will get it back to him."

"I am good for cash my husband. I have $500.00 with me. That is more than enough to get my ticket and other things I needed. I have not spent any money since I have been here. My mother took care of my cosmetic needs. Now my husband, tell me about the conversation with our daughter."

"Carmeli'ta' is not buying the reason I gave her for you not returning. She is upset more than I have seen her other than the time in high school when she could not remember the history dates for a test. She is not accepting that you are okay, she thinks I do not know where you are or you might be sick and I will not tell her. I am concerned about her Simone'. I insist that you come home this week my beauty. It will be better for everyone if you are here. You are the only one that can answer either of our questions. She has a date with Jason tonight, which I am thankful she is not alone. I asked her to come home with me tonight, but she refused promising to call me after her evening with Jason ends."

Silence on the other end of the phone, she eventually said, "I understand my husband. I plan to come as soon as I can get a flight. My father is checking tomorrow, December 6, when he is at the weekly meeting of the employees at the Airport. There are no flights on Wednesday and no reservations made; it is a day of training my husband."

"Please let me know as soon as you know tomorrow and I will let our daughter know you are on your way. She is also grieved because you have not spoken to her for almost a month now. She seemed hurt to the point of almost being angry. I will be happy when you are home and we can get our lives back to normal Simone'. This is difficult for everyone."

"I know my husband. I will discuss everything with you when I arrive and then allow you to read my Diary it will further explain everything and give answers to your questions as well."

"I will wait to hear from you my beauty after your father returns from his meeting. Oh, by the way what time is that meeting?"

"It starts at 9:00 a.m. tomorrow and ends at 3:00 p.m. I will ask him to check as soon as possible and call me with flight information and seat availability."

"Thank you my beauty. It is getting late you need to sleep and I as well. I love you Simone'. Have a good night."

"Thank you my husband, I love you. Have a restful night."

Simone's parents were waiting to hear the results of the conversation with Carmeli'ta'. They could only hear one side of it. Simone turned around from the desk and walked to where her parents were sitting near the Fireplace in her father's office. She sat on the Ottoman in front of them and said, "Roberto' said the conversation did not go well with Carmeli'ta'; she is upset and not buying the explanation that he is giving for my not returning home with him and why I have not called her. He said she was almost angry along with being upset. He insisted that I come home this week so we can get the problem solved and get our lives back to normal. I don't know if that is ever possible again."

Franco commented, "Simone' you can only deal with one problem at a time. You cannot think too far ahead that will not help the challenge any. You are borrowing trouble become it gets here."

"I agree with your father Daughter. It will be okay your husband and you have to work through this."

"I need to rest Mother and Father. I promised to call Roberto' as soon as you know if there is a seat on a flight on Thursday father. Will you call me when you get a chance after you the check the Thursday flight and check for seat availability?"

"Yes, daughter I will get that information as quick as I can."

"Thank you both, Good night."

Her parents observed her walking toward her bedroom suite noticed her movements were of a tired person having aged in the last few minutes. The challenge made her feel someone had beaten her both physically and mentally. She drew her water, took her bath, put on her negligee, went to bed, and fell asleep immediately from sheer mental exhaustion.

Roberto lay sleepless after he prepared for bed on the loveseat in their sitting room looking into the flames lost the ability to put his thoughts together in any sensible order, especially concerning his wife and daughter. He felt perplexed and pulled in three different directions; first Simone' and all the unanswered questions over the years; Carmeli'ta' and the questions she asked he could not answer and the fear that she would do something rash, but what? Then, the Farm, he could not concentrate fully on the Farm as he had done in the past. He could not leave the total responsibility of running it to Peter, his Foreman, and his cousin Amelio'.

His wife away from home with mystery surrounding her absence and his daughter questioning his truthfulness was like white water rafting, difficult to navigate, making the watery path to the truth rocky, forceful, lacking a solid area to grasp the concreteness of the entire situation, leaving him feeling undefended and open to the elements of the environment. Unable at the time to either control, nor amend any part of the situation, and feeling drained, he slept.

Carmeli'ta' waiting for Jason to arrive, contemplated what action she would take to secure the truth of the situation with her mother. Reflections went once again to almost a month ago the last night she saw her mother; her father was angry with her for no apparent reason. It was still a mystery to her why he became angry and then her mother leave without explanation. She would talk to Jason when he arrived to see what he thought about her final decision to go abroad to find her mother or at least see if she were with her grandparents. Glancing out of her Bay Window saw Jason's Beige and Black Bentley coming up the drive that led to the front of her Townhouse. She quickly went to her bathroom mirror for one last check and picked up her handbag from the lounger in her dressing room, dabbed more Chanel 5 cologne behind her ears and went back to the living room to wait for Jason's knock.

The light knock at her door had become familiar to Carmeli'ta'. Moving with speed to the door, called as she arrived, "Jason darling is that you."

Smiling at the sweet tone of her voice he said, "Yes, my lovely Carmeli'ta' it is your Jason." Jason saw a beautiful smile on her face when she opened the door she said sweetly, "I like the response you gave me sweetheart of being My Jason, because you are my heart my darling, thank you."

"I am yours my lovely one. How are you Carmeli'ta'? I hope that you are feeling a little better after your conversation with your father and have some of the answers to your questions concerning your mother and why she did not return with your father last week."

"I do not know anymore after my father and my conversation a few hours ago than when I spoke with you when I arrived at work earlier. He is planning to visit me again tomorrow after work Jason. He cannot answer my questions or he will not answer them; now, I do not know which, but they are unanswered. I am ready for dinner my love so we can spend the evening together."

Jason felt uneasy with the surface of calm and the faraway look in Carmeli'ta's eyes. He feared her making a rash decision to go abroad without the knowledge of traveling that great a distance from home. He thought of a million things that could happen to her in route to find her mother; he saw a lack of focus when normally she were more focused. His major concern was her inexperience, which could prove to be dangerous. He knew her traveling on a ship was exponentially more dangerous than the airplane; a young woman alone on the ocean for 9 days or more. He fretted within at the possibility, wondered what option she would choose or if she would tell him how she decided, she would travel.

Jason and Carmeli'ta' left for their dinner and tour of the Heyward Washington House, which was a surprise planned by Jason for Carmeli'ta'. She wanted, for some time, to tour the house and grounds of the home of Thomas Heyward, one of the signers of the Declaration of Independence. She had become an enthusiast of the magnificent Charleston-made furniture and the formal 18th century gardens of Charleston, part of the Charleston Museum Mile. Jason had arranged, as a surprise, a private tour for Carmeli'ta'.

To Carmeli'ta's astonishment, after dinner, Jason drove to Church Street and stopped in front of the Heyward-Washington House. She was amazed to see the lights on and staff on the front steps smiling waiting to start the tour. With the position she held at Madison Steel had not afforded her the opportunity to visit during regular business hours; 9:00 a.m. to 4:00 p.m. in the evening and was not open on the weekends. Jason opened her door smiling and reached for her hands to assist her in standing. She stood staring at the well-lit windows, looked up, at Jason, and exclaimed, "Jason I am excited and surprised my darling. You arranged this just for me? I love it Jason what a pleasant after dinner treat. Thank you darling, I feel very special. How did you arrange it; they are so particular about the historical homes on Museum Mile?"

"You are welcome my darling. I wanted this to be special for you because you love Charleston manufactured furniture and beautiful gardens. I like doing things that makes you smile and bring you pleasure in life my darling."

"How did you get them to open the Heyward-Washington House for you after hours?"

Smiling he hugged her and commented, "Babette D'Aubiguine, Curator and Manager, is a friend of my Father and Mother. I have known her since I was 13 years of age. She had dinner with my parents on Saturday. I asked her if she could arrange a special tour for me and she said she would see if she could arrange it and call me. She called earlier today to let me know the details; 9:30 p.m. is late, but, she has security working, her assistant manager and two tour guides are on duty, one for the house and one for the garden."

"Thank you Jason, for this special treat, my love. You say she is a friend of your father and mother Jason, how old is she?"

"She is a few years older than I am my love why you ask?"

"She is 29 years old. I just wondered. You said she was a friend of your parents and not you Jason if you have known her most of your life?"

"Her parents and my parents were friends my love, as Babette and I grew up. I was not around her that much when she went to a private school I went to Charleston High. Her father and mother are patrons of the Heyward-Washington House and Babette studies are in art and history. Therefore, after she graduated she worked at the Museum for a few years. She has an excellent and very extensive knowledge of art and history. When the position for Curator and Manager opened up the Board of Directors appointed her; she is a wise choice for manager. My mother and Babette does quite a bit of charity benefits together is why I said she is a friend of my parents. I do not have any interaction with her unless she visits my parents or I attend a function that my mother is chairing."

"I understand Jason, thank you for clarifying the relationship for me."

"She is a lovely lady Carmeli'ta' but she is not for me. My mother wanted it so, but I could consider her as a friend but never anything further than that my lovely Carmeli'ta'."

"I see. Jason, are your parents close in age to my parents?"

"I am not sure my lovely one. My mother is 46 years old and my father is 50 years old. How old are your parents?"

"My mother is 40 years old; her birthday is soon she will be 41 years old and my father is 44 years old. So, they are somewhat close in age."

"Yes, my lovely Carmeli'ta' they are somewhat. Your mother is young Carmeli'ta' 15 years older than I am. It is hard to imagine our parents being in their early or mid-40s and we are in our mid and late 20s."

"You are right it is Jason. My mother was 18 when I was born and my father was 22."

"That is amazing Carmeli'ta' they were so young when they married." She smiled and did not comment.

Jason knew his relationship with Babette was questionable in Carmeli'ta's mind. The thought made him smile. It was pleasing to know that she would be jealous of any other woman in his life. They chatted while walking toward the door, Jason held even tighter to Carmeli'ta'. He knew how she felt at the prospect of him and another woman. He felt the same way when observing Charles Meriwether watching his Carmeli'ta' causing his green-eyed monster to come alive. With just one difference, she seemed to be oblivious to Charles Meriwether watching her as a man does a beautiful woman with the look of longing in his eyes. His relating this fact, to her traveling alone, frightened him even more; she would never notice a man looking at her in that way. Innocence is a wonderful thing then again it can be dangerous to one so lovely; she has never been in a threating environment. She has been with her father and mother and never exposed to the dangers in the world; in addition, at every company function; he kept her close to him.

Anxiety and uneasiness gripped Jason's mind and heart.

This was a special night he planned for Carmeli'ta' and did not want anything to spoil her seemingly happy mood with the surprise so he said nothing just smiled and held her close as they toured the house and grounds. After an hour and a half, the tours were over. Carmeli'ta' excitedly thanked the staff and the Assistant Manager with thoughts in her mind of how she wanted her and Jason's home to have at least one room of the fascinating Charleston-made furnishing. Her mother was too an antique enthusiast, she bought the antique Armoire' from Esty Candelabra's. She thought of the quaint beauty it had and the magnificent handy work done by the wood smith.

After the tour of the house and grounds, on the way to her Townhouse Carmeli'ta' sat quietly looking at the scenery the beautiful homes on Museum Mile provided had become such a treasure in Charleston. Jason noticing how quiet she was, reached over and took her left hand, held it to his mouth, kissed it and asked, "Where are you in thoughts my sweetheart? You can share with me what is on your mind my darling."

"I am here Jason my thoughts are just in three or four different ways right now. I was thinking of the lovely evening you planned for us. I so enjoyed seeing the Heyward-Washington House I have always wanted to. I would like for one room of our home completely decorated, with Charleston-made furniture. I do love the look of it so much, what you think about one room being furnished that way?"

"I love the look of the furnishing my darling I always have; my mother has quite a bit of Charleston-made furniture in our home. You have exquisite taste Carmeli'ta' like everything else about you. It warms my heart to know that you are pleased with the evenings I planned for us my darling. I love doing it for you because I love you with everything that I am. The expression on your face tells me how pleased you are my darling. I love watching you when you are excited and surprised."

"Thank you Jason I feel so loved and cared for by you."

"Is that all you were thinking about Carmeli'ta'?"

Jason wanted to get her to talk with him about her plans without pressing her. He noticed over the months that she was not someone, though young and inexperienced, that could be pressed, has a sharp mind, and an undetermined amount of will accomplish the task before her, or get the sufficient information to form a conclusion or arrive at an acceptable answer. "No Jason I was waiting until we got to my Townhouse before I discussed with you my plans for trying to find my mother and know if she is with my grandparents since my father is not answering my questions to my satisfaction."

"What are you planning Carmeli'ta'?"

"I want to know about my mother it is worrying me more and more as the minutes pass. I plan to go to Tuscany as I discussed with you and I will go in whatever way I can get there the quickest. If I can't get a seat on a plane, then I will go by ship it will take a little longer but it is worth my efforts to know my mother is okay."

Fear gripped Jason's heart and mind at the prospect of her going whichever way was the quickest. He did not know how to comment since she did not ask him a question only stated definitely she would go it did not matter how said finally, "Carmeli'ta' my love I would like to see you take your time and talk with your father as he asked tomorrow, to see if he knows definitely when your mother will return. I am sure my love that your father is telling you everything he knows about the situation. He may not have the answer to your questions had you considered that?"

"Frankly, no I had not Jason. You may be right I do not know. What I do know is he is keeping something from me. I know my father; he is not good at hiding his feeling; he never liked secret or vagueness. He taught me as I grew that absolute honesty is always the best way to approach any subject and now he is being vague that is not like him."

"He is right my love absolute honesty is what is best and vagueness only leaves room for unanswered questions. I understand your point and need to find the answer to your mother's whereabouts and why she has not called or contacted you since she left almost a month ago. I know that I would have the same reaction and probably would; no, I know I would plan to do the same time."

"So, you do understand my darling why I must take off from work and go to find my mother and see if she is okay, at my grandparents, or just what?"

"Yes, I understand my sweet precious Carmeli'ta' that is one of the things I love so much about you, your caring personality and loving heart."

"Thank you Jason, I do love my mother we have always been so close; is one of the reasons that I don't understand her actions. Then my father we are close as well, a loving family and for them to act in this manner is logic defying to me, I have to know why, it feels so strange to me."

The minutes passed quickly. They drove back across town to her Townhouse in the residential part of the city. Jason parked the car and helped Carmeli'ta' out. She handed him her key to open the door stopped in the foyer to pull off and hang her coat in the hall closet. He held her tight and said, "I love you Carmeli'ta' and I want to see you happy and you are not because of the fear you have your mother is not okay. I know that you will not be focused until you get answers to your questions."

"So, you do not mind me taking off to go and see about my mother?"
"No, I do not mind you taking off there are people that can pinchhit for you until you return. But I will miss you so terrible my heart is aching now at the prospect of you going away from me for even a day, but an unnumbered amount of days it is hard to bear my darling."

"I know Jason, I will miss you dreadfully also my darling, but I will be back as soon as I can and I hope to have my mother with me."

"Are you planning to speak with your father before you leave?"

"Yes, I promised him that I would. I like to keep my promises my darling. I will let you know after I talk with him. He will probably call me before he goes to the farm. I may not be in early again Jason, depending on the conversation and how well it goes."

Holding her tightly he felt tears forming in his eyes, it felt as if he was losing her before she was completely his, how hard love is sometimes. He felt as if his heart was being ripped out, replied in a low whisper, "I understand."

Carmeli'ta' held tight and snuggled close to him neither of them talking because of the pain they felt that took away words from them and only emotions of their heart spoke through their embrace of love and care.

After a long while Jason looked at his watch and said, "It is near midnight my lovely. The main thing tonight is you need your rest for the long day ahead of you tomorrow. Please call me when you have spoken to your father my darling. I will be waiting anxiously my love."

Jason kissed Carmeli'ta' with a long and passionate kiss, she felt an intensity in him that she had not known before; she knew he needed her as she did him in her life, kissed him. Jason felt with the kiss the same way he did the first night they kissed, he hugged her, took her hand, walked to the door, opened it, stepped into the hallway, and waited for Carmeli'ta' to put the security latch in place knocked light and said, "Thank you my lovely Carmeli'ta'."

Carmeli'ta' undressed and prepared for bed while thoughts of her next steps occupied her mind, did not call her father it was too late after midnight he was surely sleep by that time. She freshened up, brushed her teeth, put on her gown, and slipped beneath the comfort of her blankets and prayed to God to help her make the right decision and be safe while she tried to find her mother.

The adversary in the shadows pressed Simone'!

CHAPTER
THIRTY-SEVEN

Simone' awakens Wednesday morning, December 6, at 6:00 a.m. with the situation, on her mind, as an unrelenting adversary, it tenaciously pursued her. She felt at that moment she was barely ahead of this merciless enemy of guilt that steadfastly stalked her in unseen shadows near her path, staying right outside of the light so she could not see the foes that challenged her.

She tossed and turned for a long while until she heard the sound of her mother and father's voices as they walked toward the kitchen from their bedroom three doors down the hall. She rose, bathed, and dressed for the day preparing for whatever that day's fallout would be.

Before she joined her parents in the kitchen, she pulled her luggage out of the closet and placed it on the trunk that held her childhood treasures, near the window. She wished she could open the trunk and pull out her innocence and replace it with the guilt she felt from her poor decisions made between the ages of 14-17 years old, and after she moved to America. She planned to begin packing when breakfast was over and her father left for the meeting of the Airport Managers and employees with the Tuscany Development Committee.

She joined her parents in the kitchen her mother had coffee ready.

Franco and Catarina, while the bread and Italian sausage heated in the oven, were sitting having their morning conversation and prayer over coffee before they ate breakfast.

Perplexity and tiredness was written on her face from lack of sleep when Simone' walked into the kitchen. Her parents surprised to see her so early, looked at each other without comments.

"Good morning daughter how was your night?" asked Franco.

"Good morning Mother and Father. It is good to see each of you day. My night was long and I did not sleep well. I wish now Father; I had gone home with Roberto' last Friday and I would not be worried about what my daughter would do because she is not getting answers to her questions. Mother and Father this situation has taken on a different shape than I ever expected. How can one poor decision cause so much confusion?"

Catarina poured a cup of coffee for Simone' and handed it to her across the table and smiled. "Thank you Mother", she said.

"You are welcome Daughter, please calm down Simone'. I know that this situation is eating away at you, but take your time and think so you will know how to respond to your husband when he calls in a few hours. It is difficult what you are facing, but we are with you Simone' remember that and your husband and daughter loves you."

"Mother is right, Simone' you must stay calm. I will be leaving for the Airport within the hour. I will make checking the flight schedules my priority when I arrive. Actually, I will ask the Head Reservation Superior, Gabriella De Luca, to check the seats availability for me when I arrive without letting her know why I need the information before the meeting. She will assume that it is for the benefit of the meeting we will have with her department later today."

"Thank you Father. I would appreciate knowing as soon as I can. If I can leave on the 7th of December Thursday that will be better for me than waiting for a flight on Friday, December 8th. I need to get to Carmeli'ta' as soon as I can before her suspicions go any further."

Catalina put fruit bowls, (cantaloupe, melon, mandarin oranges), bread, butter, and Italian Sausage on the table. Franco ate as quickly as he could. Simone' picked at her food, pushed it around on her plate eating very little of it. Catarina watched her daughter as flashbacks, of Simone', at a younger age, danced in front of her eyes, doing the same thing when she had something that was weighing heavy on her mind. She reached over, caught her daughter's hand, rose, then stood behind her, placing her hands on both her shoulders, and comforted her.

Franco ready to depart, retrieved his briefcase from his office, kissed his wife, and squeezed Simone's hand and left, it would take almost an hour for him to drive to the airport. Arriving at the Airport, as predictable, Gabriella De Luca was at work. Franco knocked lightly at her door and waited, 'Come in', said the voice from the other side of the door. He walked in and greeted her, "Good morning Ms. De Luca. I hope that your week has been a good one so far."

"Good morning Mr. Giovanni. Thank you my week has gone well so far. How are you?"

"All is well with me and my family thank you."

"How can I help you Mr. Giovanni?"

"I need you to check for me the number of available seats on the 3:00 p.m. flight to London on Thursday, December 7th."

"I have that information ready for the meeting Mr. Giovanni as is routine."

"I need to get that information now if you don't mind." She hesitated for a moment before speaking looked at him and finally said, "I will get it for you sir." The rule states, "Information packets are to be distributed during the meetings to Committee Members and employees." She knew it must have been of uttermost importance because he made the rule.

Franco looked at the seat availability lists and to his surprise, all flights

were full with no seats available and a waiting list had 10 passengers in event there was a cancellation. He knew Simone' would have no possible chance of getting on either the morning or evening Thursday flights to London. She would definitely have to wait until Friday. She would be upset and disappointed there were no available seats left on either of the flights on Thursday. Reservations could not be altered or changed they were set on Tuesday's for Thursday's flights. After looking at the seat availability list, said, "Thank you Ms. De Luca I appreciate you sharing the information with me."

"Is there something I can help you with Mr. Giovanni or a question I can answer about the seat availability lists for Thursday?"

"No Ms. De Luca. I will see you at the meetings later in the morning."

His request left questions in Ms. De Luca's mind; for Franco

Giovanni this was strange behavior to her. He was strict about the rules and guidelines set for the operation of the Airport for confidentiality and safety purposes for all concerned. She soon dismissed the information request from her mind and attended to the details for the meetings later that morning.

Franco walked to the Boardroom to call his home to let Simone' know about the flights to London on Thursday. Opening the Boardroom door, he was relieved to find that no one had arrived for the meeting that started at 9:30 a.m.; it was 8:30 a.m. the other board members would be arriving within the next few minutes to prepare for the meeting. He walked to the hutch, picked up the phone, and asked the operator to ring his home. Simone' waiting anxiously in the kitchen with her mother, heard the first ring, ran down the hallway, through the French Doors, and over to her father's desk, picked up the phone, and said "Hello."

"It is me, daughter", said Franco.

"Yes, father. Thank you for calling so quickly. I am eager to hear if any seats are available on either of the Thursday's flights." Simone' was holding her breath waiting for her father to speak.

"I know that you were Simone'. There are no seats on the flights for Thursday. I am sorry. I know that you are disappointed. We will call the Airport first thing Thursday morning and make a reservation. We need to keep with the rules of making no reservations on Wednesday it would violate the integrity of the Board's ruling."

"I understand Father, it will be Friday then. I will let Roberto' know when he calls in a few hours. He should be calling soon it is 4:00 a.m. in Charleston. He will probably call around 6:00 a.m. I am sure. Thank you again father. I will see you when you get home later today."

"Okay my sweet daughter. I should be there by 4:00 p.m. The meetings usually end at 3:00 p.m. unless there is an issue on the table that was not on already on the schedule to discuss."

"Thank you Father."

Simone' hung up the phone and walked back to the kitchen where Catarina was waiting. Her face told Catarina there were no available seats on the flights by the expression on Simone's face. She sat down slowly after a moment said, "Father said there were no seats on the Thursday flights. I will prepare to leave on Friday Mother. He said we could make the reservation first thing tomorrow morning."

"Yes, Simone'. The airport reservation desk opens at 6:00 a.m. on Thursdays. If you are not up by that time, your father or I can make the reservation for you my daughter. Please go rest you look tired to me. I know you are waiting for Roberto' to call; I will let you know when he does."

"It is time to start preparing lunch and dinner Mother I can help you."

"No, my Daughter I do this every day. I appreciate your offer but you need to rest and relax. Go, go my lovely Daughter. I will take care of lunch and dinner preparations. We will have fruit for lunch and I will prepare dinner."

Simone' bone weary and mentally exhausted went to her bedroom to rest and try to relax before she talked to Roberto' later. She remembered he would be seeing Carmeli'ta' before she went to work and would not call until after he spoke with her. She had at least two hours before he called.

Roberto' awake at 5:00 a.m., lay looking up at the ceiling wondering what his daughter would do as she indicated to him last night. If she would be willing to wait to see him before she left to start her workday. Unable to rest or relax, after a while, decided to get dressed and balance the Farm Accounts while he waited for Marianna to prepare breakfast. She had heard him moving around and prepared breakfast for him by 7:30 a.m. He worked on balancing the account for two hours they were current and breakfast was ready. He walked in the kitchen just as Marianna was putting it on the table, "Good morning sir. You are on time today." Smiling he said, "Thank you, good morning Marianna my time clock." He ate quickly and went back to the office and called Carmeli'ta' she should be awake and having breakfast. The phone rang at her Townhouse, "Hello."

"Good morning my lovely daughter, how are you today?"

"Good morning Father, I am fine thank you. How are you today?"

"I want to visit you before you leave for work Carmeli'ta' if your schedule will allow."

"Yes, my Father I am always glad to see you. It was late last night when I arrived home so I did not call."

"That is okay little one; I will be there in 15 minutes if that is okay."

"Yes it is Father, I am preparing breakfast. I will have coffee for you."

"Thank you. I will see you shortly."

Carmeli'ta' ate breakfast, finish dressing, tidied her bedroom and bathroom as she did each day, and went to the window to wait for her father. She saw his car turn into her Townhouse complex at 8:30 a.m., poured her father a cup of coffee, and placed it on the coffee table near his favorite spot on her couch.

Roberto' knocked softly on the door and said, "Carmeli'ta' its father."

"I am coming Father, just a moment" she replied. Opened the door, smiled, and hugged her father, "Hello Father I am happy to see you. I love you. Have you talked to my mother?"

"Hello, my precious little one, I am happy to see you. You are very precious to your mother and me Carmeli'ta'. We both love you. I have not spoken with her today. I will when I return home after our visit."

"Father I poured you a cup of coffee, I sit in on table in your favorite spot near the Fireplace. Is my mother okay? When will she come home my Father?"

Roberto' went over to the couch, picked up the cup of coffee, sipping it slowly did not know what to say to convince her that Simone' was well and she would be home later that week. After a few more sips said, "Carmeli'ta', again, your mother is well. She is with your grandparents. She will be home later this week. I just want to be sure that you know she is okay and nothing has happened to your mother. She is spending some time with her parents. You said you would decide what you wanted to do, what did you have in mind Carmeli'ta'?"

He knew by the expression on her face that his words to her were not registering. He saw tears begin to form in her eyes and run down her cheeks. He walked over to her and hugged her close to him as she sobbed. So touched by the tears of his daughter and the unanswered questions silent tears rolled down his cheeks. She said with a shaky voice, "I want to see my mother she has been gone for a long time."

He said, "I know Carmeli'ta' this is strange to you since you and your mother are so close, but she is fine and wants you to not to worry about her. I love your mother Carmeli'ta' I would never allow anything to happen to you or her. She will be home very soon. Can you accept waiting a few more days?"

Carmeli'ta' has become more upset; the more he explained trying to calm her down only made it worse, "No Father, I don't accept that answer and I have been patient. It is strange she left then did not come home and she will not talk to me. I have not heard from her; I don't think you know where my mother is but do not want to tell me."

"Please my Daughter calm down. I do know where you mother is. I talk with her twice every day. She is with your grandparents in Tuscany and will be home later this week. I want you to try and understand and trust me and your mother."

"No Father, I will not accept that, I will not accept your answer anymore. I do not understand why you and mother are acting so strangely. I will not accept your explanation anymore." In a never heard before, determined almost calculating tone of voice she said, 'I need to go to the office my Father, Jason will be waiting."

Roberto' did not know what to say to calm Carmeli'ta'. He knew any attempt to have further conversation with her at that time would be useless. He could only hope that she would calm down and talk with him later that day. Walking to the door, he turned and kissed her on the forehead and said, "Carmeli'ta' I am sorry that you are upset. I will come to see you after my workday is over, my little one."

"Thank you for coming to see me father. I need to get to work."

Simone' had awaken with a start from her short rest, thought she heard Roberto' calling her. She realized it was a dream when she was fully awake.

She freshened up and went to the kitchen where her mother was preparing dinner. Catarina put a bowl of fruit on the table for Simone' to have her light lunch it was nearing 1:00 p.m. "Did you have a good rest my daughter."

"It was okay Mother. I heard Roberto' calling me and I realized it was a dream when I was fully awake. She sat down in front of the bowl of fruit and slowly ate strawberries and blue berries with cream.

"All will be okay Simone'. It will take patience to get through this issue, but you will get through it. Remember your husband and daughter loves you and your father and I love you."

"Thank you Mother for your kind words; love has caused this issue. I have come to know over the years that love can cause both happiness and pain, awful pain in our lives."

"Yes it can my Daughter."

Simone ate her fruit wondering if Carmeli'ta' would attempt to make the trip to Tuscany.

In Charleston, Roberto' left his daughter's Townhouse with a nervous fear gripping his heart and mind hoping she would be calmer when he saw her later in the day. Arriving at home, he quickly climbed the stairs to their sitting room and called the operator, gave her the number to the Giovanni home.

Simone finished her lunch sat chatting with her mother and said, "Maybe I should try and contact Roberto'. He should have called by now." Just as she rose, walked to her father's office, the phone rang four times. Simone' picked it up and said, "Hello."

"Hello my beauty. How are you today? I hope that you had a restful and peaceful night."

"Yes, my husband it was okay. I am worried about Carmeli'ta'. How are you today? Have you spoken with her yet?"

"I am fine my beauty. Yes, I am just this minute returning from seeing our daughter. She became very upset during our conversation. She is not accepting my explanations Simone'. You must come home this week; we must think of our daughter. Your absence is causing her pain. She cried this morning while

I was there. It broke my heart to see her so upset. I love you both and want to protect you Simone'but how can I if I do not know what is causing you to be so secretive? Will you be able to get a flight tomorrow to America?"

"I understand my husband. Our daughter and her happiness is a great concern for me. I know she does not understand my absence and my not calling. I love you both and would do anything to protect either of you from pain or hurt. It only seems now that the opposite has happened. I am the cause of great pain and suffering for both the people that I love most in this world, especially for you, my husband, since Carmeli'ta' only know that I am not there. My father did check the flights and there are no seat available on Thursday (tomorrow) December 7. I will make a reservation on Thursday on one of the flight to London on Friday. I should be there by noon on Saturday and we will discuss everything my husband. I am less fearful now than when you first knew about my Diary."

"I cannot think of anything that would keep me from loving you Simone'. I just want you to come home so we can work through whatever the issue is together my beauty."

"I will my sweet husband. Please see Carmeli'ta' this afternoon and make sure she is okay. I wish she would come and stay with you until I arrive. Will you ask her to come home until after the weekend?"

"Yes, I will ask her my beauty."

"Did she mention doing anything?"

"No, she just wanted to get to work, Jason was waiting for her. I hope that her work will occupy her time so the remainder of the week can pass fast and you get home my beauty."

"It will Roberto' my love."

"I know you need to get to the Farm, so I will wait to hear from you later today. I love you my husband. Take care of yourself and our daughter until I arrive."

"I love you Simone'. I will take care of Carmeli'ta' always my lovely, you both are my life. Take care of yourself. I will be happy to see you on Saturday. I cannot wait my beauty. Bye for now."

"Bye my husband."

Carmeli'ta' drove slowly towards Madison Steel and Iron, pulled into the parking lot near the administrative entrance door about the time her father ended his conversation with her mother. Eagle-eyed Ms. Horne noticed she was not smiling and said, "Good morning Ms. Bandaci it is good to see you. You did not call; I thought you might not come to work today. Mr. Madison was not sure that you would come in today. He said you had some business to take care of away from the plant."

"Thank you for your concern Ms. Horne. I did have business to take care of away from the plant. Is Mr. Madison at his desk, if so please let him know that I am in my office."

"Yes I will. Is there something that I can assist you with Ms. Bandaci?"

"No Ms. Horne thank you for your concern and offer of assistance."

Ms. Horne smiled, nodded, and buzzed in to let Jason Madison know she was in her office. Preoccupied with the details of the Materials Contract with Meriwether Textiles replied, "Yes Ms. Horne."

"Ms. Bandaci is in her office. She asked me to let you know."

"Thank you. Let her know I will be there momentarily to see the results of the early morning meeting."

Ms. Horne called Carmeli'ta' and said, "Ms. Bandaci, Mr. Madison asked me to let you know he will be there momentarily to see the results of the early morning meeting."

"Thank you Ms. Horne. I have that information for him."

Ms. Horne assumed it was something with one of the contracts with Meriwether Textiles, which is what Jason Madison wanted her to think so he could protect Carmeli'ta' and her being late for work two morning straight without notifying Human Resources she would be out for vacation or sick leave before she took the time.

Ms. Horne walked to Jason's door knocked lightly opened it and said, "Excuse me sir, Ms. Bandaci says she has that information for you."

"Thank you, I am almost done."

Jason laid the contract down, leaned back in his chair, and prayed that she would not decide to go to Tuscany. He did not want to risk the chance of her being hurt or something worse, he shuttered to think about what could happen to her on a trip on ship and on a flight. He rose slowly and took the contract off the desk so it would appear to Ms. Horne that her off-site meeting was about the contract. Ms. Horne noticed when he stopped at her desk to instruct her as for the meeting time frame with Carmeli'ta', he had the Materials Contract in his hand he held it so she could see the title said, "Ms. Horne I will probably be a good part of an hour with Ms. Bandaci. I do not have any other appointments until after lunch. Please hold all calls and only in the event of an emergency interrupt us."

"I understand Mr. Madison it will be as you instructed."

Jason walked slowly to her office not wanting to appear in a great hurry, as he walked he look down at the contract as if he was reading. Ms. Horne watched him until he reached Carmeli'ta's office door. She observed him knocking and the door opening and him walking in.

Jason closed the door behind him and reached for Carmeli'ta' waiting for him in the middle of her office floor said, "Good morning my lovely little one. I was overanxious for you to get here; then, I was not sure that you would be coming today. Did you speak with your father before you left home?"

"Yes, he came over and we talked. He did not tell me anything different. I said to him that I could no longer accept his explanation about my mother. I am more fearful each time I speak with him. He asked me to trust him and my mother to ensure that everything is okay. He said she will be home soon hopefully by the end of the week."

"That is wonderful Carmeli'ta'."

No, it is not Jason; my father is coming by again after his workday is over. I am afraid."

"Have you decided what you want to do?"

"I will wait to talk with him when he comes after work. I do not know what I will do yet. Please forgive me my love for my indecision at this time. I just do not know Jason." She held onto him as a frighten child.

He held her tight and did not comment for a long while and said, "I love you my lovely Carmeli'ta'. I understand how you must feel. I love my mother with all my heart too."

"I know that you do Jason and that is a wonderful thing for me because I know that you will love me that way also."

"Yes I do and I will forever my lovely one."

Jason had laid the contract in the chair nearest where he and Carmeli'ta' was standing, after almost hour conversation picked it and remarked, "I told Ms. Horne about an hour, so I need to get back to my office. She thinks that it is about the contract and that is what I want her to think to protect you my lovely."

Thank you Jason, please know that I love you my darling but I have to know about my mother and why my father is acting so strange."

Jason knew she was telling him she was going without saying to him, I am going. He hoped she would not, but it sure sounded like it. He would wait to see what were the results of the meeting with her father. "We do not have a date tonight my love one, but is will call you later before you retire for the night after you have spoken with your father."

"Thank you Jason, I will see you before I leave today. They held each other and kissed passionately for a long time before he returned to his office.

CHAPTER
THIRTY-EIGHT

Wednesday, December 6, it was nearing the end of the workday Roberto' called Amelio' and asked him if he could see him on his way home. Leaving work, he drove rapidly to his office, parked the car, and went in. Amelio' sitting at his desk rose when Roberto' entered said, "Hello my Cousin it is good to see you."

"Thank you Amelio' it is good to see you also." Amelio' saw the look of worry and stress sitting on his brow and in his eyes said, "Is Carmeli'ta' and Simone' okay Roberto'? Is there something with the business that concerns you?"

"No, the business is fine as always. I may need your assistance again with overseeing my business until I can take care of the issues with my family that is before me right now."

"Of course, Roberto' I will do whatever is necessary. Please take care of your family. How is Carmeli'ta?"

"She is who I am concerned about my Cousin. She is upset she has not heard from her mother; she thinks I do not know where she is, or she is ill, and I will not tell her. I am not sure what to do. I have not convinced her that everything is okay with her mother and me."

"I understand Roberto'. Carmeli'ta' is determined she will not stop until she had an answer to her questions. Do Simone' know she is upset?"

"Yes, I told her. Simone' thinks she might try to come to Tuscany. I am not sure but I hope that she will not."

"That will be far too dangerous for her Roberto'. She is too young and inexperienced to travel that great a distance never been outside of Charleston without Simone' or you. Do you want me to talk with her?"

"I know. I try not to think what dangers she would expose herself to making a trip of this magnitude. Thank you, but I do not think she would be receptive to any conversation at this point. I heard a tone in her voice that I have not heard before determined almost calculating tone; also, in her tone I heard pain and anger; in her eyes I saw fear, confusion, and anxiety."

"I am sure that at this point she would be upset and overanxious about her mother. She is so much like you Roberto'. You get the same determined calculating tone when you are requiring answers. I have seen that many times in you over the years, even when you were young and growing up. Your father mentioned to me once, you were a person of determination gauging your every move, when we talked not long before he died."

"Thank you for mentioning what my father told you Amelio'. He knew me well. I appreciate your support. I know that I have those characteristics in me and I try never to let them get out of control when I am making a decision or looking at an issue.

" Are you on your way to see Carmeli'ta' now."

"Yes she is expecting me. I need to be on my way. I want to arrive in a timely manner and see if I can determine what is on her mind about "What she wants to do."This statement worries me more than anything does. I fear she will not think before she acts in her decisions because she is upset. I will call you later Amelio' and let you know the outcome."

"Please do Roberto'. I will expect your call. Take care of yourself. Oh, Roberto, I finalized the transfer of funds to Carmeli'ta's accounts. I was at the bank when it opened at 9:00 a.m. this morning. I have the legal papers here for you." He walked to his desk, opened the draws, took out a long brown envelope and handed it to Roberto'. He looked at the documents and noticed the transfers were dated Wednesday, December 6, 1927.

"Thank you Amelio'. I feel better having secured our family finances. I will put this in the safe with the rest of the banking information. I will let Carmeli'ta' know that her transfers are complete and safe."

"You are welcome always Roberto'. I will await your call. "Thank you. I will call you later."

Carmeli'ta' left work at 4:30 p.m. to prepare her father's favorite tea. Though she was upset, she wanted him to be pleased. Roberto' turned into the driveway leading to her Townhouse at 5:00 p.m. just as she reached the Bay Window to watch for him saw his car went to the refrigerator, took out the tea, chilled glasses with ice, and placed both on the coffee table near where her father sat during his visits. Roberto' knocked at the door. She called walking toward the door, "Is that you Father?"

"Yes, it is your father." She opened the door and smiled, hugginghim, and said, "Hello my father. How was your day?"

"It was a good day Carmeli'ta'. How was your day by sweet daughter? I am happy to see that you are more calm now my daughter. I was worried about you when I left you this morning."

"I am better my Father, thank you. I made your favorite tea would you like some?"

"Yes, thank you it will feel good after a long workday." She poured two glasses of tea three-fourth full, handing one to her father and took hers and sit in the oversized winged back chair, sipped her tea, and waited for her father to start the conversation.

Roberto' sipped his tea, smiled at his daughter, and said, "The tea is as tasty and enjoyable as always my daughter; thank you for thinking of me; it means a lot to me to know that you care enough to make a little thing like tea for me each time I visit. I stopped at Amelio's office on my way here. He has completed the transfer of your funds into the Swiss Bank account. I have the legal papers in the car. I will add them to the ones in the safe when I arrive home. You can get a copy any time you desire my lovely daughter."

"Yes, I was concerned about that my father. Thank you, for informing me the transfers for all accounts were completed." She continued, "I enjoy seeing you happy my Father and I know now that the tea with chilled glasses with ice reminds you of the first-time mother made it for you. Have you heard from mother today Father?"

"Yes, I have Carmeli'ta' and hopefully she will be here by the end of the week if nothing happens."

"What do you mean 'if nothing happens?'"

"If she gets a seat on the flight to America my lovely daughter there is always a chance that she may not get a seat on the American bound flight."

"I don't understand you are always so vague with me Father. I just cannot accept that my mother has not called me, she did not come home with you, all I get is unanswered questions, and I fear that my mother is not okay or you don't know where she is."

"Carmeli'ta' I don't want you to be upset it is like I said to you, your mother is fine and she is with her parents and will be home this weekend."

"I can't accept that father. My mother always talked to me and you never hid anything from me. I cannot accept that."

"Carmeli'ta' I would like for you to come home with me and stay until the first of the week. You do not need to be by yourself as upset as you are. You are always welcome at home my sweet daughter. What are you doing for dinner?" She was quiet for a long time just sit looking into her glass of Tea. Roberto' waited did not say anything just sipped his tea.

After a long time Carmeli'ta' looked at her father and said, "I thank you for the invitation and I feel welcome; you and mother always made me feel welcome to come home. I would like to be by myself if you do not mind Father so I can think. I am not hungry right now. I may have a bowl of fruit later in the evening just not right now."

Her answer disappointed Roberto'. He knew she was upset and angry, but did not expect her to say no to his invitation. He knew if she were at home, at least, he would know what her movements were and could possibly determine from her actions what she was thinking of doing. However, if he were not around her his fear is, she would take actions that she has not given the uttermost consideration. There are ramifications to quick actions.

Roberto' sit again took the glass of tea from the tray continued to sip it, looked at his daughter and replied, "I just don't want you to be by yourself feeling the way that you do. I will go my sweet daughter and call you before I sleep tonight. Are you going out tonight?"

"No father, I am staying home tonight, Jason may come by later he will call to let me know and see if I am up to his visiting."

"Does Jason know how you feel Carmeli'ta?" Wanting to be discreet and not say too much about what Jason knew of the situation, she knew, though her father, while he was distracted with the issues before him, was not keen on their relationship replied, "He knows I am upset and its concerning my mother."

"I see daughter. I will take my leave now dinner is waiting; it is after 6:00 p.m. I did not inform Marianna that I would be late."

"You want to call her my Father or I could call her for you to let her know you are on your way?"

"I don't think that is necessary. It only takes a few minutes traffic is slower at this time of day." Roberto' took her hand and walked to the door, turned, looked down at her, saw her sweet innocence and naivety about the dangers of the world, felt a small chill of fear invade his heart and emotions, knew he could not go any further with the conversation, none she would accept. He kissed her on the forehead and smiled.

Carmeli'ta' hugged him with a tightness of a child when they are frightened of the boogeyman. She held onto her father for a few minutes then said, "I love you Daddy." She had not called him "daddy" in a long time. He saw the girl in her again when she was young the same reactions when she did not know what decision to make.

Roberto' held her close to him as he did when she was a child comforted her and said again, "Daughter please come home with me. I want you to be safe and calm; your mother is fine and I do know where she is, please don't worry." She hugged him once more and said, "Thank you Father, I will have more tea and relax for a while. I hope you enjoy your dinner."

Roberto' left for home and dinner. Carmeli'ta' walked over to the table by the other winged-backed chair she sits in when making calls picked up the phone, dialed the operator. The phone ring five times before it was answered, Charlotte Overby said, "Charleston International Airport how may I assist you?"

"I would like to check the times of your next flights to London, Thursday, December 7, the cost of the ticket, and if there are any available seats."

"Yes, I can check those for you could you hold?" Carmeli'ta's voice sounded familiar to her but she was not sure since it had been almost four years since their graduation from the Charlotte School of Business would not chance being wrong, she would wait until she asked for her name to know for certain it was Carmeli'ta' Bandaci.

Carmeli'ta' so distracted with her thoughts did not pay attention to the voice that spoke with her from the other end replied, "Yes thank you, I will hold." Charlotte Overby checked the list, there was only one seat left and it was in First Class picked up the phone and said, "Hello Miss, there is one seat left on the flight on Thursday, December 7; Pan American Flight 2374, leaves at 11:00 a.m. each day. There is another flight Pan American 2370, later that day at 3:00 p.m.., but it is full. I could put you on the waiting list on that one if the evening flight is more convenient in the event someone's reservation is cancelled."

"No, that would not help my plans any. I will take the seat on the 11:00 a.m. Thursday flight to London."

Miss the First-Class seats are expensive. There are only six seats in First Class and they are $150.00. It does come with special service we have two attendants waiting on 3 people each." Charlotte Overby waiting for a response asked, "Miss, are you there?"

Carmeli'ta' mentally looking in her purse to determine if she had sufficient funds to buy the ticket or needed to go to the bank and be there when it opens. She would be packed and ready to go to the airport after she withdrew money from her account. She only had a small window of time between 9:00 a.m. and 11:00 a.m. Carmeli'ta' remembered she did have $300.00 she kept on hand in her Jewelry Armoire' on her dresser. Her mother put it there shortly after she moved in for emergencies in case she ran low in funds. She had only $50.00 in her purse for lunch and other things she needed during the week replied, "Yes, I am here. I will take the seat."

"What is your name Miss? I will add you to the first-class passenger list?" She thought for a moment then asked herself, "What name should I use?" She knew her father well; he was too obliging and accepting of her refusal to come home at least for dinner when he left for home.

"Miss what is your name?"

"I apologize for the distraction. My name is Noelle A. Giovanni."

"Thank you Ms. Giovanni. You can pick up your ticket at the desk tomorrow by 10:00 a.m. Passengers board 20 minutes before the flight leaves. Thank you for flying Pan American Airways Miss. I hope that you enjoy your flight."

"Can I get a flight to New York on Friday at 11:00 a.m. are there seats available?"

"Yes there are seats available Miss. Our Friday flights are never full. If you want me to place your name in one of the available slots I can Miss. If you are not here when the flight leaves it automatically cancels your reservation."

"Yes, please reserve a seat for me peradventure I miss my flight in the

morning, I can still get to New York on Friday morning."

"Your name is on the list Miss. Please remember if you are not here when the flight leave, your name will be removed from the passenger list. The cost of the flight Miss on Friday, December 8 from Charleston to New York is $40.00."

"Thank you for your kindness and patience. Bye." Charlotte Overby still puzzled because that voice was so familiar, but the name was not. During the time they attended the Charlotte School of Business she was known as Carmeli'ta' Bandaci. She let the thought pass and answered the next reservation call.

Carmeli'ta' went directly to the guests bedroom walk-in closet and took two suitcases and her cosmetic case, off the luggage rack there placed them in her suite, on the foot of the bed, and opened them. She packed lingerie', suits and shoes. In the second suitcase, she packed a few winter clothes not knowing what to expect but wanted to be prepared, for the weather in Tuscany, and two additional lighter jackets.

She would wear her dress coat winter was just beginning. Her mother told her that Tuscany was not freezing in December but had a nip in the air reminded you it was necessary to wear a coat or jacket. Finally, she packed her cosmetics, her Chanel 5, extra tube of lipstick, lotions, bath salts, pearl necklace, earrings, and lastly, her comb and brush. Her mother kept her sufficiently supplied with things she needed.

She took a black two-piece suit, a yellow blouse, and a pair of black low heel shoes from the closet to wear on the flight with a hat and gloves to match her purse. She walked over to the dresser, opened the drawer in her Armoire' retrieved the envelope under the Black Felt cloth strip that held some of her jewelry, opened it and counted the money that was there. It was $300.00 just as she supposed it would be, put it in her purse, replaced the empty envelope, Felt cloth strip, and jewelry back in place. She did a mental and physical check of her luggage to make sure she had everything she needed.

Carmeli'ta' then called the travel agency in New York to check the availability of cabins on the RMS Olympic. She waited while the phone ring hoping someone would answer, the agency did not close until 9:00 p.m. it was 8:00 p.m. the time zone is an hour ahead of Charleston. On the fifth ring an agent answered the call, "Cunard Travel, 'We Can Get You There' may I help you?"

"Yes, I would like to make reservations if possible on the RMS Olympic sailing for South Hampton on Friday. Do you have any cabins left?"

"I will check that for you Miss." Waiting for a few minutes, the agent said. "Yes, Miss we have cabins left. Let me get your name please and I will assign you to one of the empty cabins on Deck 9. I am ready when you are Miss."

"I am Noelle A. Giovanni. Can I make reservations to fly on to Tuscany from London through you?"

"Yes, we have a contract with Pan American Airlines Miss for connecting flights in the United Kingdom. Just a moment let me check the times of the flight when the ship arrives in South Hampton nine days from now, December 15 Miss. What is your age Miss? You have to be 21 years of age to sail unescorted on the Olympic?"

"I am 23 years of age. I would like to make reservations to sail Friday and then my flight on to Tuscany."

"Miss, are you a citizen of Italy or America?"

"I am a citizen of both countries. I was born in Italy and I moved to America when I was five years of age with my parents."

"Do you have proof of your citizenships Miss?"

"Yes, I have my birth certificate from Italy and copy of my immigration papers and citizenship card. My full name is on both. I only use part of my name now."

"As long as you can prove what you say Miss that will be fine. Your Cabin number is 942 Miss and if you are ready I will give you your reservation number, which is the initials of your name, your cabin number, dinner time, and Butler's number that attends your cabin, NAG942-854-301."

Carmeli'ta' wrote the reservation number on the note pad she kept beside the telephone and asked, "How nifty the process is to identify so easy. What time do I need to board?"

"The ship sails at 5:30 p.m. Miss the ship is docked in Queens. Your alphabet boards at 2:00 p.m. and the cost of the reservation is $500.00 which includes your flight to Tuscany on December 15. Miss you can pay upon arrival at the check-in desk since this is last minute reservation. Instructions, for everything else will be given to you by your butler when you check in."

"Thank you for your assistance. I understand everything."

"You are welcome Miss, have a good trip."

It was 8:00 p.m. when Carmeli'ta' completed both reservation processes. She did not know which one she would take, but she was determined to get to her mother by whatever means possible. If her father somehow discovered her plans to fly on Thursday she would have a day to get to New York to board before the ship sailed on Friday. Jason called immediately as she hung up the phone, "Hello."

"Hello, my lovely little one, how are you?"

"I am well thank you Jason, how are you? Are you home from the office yet? I know that you were working late today."

"Yes, my lovely I am home from the office. I had dinner with my parents, to their surprise, and now if you are up to it I would like to come see you tonight. I miss you so much and want to make sure that you are okay and I can only do that if I look into your eyes. Do you feel well enough for me to come over?"

"Yes, my darling I do feel well enough to see you anytime even if I was not feeling well. I will wait your arrival Jason thank you for checking on me and caring about me."

"I will be there in a few minutes my sweet Carmeli'ta'."

She went to her dressing room and bath to freshen up and prepare for Jason's visit. The phone rang again. Roberto' called after dinner to see how she was feeling. "Hello."

"Hello daughter how are you? I hope that you are calmer and more settled in mind after your relaxation and thinking."

"I am fine Father thank you for thoughtfulness and care. I love you. Jason is coming over; he called and said he completed his work and will come over tonight. I will spend a few hours with him my Father. Remember I love you always."

"I am glad that you are not by yourself tonight my darling since you did not want to come home with me. Goodnight my daughter; I will come see you after my workday tomorrow." Carmeli'ta' did not respond to her father's comment that he would come by after his workday, but only said, "Thank you Father, good night I will see you soon."

Roberto' was happy to know that Jason was spending the evening with her at least he knew she would not be making any hasty decisions. He would see her again on Thursday, December 7 after his workday ended.

Roberto' called his cousin to let him know the results of the conversation with Carmeli'ta'. Amelio' was waiting anxiously to hear the outcome. The phone rang; he rushed to the hallway to answer, picked it up, and said, "Hello."

"Hello, my cousin, I spoke to Carmeli'ta' she is still quite upset and a bit angry, but is kind always. I invited her to come home for a few days as Simone' suggested, she did not want to. She is spending the evening with Jason. I will see her again after work tomorrow. I cannot afford to ask her to be late for work for a third day straight. It will create a bad image with her position in the company."

"I understand you are right she can only be late so many times without the proper procedures. You sound as if you feel a little more relieved than when we last spoke. I am happy to hear that. We will have to take this one day at a time until your Simone' has come home. That will be soon. Thank you for keeping me informed my cousin."

"You are welcome. Thank you for your support and understanding Amelio'. I need to call Simone' it is getting late almost 1:00 a.m. there. Goodnight."

"Goodnight."

Jason arrived at Carmeli'ta's Townhouse bounded up the stairs by twos anxious to get to Carmeli'ta' and know her plans after speaking with her father. He knocked at the door, she opened it immediately so it would not worry Jason with her delayed response to his knock smiling said, "Hello my love. I am glad you came over. I did not think I would get to see you tonight."

Jason smiled back, reached, and pulled her to him, kissed her, his lips demanding and sweet took Carmeli'ta' breathe away for a moment, commented, "Hello my darling Carmeli'ta'. It is good to see you and hold you close to me. I miss you when we do not spend the evening together. How can I go on without you in my life, I would not want to my darling. How are you tonight? Did you have a good conversation with your father?"

"I am fine Jason and I did see and talk to my father, but nothing has changed I am not convinced of my mother's whereabouts and wellbeing. He asked me to go home with him for a while until the first of next week so I would not be alone. I begged off. I told him, I wanted to relax and think."

"Have you come to a conclusion about what you want to do my lovely one?"

"I have packed Jason and made reservations on both Pan American Airline for Thursday, December 7, and RMS Olympic Cruise Line out of Queens, New York, on Friday, December 8. I am not sure which one I will take. If I miss one, I will have a backup plan." Carmeli'ta' knew this was not exactly the truth of the matter. She needed to create a diversion so her father would not know she had left the country until after she was on her way. She knew her father would check the airline and if she had a reservation, he would try to stop her from traveling alone to Italy to find her mother.

Jason stood like stone for a moment, feeling as is someone punched him in his heart, he could not breathe for a few moment, nor speak. Finally able to utter, "Carmeli'ta' I was hoping that you would give this a few more days to see if your mother would be coming home as your father said. I did not expect you to leave so soon. In fact, I will take you myself the first of next week if you can wait that long. I meet with Meriwether Textiles Plant Manager on Friday to confirm the delivery contract."

"Jason, I just feel so uncomfortable not knowing or being sure about my mother it has been more than a month now or approaching it anyway. I have not spoken to her once. Can you imagine how I feel after all my life being close to my mother then she is snatched away and I do not know what is happening with her, can you understand how I feel?"

Jason pulled her to him once again saying, "Yes, yes, my darling it would tear me apart if I were not able to speak or see my mother in a long time it would have an enormous effect on my life. My mother, like yours, is the best in the world. There is nothing that she would not do for me as your mother does for you my lovely one, I understand, I am frightened for your safety especially on a ship for a long period of time."

"I am a little frightened as well as the prospect of leaving America and traveling in a country I am not familiar with. I was 5 years old when we came to America that was almost nineteen years ago. However, I do not think that I have any choice Jason. I hope that you understand my love. I love you my darling, I will miss you so terribly, but this is something I feel I must do."

"I understand my darling. I am just concerned about your safety. Please my love, stay alert and aware of your surrounding; do not spend a lot of time talking to strangers sweetheart. Stay focused; you are good at focusing. You are just so innocent and lovely. What time is your flight my lovely one?"

"At 11:00 a.m. Jason. I need to get money from the Bank. I have $350.00 cash. I am not sure that will be sufficient. I do not know what I might need in the way of cash while I am traveling. I would rather not try to make a withdrawal from my Swiss Account without the proper process. I will be at the bank at 9:00 a.m. when it opens tomorrow."

"Carmeli'ta' I can give you the cash you need. I always carry $1,000.00 on me. I will give you whatever amount you need."

"Jason thank you, but I am not sure that is a good idea. I have never taken money from anyone expect my Father. He said as long as I can remember it is better not to take money from others. I appreciate your offer, but..." She seemed compelled to take his suggestion, but then was not sure she should take money from Jason her upbringing and proper etiquette for a woman, caused her to hesitate.

"Carmeli'ta' I am not just anyone my darling. You are my future wife and I love you. If it will make you feel any better, it can be a loan until you give it back to me (Jason knew he would never allow her to pay it back). It will take the stress off your needing to stop by the bank. You are right it is better to be prepared for any eventuality my love. Will $500.00 be enough extra cash with the $200.00 that you have beyond your ticket?"

"Yes, my love that will be a sufficient amount I believe. Thank you my darling, I appreciate your encouragement and willingness to help make the stress in my preparation for my trip easier."

"Carmeli'ta' there is nothing that I would not do for you or any extent I would not go to help keep you safe. I want you to be careful. Put the money not being used in a small pocket if your purse has one or roll it up put it in a change purse. Leave available in your purse so you can reach it without pulling out all of your cash, the money for the ticket and $2.00 for a tip for the Porter."

"Yes, Jason I had not thought about that. I will do as you say. Thank you." Jason was concerned even more. She had not thought about having a large amount of cash as a danger point in her travel. He realized that is something she never think about the possibly of being assaulted or robbed, especially if someone saw the cash money. He said again, "Carmeli'ta' please, takes care and stay focused on your surroundings."

"I will Jason. I will be careful and stay alert. Thank you for caring, it makes me love you all the more my darling."

At home settled for the evening Roberto' retired to their sitting room to call Simone' it was nearing her bedtime.

CHAPTER
THIRTY-NINE

Passing the desk in their suite, he picked up their wedding photo and looked at it, called the operator to place the call to Tuscany. The operator answered said, "Hello Mr. Bandaci, are you ready to place your call to

Tuscany sir?"

"Yes, thank you. You remember my name operator?"

"Yes, sir we record each International call that we place in a daily log, the place, the time, and the phone number. I have the phone number that you have called each time sir, would you like for me to connect you or is there another number you want me to get for you?"

"No, thank you. Please dial the same phone number. Do you have the ability to listen to calls Operator?"

"No sir, once the call is placed it goes away from our line and we cannot listen. Even if we could, it is against the rules sir, we cannot violate the company's privacy policy, and if caught we will be fired. Mr. Bandaci, you can tell if someone is listening in sir; the line has a frying sound to it when it is open. I have reached the party you called; the line is ringing sir are you ready?"

"Thank you for the information. I am ready. Thanks, you again."

"You are welcome. Please hold for your party. Goodnight."

Simone' was waiting for Roberto's call at the kitchen table with her parents. On the first ring, she jumped up from the kitchen table and ran down the short hall. The phone rang three times before she reached it picked it up and said, "Hello, Roberto' my love. I was waiting anxiously for you to call my husband. How are you? How was your day? Is everything going okay with the farms? Did you talk with Carmeli'ta?"

"Hello, my love one question at a time. I am fine, my day was good, and everything is going okay with the farm. Yes, I talked with Carmeli'ta' again. I visited her after work today. How are you my beauty, your day, your evening?"

"I am fine my husband just a little anxious to hear from you. My day was good as always. My evening was good as well. I enjoy being home with my parents. They are the best in the world."

"I spoke with Carmeli'ta' my beauty. I do not think that I convinced her you are okay and coming home on the weekend. She shut down on me my beauty and would not discuss any further, but rather said that she wanted to rest and think. After dinner, I called to see if she was okay. She said Jason was coming over and he is spending the evening with her. I am glad that she has a distraction at this point, though I am not pleased with the relationship."

Simone' did not respond to his comment about their daughter's relationship with Jason. She did not want to battle the subject out over the phone being so far away. But wanted to keep the atmosphere on the line focused on what actions or decisions Carmeli'ta' would make as a result of her not getting satisfactory answers to her questions, said, "Did you ask her to come stay with you until the first of the week my husband?"

"Yes, she begged off and said she wanted to rest and think. I will be eager to know if you are successful in getting a seat on a flight to America on Friday. Will you call early my love? The reservation desk will probably be busy since no reservations were booked on Wednesday."

"Yes, my husband. My father or mother said they would call early Thursday morning, actually my husband; it is already 2:00 a.m. here. The airport reservation desk opens at 6:00 a.m. and if I were not awake by that time, they would take care of it. My father will probably be successful in getting me on a flight, my husband. I will come as soon as I can."

"Thank you my beauty your presence is desperately need." After an hour conversation Roberto' commented, "It is getting to be the wee hours in the morning my beauty, time for you to sleep. It is almost 9:00 p.m. now I have a workday tomorrow. I love you Simone'. I am looking forward to having you back in my arms again."

"Thank you my husband. I love you. I miss you. I need to feel your arms around me again. I will await your call tomorrow my darling. Oh, Roberto' did Amelio' get Carmeli'ta's account transferred?"

"We did not get a chance to talk about that. I am confident he did. I will check tomorrow when I arrive at my desk at work. Do not worry my beauty; if he said he would take care of it he did."

"I am sure my husband. Goodnight."

"Goodnight my beauty." Roberto' went into shower and prepare for bed. Simone' rejoined her parents in the kitchen waiting to hear if Roberto' was successful in convincing Carmeli'ta' she was okay, entered the kitchen, sat at the table quiet for a few minutes then said, "Carmeli'ta' did not buy into her father's attempt to convince her that I am okay mother and father. I feel like such a, well, I really do not know what I feel like to be honest with you. I do know that I feel miserable. I need to retire in order to rise early enough to call the reservation desk to be one of the first calls for a flight. Goodnight Father and Mother."

She rose to go to her suite Franco said, "Simone', I will do my best to get you a seat on the first flight out on Friday. Goodnight my precious Daughter." Catarina did not comment just smiled at her daughter as she held her husband's hand.

The night before she left for Tuscany on Thursday, December 7, Carmeli'ta' and Jason sit for a long time on the loveseat in front of her fireplace after their discussion about her traveling and the safety factors involved. Jason held her close without speaking and felt his heart breaking because she would not be in his arms for a few day or more. Jason sit forward, looked at her and said, "I love you past my heart and mind. I need you so much Carmeli'ta'. I want to love you and be close to you before you go my lovely one."

"I know Jason I feel the same way my darling; I wish that we were man and wife more tonight than I have wished it since you told me you love me. I want to be close to you and give you all my love. I know that if we do it will ruin everything for us and we will regret it my darling."

"I know that you are right my lovely one. It has been hard for me to control my emotions when I am around you and knowing that you are leaving makes it all the harder my darling."

"You are right Jason, I feel the same way it is hard, but we will be glad we waited on our wedding day."

"Yes, my darling we will. I just want you to remember when we are apart for the next days that I love you and I am waiting for you my love to come back to my arms."

"Soon my darling, when I know that my mother is okay and she is not ill, I will come back to you forever Jason. Please remember that I love and need you my love. Your heart is my home my darling. It is time for me to retire Jason. I have a long day tomorrow. I will call you before I leave my darling."

Jason was not aware that Carmeli'ta' was not using the names he was familiar with but her middle names and her mother's maiden name. Prepared to leave, it was hard for him to walk to the door. He felt as if a weight was holding him back. Sorrow and grief gripped his heart. He was not losing her, but if this is what losing her feels like he wanted no part of losing the one that he loves so much. Jason and Carmeli'ta' reluctantly kissed; they felt overpoweringly loving and warm they could not determine whether it was their love or their separation, for a short time. It did not matter the reason for the overpoweringly loving and warm feeling they held onto each other, Jason whispered, "You are my heart my darling. I hate to let you go. When I hold you in my arms, our love feels safe. There is nothing that I would not do to keep you safe."

"Thank you Jason, I feel the same way my darling in your arms our love feels safe. I will think of you every minute my darling while I am away."

"Thank you Carmeli'ta' you don't know how much what you saying means to me my lovely little one. Goodnight."

"Goodnight Jason." Carmeli'ta' closed and bolted the door. Jason tapped lightly to let her know he heard the latch being slide into place. He drove home with loneliness gripping his heart and mind knew he did not want to be without her for any length of time.

Carmeli'ta' prepared for bed slipped beneath the comforter and crisp sheets slept immediately mentally, emotionally, and physically fatigued from the long arduous day.

The next morning, in Tuscany, the alarm rang at 6:00 a.m. Franco awaken with the determination to make a reservation for Simone' on the first flight to London. He and Catarina bathed, dressed, and went quietly to the kitchen. While she made their morning coffee, Franco went to his office and called the Tuscany Airport's reservation desk. The phone ranged six times, a voice finally said, "Hello Campo di Marte, Imperial Airways may I help you?"

"Yes, this is Franco Giovanni. I would like to check the availability of

seats on your next flight to London on Friday, December 8."

"Good morning Mr. Giovanni. I can assist you with that sir." Checking the flight list for Friday, the reservation attendant said, "Mr. Giovanni the 3:00 p.m. IA Flight 2372 to London has two seats left in First Class; can I reserved one or both for you?"

"Yes, I only need one please; it is for Simone' A. Bandaci. What time is the connecting flights to New York and then to Charleston, South Carolina?"

"The flight leaves at 10:00 p.m. sir for New York. The Pan American Flight 2372 to New York arrives at 11:00 a.m.; there is a forty-five minutes layover for refueling. The flight arrives in Charleston at 1:30 p.m. There is a five-hour layover in London would you like to reserve a suite at the Premier Inn five minutes from the Airport for Ms. Bandaci?"

"Yes, thank you."

"The tickets are $150.00 for First Class sir and it comes with private service to the passengers. Ms. Bandaci's seat will be in First Class from London to New York and then on to Charleston, South Carolina. Ms. Bandaci can check with the Customer Service Desk for her hotel reservation and a cab. Please remind Ms. Bandaci she will need her Identification. Is there anything else I can assist you with?"

"The price for the ticket and the travel arrangements are fine. I want Ms. Bandaci to be comfortable on this long trip. We will pay for the ticket when we arrive. Thank you, for your patience and kindness, goodbye."

Franco hung-up stood and thought for a moment about the excellent service that he received. He was pleased that the employees were doing a good job with Customer Service. This was an opportunity to check the efficiency of the employees other than the employee's reports at their weekly meetings. Returning to the kitchen Catarina poured coffee ready for their morning conversation and prayer before they started their day. He sat down lifted his cup to his mouth took a few sipped of coffee then said, "I was successful in getting a flight for Simone' on Friday. Amazingly so my lovely wife, there were only two seats left and they were both in First Class at a premium price. I want our daughter to be comfortable and it will give her a chance to reflect, think, and plan how to explain the situation to Roberto'."

"The price of the ticket does not matter, my husband. She is worth every cent we pay for it. I do want you to pay for the ticket Franco if that is okay with you. She will object but tell her that we insist if we can't spend our money on our only child then who?"

"You are right my sweet wife spoken like a mother. I have no objection and I was planning to do that anyway. In fact, I will call the Airport and tell them to charge it to me and I will take care of it."

"That is a good idea my sweet husband. Simone' is precious to us."

Just as they ended their conversation and prayer Simone' walked in the kitchen in her dressing gown with sleep in her eyes sat in the chair next to her father. Catarina poured a cup of coffee and sit it in front of her smiled, "How are you today my Daughter? Did you have a good night what was left of it?"

"It was a good night mother. I was anxious for the day to come so I can call the Airport. I will go do that now it is 7:00 a.m. I hope there is a seat available so I can leave on Friday and get to my and husband and daughter."

Franco listened silently to their conversation smiled then said, "By this time of day on Thursday my daughter, there are no seats left on either of the flights to London on Friday." Catarina looked at her husband and shook her head; he was playful as ever smiling said, "Do not tease her, my husband, tell her."

"Tell me what father?"

Franco stood, walked over to the sink, stood next to his wife, and was silent for a moment, "I have made your reservation for Friday my lovely daughter. Your flight leaves for London at 3:00 p.m. on Friday, the connecting flight is at 10:00 p.m. a five hours layover then on to New York and Charleston you will be home by 1:30 p.m. on Saturday. You have a reservation at the Premier Inn to rest while you wait for your flight to New York."

Simone' was surprised sat for a moment and recalled how pleasant, energetic, and full of life, her father was; there was never a dull moment in their home. Laughter flowed abundantly in their home when she was a growing child. In light of the situation surrounding her sudden arrival without notice, had not given her father many occasions to express amusements. The focus was on the claim made by Vincenzo' Moretti and her Diary. She equated the situation plaguing her and their search for a solution to looking for a needle in a haystack.

Simone' after a few minutes, rose quickly and hugged her father, "Thank you Father and Mother, I will finish my packing today. Roberto' will be pleased and I can see my daughter to let her know that I am okay and her father and I are fine as well. I am suddenly hungry mother I think I can eat breakfast now." Catarina took the Bread and Italian Sausage out of the oven, dipped three bowls of Mixed Fruit, and put it on the table. Simone' ate with peace and joy in her heart as she smiled and chatted with her parents.

Her father left for his farm at 8:00 a.m., she and her mother enjoyed another cup of coffee while they talked about her returning to America. Simone' helped her clean the breakfast dishes, went to her suite, bathed, and dressed for the day, finished packing her suitcases, and chose the outfit she would wear back to America.

It was nearing lunch time and she knew Roberto' would be rising for the day it was 6:00 a.m. in Charleston. In another hour Carmeli'ta' would be getting ready to go to her office as well. She became excited at the thought of going home, but still apprehensive when it came to revealing the contents of the Diary and the twenty-four years secret she held close to her heart and hid from Roberto'.

The spectators she strived for twenty-four years to protect would soon see the theatre of her life.

CHAPTER
FORTY

Thursday morning December 7, Roberto' awakened to the birds singing in the tress outside his window and hope in his heart. His Simone' would be arriving on Saturday; he would know the secret she held for so long, but more than that she would be back in his arms once again. He planned never to let her be separated from him ever again, it was too hard. He would be wherever she was for the rest of his life, no matter the cost or the price he had to pay. His life was nothing without her by his side and him holding her every night. However, plans do go awry. Unannounced trouble was coming for his family and him very shortly.

Roberto' dressed hurriedly, returned to the sitting room, walked to the desk, picked up the phone, and dialed the operator to make an International call. Then decided to call Carmeli'ta' before he spoke with Simone'. The phone rang in her Townhouse three times, she jumped out of bed in a start, but soon realized she was at home and it was the phone. She was not sure what she thought it was she was hearing. It was Thursday morning and her flight left in a few hours. She picked up the phone and said, "Hello."

"Good morning, my beautiful daughter. How are you today? I hope you slept well."

"Good morning Father, I am fine, I did sleep well. Are you okay my Father?"

"Yes, I am fine. I wanted to call you before you went to work today and let you know I will visit you on my way from work later today. I want to reassure you once again about your mother coming home and the fact that she is okay and will possibly be home by the weekend if she is successful in getting a flight."

Carmeli'ta' listened silently. "Are you there my Daughter?"

"Yes, father I am here. I cannot accept that Father. I want to know where my mother is and see her. I am afraid she is not well and you are not telling me. I do not accept that Father." She became very emotional, her voice broke Roberto' knew she was crying, she finally said, "I have to go now Father I have a long day ahead of me." Roberto' thinking it was work related said, "I will come to see you now my Daughter. I don't want you to be upset." Calming down she knew would prevent her father from coming to her Townhouse said, "No my Father I am fine. I need to go now. Thank you for calling and checking on me. I love you."

"I love you Carmeli'ta'. I will come by after my work today. "She commented, "Yes, Father. Bye."

Roberto' thought about their conversation and her being upset for a while, picked up the phone to call Simone'.

The operator answered recognizing the number said, "Good morning Mr. Bandaci, are you ready to place your morning international call to Tuscany?"

"Yes, thank you."

"Please hold while I get your party on the line." The operator after a few minutes, said, "Sir your party's line is ringing. Have a good day."

"Thank you." The phone rang four times in the Giovanni's home. Simone' walking down the hall from her bedroom suite to the kitchen to help prepare lunch heard it, running she reached the office out of breath on the sixth rang and said, "Hello."

"Good morning, my beauty. Are you okay? You sound strange!"

"I am fine my husband. I ran when I heard the phone. I knew it was you. How was your night?"

"My night was restful, how was yours?"

"It was good my husband. Have you talked with Carmeli'ta' today?"

"Yes, I spoke with her before I called you my beauty to see if she was okay. She was upset but I think she is okay. She was preparing for a long day. Were you successful in getting a flight to America Friday my beauty?" With excitement in her voice she replied, "Yes, yes my husband. My Father called before I was awake. My flight leaves at 3:00 p.m. tomorrow, with a five-hour layover in London, then to New York at 10:00 p.m. I will rest at the Premier Inn; I will be in New York on Saturday by 10:00 a.m. and Charleston by 1:30 p.m. I am excited to be coming home to you my husband and to quiet my daughter's fears about me. My father was only able to get me a seat in first class. The tickets are expensive Roberto', $150.00."

"It does not matter the expense my beauty, if the price were a $1,000.00 it would not matter, I just need and want you home. I am miserable without you Simone'. I cannot bear this separation much longer. Do you have enough money to pay for the ticket? I can give you the Swiss Bank Account number to withdraw funds or you can borrow it from Franco. I will have it transferred back to his account."

"I have enough my sweet husband. I still have the $500.00 I bought with me. I miss you too my husband. I will be happy to be back in your arms again. I need you to love me my darling. I miss our intimacy so much."

"I know Simone' I feel the same way. I need to get to breakfast and work. I will call you tonight after I visit our daughter. I hope she will be calmer when I tell her you will be here on Saturday just two more days my darling, two more days."

"I love you Roberto' have a good day. I will look forward to talking with you later. I want to help mother with lunch, father will be here soon" turning she saw her father standing looking at her, said, "actually he is here now."

Franco had walked in the office unnoticed by Simone' stood waiting for her to finish her conversation, smiled when he heard her tell Roberto' he was home.

"Have a good lunch my beauty. I love you."

They hang up, Simone' walked over to where her father stood smiling. She smiled back as they walk back to the kitchen where Catarina was waiting with lunch prepared. It was 12:00 Noon.

Catarina asked, "How is everything in America?"

"Everything is fine mother. Roberto' is excited I am coming on Saturday. I am excited to be getting there on Saturday and back to my family and my life."

Franco did not comment but wondered if the outcome would be as exciting as Simone' thought. He was concerned about his daughter and her telling Roberto' Vincenzo's claim of parentage to Carmeli'ta' and what the possibility was that she could truly be his daughter. Right at this defining moment, he did not think that Simone' knew which one was her father. He knew this chapter had not ended yet, in fact, it has just begun. Catarina noticed her husband's expression and quiet manner did not say anything at that moment. She would wait until Simone' was not with them to ask about the frown. In her happiness and excitement, Simone' had not noticed her father's expression. He saw his wife looking at him smiled back reached and squeezed her hand.

Carmeli'ta' Thursday morning, December 7, made final preparations to leave for her journey to Tuscany dressed, made her bed, and checked the bedroom for neatness. She did not want to leave her home untidy. Her luggage was packed and ready. She had packed everything she needed, closed, and locked the suitcases the night before.

While the coffee was perking, warmed a Bagel and Italian Sausage in the oven, noticed the clock on the kitchen wall it was 7:30 a.m. She promised Jason she would call him before she left for the Airport. Walking into her sitting room with the intention of calling him, there was a knock at the door. She was surprised, not expecting anyone to come by this early. Her father was not coming, she did not think. She became a little jittery at the thought her father might come by unannounced, she would not put is past him. His nature was as determined as hers was when he faced issues that seemed to have no solution or he could find a ready answer.

She moved her suitcases back the bedroom and closed the door. He would try to stop her if he knew she was leaving the country. She had a subtle nature, much like her mother Simone'. She knew he would not go in her private bedroom suite. She walked to the foyer and said, "Who is it?"

"Carmeli'ta' it is Jason my darling." She opened the door Jason rushed in and took her in his arms holding on to her; she felt the tremble in his body, he squeezed her tight for a long time without saying anything.

Carmeli'ta' held Jason and softly said, "I love you Jason. I will miss you my darling. It is painful for me to leave you, but I must go find my mother. We will be together soon my darling, and when I return I want to be your wife without waiting."

Jason's voice broke and what he felt when he spoke came out with a sound of pain, "I understand why you are going my lovely one, and I just can't bear to be without you for any length to time. I need you so Carmeli'ta'. I know you were not expecting me to come by today, especially unannounced. I could not let you go without holding you today. I apologize for coming without calling, it is not good etiquette I know; will you forgive me?"

"Yes Jason. I am glad that you came by to see me before I leave my darling. I wanted to call you to ask you to come by my darling and here you are. I am thankful that I have you in my life, thank you for supporting me in my decision to go find my mother, and thank you for the money Jason. It makes it easier for me I can go directly to the Airport."

"I will drive you Carmeli'ta'."

"No, my love, please it is hard enough to go, if you drove me it would make it even more so. Thank you for the offer. I can leave my car at the Airport."

"Do you want me to have it picked up and bought back to your complex?"

"No Jason let me keep my plans as they are my darling."

Carmeli'ta' did not want to go to the bank. She knew there was a chance she would run into her cousin Amelio'. It was hard to fool him; he would stop her.

"If that is what you wish, I will honor your wishes my lovely one. Just hurry back to my arms. I do want to marry you as soon as you return. I would have before you left were it not for the custom of getting an okay from your parents. Thank you for wanting to become mine my darling, I love you so. I will go my darling I need to get to the plant since you are not there to direct the employees for the next few days."

Jason was torn between his call of duty and his love and need to be with Carmeli'ta'.

"Thank you for allowing me to take the time away from work Jason. I would not ask but for my mother's sake."

"You have vacation and sick leave Carmeli'ta' and you have never taken a day off work since you started and you work a lot of nights and weekends when we have special functions. So please do not think about it. Even if you did not work excess hours overtime, I would want you to go."

"You are more than kind Jason; how did I get so fortunate?"

Jason knew he must leave checked his pocket watch it was 9:00 a.m. said, "I need to get to the plant. I called Ms. Horne before I left home and told I had an errand before I came to the office today. I told her I would be there by 9:30 a.m. my lovely one."

Jason held her hand; they walked to the door, turned, pulled her to him, and kissed her lips. She felt a passionate, demand, desire, and need in his kiss. She kissed Jason so softly and sweetly it melted his heart. They held each other tight she said, "I will call you when I get to London Jason that will be 1:00 a.m. if possible, if not, I will call when I arrive at my grandparents. Take care of yourself my darling."

"I will Carmeli'ta'. Please remember what I told you about staying alert and focused. Keep your money out of sight my sweet one. I almost forgot the other reason I came by, where is your luggage my darling? I will put it in the car for you."

"It is in my bedroom Jason. Thank you for helping me with my luggage. I will remember all that you said my sweetheart. I will see you soon."

Jason opened her bedroom door picked up the three pieces of baggage; stopped, picked up her keys off the Cherry Italian Marble Top Cons Foyer Table, went quickly to her Roadster luggage box, placed the luggage there, and went back upstairs. He laid the keys back on the foyer table, kissed Carmeli'ta's right hand, pulled the door close. Jason reluctantly left, tapped on the door, waiting to hear the latch fall into place, tapped, and left with a heavy heart and fear for her safety nagging at the back of his mind. He prayed as he walked back to his car, "Father, I know that this is a selfish prayer but, please keep her safe and bring her back to me, I need her to complete my life."

Carmeli'ta' retrieved her handbag from her bedroom, placed it on the foyer table, looked around at the room, picked up the chain with her car key and door key, her coat, hat, and gloves to match her suit, locked the door, and went downstairs to her car. It was 9:15 a.m. The drive to the airport would take her forty-five minutes. Her Townhouse was further from the Airport than her mother and father's home. She knew she needed to hurry. She drove through the heart of town hoping she would not see her Uncle Amelio'. He was usually doing banking at this hour of the day. If he saw her, she would be compelled to stop; he would see her luggage rack full, question her, and prevent her from going. Being untruthful with him was not easy; he would definitely know, he would inform her father, and they would prevent her from traveling that great a distance alone.

Jason arrived at the plant at 9:30 a.m. Ms. Horne at her desk said, "Good morning Mr. Madison, Ms. Bandaci is coming in later today sir?"

"Good morning Ms. Horne. No, Ms. Bandaci will not be coming in for the next few days as she is out of town on an errand. Please call the staff and ask them to assemble in the Boardroom in thirty-minutes for redistribution of duties until she returns. She left the list with the duty assignments. You will take a greater portion of her duties Ms. Horne since you worked with her so closely and she has trained you in the Quality Control Process."

"Yes sir. I will call the meeting." Ms. Horne was baffled, but did not question Jason Madison. She did not have the Carte Blanche and he seemed distracted to her. She knew this was not a good time to ask him questions. He was kind always, but had a business side to him that she had seen many times, he could be terrible to deal with when necessary, or if pushed, as if he were by the business dealing with people with the characteristics of Charles Bienville Meriwether, so she said nothing.

Carmeli'ta' nearing the Charleston International Bank, speeded up it was 9:30 a. m. she had another thirty-minutes to drive. When she passed the bank, did not see her Uncle Amelio', felt relieved and mentally wiped the "what if" perspiration off her brow. Carmeli'ta' felt tensed approaching the Airport and heard Jason's voice in her mind warning her not to talk to strangers and stay focused. She pulled to the front of the Airport at the Pan American unloading area. A Porter in a red hat unloaded her suitcases and said, "Good morning Miss. I will wait here for you while you park your car."

"Thank you, I will return shortly."

She pulled into the first available slot in the parking lot near the front of the Airport, felt fortunate to be close to the door of the Airport would only have a short distance to walk. Before exiting the car, she pulled the $2.00 tip out of her purse for the Porter. She put the money in the pocket of her jacket, retrieved her purse, and other accessories, closed and locked the car door, dropped the keys her in her purse and pushed them to the bottom so they would not be lost, walk swiftly back to the terminal where the porter waited with her luggage.

He said, "After you Miss." She walked to the Pan American Reservation Desk, opened her purse pulled out the $150.00 and paid for her ticket, checked her luggage, tipped the Porter, and walked to the waiting area for boarding noticed the clock on the wall it was 10:20 a.m. The Pan American Flight 2370 would begin boarding at 10:40 a.m. She would be one of the first on the plane the Reservation Clerk informed her at the desk. She remained jittery while waiting, hoping she would not see anyone that knew her.

Charlotte Overby was arriving on duty as Carmeli'ta' sat waiting for her flight to leave. The voice and reservation still stuck in her mind; the voice was so familiar to her; she checked the passenger list again to see if the passenger named Noelle A. Giovanni has checked in for her flight. She looked at the passenger reservation list, a check by her name indicated she picked-up her ticket. She came from behind the counter with the intentions of checking the passenger waiting area to see the passenger named Noelle A. Giovanni. Before she could leave to check the waiting area, the phone rang for reservation information; it took fifteen minutes to complete the call and reservation. The Tech called for the first-class passengers to board then the remaining passengers.

Carmeli'ta' boarded, chose a window seat settled in with her cosmetic case in front of her on the floor. A male passenger chose seat 5 parallel to Carmeli'ta'. They were the only two passengers in first class.

The plane was pushing back by the time Charlotte Overby reached the passenger waiting area. Carmeli'ta' noticed the time 11:01 a.m. she was finally on her way. An hour later, looked out of the window, there before her was the massiveness of the Atlantic Ocean. She saw the Statue of Liberty waving as they left the shores of America. This experience was scary and exciting, both in the same paradigm. So engrossed in the magnificence of the Atlantic Ocean, did not realized the Stewardess was serving lunch. She ate very little of the Beef

Burgundy with Wine Sauce, Roasted Potatoes, Green Beans with Red Bell Pepper pieces, a roll, and a glass of iced tea. The Stewardess noticed she ate only a few bites asked, "Is the food not to your liking Miss?"

"Thank you the food was fine; I am not hungry. I don't usually eat heavy meals in the middle of the day." The Stewardess thanked her and took her tray away said, "If there is something else I can get you Miss I will be glad to do so."

"No, I am fine thank you." Carmeli'ta' closed her eyes and saw scenes of Jason and her earlier before she left to catch her flight; missed him and it had only been a few hours.

December 7 workday progressed fast for Roberto'. He was not comfortable the entire day, but stayed busy. His only thought was to see his daughter after work to know if she was okay or what plans she was making. Feeling a whimper of guilt for her being confused and upset, had to find a way to convince and ensure his daughter her mother was okay, she was not ill, and she would be home on Saturday; he had to make sure she was okay. Deep in thought, glancing in the direction of the clock on the wall it was 4:00 p.m. realized his workday was over, completed his filing, locked the files in the desk, and left at 4:25 p.m. for his thirty-minute ride to Carmeli'ta's Townhouse.

Roberto' arrived at Carmeli'ta's Townhouse at 4:55 p.m., went quickly upstairs, knocked at her door, there was no answer after three knocks. His mind went back to their conversation Wednesday evening when he spoke told her he would visit after work and she said, "Yes Father." He stood waiting outside her door, wondering where she could be this time of day especially since she was expecting him. She had been home each time he visited. He returned to his car and retrieved her door key from under the mat on the floorboard went back up the steps and opened the door. It was neat, clean, and deafly quiet he knew she was not home. He walked over to the phone intending to call her work, saw the pad with the reservations to the Charleston International Airport and RMS Olympic there. He felt hot, his heart began to pound in his ears, he could not think for a few minutes, but he knew her plans were to travel to Europe to find her mother. He decided to wait for a while for her to arrive home. He called the Airport Reservation Desk to see if she was on the passenger list of either of the daily Pan American Flights that left for London's Croydon Airport. The phone rang three times a technician answered, "Charleston International, how may I assist you?"

"Yes, I am Roberto' Bandaci I would like to check to see if my daughter caught her flight to London today?"

"Yes sir, I can check that for you. What is your daughter's name?"

"Carmeli'ta' Bandaci." The technician checked the list, picked up the phone receiver and said, "Mr. Bandaci there is no Carmeli'ta' Bandaci on either of the flights to London today. There is no one named Bandaci flying with us today."

"Thank you for your assistance." He hangs up the phone and called the RMS Olympic Travel in New York, the phone rang six times, "Good evening Cunard Travel, We Can Get You There."

"Good evening, I am Roberto' Bandaci in Charleston, I would like to check your passenger list to see if you have a reservation for my daughter as passenger on your ship for Friday, December 8."

"Yes, I will check that list for you sir, what is your daughter's name?"

"Carmeli'ta' Bandaci." The technician checked the passenger list, said, "Mr. Bandaci we do not have a reservation for a passenger by that name." Roberto' was baffled. There was sudden mystery surrounding his daughter and her plans. He went to her guest bedroom and checked her luggage rack, there were two empty places where before suitcases were stored. He checked the master bedroom closet, some of her clothes was missing, it was evident they were gone by the hole where the suits, blouses, and other clothing items hung. Panic hit and she was gone! But, where and how? She did not leave on either flight that day or was she on the passenger list to sail on the RMS Olympic on Friday. Where could she be? His first thoughts were to get to the phone and call Simone'. He looked at the time, it was around 10:00 p.m. in Tuscany. He drove faster than usual breaking the speeding law within the city limits. Arriving home, went in the kitchen where Marianna was ready to put his dinner on the table asked, "Marianna have you spoken with Miss. Carmeli'ta' today?"

"No, Sir I have not talked with Miss Carmeli'ta' today?" It was a strange question to Marianna. He had not asked her that before. "Are you ready for dinner sir?"

"Not yet Marianna, I need to make a phone call first. I will let you know when I am ready hopefully it will be before 7:00 p.m. If you will excuse me I need to make that call."

He ran up the stairs to their suite, picked up the phone, the operator said, "Are you ready to place your call to Tuscany Mr. Bandaci?"

"Yes, please." The operator informed Roberto' all the international lines were busy and she would put the call through as soon as a line was clear, asked him to hold.

After dinner at 6:00 p.m., Carmeli'ta' saw more of the majesty of the enchanting Ocean before the dark set in. The beauty and splendor reminded her of pictures she saw of different Queens and all their grandness. She saw wall-to-wall water, looking back, could barely see the Sun now behind her, began its farewell descent to the day on its journey to another part of the world. She was always amazed, as a child, when her father and mother told her, when the sun was disappearing where she could not see it day was beginning somewhere else in the world.

Her meditations went again to Jason. She wondered what he was thinking and if he missed her as much as she did him. She knew her father would be upset and furious with her for leaving Charleston without telling him and for not being honest concealing her travel by using only part of her name, remembered the message tablet she kept on the table by her phone all the information was there. He would encounter several problems of which way she traveled, but when he called the Airport Reservation Desk and the RMS Olympic Travel there would be no Carmeli'ta' Bandaci traveling.

His daughter missing, Roberto' now struggling, anxious to speak to Simone' after almost ten minutes later an international line came available, the operator rang the number to the Giovanni's home. The phone rang four times, Franco sitting at his desk completing paperwork answered, "Franco Giovanni here speaking."

"Franco, good evening, I hope you are well."

"Hello my son. I am well. You are calling early tonight. Simone' is sitting on the patio with her mother. She is excited about coming home. Her flight leaves tomorrow at 3:00 p.m. We will miss her. She has been a joy for us for the past month as she was when she was a child."

"I know the feeling Franco; she is the joy in my life. She is my life! I would not want to know what it is to live without her. If you don't mind I would like to speak with her."

"Yes, yes, of course my son, I will call her. She will be pleased you are on the phone." Waiting, but impatiently he heard Franco call for Simone' and say, "Your husband is on the phone for you my lovely daughter."

Simone' rose immediately and ran back through the kitchen, down the short hall, passed her father on the way to join her mother on the patio, and into her father's office, over to the desk, picked up the phone receiver and said, "Hello Roberto'. I am happy to hear your voice so early my love. It is your dinner time, are you not hungry yet?"

"Hello my beauty. I am happy to hear your voice. I have not had dinner yet. Marianna has it ready. I told her I would be ready before 7:00 p.m. just not right now."

"It is almost 8:00 p.m. there. You sound a little strange to me my husband, is there something wrong?"

"Yes and then no, I am not sure my beauty."

"I do not know what that means Roberto' either it is or it is not, which is it my husband? Have you spoken with Carmeli'ta' today? She is alright, I hope?"

"I am not sure if something is wrong my beauty."

"Roberto' you are beginning to worry me. Is it the account transfers, did Amelio' get Carmeli'ta's transfers completed? You had not spoken to him about it when I talked with you last night."

"It is not about the accounts my beauty; he took care of the transfer. I have the documents in the safe. I went to see Carmeli'ta' after work today", he heard her draw in her breath, but continued, "She is not there my beauty."

Simone' excited said, "What do you mean she is not there Roberto'? Was she still at work sometimes she works a little later?"

"I went into her Townhouse after I knocked three times and she did not answer I went to my car and got the keys to her Townhouse, I opened the door and went in. I saw where she checked for flights and the cabin space on the Cunard RMS Olympic. The information was there on the pad she keeps near her phone. I checked her luggage rack, two of her suitcases and her cosmetic cases were not there, and I checked her closet in the master bedroom and some of her clothes was missing. The holes were there where they hung."

"What did you find out from the airport and Cunard reservation desks?"

"Neither of them had a reservation for Carmeli'ta' Bandaci. It is baffling to me my beauty; where could she be unless she went to the airport in the next city; that is a two-hour drive. I do not believe she has ever been outside of Charleston without one of us being with her. I am very concerned for her safety."

"I know Roberto' so am I. Did you drive to the airport to see if her car is there?"

"No, my beauty I did not, but I will go right away to see if her car parked there."

"Please call me the minute you return my husband." Roberto' hung up from his wife, went downstairs to his car, and drove to the airport to look for her car. There in front of him on the first parking row was her Burgundy Roadster. He drove in front of where it was parked and used to his key to open the door, he saw no luggage or anything else just the neat and clean car as she always kept it. He locked the door and returned home, went to their suite, and called Simone' again. She had waited by the phone, pacing back and forth in front of her father's desk.

When she had not returned to the patio to give her parents an update, they came to the office. Reaching the opened French Doors, they saw her pacing up and down in front of the desk. Franco and Catarina looked at each other, knew there was a problem. Franco walked over to her and said, "Is everything okay my daughter?"

"I am waiting for Roberto' to call me back. He had to check on something." She did not want to worry her parents unnecessarily but wanted to wait to see what her husband said when he returned from the airport. Simone' thought about asking Jason Madison, but decided it was best not to mention him to Roberto'. If he knew she was leaving and did anything to encourage it, there would be no chance Roberto' could ever be convinced to give her his permission to marry him; therefore, she kept the thought to herself. It would only anger her husband and the situation was bad enough as it stood. Roberto' drove swiftly back home and called Simone' again. The operator rang the Giovanni's line again, Simone' picked up the receiver and said, "Roberto' did you find her car?"

"Yes, my beauty. Her Roadster is at the airport; but it is strange that her name is not on either of the flight passenger lists today or on the ship's passenger list for Friday. I do not understand this at all." Simone' knowing that Carmeli'ta' had her bent for secretiveness and illusiveness, when she wanted to be thought, for a minute then said, "Roberto' check the passenger list to see if Carmeli'ta' used her middle names and my maiden name, you know both are on her Immigration Papers. She could be traveling that way to avoid you trying to stop her."

"I had not thought about that my beauty. How did you know she might use her middle names and your maiden name?"

The minute he asked her the question he knew it was rhetorical; she had more of her mother's characteristics than his. His anger level begin to rise again, at the time it was tempered by his concern for his daughter's safety said, "I will call again to check and see if she used any of her other names. I will call you back my beauty."

Roberto' called the Charleston Airport Reservation desk, Charlotte Overby answered, "I would like to check to see if my daughter is on either of the flights that left today?"

"What are your name and your daughter's name sir?" asked Charlotte Overby.

"I am Roberto' Bandaci and my daughter's full name is Carmeli'ta' Noelle Angelu'cia Giovanni Bandaci."

"Hello Mr. Bandaci. I am Charlotte Overby. I attended the Charleston School of Business with Carmeli'ta'. Please hold while I check the passenger list." After checking the list, she said, "There is no Carmeli'ta' Noelle Angelu'cia Giovanni Bandaci on either of the flights today sir, we do have a Noelle A. Giovanni on the 11:00 a.m. flight this morning, could that be her sir?"

"Yes, it is thank you."

Hesitating Charlotte Overby said, "Mr. Bandaci I was on duty last night and took the reservation for this passenger. The voice was so familiar to me but I did not want to say anything because I was not sure I was correct. I have not seen her since we graduated. When I came on duty this morning, I intended to check the passenger waiting area to see if that was her, but by the time I completed a reservation call the plane was pushing back."

"Thank you for the information. I appreciate your alertness." He hung up and called Simone' again, the phone rang only once Simone' picked it up saying, "What did you find out my husband?"

"There is a Noelle A. Giovanni on the 11:00 a.m. flight to London today. I spoke with Charlotte Overby who said she attended the business school with Carmeli'ta' thought when she made the reservation last night it sounded like Carmeli'ta' but was not sure. She is on her way to Tuscany Simone' to find you because she believes I am not being truthful with her, I do not know where you are, or that you are ill, and I am hiding it from her. It is dangerous for her without any experience period to travel alone, but traveling abroad is even worse. I will be on the flight to London tomorrow if I can get one. So, this means you will need to forgo your traveling home and wait for our daughter to arrive."

"Yes, my husband I will wait. I feel that I am the blame for this situation. I should have gone home when you did my husband. If anything happens to her I would not be able to survive it." Tears begin to flow from Simone's eyes and her voice broke as she spoke with her husband. Franco and Catarina observing her knew there was trouble with Carmeli'ta' but they did not know what, came to where she was standing.

Roberto' said, "We cannot think about blame my beauty just about our daughter's safety. The plane arrives in London at 1:00 a.m. There is a five-hour layover. She has a reservation at the Premier Inn Hotel until

5:00 a.m. her plane leaves for Tuscany at 6:00 a.m. she should be there by 8:00 a.m. You can pick her at my beauty, please be there when the plane lands in the morning, and call me when it does. Please stop crying Simone, it breaks my heart to hear you cry and I am not there to comfort you makes it even worse. We will pray that she will be okay. God is with us Simone' don't forget that."

"I know God is with us my husband, but there is so much evil in the world. She is young and inexperienced in traveling especially this distance alone. I am afraid for her my husband."

"I am as well Simone', but we can only wait until we hear from her." I need to prepare my luggage and call Amelio' so he can manage our farm until I can get back. I will be there on Saturday my beauty. Please call me if you hear from her."

"I will Roberto'. I will see you on Saturday."

"I need to call and make a reservation as quickly as I can before the Friday flight list fills. Bye for now my beauty."

"Bye my love."

Simone' hang up turned to her parents and said, "Carmeli'ta' is on her way to Tuscany."

Stunned for a moment neither of her parents commented. Franco said, "You are going home tomorrow Simone' why is she coming here?"

"Roberto' could not convince her that I was okay. She used her middle names and my maiden name is why all the confusion. Roberto' had not thought about her using the other parts of her name."

Franco saw in his granddaughter what he saw in his daughter, she was cagey and misleading, he had seen hints of it the times they visited them in America, said, "It is too dangerous for her to travel alone. What was she thinking taking drastic steps like this and then hiding behind the other parts of her name? I shudder to think what could have been the outcome, if you did not know our granddaughter as you do Simone'."

She felt the guilt even stronger than before; she knew of all people that Carmeli'ta' was just like her just a younger version, she looked like her, had long legs, beautiful hair, skin, height, size and personality and her sweetness. She was quiet and humble. Simone' knew that her daughter had the same ambiguous and abstruse capabilities that she has; she was determined as a child and now as an adult, never disrespectful in any way, but determined. Once she set her mind on something, it was hard to change it, as she and her father had experienced many times when she was in her growing years.

Roberto' called the airport, Charlotte Overby answered, "Pan American Airline Reservations, how may I assist you?"

"I want to check to see if there are any available seats on either of the flights to Tuscany on Friday, December 8."

"I can check for you sir, yes, there are seats, but only in first class sir would you like for me to reserve one for you?"

"Yes, please. I am Roberto' Bandaci."

"Yes, Mr. Bandaci, I just spoke with you. I will put your name on the passenger list for a seat in first class. So far sir you are the only one on the 11:00 a.m. flight in first class. There are no seats on the later flight at 3:00 p.m."

"The 11:00 a.m. flight is fine. I want to leave as early as I can. When will it arrive in London and what time is my connecting flight to Tuscany?"

"Flight 2370, arrives in London at 1:00 a.m. Saturday morning sir, and on to Tuscany at 6:00 a.m. I can make a reservation for you at the Premier Inn Hotel if you wanted to rest while you wait."

"Yes, that will be fine."

"The ticket is $150.00 Mr. Bandaci."

"The price is fine, thank you."

"You can pick up your ticket at the Reservation Desk sir, the flight boards at 10:40 p.m. you will board first sir as the only passenger in first class. Please have your identification with you. Have a good trip, thank you for flying Pan American Airline. Good night."

"Thank you, goodnight." Roberto' knew a new chapter of his life was beginning, one that he had not expected to be written in the book of his life.

Carmeli'ta' slept after dinner for almost 5 hours, when she awaken it was 12:00 Midnight, did not realize danger lurked near. In the seat parallel to Carmeli'ta' in first class sat a man with a Khaki colored 1923 London Fog Raincoat and Hat to match. He never spoke during the flight. She, however, never noticed him, but the one of the Stewardess, Desiree, assigned to the area in First Class thought his appearance was strange noticed he constantly watched Carmeli'ta' (Noelle Angelu'cia Giovanni) the entire time with every move she made. She looked young to the passenger in the Khaki coat and hat he saw her as a pigeon ready for the plucking. She had the look of being wealthy. Desiree' reported the suspicious passenger to the Captain telling him he had watched the passenger in seat 3 parallel from him the entire evening. She explained to him that the passenger in seat 3 was a very young with the appearance of being an inexperienced traveler. The Captain asked the name of the passenger in seat 5 and the name of the young woman. The Stewardess told him, the name on the passenger list for the young woman was Noelle A. Giovanni and the suspicious looking passenger name was Jacob Warren Riley. The Captain called ahead for Airport Security to be waiting at the steps of the plane before the passengers disembarked.

In the meantime, 1:00 p.m., Carmeli'ta's (Noelle) flight was nearing the coast of London the plane approached Corydon Airport, for landing the man in seat 5 seemed to be nervous, continually moved around in his seat as if he wanted to get up before the plane landed. The Stewardess watched him; the plane landed. After the plane taxied to the terminal, the Captain came and stood near the door of the plane watched the man out of the corner of his eye, but never let the man know that he was watching. When Carmeli'ta' (Noelle A. Giovanni) stood up, the man jumped up and pushed her up against the seat and grabbed her purse. As he attempted to exit the plane; the Captain restrained him until the Airport Security, waiting at the bottom of the steps saw the Captain restraining the man, came and put him in custody and retrieved the purse he snatched from Carmeli'ta' (Noelle). The blow from the assault caused a gash in her hairline on the left side, and blood trickled down her face. The blow stunned her for a few minutes. Desiree, the Stewardess, saw blood coming from the injury grabbed a towel, applied pressure to her head, assisted her in sitting back in her seat, got a cold compress from the cool box to help stop the bleeding.

The Airport Security informed the Captain Jacob Warren Riley was a petty thief who flew on International Flights preying on women who appeared young and vulnerable. He had been on their wanted list for more than a year. After the plane was empty, the ambulance took Carmeli'ta' (Noelle) to Charing Cross Hospital for treatment, which included six stiches near her hairline on the left side of her head. The Stewardess accompanied her while she was being treated and admitted overnight for possible concussion. Pan American Security at the Airport held her luggage and other personal items, except her purse until she could pick them up.

CHAPTER

FORTY-ONE

It was 9:00 p.m. Thursday evening, December 7, Marianna was still waiting dinner for Roberto' wondered if he was okay. Roberto' called Amelio' before going down to dinner, while waiting for the phone to ring at Amelio's home felt hunger pains grip his stomach, had forgotten he had not eaten dinner. He had to pack as well and be ready to leave for his farm at 6:00 a.m. and talk with Peter, his Foreman before he left to catch his flight back to Tuscany.

He felt like a pendulum with the back-and-forth direction his life has taken in the last month. He sometimes wished he had not questioned Simone' about the contents of the Diary, but left well-enough alone. He knew that well-enough alone would only work for a while, it would never be enough. The situation was beginning to make him feel like he was peeling an onion one layer at a time. He was familiar with that concept being a farmer. Each layer peeled off another layer was there. Did this onion-like situation have an end to it? When would he get to the core of the matter?"

The mystery of the situation, like the fumes from an onion, was blinding his eyes to the point he could not see. Like the mist from the onion when peeling it, causing tears in the eyes, so was the layers he was peeling off caused tears of pain, in his heart and mind. Now his daughter was gone with mystery surrounded her as well. He knew she used her middle name and her mother's maiden name to create a diversion to get out of Charleston. She knew he would stop her if he had known her plans. She could be a Secret Agent with the covert actions she took to cover her movement before leaving Charleston without him catching her. Roberto' realized he loved two women his wife and his daughter, both had the same distinct characteristics. They were esoteric, indefinable, and surreptitious.

452

Roberto' called his cousin. He answered the phone after the sixth ring, "Amelio' Bandaci."

"Hello, my cousin, I hope I did not disturb your dinner."

"No, Roberto' you did not. I have finished and was sitting and chatting with my cook, Juanita about Bibi 'Ana, while she cleared away the dishes." He waited instinctively knowing that something was wrong. Roberto' sounded as strange to him as he does when there was a problem.

"Carmeli'ta' has gone to Tuscany." Surprised and not surprised Amelio' said, "How do you know that my cousin did she leave a note or call Marianna to let her know?"

"She left on the 11:00 a.m. flight. She did not use her first name, but both her middle names and her mother's maiden name. I went to her Townhouse, her luggage is gone, clothes are gone, and she left her car parked at the airport. I called her mother before I checked the airport she told me Carmeli'ta' probably used her middle name and her maiden name. She is traveling out of the country alone, so young and inexperienced, I am afraid for her and feel at this moment distressed and overwhelmed with the entire situation."

"I understand Roberto'. I am more than concerned about Carmeli'ta' and her insistence on knowing where her mother is, if she is safe, and her not taking your word for her mother's whereabouts worried me from the beginning. I knew she would probably take steps of this kind."

"She also made a reservation on the RMS Olympic to sail on Friday; she is so much like my Simone' in the way that she thinks and she is just as elusive and arcane, I see it now more than ever."

"I know Roberto'. I have known this about my sweet little cousin all her life. Her actions and the way that she carries herself exude mystery and that makes her difficult to read. What are your plans my cousin?"

"I have made a reservation to leave on the 11:00 a.m. flight to London tomorrow. I hope I will not be imposing on you to ask you to manage my farm again for a few days. I do not know how long I will be gone, but I will call you. I will meet with Peter early tomorrow before I leave to set the next few weeks' priorities."

"That will be no problem for me Roberto'. You do whatever you need to your family is important. Bibi 'Ana will not be here until Thursday, December 14 Roberto, is actually what I was sharing with Juanita, and other instructions to prepare for her arrival. I hope that you will be home by that time. I am excited for you to meet her again after 25 years. I have told her so much about you. She knows how important you and your family are to me. So do not worry, I will take care of the business on this end. I will come and drive you to the airport tomorrow. I will be there by 9:45 a.m. You will be back by then I am sure."

"Bibi 'Ana's coming is good news to me Amelio'. You deserve to be happy my cousin. I am sure that we will be back before Christmas Eve; it is a special time. We all look forward to spending Christmas Eve together. Thank you for taking me to the airport. I had thought of driving my car and parking it at the airport; however, if you will drive me that would be much better. Also, I would like for you to pick-up Carmeli'ta' car and park it at her Townhouse. I have the keys. Please lock it and leave the keys in the office when you bring the paperwork by for the deposits, deliveries, and to check on Marianna."

"I will take care of it Roberto' go to your family."

"Thank you Amelio' I do not know what I would do without you. Please let Brother Meriwether know I have gone back to Tuscany for a few days. I am sure he will understand."

"I will. Good night my cousin, I will see you in the morning."

"Thank you Amelio' for everything you do for me and my family. Good night."

Roberto' remembered he had not told Marianna that he would be leaving, the next day, Friday, going back to Tuscany. He went downstairs to the kitchen where she was setting the dough for bread for the next day meals. Marianna heard his approaching footsteps turned, smiled, and said, "Are you ready for dinner now or can I get you something Sir, coffee maybe?"

"No Marianna, just my dinner and no coffee for me tonight. I came down to eat and let you know that I will be flying back to Tuscany at 11:00 a.m. tomorrow." Marianna stood shocked for a moment before she spoke, "Is Miss okay sir? I hope she is not ill." He thought before he answered said,

"No Marianna Ms. Bandaci is just fine. Hopefully, I will not be gone long; Amelio' will take care of what you need as always, just let him know when or if you need anything. I am ready for my dinner."

"Yes sir thank you." He saw the perplexity and confusion on Marianna face, when she put his dinner on the table, but he did not have time or felt it necessary to explain any further. He finished his dinner, rose, turned, and walked back upstairs to the bedroom closet and took down his large suitcase lay it on the foot of the bed and opened it, went to the closet, and begin taking out slacks and shirts, suit, tie and shirt, and other sundry items needed for traveling.

After his packing was complete prepared for bed, he showered, put on his pajamas, went to the sitting room where he slept each night and lay on the sofa, closed his eyes, and prayed for his daughter to be safe and arrive in Tuscany without any trouble. Roberto' went through every possible scenario that she could encounter while traveling. He thought of the possibility of her purse being snatched, her being kidnapped; someone could easily overpower her she was so small and fragile, and her innocence, in respect to the world and the nature of people; she knows nothing about traveling abroad alone. He began to toss and turn in utter misery missing his wife and fearing for his daughter, concern for his farm, and the burden it puts on Amelio', though he said it is not, yet it was his responsibility, and not his cousin's to see to oversee the operation of his farm business. The burden of his family and his business weigh heavily upon him, like the feeling of a heavy stone placed on his back to carry.

That same evening, Jason had dinner with his parents, spent time talking with them and went back to his wing of the Mansion where he anxiously paced back and forth waiting to Carmeli'ta' to call. It was past time for her flight to have landed it was 10:00 p.m. in Charleston. It was 3:00 a.m. in London, he should have heard from her by this time.

In London at Charing Cross Hospital, after her treatment in the emergency room they settled in a private room, Desiree' asked Carmeli'ta' (Noelle), "Is there a close relative here that I can call for you Ms. Giovanni?"

"My grandparents and my mother are in Tuscany, my father and my fiancée are in America."

"I will make the call for you Ms. Giovanni. There will be no charges to you for the hospital or the phone call, Pan American will pay all cost because the injury occurred while you were traveling with us. I am thankful that the situation is not any worse as bad as it is, it could have been worse." Carmeli'ta' reached in her handbag and pulled out her black phone book and gave the number to Desiree', she called the hospital operator and gave the Giovanni's home number. Franco could heard the ringing, but thought he was dreaming, realized after the fourth ring it was his phone rushed to his office picked up the receiver and said, "Franco Giovanni speaking,"

"Mr. Giovanni, I am Desiree' Stewardess for Pan American Airline."

"Yes Desiree' how can I assist you?"

"I am calling for your Granddaughter sir she was admitted to Charing Cross Hospital in London. She is fine sir, but she was involved in an attempted robbery just after the flight landed, she has a hairline fracture on the left side of her head receiving six stitches." Franco felt his heart was running away, he could not think for a minute, and then calming down said, "Can I speak with my Granddaughter, is she able to talk?"

"Sir, the doctor wants her to stay quiet and rest until morning, so he gave her a light sedative. She will be okay and the Airline will make sure she gets the next flight to Tuscany. The hospital, hotel, food, or any other expenses incurred will be taken care of by the Airline." Franco could not reason with the danger his granddaughter was in, then he had to deal with telling Simone' and his Catarina, "Thank you Desiree', my family and I appreciate the care and concern that you have shown my granddaughter. She is the only grandchild that I have and she is precious."

"I can tell that by the short association with Ms. Giovanni. She is very sweet and so lovely. I can also tell she was not very acquainted with traveling alone. She looks so innocent and vulnerable. She will be fine. They apprehended the assailant at the time he left the plane. The Captain was proactive, called the Airport Security and reporting the suspicious character of the man. I kept noticing that he watched your granddaughter the entire flight, so I informed the Captain of my suspicions."

"You are to be commended Desiree' the Airline is fortunate to have an employee of your caliber. May I ask how long you have worked for Pan American?"

"Since the first flight Mr. Giovanni, I am 45 years old sir so I am use to traveling and moving around. I am a widow. I lost my husband during the War and I have not remarried. I was young when we married I was 20 years old and he was 25 years old. I will be with your granddaughter as instructed by the airline until she arrives in Tuscany on the next flight. I believe she will be able to travel at the 9:00 a.m. when the flight departs for Tuscany. They are holding the flight for a few hours until she can get discharged sir. I will be here with her until then so please do not worry."

"Thank you Desiree'. When the flight lands I would like to meet you and thank you personally for taking such excellent care of my precious granddaughter."

"Yes, sir, that will be my pleasure. I am to makes sure her relatives pick her up as well. I will see you in a few hours sir it is 3:30 a.m. here now. She is sleeping peacefully now the sedative has taken affect Mr. Giovanni. Good night." Franco hung up the phone and returned to his sleeping wife Catarina, turned on the bedside lamp, touched her and said, "Catarina my lovely wife wake up." She opened her eyes trying to adjust them to the light after only being sleep a few short hours and said, "What is it my husband? Why are you up so early this morning? You are not leaving for work yet are you?"

"No, my lovely, it is about the phone call that I just finished taking."

"Phone call this early in the morning Franco from who? Oh no, is Carmeli'ta' okay?"

"She will be my lovely."

"What does that mean Franco? What is wrong with my granddaughter, is she sick? This is frightening me Franco, tell me about Carmeli'ta'."

"She is in the hospital in London, she was assaulted on the plane, but she is okay." Tears begin to flow from Catarina's eyes as she listen to her husband explain what the Stewardess told him that happened, finally able to speak exclaimed, "We have to wake Simone' and tell her. This situation is already hard on her and she feels guilty enough as it is, this will only add to the misery she is going through."

"I know Catarina, but there is no choice in this matter. Let's freshen up and make coffee before we call Simone' there will be no one sleeping any further in this house. Our granddaughter will be here around 11:00 a.m. they are holding the flight until she gets out of the hospital and get to the plane. We need to be prepared to leave here for the Airport at 9:30 a.m. I want to be there before the plane lands."

"Yes, definitely my husband we will freshen up and make coffee before we call Simone'."

Back in Charleston it was 11:00 p.m., Jason had slept very little waiting for Carmeli'ta' to call and let him know she was safe. He thought since she did not call from the hotel that she would wait until she reached her grandparent's home as she said to him before she left earlier that morning, yet in all of that, he felt uneasy and anxious to hear her voice.

Catarina prepared the coffee and put the cups on the table, she and Franco walked slowly down the hall to Simone's suite, opened the door quietly, and went over to the sleeping Simone'. Franco sat on the bed beside her while Catarina softy took her right hand and said, "Simone' my daughter wake up." Simone' moved when she heard her mother's voice, opened her eyes, saw her father sitting on the bed next to her, said, "Is it time to go to the airport to get my sweet daughter?"

"No, Simone'." said Franco, it is 4:00 a.m. We have coffee ready come join Mother and me in the kitchen. We will wait for you there while you freshen up and get the sleep out of your eyes my beautiful daughter."

Simone' wondered why her parents both came to her suite in the wee hours of the morning there had to be something important. She hurried to the bathroom, brushed her teeth, washed and lotion her face, brushed the few wild locks of hair in place, put on her dressing gown, and slippers, and walk swiftly down the hall to where her parents were waiting at the kitchen table. She sat down and pulled the cup of coffee to her that her mother poured for her and said, "What is this all about Mother and Father, it is far too early to go to the Airport, or for breakfast, is father leaving for work early this morning?"

Franco said, "No my daughter none of that. I got a phone call about an hour ago now from a Stewardess who works with Pan American, well there is no easy way to tell you this my daughter."

"Tell me what Father, something happen to the airplane Carmeli'ta' was on?"

Oh no the plane did not crash! What happened Father? tell me!"

"Simone' slow down, the airplane did not crash, but Carmeli'ta' was hurt and was taken to the hospital and treated for a blow she received on her head when she was pushed by an assailant who tried to take her purse." What she was hearing was like a nightmare to Simone' almost as if someone were telling a story for entertainment, "An assailant Father what happened to my baby, tell me? I must get to my daughter. We must leave right away."

"We cannot Simone' there are no flights out this time of morning and the drive would take all day and half the night to get there she will be on the 9:00 a.m. flight out. They kept her overnight in the hospital for observation and rest. She has six stiches in her hairline, but is fine. Desiree', the Stewardess, evidently very astute, noticed this assailant watching Carmeli'ta' the entire flight and reported it to the Captain who was proactive and called Security. They were waiting for him when the plane landed. Desiree' is staying with her until she is safe with us. I talked with her a few minutes; the airline has assigned her the duty of seeing that she is safe and get on the next flight. I do not think she will have any more problems before she gets to us at 11:00 a.m. She was resting comfortably according to Desiree'. The doctor did not want her to talk but rest, so he gave her a mild sedative. We can be thankful for the efficiency of the airline and the caring heart of the Stewardess, without her noticing the surrounding it could have been a dismal outcome for our sweet Carmeli'ta' had he waited and followed her off the plane."

"This is my fault, mine alone, a direct result of the decisions I made not telling my husband and returning home with him ten days ago. I have let fear of losing my husband and the threats of a man put my family in danger. I have been selfish in my fear and not trusting that my husband would understand and still love me, though it may hurt, but I think that this is much more painful than what I wrote in my Diary. Both will hurt my husband and that I cannot stand to know the pain that he has suffered and will suffer at the decisions I made. I have hurt you as well Mother and Father both of you trying to protect me, to help me, I wish I had never met Vincenzo' Moretti."

Catarina held her hand and said, "You cannot blame yourself for this situation with Carmeli'ta' there would have been no way that you could have known that a petty thief would be on the plane, it could have been you or me or anyone that he thought would be a good target. Apparently, from what your Father said the Stewardess told him, he had been doing this for more than a year to women, because they are more vulnerable. So please calm down, she is fine and will be here in a few hours. Your father said we will leave for the airport at 9:30 a.m. for the forty-five-minute drive."

Tears of pain rolled down Simone's face, like water from a faucet. She did not seem able to control them with her thoughts going to Roberto'. She would have to call him and tell him that would be the hard. She looked at the clock on the wall; it was almost midnight there. She would wait until around 5:00 a.m. his time. If she called him now, it would make his day and his trip to Tuscany a nightmare, so she let him sleep and rest. This burden she would bear on her own and not tell him until he was awake; his day and evening had been hard with Carmeli'ta' leaving under her middle name and Simone's maiden name.

Time moved swiftly during the time Simone' and her parents sit talking. Catarina noticed it was 7:00 a.m. time for to begin preparing breakfast. Franco would go to their farm for an hour three miles away and check with his managers and return in time to leave for the airport at 9:30 a.m. to meet Carmeli'ta's plane. She made a second pot of coffee and warmed bread, cooked Italian Sausage, and scrambled eggs for breakfast. After eating Simone' and her mother cleaned the breakfast dishes. They would dress while Franco went to talk with his office manager and the farm manager. Simone' planned to call Roberto' before they left for the airport. It would be a little early in Charleston, but that was unavoidable under the circumstances, the situations was increasing unfolding more of the onion as the layers came off. Having to tell him Carmeli'ta' was assaulted would worry and anger him further. He was angry enough about the circumstances facing him.

A few hours later, it would be 4:00 a.m. in Charleston, that would be close enough to 5:00 a.m. with his plans to go to the farm before he caught his 11:00 a.m. flight.

Simone' went to her suite to bathe and dress for the long arduous day ahead. She returned to the kitchen for a fifth cup of coffee. She felt stressed and lacked energy because she had only a few hours' sleep and her mind was racing ahead of her, was exhausting and laborious. Catarina returned to the kitchen dressed, begin preparing the bread for the lunch when they returned from the airport. In anticipation of Simone' leaving on the 3:00 p.m. flight on Thursday, Catarina had prepared Roast Pork with Pickled Relish they would have for lunch before her 3:00 p.m. flight to London.

Simone' remembering she had reservation for 3:00 p.m. to fly to America said to her mother, "I need to cancel my flight to America today. If you will excuse me I will do that now Mother."

"Yes, definitely, please do. I am sure that someone is on the waiting list and will be happy to know that they can leave for their destination today."

Simone' walked to her father's office and called Campo de Marte' Airport and cancelled her seat for later that day. It was almost 8:30 a.m. Franco was on his way back from his farm office, he pulled into the driveway just as she was hanging up from cancelling her reservation. He walked into the office, smiled at his daughter, and said, "How are you feeling today my daughter you must be tired from lack of sleep."

"Yes, Father I am a little weary, I was just now cancelling myreservation back to America."

"That is a good idea Simone'. I thought about that on my way back from the farm intending to do that very thing myself without you having to worry with it at all."

"You are kind Father, thank you it is all taken care of. I am anxious to leave for the airport to be there when Carmeli'ta's plane arrives. Before we go, I will call Roberto' and let him know about Carmeli'ta' and reassure him that she is not in any danger at present. He was expecting me to call when she arrived anyway. It will be difficult to tell him with everything else he has to deal with and now this."

"There is nothing you can do about that Simone' bad thing often happen to good people as it did our granddaughter; but she must understand that she cannot ever again do what she did yesterday traveling under only part of her name. What must she been thinking of; nothing is that serious that she would take such steps and put herself in danger as she did."

"I know Father. I intend to give her a stern talking to when she arrives after a few days once she is okay and back on her feet. I know her father will not be pleased with her and she will feel some of his wrath especially with the steps she took and put herself in danger and then would not take his word I was okay. This is the last straw and it will try his patience with her."

"He should be firm with her, she was blessed that the Stewardess was alert and astute. I am thankful for that; I only have one grandchild and will never have another."

"That is true Father, I was not able to have another child so Carmeli'ta' is doubly precious to me. Roberto' and I wanted a son and tried for five years, but the doctor said I was unable to have another child. It broke our hearts, which makes us all the more thankful for our sweet daughter. We hope to have a grandson one day in the near future."

"I will look forward to that day, a great grandson. Let us join Mother in the kitchen while we wait for the time to leave. I am sure that she is waiting for us. I look forward to seeing my beautiful, sweet wife each time I arrive home. I could not have married a sweeter more beautiful woman than your mother, and that is inside and outside."

"I agree Father, my mother is the best in the world to me. I will wait until 9:15 a.m. to call my Roberto'. I do hate to wake him so early, but if I do not tell him before we go to the airport, he will be angry with me and I never want to hide anything else from him again."

"It is best to be completely honest with your husband Simone'. There is a saying that I love, always be honest with your parents, your lawyer, and your doctor those three can get you out of trouble."

Smiling Simone' replied, "I like that Father." They walked to the kitchen to join her mother while waiting to call Roberto'.

CHAPTER

FORTY-TWO

Desiree' awakened Carmeli'ta' at 6:30 a.m. to see how she was feeling; still a little dazed from the ordeal, after fifteen minutes or so she was fully alert, but realized she had a mild headache. Desiree' walked to the nursing station and asked for a doctor to check her, get mouthwash, toothpaste, and toothbrushes, for both of them, and ask for something for her headache. She returned from the nurse's station with the personal items and said, "Dr. Thimmons will be here in a few minutes to check you Ms. Giovanni. He will let us know if you are well enough to be released for traveling on the 9:00 a.m. flight to Tuscany."

Carmeli'ta' (Noelle) replied, "I feel a little tired but I am fine thank you. I have a mild headache, but I do not feel dizzy anymore as I did when I first arrived last night." Looking at the clock on the wall she continued, "It is almost 7:30 a.m. I need to freshen up and get dressed. We will not make the 9:00 a.m. flight there is not enough time."

"We will be fine Ms. Giovanni, the flight is not leaving until we get there, so please stay calm remember your head injury. The doctor will be her in a few minutes."

Carmeli'ta' (Noelle) freshened up in the bathroom, dressed, and sits on the side of the bed waiting for the doctor. Her thoughts went to Jason. She hoped he was not too worried. She promised to call him from the hotel or her grandparent's home. She would call him as soon as possible when she arrived in Tuscany. Dr. Thimmons came through the door just as Carmeli'ta' handed Desiree' her brush to help with brushing her hair. She brushed it carefully not to disturb the injured area.

"Good morning ladies, I hope your night was restful and pleasant what was left of it anyway. Ms. Giovanni, I am Dr. Thimmons. I attended to your wounds earlier this morning. We got you stitched up and on the way to recovery. How are you feeling?"

"I am fine Dr. Thimmons, just a mild headache. Can I have something for the pain?"

"I would rather that you not take a sedative Ms. Giovanni. A mild headache is a recurrent side effect of a blow to the head like the one you received Ms. Giovanni. It should subside in a few hours, if it has not gone in 24 hours please ask your grandparents, I believe is who you are visiting from America, to get you to a doctor in Tuscany, but I think you will be fine, you are young and strong. I am releasing you from the hospital. The Stewardess with you was very concerned about you and insisted on the most excellent care that we could provide."

"Yes, I appreciate all she has done for me. I can never thank her enough for her kindness."

"She tells me that you were traveling from America alone. I must caution you against doing this ever again until you are a more experienced travel and a lot older than an apparently very young 23 years of age."

"Thank you Dr. Thimmons I will remember. This experience has taught me a lot. I know now why my Fiancée' was concerned about me traveling alone."

"He was right you should listen to those who know best. Goodbye. It was nice meeting you and I am thankful that your injury was not any severer."

"Thank you doctor. Goodbye." Desiree' called Airport Security to pick them up at the front entrance to Charing Cross Hospital, for the thirty-minute ride back to the Airport. Pan American Airline Security picked them up at 8:50 a.m. to board the waiting flight to Tuscany.

In Tuscany, Simone' looked at the kitchen clock, saw the time was almost 9:00 a.m. in Tuscany and 4:00 a.m. in Charleston. She excused herself and went to the office to call Roberto'. The phone rang at the Bandaci's home six times before he answered. Unable to sleep for many hours had just drifted off to sleep after counting the sparkling golden circles that dawned their sitting room ceiling. He was thinking of the events that transpired in the last few weeks over one small black book locked with no key to it, as he had no key to the intimate depths of the mind of either his wife or his daughter. Realizing it was the phone ringing, he moved quickly from the couch to the desk in their sitting room picked up the receiver and said, "Hello." "Roberto' my husband, I am sorry to wake you so early. I wanted to talk with you before we left to pick up Carmeli'ta' from the airport."

"Good morning, my beauty. It is okay that you call. I have not slept much anyway. It is pass time for you to pick up Carmeli'ta' her plane arrived at 8:00 a.m. it is 9:00 a.m. there my beauty what happened was the plane delayed?"

"No Roberto'. We had a call from the Airline earlier this morning in London, Carmeli'ta' was the victim of a petty thief who tried to take her purse." Roberto' could hardly believe what he heard; feeling weak, reached for the chair to sit yet he could believe it Carmeli'ta' being so young and experienced spoke with excitement and anxiety in his voice, "Is our daughter okay Simone'? Where is she? Let me speak to her?" Simone' could hardly get a word in edge wise finally said, "Roberto' she is not here, she was taken to the hospital in London with a head injury, and she received six stiches and spent the rest of the night there for observation."

"Simone' this is more than I can bear. What else can happen? I feel like I am in a strong turbulence with no way out. Are you flying to London today or what?"

"No, Roberto' she will be arriving on the 11:00 a.m. flight. The Airline is holding the plane until she is able to travel this morning. I am sure by this time they are on their way to the airport."

"Who is the "they" you are referring to Simone'?"

"The airline sent Desiree', the Stewardess, to care for Carmeli'ta' until she was released and she is safe with us. It was the alertness and astuteness of this Stewardess that lessened the severity of her injury. She informed the Captain of the suspicious man, he called Airport Security, and they were waiting for him. However, before the passengers started to embark from the plane, which Carmeli'ta' would be one of the first ones, the Captain was standing at the door and prevented him from leaving after he snatched her purse and pushed her against the seat. She hit her head and caused the gash. The petty thief, the Stewardess told Father, had been on the Airline's Most Wanted List for a while. He preyed on women who were apparently vulnerable and unsuspecting. Desiree', I understand is 45 years old and had been traveling with this Airline since it began."

"I am thankful it is not any worse, but even at that it is bad enough."

"I am thankful for Desiree'. We will get to meet her when she brings Carmeli'ta' to us when the plane arrives. I feel very, very blessed that she was not hurt any worse. However, Roberto', Carmeli'ta' cannot be allowed to do this without us letting her know how we feel about it and how much danger she was in using her middle name and my maiden name."

"You are right, my beauty. There is more to her actions than just the secretiveness and ambiguousness about her actions. I am afraid she has gone a little too far this time. She is an adult, but still our daughter."

"I know you are right Roberto' we have to talk with her. She could have been killed, injured permanently, or disappeared completely and we would have not known where to look for her had she not written on the pad the reservations she made and Charlotte Overby was not alert when the reservation was made and recognized her voice."

"I will be on the 11:00 a.m. flight this morning. I will see you tomorrow. If I get an opportunity, I will call you from the hotel when I arrive in London. I need to get moving my beauty; the time is getting away from me."

"Are you angry with me Roberto'?" She heard him breathe in, he said, "No I am not angry with you Simone'. I am more confused about your actions. You had nothing to do with what Carmeli'ta' did. However yes, I am angry with Carmeli'ta' to worry us this way."

"I love you Roberto'. I am anxious to see you. I miss you so much."

"I know, I feel the same way, I just want to be near you and hold you. I need you to love me Simone'. My days have been long and lonely."

"I will see you tomorrow my husband."

It was almost 9:30 a.m. Franco was standing in the office door motioning to Simone' it was time to leave. She put the phone on the hook, grabbed her jacket, the air had a crisp feel in it, and walked to the car with her father. Catarina was waiting for them, smiled when she saw her daughter approaching the car. Franco opened the door and she got in the back seat, and they left for the airport.

On their drive, Catarina asked, "How did Roberto' receive the news about Carmeli'ta's injury?"

"He was upset, worried, thankful, feels blessed; we both do, she was not injured any worse. He said that Carmeli'ta' has gone too far with this and her actions has to be addressed because more than her safety was involved in what she did. She did not consider what the effect that it would have on her family in an overall manner. I sometimes wish I had called, but I wanted to avoid answering any questions from her."

Franco listening to Simone' and Catarina's conversation commented, "Simone', your decision to stay here and not call Carmeli'ta' was your right as her mother to decide what was best for you. She is no longer a child, nor is she in your home anymore. Roberto' told her you were okay, you were not ill, and you wanted to visit with your parents for a while. Her father has never lied to her about anything, she has trusted him up to this point, and she should have continued to trust him and waited until Saturday, when she was told you were arriving; beside all that, she could have called to find out if you were here if she wanted to."

He continued, "Had you not come by Saturday then, it would have been feasible for her to really question your absence, but she did not take his word and then hid what she was doing. She traveled under an assumed name, though it is part of her name. She is not known among her friends and peers by either her middle names or your maiden name. This fact tells me she knew she was doing something she should not have done without discussing it with her father. She knew he was coming after work yesterday to see her, and she indicated to him okay, as if she would be there to greet him as usual. She was planning to leave then."

He smiled, almost laughed out-loud, and added, "I am angry with my granddaughter, but not disappointed, she has the same sharpness of mind that our daughter has Mother."

"You are right my husband she is like our Simone' in every way; mysterious, illusive, a brilliant young woman who we are very proud of, as we are you Simone'. However, she had to be made aware of what the long arm of affect her actions could have had if not for the alertness of the Stewardess." Simone' listening but thinking of Roberto' at that time smiled and said, "Thank you Mother and Father, she is definitely, my daughter."

Early morning in Charleston, Roberto' checked his luggage to be sure he had the necessary items and clothes he needed while away from home. Picked up his luggage and coat went down to the office and placed them near the door, went to the kitchen for breakfast. Marianna was preparing his breakfast, he sat at the table, she poured him a cup of coffee, he sipped it looking at the clock on the wall noticed it 10:30 a.m. in Tuscany, Carmeli'ta' plane would be landing shortly. He finished his breakfast and left for the farm at 6:45 a.m. to set the next few weeks' priorities with Peter, his Foreman, in the event his trip was longer than expected. He hoped it would only take a few days to get his wife and daughter and return home. While driving, Roberto' thought about the danger his daughter faced, knew women traveling alone was not the best idea at any time, especially when they are young and inexperienced like his daughter who had never gone one hundred miles outside of Charleston alone.

Amelio' left for his Farm Office at the same time Roberto' did so he could get there and back to drive him to the airport. Roberto' arrived at his office, talked with Peter about the deliveries to the Madison and Meriwether Mansion, especially ensuring that the deliveries were on time and the quality of the vegetables were consistent. Time passed swiftly as he worked with Peter to meet the 8:30 a.m. deadline he set for himself to leave on the thirty-minute drive back to his home. It was Friday and Charleston was busy on Friday, traffic was heavy and people were out shopping, visiting, and just generally moving around as was the custom on Fridays.

In Tuscany, Friday morning, December 8 Franco, Catarina, and Simone' were approaching the airport at 10:45 a.m.; after parking the car they walked into Camp di Marte at 10:55 a.m. to wait in the Pan American Flight 2370's passenger embarkation area. Simone' was anxious to see her daughter after more than a month. Franco standing by the window saw the 11:00 a.m. Pan American flight approaching, with excitement growing in him, Simone', and her mother waited anxiously near the door knowing that Carmeli'ta' would be the first passenger to come off the plane. The plane taxied to the disembarkation area. Carmeli'ta' felt excited she would see her mother and know she was safe.

Desiree' retrieved her cosmetic case from overhead and assisted her in standing until she was sturdy on her feet. Carmeli'ta' smiled and said, "Thank you Desiree', you are kind. I am excited for you to meet my mother and my grandparents."

"I am looking forward to it Ms. Giovanni."

"Please call me by my first name."

"Thank you I will Noelle."

"No, my first name is Carmeli'ta'. Noelle and Angelu'cia are my middle names and Giovanni is my mother's family's last name."

"I see. I will call you Carmeli'ta' you have a beautiful name."

By this time, the plane taxied and stopped at the passenger exiting area; Charlemagne, the other Stewardess in first class, opened the door and helped Desiree' get Carmeli'ta' down the steps before she allowed the other passengers to exit the plane. Franco saw her as she descended to the bottom step then up to the second floor to the passenger waiting area with Desiree' holding her around her waist and assisting her up the eight steps to the passengers waiting zone. Simone' standing at the entrance door into the airport waiting zone, saw her daughter smiled, ran to her, and held her tight and said, "Hello my beautiful Daughter. I am thankful that you are okay. It is so good to see you. I have missed you my sweet Carmeli'ta'. I was worried when we learned that you have been assaulted."

"Carmeli'ta' overcome with tears could not speak for the joy that she felt seeing her mother and knowing that she was safe and well, held onto her after a long time said, "Hello mummy it is so good to see you. I have missed you so much. I thought you were sick or father did not know where you were." She continued to hold on to her mother with uncontrollable tears flowing from her eyes. Simone' held her tight and comforted her until her the tears that bought her relief from her fears ceased. After what seemed like an eternity to Franco, Carmeli'ta' looked past her mother and saw her grandfather and her grandmother standing smiling, waiting patiently for her to greet her mother. Carmeli'ta' ran to her grandfather, hugs him tight, then her grandmother, and said to both of them, "I am so glad to see you Grandmother and Grandfather. Grandmother my mother looks so much like you. She is beautiful like you are."

"Thank you Carmeli'ta' you are a sweet granddaughter and very precious to us. We are thankful that you are safe." Carmeli'ta' walked back to where Desiree' was standing waiting to fulfill her duty in getting her to grandparents said, "Desiree', I want to you meet my mother, Simone' Angelu'cia Giovanni Bandaci, my grandmother Catarina Giovanni, and my grandfather Franco Giovanni. Everyone this is Desiree'. She has been with me through the entire incident." Desiree' Hammonds is a beautiful, slim, 5'6"; 45 years old woman with fiery red hair pulled back in a French bun, with a pleasant face, melodious voice, with dancing eyes and an eternal smile.

Simone replied, "Desiree' thank you for keeping my daughter safe and for your alertness. We are all very thankful that you were on the flight or it could have been a lot worse."

"You are all welcome. I can see that you are Carmeli'ta's family you all look alike. I am so pleased that I could be of assistance to Carmeli'ta' she is sweet and gentle. I know you must be proud of her; she has been a trooper through this ordeal and has not allowed it to affect her at all. She has a slight headache. Dr. Thimmons, at Charing Cross Hospital, told her it would dissipate in a few hours, if it has not within the next twenty-four hours, get her examined by a doctor here at the hospital in Tuscany. She did well with the headache on the flight with both takeoff and landing. I was happy to help and get her safe to you. I have to leave you now and I hope to see you soon."

Franco asked, "Can you visit a while and have lunch with us Desiree'?"

"That would be wonderful Mr. Giovanni; however, I am scheduled on the next flight at 3:00 p.m. back to America. I need to file my reports for this incident with the airline so I am off to do my paperwork. I hope to see you again the next time that I am in Tuscany, if my schedule permits."

Franco said, "Yes, please let us know and we will be more than happy to have you visit us." He pulled out one of his business cards from his card file and handed it to her. She looked at it and said, "Yes, Mr. Giovanni, I have seen you in some of the meetings that are held every Wednesday. I thought I recognized you. I had not spoken with you personally but am always impressed with your required level of efficiency for all pilots, stewardess, airport ground staff and managers, as well as your insistence on rules and regulations being followed to the letter."

"I am thankful that Pan American has employees like you Desiree'. I will see you soon then." Desiree' hugged Carmeli'ta' and said, "Don't travel by yourself until you are a more experienced traveler; it is very dangerous for you being young and beautiful; you are a target for people like the man that assaulted you."

"I will remember. Thank you for all you did for me, staying with me at the hospital, and then getting me safely to my family. I will never forget what you did for me."

"I have a daughter, Chandler; she is your age Carmeli'ta'. She is precious to me as you are to your family. I lost her father during World War I and raised her by myself. I would want someone to be kind to her if she was ever in trouble. Take care of yourself little one." Desiree' waved goodbye to them and went to the Pan American office to file her report.

Franco waited at the baggage area to get Carmeli'ta's bag, loaded it in luggage rack on the back of the car, and they left the airport for the 45-minute drive back to their little valley. Carmeli'ta' sit snuggled under her mother as she held her close to her. Simone' closed her eyes and thanked God for the safety of her daughter. After a while, Carmeli'ta' sit up and looked out the window and the sights she saw were bravura and staggering.

Taken by surprise, she could not believe the splendor before her eyes said, "Mother I have never seen astonishing beauty like this anywhere in Charleston. No artist could capture the exquisiteness."

Simone' smiled and listened at her daughter's admiration of the countryside. When they approached the valley, the landscape sparkled like diamonds, the hillside embellished with beautiful white cottages reeled with ultra-antiqueness, at the same glance the surroundings were fashionable and well placed among the loveliness of the over-hanging hills that divided and defined the land replied, "Mummy, Jason would love to see this wonderful countryside."

"How is Jason my darling daughter?"

"He is fine Mummy. I need to call him when I arrive at my grandparents' home. I know he must be worried by now. Did you tell him I was hurt?"

"No, my darling daughter, that is something you will need to do. He is your Fiancée. You have not called me Mummy since you were ten years old Carmeli'ta'. Then, as I remember, it was when you were not feeling well or you were frightened. We will get you home and eat lunch and then you can rest after you speak with Jason. Maybe a warm bath will help you relax and sleep better."

"Yes mother, I have not had a warm bath since I left home. I just freshened up the best I could in the Hospital this morning." Franco and Catarina listened to their daughter and granddaughter's conversation, but did not comment they knew it was not the appropriate time or place so they were silent glancing at each other and smiling at the pleasantness between a mother and her daughter. At length, they reached home, Franco pulled into the driveway, excited Carmeli'ta' exclaimed, WOW! Grandfather, Grandmother your house is beautiful, mother described it to me, but seeing it looks much like a picture painted by an artist."

"Thank you my sweet granddaughter, we enjoy our home. It is much like the one that your father purchased for your mother, the only difference is yours is not white in color, but nonetheless lovely."

"Yes, my father bought it especially for my mother because he loves her so; he said it to me many times over the years."

Franco took Carmeli'ta's luggage to the guest bedroom on the other side of the kitchen facing the street. Catarina quickly washed her hands and begin warming the food for lunch while Simone' helped Carmeli'ta' settle into her bedroom, change into a dressing gown, and then returned to the kitchen to help her mother with the final lunch preparations.

Franco sat at the table and chatted with his wife and daughter. Carmeli'ta' entered the kitchen and asked, "Grandfather, may I use your phone? I want to make a call back to America."

"Yes of course, Carmeli'ta' I will show you the office the phone is there. He took his granddaughter by the hand and walk slowly to his office opened the French doors, pointed to the desk, and said, "There my little sweet one. I will let you have your privacy."

"Thank you. Please tell mother I will not be long." Carmeli'ta' picked up the phone and called the operator gave her the number to Jason's office; she knew would still be there. In the meantime, Jason was pacing nervously back and forth in his office praying that Carmeli'ta' was okay. He thought to himself, "She should have arrived at her grandparents long hours ago. Where could she be?" The phone rang at his desk, not expecting a call was slow about answering, but finally after the fifth ring picked it up answering,

"Jason Madison." The operator said, "Mr. Madison I have an international call for you from Carmeli'ta' Bandaci may I put her through?"

"Yes, yes, please do." She said again, "Your party is on the line sir."

"Thank you."

Carmeli'ta' said, "Hello Jason my darling, how are you? I know that you must be worried by now because there was a delay in my calling. I hope that you are not too upset. I have reached my grandparent's home and my mother is fine." She hesitated for a few seconds. Jason realizing by the tone in her voice there was something she was not saying said, "Why did it take you so long to call me sweetheart?"

"I am just arriving with the last thirty minutes to my grandparent's home."

"Carmeli'ta' what happened you are so late calling me? I was beside myself with worry and anxiety thinking you suffered a serious injury, or something happened to the plane. There is something you are not saying, what happened?"

"There was an incident on the plane Jason, a thief snatched my purse and pushed me against the seat injuring my head a little. I spent the remainder of the night in the hospital in London. I have six stiches in my hairline, but I am fine. They apprehended the petty thief."

"I had a bad feeling about you traveling Carmeli'ta' alone young and inexperienced especially abroad. I wish you had waited to see what tomorrow (Saturday) would bring in reference to your mother." Feeling a little annoyed with her he continued, "How is your head today? I hope that you did not have a concussion from the blow."

"No Jason the doctor at Charing Cross Hospital in London said I did not and my headache should subside in a few hours if not Mother will take me to the doctor here. I am sorry that I worried you Jason, I felt I had to find out about my mother."

"I am thankful that you are okay Carmeli'ta'. We will talk more of it later. I know that you need to rest; I will call you later tonight before I go to bed. I have your grandparent's phone number you gave me earlier this week at home."

"Thank you Jason, I do need to eat and rest. I will look forward to hearing from you later. I know that you must be annoyed with me. I love you Jason."

"I am more concerned than annoyed my lovely Carmeli'ta'. I love you."

They hang up the phone and Carmeli'ta' walked into the garden from her grandfather's office to admire its beauty. She sat on the garden chair, looked down, holding her head, and thought about the last hours of her life realizing that she could have been injured or killed. Lunch ready, Simone' and her parents sit silently at the kitchen table waiting for her to return, saw her walking and then sit, wondered if she was okay. Simone' went into the garden, sat next to her daughter, and asked, "Carmeli'ta' are you okay? Your head is not bothering you, or you are not feeling dizzy are you? Were you able to talk to Jason?"

"No mother, I feel okay, just a little weak from not eating probably. Jason is okay. I can tell he was a little annoyed with me. He did not want me to travel by myself. I had to know if you were okay Mother. It was not my intention to worry anyone."

Simone' listened silently to her daughter smiled and said, "We will talk more about it later Carmeli'ta'. But you must eat now so you can rest, this ordeal has taken a toll on you, come your grandparents are waiting; lunch is ready."

"Thank you Mother. I am ready to eat. I feel weak and hungry." They went into the kitchen to have lunch, afterwards Carmeli'ta' got a warm bath and rested so she would be strong again.

In the intervening time period, Roberto' left his farm it was nearing 8:00 a.m. He left for his home to get his luggage and meet Amelio', who had left his farm office at the same time Roberto' left his. Depending on the flow of traffic, they had a twenty-to-thirty-minute drive back to 15 Rue de' Mellencamp. Amelio' lived three streets down at 21 Rue Laved, he purchased the year before Roberto' and Simone' moved to Charleston. Both were rushing to meet the deadline of getting to the airport by 10:00 a.m. Roberto' and Amelio' arrived at his home at the same time. Roberto' went in to let Marianna know he was leaving and get his luggage, "Marianna, I am on my way. Please remember to let Amelio' know of anything that you need or any other situation that come up concerning our home while I am away."

"Yes, Mr. Bandaci I will take care of your and Miss home while you are way. Thank you. I hope Miss is okay sir and she will be home soon."

"Yes, we should be home soon Marianna. Take care of yourself, goodbye." Amelio' waited for Roberto' in his car, asked when he put his luggage in the luggage rack, "Did you remember the keys to Carmeli'ta's car? I will take Juanita, my housekeeper and cook, and have her to drive Carmeli'ta's car back to her Townhouse. She is a good driver." Roberto' had forgotten the keys in his rush to get to the airport and to his family replied, "No, I will get them they are in my car." Finally on their way to the airport, Amelio' did not say anything to him as they rode along. Roberto' felt tensed and waterlogged with the contagious circumstances and mystery surrounding his wife and now his daughter.

Arriving at the airport at 10:00 a.m. Roberto' remembered he had not talked with Amelio' about the weekly transfer of funds to their Swiss Bank Accounts asked, "The transfers are going well each week Amelio'? I did not seem to be home long enough to get anything done before I need to leave again."

"Yes, the transfers are going well each week. The Finance Manager at Charleston International Bank is making the weekly transfers per our instructions into all the accounts. I will need to check with Carmeli'ta' to know when her next check will be deposited in the bank. Will you confirm this for me and let me know when you arrive?"

"Yes, I will ask her and let you know. Thank you Amelio' you are a faithful friend and loyal cousin. I love and appreciate you more than you know I could not do any of this without you."

"No thanks necessary Roberto' I am happy to do it. We are family and you would do the same for me were the cases reversed."

Roberto' assured him, "Without a moment's hesitation, all you need to do is ask." Roberto' thought as he exited the car, 'Amelio' is more than a special person. He can be trusted, and for this fact I am thankful. There has never been one false move on his part, nor one penny missing from my accounts, in fact, Amelio' used his own money to open the Swiss accounts and did not require it back though I gave it to him.' Roberto' paid for his ticket, checked his luggage, and went to the passenger waiting area. He had fifteen minutes before he boarded, sat next to Amelio' and said, "I wish I could tell you the details of what is going on with this situation with my wife and daughter, but I am afraid my cousin, I don't know the details. I feel frustrated and confused with the entire matter."

"I know that you must be at a loss for a reasonable answer to this Roberto', but there is always an answer. In your frustration, remember to keep your temper under control and listen with an open mind to what your wife and daughter have to say to you. They both love you remember that and so do I."

By this time, the Technician was calling for boarding of the First-Class passengers. Both stood, Roberto' looked at his cousin, shook his hand, and replied, "I will remember your advice to me Amelio'. Thank you again for all that you do to help my family and me."

"Take care of yourself Roberto' and your family and the difficult situation will work itself out in the end." With that statement Roberto' walked out the door down the steps to the plane and boarded, looked back when he reached the top step smiled and waved to Amelio' standing watching him from the window. Amelio' left the Airport on his way home to get Juanita to drive Carmeli'ta's car from the airport parking lot and park it at her Townhouse.

Roberto' settled in his seat in First Class, leaned back, and closed his eyes, felt he wanted to run ahead of the plane to get it in the air. He could not wait to see his family and be near his wife he missed her for the past ten days since he came home. Visions of Simone' and him making love danced in his mind as the plane begin to pushback and finally in the air he would see her soon.

In Tuscany, Carmeli'ta' and Simone returned to the kitchen where Catarina and Franco waited for them to eat lunch. They sat and ate, laughing and chatting with each other. Carmeli'ta' was still feeling overjoyed to see her mother and know that she was well.

Carmeli'ta' looked at the clock and remembered she had not cancelled the reservation on the RMS Olympic for 5:30 p.m. sailing that afternoon from New York said, "Excuse me I need to make another call to cancel a reservation that I have to sail today at 5:30 p.m. She rose from the table, went to her bedroom to get the information from her purse, went into her grandfather's office, called the New York Travel Agency, and canceled her trip. While she was out of earshot Franco asked, "Simone' does she know her father is on his way here to Tuscany?"

"No father, I have not mentioned it to her yet."

"I think that you need to do that when she returns from making her latest phone call. It does not need to be a surprise. I think that we have had enough surprises for the last little while don't you? Her father is on his way here and he is not coming just to be coming. He is upset about this entire situation and she needs to be aware that he is not pleased with her for not telling him her plans."

Catarina nodded in agreement and said, "Your father is right Simone' she needs to know her father is on his way."

"You are right Father and Mother. I have seen Roberto' upset with Carmeli'ta' a few times when she was growing, but I don't think she has ever pushed him over the top like she did this time, not even with her relationship with Jason Madison."

Franco replied, "I heard her mention his name on the drive back to the valley, who is he? She said he is her Fiancée?"

"Yes, Father her Fiancée. He is the President and CEO of the largest Steel and Iron Company in Charleston, actually one of the largest in the South period."

"She works for him is that correct?"

"Yes, for almost three years now and she is doing well. She is the Office Manager and Hostess for the entire plant and is next to Jason in authority.

They love each other and it did not happen overnight, but took a long time."

Franco said, "I see. I know she was doing well in her job, but did not connect her relationship with her boss. Am I to understand that Roberto' does not approve of this engagement or love that is between them?"

"That is correct Father. He does not approve of it, but wants her to marry Alberto Gambani. You remember the Gambian's do you not Father?"

"Yes, I remember the Gambian's, but would not have thought he would be a good match for my granddaughter. When he was growing, he seemed a little weak spirited and stayed under his mother too much for my taste for a male. But maybe he is different now."

"She does not love Alberto'. They have been friends all their young lives, but that is all. He is different now from what he was when he was younger. He is a strong man, with a good mind for business, but she does not love him. I cannot say that I would want her to marry someone she does not love, but only care for as a friend. She says it can never be anything else but friendship."

"I understand my Daughter. Nevertheless, that is between her, Roberto' and you. I chose for you, that is a little different twenty-four years ago, you were raised in Tuscany under those customs when the father pick for his daughter or son. Carmeli'ta' was raised in a different culture, the western culture where women and men choose who they want to marry."

"So, you do understand her wanting to choose for herself?"

"Yes, of course Daughter, but I will have no comments on the matter. Roberto' is her father and proprietaries must be observed no matter where you live in the world."

"Thank you Father I appreciate your insight. I will tell her when she returns from making her phone call her father is on his way. Actually, I am a little nervous as well. He will be expecting an answer when he arrives about the Diary as well?"

"Then you will give him the answer that you decided on Simone', the truth of the matter."

At that moment Carmeli'ta' walked into the kitchen and asked, "What Diary is he referring to Mother? I have no Diary!"

Simone' paused then said, "Carmeli'ta' your father is on his way to Tuscany. He is probably halfway here by now his flight left at 11:00 a.m. and it is now nearing 4:00 p.m. He will be here by 8:00 a.m. tomorrow morning." Simone' saw a look of concern dart across her brow. Carmeli'ta' walked to the French Doors leading into her grandmother's garden and said, "He is angry with me isn't he Mother because I mislead him about my plans. I don't know what to tell him when he gets here."

"He is angry that you put yourself in danger and did not take his word I was well and safe with my parents Carmeli'ta'. Your father has never lied to you before, why would you not believe him in this instant?"

"I wanted to Mother, but I was afraid you were not okay so I came to see for myself. I think I want to rest now; it has been a long day and I am feeling very tired."

Carmeli'ta' walked to her bedroom suite. Simone' pushed her chair back from the table and followed her, closed the drapes, and turned down her bed. Carmeli'ta' went in drew her bath water, bathed, lotion her body, brushed her teeth, and put on a pair of Brushed Pink Silk Pajamas with matching Robe and Slippers, brushed her hair, got into bed, and snuggled beneath the warmth of the sheets and the comforter.

Simone' sat next to her and smiled and said, "Sleep my beautiful Daughter I will wake you for dinner. I need to help mother finish preparing it. We will eat around 7:00 p.m. that will give you enough time to sleep and refresh yourself." She leaned forward and kissed her daughter on the forehead, left the bedroom, turning out the light as she closed the door. Simone' knew that after today, their lives would take a new direction with the revelations that would come out when Roberto' arrived. She could only imagine what he might be thinking or asking himself at this moment in time. She went back to the kitchen to help her mother finish dinner.

Franco decided to walk in the garden since he never quite made it to the farm to check on the day's activities with either of his managers. While walking, he contemplated what might be the result of the matter when his son-in-law arrived on Saturday. He worried more about his daughter and her situation than his granddaughter. With Carmeli'ta' it was a matter of inexperience, and upset over the fact that she had not spoken with her mother. He could well understand her feelings Simone' and she had a close mother daughter relationship all their lives. Even though he knew that both situations were created was with "absence of malice" on Simone' and Carmeli'ta' parts. Strangely, both his daughter and granddaughter were trying to protect their loved one. He thought of Roberto' his kind and loving son-in-law, who he knew loved his family with his entire being and would give his life if necessary for either or both of them. He did not want to see him hurt by this situation, though he knew that he would be. It was not something that he could control. He thought of his daughter and her innocence at that time in her life, 14 years of age and knew she was not mature enough to make a sound decision when all the rages were overshadowing her.

His main concern was Vincenzo's claim that Carmeli'ta' was his daughter. More than that Simone's lack of confidence in who was the father at this present-time was the elephant in the room. His being quaked when he thought of what Roberto' would do to Vincenzo'. He was a patient man, but not in reference to his family if, he thought they had been threatened or harmed in some way. Franco felt a huge amount of discomforting disconcertedness over the entire chain of events surrounding his family. Vincenzo' was told, by Simone' more than once Carmeli'ta' was not his, why would a man insist on claiming that child? Then again, there was the uncertainty in the air of this truth that hung like the Ax of a Guillotine.

During Franco's visit with Vincenzo' at the Moretti Estate, to speak with him concerning his daughter and granddaughter, he realized that Vincenzo' was so sure he was Carmeli'ta' father. Franco remembered the look in his eyes and the pain that it was causing him at the thought of never seeing Carmeli'ta' again. He knew he loved Simone' it was evident in the heartbreak he saw in his face when he spoke of her. He could not or would not admit this to Vincenzo' or Simone' but he knew that the love he had for Simone' was genuine and true. He played his best hold card and lost because of the train of thought about societal position in Tuscany, at that time, that no classes would mix in marriage whether they were wine kings, farmers, storeowners, shoe doctors, musicians, restaurants managers, or owners of an Allevamento di polli (chicken farmer). A large number of these were wealthy, but it did not matter, they were not to intermarry, no parent would give his son or daughter permission to marry outside their class. Franco in deep concentration had walked a long way.

He realized after a while he was nearing the Bandaci Farm Amelio' had repurchased when he came to visit a few years back. The cottage was still as beautiful as ever. The caretaker and his wife did an excellent job of working the farm and taking care of the house and grounds. He felt his family's life had become like a smorgasbord, to wide a range of dishes for his taste. He pulled out his pocket watch as he walked back towards home noticed the time 7:00 p.m. knew it was well pass time for dinner. He hurried along, thought also parts of his life had become like a smorgasbord. The dishes served were not attractive with appearances hanging around like a black cloud: doubt, blackmail, coercion, fear, and apprehension were all rancid and distasteful.

It was 7:30 p.m. when Franco reached home. Catarina worried he was gone more than three hours, stood looking into the garden. Simone' watched her mother's face, saw the worry crowd out the beautiful smile in her eyes, said, "Mother I am sure that father is fine, he probably walked further than he planned and did not notice the time."

Catarina turned smiled and said, "You are right Simone' but you know your father, he is very time conscious." At that moment, she saw him coming, flung the French Doors open, and ran to him. He saw her coming thought what a beautiful wife I have, she has eternal youth, smiled, stopped, and waited until she reached him, held out his arms to her; she hugs him tight saying, "Franco, my husband I begin to worry you were not here on time for dinner."

Smiling, he looked down at her and replied, "I walked further than I intended thinking of this situation with our daughter especially. Then, my lovely wife, it was worth my being late to see you run to me as you did. I love you my Catarina more than life itself. I feel blessed by God every day that we are together. You are a wonderful and loving wife." She did not reply, just kissed him snuggling close to him; they walked back to the house for dinner. Simone' waited at the door watching her mother and father together bought tears to her eyes, she wanted Roberto' and her to have what they have when they reached their later years. She saw the passion and desire still between her father and mother and knew their hearts still burned for each other, as Roberto' and hers did for each other.

When they came to the door Simone' opened it and smiled and said, "Father and Mother you are beautiful together, not in looks although you have more than your share of good looks both of you. I reel when I think my mother only eighteen years older than me and I seventeen years older than Carmeli'ta'; it is the love and passion that I see between you that I love and I want too for Roberto' and me and for Carmeli'ta' and her husband."

They both smiled and said, "Thank you Daughter you are a precious and unique person we are thankful to have a daughter of your caliber."

"Thank you both. I will wake my Carmeli'ta' she must be famished, as we all are. I will return in a few moments if you will excuse me."

Simone' hasten down the hall, quietly opened the door to her daughter's bedroom, and saw she was lying very still sleeping peacefully. Simone' stood for a few moments looking at her and the small gash that was in her hairline, hoped that it would not leave too visible a scar. She would treat it, when healed, with Cocoa Butter Extract. She bent forward and softly called her name, "Carmeli'ta' wakeup it is time for dinner."

She stirred at the sound of her mother's voice, opened her eyes, and looked up at her. It took a few minutes for her to focus and get her bearing she was still a little groggy from the blow she received her head felt a little light, sit up in the bed and replied, "I am awake Mother; is it time for dinner?"

"Yes Carmeli'ta' it is past time. Your grandfather went for a walk and was later getting back then he planned so hurry my daughter, get the sleep out of your eyes, your grandparents are waiting. Are you hungry? How is your head feeling, the pain gone? Sit on the side of the bed for a few seconds to get your bearing before you stand."

She sits up on the side of the bed for a few seconds, slowly stood then replied, "I feel fine Mother, and I do not have a headache now. I felt a little lightheaded when I first awaken and that is gone as well now that I am standing up."

"Hurry Carmeli'ta' I will wait for you to freshen up your face."

She went into the bathroom to wash her face and brush her hair back into place. In the meanwhile, Simone' straightened her bed and turned it back down in preparation of her retiring for the night later after dinner. Carmeli'ta' emerged from the bathroom all freshened, well-groomed, put on her robe that matched her pink silk pajamas, pink bedroom slippers and walked behind her mother back to the kitchen where dinner was waiting hot and ready. She smelled the delicious aroma flowing deliciously into her nose, whetting her appetite. The aroma was one that she was familiar with when growing up. Marianna prepared the dish for them, Baked Chicken with Rosemary, red potatoes, and carrots, seasoned with garlic, Insalata, garnished with warm oil and vinegar dressing with cracked black pepper, hot bread, and tea. When they entered the kitchen Franco said, "Good evening sleepy head. How is that head of yours, pain gone?"

She smiled and said, "Hello Grandfather and Grandmother, I am fine, the pain is gone. Grandmother, dinner smells scrumptious and mouthwatering, I feel hungry."

"Thank you my lovely one, your mother prepared it especially for you. She said it was one of your favorite dishes Marianna prepares for you I only helped her today, and prepared the dessert, she did the rest."

"Thank you Mother, I miss your cooking. This will be a treat. It is not often that you cook anymore with the extensive bookwork connected with your and father's farm."

"I do cook, but rarely Carmeli'ta'. I do the Bookkeeping; it is not so much I cannot cook. Your father prefers that I do other things of my interest. He feels I have done enough hard work in my life and wants me to relax more, so Marianna does most of the cooking. Sometimes I prepare the meals, but he is not aware of it. He thinks that Marianna does it all. I enjoy the change. I think that he knows that I do, in the way that he comments on the meals. Otherwise, he says nothing he is happy because I am happy doing whatever I want to."

"Thank you for the special dinner just for me mother, you make me feel special."

"You are special Carmeli'ta'. Now sit, let's eat." They sat eating and enjoying the meal prepared my Simone'. The art of cooking taught Simone' was still evident to both Catarina and Franco, the Chicken was fall-off-the bone tender, the potatoes and carrots were firm, yet not too hard, the bread had a sweet honey taste to it enhancing the taste of the meal. Carmeli'ta' remembered her mother would mop the dough in the pan lightly with honey before she baked it. Catarina prepared Vanilla Pinafores garnished with strawberry glaze for dessert. They would have their dessert around 10:00 p.m. After dinner, Simone' and Carmeli'ta' cleared the table and did the dishes while her mother and father went for their evening walk together. She noticed they did not leave the garden area, but walked around and looked at Catarina's flowers and talked. Franco's face told Catarina that he felt a storm brewing.

CHAPTER
FORTY-THREE

Simone' chatted with Carmeli'ta' and set up the coffee pot, while they were waiting for her parents to return from their walk for dessert and coffee, prepared the plates for dessert, while Carmeli'ta' took down the cups for the coffee. She came and stood near her mother and said, "Mother may I ask you a question?"

Simone' had waited for her daughter to get to this point of questioning why she had not heard from her since she left replied, "Of course, ask my Daughter."

"I don't understand why I did not hear from you after you left and why you never told me you were leaving? Father said you decided at the last minute to visit grandmother and grandfather, and then he left without explanation and returned home ten days later without you with him. He seemed so vague each time I asked him about you. It is not like either of you to do something of this nature; we always talk as a family."

Simone' listened to her daughter smiled and said, "Carmeli'ta' I know that you don't understand my darling daughter, there are times in an adult's life when they feel the need to get away and relax. I had not seen my parents in four years that is a long time. You understand that you feel the way I felt. I wanted to see my mother and father. I decided to visit them at the last minute. When I called you, I did not want you to be upset so I asked your father to let you know. He decided to come that Monday we spent six beautiful days in the cottage where we had our honeymoon. I am glad we decided to have a second honeymoon and my parents are getting older and I wanted to spend time with them, I hope you understand."

"The night you left my Townhouse father was upset with you and me both; I never understood what you said and did to make him upset. You only wanted me to be happy with someone of my choice in love as if you were his choice. I thought he had made you go away."

"No, Carmeli'ta' your father did not make me go away. He was upset about your and Jason's relationship and him not knowing about it. You asked me not to tell him so I did not; he was upset about that with good reason. Your father loves you and wants the best for you. He only acts out of love for both of us remember that Carmeli'ta'."

"Mother are father and you...she paused; you are not planning to be apart are you?"

Simone' plugged in the electric coffee pot replying, "No, Carmeli'ta' that is the last thing on our minds. I love your father and he loves me. What is between a husband and wife is not be freely discussed, even with my lovely daughter. You will know this once you are married. What is between a man and woman is too private to share only with each other my sweet one. No more questions tonight, let your grandparents know dessert and coffee are ready."

Not completely satisfied with her answers said, "Thank you for talking to me mother, I will let my grandparents know we are ready for dessert."

On the plane, dinner was being served, Roberto' was not hungry but ate a small amount of the roast beef with potatoes and sweet peas with a roll. He thought of Simone', how much he needed her. The intensity grew as the plane flew toward London. After dinner, he watched the sun setting in the western sky from his window. The sunset and the sky turned to grey, this scene reminded him of Simone' and his wedding night. His desire to be near his wife, like a fever, rose to an exhausting level, his memory of the warmth of her and how she made him feel raced across his mind. He drifted off to sleep, saw Simone' with both hand stretched out to him. He could not tell whether it was reality or his imagination slept after being awake since 4:30 a.m. that morning.

Simone', Carmeli'ta', and her parent's had dessert at 10:15 p.m. just as darkness set-in in their little valley. After the dessert and the dishes were cleared away Carmeli'ta' still feeling weary from the ordeal said, "I think I will call Jason and then retire for the night good night everyone." She kissed her Mother, and grandmother then stood behind her grandfather and hugged his neck kissing him on the cheek.

Carmeli'ta' called Jason waiting in anticipation of her call. It was near his dinner time, but wanted to talk with her before he joined his parents for dinner. The phone rang in his suite, "Hello."

"Jason my darling how are you this time?"

"Hello, my lovely one, I was waiting your call before I joined my parents for dinner. How are you feeling? Has your headache gone?"

"I am feeling better Jason, still a little groggy and lightheaded when I first wake up. I am tired probably from the long flight and the assault, but I am getting better. The cut on my head is stinging a little. How are you?"

"I am fine my lovely little one. I miss you and love you more than you know. I hope you will come home soon my darling Carmeli'ta'."

"I will Jason very soon. I miss you and love you with all my heart. I will not talk long Jason. I want to rest and I will look forward to talking to you tomorrow."

"I completely agree you need to rest and take care of yourself so you can recover fast my sweetheart."

"Thank you for understanding. I apologize for worrying you. I hope you will forgive me."

"You are welcome Carmeli'ta'. There is nothing to forgive. All I want is for you to be okay and recover fully. One thing before you go my sweet, I am having the Finance Manager transfer your salary to your account each week."

"Thank you Jason for you thoughtfulness. I love you. Bye for now."

"Pleasant dreams my lovely. Goodnight."

Carmeli'ta' returned to the kitchen smiled and said, "Good night everyone. I love you."

Franco and Catarina smiled and said, "Goodnight granddaughter."

Simone' went with Carmeli'ta' to her bedroom, tucked her in as she did when she was a growing up and said, "Rest my lovely little one, tomorrow is another day and you are safe with us. I will be here when you awaken in the morning." Carmeli'ta' did not comment just smiled and closed her eyes and before Simone' turned off the lamp she had drifted into a peaceful sleep.

Returning to the kitchen where her parents sat talking when she entered said, "Father we did not get a chance to talk about Shakespeare's Sonnet 116, I do so love it so much."

"You are right my daughter we did not, is now a good time before we retire for the night?"

"Yes father lets. I want to know your view of what he said about love and marriage."

Franco paused for a moment, settled back in his chair, looked at his daughter and said, "When two people marry Simone' it is for life. There are times when winds blow, wave's crash, and dark and uncertain times come along in a couple's life. In all of this, time should not be the culprit, but rather time should be the factor that is the healing agent. It is a marriage of the mind more than it is of the body. As we age, we should not lose interest in that love one, but our love should have grown to the point where we love them even more because of the trials that come into their lives and they weathered them together. Our faces change, our skin wrinkle, sometimes pounds come for no reason other than age, our bodies, and minds age, but never our spirit or soul; it has eternal youth my lovely Daughter, if we don't know these things, I feel as Shakespeare does, you never knew love in the beginning."

She sat astonished at the summation of what Sonnet 116 meant to her father; after a while commented, "Father that is beautiful, those are my exact sentiments, romanticisms, and inspirations about Sonnet 116. That particular Sonnet is one of the most beautiful ones I have ever read. It is a revealing of the heart and soul. When you can love someone time without end, on a continuum, love is as strong as death to me father, it holds your heart forever to that person, how do you stop loving someone that you care for so much in life?"

"You can't stop loving them Simone'. Your mother and I discuss this Sonnet quite often. You see them all your life like the first time you saw them; in your eyes they never change that is what true love can do to the mind's eye. Our physical eyes may dim because of time, but the mind's eye with all the memories never dims nor age; it is in a fixed state, with love as the light."

"Thank you for sharing your thoughts with me Father. You give me courage to know that my husband and my marriage will overcome this situation, it might take some time, but it will happen."

"I am happy that you realize that Simone'. It is bedtime, Saturday is here my beauties; it is after midnight. My lovely wife, are you ready?"

"Yes, Franco I am ready and a little weary, it has been a long day."

"I will wait to see if my Roberto' call. He should be landing in just a bit." Glancing at the clock on the wall it was 12:45 a.m. continued, "If he has not called by 1:30 a.m., he will not call-in fear of waking everyone. Goodnight Mother and Father, I will check on Carmeli'ta' again before I retire."

Within the hour, the Pan American Flight 2370 approached the coast of London and Croydon Airport. The Stewardess said, "Mr. Bandaci we making our descent into Croydon Airport sir. We will land in fifteen minutes, please prepare yourself."

"Thank you, I will." He woke himself up completely, checked his seat belt, looked at his pocket watch, the time was 12:45 a.m. then peered out of the window. Below he saw the City of London lit up as if it was day. His thoughts went to the time in Tuscany, knew that his family would be sleeping by the time he retrieved his luggage and got checked into at the Premier Inn, determined that he would wait until he arrived in Tuscany. He wanted to arrive before Carmeli'ta' awaken so he would have some time with Simone'. He will be at Franco's by 8:00 a.m. The Stewardess informed the passengers that the flight would leave for Tuscany at 5:00 a.m. an hour earlier than scheduled. This fact made him happy to know he would only need to wait for three hours rather than five. His eagerness grew at the time the plane taxied to where the passengers exited. In the airport, Roberto' checked with customer service to see if his reservation was confirmed at the hotel, called for a taxi, retrieved his luggage for the five-minute ride to Premier Inn.

Simone' in the meantime, checked to see if Carmeli'ta' was resting well, opened the door noticed she had kicked the covers off, pulled them up around her again. She snuggled under the comforter, Simone' knew she had gotten cold. It was 1:30 a.m., Roberto' had not called her, went to her suite, drew her bath, stepped into the Lavender fragrant bubbles, and relaxed for a few minutes as thoughts of Roberto' and her danced in her mind. Excitement grew equally with the thought of being near him in a few hours after the long days she had suffered being apart from him, and them not being together. Stepping out of the bath, she snuggled dry in a white terry robe, lotion her body, slipped into a black negligee, one of Roberto's favorites. She brushed her hair, dabbed on Chanel 5 behind her ears, in her armpits, on the back of her knees, and wrist, snuggled into the warm comfort of her bed letting her mind drift with thoughts of the situation, slept.

Roberto' arrived at the hotel at 1:35 a.m. checked in, freshen-up, and relaxed on the bed with his passion and desire growing to be near Simone' in a few hours. He asked the hotel clerk to call him at 4:00 a.m. so he would have the opportunity to shower, dress, and get his taxi back to the Corydon by 4:40 a.m. boarding time. He slept for the few hours. What seemed like a few minutes later to him, the phone rang, the clerk said, "This is your wakeup call Mr. Bandaci it is 4:00 a.m. I have called for the Taxi; it will arrive at 4:35 a.m. sir."

"Thank you, I will be downstairs at that time." He hurriedly opened his suitcase took out a pair of brown slacks, brown and blue shirt to match, brown socks, and shorts and tee shirt, and went into the bathroom. He shaved, showered, splashed on Boellis Panama 1924 aftershave and cologne, dressed, packed the clothes back in his suitcase, closed, and locked it. Then picked up his attaché' case with accounts to be rectified in it, looked at his watch, it was 4:30 a.m., retrieved the room key from the nightstand, went downstairs to checkout to pay his bill and wait for the Taxi to arrive. He noted though he was in resident in the room, for only a few hours he paid the full amount $20.00 per night thought it excessive for the quality of the room.

The taxi pulled up to the door. The driver exited the taxi, reached for his suitcase, and put it in the luggage rack, opened the back door, he got in for the few minutes ride to the airport, arriving he paid the fare and rushed to the boarding door. The plane was boarding when he arrived. The airport technician at the boarding door said, "You are last Mr. Bandaci, your seat is waiting. The flight leaves in ten minutes."

"Thank you."

Pan American Flight 2370 left on time arriving in Tuscany two hours later at 7:00 a.m. Roberto' was the first passenger to exit the plane. He waited anxiously to pick up his luggage in the baggage area for passengers, went back to the Customer Service Desk to have a taxi called for the forty-five-minute ride to the Valley.

Franco and Catarina awaken at their usual time 6:00 a.m. to prepare coffee, have their Morning Prayer, and breakfast. Franco wanted to check the farm and arrive home by lunchtime. He knew Roberto' would be there by the time he returned. Catarina said, "Franco, it would be nice to take Carmeli'ta' with you that will give her mother and father some time alone, they need a few hours together after such a long time apart. I will do some marketing this morning for a few hours so they will have the house to themselves for a while, what do you think?"

"I think it is a wonderful idea my beauty. Wake our granddaughter and tell her I want her to go with me this morning, we will return around lunch time or a little while after." Catarina went to Carmeli'ta' bedroom, opened the door quietly, went in, walked over to her bed, saw her granddaughter awake said, "Good Morning. Carmeli'ta' your grandfathers wants you to go with him this morning and see the farm and maybe some of the valley it is beautiful this time of morning, would you like that?"

"Good morning grandmother. I would love it. I will get dressed and be right there give me twenty minutes. I am excited, I want to see everything, and it is so beautiful here. We have nothing like this in Charleston."

Catarina returned to the waiting Franco and said, "She is excited and looking forward to it. I will prepare your and her fruit bowls with bread, sausage, and coffee. She, especially, needs to eat before she leaves."

Twenty minutes later Carmeli'ta' appeared in a navy blue comfortable leisure suit and low hill shoes with her hair pulled back in a ponytail.

While she and her grandfather ate breakfast and chatted, Franco said, "Thank you for going with me granddaughter; it will be a treat and honor for me to have you meet my staff and some of my workers. We will tour the valley a little before we return for lunch. Your grandmother has some marketing to do this morning, your mother is resting she was late going to bed last night."

Carmeli'ta' did not notice that everyone was leaving the house that morning except her mother, she was too excited about the trip and the sites she would see while out. After breakfast, Franco and Carmeli'ta' left in his work truck at 7:10 a.m. It was agreed that Catarina would wait until Roberto' arrived around 8:00 a.m. before she left for the market so Simone' would not be disturbed by her husband knocking on the door.

Roberto' left Campo di Marte at 7:10 a.m. at the time Carmeli'ta' and Franco left for his farm. The ride to the Valley was quiet and faster than he had anticipated. It was Saturday morning and citizens were slow about moving around on Saturday's it was usually a day of rest for everyone except the Farmers who delivered their vegetable and produce before noon. Their clients doubled his or her orders on Saturday, no one worked on Sunday's anywhere in the Valley, and it was a family day. When the taxi approached the valley and on the descent downward, the beauty of this little valley was like seeing it for the first time. He gave the taxi driver the street address to his in-laws home. The taxi reached his in-laws home, he saw only Franco' car, knew he was at the farm that morning. He paid the fare, took his suitcase from the luggage rack, and sit it near his attaché' case on the front lawn. Catarina was watching for him at the Bay Window in the Parlor so his knock would not awaken Simone'.

Roberto' knocked lightly at the door, Catarina opened it, smiled, hugged him, and said, "Hello my dear son, how are you today? I hope you had a good trip."

Roberto' kissed his mother-in-law on her cheek and replied, "Yes, it was good Catarina. I was over-anxious I think to get here and see my wife and daughter."

"I am sure. They are both fine Roberto'. Would you like to eat something or have a cup of coffee? Simone' is still sleeping."

"Some coffee would be good. I had breakfast on the plane. Where is my sweet daughter?"

Catarina sit the cup on the table and poured his coffee answered, "She went to see the farm and tour some of the Valley with her grandfather. They will return by noon or a little after. I am on my way to do some marketing this morning and should return by lunchtime or a little after. I will pick up something for lunch from the Boulangerie' Viennoise; it has been a long day and night my dear son-in-law, but we survived."

Roberto' smiled saying, "Thank you Catarina, I appreciate you and Franco giving my beauty and me time to be alone. I have missed her these days we have been apart. Thank you for understanding and entertaining my sweet daughter for a while."

"You are welcome Roberto'. Franco and I know how you and Simone' feel. She is anxious to see you as well. I am off to the market and probably will visit friends for a while for our Saturday morning coffee and chat; until later then my dear!" With a slight wave of her hand, she left. Roberto' washed his coffee cup, put it away, took his luggage, and walked quietly to the end of the hall to Simone's suite, opened the door, and saw his beautiful wife still sleeping, the scent of her Chanel 5 hung heavily in the room invited in thoughts of love and romance. He put his suitcase near the window, he took off his jacket, turned the lock on the bedroom door, walked over to the bed sit, leaned over, and kissed Simone'. Feeling his touch, she slowly awakens, turning saw her husband sitting near her smiled and said, "Hello my husband, I am so happy to see you."

Without commenting, Roberto' smiled and lay next to her, pulled her close to him, and held her tight. Her skin to Roberto' was like cotton, her velvety silky hair fell on his chest, her left hand felt warm, she gently stroked his right arm, her body firm, delicate, and strong felt delicious next to his. He basked in her beauty and softness for a long time before he spoke, "Good morning my beauty. I have missed you more than you know. It is maddening to come home and you are not there to greet me. The nights were the worse for me. I missed the smooth feel of your hands when they touched me, the mellow feel of your lips while you kiss me, the fragrance of your Chanel 5 when I walk into our home each day, and I missed your beauty light as a feather to embrace my heart Simone'. It is torture without you being near me at night when I sleep. The warmth of your body whilst you lay tenderly against me at night, I can feel your soothing warm breath on my back as you sleep my beauty hung about me while we were apart. These scenes of us haunt me day and night. I wanted you to visit your parents, decide how you want to share what you have held in your heart for so many years, I wanted you to have that time. But, Oh my lovely precious Simone', time became an enemy to me and not a friend. How can I go on without you with me?"

"I know my sweet husband I feel all these things and more that you just spoke to me from your heart my husband. I can feel the pain and heartache in the tone of your voice. I know how much you missed me by the way you hold me ever so tightly my husband. I do not like being away from you. It was tormenting for me in more than one way; it bothers my heart, mind, and body, my Roberto'. I love you more now than ever. Thoughts of you consumed me while I was away from you the week before you came the first time and the weeks after you left.

I cannot picture facing life without you my husband. I want you; I love you; I need you; I cherish our love; you are the strength I need to lean on, the passions and desires that you awaken in me rages out of control, my husband. I think about that lock of hair that dances on your forehead even when you are sleep. The sweet mint taste of your kisses lingers in my mouth, the fresh, inviting scent of your aftershave and cologne drifts gently into my nose and then the look in your soft brown eyes tell me of the passion you feel for me. I cannot explain in words how and what you make me feel. You make me happy Roberto', filling my heart and my life, you are the only one I need."

After a while, Simone' slipped from his warm embrace and went to the bathroom to freshen up, brush her teeth, gargle, and daub on more cologne. Roberto' watched her cross the floor with the same moves, which makes her the sexiest woman in the world. The look of her body through the black negligée sent hot waves across his body and mind. He felt the heat of passion cover him like a carpet to the point he felt he would suffocate if he were not near her, rose from the bed and undressed sit on the bed waiting for her to return. She walked back towards him, saw the moves of her body that told him how much she needed him, and wanted to make love to him. Simone' back in bed, leaned back on one of the pillows smiled at him. Her smile captured his heart. Roberto' saw the passion by the way she looked at him was fluid as her watery mysterious eyes. He picked up his shaving case went in to freshen up, brush his teeth, gargle, and refresh his Boellis Panama 1924 aftershave and cologne. Before going back to his waiting wife, he stood for a few minutes looking in the mirror with visions of her beauty dancing before him, thought of the moments like these over the years he had with Simone' mused, "She is sensual, loving, her womanish ways, so unusual, she is a mystery I have not been able to solve. The more mysterious she is the more I love her. Her love drives me crazy. I do not know how to cure myself. She gives me an ache in my heart, body, and mind that is painful, wonderfully painful."

Roberto' felt he was with Simone' for the first time again, thought of the fresh smell of her body, like the air when a Spring Shower sweetens it. The fragrance she wears floats into his nostrils then to his taste buds, the look of her smooth silky skin, the watery eyes that pulls him in, and the way her eyes moves when she is excited. Her sexy smile causes him to be weak in the knees. The silkiness of her hair, black as coals, the glow of her skin on her face, the way she touches his face, brush back the lock of hair that dances on his forehead, caresses his legs at the same time they talk and chatted endlessly, and the quickness of her mind, gets him lost in her love. These thoughts gave him butterflies in his stomach, he felt like a pupil again. He felt needed and wanted by her the most beautiful woman in the world. He whispered, "I want her with all my heart; she makes me feel a lust, passion, and desire raging in my heart which blinds me. She makes me feel like a man, a sexy desirable man. She completes me in every way."

Simone' called to Roberto' saying, "My love I am waiting with anticipation for you. I want to be near you." The sound of her voice intensified his desires. He smiled in the mirror at her statement, brushed back his hairs, and walked away from the mirror and back toward his beautiful wife waiting for him.

She looked more beautiful to him than ever as she sat smiling. He crossed the room to join her in bed and saw the cold black lock of hair dancing on his forehead, his firm strong body, moving toward her. He sat on the bed near her, lifted both her hands kissed them on the inside and said, "I love you Simone', I need you to love me and let me love you. I feel a terrible burning passion that has held my body hostage for days. When I think of you it makes me boil on the inside, my blood feels hot like it is on fire. Love me Simone', love me, I want to feel your warmth.

"Your love is the valve that relieves the pain that I feel in my body and heart. I yearn for your love and comfort my sweet wife."

He continued, "Simone', the way you look, your eyes tells me how much you want me. I love that, it makes me know you care and love me. The sounds of pleasure I hear when I make love to you, when you call my name, and whisper how I make you feel, all this love melts me on the inside. When you give yourself to me never denying me when I want to make love, plays like music in my heart and mind. I know there were times when you were not in the mood or you had a long day, especially when we were first getting the farm started, you never said no. There were times when I knew you must be weary, those were the times I noticed you were the most loving. You put my needs ahead of yours when stress and anxiety overtook my being trying to start a life in a new country with new laws and culture we did not always understand, you were there for me, my balancing beam. You were calm and had faith in the new country, in Amelio's wisdom and vision of a new life, and especially in me my love. Do you know how much that pole-vaulted me to success? When I wanted love and intimacy, I knew continually asking you each night, I was selfish in my need my beauty. Yet, you never refused me, which that very fact has meant more to the success of Roberto' Bandaci than anything else. I love you Simone'."

Roberto' learned forward kissed her and added, "My love for you is like a fever creating a thirst in me, no matter how much of your love I drink it does not quench my thirst. It brings to me misery, joy, peace and then it tears me apart when I cannot know all of you. I need to know you love me, I want to know all there is of love and I want to know it with you my beautiful Simone'! You never seem to mind my selfishness when it came to making love to you, in the middle of the day, the afternoon, night, or early morning. You are an amazing woman, wife, mother, partner, friend, and lover. You care for Carmeli'ta', Marianna, me, our Church Family, even the workers on our farms. You are forever kind my beauty watching you astounds me. Your goodness spreads to everyone that is around you. I feel as if I am the most blessed man on earth. Your love and example is why I am a Christian today. You met our Minister at the Lafayette Street Church of Christ and became a Christian not long after we arrived in America and your faithful example bought me to the Lord, for this I am most thankful. Though Amelio' talked to me many times about Salvation, it never took, but watching you, I finally knew he was right, both he and Brother Meriwether. Thank you for that more than anything else. My world would look different without you in it. It was torture for me when I returned home without you. When speaking to Carmeli'ta' about your whereabouts, I could hardly contain my tears my heart ached so for you."

Simone' listened patiently, he held her hands, looked into his kind beautiful brown eyes, she reflected on all the scenes he spoke of like a picture show, scrolled across her mind replied, "Of all the life we have seen together my husband, where we have arrived today is more of a blessing than I can ever tell you. There are no words to describe how I feel about the life we have together. You have given me, the care, the concern, the love, and the understanding far above what any woman would expect."

She added, "You have shown me a glance into Paradise my sweet husband and lover. I want to let you know all those times you thought you were being selfish; I was thankful for your selfishness; I wanted and desired you as much as you needed me, but I did not want to ask because of the stress and anxiousness associated with the new life we started. I felt one more demand would be selfish, unnecessary, and additional pressure. I wanted you so my body ached for your touch each day. You are a handsome sexy man my darling and I love the way you make me feel, the way you move with tenderness and precision, exploring every part of me, when we make love."

"Our intimacy Simone' is what helped me most; you were there when I needed you and you were always so giving." He pulled her to him and slowly removed the black negligee untying the ribbon on the duster, removed the sleeves from her arms one at a time slow and meretriciously, and then her gown the same way, pulling it over her head while she held her arms in the air.

Seeing Simone' after 10 days, Roberto's mind went back to their Honeymoon the first night; that night, she turned his world upside down and drowned him with her beauty and womanliness. When he saw her body for the first time thought she was beautiful, but now her beauty had increased over the years to an elegance that was more than sensual. He pulled her to him and kissed her with slow, deep, long kisses until Simone's breath was completely gone. She felt her heart in her chest beat faster. The intensity he made her feel was like nothing she felt before. The sweetness of his kisses was like magic to her being, felt as if she dissolved into Roberto'. He faintly heard her say, "Roberto, Roberto' my darling husband." The passion and pure ecstasy he heard in her voice for a brief moment seemed he could not catch his breath felt hot; feverish kissed her more and more. Her body quivered under his touch, the silky softness of her skin as his hand glided over her body lit a fire in him that became a burning flame.

Her touch gave Roberto' a sensation he had not known before it was unfamiliar and intriguing as their needs and desires for each other grew to the intensity like the flames of a burning furnace. He whispered, "Simone your kisses are like music that enraptures my heart and mind. Your kisses bring beauty to my life as the glistening stars bring wonderment and glamour covering the Heavens above; your kisses cover my mind like the celestial blanket in the sky at night. "

Simone' replied with a low delicious moan of pleasure. The kisses became intoxicating until their lips and bodies seem to turn to liquid together. Tears flowed from Roberto's eyes he softly said, "You open the door to a passion paradise for me Simone', and its beauty adds *joie de vivre* and exuberance to my heart."

She did not speak, but moved to allow him to lie beside her. Sitting up, she turned and smiled, pushed the lock of hair back that was dancing on his forehead, the look in Roberto's eyes said what his mind was thinking of love. Surrendering himself to her touch murmured a little incoherently and fragmentally saying, "Love me, love me, your love makes me feel that we are on an island and there is only you, me, and love. My cup of love has been so empty since I left 10 days ago, fill it up again Simone' as only your love can, I want to fill full again, love me my darling wife."

Simone's love warm and inviting, Roberto' slipped into a daze as their bodies met in the passion and desire built over the 10 days they were apart like the steam does in a volcano, erupting in a hot and burning pleasure. Fear, like a thief, still found a small crack in her mind crowded its way through and hung in the air, at the same time she gave her body to him. His body slowly slipped into hers, he heard her gasp for breath, panting softly. She held onto Roberto' when his body moved closer to her deepest desire, he felt the tightness of her body as she gripped his putting him in a daze, she loved and gave herself to him, but not completely not yet...

Roberto' and Simone' loved each other, holding onto the moments they had together. Yet, he noticed still tensed, she did not allow him to reach her deepest need, held her and whispered, "Simone' you make me feel like a king when you love me the way you are now. The physical part of our love is more than wonderful my darling wife, I cannot tell you how warm and inviting your feel to me. When we come together, the warm flow of your love absorbs my entire being."

She softly said, "Thank you my sweet husband. What I feel for you and how you make me feel lifts me to the clouds and I never want to come down my darling. Your love is sweet to me. There is no dessert that I have ever tasted compares to how sweet your love is to me. It soothes me and bathes me in gentleness my husband. I love you Roberto', I love you with everything in me."

"I love you sweet Simone'. I want and need no other. You are part of my soul, the best part. More than the physical part of our relationship, which is wonderful, the emotional and psychological part is what and where I always want to be with you. Your expressions to me of how I make you feel and how much I satisfy your needs is much more important to me. A man being able to satisfy his wife as a lover makes him feel he could conquer the world. You do that for me Simone', you fulfill my emotional and psychological needs. A wife's love can either make or break that man. It is important to me you see me as a desirable man and lover to you. You have given me everything I need to feel like a man. I am jealous of anything I do not know about you Simone'. I love you that much and need to be completely one with you."

"I know my husband and we will. I have resolved to share everything with you, even though I have fears, our love and relationship is important to me. I want to conquer the fear surrounding it by telling you everything and allowing you to read my Diary my darling."

"Thank you Simone'."

He pulled her to him and kissed here deeply she felt as if her heart would jump out of her chest with the feelings of passion his lips gave her. It was three hours later, nearing lunchtime and the return of their family.

They decided to bathe and dress before the family returned. He said, "I am thankful for the foresight of your parents to leave us alone for a while so we could love each other without distractions."

They bathed, dressed, and went to the kitchen. Simone' set the table for lunch. Roberto' mentioned to her Catarina was bringing lunch from the Boulangerie' Viennoise. They walked into the garden to enjoy the crisp cool of the December day. Roberto' hugged her close to him, and then picked her up and sits in the garden chair with her in his lap, she snuggled close to him for his warmth. There was a still crispness in the December air announcing the arrival of winter in the Valley.

Roberto' held onto his wife firmly and yet so gently he knew within his heart that the time was coming for all cards to be lain on the table. He wondered within himself what the hold card Simone' would have to show when it was her time to lay her cards on the table. And then there was the situation with Carmeli'ta', she was not a child any longer, but a 23-year-old adult out on her own, but yet tied to her family fully by love, blood, dedication, faithfulness, and respect. He could not allow her to continue with the actions that she displayed over the past month with the situation with her mother not being where she could put hands on her, as she has been able to all her life.

Parents have a right to act without informing their children, especially if they are an adult or even if they are still a child in their home. She put herself in danger as well as violated a principle taught as she grew, "respect", for your parents. He knew that though it was not her intentions, she violated that principle without thinking it through as a danger to herself and unnecessary stress and worry for her parents and grandparents. She did not stop to consider everyone involved. He had never lied to his daughter, so she should have taken his word no matter what she thought. He would deal with the question of respect and authority in her life now before she was married and created the same situation with her husband. The path she was on just could not be the one she needed to take. She owed her father and future husband a certain amount of respect. Therefore, he would deal with it from that angle, the basis of respect and truth. Time was nearing for her to return with her grandfather. He said, "Simone'."

Laying so comfortable against him listening to his heartbeat and thinking of the morning and the love and passion that passed between Roberto' and her thoughts were floating on a path alone in a sea of quiet, serene satisfaction was mentally bought back to reality by him calling her name replied, "Yes my husband are my parents here yet?"

"No not yet my beauty. I want to discuss with you what we are to say to Carmeli'ta' about her actions and lack of respect and trust. We need to approach her in the manner of one adult to another so much so because she is not a child any longer."

"I understand, and you are right my husband, we must remember that when we are talking to our daughter. Though you still holding to our traditions here, she will not understand all that you tell her because we did not raise her in this country with the traditions that we had in our lives. Though they are beautiful Roberto', it is twenty-four years later and we live in America. I say this more so for Carmeli'ta than for us. We need to find a balance when we are speaking with her about the decisions she made and the way she made them in an unorthodox and chaotic manner contrary to her teachings. We need to think for a few minutes about the direction of the conversation."

"You are right. Let's walk and think about it for a few minutes we still have almost an hour before the family returns." Roberto' and Simone' walked arm and arm thinking of the situation with Carmeli'ta'. They walked toward the Bandaci Farm a few miles away, exchanging thoughts and views of the approach needed to address the two issues before them.

Earlier that morning, Franco and Carmeli'ta' visited the farm and he introduced her to his Office Manager, Produce Manager, and his workers. They were mystified with her looks; she was so much like Catarina, her grandmother, beautiful, just a younger version. The freshness of her beauty astounded them as they observed her smile, the glowing lusciousness of her hair in a ponytail hanging down her back, her misty, compelling, and robust eyes framed by long black eyelashes fluttered like a beautiful butterfly in flight when she spoke and the sweetness of her overall personality. Later that morning around 10:00 a.m., Franco and Carmeli'ta' took a tour of the breathtaking Wine Country from the hillside overlooking the *Val de Greve River.*

Carmeli'ta' excitingly said, "Grandfather the vineyards hang in a manner that brings to mind the historical account of the Hanging Gardens of Babylon in history, one of the Seven Wonders of the World."

"Franco smiled and held onto her arm while standing near the cliff above the river replied, "Yes my sweet granddaughter that is my very thought each time I visit this site. This is your father and mother's favorite place to come during the time they were courting and now. It is beautiful indeed."

"I would not mind living here Grandfather. I do so enjoy beauty."

"Yes, you are so much like your mother Carmeli'ta' she enjoys beauty also. Come let us go I want you to see the Marketplace before we return home for lunch."

"Yes please I want to see everything. I love it. Grandfather, may I ask

your opinion of something?"

"Of course, you can ask me anything Carmeli'ta'." Franco drove slowly so she could see the beauty of the valley waited for her to continue. Hesitating for a few seconds she asked, "What do you think my mother and father will say about my coming to Italy and misleading them and not listening to my father when he assured me that mother was okay and he knew where she was?"

"I think that your father and mother has reason to be upset with you Carmeli'ta' more because you put yourself in danger and used a name that you are not known by. Do you have any idea what could have happened to you had your mother not known you the way she does? Your life could have been lost, been injured permanently, kidnapped, or assaulted even worse than you were. You cannot conduct yourself in such as manner; simply my sweet granddaughter your actions had a long arm of consequences from Charleston to Tuscany. What is your own opinion?"

"I realize now grandfather that I did not think it through and should have listened to my father when he told me my mother was safe and he knew where she was. I was so worried she was ill and he would not tell me or something worse."

"Carmeli'ta' your father would never harm your mother and moreover, he has never lied to you about anything has he? Do you realize he loves her? He would give his life for your mother's and yours! The same as I would do for your grandmother, my Simone' and you. That is just a man's attitude that loves his family nothing is too good for them in his eyes even death."

"Thank you for sharing your thoughts with me. I will have to face mother and father with what I have done to cause my family upset and anxiety as well as Jason. He did not want me to come by myself."

"Tell me of Jason. Do you love him Carmeli'ta'?"

"Yes, I love him with my entire heart grandfather. He is a wonderful Christian Man and so good to everyone around him and me. Mother likes him."

"And your father, how does he feel about Jason?"

"He wants me to marry Alberto Gambani. I do not love him, not that way grandfather only as a friend and nothing more. However, father said he did not want me to be hurt so he felt he had to choose for me. I know that is the tradition here; except, they raised me to choose for myself Grandfather. I do not know or understand this custom. Then again, I know how my heart feels. Do you believe that we can use the same customs in America they live by here?"

"Carmeli'ta' that is a hard question to answer. I am sure Jason is a wonderful man. Your mother says he is and she is astute in reading people even as a child. As far as the customs of one country opposed to the other, I understand both points yours and your fathers and to that, I will beg off from giving my opinion. Roberto' is your father and that will need to be discussed with your parents adding a third opinion to it will serve no purpose at this time."

Franco drove to the marketplace, parking the truck decided to walk with her through the marketplace asked, "Do you feel well enough to walk granddaughter?" Carmeli'ta' delighted at the colors and activity at the Market answered, "Oh yes let do walk." The beauty of the flowers glowed with red, yellow, brownish orange, and blues like the colors of the rainbow. The citizens of the valley looked like pictures painted by artists with the different array of outfits with colors that blended with the surroundings and the flowers that sit everywhere in the marketplace.

Violin Music hung thick in the air and some of the people danced in the street. She saw happy children smiling, running, and playing among the merchants. Scents of spices seem to resonate from everywhere and skate along the street. The faces of the men were handsome and the women were beautiful reminded her of her mother and grandmother; good looks seem to be the norm in this little valley. Her heart raced with excitement at what she experienced. She continued to comment, "We have nothing like this in Charleston grandfather."

"You are right my sweet little one. Nonetheless, your town is quaint and beautiful also. Each town has its own beauty Carmeli'ta' remember beauty is in the eye of the beholder." After an hour of touring the marketplace Franco said, "I think you have walked enough for one day with the head injury you have. Let us go it is nearing lunchtime and your father and mother will be waiting for you I am sure."

"I am ready. I do feel a little tired. Maybe I am not as strong as I thought." Franco held her hand and they walked slowly back through the marketplace to his truck, getting in Carmeli'ta' expressed, "I understand what you meant about mother and father being upset and me not thinking before I acted. Thank you for talking with me grandfather." Nearing the Boulangerie' Veinnoise Carmeli'ta' saw Catarina car said, "Look Grandfather isn't that grandmother's 1925 Chrysler? And there is Grandmother going into a Boulangerie' Veinnoise, is that how you pronounce it? What is it my Grandfather?"

"There is my lovely wife and that is her car and yes, Boulangerie Viennoise is the correct pronunciation. It is a bakery and deli. She is picking up lunch for us. We should hurry home and be there when she arrives. I know that your father is anxious to see you. Are you ready to face your parents after lunch Carmeli'ta'?"

She smiled and said, "I don't have a choice grandfather." The ride back from the village took them by the Moretti Vineyard and Mansion one of the most stunning sites in the valley, the vineyards stood as soldiers on duty so strong, silent, and straight; the Moretti Mansion had the appearance of the Chatsworth House in England when she saw it exclaimed, "Oh my, what a beautiful vineyard and mansion. Do you know the owners grandfather?"

Anger rose in Franco remembering his and Vincenzo's conversation about her parentage replied, "Yes, they are the largest wine makers in the valley."

On their climb up the long hill to the top from the valley, Carmeli'ta' saw its beauty the way it curved and twisted in their ascent to the top. The hillside graced with the loveliness of Flora and Fauna; nature's beautiful fall flowers still in bloom, lent color to the landscape of the hillside. The patterns the flowers made looked as if they created a map of beauty in the natural surroundings of the hillside. The hill was not very steep the curving of the road made it dangerous to drive if you were not familiar with it.

Franco and Carmeli'ta' arrived home at 12:30 p.m. just as Roberto' and Simone' were returning from their walk. Franco parked his truck, opened the door took her hand, she stepped out saw her father standing and smiling looking at her; ran through the garden into his waiting arms said with a softness in her voice, "Hello my Father, I am so happy to see you. I love you my Father."

"I am happy to see you too my sweet Daughter and know that you are safe. I love you." He hugged her tight and kissed her on the forehead moved back a little to see the small gash on her head, hugged her again say, "I am thankful to God that you are safe and not injured badly Carmeli'ta'."

"Thank you Father I am thankful I was not injured any worse. I feel a little lightheaded, maybe I should have not run." Roberto' and Simone' put their arms around her waist to support her. She stood between her mother and father with her arms around their waist added, "It is good to be back together again. I have missed us being together. It seems like it has an eternity."

Franco stood watching them waiting for Catarina to arrive to carry the lunch items inside, smiled and waved when they looked his way and said, "Hello Roberto' my son. I will be there in a minute I am waiting for my Catarina. We saw her in the village picking up lunch she should be here in a few minutes."

Roberto' waved and called, "Hello Franco, I will come and help you carry the lunch inside."

At that time Catarina drove into the driveway, parked the car, Roberto' opened the door for her. She exited the car, in her excitement to have her family together again, left the key in the switch. Franco began taking the lunch off the seat and did not notice the key in the switch. Simone' and Carmeli'ta' went in to get the ice-chilled glasses from the refrigerator for the tea and placed them on the table. Simone' noticed Carmeli'ta' had a strange expression on her face and asked, "Are you okay my little one? Did you enjoy yourself? Are you still feeling a little lightheaded?"

"Yes mother I am okay. I do not feel lightheaded right now just a little tired. Oh yes, I enjoyed myself so much. I love this valley. It has beauty like none I have ever seen. The people are as beautiful as the valley mother." Looking out into the garden asked, "I am in trouble with father and you, am I not? My father is especially not pleased with me and my actions over the past ten days is he?"

"Let us enjoy lunch and being together Carmeli'ta' your father and I are happy to see you, so let's enjoy it for now and we will talk later, maybe after you rest for a while. You had a long morning; it is good that you enjoyed yourself."

"Thank you mother, I am happy to see him also. I love you both so much. Yes, I did enjoy especially being with my grandfather. He reminds me of you mother. You look like grandmother, but you act like grandfather. Mother, Grandfather is such a wonderful person and he is so wise and kind."

"Yes he is a wise and kind man, the best father in the world, like your father Carmeli'ta'. And we love you never forget that my little one."

Catarina washed her hands in the hall bath and joined them in the kitchen began unwrapping the food items for lunch.

"Mother I need to call Jason before I eat. He should be at the office by now. I need to check-in with Jason and ask him about Ms. Horne to see how things are progressing in my absence. Will you please excuse me and let everyone know I will not be long?"

"Yes of course. It is only right you check in with your office because of your position."

Catarina did not comment looked at Simone' and Carmeli'ta and smiling, continued to work at getting lunch on the table in a timely manner since it was past lunchtime. She knew Franco and Roberto' both must be starved by this time, especially her Franco.

Franco and Roberto' went to freshen up while Catarina and Simone' unpacked lunch. Roberto' said, "I like Catarina's car Franco it is a 1925 Chrysler isn't it? The tan and black color with light color interior and seats gives it the look of a car whose owner is female."

"Yes, it is my son and yes it does. I did not want to order a dark color for her. I ordered it and it arrived 2 months ago. It is large, in comparison to the other car I bought her. It takes a bit of getting use to the way it drives, especially the first time. My Catarina had a bit of a time getting use to the way it handled on the road, especially around the curves going to the valley below, but now she has driving it down to a science."

Catarina and Simone' put the delicious looking lunch on the table, Panini with Salami, Mortadella, Tomatoes and Lettuce with Formaggi e frutta (Italian Cheese and Fresh Seasonal Fruit) and placed it on the table with the iced tea in chilled glasses with ice.

Carmeli'ta' went quickly to make her call to Jason. It was 7:00 a.m. in Charleston on Saturday morning, though the plant was closed, she knew he would be at his desk and waiting for her to call him. She gave the operator the number to Madison Steel, and while waiting for the call to go through she saw her father and grandfather walk back out in the garden from the kitchen. She knew they were waiting for her to return to the kitchen. The call finally through Jason pacing anxiously to hear from Carmeli'ta' when the phone rang ran over to the desk, picked up the receiver, and said, "Jason Madison." The voice on the other end was what he waited and prayed for with a sigh of relief heard, "Jason darling, how are you today?" He breathed and said, "Carmeli'ta' my beautiful Carmeli'ta' how are you feeling today darling? I miss you so much and am beside myself with worry and aggravation over your being away from me and then being assaulted."

"Jason, darling I am fine. I had a little dizziness this morning and feel a little tired but otherwise I am fine. I wanted to check in with you. How are things going? How is Mrs. Horne getting through the list of duties did she have questions after I left last week?"

"She is fine Carmeli'ta' to your credit you trained her well. She is working with the Quality Control it is a little tricky but I will help her with it when necessary and so can the plant manager. You take care of yourself I will oversee what needs to be done here. My father can always come in if I need him. In fact, he is coming next week. I plan to join you on Wednesday. I am leaving on Tuesday morning if I can get a flight if not that evening."

Carmeli'ta' excitement growing said, "Oh my darling, that is wonderful it will be so good to see you. You will love this Valley it is breathtaking. I will be happy to see you my darling. I will let mother and father know you are coming. Maybe you can talk to father while you are here."

"Yes, I planned to do that Carmeli'ta'. I love you my lovely one."

"I love you Jason with all my heart and miss you terribly. My family is waiting to eat lunch. I will call you after Church tomorrow my darling."

"After Church tomorrow, I will have lunch and then home. I will be waiting my darling. Please take care of yourself for me until I arrive. Bye for now."

"I will Jason, you take care also. I love you never forget. Bye."

Carmeli'ta' hung up and returned to the kitchen. When Franco and her father saw she had returned they came in from walking and enjoying the crispness of the afternoon air and beauty of the day. Franco blessed the food. Everyone sit and enjoyed the lunch smiling, laughing, delighted they were together as a family.

Roberto' looked at Simone' smiled and said, "I promised Amelio' I would let him know that I arrived safely and our sweet daughter is okay. I will call him after lunch."

Carmeli'ta' remembered Jason told her he had his Finance Manager transfer her salary to her account each week until she return said, "Father before you go to talk with Uncle Amelio' let him know that my salary is being transferred into my account each week."

"Thank you daughter, that will make it easier for Amelio' to handle. I will let him know." He looked at Simone' and said, "I will not be long my beauty."

"Yes my sweet husband he will be worried if we do not call. Carmeli'ta' needs to rest for a while she had a long day. I will help mother with dinner while she rest."

"That is okay my beauty. I will talk with Franco after my call to America."

Tension rises....

CHAPTER
FORTY-FOUR

After lunch, Roberto' took permission from Franco to make a call to America. Franco chatted with Catarina and Simone' for a few minutes before he went into the garden and sit waiting for Roberto' to finish his conversation with Amelio'.

Roberto', while waiting for the operator to put his call through to Charleston, looked at his watch, Amelio' would be at his office it was 8:00 a.m. Amelio' sitting at his desk enjoying the quiet of the morning realized the phone was ringing, answered, "Bandaci Farms, Amelio' Bandaci."

"Hello, my cousin, how are you today?"

"Hello Roberto' I was expecting your call. How was your trip" How are Simone' and Carmeli'ta'? Both are well I hope."

"Yes my cousin everyone is fine. Carmeli'ta' is recovering from the assault; she is resting now but getting better. The scar does not look too bad, just red. The stitches she has will come out in another 4-5 days and Simone' is beautiful as always. Did you get a chance to mention my visit to Tuscany to Brother Meriwether?"

"Yes, he understands and sends his well-wishes and asks me to let you know his prayers are with you my cousin. It is good to know that everything is well with your family. That was my constant prayer for you."

"How are you doing Amelio'?"

"I am fine Roberto'. I am taking care of everything as usual, which is not hard to do. I have efficient help with your and my managers taking most of the responsibilities. I concentrate on collecting the accounts, making the weekly deposits, and keeping up with the weekly transfers and deposits into our Swiss

Accounts. I checked on Marianna today; she is doing well as always. She takes excellent care of your home. She is only away from your home when she goes to Church Service on Wednesday and Sunday or to the market."

"How is Bibi' Ana have you heard from her?"

"Bibi' Ana is doing fine my cousin. I talked with her last night for a long time. She is nearing the end of the sale on her home in Rome. The papers will be ready for signing in 3 days my cousin and she will be on her way to America and to me. I hope that you will be able to return by that time. I am anxious for our families to get to know each other."

"I am looking forward to seeing Bibi' Ana after all these years and welcoming her to our family. I am happy you got the chance to be with the love of your life. Only God can answer prayers. Please let me know if there are any problems with my farm or the deposit collections Amelio'. Thank you again for helping me and my family."

"You are welcome Roberto' anytime. We are here for each other Roberto'. I appreciate all that you do for me as well more than you realize. Tell Simone' and Carmeli'ta' I said I send my love. Say hi to Franco and Catarina for me."

"Thank you Amelio'. I will tell Franco and Catarina hello for you. I will give Simone' and Carmeli'ta' your love and you know we all love you. I will call you after Church tomorrow if I get the opportunity, if not then Monday. Amelio' one more item, Carmeli'ta's salary is being transferred into her account each week until she returns."

"Thank you for giving me the information about her salary. I will take care of the transfers on schedule. Bye for now."

Roberto' hang up from speaking with Amelio' walked back to the kitchen to where Simone' and her mother was preparing the vegetables for Soup, and the dough for bread for dinner later. Simone' smiled at her husband when he walked back into kitchen and said, "How is Amelio' and everything at home my husband?"

"He is fine my beauty and everything is going well as always. He said Bibi' Ana will be there in three days she is almost through with the sale of her home in Rome. He is excited, I could tell by the tone in his voice." "That is wonderful my husband it will be good to see Bibi' Ana after twenty-five years. I am happy for Amelio' he deserves to find happiness in his life. He has worked hard and helped guide our lives as well to the success we enjoy now my sweet husband."

"I am glad that you realize that my beauty. My cousin is precious to me and I want all the best for him. I could not have asked for a closer or better friend and father figure than he has been to me all of my life. Combined with, helping raise our daughter as if she were his."

Simone' rinsed and dried her hands and walked over to her husband and put her arms around his waist, looked up at him pushing the black lock of hair that danced on his forehead back from his face. He leaned forward, kissed her, and whispered, "I love you. The love you gave me this morning is so fresh on my mind my love, thank you for sharing the warmth with me from your heart my beauty."

Simone' smiled and whispered back, "You are a wonderful lover Roberto'. I never tire of being near you and you loving me. I need you so much my darling husband. I don't ever want to know what it is to live without you."

"You will never have to know what it is to live without me in your life Simone'. I love you and need you. I cannot wait until tonight my darling when we are alone again so I can be near you, hold you and you love me again. I will join Franco now as I promised. When Catarina and you have finished the preparations join me in the garden for a while before dinner if time permits."

"Yes, I will my darling."

Roberto' and Simone' so involved in a romantic moment did not notice Catarina had walked into the garden to join Franco to give them privacy said as he reached for her to sit next to him, "I did not want to disturb the beautiful moment between our children. They are so much in love my Franco. It reminds me of us when we were their age."

Franco smiled and said, "When we were their age my lovely Catarina. I still feel the same way about you now as I did then my darling more so because time and maturity has bought with it new excitement, passion, and a higher level of love between us. You are as beautiful and as desirable to me as you always were. I feel a love from you that completes me in every way.

The best decision I ever made was marrying you. I have never regretted it one day, even when times were hard for us in the early years of the farm. You were always there for me, a man needs that from his wife my lovely, to know she is there and supporting him. Her support makes him strong and he feels as if he can move a mountain. The love of a good woman is a blessing my beautiful wife."

"You are a wonderful husband Franco. I love you and I have never regretted one day that I married you. You are my best friend, my companion, my strong rock to lean upon when storms in life come. Thank you for the wonderful compliments my husband; you make me feel wonderful. I love you and I always will. Yes, I still feel all the passion for you as I have since the first day I married you forty-two years ago my sweet husband. I have a beautiful, easy life. I would not exchange what we have for anything. Every woman should be blessed enough to have the sweet and loving husband you are to me." Franco pulled her close and held her tight; they sat and looked at the garden enjoying the beauty of it, the afternoon, and watching Roberto' and Simone' through the French Doors in the kitchen.

Roberto' and Simone' realizing they were alone in the kitchen, sit at the kitchen table to discuss when they would talk to Carmeli'ta'. Simone' said, "My husband, I would rather wait until Monday to talk with Carmeli'ta' or at least until after Church tomorrow. She still seems a little fragile to me. I want her to be stronger when we talk with her."

"You are probably right my beauty; she is still weak and not feeling quite up to a long conversation. We can wait until Sunday or Monday. Let's see how she feels when we return from Church tomorrow." He reached for her hand, looked into her eyes continued, "I can't wait until tonight my beauty when we are alone. I need you so much."

"I know my husband; I feel the same way. I want to get dinner ready so, we can eat on time. Are you joining father?"

"Yes, I am. I want to keep my word." Roberto' kissed Simone' on her forehead and walked into the garden and over to where Catarina and Franco sit smiling as he approached. Catarina said, "You are a good husband and father Roberto' thank you for caring for our precious Simone' and Carmeli'ta'."

"I love my wife and daughter they are my world. Simone' is my life. She is every breath I take."

Catarina excused herself, went to the kitchen, and helped Simone' in the final preparations of dinner; Roberto' and Franco talked for a while about the improvements made in the Valley, the modernization of the Campo di Marte' Airport, the slow, but finally positive change in the cultural horizons that existed for so long, and the Bandaci Farms. The conversations flowed smoothly with the ebbs and flows of the modern times that were coming into their once structured lives. It was getting late in the evening.

Simone' and Catarina finished the vegetable soup, bread, salad with oil and vinegar, Iced Tea and Schiacciata Florentine, a popular winter dessert for later with coffee. The table was set for the dinner. Realizing their wives would not get to join them in the garden before dinner, Roberto' and Franco walked up the path leading to the entrance to the kitchen smelled the delicious aroma of the meal hovering drifted through their nostrils and into their taste buds. Simone' went to check on Carmeli'ta' and let her know dinner was ready, opened the door and saw she was still sleeping peacefully, walked quietly over to the bed, and looked at her, touched her on the right shoulder, "Carmeli'ta' my little one." She opened her eyes and asked, "Mother, Is dinner ready? I feel a little hungry. What time is it?"

"Yes, dinner is ready Carmeli'ta' it is 6:40 p.m. you slept for 5 hours my little one. How are you feeling? Freshen-up and come join us. I will wait for you my daughter."

Carmeli'ta' smiled and replied, "Thank you mother, I feel okay just still a little tired. I don't seem to be able to shake the tiredness." Continuing she added, "I am so glad to see you and have you near me again. I missed you so when you were gone. I felt lost without my mother being near me. I love you so much. I will freshen-up. It will only take me a minute."

Simone' smiled at her and did not comment, but sit in the winged-back chair near the window that looked out on the Moretti Vineyard and Winery. She thought as she waited, 'It is so massive and takes up so much of this part of the valley. I wish that my decisions had been different or I had been mature enough at that time to make a different decision."

Lost in thought, did not notice Carmeli'ta' standing near her. She touched her mother on the shoulder asking, "Mother are you okay, I called you and you did not hear me? What is taking you so far away you seem to be worried; I noticed the same look on your face when I arrived yesterday you seemed so distracted."

"I am fine Carmeli'ta'. I was just reflecting on my childhood, growing up, and making wise choices. How are you feeling now since you moved around, still a little tired?"

She said, "I feel a little better, but not great. Maybe I lay down too long", then added, "Mother you can talk to me about what is bothering you. I will understand."

Simone' rose, smiled, hugged her, and replied, "I am fine my little one. It is good to reflect on life, past and present; it helps keep us balanced and reminded of whom we are, and where we got our roots. Our family is waiting for us to join them. I am sure your father wants to see you. He loves you so much Carmeli'ta', we both do and want the best for you."

"I know Mother, I love you and father. I cannot imagine anyone else being my parents you both are so wonderful always have been to me. I have the best father in the world. I am just sorry that I upset him and made both of you worry."

"We will talk about that one day soon Carmeli'ta'. However, I am sure, by this time, your grandfather and father are hungry; it is 7:00 p.m. Let us join them."

They walked down the hallway to the kitchen and their waiting family.

Roberto' stood by the French Doors looking out into the garden thinking of what he would say to his daughter about her actions over the last few weeks. He knew that letting it pass and not addressing the issue would be a problems later. Hearing Simone' and Carmeli'ta' chatting as they approached the kitchen, turned, and smiled. Simone' walked over to where he stood, smiled, and asked, "Are you ready for dinner my husband. Our sweet little daughter is rather hungry, but still tired. Let us eat so she can retire for the night as soon as she can." "I am ready my beauty."

Roberto' walked over to where Carmeli'ta' stood watching he and her mother asked, "How are you my precious daughter? Mother says you are still tired. We will finish dinner and you can rest my daughter. I want you to recover as soon as you can."

Carmeli'ta' hugged him and replied, "Thank you father. I am happy to see you and mother together again. I am glad to be here with all of you. I feel very blessed to have such wonderful parents and grandparents that care so much about me. I love you all."

Roberto' held her close to him closed his eyes for a second and thanked God for the safety and health of his daughter finally commented, "I am thankful that you are okay Carmeli'ta'. I only have one child and could not bear to lose you for any reason."

He kissed her on the forehead and said, "Let's eat we are all hungry and you need to get to sleep again as soon as possible."

They chatted and laughed while enjoying their dinner. Even though Carmeli'ta' enjoyed the dinner she did not eat much she felt tired and sleepy. Roberto' noticed that she was not up to par worried that her head injury might be more severe than first thought.

Franco observed Roberto' watching Carmeli'ta' said, "Do we need to visit the hospital and let the doctor check out our sweet little one?"

"No grandfather, I think I am just tired from the long trip and then getting a head injury just compounded the matter. I will see how I feel tomorrow; if I do not feel better then I will go. Dr. Thimmons said I should give it time. I think I will prepare for bed after my food digest a little father and grandfather. We have church tomorrow I don't want to miss attending Lord's Day Service with my family."

Simone' listening to the exchange of conversation said, "I think she needs rest. She also had a long day and with all the excitement she had and the sights she saw are adding to her tiredness I am sure. I will get her in bed in a while and see how she feels tomorrow morning."

Finishing dinner, Simone' and Catarina cleared the table, put up the food, washed the dishes and set the plates for dessert while the coffee was making.

Roberto' sat chatting with Carmeli'ta' waiting for dessert. Schiacciata Florentine was one of his favorite desserts especially this time of year. He seldom had it in Charleston. It was approaching 9:00 p.m. when they finished their dessert and coffee, Simone' helped Carmeli'ta' prepare for bed tucked her in, kissed her on the cheeks and said, "I will see you in the morning my little one. Good night." Carmeli'ta' commented, "Mother I had not gotten a chance to tell you and Father Jason will be coming on Wednesday. He is leaving Charleston on Tuesday. Do you think grandfather would mind him staying in his guest house?"

Simone' smiled and said, "You will need to let your father and your grandparents know my little one. I am happy to know that he cares that much that he would leave his empire and come to see about you my daughter that will be good for both of you in the end. I am sure your grandfather will not mind Jason staying in the guest house."

"Thank you mother for supporting me, I love you. Goodnight. I will be ready to attend service in the morning."

"Good night Carmeli'ta' pleasant dreams." Catarina and Franco left for their evening walk before the darkness set-in.

Simone' turned off the bedside lamp, closed the door and walked back to where Roberto' was waiting for her at the kitchen table. He smiled when he saw her walking back toward him, asked, "Is Carmeli'ta' okay, my beauty? She seems so tired to me. I hope there are no serious problems with her head injury."

"I don't think so my husband. I think that she just had too much activity too fast. She still has the stiches. She probably needs to slow down a little and not try to see the entire valley in one day as she did today. By-the way Roberto', Carmeli'ta' has something she wants to tell you tomorrow. I thought I would mention it; but rather she talk to you about it."

"I will wait for her to talk to me about whatever it is. Concerning her injury, you may be right my beauty as always you know our daughter well. I am thankful for you in my life Simone'. How could I go forward without you? I never want to know what that would be like. I know how my mother felt after she lost my father; she did not last 6 months. She loved him with all her heart and soul. I do need you so much my beauty."

"Thank you Roberto' my sweet husband. I do love you my darling. This is the first time in twenty-five years that you have mentioned the loss of your mother after your father's death. Thank you for sharing something that is so painful for you to talk about Roberto'. I liked both of your parents the few times I saw them at the market as I grew up. It was strange I never saw you my husband. I am ready to go to our bedroom my darling. Mother and father will be a while I am sure. It is getting late my love."

He commented, "It hurt so much when I lost both my parents 6-month apart Simone'. It was many years before I could bear to think about it. I am glad that I had my cousin Amelio' in my life as a father figure and friend. Then I met you my beauty. I knew I had found someone who I could love and hold dear to my heart. I do love you with all my being Simone'. You give me what every man needs from a woman my darling, true love. I just want to know all of your love my darling."

She stood, held her left hand out to him, invited him to start their night of intimacy; he took her hand, stood, pulled her to him kissing her passionately, picked her up and walked down the hall to their bedroom suite. Simone' snuggled under his neck and whispered, "Thank you for the lovely compliment my husband. I want you to love me my darling. I need to feel your closeness. I have missed you so much in the last few weeks we were apart."

Roberto's thoughts went to earlier that morning after his arrival and the love and intimacy they shared for the hours while they were alone. His desire to be with Simone' flooded his mind and body consuming his thoughts shut out everything else. He opened the door to their bedroom, let Simone' slide gently to the floor, and lock the bedroom door. Simone' turned for him to unzip her dress; he gently moved the silky beautiful lock of hair aside and leisurely slid the zipper down enjoying the beauty of her hair and skin when she slipped out of the dress. She walked to the closet hung her dress and put on her dressing gown. Roberto' met her halfway the room as she walked back toward him and took her in his arms. The fresh inviting scent of her cologne encircled them, he held her tight; he never wanted to let her go, kissed her with the same depth of passion she felt earlier in the morning. Gradually letting her go, held her face in his hands said, "I will draw our bath my beauty so we can enjoy the warmth of the water together."

While preparing to take their bath, they heard voices, knew that Franco and Catarina had returned from their evening walk. They were laughing and talking as they walk to their bedroom down the hall from Simone's Suite.

"You are so sweet and romantic Roberto' which makes me love you all the more my darling husband. You are an exciting lover."

Roberto' kissed her again and did not comment. He went in and drew their bath while she pinned her hair up. She went into the bathroom took off her dressing gown, stepped into the warm lavender bath of bubbles, and waited for him to join her.

He undressed and stepped into the tub, sitting opposite her smiled and massaged her legs and said, "You are lovely in every way my beauty, not just your body; but also, your mind, your heart, your words, and your palatable personality. I am thankful that you are mine my darling all mine."

Simone' did not comment just smiled, leaned forward, and massaged his legs noticed how muscular he was, his chest, his stomach, his thighs, and his legs said, "Hmmmm, my husband, I love us taking a bath together being near each other, it feels so good. Being with you soothes my heart and my mind darling and lets me know how much you do love me."

"I do love you Simone' there are no words that can describe what I feel for you and how you make me feel my darling. It feels like the sunrise on the horizon in early morning, the beauty of it is incomparable, it is like seeing a bouquet of Red Roses fresh and alive with the petals so delicate you want to cherish them as long as possible and continue to water them until the last petal is gone. "I love you is never enough but is as close to perfect as any human being can say to describe their feeling for their mate. I fall in love with you more and more each day Simone'. Your personality, your feminine qualities fills my mind with pleasure. The fragrance of your love is in the mysterious fluidity of your gorgeous eyes my beauty. Your love, like a swaddling band, binds me and wraps me in rapture and excitement. How can words ever describe how I feel about you? Love is such a mystery in-and-of itself Simone' and it takes a different shape and form for everyone that experiences it; especially the love between a man and woman or a husband and wife."

Simone' listening intently replied. "Let us finish our baths my husband and love each other. You are right words cannot express what I feel and how much I want and need you."

Roberto' smiled, finish bathing, kneeled up, and tenderly washed her back and neck. He stepped out of the tub put on his terry bathrobe and held the matching terry robe, she stepped into it, and snuggled dry. Then lotion her body, brushed her teeth and gargled to freshen her mouth, brushed her hair, splashed on Chanel 5, put on her dressing gown, and went into Roberto' waiting anxiously in the bedroom for her to come to him for a beautiful night of passion. They fulfilled each other's desires and needs until they were both exhausted, drifting into a blissful sleep Roberto' commented, "Your love tonight takes me back to our wedding night my beauty. You are so sweet and loving. You are the embodiment of elegance and ecstasy Simone'." He held her close and they slept wrapped in each other's love.

Morning approached quickly.

CHAPTER
FORTY-FIVE

Carmeli'ta' lying awake for a long time, looked at the clock on the nightstand it was 5:00 a.m. She knew that everyone was still asleep. Jason and their relationship danced in her mind and his coming to Tuscany wondered how she could tell her father that he was coming to Tuscany.

In the Master Suite, the alarm sounded at 6:00 a.m. as it did each day signaling Franco and Catarina a new day has arrived. As was their custom, they bathed and dressed. Catarina put on a duster over her suit. They went to the kitchen for their morning coffee, talk, and prayers.

It seemed to Carmeli'ta' an eternity has passed; she checked the time again it was 6:45 a.m. still early heard her grandparents talking, decided to join them after she bathed and dressed for Church. Roberto' and Simone' were still sleeping snuggled together, did not hear the movement in the kitchen. Carmeli'ta' made her bed, slipped on her bedroom slippers, brushed her hair, and went to the kitchen. Franco heard her light quick footsteps turned and looked down the hall. When he saw her coming said, "My lovely wife here is our sweet granddaughter awake and dress for Church Service. How are you feeling granddaughter? Are you stronger today?"

She walked over to the table kissed him and then over to the sink, kissed her grandmother and said, "Good Morning my sweet Grandparents. I am fine. I feel much better this morning. I am still a little tired and my head is stinging where the stiches are, but I am fine otherwise."

Catarina replied, "That is good to hear Carmeli'ta' we grew more than concerned about you yesterday. I am glad to see you begin to improve. I will pour you a cup of coffee if you want to join your grandfather at the table."

She walked to the kitchen table and sit opposite her grandfather so she could see both of her grandparents while they talked replied, "I would love to join my sweet grandfather and you grandmother for coffee. Mother and father are still sleeping I am sure."

Franco commented, "Yes, I am sure they are Carmeli'ta'. They will be awake by 7:30 a.m. It is just 7:00 a.m. We will wait breakfast for them. Your grandmother and I spend this time together having our morning coffee, talking, and in prayer. We are happy that you joined us. I like your Winter White Coco Chanel Suite and blue paisley blouse. Your outfit is in good taste; it looks classy granddaughter. You are so much like your mother and grandmother."

"Thank you Grandfather that makes me feel good. You are aware of fashion?"

"Yes, I am my sweet Granddaughter. Your grandmother has a Winter White Coco Chanel Suite."

Catarina sat with her coffee next to her husband smiled and nodded in agreement with her husband. They held hands while Franco said prayers of thanksgiving for blessings for their family and petitions to God for the sick and other needs of the people the world over.

Carmeli'ta' looked at her grandfather smiling and asked, "Grandfather would you mind if Jason stayed in your and grandmother's guesthouse? He is coming to Tuscany on Wednesday."

Franco quiet for a moment looked at Catarina, then back at Carmeli'ta' and asked, "Do your father know he is coming here my Granddaughter?"

"Not yet Grandfather. I did not get a chance to tell my father. My mother knows. I told her last night after I talked with Jason. She said I need to tell father, but before I spoke with him, wanted to know how you and grandmother felt about him staying in the guesthouse."

"I don't foresee any problem with him staying in the guesthouse or even in the house Carmeli'ta'. We have a guest bedroom up front near my office that gives our guest privacy as well as the family. So, let's plan for him to stay in the house and he is as welcome here as you are my Granddaughter."

Catarina added, "Definitely he can stay here with us Carmeli'ta' it will be a pleasure to meet him and get to know the man that our granddaughter is in love with. I know he loves you or he would not bother to make a trip here."

"Grandfather, I did not know there is another suite in your home. I did not notice. I would love to see it sometimes. You have so many bedrooms. There are three on the hallway and then mine. Five, grandfather, is a lot of rooms, plus the guest house."

"Yes, my Granddaughter, we planned it so for times like this when we have a lot of guests. We do not want to be on top of each other, but comfortable so we can move around. Each one has a private bath except the one on the hall. It is smaller; the bath is next to it on the hallway. The guest suite beyond my office is a littler larger than the one you are in. It is comfortable and your grandmother has it well-decorated for a man or woman to feel comfortable and at home."

"Thank you both. I love you." They both smiled a 'you are welcome' smile to her.

Roberto' heard voices as he lay between sleep and awake turned looked at the bedside clock it was 7:10 a.m. time to prepare for breakfast and then leave at 9:20 a.m. for Bible Study and Morning Worship Service. He turned looked at Simone' still sleeping leaned over kissed her, took her in his arms and held her until she awaken smiled, kissing her as the memory of last night danced before him whispered "Good Morning my beauty, how was your night?"

"Good morning, my husband. My night was fine. I rested last night more than I have since you left 2 weeks ago. The love you gave me last night took away all my stress. How are you my darling?"

"I am fine. I feel refreshed and destressed today my beauty. Thank you for the wonderful evening we shared. I hear voices, we must hurry to bathe and dress for Church. Your parents are waiting. I hope Carmeli'ta' feels better today."

Smiling at his comments of their evening hugged him replied, "I am sure she does Roberto'. She is young and strong. A blow on the head will make the strongest of people feel bad for a day or so I am sure."

They went in bathed and dressed. Simone' dressed in a Winter White Coco Chanel Suite with black trim on the pockets, the neck, and sleeves with black sling-back shoes, flesh-tone stockings and pearl neck and earrings and the final touch she opened her jewelry box and slipped on the Ruby Ring Roberto' gave her twenty-four years ago. She hurriedly made the bed while Roberto' put on his Navy-Blue Pin Stripped Suit and vest, white shirt, blue bow tie, blue silk socks and black shoes.

Roberto' hugged Simone' saying "You are so lovely my beauty. Your suit is picture perfect you take my breath away."

"Thank you Roberto' my husband you look handsome as always. I am ready to join the family for breakfast. I know they are waiting it is 7:45 a.m."

They walked hand-in-hand down the hall to the kitchen and their waiting family. Carmeli'ta' saw her mother and father coming, noticed she had on a similar suit the same color of hers expressed, "Wow, Mother you are beautiful and we are dressed alike."

Catarina heard Carmeli'ta's comment, poured two more cups of coffee. Simone' and Roberto' said, "Good morning everyone." Happy to see her parents, Carmeli'ta' jumped up from her chair and rushed to where her parents were standings and hugged them together.

"Thank you my sweet little one, you are pretty in your Winter White suite. It seems as if we were thinking alike this morning" Her mother commented.

Franco added, "You both look adorable. Beauty is a blessing in my family all three of you look so much alike."

They held her tight. After a few minute Roberto' asked, "How are you my lovely Daughter? Are you feeling better today?"

"Yes, father thank you; I still feel a little tired and my head is tingling where the stitches are, but much better my father. How was your and mother's night? Did you sleep well?"

"Yes we did Carmeli'ta' we all had a long day yesterday."

Catarina had prepared breakfast after their morning prayers and was waiting for the bread to warm in the oven. She put the Italian Sausage, fruit, and bread on the table. They ate talking and chatting as they do during meals. Carmeli'ta' looked at her father and said, "Father, Jason is leaving Charleston on Tuesday and will be here on Wednesday. I asked grandfather and grandmother if he could stay in their guesthouse. They both said that he would be welcome to stay in the guestroom up front. Do you have any objection to him visiting me here?"

Simone' sitting at the table after helping her mother clean the breakfast dishes, waited, felt nervous anticipation of what her husband would say. Knowing how he felt about the relationship between them, did not want to comment, and saw her father watching her smiling.

Roberto's silence was an eternity to Carmeli'ta' looked at her and said, "If your grandparents don't mind and welcomed him, then I have no objection to him visiting."

"Father thanks you."

Continuing he added, "Carmeli'ta' let me be clear with you about something. I have no reason number one, to dislike Jason Madison, Jr. In addition, number two, the Madison family is one the finest most respected honorable families in Charleston. There is not one iota of a scandal or anything negative associated with Madison Steel and Iron, nor is there any negative talk about Jason and the way his company conducts business. In fact, my sweet Daughter, he has a reputation of being a Gentleman in the business community, as well as among the Brethren of the Church. He does not have the reputation of being a Ladies man, but have worked hard all his life and learned his family's business. He is well-liked and respected by the business world and by me Carmeli'ta'. The only point that I have is what we discussed last month."

Simone' breathed a sigh of relief and thanked God.

Moved by his discourse, Carmeli'ta' excitedly replied, "Thank you Father. I am so glad to know Jason's reputation as an honorable man and Gentleman." She hugged and kissed her father.

Simone sit silent without a comment. Franco nodded and smiled. Catarina standing behind Franco said, "The clock is showing we have 30 minutes to get to Sunday Worship."

Simone' said, "Mother do you need me to help you dress. We are all dressed except you. We must hurry."

Catarina smiled, unbuttoned her duster, and under it was a Winter White Coco Chanel Suite with Navy Blue trimming on the cuffs and pockets, and navy ribbing around the collar of the Jacket. Simone' and Carmeli'ta' looked in amazement because all three had on the same color and style of suit.

Franco said, "My son have you seen a lovelier sight? We have the three most beautiful women in the world."

"Yes, Franco it is like looking at the same picture three different times, they all look alike. Simone' has her mother's features and Carmeli'ta' has features of my Simone's. We are ready. We don't want to be late getting to the Church building."

Carmeli'ta went to her suite left her bedroom slippers on the dressing bench at the foot of her bed, put on her black sling-back shoes; Catarina slipped her feet into her blue sling back heels, put on her blue hat, picked up her and handbag and gloves matching her suit and hat off the window seat in the kitchen. Franco and Roberto' looked handsome in their blue tailored suits. The Giovanni and Bandaci families arrived at the Tuscany Valley Community Church of Christ at 9:20 a.m. The church community marveled at the sight of Simone', Catarina, and Carmeli'ta' because of their striking resemblances to each other seeing the same face three times.

After Church Services, arriving home, they all changed into leisurewear, and had lunch prepared by Catarina on Friday. Roasted chicken, oven roasted Red Potatoes, Italian Green Beans sautéed with Garlic and Butter, Bread, Green Salad sprinkled with Balsamic Vingerette Dressing and Olive Oil and Iced Tea in chilled glasses.

After lunch, Simone and Catarina cleared the table, cleaned, and put away the dishes. Franco and Roberto walked in the garden. Carmeli'ta' went to her suite to rest. Simone' concerned about the constant tiredness, followed her, opened the door, and asked, "Are you okay Carmeli'ta'?"

"I am mother, just tired and still have a little headache."

Simone' growing uneasy, the headache should have been gone by this time said, "Carmeli'ta' maybe we should let the doctor check your head."

"I don't think so mother. I want to rest for a while and then see how I feel when I get up later. Do you mind if I sleep for a while?"

"No, not at all Carmeli'ta' I will check on you after a few hours. I will let your father know that you are still a little tired and want to rest this afternoon."

"Mother did father have something he wanted to tell me or talk with me about? I can wait to rest."

"He wants to talk with you and so do I about your trip to Tuscany. I am sure that you know we need to have that discussion. Your father is a patient man Carmeli'ta' but there are somethings he cannot let pass and this is one of them. We only have one child and the possibility of us losing you for any reason scares both of us to death especially if it is something that we can avoid. You rest we will talk later or tomorrow."

"Thank you mother I will see you later. Tell father I am sorry and I will be up in a few hours."

Carmeli'ta' lying on the bed fell asleep immediately. Simone' watched her for a while to see if her breathing was even and there was any sign of severe pain by her facial expressions. Carmeli'ta' slept peacefully and her breathing was even. Her face showed no signs of pain. Simone' felt relieved walked back to the kitchen looking for her mother saw she had joined Roberto and her father in the garden. Simone' walked through the open French Doors over to where they were, Roberto' who stood after giving Catarina his seat, touched his arm. He smiled looking down at her, pulled her close to him.

She said, "Carmeli'ta' is not feeling well right now. She wants to rest. She fell asleep immediately when she lay down. I asked her about going to the doctor. She wants to wait until later and see how she feels after she awakens. I am a little concerned about her my husband."

"We will keep an eye on her my beauty. I hope that she does not have a concussion from the blow to her head. I need to call Amelio' and check with him about the farm and Marianna. Will you join me while I make my call my beauty?"

"Yes my husband. Mother and Father excuse us we will be back in a while."

Franco commented, "Of course my children. Mother and I will take a walk to our neighbor's home we visit with on Sunday afternoons. We shall return in a few hours."

Roberto' and Simone' went to her father's study. While Roberto' talked with Amelio' Simone sit in the large comfortable wing-backed chair and read Shakespeare's Sonnet 116 again.

Roberto' finished his phone call and joined her. She asked, "How is everything with the farm, Amelio' and Marianna my husband?"

"Everything is going well as always. He is not having any problems. He is excited Bibi' Ana will be in Charleston on Wednesday, 13th of December."

"That soon Roberto' that is exciting to hear about for our Amelio'. I will be happy to be home and have our life settled again. After we talk with Carmeli'ta' tomorrow Roberto' I want us to talk and then I want you to read my Diary and discuss any questions that you might have about what you read."

"Yes my darling I want that very much so I will know what is taking you from me and have kept you hostage all these years we have been married. I was not aware of the level of pain and suffering you were experiencing with this heavy burden whatever it is."

"I wanted to share my fears with you many times my husband, but just could not tell you for fear of hurting you and losing you. I love you more than life itself. I could not bear the thought of hurting our daughter or you."

"Come beauty. Let us not discuss this anymore today until we have dealt with the question of our daughter putting herself in danger. I want to check to see if she is okay then go for a walk around the garden. I do not want to leave her here alone sleep since her grandparents are not at home right now. She is in a strange country and place, and do not know her way around and that is dangerous. She needs protecting more than she realizes my beauty. She is so innocent and inexperienced that is why I worry about her relationship with Jason Madison, Jr." Simone' did not comment as they walked to the Suite where Carmeli'ta' was sleeping, opened the door quietly, walked over to the bed, and looked at their daughter sleeping peacefully. Roberto' said, "She looks like an angel my beauty. She looks the same as she did when she was girl of 15 years old. Do you remember when she walked home from school in the rain? April, Alberto', and her because they wanted to see how early summer rain felt. Actually, it was the last day of school and by the next morning, she was burning up with fever and the doctor came to treat her."

Simone' smiling said, "Yes my husband, I remember she was pretty terrible sometimes as a growing child, her determination was unmatched by anything I ever saw in a youth her age."

"Apparently my beauty it still is or we would not be here now, but in Charleston at our home. I want to get back home soon my beauty. I miss our life and our privacy, and our Church Family."

"I miss our life and church family and also my husband. Father and Mother should be returning in a few minutes. They never visit long since I have been here. We will probably have soup and salad for dinner my darling or leftovers from the Boulangerie' Veinnoise. I want to rest for a while my husband would you like to join me?"

"Always my beauty I want to be wherever you are no matter the situation."

Carmeli'ta' sleeping soundly she did not hear their conversation. Nor did she know when they entered or left the room. Simone' and Roberto' went to their suite to rest for a while. They took a blanket and rested in front of the Fireplace.

Roberto' said, "This reminds me of the last night of our honeymoon my beauty."

"Yes, it does my husband. I remember that night so well. I love my Ruby Ring. I keep it in my jewelry Armoire when I am helping mother with dinner or the cleaning."

"I noticed you wore it to Church Service today my beauty. Thank you for taking care of it. It is special to me as you are." Roberto' lay back and pulled Simone' next to him; they snuggled, chatting, and enjoying their private time. Roberto' checked the time, it was 3:00 p.m.

Two hours later Carmeli'ta' awakens to the quietness of the house. She walked through the kitchen, looked in the garden, and in her grandparents open bedroom door, they were not there. She went down the hall to her parent's bedroom heard them laughing and talking decided not to disturb them. She wanted to call Jason he should be home from Church Service by 11:30 a.m. She called the operator to connect her transatlantic call.

Jason just walking into his wing of the Mansion answered the phone on the third ring, "Hello, Jason Madison." The voice said, "Please hold for Carmeli'ta' Bandaci." He said, "Thank you."

"Hello Jason darling. How are you?"

He replied, "Hello my lovely Carmeli'ta', how are you?"

"I am okay Jason just a little tired. My head is tingling. I guess from the stitches. How was service today Jason?"

"Good my lovely as always. I missed you. Father said tell you hello."

How are your parents and grandparents?"

"Everyone is fine Jason. I am so happy to see my mother."

"I am thankful you are okay. Are you getting checked by a doctor soon Carmeli'ta'?"

"Yes, the stitches will come out in two more days."

He said, "I am leaving on Tuesday Carmeli'ta'. I will be there on Wednesday. Is there a hotel in Tuscany Valley?"

"Yes, I think so. I believe I saw one yesterday when I was sightseeing with my grandfather. The one I saw was the Vineyard Garden Inn is the name. Why do you ask?"

"I need to reserve a room while I am there visiting."

Excited she replied, "No Jason, grandfather said you could stay here with us in the guest bedroom. It is private and you are welcome. He also has a guesthouse. I want you to stay in the main house with us."

Hesitating asked, "Your father said what?"

Carmeli'ta' smiling from sheer delight continued, "He said if grandfather did not mind he does not either. Actually, Jason, he has a lot of respect for you. He said that this morning before Church, but he still holds to his tradition of choosing a husband for me."

"Thank you for telling me my lovely. I will not give up on changing his mind. I love you too much to let you go."

Feeling flushed with the love for Jason that rushed over her as a hot wave whispered, "Thank you Jason. I love you and I don't want to lose you."

His desire to be near her grew stronger commented, "You will not lose me Carmeli'ta'. Only death will part us, this is my Vow to you."

"Thank you Jason. I Vow the same to you. I hear my grandparents coming in so I will talk with you tomorrow my sweet love. Be sure to tell your father and mother hello."

"I will tell father Carmeli'ta'. It is best not to talk to mother about you too much right now as my father warned me. She thinks I am coming abroad to connect with new industry, which I have a contact there in London someone father wants me to see before I return to America. I will do that on our way back. I want you to go with me when I visit the company. You will be a key player in this idea that my father has to increase our holding on that side of the Ocean. I will see you safely home. Your parents will not need to worry about that you will be with me."

"Thank you Jason that is a great honor for me and an opportunity for me to grow and learn. Oh Jason, one more question."

"Yes, my darling."

"How is Mrs. Horne managing?" He replied, "She is doing well. I assist her and so does the Plant Manager. Have fun Carmeli'ta' and relax and heal my darling. Do not worry task here are being executed. My father will take the helm until I return."

"How long will you stay Jason?"

"It is my plan to stay at least 7-10 days or when you return unless there are unforeseen complications."

She happily said, "That sounds wonderful it is beautiful here. You and I can take in the sights of this beautiful valley my darling. I love you. Bye for now."

He replied, "Bye my sweet Carmeli'ta'. Take care of yourself and call me if you are not feeling well or ask your mother to call, promise me."

She agreed, "I promise, bye."

Jason and Carmeli'ta' did not know that unforeseen complications were already in the works and it would alter their plans completely changing the course of their lives for a while. As a river changes it course and cuts its way through to a new path to the sea, so would their lives and the events that was shortly taking place. More than one life changing revelation would surface in a few short days. Like the game of chess, there is only one King and one Queen in a game; as the players get closer to the end of the game it will end in a draw without the King in captivity. The King is the most important player as well as the weakest in a game. In this game of Chess, the King is Vincenzo' Alessandro Moretti.

She hung the phone up just as Franco and Catarina walked into the office. Franco asked, "You are feeling better Granddaughter?"

"Yes, Grandfather lots better. I am to see the doctor and have the stitches out on Tuesday as Dr. Thimmons told me before I left London on Friday. Who is your doctor Grandfather?"

"His name is Christian Panniche', Jr. His father was Christian Panniche' Sr. he delivered our Simone'."

"He is old Grandfather?" He smiled and answered, "No my granddaughter, he is in his 60's. He and his father have delivered most of the babies in this community. He took over his father's practice and is familiar with everyone's medical history here in this little valley. He was young when he graduated from Medical College. He is a brilliant man. He advanced in his schooling two grades at a time." Listening and amazed remarked, "WOW, that is amazing." Her grandfather continued, "He graduated from high school when he was 16 years old like you my granddaughter and is a well-respected member of the community and head of the Tuscany Valley Medical Hospital. He is a close friend of mine." Carmeli'ta' pondering, "Did he deliver me my Grandfather?" Franco smiled, "As a matter of fact he did, just as his father delivered your mother and father."

She replied, "That is so amazing to me. I want to meet him grandfather. You think he remembers me?"

"You will meet him my little one. He will be there when we take you on Tuesday to get your stitches out. He remembers that I have one granddaughter, but you were 5 years old when you left, but we will see. Your face is still as pretty now as it was when you were a baby. He said when he saw you, 'you looked like a doll. He had not seen a more beautiful baby in his medical career." Continuing Franco added, "I called him on Saturday to let him know we needed his services. Your appointment is at 12:00 Noon on Tuesday."

"Thank you Grandfather I will tell mother and father."

He inquired, "Your parents still resting?"

"Yes I walked to their room and they were laughing and enjoying themselves." She added, Mother said, 'Father wants to talk with me."

Taking a more serious tone Franco replied, "I am sure he does my Granddaughter. I believe we all do."

Carmeli'ta did not say anything but looked at her grandmother. Catarina smiled and squeezed her hand and went to the kitchen to prepare to the dinner. Franco and Carmeli'ta' went in and sat at the table chatting as Catarina began to prepare the dinner.

Simone' and Roberto' heard voices and movement in the kitchen; he checked his watch it was 5:00 p.m. turned to Simone' and said, "Let's see if our daughter feels like a chat my beauty. Were you planning to help your mother with dinner?"

Simone' folded the blanket laid in back on the Chaise Lounge replied, "I will see my husband what she says. She is just warming it. Dinner will be soup we had on Saturday. They both freshened-up Simone' left for the kitchen to see if her mother needed help with the dinner preparations. Carmeli'ta's and her grandfather joined Catarina in the kitchen while she was warming dinner sit chatting with them while waiting for dinner. Simone' helped her mother. Roberto' joined them said, "It is good to see you up my sweet Daughter. You are feeling better?"

"Yes, Father I am feeling a little better. Grandfather said he called and made an appointment with Dr. Panniche' for me Tuesday at 12:00 Noon. He told me Dr. Panniche' delivered you, Mother, and me that is so amazing to me."

"I am sure it is my daughter; however not really if you think about it. He started his practice when he was 20 years old as an Intern."

"Dr. Panniche' Sr. was our doctor. The one that you will see is the son. His father is retired isn't he Franco?"

"He is semi-retired my son. He still comes into the office two days a week. He is 83 years old; I believe; but you cannot tell it by looking at him and the way he gets around. He looks maybe 60 years old. He is as sharp as ever. His son, Christian Jr. looks maybe 50 years old, if you can get that high in age with him."

Simone' and Catarina listened to the conversation while they heated the dinner. There was tenseness in the environment felt by the entire family. It hung thick around Carmeli'ta' thick enough to cut with a knife. Feeling a discomforting pressure, she excused herself and walked to the garden. The pressure bound her like a cord sit on the garden bench beneath the Rose Trellis. Roberto' followed her, when she watched him approaching smiled and said, "Hello my Father you are so handsome and mother is so beautiful. I am proud to have you as my parents."

He sat next to her, "Hello my sweet Daughter. Thank you we are proud to have you as a daughter. Are you feeling stronger?"

"Yes, my Father. I am better a little tingling near the scar, but I think it is from the stitches. I am glad that grandfather called the doctor so I can get the stitches taken out."

"Yes, I am anxious for them to come out as well Carmeli'ta'. What I can see of the gash it is healing well. Do you feel like chatting with me this afternoon? Or we can wait until tomorrow when you are a day and night stronger."

"If you don't mind father, I would like to wait until tomorrow. After dinner I want to go to bed if that is okay with you and mother."

"That is fine with me Carmeli'ta'. I want you up to talking with us, not tired or not feeling up to par yet. Let us go in my Daughter. Dinner is ready by now and it is getting cold and you don't need any complications as a result of getting cold."

He stood, held his right hand to help her stand. They walked arm in arm back to the kitchen to join their family. Just as they arrived at the French Doors leading into the kitchen, Catarina, and Simone' were putting dinner on the table for their evening meal at 5:45 p.m. on Sundays, December 10. Dinner for the family was lively as usual chatting and laughing inherent to the Giovanni and Bandaci families as a whole. They were a happy family with trouble on its way and it would not be many hours away. Simone', though happy and smiling to have her family with her, knew that tomorrow would be a defining factor in all of their lives. They first would deal with the issue that Carmeli'ta' bought to the table. And, then there was the issue of the Diary to be read by Roberto'. She was not ready to face the pain that she would see in her husband's face.

Nonetheless, she knew it was inevitable. It would not be so much what she did but why and the length of time she allowed it to prolong. She knew that Roberto' would want to hurt Vincenzo' for his ungentlemanly behavior in this situation. Actually, he would be the one that caused the entire deception with his insistence on seeing Carmeli'ta' and Simone' over the years. Uncertainty at this point, of who the father was would be more than her husband could take. She did not know what his reaction would be.

Simone' could only pray. Franco saw the far-away look in her eyes, patted her on her left hand and smiled as if he knew what she was thinking, for he too knew that time was approaching for the mystery to be revealed to Roberto'. He felt for his daughter and the dilemma she faced with the contents of the Diary and the truth; the whole truth revealed. As he pondered the details, decided that definitely, Carmeli'ta' did not need to know just yet.

Dinner over, Franco and Catarina went for their evening walk, Carmeli'ta' went to her bedroom suite to bath and go to bed for the night, she still felt a little tired from the accident. Simone' went in to help her and make sure she was okay and not dizzy with the tingling that resulted from the accident and having stitches. Roberto' walked into the garden while Simone' helped Carmeli'ta'. After she was in bed, Simone' noticed the clock on the bedside stand, it was 8:00 p.m. Roberto' and Franco would be expecting dessert and coffee at 9:00 p.m.

Leaving Carmeli'ta's room to prepare for dessert and coffee saw her husband standing under the Weeping Willow Tree looking in the direction of the kitchen as if he were looking for her. She hurriedly set up the pot with coffee, placed the dessert saucers with silverware on the table, and took the Schiacciata Florentine from the refrigerator to get to room temperature, walked into the garden to join her husband waiting. He saw her coming, met her halfway the garden, looked down at her and smiled, hugged her, kissed her snuggling her close to him because of the chill in the air and said, "Hello my beauty, I was waiting for you. I wanted to spend some time alone with you before we have dessert. Your expression at dinner said that you were worried about something my beauty; please share with me what is on your mind."

She thought, "He never misses anything about me. 'What a wonderful loving, caring husband he is noticing every expression."

Holding onto Roberto' Simone' was silent for a few minutes finally said, "I was thinking about talking with Carmeli'ta' tomorrow and what her reaction would be. We have never had to deal with her on an issue of defiance and putting herself in danger by using a name that is not familiar to many my husband. She probably will not see it that way because she is an adult, but that is what it is defiance and without a sound reason. She knew that she could trust you and should have known that I was okay. She could have called her grandparents if she had wanted to know if I was here without asking them."

"All of what you said is true my beauty and those were my exact opinions about the situation. Her reasoning in this was not as sound as it should have been and then putting herself in danger is the factor that worries me. I could have lost my only child in this world. I don't think I could have survived that Simone' not in the way that she went about it. I know that life is fleeting and uncertain. We all have an appointed time, the Scripture tells. However, to put self in a position to cut her life short would be more than either one of us could have stood."

"You are right my husband and that is exactly what I mean. When I saw her getting off the plane that was one of the happiest moments I have ever experienced in my life to know that my daughter was still among the living and she had not suffer any brain damage."

"Was that all on your mind at the time Simone'? Tell me everything don't hold anything back from me, please."

"I was thinking of you reading the Diary my husband and us having the conversation before you read it. I just want you to understand where I was at every point in my life since I was 13 years of age my husband."

"I am afraid I don't follow you Simone', please add some details for me."

"I don't want to go into the details now Roberto', it would take telling you everything tonight for you to know the place that kept me bound for so many years my husband. May I get leave from you to wait until we have spoken with Carmeli'ta' before we discuss us my darling. It will take more than a few minutes for me to explain to you the details and for you to read my Diary."

"I will be patient my beauty until after we talk with our daughter tomorrow, but I don't want to wait any longer. It has been too long as it is my beauty. I can't accept being shut out any longer, I can't Simone' it is destroying me. I need all of your love. I don't want you to hold back a part of you from me, I love you, and I want to feel you love me the same way that I love you my beauty."

Tears were flowing from her eyes as he spoke his heart to her. She held him even tighter. He felt her body quiver and shake as if she was in terrible fear and pain, held her close and whispered, "Please don't cry Simone' I love you and I know that you love me, but I want to feel all of your love and desire that you have, is that asking too much?"

She whispered a barely heard, "No my husband you have every right

to know all of me and my passion and desire I feel for you. Thank you for understanding and being patient Roberto'. I love you my husband with every ounce of breath that is in me. I never wanted to hurt you that were never my intention; but I wanted to protect you and Carmeli'ta."

"I will try and understand Simone', I love you, and I will try to understand."

It was nearing 9:00 p.m. the grey darkness lost it light and the cover of dark cloud began to blanket the sky. Franco and Catarina walked back to the garden and saw, Roberto' and Simone' standing silently holding on to each other, did not disturb them, walked toward the front of the house, and went in that way. Catarina freshened up and went to the kitchen. She saw the coffee pot ready and the table set, the dessert on the counter, plugged the coffee pot in. She and Franco sat and looked at each other, he said, "Our daughter is getting close to the time when she will tell her husband why she ran away from him almost two months ago my lovely. It is weighing heavy on her mind. I could see it at dinner."

"I know Franco; I saw the same expression on her face. She is struggling, my husband, and I don't know what we can do to help her."

"We have done everything we can my lovely. She knows that we are here and that is comforting to her. We will pray for them; they will need to work it out themselves."

"I know my husband, I know."

Simone and Roberto' saw her parents sitting at the table, Roberto' pulled out his Pocket Watch, checked the time, it was 9:05 p.m. looked at her smiled and said, "It is time we go in my beauty. Your parents are waiting and I want my dessert and coffee. I want to enjoy the rest of the evening loving you my beauty. I need to be close to you tonight."

"I am ready my husband to go in for dessert and coffee. I want to be near you and have you love me. I will check on Carmeli'ta' before we have dessert. If she is awake she may want to join us if not that is even better."

They walked to the kitchen, Roberto' pulled the chair out to sit and asked Franco, "How was your walk? The chill in the air tonight is definitely announcing the arrival of winter."

"Yes, my son the temperature is dropping tonight. I am looking forward to the winter, right after is spring again and time to prepare the soil for planting for the summer produce."

"Yes that is always my thought as well."

Catarina poured the coffee and put the dessert tray on the table. Simone', in Carmeli'ta' suite, tipped over to the bed and saw her sleeping soundly and peaceful did not want to disturb her left quietly and joined her parents and husband at the table. They laughed and talked as they enjoyed their evening dessert and coffee before retiring as was their custom. The dishes done and put away Simone' and Roberto' said goodnight and went to their suite. She asked, "Are you planning to talk with Amelio' today my husband?"

"No, my beauty he went back to Worship Service today, it is nearing time for service to start I am sure he is on his way. I will wait until tomorrow after we speak with Carmeli'ta' so I can tell him about our conversation with her. Right now, I want to draw our bath so we can enjoy the rest of the evening. I only have loving you on my mind right now my beauty." She did not comment but smiled went to the closet, undressed put on her dressing gown, pinned up her hair, and joined him the bathroom for their warm bubble bath.

The evening passed quickly and morning approached before Simone wanted it to.

CHAPTER
FORTY-SIX

Still early evening in Charleston, after worship service, Jason visited with his parents, for a while, enjoying evening coffee. He wanted to talk with them before retiring to his wing of the mansion said, "Mother, I will be leaving on Tuesday for London for the appointment with the Langley Mills to discuss a contract proposal for Madison Steel to supply their steel and iron needs and expand our industry to include textiles. I will take this opportunity while I am there to visit some of the surroundings countries. I have always wanted to see Tuscany, the City of Rome, and a few other places."

"Yes Jason, your father told me. Son you have other staff persons that can operate the business while you are away. Carmeli'ta' Bandaci and the Plant Manager can take the helm for a few weeks can't they without asking your father to guide the company while you are away?"

"Yes, mother, the Plant Manager and Accountant both can manage; however, I want father to help me while I am away from the office. We are still dealing with Charles Meriwether and that can be tricky. I would not want to place this measure of responsibility on Carmeli'ta' Bandaci; therefore, I asked father to oversee everything while I am away and he agreed to help me out."

"How is Carmeli'ta' doing Jason? I hear wonderful things about her level of efficiency and likeability. I will visit her very soon Jason, probably after the holidays."

"That would be nice Mother. She is efficient and a key player in the Meriwether and Madison Co-op. However, I think she will be vacationing with her parents and grandparents soon maybe over the holidays. It is a busy time right now."

Neither Jason nor his father wanted to feed into her questions especially about Carmeli'ta. Her knowing the other reason he was going abroad at this time would open a 'can of worms' and that would be trouble. Jason looked at his father with the look 'help me' in his eyes. His father commented, "I am looking forward to being at the office again Juanita my lovely. I will not be there all day every day but enough to know what is going on. Jason has a reliable staff, which of course you know because they were our staff."

"Thank you Father he said, the staff are some of the best in the surrounding area."

Juanita smiled and replied, "You are right my husband the staff are efficient. I will wait until after the holidays to visit the plant and Carmeli'ta' Bandaci. I have many other functions on my calendar for the holiday season. Especially, the one function where we are raising money for the gift tree for the children in the Charleston Orphanage."

"That is good Mother let me know what the donation levels are and I will write the check and get it to you before I leave. I will retire now and start packing for my trip. I am looking forward to flying abroad opposed to taking a ship this time."

"Thank you Jason for your donation."

He said, "You are welcome." Jason kissed his mother, smiled, and nodded thank you to his father, and went to his living area. After bidding him good night Juanita asked, "Is there something you are not telling me my love about this trip it seems so mysterious?"

"No, my lovely it is not a mystery. Jason is meeting with the powers to be at the Langley Mills to try to secure their business and look at expanding our holdings abroad. He will be back in 7-10 days. There is no mystery. It is getting late Juanita time for bed. It is almost 8:00 p.m. I want to be at the office early tomorrow to go over the schedules with Jason and the Plant Manager."

Monday morning came quickly in Tuscany.

Monday December 11, Carmeli'ta' awakens at 5:00 a.m. lay awake thinking of what tone the conversation might take between her parents, her grandparents and her, especially her father. She knew her mother, in this situation, would agree with the thoughts of her father. She dozed off to sleep, after a while awaken to the sound of her grandparents in the kitchen. Franco and Catarina were having their coffee and Morning Prayer. She decided to join them, especially since the coffee smelled so inviting. Freshening up, she put on her dressing gown and slippers, pulled her hair back in a ponytail and walked with cat-steps down the hall. Her grandparents did not notice she was coming until she walked up to the table where they were chatting and having coffee.

She said, "Good morning Grandmother and Grandfather. How are you today?"

Franco and Catarina smiled. She stood and hugged Carmeli'ta' and said, "We are fine my sweet little one. How are you feeling today? Your head is feeling better?"

"Yes, it is feeling much better. It is still itching around the stitches. I don't feel as tired this morning as I did the last two days after I got here."

Franco smiling looking at her said, "Rest is the best medicine for what

happened to you Granddaughter and the long flight did not help. I am happy to know you are feeling okay today. Dr. Panniche' should give us a good report tomorrow around Noon after he examines you."

"Yes, grandfather, I am looking forward to meeting him and getting the stitches out. They are uncomfortable now since my head is getting well." She changed the subject and commented, "Father and mother is still sleeping. They will want to talk with me soon after breakfast I am sure."

She seemed a little nervous to Franco and he added, "Yes, Granddaughter, they will want to talk with you. It will be okay. I think it is more concern for you than anything else, Carmeli'ta'. What you did and the decision to use your middle names was not wise. You could have disappeared or been lost to us period. How would we know where to look or who to ask about your whereabouts? You can never do anything of this nature again regardless; there is no reason to make such decisions and follow through with such drastic actions."

"Yes, grandfather I know that now. I just wanted to know where my mother was and if she was okay. I should have not doubted my father. He has never said an untruth to me." Catarina hugged her and said, "Take heart my little one. It is only because they love you that they want you safe and so do we."

Roberto' awakened prop himself up on his left elbow, looked at his beautiful sleeping Simone', leaned forward and kissed her on the forehead and whispered, "Wake up my beauty it is getting late in the morning almost 7:00 a.m." Simone' sighed moving closer to him, snuggling under his arm held onto his waist and whispered, "I am awake my husband. How are you today? The love you gave me last night was wonderful. I love you more each day."

"I love you my darling and enjoy our intimacy past my ability to put it into words. It is time we bathed and dressed and join your parents in the kitchen and see how our little sweet Carmeli'ta' is feeling today."

"Yes, I am ready to get up my darling."

She moved the sheet aside reaching for her dressing gown, Roberto' reached it first, walked to the middle of the room stood and watched while she walked to him and slipped her arms into the sleeves. He held her tight for a moment as if he never wanted to let her go.

Carmeli'ta's mind flipping back and forth with the conversation with her grandparents and thoughts about the conversation with her parents, said, "Thank you for your support Grandmother and Grandfather. I love you. I think I will go see father and mother now if you will excuse me."

Carmeli'ta' walked slowly down the hall to her parent's bedroom suite, knocked lightly, Roberto' let Simone' slip out of his embrace, put on his robe, and answered the door; to his surprise, stood his sweet daughter said, "Good morning Carmeli'ta' my sweet little one. How is your head? Are you still a little tired today?"

"No Father, I feel much better thank you. The stitches are pulling otherwise I am fine. I do not feel as tried today. I was just telling my grandparents that I felt better. Where is mother? Is she awake yet? I hope I am not disturbing you?"

"Your mother is fine my daughter; she is in the bathroom. Moreover, no, you are not disturbing us. You are our daughter how could a visit from you disturb us in any way? I am happy to see you always my daughter and so is you mother. We love you Carmeli'ta'. You are the only child that we have in this world."

"Thank you father, I love you and mother with all my heart." Simone' heard her voice opened the bathroom door and said, "Good morning my precious little one. How are you today? Your head feeling better are you still tired?"

"No Mother. I was just telling father the only thing bothering me now is the stitches stinging a little, but not unbearable. How are you? You always look so fresh Mother. When father opened the door, I could smell the freshness of your Chanel 5. I have wanted to be like you all my life."

"That is a precious thing for you to say Carmeli'ta' thank you. I am thankful for you my darling Daughter. I know breakfast must be ready by now, as soon as we dress we will join the rest of the family."

Carmeli'ta' hugged both her parents around the waist standing between them smiled and said, "I will wait until you are ready."

Roberto' said, "Simone' this reminds me of when Carmeli'ta' was growing up she waited in our suite lots of days while we dressed."

"You are right my husband it does."

Carmeli'ta' sat on the side of the bed while her father and mother dressed in their dressing room off from the bath. Dressed they walked down the hall to kitchen. Catarina saw them coming and poured three cups of coffee just as they reached the table said, "Good Morning, our children it is a blessing to see you and know each of you are well today."

Franco added, "Yes, Mother it is good to see them. I hope you sleptwell."

Simone' listening to her parents did not comment.

Roberto' replied, "Yes we did it is good to be home in Tuscany again and have my daughter and wife with me." Catarina had prepared breakfast as usual they ate with happiness and joy of being together. Roberto' thought while observing his family from where he was sitting, "the only one missing is Amelio'. He would call him later when he was at his desk to check on him, the farm, and the deposit collections."

It was a brisk breeze blowing Monday morning, December 11 in Tuscany. Franco rose to prepare to leave to check with his Farm Managers and the day's priorities, said bye to his family. Carmeli'ta' thought about going with him to see more of the sights, not ready to face what her parents would say to her, especially her father. She knew how her grandparents felt when they talk with her at breakfast. She did not want to mention it to her grandfather because he would remind her she had a conversation overdue with her parents. Simone' and Roberto' went back to their bedroom to make the bed and neaten it up.

Catarina walked Franco to the door. After he left she returned to the kitchen and looked for Carmeli'ta' and noticed she had walked into the garden. Catarina planned to go to the village for her early Monday morning visit to the market so she would be out of the house to give Carmeli'ta's parents privacy when they talk with her. She picked up her jacket, car keys, and purse walked through the garden on the way to her 1925 Chrysler said, "Carmeli'ta' I am going to the market to get something I need for the house. I should return in a few hours probably by 11:00 a.m. would you let your parents know for me?"

"Yes, Grandmother, I will tell father and mother what you said. Have a safe trip. I will see you soon." Catarina hugged her smiled and left. Carmeli'ta' went into her bedroom suite, bathed, and dressed readying herself to talk with her parents.

Five miles away at the other end of the Moretti Vineyard, Vincenzo' was talking with the overseer of his vineyard checking the vines because of the cold to ensure that they were safe and the furnaces were lit to warm the vines until the sun rose higher in the sky.

Roberto' and Simone' finished their cleaning chores in their suite and returned to the kitchen to look for Carmeli'ta. She was not there, they looked in the garden, she was not there, they knew she was dressing. They sit at the kitchen table chatting while they waited for her to come to talk with them. At long last, Carmeli'ta' reluctantly opened her bedroom door and walked slowly down the hall to where her parents were waiting.

She walked to the table and sat across from her parents and said, "I am ready to talk my Father." Roberto' quiet for a long period-of-time, wanted to control his words and mannerisms, so he could keep it on an adult level and not speak to her as is she was 15 years old replied, "Thank you Daughter for talking with us. We want to discuss your actions over the past few weeks, when I returned from visiting your mother now 3 weeks ago, the fact that you questioned my truthfulness, and your decision to travel and use a name that you are not recognized by anywhere in the world became an issue. Your two middle names are not registered anywhere except on your immigration papers and with the American Government."

"I realize now Father I should not have used my middle names and mother's family name. At the time, I did not think about the danger. I just wanted to come to see if my mother was okay."

"I told you your mother was okay Carmeli'ta'. Have I ever misled you my daughter? Your mother and I have a right as your parents to decide what we want to do. You are not a child any longer Carmeli'ta' but an adult out on your own. You are not living in our home anymore. One, your mother can go and come at her leisure without explanation. She is your mother that is her right. If she had been in danger, I would have never returned to Charleston. To that end, I would never harm her in any way Carmeli'ta'. I love your mother too much to consider harming her in any way. What is between us is our private business. You, as our daughter, do not have the right to question our decisions. Two, you knew I was coming to see you last Thursday after my day ended and you allowed me to believe you would be there, what I found was reservations on Pan American Airline and the RMS Olympic Cruise Ship. I called both and there was no Carmeli'ta' Bandaci with reservations on either."

Carmeli'ta' sat quietly as her mother held her right hand nodding her head in agreement with her father. He continued, "I called your mother, if she did not know you as well as she does the situation would have been worse. If you received injuries as results of an accident and identification is required, where would the airline call? Just think if that thief has been successful in taking your purse your papers and documents would be gone. Luckily, she knew you would use your middle names and her family's last name. I went to the airport and there was your car. I check the airline. The passenger list on either of the daily flights to London did not have you registered as a passenger."

He continued,"I also checked the passenger list of the RMS Olympic I got the same results no passenger using your name."

"I know Father and Mother, I apologize for my actions, and not taking your word mother was okay. Please forgive me."

Simone' with a stern tone in her voice Carmeli'ta' had not heard in years said, "It is not a matter of forgiveness my sweet Daughter, it is a matter of you realizing the danger you were in; plus, your show of total disrespect to your father in questioning his word, this is absolutely unacceptable to me, period! I made the decision to come to see my parents and the decision to stay and visit with them for a while. Your father did not object and he has the right to."

Carmeli'ta' careful with her words and facial expressions in her mother's presence humbly said, "Yes, Mother you are right." She saw a side of her mother she knew existed, but rarely did she let it come out. She knew her mother could be just as terrible as she was good. Carmeli'ta' remembered when she was growing up her mother became both beauty and the beast especially times when she did not adhere to her mother's training, and punishment was forthcoming.

"Roberto' added, "When your mother called me and told me you had been assaulted, I cannot tell you the horror that enveloped my mind and heart. I could barely breathe until I knew you were safe. I almost went out of my mind with worry and so did your mother. Fear is a terrible place to be Carmeli'ta'. You are my only child in the world. I will never have another not this late in life. Your mother and I are both past 40 years of age. We are not old my Daughter, but too old to consider having another child. God did not bless us but with one, you. We prayed years ago for a son, but it did not happen so we are pleased with His blessing us with one child. I hope you understand our points to you."

"I am so happy that you are both my parents my Father. I will never do anything like this again."

Her father continued and, "Third, You cannot afford to make decisions of this nature alone Carmeli'ta'. You will be married one day soon. When you are with your husband every decision you make will affect him as every decision he makes will affect you. You and he are one, a part of each other. Weight all options my Daughter before you make a move. The fact that you came to Tuscany is not an issue, the issue is that you used a name to hide what you were doing. I cannot let it go and not tell you about the danger of it. Now you know the danger of traveling alone, using another name. You are too young and too lovely my Daughter to travel alone and above all you have never left Charleston without your mother or me being with you; these circumstances poses more danger than anything else. I will sum it up as inexperience and until you have the wherewithal to move around the world by yourself; it is best to think before you act. You are a long way from home and in a country and a part of the world that is entirely unfamiliar to you. We moved from Tuscany to America when you were 5 years of age. You can barely remember being here."

"You are right, I remember how happy I was playing in the yard. I do remember the white cottages on the hillside and our white cottage. Thank you Father and Mother for being patient and being kind, I know that you are upset with me Father and Mother. I love you both for loving me so much."

Roberto' stood and reached for her hand to help her up, hugged her close and kissed her on the forehead and said, "You and your mother are my life Carmeli'ta' everything that I do is for both of you and your security and comfort, so please Daughter don't worry us this way ever again."

"I promise Father, I will always talk with you and mother before I do anything. I know my telling mother not to tell you what I discuss with her causes a problem. She is a wonderful mother to keep my secret even at the risk of you being upset with her. For that, I am sorry mother. I know it is a difficult position to be in for you. I never want to come between you and father."

Her mother replied, "Thank you Carmeli'ta' we appreciate your concern. You can talk to me anytime. Mothers and daughters have things they talk about, but when it comes to anything else that will affect the entire family it would be better if you told your father and me together or at least give me leave to discuss what you told me with him."

"I understand fully now Mother and Father. I apologize again."

Roberto' still hugging her commented, "That is okay Daughter we have everything out in the open now and a clearer understanding so we go forward from here."

Simone' rose stood next to Carmeli'ta' and smiled squeezing her hand. She said, "Mother and Father, grandmother asked me to tell you she went to the market in the valley and will be back around 11:00 a.m. for lunch. She should be here in a little while since it is 11:00 a.m. now."

Simone' said, "Thank you daughter." Roberto' excused himself and went to the office to call Amelio' before he left for the farm. It was 6:00 a.m. in Charleston. He would be awake and waiting for his housekeeper and cook, Juanita to prepare his breakfast. He rang the long-distance operator, gave her his home number. She placed the call when the phone rang, said, "Your party's line is ringing sir. I will wait for the connection and then hang-up."

"Thank you."

The phone rang four times before Amelio' picked up, "Hello."

"Amelio', good morning how are you cousin? Is everything going well, there with you and the farms?"

"Good morning Roberto'. I am fine thank you. How are you and your family?"

"Everyone is well, Simone' and our sweet, Carmeli'ta' is doing okay much better now. She get the stitches out tomorrow at Noon. Franco and Catarina are as they have been excellent in-laws and grandparents."

"And you Roberto' you did not mention yourself."

"I am well my cousin, anxious to get home and get back to my life there with my family."

"I understand. I am sure it will be soon."

"Yes it will. Carmeli'ta' is doing much better. We will start making our plans in a few days to return. Simone' and I still need to talk about what is frightening her. We spoke with Carmeli'ta' this morning about her actions over the past few weeks and traveling under her middle names and her mother family name. I think she understands now. She took it well. She did not say very much and you know she will not when she is upset about something."

"I am sure she will be fine. It may take her some time to shake-off a scolding by her parents; she will be okay. The farms are doing well, accounts are collected, deposits are made, transfer to the bank in Switzerland is being sent in a timely manner, and Marianna is doing well as always."

"Thank you Amelio' once again for making my trip possible. How are plans progressing with Bib' Ana and her move to America?"

"She is doing well, the house sale is done, she has her immigration papers from the U.S Embassy, she is packing China, Silverware, and other items she want to have with her and shipping them tomorrow. She will be on the flight to America and me on Thursday, December 14th. We had said Wednesday the 13th, but the flight was full for that day, so she took the next available one. I cannot wait until I see her again. I do love her so much my cousin, I have all of my life."

"I know how it feels to love and want that person to be with you. I am happy for you Amelio', so pleased that you have love in your life. I will tell Simone' and Carmeli'ta'. I will let you get your breakfast and get to work. Thank you, Amelio', take care of yourself."

"I will Roberto' you do the same and say hello to Simone' and my little sweet cousin for me. Tell them I send my love. Bye for now."

"Bye Amelio." They both hang up. Amelio' felt a sense of danger nagging at him for some reason. He did not understand it. He thought about Bibi' Ana, Roberto' and his family. He shook it off, went into breakfast, leaving for the farms at 7:30 a.m. He noticed as he walked out of the door the briskness to the morning.

Not able to shake the danger nagging at him, continued to pray as he drove to work so that all was okay with his loved ones.

CHAPTER
FORTY-SEVEN

Monday morning, December 11, in Charleston, Jason and his father arrived early at Madison Steel before the office staff arrived. They went over the protocol of each of the duties critical to the running of the plants. The quality control process, the duties of Mrs. Horne and finally the next phases of the contracts with Meriwether Textiles and Madison Steel and Iron Co-op. Pleased with what he saw, Jason's father said, "This is excellent son, I am proud of the way that the company has grown under your leadership."

"Thank you Father, that means a lot to me. I credit 80% of the success of this company in the last 3 years to Carmeli'ta'. She is a gem and proposed and implemented efficient practices and ideas that stimulated both growth and prosperity."

"You have what I have with your mother in Carmeli'ta', Jason. Your mother helped me a lot in the first years of this business. The plant operations were largely her idea."

"You never told me that Father."

"It wasn't necessary Son. The point is you have someone who will be behind you every step of the way, cherish her, do not let her get away Son."

"I will not Father is why I am going to Tuscany tomorrow. I need to get home, finish packing, and write mother the check for my donation to the Charleston Orphanage. It is mid-morning now sind I need to hurry. I will see you at home tonight before I leave on the 11:00 a.m. flight tomorrow."

"See you then Son. I will be along in early afternoon as I told my Juanita before I left."

In the meantime, in Tuscany, Carmeli'ta' went to her suite to get a jacket to take a walk and look at some of the valley on foot. She said to her mother and father, "I want to take a walk and see some of the beautiful vineyard. I will not be long."

Simone' did not care for the idea of her walking in the Moretti Vineyard for the fear she would see Vincenzo'. She always feared he would carry out his threats to tell her he was her father. She said, "Would you like for me to come with you little one? I would not want you to get turned around it is a large vineyard."

"No Mother, I plan to walk near the road. I can see our house from a long way. I noticed that Saturday when grandfather and I were returning from sightseeing. I will keep the house in sight."

"Okay my lovely Daughter, do so please. It is a little nippy outside. I can see from the window that the furnaces are lit to warm the vines so don't venture near those areas."

Carmeli'ta' smiled kissed both her parents, put on her jacket, and walked out the French doors toward the road that ran along the vineyard and down to the village in the valley below. She walked looking around enjoying the crisp clean air and the beauty of the vines that looked as if they were suspended. It looked like a green forest hanging in the air.

Roberto' and Simone' watched until she was out of sight. Simone' said, "I want to talk about us now my husband and what is in "secret" that has been hidden in me since I was 13 years old. I want to try and make you understand why I kept these things hidden in me all our married life."

"I am listening, my beauty. I will do my best to understand and keep an open mind."

"Thank you Roberto'. It is not easy for me to tell you, When I was 13 years of age, I realized there was something different about me. I felt something inside of me that I did not understand. It was like a force that kept me hostage within myself. I did not know how to tell my parents; I did not understand the feelings I had when I was only 13 years old so I kept them to myself for an entire year. I spent a lot of time alone my husband walking, and in my room. I did have but one friend, Bibi 'Ana

Nunnarelli. She and I played together a lot when we were growing up, then in primer school, then high school. She was a grade ahead of me, but that did not make any difference to us were close friends. I could not talk with her she could not help me, so I tried to manage what I was feeling alone."

"Simone I hear what you are saying my beauty, but I am not following you not yet. What does this have to do with and you not letting me know and share all of you?"

"I know that you don't understand at the present time Roberto', but you will as I explain more, if you will be patient just a little while longer. This is hard for me my husband. I do not want to hurt you."

"I am hurt more by you not sharing all your love with me Simone', but go on my sweet wife, I will be patient regardless of how long it takes." Looking at his watch saw it was 10:45 a.m. nearing the time for Catarina to return, said, "Your mother should be here in a few minutes. Let us continue and we will go to our private suite if necessary."

"Thank you my husband. I want to get the Diary before I start talking to you again. Please excuse me my sweet husband I will be right back." She went to their suite and took the Diary and the key from inside her Lingerie Armoire under her gowns and returned to the kitchen where Roberto' was patiently waiting. She sits at the table and placed the Diary in front of Roberto' but kept the key in her pants pocket intending to give it to him when she completed her explanation to him. He smiled as she sits down again, but said nothing.

In the Moretti Vineyard, Vincenzo' still working with his vineyard workers to keep the vines warm, walked back toward the front of the Vineyard that looked in the direction of the Giovanni home, his thoughts went to Simone' and hoped she had a safe return home. He knew by what Franco said when he visited him two weeks before she was still in Tuscany. By this time, she was surely gone.

Carmeli'ta' walked along slowly looking at the beauty of the vineyard. She saw her grandmother's car approaching, waved as she slowed down and stopped. Catarina said, "Hello my sweet Granddaughter you are not lost are you? You are a distance from the house now, are you aware of that?"

Carmeli'ta' looked around she had walked further than she thought said, "Hello Grandmother. I did not know I had walked this far. It is beautiful out her today. I am not lost I know the way back. I am staying near the road so I will be fine. I will walk back soon probably around lunch time."

Catarina smiled and said, "Be careful Granddaughter I see the furnaces are lit in the vineyard so don't go near them the flames jumps and shoot out heat I would not want you to get burned. I will see you in about an hour."

"Yes, thank you Grandmother, I will be careful. Tell father and mother I will be there shortly. I want to walk just a little further maybe to the bottom of the hill. I can see it from here."

"Okay. It is not far maybe a 1/4 of a mile or more see you soon."

Catarina waved and drove off looking in her side mirrors saw her go under the hill, drove to her home, and into the yard, retrieved her packages from the front seat, walked through the garden toward the kitchen. Simone' saw her approaching said, "Mother is coming with package my husband, would you help her?"

Roberto' quickly met Catarina in the garden and took the packages from her. She smiled at him and walked ahead of him to the kitchen and said, "I saw my granddaughter a minute ago. She asked me to tell you she will be here shortly. She is walking to the bottom of the hill then she will return for lunch."

Simone' picked up her Diary and held it as her mother talked with Roberto' and her. She said, "Mother I will help you prepare lunch if you need to me." Catarina replied, "Help is not necessary Simone'. I stopped and picked up fresh bread, we will have some of the Vegetable Soup from Saturday again, for lunch and cook a heavier meal for later. I am only heating up; your father will be here in another hour. He will be hungry. You and Roberto' enjoy your time together. I do this every day my children it is no problem for me."

Simone' and Roberto' walked down the hall to their bedroom suite to continue their conversation.

In the meantime, Carmeli'ta' reached the bottom of the hill and stood looking at the vineyard and the furnaces as they heated the vines did not see the car approaching the top of the hill. The driver, Ramon' Allavera' de Antoine, a tourist from London, was driving erratically. He was not familiar with the winding and the twisting of the road was losing control the car as it advanced in speed toward the bottom of the hill.

Vincenzo' busy checking the vines did not see or hear the car nor did he realize there was anyone near the vineyard. Carmeli'ta' standing near a small oak tree only saw the car when it was right near where she was standing. The driver swerved, but not in enough time, the left front light hit Carmeli'ta' and knocked her back into the small oak. She screamed when the car hit her fainted, slumped, and falling to the ground. The blow immediately broke open the stitches on her head and small streams of blood trickled down her face.

Vincenzo' heard the scream, running he reached the small oak and saw the small body lying still with blood on her forehead and in her hair. Leaning over he saw her face, the face of Simone' Bandaci. He panicked, his heart racing said, "Simone'."

By the time he reached Carmeli'ta', Ramon' stopped the car and ran back to where she was lying still as stone. Vincenzo' still panicking said, "Get me a blanket. She will go into shock in this cool weather. Do you have a blanket in your car?"

"Yes, I have one I will be right back. He ran to his car got the blanket from the back seat and ran excitedly back to where she was laying. Vincenzo' looked at her again knew it was not Simone' but Carmeli'ta, with tears in his voice, cried out in pain, "No, no, not her, not her, please not her."

He said, "Go get a doctor. The hospital is at the foot of the hill five minutes away. Hurry, oh please hurry." He took his handkerchief from his pocket and dabbed the blood he saw on her head and face. Tears begin to flow from his eyes as he kneeled near her patting her hand said, "Carmeli'ta', Carmeli'ta' can you hear me?" She moaned in pain murmuring "Mother, mother where are you? I hurt mother; my left side is hurting so badly. Help me mother, help me." The whimpering sounds, cries for help, and pain in her voice broke Vincenzo's heart. He finally heard the ambulance coming said, "Don't move Carmeli'ta', don't move. Help is on its way."

The ambulance arrived, Dr. Panniche. Jr. rushed from the ambulance and examined her, saw the swelling on her left side said, "We have to get her to the hospital this child is bleeding inside. Tell me Vincenzo' did she have any of these signs: blurred vision, confusion, light-headedness fainting, signs of shock, restlessness, anxiety, nausea, and paleness?" Vincenzo' said, "Yes, she seemed confused calling for her mother, she seem to not be able to see, she fainted, she has been restless, in pain, she looked pale like the blood drained from her face."

"He looked her and said, "She looks like Simone' Giovanni, but that can't be." Vincenzo' said, "No Christian, this is Simone's daughter. Please you have to save her." Dr. Panniche' looked at Vincenzo' and replied, "I will do everything I can. We need to call Franco Giovanni to let him know his granddaughter is hurt and on the way to the hospital."

Vincenzo' replied, "We can do that after we arrive can't we Christian? At this moment, she is the most important." They carefully lifted Carmeli'ta' on the stretcher, put her in the ambulance. Dr. Panniche' continued to examine her while they made the five-minute trip to the bottom of the hill. Ramon' followed closely with Vincenzo' riding on the passenger side.

Arriving at the hospital, they took Carmeli'ta' to the surgical ward to prepare for X-ray images to determine the extent of the injury. While they took X-ray images, Dr. Panniche went to his office to call the Giovanni's home. Roberto' and Simone' checking the time knew that Carmeli'ta' should have returned by that time, walked through the kitchen into the garden to wait for her. At the same time, Franco, was driving in the yard, parked his truck got out and waved, "Hello my children." The phone begin to ring, he said, "I will be there let me answer the phone." He walked into his office over to the desk and said on the sixth ring, "Hello, Franco Giovanni here."

"Franco, this is Christian."

"Hello Christian, we will see you tomorrow at 12:00 Noon or a little before. How are you today? It is good to hear from you."

"Franco."

The tone in Dr. Panniche's voice told him something was wrong, asked, "What is wrong Christian? Is there trouble at the hospital of some kind? I can come right away."

"Franco, I have a young lady here that looks like your Simone'. She is injured; she is semi-conscious and calling for her mother. She is bleeding internally. The stitches on her head, has burst open and is bleeding. However, that is a minor problem; her bleeding internally is what concerns me. Is her mother and father in Tuscany?"

"Yes they are Christian they are outside. I will get them."

"No Franco, there is no time for more conversation. They need to come right away. We need permission to treat her even if she is of age she is not aware enough to give us permission." Vincenzo' Moretti was with her. He was working in his vineyard near the road. He told me, as I treated her at the scene, he heard her scream and the screeching of car tires. Apparently when she was hit, knocked her against a small tree and her left side caught the blow. Hurry my friend."

Franco walked into the kitchen and the expression on his face said to Catarina it was Carmeli'ta'. She said, "What is it my husband?"

"Carmeli'ta' has been hurt we need to tell Simone' and Roberto'. The walked quickly to the garden, Simone's saw them coming knew the expression of trouble on her father's face asked, "What is the matter Father, what is it?"

"It is Carmeli'ta' my children, she has been injured and is in the hospital. Christian wants us to come right away." Roberto' could not believe what he was hearing said, "What happen to her was she attacked, what Franco?" He replied, "I will explain on the way let us hurry." They all rushed and got into the car.

Answering, he replied, "No my son, she was not attacked, she was injured when the driver lost control of his car on that steep curve before you get to the bottom of the hill near the Moretti Vineyard. The driver, I understand, swerved to keep from going off the hill, but did not see Carmeli'ta' standing there. The left front bumper or light of his car hit her knocking her against a small oak. She is bleeding internally, and her stitches are open and her head is bleeding. He said that the stitches being open, isn't the issue but the internal bleeding is."

Simone' felt numb looked down realized she was still holding her Diary. She could not feel anything at that moment. She saw her life flash in front of her face, prayed that her daughter would not die from the internal bleeding, not her beautiful little sweet Carmeli'ta'.

Uncontrollable tears rolled down her face. Roberto' held her close with his eyes closed prayed to God to let his only child would live. The trip took fifteen minutes to get to the hospital. It seemed to Simone', Roberto', Catarina', and Franco that it was one of the longest fifteen minutes they had experienced in their lives. The silence on the ride to the hospital was deafening. At the hospital, Franco parked the car at the front entrance and they all went in.

Dr. Panniche met them at the front desk with the x-ray film, said, "Hello Simone', Roberto' it is good to see both of you again. I regret it had to be under these circumstances. Franco, Catarina, good to see you."

Roberto' impatient with the greeting asked, "How is my daughter Dr. Panniche?" He replied, "She has internal bleeding. Her X-ray shows when the car knocked her against the tree, the blow cracked the seventh rib on her left side, and it punctured her Spleen. She is bleeding and I need to get your permission to do surgery to stop the bleeding."

"Yes, Doctor what is the success rates with this type of surgery? Have you done this surgery before? I want to see my daughter."

"Roberto' yes, I have done this surgery before and the success rate is 90%. My father perfected this procedure years ago once we got X-ray imaging technology thanks to your father in-law. I need you to sign the papers so I can get started. I would prefer you not see her before surgery. She has already been prepared for the procedure. I did not want to wait to do all of this so while you were on the way we took care of the preliminaries. I will tell her before we put her to sleep you are here."

Dr. Panniche waiting for Roberto's response, which was only a minute, seemed longer said, "I need to get started Roberto' time is the important factor here." Roberto' quickly read the permission form and signed it. Dr. Panniche handed the form to the charge nurse and rushed to the Surgical Room 3 where Carmeli'ta' was ready for the procedure asked, "Carmeli'ta' can you hear me?" Barely above a whisper said, "Yes, where is my mother?"

He took her hand and replied, "both your parents and grandparents are here, Carmeli'ta'. You are in the hospital and have been injured, I am taking care of your injury when you wake up your parents will be here." Tears rolled from her eyes as she closed them from the effect of the Anesthesia. The Head Surgery Nurse said, "She is sleeping Dr. Panniche we are ready to begin." Ramon' and Vincenzo' were in the Waiting Room when Roberto', Carmeli'ta', Franco, and Catarina walked in.

Ramon' walked over to Simone' and said, "I know she is your daughter she is the spitting image of you."

She said, "Who are you?"

"I am Ramon' Allavera' de Antoine. I was driving the car that caused the accident. I did not see your daughter standing near that tree. When I came around the curve, my car went out of control. When I did see her I swerved, the left bumper light hit her knocking her against the oak tree and she fell. I stopped as soon as I could and ran back. Mr. Moretti, sitting over there, had gotten to her by that time. I got a blanket from my car he covered her to keep her from going into shock, and sent me for a doctor. I am not from this area, Miss. I would give my life if it would help her. I have a daughter her age in her mid-twenties and she is precious to me as I know your daughter is precious to you."

Roberto' walked over to where Ramon' was standing talking with Simone' who heard him, but felt numb. She could not think. Trying to process all of the events, in the last hours, was overwhelming. Ramon' continued, "I am sorry, so sorry I will pay for all the expense. I want to stay here until I know she is okay if that is agreeable with you."

Roberto' said, "We appreciate your kindness thank you."

Franco stood near Simone' as her mother Catarina held onto her. It was a nightmare that seemed to have no end first, the attack on the plane and now the accident. How could this be happening all in a short period-of-time?

At that moment, the police officers walked into the waiting room and

over to Franco, the Captain said, "Hello Franco, tell us what happened with the accident. Dr. Panniche reported the accident as is the rule for any major injury that is treated here."

Franco sat with Captain Marche' and gave him the facts as they were explained to him by Ramon' and Vincenzo' while he filled out the report.

Vincenzo' did not approach Simone' or Roberto'.

Franco when done with the report went over to Simone' and Roberto', "I have taken care of the police report for this injury." Simone' said, "Thank you Father." She looked in Vincenzo's direction. He sat looking at her, his heart skipped a beat and butterflies was in his stomach as he watched the woman he has wanted for all times stand in pain with tears in her eyes, could not do anything to comfort her. He wanted to go to her, but knew it would be detrimental for him.

Franco saw Vincenzo' watching Simone', walked over to him and said, "Thank you Mr. Moretti for helping my granddaughter. Your quick thinking might have saved her life according to Dr. Panniche. I appreciate your kindness."

Vincenzo' replied, "You are welcome. I will wait to hear the result of the surgery. I would like to speak to Simone' if I may."

Franco felt his anger level rising replied, "I don't think that that would serve any purpose at this time Mr. Moretti. I would prefer you not talk with my daughter as we discussed two weeks ago. She has enough to contend with right now without you adding more stress to the situation."

Roberto' observed the expressions on Franco' face knew he was angry, but why?

Roberto' walked over to where they were standing talking said, "Mr. de Antione said, you helped my daughter Mr. Moretti, I appreciate your kindness." Roberto' continuing, made a statement rather than ask the question commented, "I have not seen you in years. I saw you last here in this hospital when my daughter was born you were visiting someone in your family also."

Vincenzo' shivering deep within his soul knew caution was the rule of the day guarded his words and tone of his conversation, realized he had his hand in the Lion's mouth and needed to ease it until he got it out. Looking at the height and statue of Roberto', he felt short in comparison to him and his father-in-law Franco, their height and physical strength was foreboding. They were both 6'4" and 6'5" tall; he was 5'10" tall and slimmer built said, "Hello Mr. Bandaci. It has been many years since I have seen you. I am sorry it has to be under these circumstances."

Roberto' looked at him put emphasis on his words commented, "It is unfortunate Mr. Moretti citizens of the same community are divided by status."

Simone' watching her husband and father in conversation with Vincenzo' saw anger on both their face, felt a wave of crushing fear like an anvil hit her, turned to her mother, and said, "Mother, father and Roberto' look so angry. What could they be saying? You don't think Vincenzo' is telling them he believe he is Carmeli'ta's father do you?" "No, my Daughter, he did not." Simone' not convinced asked, "How do you know mother, how can you tell?"

"Simone', Vincenzo' Moretti is still standing and he is still alive that is how I know." Simone' calming down agreed, "You are right Mother. My daughter and how she is doing is the only thing I can think about now. What is taking so long? When will the doctor come to tell us something? Anything would be better than this horrible waiting." Roberto' and Franco saw the expressions on Simone' and Catarina faces, walked back to where they were.

It was a five hours since Carmeli'ta' surgery began. Roberto' sat holding Simone' close to him as she held tight to her Diary, closed her eyes, and prayed for strength. The hour grew late. Finally, Dr. Christian Panniche, Sr. walked into the waiting room.

When Roberto' and Franco saw him, they stood, he walked over to where Roberto' and his family were sitting and said, "Hello Franco, Roberto', Simone', Catarina. I assisted with Carmeli'ta's surgery today, she is in recovery, she came through the surgery okay. It was a little tricky. The puncture was not as severe as it could have been. We were able to repair it and stopped the bleeding. The 7th rib on her left side is cracked, but that will heal with time." He paused... Franco said, "What are you not telling us about our child Christian?"

He continued, "She lost a lot a blood before we could get the surgery done. Right now, she is holding her own, very weak, but her vital signs are good. We will watch for a few hours; she may need a blood transfusion. If so, it needs to come from one of her parents, but we might have to test others to see if we can match. In this case blood transfusion from a man would help her most."

Roberto' said, "That is no problem whatever you need to do to save my daughter's life is what we want. I will give her all the blood she needs." Simone' stood shivering with pain gripping her heart and mind, was past speaking. Franco looked at Dr. Panniche, Sr. and asked, "Is there a problem Christian, you keep hesitating, what is it?" When we tested Carmeli'ta' blood, the test shows that she has a rare blood type "AB Negative" this blood type is found in a very small population of people in any society. She can only have blood with integrin's factors that are Rh-negatives. We will let you know if the transfusion is necessary."

Franco, Catarina, Ramon', and Vincenzo' all volunteered for the test for possible donors, if needed. This revelation of Carmeli'ta' rare blood bought the last twenty-four years flooding into her mind. She did not know what to think or how to think. Her mother and father looked at each other with concern on their faces. The next few hours would be the hardest they would spend waiting to see if Carmeli'ta' would pull through. Roberto' asked, "Can we see our daughter Dr. Panniche?" He said, "I will ask her attending physician." He excused himself and left the waiting room.

Carmeli'ta's family and Vincenzo' Moretti waited in fear and horror.

CHAPTER
FORTY-EIGHT

Christian Panniche, Jr. came in a few minutes later to speak with Carmeli'ta's family.

He walked over to Roberto' and Simone' and said. "I will allow you to see her for only a few minutes. The next few hours are critical. You can follow me she is in the Critical Care Unit. Please be very quiet we do not want her to suffer any sudden traumas. She is conscious, alert, understands questions I asked her, her vision is not blur, her color has returned a little, she is not nauseated, but she is very weak. She does not need to see you upset Simone' she called your name when she awakens as the anesthesia wore off. You have to be strong and not cry or you Roberto'. She thinks you may be upset with her because she stayed too long on her walk. She talks about you both in her delirium. She loves you both deeply. It will affect her recovery if she does not see you; it will also affect her recovery if she thinks you are upset and worried. Can you maintain your composure? If not I prefer you not see her."

Simone' and Roberto' said, "Yes, we will do what is best for our daughter."

Dr. Panniche continued, "I require the same composure from you Franco and Catarina it is hard but it is best for that child lying there fighting for her life."

Franco said, "We will all do what is best for our baby she is our heart."

Reaching the Critical Care Unit, they walked quietly in behind Dr. Panniche, Jr. When they arrived, Dr. Panniche Sr. was monitoring her vital signs motioned for them to come over. Simone' walked over to her bed, leaned over her, took her right hand, and said, "Carmeli'ta' it is Mummy. Can you hear me my daughter? Your father and grandparents are with me.

We are all here and love you."

Carmeli'ta' though very weak, when she heard her mother's voice opened her eyes and smiled weakly, "Mummy, I love you. I am sorry to upset you and father. I only wanted to take a walk to see the sights."

Roberto' walked to the other side of her bed and said, "Carmeli'ta' my precious daughter we are not upset period, and especially not about you taking a walk. We are thankful to God you are okay. You will be well soon and home with us. Your mother and I will be right here. We will not leave you. We love you. We want you to rest and sleep so you can get well my darling Daughter."

She smiled and whispered, "Thank you Father and Mother, I love you both and my grandparents. Mother will you call Jason and let him know tonight so he will not be surprised when he get to Tuscany on Wednesday. Tell him I love him for me Mother please."

"Yes, Carmeli'ta' I will call Jason and your father will call Amelio' to let him know also. Yes father, tell Uncle Amelio' I love him and will see him soon."

Simone' barely able to hold back tears said, "I will my Daughter, I will. Rest now and we will come again soon to see you." She kissed her and gently laid her hand back by her side. Roberto' stroked her hair and said, "Sleep my beautiful Daughter."

Franco and Catarina both kissed her and smiled. She closed her eyes like a flittering butterfly and slept.

They left the room and walked back into the hall to talk with Dr. Panniche, Jr. and Sr. they said, "We will watch her now to see if her vital signs get stronger, if not we will need to do the transfusion right away."

Dr. Panniche, Sr. went back in to continue his monitoring her progress. Franco asked, "Can we get rooms here for the night or stay in the doctors quarters Christian?" He replied, "Yes, Franco, we have the executive quarters open it has a sitting room and two bedroom you can use them for tonight. I will make the arrangements."

Franco said, "Thank you Christian you cannot know what your help means to my family." He replied, "I know Franco, believe me I know my friend. I need to get back into my patient. I will let you know of any changes."

Roberto' Simone', Franco, and Catarina walked back to the waiting room. Simone' still holding her Diary tight sit and tears flooded her eyes as she cried aloud in the waiting room. Roberto' held her and said, "Please my beauty I cannot stand to see you cry. I know this is breaking your heart. I do not think I have ever felt this kind of pain that is gripping my heart. I cannot reason with my daughter being in critical condition and just a few hours ago she was fine and we were talking."

Simone' through broken tears said, "I know my husband, I know."

Vincenzo' and Ramon' standing anxiously waiting asked Franco, "How is she?" He said, "She is weak, but holding her own. Now, the doctors are monitoring her progress. If you will excuse me my family and I need to prepare to stay the night." He walked over to where they were sitting.

Franco said, "We need to go home and get ourselves situated to spend the night here. Mother and I will go first and return. We will stay while you and Simone' go and prepare to spend the night. We can get dinner here in the hospital cafeteria."

Simone' said, "I think Roberto' and you should go father, so he can call Amelio' and our Minister to let them know and then Mother and I can go and prepare. I need to call Jason for Carmeli'ta'. I don't want her to wake up and ask me if I called and I have not done so." Roberto' said, "That sounds okay to me Franco if you are in agreeance."

He replied, "Yes, that is fine let us go it is getting late almost 6:00 p.m." He and Roberto' left the waiting room. Catarina sit next to Simone' and said, "She is still with us Simone' we are not thinking any other way."

She replied, "You are right Mother, thank you."

Vincenzo' took the opportunity to speak with Simone' since both Roberto' and Franco left. He walked over and said, "Hello Simone'. I don't know what to say, when I saw Carmeli'ta' lying there unconscious..." He shook his head and continued, "I would give anything if she were not hurt and this was not causing you any pain. I will do whatever it takes to make sure she is okay. I love her Simone' I can't think of anything else."

She looked up at him and saw the expression of pain in his face and said, "I appreciate your concern for my husband and my daughter. You are kind to wait here with us, and offer to give blood. Thank you for all that you did, she might have died had you not been working in your vineyard. I will forever be grateful for that."

He replied, "Thank you is not necessary Simone'. I love Carmeli'ta' as I love..." He stopped short before he finished his sentence.

The look on Simone's face told him what she was feeling at that moment. He saw anger and fear in her eyes and said, "I would do anything if to prevent you from suffering Simone'. I cannot let my daughter go, I just cannot."

She said, "I will not discuss that with you again Vincenzo'. My only concern is the health of my daughter at this time. I do not want to think of anything else."

Catarina watching them from across the room saw anger in her daughters face. She walked over to where Ramon' Allavera' de Antoine was sitting and said, "Mr. de Antoine we appreciate you waiting with us. I appreciate the fact that you stopped and tried to help our child. She is indeed precious to us. Simone' tell me you have a daughter our Carmeli'ta's age."

He said, "Yes, Mrs. Giovanni, I do she is 25 years old and very precious to me. She is a beautiful young woman as is your granddaughter. I hate that I was the cause of this pain to your family."

"Thank you for your concern. We appreciate you staying with us, it is not necessary we will let you know how she is doing. If you want to leave your number at the Nurses Station we will call you and let you know."

"I will be in Tuscany for a few more weeks Ms. Giovanni. My daughter and wife are joining me next week. I cannot leave Tuscany anyway right now. The Police Captain said that I needed to stay until they know the outcome of your daughter's health. They are not certain there will not be charges in this case."

She nodded and said, "I understand. I will call you please leave your number."

He went to the Nurses Station and left his contact information to his suite at the Tuscany Valley Vineyard Hotel and Suites, located on the Northside of the Valley. He said goodbye to Simone', Catarina, and Vincenzo' and left.

Vincenzo' still sitting with Simone' she said, "Vincenzo' your family must be concerned about your whereabouts by now will they not? It is not necessary for you to wait there is nothing for you to do here. Please go to your family. I am sure your wife is wondering where you are by now."

"I called my father earlier my family knows where I am."

"She replied, "I am sure that your family is wondering why you are so concerned with a Farmer's Daughter don't you think?"

"No, I don't think and at this moment Simone' I don't care whether they are concerned about why I am at the hospital. I explained the reason to my father."

"Really, you explained to your father and he had no questions."

Seemingly annoyed he replied, "Yes, he had questions and wanted to know what I had to do with the Giovanni family. I told him that Franco's granddaughter was hurt on our property and I want to take any responsibility that is necessary because she was on our property. He agreed and said he would let the family know that was the end of the discussion."

"I see. I want to think Vincenzo'. I would like to be alone if you don't mind and my husband and father should be returning in a little while."

"I understand. I will be here if you need me Simone'." She did not reply just continued to look out of the window into the garden outside. Catarina observed her went and sit near her without commenting.

Franco and Roberto' arrived at home. Franco noticed that the soup was still on the stove. He put it back in the refrigerator and the bread in the cabinet. He went took a bath, dressed; put his personal items into his shaving satchel. Catarina would pack his robe, slippers, and a change of clothes and bring them with her.

Roberto' went to call Amelio'. He waited nervously while the phone rings at Amelio's office. It was 1:00 p.m. and he knew he would be having his midday meal at that time. The phone rang four times the voice answered, "Bandaci Farms can I help you?" It was not Amelio'; but his Farm Manager.

Roberto' said, "this is Roberto' Bandaci is Amelio' there?"

"Yes Mr. Bandaci, he stepped outside for a minute to talk with the Produce Manager, I will get him for you." A few moments later Amelio' picked up and said, "Hello Roberto' I am pleased you called today, but surprised, I expected you to call later tonight. How is everything going?"

He paused and said, "Amelio." Immediately he knew something was deathly wrong by the tone in his voice. His not being able to shake the feeling something was wrong gripped him even stronger asked, "What is wrong Roberto', tell me what has happened."

"Carmeli'ta' is in the hospital cousin. She was in an accident today and had to have surgery."

"Surgery, what from a gash on her head that is impossible Roberto'."

He replied, "No Amelio' she was hit by a car when she was walking near the Moretti Vineyard. A car lost control on that steep hill leading into the valley. The car knocked her against a small oak and the blow when she hit the tree cracked her rib on the left side and punctured her Spleen. She was bleeding internally. They did surgery and stopped the bleeding, but she lost a lot of blood in the process. She is very weak and might need a transfusion. The doctors are monitoring her now."

Amelio' not believing what he was hearing said, "This is impossible Roberto'. I can hardly get this in my head. Who is the doctor? Is it Christian Panniche, Sr.? He would be too old now to be still practicing wouldn't he?"

"It is Dr. Panniche, Jr. the one who delivered Carmeli'ta'. His father is still practicing; in fact, he assisted with the surgery earlier. He perfected the procedure that they performed. I was glad to know he was there to assist his son."

"I was not as familiar with his son as I was with the senior Dr. Panniche. What is the prognosis, for recovery time?"

"They are monitoring her now Amelio' if her vital signs do not get better and she does not show signs of improvements within the next twenty-four hours they will need to do a blood transfusion. Carmeli'ta', they discovered, has a rare blood type. We will all give blood samples to see whose blood type matches hers. The doctor says a male's blood, her grandfather, or mine whichever of ours match, would be better for her. It is a difficult situation at best Amelio'."

"Simone', Roberto', how is she holding up?"

He paused, "I wish I could say she is being strong; she is not Amelio'. I am worried about my wife to be frank with you. This has taken a toll on her. She acts as if she thinks this is her fault. That is just something I observed with the look she has on her face."

"Did you and she ever talk Roberto'?"

"We started to talk this morning after we spoke with Carmeli'ta', but did

not finish. We had several interruptions then the accident. It has something to do with a Diary she has kept all these years and what I can get from it, whatever it is started when she was very young. I still do not know what is keeping my wife upset and distance sometimes. But now, I am concerned with Carmeli'ta' and Simone's health. I don't know if we could bare it if." He stopped short of finishing his statement.

Amelio' said, "We are not thinking negative Roberto'. Carmeli'ta' is young and strong she will bounce back from this and Simone' is strong also probably more than you are aware. We will pray for God's intervention in her recovery and Simone's strength."

"Thank you Amelio'. Would you please let Brother Meriwether know so he can tell the congregation to pray for my baby girl? I think it best to wait to tell Marianna until it is necessary to tell her."

"Yes, I agree Roberto' please keep me informed about her progress and the blood transfusion. I am sure that she probably has your blood type. We never thought about knowing about blood types until now. It is a critical factor in a person's health. I hope they are careful and precise in their testing and matching her since her blood is a rare type."

"Thank you Amelio'. I need to get a bath, changed, and go back to the hospital so my wife and mother-in-law can come make necessary preparations for spending the night in the hospital. Dr. Panniche is arranging the Doctors Executive Suite for us tonight. I will call you with a progress report on my sweet daughter. Carmeli'ta' asked me to tell you she loves you. Bye for now."

Amelio' replied, "Tell my sweet niece I love her with all my heart. Take heart, my cousin, bye for now."

Roberto' hung up and went to their bedroom suite and bath, changed his clothes, gathered his shaving case with his cosmetics, walked back to the kitchen. Franco was waiting at the table for him ready to leave. They returned to the hospital. On the ride back, Roberto' checked the time it was 7:00 p.m. It would take Simone' and Catarina at least an hour to get home and back to the hospital. They arrived, walked back in the waiting room.

Franco saw Vincenzo' still waiting went to Catarina and asked, "Has he bothered Simone'?" She looked down then replied, "He talked with her for a few minutes. She did not entertain him in a conversation very long. He returned and sat where you see him now. My fear my husband is that sooner or later Roberto' will question his purpose for being here."

Roberto' hardly noticed that he was there, sit behind Simone' and held her around the waist and said, "How are you holding up my beauty? You must be tired and hungry by now. Please go and prepare yourself and come back so we can get dinner before the cafeteria closes at 10:00 p.m. or we can go to the Boulangerie' Viennoise across the square. They are open until 11:00 p.m. at night."

She turned and looked her husband snuggled against him and replied, "Either of them will be okay my husband. I know by now, Father, Mother, and you are hungry. I need to eat so I can have strength to help my daughter. Mother and I will be as quick as is possible."

He asked, "Would you like for me to drive Catarina and you? Franco can stay with Carmeli'ta'."

"No, my love, we will be fine stay with my father. I am concerned about him he seems angry for some reason."

Roberto' walked Simone' and Catarina to the car. They left for home to return within the hour. Dr. Panniche, Jr. came to the door of the waiting room and beckoned to Franco and Roberto'. Worried that there was change in Carmeli'ta', they picked up their personal cases and walked to the door and into the hallway.

He said, "Roberto', Franco, I have arranged one of the Doctors Executive Quarters for you during your stay while Carmeli'ta' is in the hospital. I also asked them to prepare dinner for you and bring it to your suite at 9:00 p.m.

I know you have not eaten today. I asked Catarina she said you had only breakfast. You can get coffee while you are waiting. It is fresh and kept there for the doctors all the time. I will show you the way."

He looked at Vincenzo' and asked, "I wonder if he want to join you for a cup of coffee? He has been here all day."

Franco said, "I would not think so Christian."

Dr. Panniche understood what he meant. He knew the Wine Kings did not want to associate with Farmers that had not changed in their little valley, at least publicly anyway.

He replied, "I will have coffee bought to him if he wants it. I will have the Charge Nurse check and get him what he needs."

He escorted Franco and Roberto' to the Doctors Executive Suite down the hall from the Waiting Room. The aroma of fresh brewed coffee met them as they opened the door. The suite was comfortable and well decorated. They put their shaving cases in the bathrooms and Franco poured coffee for both of them.

Settling in the comfort of the suite Roberto' leaned forward on the couch, looked at Franco, and asked, "Why is Vincenzo' Moretti still here? Does it not seem strange to you that he would stay here the entire day?"

Franco uncomfortable with the question did not show any emotion. He knew the sharpness of his son-in-law replied, "I guess he feels some responsibility because our baby was hurt on his property and they fear repercussions from the family."

Roberto' took his cup and leaned back again sipping his coffee avowed, "Maybe, that has a somewhat reasonable rationale to it, I am not sure. It is just strange. I doubt he cares that much about our family."

Franco wanting to change the subject stated, "I am getting more coffee, it is good or I am hungry maybe both; would you like me to refresh your cup?"

Roberto' still in thoughts of why Vincenzo' sit all day uttered, "Yes, I would like more coffee and it is good, thank you Franco."

By the time Roberto' and Franco settled into the Doctors Executive Suite, Simone' and Catarina arrived home. Simone' went into Carmeli'ta' bedroom suite retrieved her phone book from the nightstand, went into her father's office, laid her Diary on the desk, and phoned the International Operator. She gave the number to Jason Madison Jr. home first just in case he was packing and preparing to make his trip. The phone rang 4 times,

Jason answered saying, "Jason Madison."

Simone' replied, "Mr. Madison, this is Simone' Bandaci. How are you today?"

He replied, "I am fine Ms. Bandaci how are you?"

He thought in the seconds that he spoke with her why would Carmeli'ta's mother call me unless she is not doing well? He held his breath while waiting for her to continue. She said, "Jason, Carmeli'ta' has been in an accident, was severely injured, and is in the hospital in Tuscany."

Jason knees went weak. He dropped down to the floor where he was standing near his bed packing his luggage and could not speak for a moment. Simone' said, "Mr. Madison you there? Hello."

He in a breathless manner, "She is not..."

"No Jason she is not near death. She had surgery for a cracked rib that ruptured her Spleen. She was bleeding internally from the blow."

He had a hard time accepting what she was saying asked, "What happen that she would be in such a severe accident?"

"She was walking right before lunch near a Vineyard, a car lost control, the driver tried to miss her, when he swerved the front of the car knocked her against a small oak tree. The blow fractured her rib, which damaged her Spleen."

"What is the prognosis Ms. Bandaci?"

She paused, and then continued, "She is being watched now. If her vital signs do not improve over the next twenty-four hours, she will need a blood transfusion, and there is a little problem with that, we have to match her blood type; she has a rare blood type. The doctor would prefer it be a male. Carmeli'ta' asked me to call and let you know so you would not be surprised when you arrived on Wednesday."

"Ms. Bandaci. I love Carmeli'ta' with everything in me. I cannot lose her, I just cannot. I will not be there until Wednesday. I will gladly give her my blood if it matches hers. My flight leaves at 11:00 a.m. tomorrow. Please tell Carmeli'ta' I love her and I am coming will you tell her for me?"

"Yes Jason I will tell her. I hope that her knowing you are coming and is aware of her being in the hospital will help her. Thank you for caring for my daughter Jason. I need to get myself prepared for the night and get back to the hospital; take care. Please pray for Carmeli'ta'. I will see you soon. You have the address to my parent's home?"

"Yes, I have the address, Carmeli'ta' gave me contact information for all her family months ago. I will pray for her and the entire family, Ms. Bandaci. I do not know what to say. I know how hard it must be. Thank you for calling and letting me know. She means the world to me. Bye for now."

"Bye Jason. We look to see you soon."

Simone' hung up the phone, picked up her diary, and the phone book and replaced Carmeli'ta's phone book back in her suite, went to her bedroom, bathed, dress, packed gowns, slippers, and a change of clothes for she and Roberto', and other personal items needed for overnight stay. Catarina, while she was speaking with Jason, bathed, dress, packed for Franco and herself went back to the kitchen to wait for Simone'.

Simone' was ready by 8:10 p.m. She and her mother loaded the car and left for the 15-minute drive back to the hospital. On their way Catarina inquired, "What was Jason's response to the news of Carmeli'ta'?"

"Mother, I thought he was having a heart attack when I told him. He could not speak for a while. I could tell he was more than upset; he was beside himself with worry. He loves her with all his heart mother and Roberto' wants her to marry Alberto Gambani. I want her to have the choice to choose who she loves and she has. She is not a child, but a 24 years old woman, who knows her mind. She has always known what she wanted to do and did it sometimes at a great cost to her, just as she did last week when she traveled here."

"I know Simone' she is like you in many ways my darling daughter. She is strong like her father and has the mind of both of you. She is an amazing young woman to have come so far in such a short length of time."

"I agree mother."

Catarina added, "Simone' if it comes down to Carmeli'ta' needing a blood transfusion, have you thought about what you will say to your husband. She has a rare blood type. Naturally, Christian will check yours and her father's first. Vincenzo' is still waiting at the hospital. Eventually Roberto' will question his presence, if he has not done so already, what will you say to your husband?"

"I don't know Mother. All I know right now is I want my daughter to live and be healthy. I will deal with anything else when it comes up."

"I see you are still holding your Diary Simone' is that what will tell Roberto' what he wants to know or at least give him an explanation?"

"Yes, Mother it has all the facts about my past life here from when I was 13 years old until a few years after I moved to America. I tried to explain my actions over the years, earlier today after Carmeli'ta' went for a walk, but did not get an opportunity to finish. My explanation did not even touch the issue, you returned, and then the accident happened. Vincenzo' being at the hospital is not a wise idea for him right now. I know you were right when you said earlier he had not told my husband his claim of being our daughter's father, he would have killed him I know he would have or injured him. The way that Roberto' is feeling today and worried about Carmeli'ta' he would have hurt Vincenzo'."

"I know Simone'. I could see the anger in Franco's face the entire time he spoke with Vincenzo'. Between he and Roberto' Vincenzo' would not have a chance. Franco is so adamant about Vincenzo' and his ungentlemanly ways over the years in coming America and threatening you with fear of revealing what he thinks is the truth. I cannot accept his truth, even if it was true, she is your and Roberto' daughter in my mind."

They reached the hospital Catarina parked the car and they went in.

The Charge Nurse showed them to the Doctor's Executive Suite where their husbands were waiting. They knocked lightly at the door, Roberto' opened it calling back to Franco. "Here are our sweet wives Franco."

They walked in, Franco met Catarina halfway in the room and said, hello my lovely wife. "Can I get you a cup of coffee it is fresh and delicious."

She smiled and replied, "Yes, thank you my husband that would be nice. "Looking around she commented. "This is a beautiful suite and comfortable."

Simone' leaning back on Roberto' agreed, "Yes, it is. It reminds me of our sitting room at home Roberto', it is spacious, elegant, and comfortable."

Roberto' said, "It is true my beauty. It is like our suite at home. I will get the suitcases from the car. Our bedroom suite my beauty is the one to the left of the kitchen is also nice and comfortable."

Franco handed Catarina her cup of coffee, walked toward the door and replied, "I will assist you my son. We will be back shortly. Christian has arranged for us to be served dinner here at 9:00 p.m. We are all hungry I know. We need our strength."

They left to get the luggage. As they passed the waiting room Franco noticed that Vincenzo' was still sitting waiting to hear more about Carmeli'ta'.

His thoughts went to his and Vincenzo's conversation now almost 3 weeks ago, when he was sure of being Carmeli'ta's father. He could not reason with the thought that he might be her father, but had to face the reality that he could be with everything his daughter said when they talked in November 1905. Upset as she is even she is not sure of anything right now. He decided to stop and chat with Vincenzo' when he came back through.

Roberto' and Franco took the luggage from the car, walked back to the lobby. Franco said, "My son I want to stop here for a minute, could you take the bags. Tell mother I will be there in a few minutes; I want to check on something. Roberto' nodded took the bags and went back to his waiting Simone'.

Vincenzo' looked up saw Franco walking toward him stood and asked, "Is there news about Carmeli'ta'?"

"No, Mr. Moretti we have not heard anything else it has not been enough time just a couple hours now. Christian will let us know of any changes in her condition. I want to let you know again we appreciate your help and I will call you personally if anything happens or if a blood transfusion is need. I know you volunteered to be a donor. We will be having dinner shortly and retire for the night."

Vincenzo' looked at him for a moment then replied, "I do need to go to see my family and get some dinner. I will look to hear from you if there is a change in Carmeli'ta's condition. I appreciate you saying you would call me. I do want to rest just in case my blood is needed." Franco boiling inside nodded and said, "Goodnight Mr. Moretti." Vincenzo' did not comment further just walked out of the waiting room into the lobby, out of the hospital, across the street, and through the square, the Moretti Mansion was less than a mile away.

Franco joined his family in the doctor's suite to relax and wait for dinner from the cafeteria. A knock at the door bought Roberto' to his feet. He knew it was not time for dinner it was 8:40 p.m. Opening the door, he saw Dr. Panniche, Jr. standing waiting. He said, "Good evening everyone. I wanted to give you an update on Carmeli'ta'. She is still holding her own. Her vital signs are maintaining their levels at the moment, but it has only been 3 hours since the surgery."

Roberto' said, "Thank you for the update. Is she awake, can we see her?" Simone' quiet the entire time did not say anything just listened.

"No Roberto' she is not awake, Sleep is the best thing for her right now she will get stronger if she is not expending energy awake and trying to talk. I want her quiet and still. She is lightly sedated just enough to keep her calm. My father has not left her side since the surgery. I cannot get him to go home, mother called; he usually listens to her; she could not get him to come home either. He had dinner there near her room at 7:00 p.m., but will not leave the hospital."

Franco said, "Christian your father has always been an amazing man. You know how much he cared about our Simone' and Roberto' when they were growing up. He told me so they were two of his favorite people in this valley. We appreciate his vigilance. He is welcome to join us here if he wants to rest. Roberto' and I can bunk here in the sitting room and let him have one of the bedrooms."

"No, my friend that will not be necessary there are several other suites here as you well know, he can rest in one of them if necessary."

A knock on the door ended the conversation. Dr. Panniche opened the door and a cart of food was wheeled in by a handsome, 5'7" tall, petite woman in her late 40s, dressed in a white uniform with a chef's hat on. He said, "This is Arabesque' our Cafeteria Manager, she prepared the meal for you herself. I believe she knows your wife Franco."

Catarina said, "Yes, Christian, I see Arabesque' at the market on Saturday's. She and I are in the same Saturday Morning Coffee with Friends Group that meets at the Boulangerie' Veinnoise at 9:00 am. How are you Arabesque'?"

She smiled and said, "Hello Catarina, I am fine, hello everyone."

Dr. Panniche finished his introductions and said, "We will leave you to your meal. I need to get back to my patients and plus check on my father. Just leave the cart in the hallway there someone will take it away."

Franco said, "Thank you Christian, thank you Arabesque', this makes our lives a lot easier. Thank you."

He said "It is my pleasure my friend. We could not do less for anyone, but especially for my friends and Franco you are a key person in getting this hospital on the cutting edge with the new medical equipment we have and the improvements everywhere here. Everyone is appreciative of your efforts. We are able to do a lot more for our patients. I am thankful we have the x-Ray Machine; it was instrumental in helping get Carmeli'ta' the fast treatment she received and identity the problem areas; it eliminated guess work."

Roberto' replied, "Thank you Dr. Panniche, my father-in-law is an amazing man who never says anything about anything he knows or does."

"Yes, Roberto', he is a good man and a good friend. Remember, Carmeli'ta' is one of my babies I delivered. I will talk with you later. Are you ready, Arabesque'?"

"Yes Dr. Panniche. "I need to finish my preps for tomorrow and get home to my family."

Roberto' said, "Thank you Arabesque'. The dinner smells delicious."

Dr. Panniche and Arabesque' left. Simone' and Catarina covered the table in the middle of room with the tablecloth on the cart, set and put the food on the table. They sat down to a meal of "Parsley Roasted Chicken with Red Potatoes, Italian String beans with Garlic, Green Salad with Oil and Vinegar dressing, Fresh baked bread, butter, and Iced Tea. And for dessert,

Simone' noticed Arabesque' left on the kitchen counter near the coffee pot, a tray of small Lemon-pudding filled Italian cakes. They ate and enjoyed their meal. Simone' realized she was hungrier than she thought. They finished their meal, and pushed the cart and the dishes outside their door.

Vincenzo', on his way home at the time the Giovanni's and Bandaci's ate dinner, walking as swiftly as he could, cut through the vineyard near the cabin where he and Simone' always met during their years together. He stopped for a moment and reflected on the day they met she told him that she was having a baby. He could still feel the joy in his heart he felt that Thursday morning twenty-four years ago when knew he was a father. His dream had come true, he would have a part of Simone' forever they had a child together. It had not gone as he planned. He did not think about his telling Simone' when he visited America he would do anything to see his daughter seemed as a threat; it never occurred to him to threaten her. He knew he still loved Simone' and loved Carmeli'ta' who he knew within his heart for his daughter. Vincenzo' realized that tears were flowing from his eyes because of the hurt and pain he felt for losing Simone' and sit for hours watching her with her husband knowing she did not love him but loved her husband Roberto' it was evident to him from her actions. He felt pain for the child that lay weak trying to hang on to life wondered what the outcome would. Then there is his wife, waiting for him at home, not knowing anything about the situation, just that she knew he did not care for her, as he should.

He felt pain for the years that he had not loved her. They were in an arranged marriage as Roberto's and Simone's were, but theirs ended in love. His marriage had not up to this point ended in love, as least not for him. He knew he had not given it a chance because he dreamed of a life with Simone' once now he knew he would never have. Then his father is suspicious, his mother never says anything, but he knew within him, she was more aware than anyone at the Moretti Mansion what was taking place in her family's lives at and away from their home. He knew his mother was aware of his feelings and his pains over the years. But could she know about Simone'? Knowing his mother, astuteness, and powers of observation, he would not be surprised. The question glared at him as the sun does on a hot Tuscan day. His mother and Franco Giovanni had a lot in common. They knew about everything but said nothing about anything. He thought, "Go figure."

It would not be a stretch to assume she knew whom the woman is he loved with all his heart. Then there is Franco Giovanni, who he knew did not care for his presence in his daughter's life nor did he want him around his granddaughter how could he expect him not to want the only child he had in the world. His wife, though ten years younger, he could have children with, but that had not happened in the years they have been married. Vincenzo's life flashed across his face as he thought of the division of status in the valley among the people, wine kings and farmers was always the tone of the conversation one he never cared for, but his father did at one time, but now even that has changed for his family anyway. However, the years gone by and the separation into classes had damage the relationships with the farmers and other citizens of the valley.

At this point, was reparation possible?

Darkness begins to fall as he gained self-control and walked into the yard that led to the back of his home. He went in through the kitchen. Fabio, their Butler was there, asked, "Mr. Vincenzo' you look tired sir, would you like dinner? I have been waiting for you to come. The rest of the family had dinner about 8:00 p.m. They waited for you."

He replied, "Yes, thank you Fabio, I am hungry. I will freshen-up and return."

He smiled and said, "I will have it on the table when you return sir."

Vincenzo' walked to the bathroom in the hall near the kitchen and washed his face and hand and was drying them ready to return to the dining room when Francisco, his father, listening for him to come home, went to the dining room to talk with him during dinner. He returned to the dining room as he entered he saw his father sitting in the chair next to the place Fabio placed his plate, greeted him, "Good evening Vincenzo' I was not sure you would come home tonight. I want to talk with your son, to finish that conversation we started when Franco Giovanni came to see you 3 weeks ago now. You want to tell me the details that you are hiding. Why did you staying the hospital so long today? Our lawyers could have taken care of the matter. I want to take responsibility for whatever happened to Giovanni's granddaughter on our property, we have done so before when people have gotten hurt. Why do you have a special interest in this family?

Can you share that with me?"

Vincenzo' feeling annoyed asked, "Father, Mother and my wife are where?"

"They went out tonight to the Art Museum. The Art purchased for the museum arrived and was hung today. It is now on display to the public. They are having a reception and wine tasting event there tonight."

"I thought you would have gone to this function Father since the Moretti family was instrumental in bringing in the art collection to the museum."

He frowned and said, "I wanted to talk with you while no one was in the house except you and me my Son. I want you to tell me what is going on with you and the Giovanni family. Franco Giovanni is an intelligent man, a good man, he is quiet, a fine neighbor, and instrumental in the growth in this valley. He never says anything unless he has a reason. I have known him all his life Vincenzo'. I knew his father Franco, Sr. He was the same type man his son is. I know when he says something there is validity to it. Because the farmers and the wine makers do not mix does not mean I am not aware of what is going on in this valley and with you."

Vincenzo' ate his dinner without commenting, he was hungry and tired. He looked at his father and looked down again at his plate his voice broke and he whispered, "I don't have anything that I can share with you Father. I am tired. I want to bathe and go to bed if you don't mind." He pushed his plate away from him, pushed back his chair, and called, "Fabio I am done with dinner you can take the plate now." Fabio appeared cleared away the plate and exited the room.

Francisco not accepting another put off said, "No Son, I do mind you not sharing with me what are causing you the pains I see in your face."

"Father, there is nothing that I can tell you at the moment other than, a young woman was hurt on our property, I helped her, sent for the doctor, and waited at the hospital with the family. I volunteered to give blood if needed. I will return tomorrow or when Franco Giovanni calls me that is it. If you will excuse me, I want to retire for tonight."

Francisco insisting, "No, I will not excuse you for tonight. I want to know what connection you have with the Giovanni family it is not as simple as you stated it son. I have noticed over the years your look of unhappiness and sometimes lack of interest in the family business it all seem to start when you would disappear for hours at a time or stayed to yourself. I know that losing your twin sister affected you, but I did not think that your reaction years later would surface in the conduct that it have now for years."

He continued, "Son, you, and Valantina were 10 years of age when she died, as a result, of Scarlet Fever. You do not need to carry this burden whatever it is any longer without sharing it with me. I will do whatever I can to help you. Your mother and I love you. You are our life and future. Your wife needs you. She cares for you. Your actions and lack of attention has hurt her a lot and over the years she deserves better from you. She is a fine woman, a good daughter in-law and has waited for you all these years. She wants to be a mother. If you and she cannot have a child, I want you to think about adopting a child so we can enjoy a grandchild before we get too much older."

"Father, love has not served me well over the years. I am thankful that you and mother love me, and I love you as well. Love only breaks your heart, tears you apart, and causes separation. Love is fleeting father; it does not get you what you want in life Father it does not! I do not want to discuss anything further tonight, please excuse me." He walked away, up the stairs to his bedroom suite adjoining his wife. They had never slept in the same bedroom all the years of their marriage.

Francisco baffled at his son's statement about love walked back to the family room to finish his coffee. Fabio had refreshed it during his conversation with Vincenzo'.

At that time, his wife Concetta and daughter in-law Antonia walked in from the art show and reception. Concetta asked, "Francisco has Vincenzo' come home yet? I worry that he has not eaten today. He missed two meals with his family."

Francisco answered, "He is home, has had dinner, and is has retired for the night. I am sure by this time he is sleep. He looked worn when he arrived. His concern is for the young woman injured on our property today. That should be everyone's concern we have seen repercussions from injuries on our property before. I am thankful that he gave this his undivided attention today."

Antonia asked, "Did he tell you why he stayed at the hospital today so long Father?"

Concetta looked at her husband knew he was only stating half-truths something went on between him and their son he did not mention. Antonia feeling annoyed knew he did not care to spend that much time with her and give his full attention to their marriage responded, "I think I will skip coffee tonight and retire. I am feeling a little tired and sleepy. Goodnight Father and Mother. I will check on my husband before I sleep."

Antonia climbed the stairs to her suite, went over to the adjourning door that opened into Vincenzo's bedroom walked in and over to the bed, looking down at her sleeping husband she saw, even as he slept, the face of an unhappy and stressed man who she knew did not love her, as a husband should. Turning to leave dropped her purse, Vincenzo' dreaming he was at the hospital still, woke with a start, and said, "Who is it?"

Antonia replied, "It is me my husband. Father said you had come home. I wanted to see if you were okay and resting."

"I am fine thank you Antonia. If you do not mind, I would like to get back to sleep. I have another long day tomorrow."

"I do mind Vincenzo' that is the point, I do mind. I have for these many years, I do mind my husband."

She turned and walked back to her suite closing the door behind her. He lay back on his pillow and looked at the ceiling and did not care about anything at that time except whether Carmeli'ta' survived. He tossed and turned until he fell asleep again.

The approaching morning at the Tuscany Valley Hospital started like a grey hazy day with a murky, blinding fog.

CHAPTER

FORTY-NINE

Dr. Panniche, Jr. checked his pocket watch for the time; 7:00 a.m. went into Carmeli'ta's room. His father was still sitting in the comfortable chair, by her bedside. Carmeli'ta made it through the night; her vital signs seemed to improve just a little. At that point, Drs. Panniche was hopeful. They walked over to her bed and checked her incision, it was draining okay, she did not have a fever at that point, but her color was not very good. Dr. Panniche, Jr. lifted her right hand and looked at the tips of her fingers. He squeezed her forefinger at the tip to see how much pink would show that would tell him a little about her blood levels. He did not get the pink color to her finger he had hoped.

Carmeli'ta' feeling his touch opened her eyes, could not focus at first said, "My Father is that you. I cannot see you."

Concerned about her statement Dr. Panniche said, "No Carmeli'ta' it is your doctor. You remember me from yesterday. How are you feeling?"

"I feel weak. I cannot focus well. Where are my father and mother are they gone?"

"No Carmeli'ta' they are here. They stayed in the hospital last night. I will allow you to see them in just a while. Tell me about your vision."

"It looks blurred. I cannot focus well. What is happening?"

"I want you to stay calm Carmeli'ta' and listen to me. Sometimes when a patient have surgery as extensive as you did yesterday and when they sleep a long time, plus the effects of the anesthesia, and the fact you are weak, can cause a temporary blur in vision. As the morning progresses, the blurred vision should get better."

581

He looked at his father and shook his head. Dr. Panniche, Sr. added, "Carmeli'ta', I am Dr. Panniche's Father and your other doctor. We want to leave you for a few minutes and talk with your parents and then let them visit with you for a while. We will talk with you a little later."

He walked outside her room to wait for his son to come for the decision they needed to make about the next steps to take.

He stood at her bedside checking her vitals sign she said weakly "Okay Dr. Panniche. I want to see my mother and father, please let me see them."

"We are going now to talk about your case and then let your parents see you. I want you to stay calm for me Carmeli'ta' and not expend too much energy you are still weak. Will you do that for me?" She whispered, "Yes, I will do as you ask me. Will you get my parents?"

"Yes, I am on my way now." He joined his father in the hallways and asked, "Give me your assessment of our patient doctor."

His father said, "We can't wait more than a few more hours. This child is not progressing, as she should. Her body is not building the Red Blood Cells, as it should. She is so tiny and which adds to her lack of strength as well. We need to talk with Franco, Catarina, and her parents right away."

On the other side of the hospital in the residence wing, Roberto', Simone', Franco, and Catarina were dressed and breakfast had been bought to them. They ate quickly wanting to be ready to see Carmeli'ta' as soon as possible. Drs. Panniche left orders with the nurse attending Carmeli'ta' to take her vital signs every 10-minutes and keep a journal so they could know her progress.

Arriving at the suite, they knocked at the door. Roberto' opened it, they said, "Good morning Roberto'." He replied, "Good morning, doctors my daughter is how today?"

Dr. Panniche, Sr. answered, "That is why we are here to discuss with you Carmeli'ta' progress." Walking in, they greeted the rest of Roberto's family.

Simone' nervous knew within herself that her daughter was not doing as well as the doctors expected her to, inquired, "How is my sweet daughter today doctor? Is she awake and asking for us?"

"Yes Simone' she is. She has made that request twice within the last 20 minutes. I told her I was on my way to get you. However, before you see her we need to discuss the next phase in her treatment." He continued, "Carmeli'ta' awakened with blurred vision, she is weak, and her blood levels are not building very fast, which we attribute to her size and weight. She is tiny and it takes longer for a small person's body to generate red blood cells. She is even smaller than Simone'."

Dr. Panniche, Jr. added, "I did the finger check for pinkness and it is barely there."

Roberto' questioned, "The finger test. I am not clear on this what does that mean?."

Dr. Panniche, Sr. answered, "When you squeeze the end of your finger you should get an accumulation of blood at the tip it should be a deep pink more than normal, we did not get this with Carmeli'ta' this morning."

Franco stood and inquired, "So what your next phase in her treatment Christian we need to wait for how long?"

"We are not waiting any longer. We need to start looking towards the transfusion and matching the donor. The next few hours are critical. We cannot afford for her to slip into a coma so we must act quickly."

Dr. Panniche, Jr. reminded them, "I want you to visit her, I promised she could see you, but please do not get her excited, remain calm and let her see you smile. She will be hopeful that way. God only know what is going on in that sweet child's mind right now. I know she is frightened she wants to see her mother and father so go to her and remember my caution to you."

He continued, "In the meantime, I want to get the blood donor volunteers back in here and test them one at a time so there will not be any mix-up in the samples, it can happen. I do not want any mistakes in this. I will have my nurse to call Vincenzo' Moretti and Ramon' Allavera' de Antoine and have them come in. We need to get started. I will see you later. Stay only a while with her. Try to encourage her not to talk."

Roberto' heart dropped and fear gripped his mind he stated, "We need to get to our daughter Simone' she needs us. Franco and Catarina are you coming with us?"

Franco quickly replied, "Yes, yes, of course. We are ready." They walked to the other side of the hospital to the Critical Care Unit and into their daughter's room. Simone' went overtook her right hand kissed it and called quietly, "Carmeli'ta' my lovely daughter mummy is here." She opened her eyes, smiled, and replied, "Hello mummy, I missed you. I thought you left me. Where is my father?"

Roberto's heart breaking, cried tears of pain within his soul said, "I am here Carmeli'ta'." He held her left hand and she slowly turned her head and said, "Hello my Father, I love you. I am glad to see you and my mother. Where are Grandfather and Grandmother?"

Standing at the foot of her bed they said, "We are here Granddaughter we are all here and will not leave you."

She whispered, "Mother did you call Jason? What did he say? Is he coming still?"

"Yes, Carmeli'ta' he is coming. He leaves at 11:00 a.m. today; he is possibly on his way in a bit and will be here by Wednesday. He said tell you he loves you and send you these kisses." She leaned over and kissed her daughter on her check and forehead. She kissed her again and said, "And this one is from your mummy."

"I love him so much. I want to see him; thank you mother for calling him."

Roberto' leaned over kissed her on the forehead and quietly said, "He will be here my daughter. Please stay quiet and save your strength."

Dr. Panniche, Sr. came in and said, "Time for you to sleep young lady. Your parents and grandparents will not be far away."

Tired from the effort of conversation she gave in to his command, "Yes doctor I will sleep I am so tired mummy; I am so very tired mummy." She drifted off to sleep.

They all left the room walked back to their suite, Simone' could not contain her tears any longer fell to her knees and prayed, "God in Heaven, please help my daughter, I don't want to lose her. She means the world to me. I only have one child please help her."

She felt guilt flood her, she blamed herself for her being there in Tuscany said to Roberto', "This is all my doing, I should have called my daughter and let her know I was okay. Forgive me Roberto', it is my fault I should have gone home with you when you asked me. I have been selfish in staying here."

Roberto' could not bear her tears kneeled beside her and said, "Simone' this is not your fault, it was an accident my beauty, please. You are the least selfish person I know; but have given your life to our daughter and me. I cannot bear to see you hurting this way, blaming yourself for something you had no control over."

Tears flowed from his eyes, he held Simone' stood, lifted her in his arms, went to the couch and sit, held her in his lap, snuggled her near him until she calm down. Franco and Catarina watched hurting for their daughter, granddaughter, and son-in-law. In a moment's time, all Franco's anger burned like lava from a volcano for Vincenzo' Moretti. Had it not been for his involvement in her life she would never had anything to run from or nothing frightening her.

Dr. Panniche, Jr. checked the time. It was 10:00 a.m., he asked his Nurse to get Vincenzo' Moretti on the phone. The phone rang in the Moretti's Mansion, Fabio answered, "Moretti residence."

The Nurse asked, "Is Vincenzo' Moretti there?"

Fabio answered, "Yes, hold please."

He handed the phone to Vincenzo'. The nurse held the phone up indicating he was on the line. Taking the phone Dr. Panniche, Jr, said, "Vincenzo' this is Christian Panniche, I need you to come to the hospital right away. I want to get a blood sample from you."

Vincenzo's felt his heart in his throat said, "Is Carmeli'ta' worse Christian?"

With caution he replied, "She is not getting strong as we thought she would by this time; her blood levels are too low. Can you be here in the next 20 minutes? That would help me a lot."

He said, "I will be there in 10 minutes Christian, I was coming anyway."

He hung up and walked into the office where his father and he were meeting to establish the next week's priorities asked, "Father, will you complete the priority list? Christian wants me to come for a blood sample. I volunteered to be a donor for Franco's granddaughter if necessary."

His father baffled replied, "Yes, I can complete the list son. I do not understand why the interest in this family. Does this have something to do with what you and Franco Giovanni talked about when he was here three weeks ago?"

"Father, I do not have time to discuss any points with you I need to be there in 10 minutes."

"What shall I tell your wife and mother?"

Feeling annoyed with the insistence replied, "Tell them the truth; I went to the hospital to give blood."

He walked out the door, got into his car, and drove quickly to the hospital, parked, and went in. Dr. Panniche was waiting for him at the front information desk exclaimed, "Come with me Vincenzo' the Lab Technician is waiting for you."

Walking next to the doctor he asked, "Has her father been tested yet?" He did not say anything just shook his head no and wondered why he was so interested in whether Roberto' been tested. He and his family never cared for the farmers; at least they acted like it anyway. They walked to the lab. Dr. Panniche. Jr. assisted the lab tech in taking and labeling the sample. His father would test and compare each sample as they came to the lab. Dr. Panniche Sr. was sitting with the microscope waiting to get started.

In Charleston, Jason awaken at 6:00 a.m. and readied himself for his long arduous flight and even more so because Carmeli'ta' was injured and he felt she was not doing well. He went to his father and mother's wing of the mansion with the check for $1,000 for the Charleston Children Orphanage. His father was in his office dressed and working ready for breakfast and then to the office at the plant. Jason greeted him,

"Good morning Father, you are how today?"

"I am good today son, how are you?"

"I am doing okay. I wanted to leave this check for Mother for the Orphanage Fundraiser. I will be leaving for the airport at 9:00 a.m. Do you have any questions for me especially about the Madison Steel and Iron and Meriwether Textiles Alliance? I hate to leave you with this responsibility right now. I hope that all goes well?"

"Everything will be fine son, go and see Carmeli'ta' and enjoy yourself. I will take care of any situation that arises. I have a few hold cards just in case Charles Bienville Meriwether gets difficult. I am not without resources." He smiled.

"Father, I will not ask you what those resource are right now. I am not sure I want to know." He smiled at his father then added, "Tell mother I will see her before I leave for the airport." Jason Sr. pondering, "Son would you like for your mother, me, or Ashton our chauffeur to drive you to the airport?"

"No father that will not be necessary. I will leave the keys under the floor mat. Please have my Roadster picked up for me and parked under my carport."

"I will take care of it son. I have my set of keys here for your vehicles. Juanita and I will take care of it. You have a wonderful trip and tell Carmeli'ta'; I said hello. Let us hear from you after you get situated."

"I will father, thank you. Bye until I return. I will call you soon."

In the Hospital Lab after the blood samples was drawn from Vincenzo' Dr. Panniche Jr. asked him to wait in the Waiting Room. He instructed the Duty Nurse to get him water and see that he drank two glasses. A few minutes later Ramon' Allavera' de Antoine arrived and gave a sample of blood. Dr. Panniche called to the Suite and asked Franco to come to the lab to give a sample. He asked him to send Catarina next. Franco walked back to the lab with his wife to show her the way. Dr. Panniche Sr. tested each sample and completed his report on each before starting another. Finally, everyone was tested except Simone' and Roberto'.

As the morning progressed, Simone' felt nervous and antsy. She seemed to Roberto' more fidgety than normal. She hung on to her Diary even after she calmed down and regained control of herself, paced back and forth in the suite as a caged animal as if the moment the cage door was opened would bolt and run away.

Roberto' continued to observe her and wondered why she hung on to her Diary. He wondered what the connection was to all of this. He could not reason it out in his mind his distraction with the seriousness of his daughter was in the forefront.

At length, Dr. Panniche, Jr. asked Simone' to give a blood sample first. She left the suite taking the Diary with her.

Roberto' approached Franco and asked, "Franco is there something in this situation I do not know about?"

Franco measuring his words answered, "I am not sure what you mean my son. Everyone's concern is Carmeli'ta' right now my son."

Catarina stood by her husband's side and did not comment. Roberto' did not comment any further. Simone' returned from giving a sample of her blood. She informed Roberto' Dr. Panniche, Jr. was waiting for him in the lab to get a blood sample.

After Roberto' left she looked at her parents watching her from across the room and asked, "Is there something you want to say to me Father and Mother?"

Her father said, "Simone', Roberto' is wondering what is going on. He feels that something is out-of-sync here with all of this. He asked me was there something he needed to know. This situation could easily get out of hand my daughter. Vincenzo' Moretti is still here in the hospital. Christian asked that he wait until all sample were tested in case any of the sample were tainted while being test and it would be necessary to get another sample of blood."

"I know Father, at this point I do not know what to do. This is not a good time to tell Roberto' about the situation. He would hurt Vincenzo' with the way he is feeling now."

"No daughter we would hurt Vincenzo'. It is all that I can do to keep my anger from spilling over into a confrontation."

In Charleston, it was approaching 9:00 a.m. time for Jason to leave for the airport, went to say his goodbyes to his mother, Juanita. He knew she would be in her garden went through his father's office to where she was pruning her flowers, walked over to her hugging her said, "Mother I am on my way to London. My plans are to return in 7-10 days unless something unexpected happens. I left the donation I promised you with father."

"She smiled and said, thank you son. Your donation is generous, but you have always had a generous spirit about you. I will miss you while you are away."

He said, "I will miss you also Mother, take care of yourself and my father." He looked at her smiled continued,"You are like a picture in a frame Mother; your beauty is timeless."

"Thank you Jason. I will see you when you return."

He loaded his luggage and left for the airport anxious to get to London then to Tuscany to see Carmeli'ta'. He felt fear grip him at that moment. He knew somehow Carmeli'ta' was not doing well.

At the Moretti Mansion, Antonia started her day looked for her husband, when she did realized he was not in the house went to the office in their home asked Francisco, "Father, where is my husband this morning. He left before I awaken?"

Hesitating Francisco answered, "He went to the hospital to give blood this morning. Christian Panniche, Jr. called and asked him to donate blood."

"I am not sure I am clear on what is happening here Father! I will go and see my husband there."

Francisco tried to discourage her from going she insisted and left. Antonia arrived at the hospital, walked in, asked the Charge Nurse where she could find Vincenzo' Moretti. The nurse walked her down the hall to the waiting room. To Vincenzo's surprise, she walked in and over to where he was sitting talking with Ramon' said, "Good morning my husband. You left before I awaken this morning. I decided to come and see why you are back in the hospital a second day without explanation."

Vincenzo' feeling annoyed replied, "I am giving blood my lovely Antonia, father explained my absence to you," he said declaratively!

She hissed back, "Of course Father told me, but that is not enough explanation for me Vincenzo'. I want to know what you have to do with this situation."

"I would appreciate it if you went home and waited for me there we can discuss whatever you think you want to talk about then."

She looked annoyed then replied, "No my husband, I intend to wait here with you."

Ramon' sensed a thick antagonistic heaviness to the air around them excused his self and went across the room to sit and wait, picked up a magazine, "All Wine" and flipped through it.

In all the years of marriage between Vincenzo' and Antonia, Franco and Catarina had never seen her once. She stayed out of the valley with her parents off and on for the first few years of their marriage. When she was in the valley, they traveled in different social circles.

Roberto' back from giving his blood sample in the lab walked in and over to Simone' standing looking out the window right into the lower end of the Moretti Vineyard. It was as overwhelming as the situation with Carmeli'ta', held her around the waist, and kissed the back of her head and said, "How are you my beauty?"

She turned and said, "I don't know what to think or do my husband. I am so afraid for Carmeli'ta'."

Before she could complete her statement a knock came at the door, Franco standing near it rushed to open it expecting to find Christian Panniche, Jr. instead it was the maid Desiree' coming to clean the suite. She said, "I would like to clean if you will permit me." She continued, Dr. Panniche, said, "You would not mind sitting in the waiting room until I finished; he would see you there."

They left and went to the other side of the hospital to the waiting room. As they approached, Simone' knowing Vincenzo' Moretti was waiting there felt uncomfortable, more so than she did on Monday, they were one day closer to knowing what the blood test would reveal.

She had desperately hoped Carmeli'ta' would not need a blood transfusion and she would have time, but now the sands in her hourglass of time seemed to be running out; time was ticking; she wanted it to stand still.

Vincenzo' and Antonia were standing looking out the window when they walked in the waiting room. Simone' noticed a petite, approximately 5'6" tall woman standing next to Vincenzo' with long straight black hair glistening and sparkling under the light, dressed in a Yellow Jacket she knew was from Worth's in London trimmed in black with a pair of black slack to match, and black sling back heels. When they walked in Vincenzo' heard the movement and turned to see Simone' dressed in a Navy-Blue Leisure Suit with black low-heel shoes and felt his heart skip a beat.

At the same moment, Antonia turned and looked in their direction, it was Deja vie to Roberto', Franco, and Catarina. There in front of them stood almost a replica of Simone'. Roberto' gazed at her in amazement, Franco could not believe what he saw; Catarina gasped and said, "Oh my goodness." Simone', did not notice how she looked. She was focused on Carmeli'ta' went and sat on the opposite side of the room from where Vincenzo' and Antonia were standing. She intended to avoid speaking with him if she could.

Vincenzo' took his wife's hand, walked over to where Franco, Catarina, and Roberto' were standing to make proper introductions, "Mr. Giovanni, Mr. Bandaci. Ms. Giovanni, this is my wife Antonia."

She said graciously, "It is good to meet you. I am sorry to hear about your daughter Mr. Bandaci. I hope that she will be okay."

Roberto' still baffled at her resemblance to his Simone' replied, "Thank you Ms. Moretti. I appreciate your kindness."

Simone' watched from across the room and noticed Antonia was looking at her in a strange manner. Antonia asked Vincenzo' after they walked back to the window, "Who is the woman sitting by herself?"

He answered, "Roberto' Bandaci's wife, Franco, and Catarina's daughter."

Catarina walked over to Simone' left Roberto' and Franco chatting and said, "How are you my sweet Daughter?"

She replied, "I don't know Mother, I fear for my daughter. What we will do if…?" she stopped short with Catarina catching her hand commented, "Simone' we are not letting those kinds of thoughts come into our mind. Carmeli'ta' is still with us my darling Daughter. We will continue to pray for God's mercy."

"I know Mother it is so hard for me."

Wanting to take her mind off the negative thoughts about Carmeli'ta' for a moment Catarina said, "Simone' have you not noticed Vincenzo's Moretti's wife?"

She said, "No Mother, I saw a woman standing near him, why you ask?"

Simone', look at her my daughter, she looks so much like you, just not as pretty. Can't you see what Vincenzo' did? When he could not have you, he married someone that looks just like you."

Simone' for the first time looked at Antonia and exclaimed, "Mother you are right she looks like you as well. She could be your daughter." Catarina replied, "Roberto' noticed that my Daughter."

She asked, "How does her looks matter? No one is responsible for the way they look."

"Simone' if it were any other man except Vincenzo' Moretti I would say it does not matter, but in this case it does, he was trying to replace you in his life."

"I had not thought about it like that Mother."

More fear gripped here heart sat with her Diary hugged to her chest. Roberto' joined her and sat next to her and said, "I had not thought that I would ever see anyone that looks like you my beauty. She is almost as pretty as you are with the same face. Franco has never met her before in all the 12 years she and Vincenzo' has been married. He was surprised as was your mother."

She barely whispered, "I see my husband."

The storm clouds begin to gather, at 2:45 p.m. in Tuscany, Dr. Panniche, Jr. was on his way to the Waiting Room with the results of the first round of test.

CHAPTER

FIFTY

In the interim, Jason arrived at the airport at 9:45 a.m., checked his luggage, confirmed his reservation, and walked to the passenger boarding area to wait. He would be on his way in less than an hour to his Carmeli'ta'. His heart felt heavy, he sat and prayed she was okay. He did not know at that time the seriousness of her condition was deteriorating by the hour while the doctors frantically and with elevated speed, tested the blood for a match.

Dr. Panniche, Jr. walked in the Waiting Room; Simone', Catarina, Franco', and Vincenzo's heart were in their throats for different reasons.

They did not know which of the test he had or what they would reveal. Dr. Panniche walked over to Roberto' and Simone' and said, "My father finished the first rounds of test." Simone' held her breath. "These are the first findings, Ramon' Allavera' de Antione blood type is an O+ we cannot use him as a donor. I will let him know that he can leave it will not be necessary for him to be tested a second time. Catarina's blood type is an A+, there is no chance we can use her blood either, even with her being the grandmother. These are the only two people at this point we have eliminated for possible donors. Franco's blood is a B+, so he cannot be a donor either, but we want to test him again. She has to have a donor with AB-, B-, A-, or O- so far this has not happened with our testing. I will let you know the next round of results."

Roberto' afraid said, "How is Carmeli'ta' Christian?"

He paused for a moment and said, "She is weak Roberto' very weak, we are working fast as we can but we have to be sure about the blood test results or the wrong transfusion will be certain death for that child.

I need to get back to the lab. I will let you know as soon as I can. "Simone' asked, "Can we see her."

He said, "She is sleeping now, I want her to sleep, it preserves her strength. I am afraid if you go to her room, she will sense you are there and try to talk." He left and almost ran back to the lab.

Vincenzo' walked over and said, "What did Christian Panniche say about your daughter?"

Roberto' said, "No matches yet Mr. Moretti, we appreciate your concern."

He turned back to Simone' and said, "She will be fine my beauty, I will not believe anything else."

Simone' sat feeling numb as if the life had drained out of her. Roberto' continued to look at Antonia. He could hardly believe he was seeing the same face his wife had sitting across the room.

Antonia asked, "What were the results Vincenzo'?" When will we leave for home?"

He stood and looked down at her and replied, "You may go anytime you wish my lovely Antonia, waiting seems to inconvenience you." He moved to the window and stood looking out into his vineyard.

At the Charleston Airport Jason boarded his flight at 10:40 a.m. At 11:00 a.m., Pan American Flight 2742 pushed back and taxied to the Tar Mat for takeoff. Finally on his way; out over the Atlantic, he would be at Carmeli'ta's side in less than 24 hours.

In the lab Dr. Panniche, Sr. tested, Simone' blood next. He was surprised at the findings of her blood Rh factor. Dr. Panniche, Jr. was on his way to give them the results of the test stopped by Carmeli'ta' room to check her heartrate she was sleeping. He checked the Sodium Nitrate drip that kept her from dehydration. He lifted her hand and she moaned and said mother, I am so tired, help me mother. He said, "Carmeli'ta' it is Dr. Panniche, Jr. your parents and grandparents are down the hall you are fine right now, I want you to preserve your strength so try not to talk." She did not open her eyes, but nodded her head yes. He hurried down the hall to update them on her condition and give the results of Simone's blood test. He walked into the Waiting Room, Roberto', when he saw him, sprang to his feet, and met him in the middle of the room asked, "How is she Christian?"

"She is still holding her own, but getting weaker. My father and I are almost done with the last two tests; it will be within the next hour. We will start the transfusion right away and then after than it is in the hands of God and the will that child has to fight to live. I want you to see her for just a minute, but do not stay long. She needs to know you are still here. In her weak condition she will think you are gone if she does not see you and that will not be good." He continued, "Now to the blood test results. We tested Simone's blood her RH factor is an AB."

Before he could complete his statement Roberto' exclaimed, "Then her mother matches, thank God."

Dr. Panniche held up his hand in a stop position, "Simone's blood Rh factor is an AB+, she does not match remember we need a person whose blood RH factors are negative. A person with AB- RH factors can give blood to anyone; but, when it comes to getting blood, it becomes a horse of a different color. I am not surprised, it not strange for both parents to have the same AB factors in their blood that a child does. I see now why it is so hard to match. It is so much better for her if she has a male's blood. I will walk with you to her room on the way back to the lab to test Roberto' and Vincenzo' Moretti's blood."

In the Waiting Room, Franco and Catarina was in agony over uncertainty of the blood results for Roberto' and Vincenzo'. They sat together holding hands and prayed for their granddaughter to survive no matter whose blood she had in her veins, to them they loved her and that was all that mattered.

Carmeli'ta' in a weaken condition, but awake, kept her eyes closed, saw herself walking down the aisle in their congregation building toward Jason in a beautiful white lace gown like the one her mother showed her she wore when she married her father. She saw Jason smiling and holding out both arms to her as she reached the Alter. They turned after they took their vows, run through the meadow, and field happy to be together. She saw him and her running, running, toward a mountain, each time they got close to the mountain it moved farther and farther away than fading. She could not see any farther kept her eyes closed trying to see what happened and if the mountain stopped moving and they caught up with it.

Roberto', Simone', and Dr. Panniche, Jr. arrived at Carmeli'ta's room. He warned them again to encourage her. Simone' tipped over to her bed leaning over whispered, "Mummy is here my darling Daughter. I love you; your grandparents loves you."

She opened her eyes for the first time since early morning and asked, "You did not say father loves me Mother, where is my father?"

Roberto' standing on the other side of her bed said, "I am here my darling Daughter. I love you with all my heart, you are my baby girl, I will always love you, and we will be right here until you are well my lovely Daughter. You are as pretty as ever. We want you to sleep so you can get well, will you do that for us?"

She nodded her head again yes, closed her eyes, and slept. Dr. Panniche, Sr. in the lab looked at both Roberto' and Vincenzo's test results. He could not believe what he saw. He asked the nurse to get Vincenzo' medical chart, he looked at the test results again and said to his son, "The factors of one of these test is strange and unusual. I checked Vincenzo's medical records and there is something there I am not sure he is aware of from the last test that we did 5 years ago during a check-up. Now his test shows something different today. And then there is Carmeli'ta' father's test, this is so unusual, really unusual."

Dr. Panniche, Jr. studied the chart and then the test and said, "I see what you mean. I do not know if this is good or bad, but now we need to go to the Waiting Room to talk with her parents. Can Vincenzo' Moretti's Chart be accurate father?" he asked.

"Yes, yes, I did the test myself and stood there while the Lab Tech took the sample and looked at it, he handed me the results. I could not believe the results he handed me, even with me standing there looking at him. I looked at the samples myself, so there is no chance of it being a mistake."

Dr. Panniche, Jr. looked at his pocket watch, did not offer further comments on the chart and results of the tests, but added, "It is 2:45 p.m., and our patient will start losing ground in another hour. We can only deal with one situation at a time. But father I must ask you what will the results of one of the tests do in the lives of that family?" He continued, "But nonetheless, Carmeli'ta' Bandaci's life is hanging in the balance and that is more important. I would like to stop to see her before we give her parents the results of the tests."

His father replied, "My exact thoughts. I am ready."

They stopped by the Nurse's Station and asked the Charge Nurse to tell Carmel'ta's family they would be there in about 10-minutes as soon as they checked their patient. Entering her room, approaching the bed, saw that she had lost more color, knew she was getting weaker, the next 2-hours would be critical. They had to move fast before she slipped into unconsciousness.

December 12, Jason's flight out over the Atlantic, was into the first 5-hours of his journey sat looking out the window his heart grew heavier, saw the vastness of the ocean, felt his heart and the love he had for Carmeli'ta' was as huge and overpowering as that ocean. The closer he got to London, the more overcome with nervousness he felt, did not know what the condition of her health would be when he arrived. The woman he loved with all his heart and soul, the one who held his heart. Would she survive? This question taunted him.

Roberto' and Simone', 15-minutes later, after visiting with Carmeli'ta' returned to the Waiting Room sat with her mother and father. Franco inquired, "How is my granddaughter?" Simone' said, "She is weak father I am so afraid, so afraid." She sat trembling uncontrollably.

From across the room Vincenzo' watched Simone' saw her shaking, asked his wife to excuse him went over and said, "are you alright Simone'?"

She did not reply, Roberto' said, "You seem to be overly concerned with the state of my wife's health, Mr. Moretti."

Franco had stood by that time and said, "We appreciate your concern Mr. Moretti this is a very hard time for us. We thank you for your support and concern." Franco felt as if he would explode inside continued, "It is hard for my daughter to talk right now, I am sure you can understand so if you will excuse us."

Except for Carmeli'ta' family and Vincenzo' and his wife, the Waiting Room was empty. The Charge Nurse entered. Roberto' stood, Vincenzo' stood, Franco' stood, she said, Mr. Bandaci, Drs. Panniche will be here in 10-minutes with the results of the last two test, they are checking the patient before they come."

Vincenzo' joined his wife again, sat, put his hands together in a prayerful manner, and looked down at the floor. When he sat next to her she asked, "I still want to know why you are so concerned with this family's daughter? It is as if you had some ties to them my husband. I noticed over the years your strange behavior, distance, and lack of interest in almost anything, what is different about this? We have talked about your aloofness before and you had no response."

He did not look up said, "Why don't you go home Antonia, you are not needed here. There is nothing you can do here."

Feeling annoyed, Antonia replied, "When you go, I will go. There is something that is missing in this Vincenzo' like a piece of a puzzle missing or under something, as if it is hiding from the seeker."

He looked at her and replied, "You lost me somewhere between the puzzle's missing piece and its hiding from the seeker." Vincenzo' felt uncomfortable with the questions his wife asked him. He felt transparent at that moment more than he had in his lifetime.

Franco and Catarina tried to comfort Roberto' and Simone' with words of encouragement said, "Our children, this situation with our sweet Carmeli'ta' is not as bad as it can get, she is still hanging on, the will to fight she has in her comes from both her mother and her father. You have given her so much strength to draw from and the will to go forward. I will not believe that she will give up. She knows you are here and that is a plus. The test being completed is a step in a positive direction."

Simone' could not sit still she had 10-minutes and her life would fall apart. Her daughter's life was hanging in the balance, whether she lived or died depended on one of the other of her husband or Vincenzo' Moretti. Fear gripped her covering her like a blanket she paced like a caged animal.

Franco and Catarina sat silent as stone praying, not knowing what the test results would reveal.

In Charleston, Tuesday afternoon December 12, at 3:00 p.m., Jason Madison, Sr. first meeting with Charles Bienville Meriwether was tense but successful. It was as if he was punishing Jason, Sr. for two reasons: he married the only woman he ever truly loved; and he expected to see Carmeli'ta' Bandaci in this contractual meeting. In his disappointment, his Alter Ego appeared. He was his confidant and best friend, the other version of his personality accompanied him to the meeting and sprang into action when he realized the meeting was with Jason Madison, Sr. Charles Meriwether's other him, usurped his good manners. Those good manners lost to him at that meeting had contributed to his reputation of respectability in the Charleston community.

Jason Madison, Sr. with the reaction of Charles Meriwether at the meeting, though his outward appearance was calm and collected in the meeting, mentally put the strategy in place that Charles Meriwether was not aware of that would have an adverse effect on his business and the future of Meriwether Textiles. As Jason, Sr. said to his son before he boarded the plan to go to Carmeli'ta'; 'He was not without resource and power to stop Charles Meriwether.'

Vincenzo' sat stalking Simone' with his eyes, watched bewilderment paint the pain of uncertainty on her face thought, "She is to me the same today as when she was 14 years old when I met her for the first time. She was pretty in her teens, but now she is a beautiful and even more desirable woman. I loved her then and I still love her now. My wife Antonia deserves better from me than I have given her. She loves me and I know she does, but is angry, as she should be because she knows that I do not love her the same way. I admire her beauty, she reminds me of Simone', she is warm and kind to my parents and I respect her for that, because I love them with all my heart. My father knows there is some connection but do not know what and my mother, well my mother knows I am almost certain of it, but would never say anything. She never like the separation in classes of people, but was powerless to do anything about it. I don't think my father liked it either, but adhered to tradition feeling he had no choice at that time."

Roberto' saw Vincenzo' visual stalking his wife wondered why he watched her so closely thought, "Maybe he is as amazed our wives have the same face just my Simone' is prettier and lovelier in every way in my mind." However, he left the question of "Why?" on his mental table of problems to solve.

Antonia felt lost in the situation. She had no answers from her husband, and she had the same face as the woman across the room. She felt a quick pain of envy, "Simone's husband's actions say she is the most precious person in the world to him my husband, Vincenzo' acts sometimes as if he does not know I even exist. I have fallen in love with my husband. I need his love and want children so badly, our children, so we will have children from both of us to love and care for them. I need him so much but he does not need me. When we are man and wife in an intimate way, I know it is sometimes out of his need as a man, but it is not the kind of love I want or need. Even with knowing this, he fulfills the desires and needs I have as a woman and I love being close to him; he feels so strong to me." She fought the mental turmoil that has haunted her since their marriage twelve years ago.

Roberto', perplexed, watched Simone', what he knew and what his instinct was telling him was two different things. Why did she not let that Diary out of her sight? What did it have to do with Carmeli'ta' and this situation? What was the connection?" He felt as if he was dealing with an octopus with tentacles going in all direction with the one head to give direction and that head was his lovely Simone'. Questions swirled around in his head like winds of a violent storm. He felt at that moment, the situation in his life was as dark and frightening with the all the violent of a Tornado and he was caught up the Vortex. The Diary was the elephant in the room. She was holding both, the Diary and the key that opened it with the answers he needed.

They knew the doctors were on their way with the test. The atmosphere in the Waiting Room became a death watch and Carmeli'ta' Noelle Angelu'cia Bandaci's life was uncertain.

Vincenzo' test results would give him hope; however, would this hope bring him the success desired? His actions over the years were equal to a bull in a China Closet.

Roberto' was certain that he would have the RH negative factors in his blood that matched his daughter Carmeli'ta', no other thought entered in his mind. Would his blood type match his daughter's AB- blood type?

How can one person's actions twenty-four years before touch so many lives? Directly or indirectly, all roads, far or near, led to one small black book with a key. It had answers to the confusion and twenty-one and a half old decades of hidden secrets. Simone' felt trapped. Everyone needed the key to open the door to get in to solve the mystery. But not Simone', she needed the key to get out?

Her jailers were there, was she ready to face the danger that lies beyond the bars she locked herself behind since she was 13-years of age? The only two people that she cared to protect with this Diary were her husband and her daughter. At that time, she could not help her daughter, her blood RH factors was AB+; nor, could she tell her husband the truth behind a twenty-four years old mystery at that moment. He would hurt Vincenzo', her father would be involved, and she did not want that, it was a catch-22.

Trying to mentally push the plane forward, Jason heart full of sorrow,pain, and uncertainty, headed to Tuscany and his Carmeli'ta', was not aware of the emotional storm brewing in this beautiful little valley.

In Charleston, Amelio' felt as if he was sitting on pins and needles while he waited to hear the fate of his sweet niece. Events were not shaping up as he thought. His Bibi 'Ana would be there in two days, Thursday, December 14. He would pick her up from the airport at 4:00 p.m. Amelio' knew only God could help, prayed fervently for his family they would find the right donor and the success of the transfusion would be in time to save his beautiful niece whom he loved as a daughter. He knew he would lose Roberto' and Simone' both if Carmeli'ta' did not survive, it would kill them, fell to his knees, and prayed to God for his mercy. He could not process the thought of the possibility of his losing all of his family at the same time.

Alberto Gambani, Monday, December 11, feeling puzzled and dismissed by Carmeli'ta' could not process the feeling of disappointment enveloping his mind and heart, returned to the University for his Semester Exams. January 15, 1928, he would begin the last six months of study for his degree in Business. His spirits fallen knew his chances to have the woman of his dreams was getting slimmer with each day that passed. Carmeli'ta' was out town he did not know if he would see her during the holidays when he returned, December 20, for the two weeks break for Christmas. He desired to tell her how much he cared for her. He called her parent's home and Marianna told him Mr. and Ms. Bandaci were not in town and she did not know when they would return. He knew she must be with her parents. His hope, like snow after the winter was melting away. Would he have the wherewithal to compete for her affections?

Brother Meriwether, Roberto', Simone's, and Amelio's Minister waiting to hear if his friends and spiritual family member's daughter, and niece would survive mentally reflected on the conversations with Simone' and Roberto' were prayerful, asking for God's mercy upon them and the situation he knew was at this point was past any human management.

Tuesday evening, December 12, after leaving the meeting with Jason Madison, Sr., Charles Bienville Meriwether began plotting. His conversation with Vincenzo' encouraging him and his father to join the co-op that would supply iron and steel to their expanding interest abroad planned to use him as a Segway to try and destroy the Madison's. It could backfire!

Tuesday evening, December 12, with tension running high in the Tuscany Valley Hospital, Carmeli'ta' was hanging between life and death. Vincenzo' sure he was the father could not accept any other truth. Roberto' knows he is the father; he raised his daughter. Simone' felt nervous and sick; Franco and Catarina grew increasingly afraid by the minute. Antonia sit lost and puzzled in this sea of tumult and tension she felt so thick it could be cut with a knife did not understand any of it and her husband would not answer her questions.

At the Moretti Mansion Francisco determined to know why his son acted so strange the last two days more than usual, left for the hospital to get answers to the questions that haunted him about his son since he was 17 years of age. He had noticed when he reached the age of 17 years old his personality and entire demeanor changed overnight almost into a budding young man, he wondered what was behind the transformation then and afterward the sinking back into anger and secrecy.

Love, as a hungry Lion was ripping and tearing into these families lives, gobbling them up. The winds of change blew silently across the lives of the Bandaci, Giovanni, Madison, Meriwether, and Moretti families.

The Doctors Chistian Panniche, Jr. and Sr. arrived at the waiting room, opened the door, and walked into deadly silence. Roberto', Franco, Catarina, Simone' and Vincenzo' rose, Dr. Panniche Jr. said, "Mr. Bandaci, we have the results of the test..."

Simone' gripped her Diary even tighter to her chest as if to suppress the truth!

For who will Twenty-four years of heartache begin anew? Or heartache will begin for whom?

BIBLIOGRAPHY

American Civil War, (1861-1865),

> *https://en.wikipedia.org/wiki/ Naming _ the_ American _Civil _War*

Apennine Mountains,

> *https://en.wikipedia.org/wiki/Apennine mountains*

Ave Maria, Schubert, Franz, (1825).

> *https:www.britannica.com/topic/ Ave Maria-song-by-Schubert.*

Blood types, (Ab-, Ab+, B-, 0-, 0+, B+),

> *https://en.wikipedia.org/wiki/ Blood type.*

Boellis Panama (1924),

> *www.smallflower.com/boellis/panama-1924- coffret-shave-soap-250g*

Borneo Serge Lutens Cologne and Aftershave,

> *(1834), www.perfume. com/serge-lutens/borneo-1834/men-cologne*

Boulangerie Veinnoise in Tuscany (1920's),

> *bing.com/images*

Campo di Marte Airport,

> *https://en.wikipedia.org/wiki/Florence Airport*

Chanel 5, (1921)

> *https://en.wikipedia.org/wiki/Chanel No. 5*

Charleston-Made Furniture, (1772)

> *www.charlestonfurniture.com*

Chateau Margaux Bordeaux Winery, (1572),

> *www.chateaumargaux,com/en Chatsworth Mansion, www.chatsworth.org*

Cocoa Butter Extract,

> *www.livescience.com/36626-cocoa-butter-chocolate-lotion-benefits.html*

Croydon Airport London, (1920-1930),

> *https://en.wikipedia.org/wiki/Croydon Airport*

Cunard Line, (1902),

> *RMS Olympic and Mauretania Cunard Line*
>
> *https://en.wikipedia.org/wiki/RMS Mauretania (1906)*

Detaille, (1905),

    www.eaumg.net/detaille-aeroplane-edt-fragrance-review

Duck à L'Orange, (Canard1820)

    https://en.wikipedia.org/wiki/Duck_ à l'Orange.

Egyptian Cotton Towels, History of,

    elsatex.com/history-of-the-towel

Enotris, "Land of Wine",

    www.tuscany-wine.com/history.html

Fruit and Vegetables grown in Italy (1900),

    https://en.wikipedia.org/ wiki/Italian food

Fur Elise' (1867) Ludwig Van Beethoven,

    https://en.wikipedia.org/ wiki/Für Elise

Golding, B, (1818). Charing Cross Hospital, London

    www.ezitis.myzen.co.uk/charingcross.html.

He that findeth a wife, Proverbs 18:22.

    (Master Study Bible, NKJV 2001).

Here Comes the Bride, Felix Mendelssohn, 1858,

    https://en.wikipedia. org/wiki/Bridal Chorus.

Heyward-Washington House, (1772),

    www.charlestonmuseum.org/historic-houses/heyward-washington-house.

History of the City, Charleston, South Carolina

    www.charleston-sc. gov/index.aspx?nid=110

House of Worth (1858)

    https://en.wikipedia.org/wiki/House of Worth

Images of Tuscany valley, Italy history,

    bing.com/images

Imperial Airways,

    https://en.wikipedia.org/wiki/Imperial -Airways (1924-1939)

Langley Mills.

    www.picturesofengland.com/history/london-history.html

Liszt, Franz, Liebestraume, (1850),

    https://en.wikipedia.org/wiki/ Liebesträume

Master Study Bible,

    (NKJV, 2001).

Meet your Waterloo (1815),

    www.phrases.org.uk/meanings/245800.html

Nivea Crème and Lotion (1911)

    https://en.wikipedia.org/wiki/Nivea

'O Sole Mio' Di Capua, Eduardo (1898)

    www.classicalmusic.about.com

Pan American Airways, (1920's),

    https://en.wikipedia.org/wiki/Pan American Airlines

Reconstruction (1863-1877).

    www.history.com/topics/american-civil-war/reconstruction.

Roadster, Hot Rod, and Bentley Cars

    www.1920-30.com/automobiles

Romance,

    www.thesaurus.com

Song of Solomon,

    Chapter 5:10-16 and Chapter 7:1-19.

    (Master Study Bible, NKJV, 2001.)

Sonnet 116,

    www.Shakespeare.com, (1609)

Swiss Bank, (1879)

    www.swissbank https://en.wikipedia.org/wiki/Swiss Bank Corporation

The Ghost, Shakespeare (1762) Discretionistheetterpartofvalor;

    www.goodreads.com/quotes/46820-direction-is-the-better-part-of-valor.

Tuscany,

    https//en.wikipedia.org/wiki/History_of_Tuscany

Val di Greve River,

    www.chianti.info/chianti/val-de-greve-in-central-tuscany.

World War I, (1914-1918)

    www.worldwar-I.net.